Mildred Arkell by Mrs Henry Wood

COMPLETE IN THREE VOLUMES

Ellen Price was born on 17th January 1814 in Worcester.

In 1836 she married Henry Wood, whose career in banking and shipping meant living in Dauphiné, in the South of France, for two decades. During their time there they had four children.

Henry's business collapsed and he and Ellen together with their four children returned to England and settled in Upper Norwood near London.

Ellen now turned to writing and with her second book 'East Lynne' enjoyed remarkable popularity. This enabled her to support her family and to maintain a literary career.

It was a career in which she would write over 30 novels including 'Danesbury House', 'Oswald Cray', 'Mrs. Halliburton's Troubles', 'The Channings' and 'The Shadow of Ashlydyat'.

Sadly, her husband, Henry died in 1866.

Ellen though continued to strive on. In 1867, she purchased the magazine 'Argosy', founded two years previously by Alexander Strahan. She was a prolific writer and wrote much of the magazine herself although she had some very respected contributors, amongst them Hesba Stretton and Christina Rossetti. Although she would gradually pare down writing for the magazine she continued to write novel after novel. Such was her talent that for a time she was, in Australia, more popular than Charles Dickens.

Apart from novels she was an excellent translator and a writer of short stories. 'Reality or Delusion?' is a staple of supernatural anthologies to this day.

Ellen Wood died of bronchitis on 10th February 1887. He estate was valued at a very considerable £36,000.

She is buried in Highgate Cemetery, London.

A monument to her in Worcester Cathedral was unveiled in 1916.

Index of Contents

CHAPTER I

WHICH IS NOTHING BUT AN INTRODUCTION

I am going to tell you a story of real life—one of those histories that in point of fact are common enough; but, hidden within themselves as they generally are, are thought to be so rare, and, if proclaimed to the world in all their strange details, are looked upon as a romance, not reality. Some of the actors in this one are living now, but I have the right to tell it, if I please.

A fair city is Westerbury; perhaps the fairest of the chief towns in all the midland counties. Its beautiful cathedral rises in the midst, the red walls of its surrounding prebendal houses looking down upon the famed river that flows gently past; a cathedral that shrouds itself in its unapproachable exclusiveness, as if it did not belong to the busy town outside. For that town is a manufacturing one, and the aristocracy of the clergy, with that of the few well-born families time had gathered round them, and the democracy of trade, be it ever so irreproachable, do not, as you know, assimilate. In the days gone by—and it is to them we must first turn—this feeling of exclusiveness, this line of demarcation, if you will, was far more conspicuous than it is now: it was indeed carried to a pitch that would now scarcely be believed in. There were those of the proud old prebendaries, who would never have acknowledged to knowing a manufacturer by sight; who would not have spoken to one in the street, had it been to save their stalls. You don't believe me? I said you would not. Nevertheless, I am telling you the simple truth. And yet, some of those manufacturers, in their intrinsic worth, in their attainments, ay, and in their ancestors, if you come to that, were not to be despised.

In those old days no town was more flourishing than Westerbury. Masters and workmen were alike enjoying the fruits of their skill and industry: the masters in amassing a rich competency; the workmen, or operatives, as it has become the fashion to call them of late years, in earning an ample living, and in bringing up their children without a struggle. But those times changed. The opening of our ports to foreign goods brought upon Westerbury, if not destruction, something very like it; and it was only the more wealthy of the manufacturers who could weather the storm. They lost, as others did, a very great deal; but they had (at least, some few of them) large resources to fall back upon, and their business was continued as before, when the shock was over; and none in the outer world knew how deep it had been, or how far it had shaken them.

Conspicuous amidst this latter class was Mr. George Arkell. He had made a great deal of money—not by the griping hand of extortion; by badly-paid, or over-tasked workmen; but by skill, care, industry, and honourable dealing. In all high honour he worked on his way; he could not have been guilty of a mean action; to take an unfair advantage of another, no matter how he might have benefited himself, would have been foreign to his nature. And this just dealing in trade, as in else, let me tell you, generally answers in the end. A better or more benevolent man than George Arkell did not exist, a more just or considerate master. His rate of wages was on the highest scale—and there were high and low scales in the town—and in the terrible desolation hinted at above, he had never turned from the poor starving men without a helping hand.

It could not be but that such a man should be beloved in private life, respected in public; and some of those grand old cathedral clergy, who, with their antiquated and obsolete notions, were fast dropping off to a place not altogether swayed by exclusiveness, might have made an exception in favour of Mr. Arkell, and condescended to admit their knowledge, if questioned, that a man of that name did live in Westerbury.

George Arkell had one son: an only child. No expense had been spared upon William Arkell's education. Brought up in the school attached to the cathedral, the college school as it was familiarly called, he had also a private tutor at home, and private masters. In accordance with the good old system obtaining in the past days—and not so very long past either, as far as the custom is concerned—the college school confined its branches of instruction to two: Greek and Latin. To teach a boy to read English and to spell it, would have been too derogatory. History, geography, any common branch you please to think of; mathematics, science, modern languages, were not so much as recognised. Such things probably did exist, but certainly nothing was known of them in the college school. Mr. Arkell—perhaps a little in advance of his contemporaries—believed that such acquirements might be useful to his son, and a private tutor had been provided for him. Masters for every accomplishment of the day were also given him; and those accomplishments were less common then than now. It was perhaps excusable: William Arkell was a goodly son: and he grew to manhood not only a thoroughly well-read classical scholar and an accomplished man, but a gentleman. "I should like you to choose a profession, William," Mr. Arkell had said to him, when his schooldays were nearly over. "You shall go to Oxford, and fix upon one while there; there's no hurry." William laughed; "I don't care to go to Oxford," he said; "I think I know quite enough as it is; and I intend to come into the manufactory to you."

And William maintained his resolution. Indulged as he had been, he was somewhat accustomed to like his own way, good though he was by nature, dutiful and affectionate by habit. Perhaps Mr. Arkell was not sorry for the decision, though he laughingly told his son that he was too much of a gentleman for a manufacturer. So William Arkell was entered at the manufactory; and when the proper time came he was taken into partnership with his father, the firm becoming "George Arkell and Son."

Mr. George Arkell had an elder brother, Daniel; rarely called anything but Dan. He had not prospered. He had had the opportunity of prospering just as much as his brother had, but he had not done it. A fatal speculation into which Dan always said he was "drawn," but which everybody else said he had plunged into of himself with confiding eagerness, had gone very far towards ruining him. He did not fail; he was of the honourable Arkell nature; and he paid every debt he owed to the uttermost penny—paid grandly and liberally; but it left him with no earthly possession except the house he lived in, and that he couldn't part with. Dan was a middle-aged man then, and he was fain to accept a clerkship in the city bank at a hundred a year salary; and he abjured speculation for the future, and lived quietly on in the old house with his wife and two children, Peter and Mildred. But wealth, as you are aware, is always bowed down to, and Westerbury somehow fell into the habit of calling the wealthy manufacturer "Mr. Arkell," and the elder "Mr. Dan."

How contrary things run in this world! The one cherished dream of Peter Arkell's life was to get to the University, for his heart was set on entering the Church; and poor Peter could not get to it. His cousin William, who might have gone had it cost thousands, declined to go; Peter, who had no thousands—no, nor pounds, either, at his command, was obliged to relinquish it. It is possible that had Mr. Arkell known of this strong wish, he might have smoothed the way for his nephew, but Peter never told it. He was of a meek, reticent, somewhat shy nature; and even his own father knew not how ardently the wish had been cherished.

"You must do something for your living, Peter," Mr. Dan Arkell had said, when his son quitted the college school in which he had been educated. "The bank has promised you a clerkship, and thirty pounds a year to begin with; and I think you can't do better than take it."

Poor, shy, timid Peter thought within himself he could do a great deal better, had things been favourable; but they were not favourable, and the bank and the thirty pounds carried the day. He sat on a high stool from nine o'clock until five, and consoled himself at home in the evenings with his beloved classics.

Some years thus passed on, and about the time that William Arkell was taken into partnership by his father, Mr. Daniel Arkell died, and Peter was promoted to the better clerkship, and to the hundred a year salary. He saw no escape now; he was a banker's clerk for life.

And now that all this preliminary explanation is over—and I assure you I am as glad to get it over as you can be—let us go on to the story.

In one of the principal streets of Westerbury, towards the eastern end of the town, you might see a rather large space of ground, on which stood a handsome house and other premises, the whole enclosed by iron gates and railings, running level with the foot pavement of the street. Removed from the bustle of the town, which lay higher up, the street was a quiet one, only private houses being in it—no shops. It was, however, one of the principal streets, and the daily mails and other stage-coaches, not yet exploded, ran through it. The house mentioned lay on the right hand, going towards the town, and not far off, behind various intervening houses, rose the towers of the cathedral. This house lay considerably back from the street—on a level with it, at some distance, was a building whose many windows proclaimed it what it was—a manufactory; and at the back of the open-paved yard, lying between the house and the manufactory, was a coach-house and stable—behind all, was a large garden.

Standing at the door of that house, one autumn evening, the red light of the setting sun falling sideways athwart his face, was a gentleman in the prime of life. Some may demur to the expression—for men estimate the stages of age differently—and this gentleman must have seen fifty-five years; but in his fine, unwrinkled, healthy face, his slender, active, upright form, might surely be read the indications that he was yet in his prime. It was the owner of the house and its appendages—the principal of the manufactory, George Arkell.

He was drawing on a pair of black gloves as he stood there, and the narrow crape-band on his hat proclaimed him to be in slight mourning. It was the fashion to remain in mourning longer then than now. Daniel Arkell had been dead twelve months, but the Arkell family had not put away entirely the signs. Suddenly, as Mr. Arkell looked towards the iron gates—both standing wide open—a gentlemanly young man turned in, and came with a quick step across the yard.

There was not much likeness between the father and son, save in the bright dark eyes, and in the expression of the countenance—that was the same in both; good, sensitive, benevolent. William was taller than his father, and very handsome, with a look of delicate health on his refined features, and a complexion almost as bright as a girl's. At the same moment that he was crossing the yard, an open carriage, well built and handsome, but drawn by only one horse, was being brought round from the stables. Nearly every afternoon of their lives, Sundays excepted, Mr. and Mrs. Arkell went out for a drive in this carriage, the only one they kept.

"How late you are starting!" exclaimed William to his father.

"Yes; I have been detained. I had to go into the manufactory after tea, and since then Marmaduke Carr called, and he kept me."

"It is hardly worth while going now."

"Yes, it is. Your mother has a headache, and the air will do her good; and we want to call in for a minute on the Palmers."

The carriage had come to a stand-still midway from the stables. There was a small seat behind for the groom, and William saw that it was open; when the groom did not attend them, it remained closed. Never lived there a man of less pretension than George Arkell; and the taking a servant with him for show would never have entered his imagination. They kept but this one man—he was groom, gardener, anything; his state-dress (in which he was attired now) being a long blue coat with brass buttons, drab breeches, and gaiters.

"You are going to take Philip to-night?" observed William.

"Yes; I shall want him to stay with the horse while we go in to the Palmers'. Heath Hall is a goodish step from the road, you know."

"I will tell my mother that the carriage is ready," said William, turning into the house.

But Mr. Arkell put up his finger with a detaining movement.

"Stop a minute, William. Marmaduke Carr's visit this evening had reference to you. He came to complain."

"To complain!—of me?" echoed William Arkell, his tone betraying his surprise. "What have I done to him?"

"At least, it sounded very like a complaint to my ears," resumed the elder man; "and though he did not say he came purposely to prefer it, but introduced the subject in an incidental sort of manner, I am sure he did come to do it."

"Well, what have I done?" repeated William, an amused expression mingling with the wonder on his face.

"After conversing on other topics, he began speaking of his son, and that Hughes girl. He has come to the determination, he says, of putting a final stop to it, and he requests it as a particular favour that you won't mix yourself up in the matter and will cease from encouraging Robert in it."

"I!" echoed William. "That's good. I don't encourage it."

"Marmaduke Carr says you do encourage it. He tells me you were strolling with the girl and Robert last Sunday afternoon in the fields on the other side the water. I confess I was surprised to hear this, William."

William Arkell raised his honest eyes, so clear and truthful, straight to the face of his father.

"How things may be distorted!" he exclaimed. "Do you remember, sir, my mother asked me, as we left the cathedral after service, to go and inquire whether there was any change for the better in Mrs. Pembroke?"

"I remember it quite well."

"Well, I went. Coming back, I chose the field way, and I had no sooner got into the first field, than I overtook Robert Carr and Martha Ann Hughes. I walked with him through the fields until we came to the bridge, and then I came on alone. Much 'encouragement' there was in that!"

"It was countenancing the thing, at any rate, if not encouraging it," remarked Mr. Arkell.

"There's no harm in it; none at all."

"Do you mean in the affair itself, or in your having so far lent yourself to it?"

"In both," fearlessly answered William. "I wonder who it is that carries these tales to old Carr! We did not meet a soul, that I remember; he must have spies at work."

The remark rather offended Mr. Arkell.

"William," he gravely asked, "do you consider it fitting that Robert Carr should marry that girl?"

William's eyes opened rather wide at the remark.

"He is not likely to do that, sir; he would not make a simpleton of himself."

"Then you consider that he should choose the other alternative, and turn rogue?" rejoined Mr. Arkell, indignation in his suppressed tone. "William, had anyone told me this of you, I would not have believed it."

William Arkell's sensitive cheek flushed red.

"Sir, you are entirely mistaking me; I am sure you are mistaking the affair itself. I believe that the girl is as honest and good a girl as ever lived; and Robert Carr knows she is."

"Then what is it that he proposes to himself in frequenting her society? If he has no end at all in view, why does he do it?"

"I don't think he has any end in view. There is really nothing in it—as I believe; we all form acquaintances and drop them. Marmaduke Carr need not put himself in a fever."

"We form acquaintances in our own sphere of life, mind you, young sir; they are the safer ones. I wonder some of the ladies don't give a hint to the two Miss Hughes's to take better care of their sister—she's but a young thing. At any rate, William, do not you mix yourself up in it."

"I have not done it, indeed, sir. As to my walking through the fields with them, when we met, as I tell you, accidentally, I could not help myself, friendly as I am with Robert Carr. There was no harm in it; I should do it again to-morrow under the circumstances; and if old Carr speaks to me, I shall tell him so."

The carriage came up, and no more was said. Philip had halted to do something to the harness. Mrs. Arkell came out.

She was tall, and for her age rather an elegant woman. Her face must once have been delicately beautiful: it was easy to be seen whence William had inherited his refined features; but she was simple in manner as a child.

"What have you been doing, William? Papa was speaking crossly to you, was he not?"

She sometimes used the old fond word to him, "papa." She looked fondly at her son, and spoke in a joking manner. In truth, William gave them little cause to be "cross" with him; he was a good son, in every sense of the term.

"Something a little short of high treason," replied William, laughing, as he helped her in; "Papa can tell you, if he likes."

Mr. Arkell took the reins, Philip got up behind, and they drove out of the yard. William Arkell went indoors, put down a roll of music he had been carrying, and then left the house again.

Turning to his right hand as he quitted the iron gates, he continued his way up the street towards the busier portion of the city. It was not his intention to go so far as that now. He crossed over to a wide, handsome turning on the left, and was speedily close upon the precincts of the cathedral. It was almost within the cathedral precincts that the house of Mrs. Daniel Arkell was situated. Not a large house, as was Mr. Arkell's, but a pretty compact red-brick residence, with a small garden lying before the front windows, which looked out on the Dean's garden and the cathedral elm-trees.

William Arkell opened the door and entered. In a little bit of a room on the left, sat Peter Arkell, deep in some abstruse Greek play. This little room was called Peter's study, for it had been appropriated to the boy and his books ever since he could remember. William looked in, just gave him a nod, and then entered the room on the other side the entrance-passage.

Two ladies sat in this, both of them in mourning: Mrs. Daniel Arkell, a stout, comfortable-looking woman, in widow's weeds; Mildred in a pretty dress of black silk. Peter and William were about the same age; Mildred was two years younger. She was a quiet, sensible, lady-like girl, with a gentle face and the sweetest look possible in her soft brown eyes. She had not been educated fashionably, according to the custom of the present day; she had never been to school, but had received, as we are told of Moses Primrose, a "sort of miscellaneous education at home." She possessed a thorough knowledge of her own language, knew a good deal of Latin, insensibly acquired through being with Peter when he took his earlier lessons in it from his father, read aloud beautifully, wrote an excellent letter, and was a quick arithmetician, made shirts and pastry to perfection, and was well read in our best authors. Not a single accomplishment, save dancing, had she been taught; and yet she was in mind and manners essentially a gentlewoman.

If Mildred was loved by her own mother, so was she by Mrs. George Arkell. Possessing no daughter of her own, Mrs. George seemed to cling to Mildred as one. She cherished within her heart a secret wish that her son might sometime call Mildred his wife. This may be marvelled at—it may seem strange that Mrs. George Arkell should wish to unite her attractive, wealthy, and accomplished son with his portionless and comparatively homely cousin; but she knew Mildred's worth and the sunshine of happiness she would bring into any home. Mrs. George Arkell never breathed a hint of this wish: whether wisely or not, perhaps the sequel did not determine.

And what thought Mildred herself? She knew nothing of this secretly-cherished scheme; but if ever there appeared to her a human being gifted with all earthly perfections, it was William Arkell. Perhaps the very contrast he presented to her brother—a contrast brought palpably before her sight every day of her life—enhanced the feeling. Peter was plain in person, so tall as to be ungainly, thin as a lath, and stooping perpetually, and in manner shy and awkward; whilst William was all ease and freedom; very handsome, though with a look of delicate health on his refined features; danced minuets with Mildred to perfection—relics of the old dancing days, which pleased the two elder ladies; breathed love-songs to her on his flute, painted her pretty landscapes in water-colours, with which she decorated the walls of her own little parlour, drove her out sometimes in his father's carriage—the one you have just seen start on its expedition; passed many an evening reading to her, and quoting Shakespeare; and, in short, made love to her as much as it was possible to make it, not in words. But the misfortune of all this was, that while it told upon her heart, and implanted there its never-dying fruit, he only regarded her as a cousin or a sister. Brought up in this familiar intercourse with Mildred, he never gave a thought to any warmer feeling on either side, or suspected that such intimacy might lead to one, still less that it had, even then, led to it on hers. Had he been aware of his mother's hope of uniting them, it is impossible to say whether he would have yielded to it: he had asked himself the question many a time in his later life, and he could never answer.

The last remains of the setting sun threw a glow on the room, for the house faced the west. It was a middling-sized, comfortable apartment, with a sort of bright look about it. They rarely sat in any other. There was a drawing-room above, but it was seldom used.

"Well, aunt! well, Mildred! How are you this evening?"

Mildred looked up from her work at the well-known, cheery voice; the soft colour had already mantled in her cheek at the well-known step. William took a book from his pocket, wrapped in paper.

"I got it for you this afternoon, Mildred. Mind and don't spoil your eyes over it: its print is curiously small."

She looked at him with a smile amidst her glow of blushing thanks; she always smiled when he gave her the same caution. Her sight was remarkably strong—William's, on the contrary, was not so, and he was already obliged to use glasses when trying fresh pieces of music.

"William, my dear," began Mrs. Daniel, "I have a favour to ask your father. Will you carry it to him for me?"

"It's granted already," returned William, with the free confidence of an indulged son. "What is it?"

"I want to get over to see those children, the Carrs. Poor Mrs. John, when she was dying, asked me if I would go over now and then, and I feel as if I were neglecting the promise, for it is full six months since I was there. The coaches start so early in the morning, and I thought, if your father would let me have the carriage for the day, and Philip to drive me; Mildred can sit in the back seat—"

"I'll drive you, aunt," interrupted William. "Fix your own day, and we'll go."

But Mildred had looked up, a vivid blush of annoyance on her cheek.

"I do not care to go, mamma; I'd rather not go to Squire Carr's."

"You be quiet, Mildred," said William. "You are not going to see the squire, you are going to see the squire's grandchildren. Talking about the Carrs, aunt, I have just been undergoing a lecture on their score."

"On the score of the Carrs?"

"It's true. I happened on Sunday to be crossing the opposite fields, on my way from Mrs. Pembroke's, and came upon Robert Carr and Miss Martha Ann Hughes, and walked with them to the bridge. Somebody carried the news to old Marmaduke, and he came down this evening, all flurry and fire, to my father, complaining that I was 'encouraging' the thing. Such nonsense! He need not be afraid that there's any harm in it."

Mrs. Dan Arkell gave her head a shake, as if she were not so sure upon the latter point as her nephew. Prudent age—impulsive youth: how widely different do they judge of things! William was turning to the door.

"You are not going?" said Mrs. Dan, and Mildred looked up from her work, a yearning wistfulness in her eye.

"I must, this evening; I asked young Monk to come in and bring his violin, and he'll be waiting for me, if I don't mind. Good-bye, Aunt Dan; pleasant dreams to you, Mildred!"

But as William went out, he opened the door of Peter's study, and stood there gossiping at least twenty minutes. He might have stood longer, but for the sight of two gentlemen who were passing along the road arm-in-arm, and he rushed out impulsively, forgetting to say good-evening to Peter.

CHAPTER II

THE MISS HUGHES'S HOME

Marmaduke Carr, of whom mention has been made, was one of the Westerbury manufacturers—a widower, and a wealthy man. He had only one son living—Robert; two other children had died in infancy. Robert Carr, about thirty years of age now, was not renowned for his steadiness of conduct;

indeed, he had been a sad spendthrift, and innumerable unpleasant scenes had resulted therefrom between him and his father. It could not be said that his heart was bad; but his head was certainly light. Half the town declared that Robert Carr had no real evil in him; that his faults were but the result of youth and carelessness; that he would make a worthy man yet. The other half prophesied that he would be safe to come to a bad ending, like wicked Harry in the spelling-book. One of his escapades Mr. Carr was particularly sore upon. After a violent quarrel between them—for each possessed a temper of his own—Robert had started off clandestinely; that is, without saying a word to anyone. At the end of a month he returned, and bills to the amount of something like a hundred pounds came in to his father. Mr. Robert had been seeing life in London.

In one sense of the word, the fault was Mr. Carr's. There cannot be a greater mistake than to bring up a son to idleness, and this had been the case with Robert Carr. He would settle to nothing, and his father had virtually winked at it. Ostensibly, Robert had entered the manufactory; but he would not attend to the business: he said he hated it. One day there, and the other five days away. Idling his hours with his friends in the town; over at his uncle's, Squire Carr's, shooting, fishing, hunting; going somewhere out by the morning coach, and in again; anything, in fact, to avoid work and kill time. This should have been checked in the onset; it was not, and when Mr. Carr awoke to the consequences of his indulgent supineness, the habits had grown to a height that refused control. "Let him take his pleasure a bit," Mr. Carr had said to his own heart at first, "youth's never the worse for a little roaming before settling down. I have made plenty of money, and there's only Bob to inherit it." Dangerous doctrine; mistaken conclusions: and Mr. Carr lived to find them so.

Squire Carr was his elder brother. He was several years older than Marmaduke. He possessed a small property, and farmed it himself, and was consequently called "Squire" Carr—as many of those small landed proprietors were called by their neighbours in the days now passing away. Squire Carr, a widower of many years, had one son only—John. This John had made a marriage almost in his boyhood, and had three children born to him—Valentine, Benjamin, and Emma, and then his wife died. Next he married a second wife, and after some years she died, leaving several young children. They all lived with the squire, but the three elder children were now nearly grown up. It was to this house, and to see these younger children, that Mrs. Dan Arkell purposed going, if she could borrow Mr. Arkell's carriage. They lived about eight miles off, near to Eckford, a market town. By the coach road, indeed, it was considerably more.

Squire Carr and his brother were not very intimate. The squire would ride into Westerbury on the market day, or drive in with his son in the dogcart, but not once in three months did they call at Marmaduke's. There was no similarity between them; there was as little cordiality. The squire was of a grasping, mean, petty nature, and so was his son after him. Marmaduke was open-handed and liberal, despising meanness above every earthly failing.

Robert Carr had plunged into other costly escapades since that first one of the impromptu sojourn in London, and his father's patience was becoming exhausted. Latterly he, Robert, had struck up an acquaintance with a young girl, Martha Ann Hughes; and there is no doubt that this vexed Mr. Carr more than any previous aggression had done. The Carrs, in their way, were proud. They were really of good family, and in the past generation had been of some account. A horrible fear had taken hold of Mr. Carr, that Robert, in his infatuation, might be mad enough to marry this girl, and he would have deemed it the very worst calamity that could fall upon his life.

For Robert was seen with this girl in public, and the girl and her family were, in their station, respectable people; and the other evening, when Mr. Carr had spoken out his mind in rather broad terms, Robert had flown in a passion, and answered that he'd "shoot himself rather than hurt a hair of her head." The fear that he might marry her entered then and there into Mr. Carr's head; and it grew into a torment.

The two gentlemen, passing Mrs. Dan Arkell's house as William flew out, were Robert Carr and a young clergyman with whom he was intimate, the Reverend John Bell. Mr. Bell had had escapades of his own, and that probably caused him to tolerate, or to see no harm in, Robert Carr's. Certain it is they were firm, almost inseparable friends; and rumour went that Mr. Bell was upon visiting terms at Miss Hughes's house, introduced to it by Robert. The Reverend John Bell had had his first year's curacy in Westerbury; he was now in priest's orders, hoping for employment, and, meanwhile, helping occasionally in the services at a church called St. James-the-Less, whose incumbent, one of the minor canons, had fits of gout.

William joined them. He did not say anything to Robert Carr then, in the presence of Mr. Bell; but he did intend, the first opportunity, to recommend him to drop the affair as profitless in every way, and one there seemed to be trouble over. They walked together to the end of the old cathedral outer wall, and there separated. William turned to the left, which would lead him to his home; while Mr. Bell passed through a heavy stone archway on the right, and was then within the precincts of the cathedral, in a large open space, surrounded by the prebendal and other houses; the deanery, the cloisters, and the huge college schoolroom being on one side. This was the back of the cathedral; it rose towering there behind the cloisters. Mr. Bell made straight for the residence of the incumbent of St. James-the-Less, the Reverend Mr. Elwin—a little old-fashioned house, with no windows to speak of, on the side opposite the deanery.

Robert Carr had turned neither to the right nor the left, but continued his way straight on. Passing an old building called the Palmery—which belonged, as may be said, to the cathedral—he turned into a by-street, and in three or four minutes was at the end of the houses on that side the town. Before him, at some little distance, in the midst of its churchyard, stood the church of St. James-the-Less, surrounded by the open country. The only house near it, a poor little dwelling, was inhabited by the clerk. That is, it had been inhabited by him; but the man was now dead, and a hot dispute was raging in the parish whether a successor should be appointed to him or not. Meanwhile, the widow benefited, for she was allowed to continue in the house until the question should be settled.

Robert Carr, however, had no intention of going as far as the church. He stopped at the last house but one in the street—a small, but very neat dwelling, with two brass plates on the door. You may read them. "Mr. Edward Hughes, Builder," was on one; "The Misses Hughes, Dressmakers," was on the other.

Yes, this was the house inhabited by the young person who was so upsetting the equanimity of Mr. Carr. Edward Hughes was a builder, in business for himself in a small way, and his two elder sisters were the dressmakers—worthy people enough all, and of good report, but certainly not the class from which it might be supposed Robert Carr would take a wife.

Two gaunt, ungainly women were these two elder Miss Hughes's, with wide mouths and standing-out teeth. The eldest, Sophia, was the manager and mistress of the home, and a clever one too, and a shrewd woman; the second, Mary, not in the least clever or shrewd, confined her attention wholly to her business, and went out to work by day at ladies' houses, and sat up half the night working after she got home.

She had been out on this day, but had returned, by some mutual arrangement with her patrons, earlier than usual; for it was a busy time with them at home, and the house was full of work. They were at work at a silk gown now; both sisters bending their heads over it, and stitching away as fast as they could stitch. The parlour faced the street, and some one else was seated at the window, peeping out, between the staves of the Venetian blind.

This was Martha Ann, a young girl of twenty, pretty, modest, and delicate looking; so entirely different was she in person from her sisters, that people might have suspected the relationship. Perhaps it was from the great contrast she presented to themselves that the Miss Hughes's had reared her in a superior manner. How they had loved the pretty little child, so many years younger than themselves, they alone knew. They had sent her to school, working hard to keep her there; and when they brought her home it was, to use their own phrase, "to be a lady"—not to work. The plan was not a wise one, and they might yet live to learn it.

"I wish to goodness you could have put Mrs. Dewsbury off for to-morrow, Mary!" exclaimed the elder sister.

"But I couldn't," replied Mary. "The lady's-maid said I must go to-morrow, whether or not. In two days Mrs. Dewsbury starts on her visit."

"Well, all I know is, we shall never get these dresses home in time."

"I must sit up to-night—that's all," said Mary Hughes, with equanimity.

"I must sit up, too, for the matter of that," rejoined the elder sister. "The worst is, after no bed, one is so languid the next day; one can't get through half the work."

Martha Ann rose from her seat, and came to the table.

"I wish you would let me try to help you, Sophia. I'm sure I could do seams, and such-like straightforward work."

"You'd pucker them, child. No; we are not going to let your eyes be tried over close sewing."

"I'll tell you what you can do, Martha Ann," said the younger of the two. "You can go in the kitchen, and make me a cup of coffee. I feel dead tired, and it will waken me up."

"There now, Mary!" cried the young girl. "I knew you were not in bed last night, and you are talking of sitting up this! I shall tell Edward."

"Yes, I was in bed. I went to bed at three, and slept till six. Go and make the coffee, child."

Martha Ann quitted the room. Mary Hughes watched the door close, and then turned to her sister, and began to speak eagerly, dropping her voice to a half whisper.

"I say, Sophia, I met Mrs. Pycroft to-day, and she began upon me like anything. What do you think she said?"

"How do I know what she said?" returned Miss Sophia, indifferently, and speaking with her mouth full of pins, for she was deep in the intricacies of fitting one pattern to another. "Where did you meet her?"

"Just by the market-house. It was at dinner-time. I had run out for some more wadding, for me and the lady's-maid found we had made a miscalculation, and hadn't got enough to complete the cloak, and I met her as I was running back again. She never said, 'How be you?' or 'How bain't you?' but she begins upon me all sharp—'What be you doing with Martha Ann?' It took me so aback that for a moment I couldn't answer her, and she didn't give time for it, either. 'Is young Mr. Carr going to marry her?' she goes on. So of course I said he wasn't going to marry her that I knew of; and then—"

"And more idiot you for saying anything of the sort!" indignantly interrupted Sophia Hughes, dropping all the pins in a heap out of her mouth that she might speak freely. "It's no business of Mother Pycroft's, or of anybody else's."

The meeker younger sister—and as a very reed had she always been in the strong hands of the elder—paused for an instant, and then spoke deprecatingly.

"But Mr. Robert Carr is not going to marry her that we know of, Sophia. Where was the harm of my saying the truth?"

"A great deal of harm in saying it to that gabbling, interfering Mother Pycroft. She has wanted to put her nose into everything all these years and years since poor mother died. What do you say?" proceeded Miss Sophia, drowning her sister's feeble attempt to speak. "'A good heart—been kind to us?' That doesn't compensate for the worry she has been. She's a mischief-making old cat."

"She went on like anything to-day," resumed Mary Hughes, when she thought she might venture to speak again; "saying that young Mr. Carr ought not to come to the house unless he came all open and honourable, and had got a marriage-ring at his fingers' ends; and if we didn't mind, we should have Martha Ann a town's talk."

Sophia Hughes flung down her work, her eyes ablaze with anger.

"If you were not my sister, and the poorest, weakest mortal that ever stepped, I'd strike you for daring to repeat such words to me! A town's talk! Martha Ann!"

"Well, Sophia, you need not snap me up so," was the deprecating answer. "She says that folks are talking already of you and me, blaming us for allowing the acquaintance with young Mr. Carr. And I think they are," candidly added the young woman.

"Where's the harm? Martha Ann is as good as Robert Carr any day."

"But if people don't think so? If his folks don't think so? All the Carrs are as proud as Lucifer."

"And a fine lot Robert Carr has got to be proud of!" retorted Sophia. "Look at the scrapes he has been in, and the money he has spent! A good, wholesome, respectable attachment might be the salvation of him."

"Perhaps so. But then—but then—I wish you'd not be cross with me, Sophia—there'd be more chance of it if the young lady were in his own condition of life. Sophia, we are naturally fond of Martha Ann, and think there's nobody like her—and there's not, for the matter of that; but we can't expect other people to think so. I wouldn't let Martha Ann be spoken of disparagingly in the town for the world. I'd lay my life down first."

Sophia Hughes had taken up her work again. She put in a few pins in silence. Her anger was subsiding.

"I'll take care of Martha Ann. The town knows me, I hope, and knows that it might trust me. If I saw so much as the faintest look of disrespect offered by Robert Carr to Martha Ann, I should tell him he must drop the acquaintance. Until I do, he's free to come here. And the next time I come across old Mother Pycroft she'll hear the length of my tongue."

Mary Hughes dared say no more. But in the days to come, when the blight of scandal had tarnished the fair name of her young sister, she was wont to whisper, with many tears, that she had warned Sophia what might be the ending, and had not been listened to.

"Here he is!" exclaimed Sophia, as the form of some one outside darkened the window.

And once more putting down her work, but not in anger this time, she went to open the front door, at which Robert Carr was knocking.

CHAPTER III

THE ADVENT OF CHARLOTTE TRAVICE

Mrs. George Arkell sat near her breakfast-table, deeply intent on a letter recently delivered. The apartment was a rather spacious one, handsomely fitted up. It was the general sitting-room of the family; the fine drawing-room on the other side of the hall being very much kept, as must be confessed, for state occasions. A comfortable room, this; its walls hung with paintings in water-colours, many of them William's doings, and its pleasant window looking across the wide yard, to the iron railings and the street beyond it. The room was as yet in the shade, for it faced due south; but the street yonder lay basking in the bright sun of the September morning; and Mrs. Arkell looked through the open window, and felt almost glad at the excuse the letter afforded her for going abroad in it.

Letters were not then hourly matters, as they are now; no, nor daily ones. Perhaps a quiet country lady did not receive a dozen in a year: certainly Mrs. Arkell did not, and she lingered on, looking at the one in her hand, long after her husband and son had quitted the breakfast-table for the manufactory.

"It is curious the child should write to me," was her final comment, and the words were spoken aloud. "I must carry it to Mrs. Dan, and talk it over with her."

She rang the bell for the breakfast things to be removed, and presently proceeded to the kitchen to consult with the cook about dinner—for consulting with the cook, in those staid, old-fashioned households, was far more the custom than the present "orders." That over, Mrs. Arkell attired herself, and went out to Mrs. Daniel Arkell's. Mrs. Dan was surprised to see her so early, and laid her spectacles inside the Bible she was reading, to mark the place.

"Betty," began Mrs. Arkell, addressing her sister-in-law by the abbreviation bestowed on her at her baptism, "you remember the Travices, who left here some years ago to make their fortune, as they said, in London?"

"To be sure," replied Mrs. Dan.

"Well, I fear they can't have made much. Here's a letter comes this morning from their eldest girl. It's very odd that she should write to me. A pretty little thing she was, of about eight or ten, I remember, when they left Westerbury."

"What does she write about?" interrupted Mrs. Dan. "I'm sure they have been silent enough hitherto. Nobody, so far as I know, has ever heard a word from any of them since they left."

"She writes to me as an old friend of her father's and mother's, she says, to ask if I can interest myself for her with any school down here. I infer, from the wording of the letter, that since their death, the children have not been well off."

"John Travice and his wife are dead, then?"

"So it would seem. She says—'We have had a great deal of anxiety since dear mamma died, the only friend we had left to us.' She must speak of herself and her sister, for there were but those two. Will you read the letter, Betty?"

Mrs. Dan took her spectacles from between the leaves of the Bible, and read the letter, not speaking immediately.

"She signs herself C. Travice," remarked Mrs. George; "but I really forget her name. Whether it was Catherine or Cordelia—"

"It was Charlotte," interposed Mrs. Dan. "We used to call her Lottie."

"The curious thing in the affair is, why she should write to me," continued Mrs. George Arkell. "You were so much more intimate with them, that I can only think she has made a mistake in the address, and really meant the letter for you."

A smile flitted over Mrs. Dan's face. "No mistake at all, as I should believe. You are Mrs. Arkell, you know; I am only Mrs. Dan. She must remember quite well that you have weight in the town, and I have none. She knows which of us is most capable of helping her."

"But, Betty, I and George had little or no acquaintance at all with the Travices," rejoined Mrs. Arkell, unconvinced. "We met them two or three times at your house; but I don't think they were ever inside ours. You brought one of the little girls to tea once with Mildred, I recollect: it must have been this eldest one who now writes. You, on the contrary, were intimate with them. Why, did you not stand godmother to one of the little ones?"

"To the youngest," assented Mrs. Dan, "and quite a fuss there was over it. Mrs. Travice wanted her to be named Betty; short, after me; but the captain wouldn't hear of it. He said Betty was old-fashioned— gone quite out of date. If you'll believe me it was not settled when we started for the church; but I decided it there, for when Mr. Elwin took the baby in his arms, and said, 'Name this child,' I spoke up and said, 'Elizabeth.' She grew to be a pretty little thing, too, meek and mild as a lamb; Charlotte had a temper."

"Well, I still retain the opinion that she must have been under the impression she was addressing you. 'I write to you as an old friend of papa and mamma's,' you see, she says. Now that can't in any way apply to me. But I don't urge this as a plea for not accepting the letter," Mrs. George hastened to add; "I'm sure we shall be pleased to do anything we can for her. I have talked the matter over with George, and we think it would be only kind to invite her to come to us for a month or so, while we see what can be done. We shall pay her coach fare down, and any other little matter, so that it will be no expense to her."

"It is exceedingly kind of you," remarked Mrs. Dan Arkell. "And when you write, tell her we will all try and make her visit a pleasant one," she added, in the honest simplicity of her heart. "Mildred will be a companion to her.'

"I shall write to-day. The letter is dated Upper Stamford-street: but I'm sure I don't know in what part of London Upper Stamford-street lies," observed Mrs. Arkell, who had never been so far as London in her life, and would as soon have thought of going a journey to Cape Horn. "Where's Mildred?"

"She's in the kitchen, helping Ann with the damson jam. I did say I'd not have any made this year, sugar is so expensive, but Mildred pleaded for it. And what she says is true, that poor Peter comes in tired to death, and relishes a bit of jam with his tea, especially damson jam."

"I fear Peter's heart is not in his occupation, Betty."

Mrs. Dan shook her head. "It has never been that. From the time Peter was first taken to the Cathedral, a little fellow in petticoats, his heart has been set upon sometime being one of its clergy; but that is out of the question now: there's no help for it, you know."

Mildred came in, bright and radiant; she always liked the visits of her aunt George. They told her the news about Miss Travice, and showed her the letter.

"Played together when we were children, I and Charlotte Travice," she said, laughing; "I have nearly forgotten it. I hope she is a nice girl; it will be pleasant to have her down here."

"Mildred, I should like to take you back with me for the day. Will you come? Can you spare her, Betty?"

Mildred glanced at her mother, her lips parting with hope; dutiful and affectionate, she deferred to her mother in all things, never putting forth her own wishes. Mrs. Dan could spare her, and said so. Mildred flew to her chamber, attired herself, and set forth with her aunt through the warm and sunny streets— warm, sunny, bright as her own heart.

Very much to the surprise of Mrs. Arkell, as she turned in at the iron gates, she saw the carriage standing before the door, and the servant Philip in readiness to attend it. "Is your master going out?" she inquired of the man.

"Mr. William is, ma'am."

"Where to, do you know?"

"I think it is only to Mr. Palmer's," returned Philip. "I know Mr. William said we should not be away above an hour."

William appeared in the distance, coming from the manufactory with a fleet step, and a square flat parcel in his hand.

"I am going to Mr. Palmer's to take this," he said to his mother, indicating the parcel as he threw it into the carriage; "it contains some papers that my father promised to get for him as soon as possible to-day. He was going to send Philip alone, but I said I should like the drive. You have just come in time, Mildred; get up."

The soft pink bloom mantled in her face; but she rather drew away from the carriage than approached it. She never went out upon William's invitation alone.

"Why not, my dear?" said Mrs. Arkell, "it will do you good. You will be back in time for dinner."

William was looking round all the while, as he waited to help her up, a half laugh upon his face. Mildred's roses deepened, and she stepped in. Philip came round to his young master.

"Am I to go now, sir?"

"Go now? of course; why should you not go? There's the back seat, isn't there?"

Perhaps Philip's doubts did not altogether refer to seats. He threw back the seat, and waited. William took his place by his cousin's side, and drove away, utterly unconscious of her feelings or the man's thoughts. Had he not been accustomed to this familiar intercourse with Mildred all his life?

And Mrs. Arkell went indoors and sat down to write her letter to Charlotte Travice. Westerbury had nearly forgotten these Travices; they were not natives of the place. Captain Travice—but it should be observed that he had been captain of only a militia regiment—had settled at Westerbury sometime after the conclusion of the war, and his two children were born there. His income was but a slender one, still it was sufficient; but it came into the ex-captain's head one day, that, for the sake of his two little daughters, he ought to make a fortune if he could. Supposing that might be easier of accomplishment in the great metropolis, than in a sober, unspeculative cathedral town, he departed forthwith; but the fortune, as Mrs. Arkell shrewdly surmised, had never been made; and after various vicissitudes—ups and downs, as people phrase them—John Travice finally departed this life in their lodgings in Upper Stamford-street, and his wife did not long survive him. Of the two daughters, Charlotte had been the best educated; what money there was to spare for such purposes, had been spent upon her; the younger one was made, of necessity, a household drudge.

Charlotte responded at once to Mrs. Arkell's invitation, and within a week of it was travelling down to Westerbury by the day-coach. It arrived in the town at seven o'clock, and rarely varied by a minute. Have you forgotten those old coach days? I have not. Mr. Arkell and his son stood outside the iron gates, Philip waiting in attendance; and as the coach with its four fine horses came up the street, the guard blew his horn about ten times, a signal that it was going to stop to set down a passenger—for Mr. Arkell had himself spoken to the guard, and charged him to take good care of the young lady on her journey. The coachman drew up at the gates, and touched his hat to Mr. Arkell, and the guard leaped down and touched his.

"All right, sir. The young lady's here."

He opened the coach door, and she stepped out, dressed in expensive mourning; a tall, showy, handsome girl, affable in manner, ready of speech; altogether fascinating; just the one—just the one to turn the head and win the heart of a young fellow such as William Arkell. They might have foreseen it even in that first hour.

"Oh, how kind it is of you to have me!" she exclaimed, as she quite fell into Mrs. Arkell's arms in the hall, and burst into tears. "But I thought you had no daughter?" she added, recovering herself and looking at the young lady who stood by Mrs. Arkell.

"It is my niece Mildred, my dear; but she is to me as a daughter. I asked her to come and help welcome you this evening."

"I am sure I shall love you very much!" exclaimed Miss Travice, kissing Mildred five or six times. "What a sweet face you have!"

A sudden shyness came over Mildred. The warm greeting and the words were both new to her. She returned a courteous word of welcome, drew a little apart, and glanced at William. He seemed to have enough to do gazing at the visitor.

Philip was coming in with the luggage. Mrs. Arkell took her hand.

"I will show you your room, Miss Travice; and if—"

"Oh, pray don't call me 'Miss Travice,' or anything so formal," was the young lady's interruption. "Begin with 'Charlotte' at once, or I shall fear you are not glad to see me."

Mrs. Arkell smiled; her young visitor was winning upon her greatly. She led her to a very nice room on the first floor.

"This will be your chamber, my dear; it is over our usual sitting-room. My room and Mr. Arkell's is on the opposite side the corridor, over the drawing-room. You face the street, you see; and across there to the right are the cathedral towers."

"What a charming house you have, Mrs. Arkell! So large and nice."

"It is larger than we require. Let me look at you, my dear, and see what resemblance I can trace. I remember your father and mother."

She held the young lady before her. A very pretty face, certainly—especially now, for Charlotte laughed and blushed.

"Oh, Mrs. Arkell, I am not fit to be seen; I feel as dusty as can be. You cannot think how dusty the roads were; I shall look better to-morrow."

"You have the bright dark eyes and the clear complexion of your father; but I don't see that you are like him in features—yours are prettier. But now, my dear, tell me—in writing to me, did you not think you were writing to Mrs. Daniel Arkell?"

"Mrs. Daniel Arkell! No, I did not. Who is she? I don't remember anything about her."

"But Mrs. Daniel was your mother's friend—far more intimate with her than I was. I am delighted at the mistake, if it was one; for Mrs. Dan might otherwise have gained the pleasure of your visit, instead of me."

"I don't think I made a mistake," said Charlotte, more dubiously than she had just spoken; "I used to hear poor mamma speak of the Arkells of Westerbury; and one day lately, in looking over some of her old letters and papers, I found your address. The thought came into my mind at once to write to you, and ask if you could help me to a situation. I believe papa was respected in Westerbury; and it struck me that somebody here might want a teacher, or governess, and engage me for his sake. You know we are of gentle blood, Mrs. Arkell, though we have been so poor of late years."

"I will do anything to help you that I can," was the kind answer. "Have you lost both father and mother?"

"Why yes," returned Charlotte, with a surprised air, as if she had thought all the world knew that. "Papa has been dead several months—twelve, I think, nearly; mamma has been dead five or six."

"And—I suppose—your poor papa did not leave much money?"

"Not a penny," freely answered Charlotte. "He had a few shares in some mining company at the time of his death; they were worth nothing then, but they afterwards went up to what is called a premium, and the brokers sold them for us. They did not realize much, but it was sufficient to keep mamma as long as she lived."

"And what have you done since?"

"Not much," sighed Charlotte; "I had a situation as daily governess; but, oh! it was so uncomfortable. There were five girls, and no discipline, no regularity; it was at a clergyman's, too. They live near to us, in Upper Stamford-street. I am so glad I wrote to you! Betsey did not want me to write; she thought it looked intrusive."

"Betsey!" echoed Mrs. Arkell.

"My sister Elizabeth—we call her Betsey. She is younger than I am."

"Oh yes, to be sure. I wondered you did not speak of her in your letter; Mrs. Daniel Arkell is her godmother. Where is she?"

"At Mrs. Dundyke's."

"Who is Mrs. Dundyke?"

"She keeps the house where we live, in Stamford-street. She is not a lady, you know; a worthy sort of person, and all that, but quite an inferior woman. Not but that she was always kind to us; she was very kind and attentive to mamma in her last illness. I can't bear her," candidly continued the young lady, "and she can't bear me; but she likes Betsey, and has asked her to stop there, free of cost, for a little while. Her daughter died and left two little children, and Betsey is to make herself useful with them."

"But why did you not mention Betsey? why did you not bring her?" cried Mrs. Arkell, feeling vexed at the omission. "She would have been as welcome to us as you are, my dear."

Miss Charlotte Travice shook back her flowing hair, and there was a little curl of contempt on her pretty nose. "You are very kind, Mrs. Arkell, but Betsey is better where she is. I could not think of taking her out with me."

"Why so?" asked Mrs. Arkell, rather surprised.

"Oh, you'd not say, why so, if you saw her. She is quite a plain, homely sort of young person; she has not been educated for anything else. Nobody would believe we were sisters; and Betsey knows that, and is humble accordingly. Of course some one had to wait upon mamma and me, for lodging-house servants are the most unpleasant things upon earth, and there was only Betsey."

Mrs. Arkell went downstairs, leaving her young guest to follow when she was ready. Mrs. Arkell did not understand the logic of the last admissions, and certainly did not admire the spirit in which they appeared to be spoken.

The hours for meals were early at Mr. Arkell's; dinner at one, tea at five; but the tea had this evening been put off, in politeness to Miss Travice. She came down, a fashionable-looking young lady, in a thin black dress of some sort of gauze, with innumerable rucheings and quillings of crape upon it. Certainly her attire—as they found when the days went on—betrayed little symptom of a straitened purse.

She took her place at the tea-table, all smiles and sweetness; she glanced shyly at William; she captivated Mr. Arkell's heart; she caused Mrs. Arkell completely to forget the few words concerning Betsey which had so jarred upon her ear; and before that tea-drinking was over, they were all ready to fall in love with her. All, save one.

Then she went round the room, a candle in her hand, and looked at the pictures; she freely said which of them she liked best; she sat down to the piano, unasked, and played a short, striking piece from memory. They asked her if she could sing; she answered by breaking into the charming old song "Robin Adair;" it was one of William Arkell's favourites, and he stood by enraptured, half bewildered with this pleasant inroad on their quiet routine of existence.

"You play, I am sure," she suddenly said to him.

He had no wish to deny it, and took his flute from its case. He was a finished player. It is an instrument very nearly forgotten now, but it never would have been forgotten had its players managed it as did William Arkell. They began trying duets together, and the evening passed insensibly. William loved music passionately, and could hardly tear himself away from it to run with Mildred home.

"Well, Mildred, and how do you like her?" was Mrs. Dan's first question.

"I—I can hardly tell," was the hesitating answer.

"Not tell!" repeated Mrs. Dan; "you have surely found out whether she is pleasant or disagreeable?"

"She is very pretty, and her manners are perfectly charming. But—still—"

"Still, what?" said Mrs. Dan, wondering.

"Well, mother—but you know I never like to speak ill of anyone—there is something in her that strikes me as not being true."

CHAPTER IV

ROBERT CARR'S REQUEST

The time went on. The month for which Charlotte Travice had been invited had lengthened itself into nearly three, and December had come in.

Mrs. Dan Arkell (wholly despising Mildred's acknowledged impression of the new visitor, and treating her to a sharp lecture for entertaining it) had made a call on Miss Travice the following morning, and offered Mildred's services as a companion to her. But in a very short time Mildred found she was not wanted. William was preferred. He was the young lady's companion, and nothing loth so to be; and his visits to Mildred's house, formerly so frequent, became rare almost as those of angels. It was Charlotte Travice now. She went out with him in the carriage; she was his partner in the dance; and the breathings on the flute grew into strains of love. Worse than all to Mildred—more hard to bear—William would laugh at the satire the London lady was pleased to tilt at her. It is true Mildred had no great pretension to beauty; not half as much as Charlotte; but William had found it enough before. In figure and manners Mildred was essentially a lady; and her face, with its soft brown eyes and its sweet expression, was not an unattractive one. It cannot be denied that a sore feeling arose in Mildred's heart, though not yet did she guess at the full calamity looming for that heart in the distance. She saw at present only the temporary annoyance; that this gaudy, handsome, off-hand stranger had come to ridicule, rival, and for the time supplant her. But she thought, then, it was but for the time; and she somewhat ungraciously longed for the day when the young lady should wing her flight back to London.

That expression we sometimes treat a young child to, when a second comes to supplant it, that "its nose is put out of joint," might decidedly have been now applied to Mildred. Charlotte Travice took her place in all ways. In the winter evening visiting—staid, old-fashioned, respectable visiting, which met at six o'clock and separated at midnight—Mildred was accustomed to accompany her uncle and aunt. Mrs.

Dan Arkell's visiting days were over; Peter, buried in his books, had never had any; and it had become quite a regular thing for Mildred to go with Mr. and Mrs. Arkell and William. They always drove round and called for her, leaving her at home on their return; and Mildred was generally indebted to her aunt for her pretty evening dresses—that lady putting forth as an excuse the plea that she should dislike to take out anyone ill-dressed. It was all altered now. Flies—as everybody knows—will hold but four, and there was no longer room for Mildred: Miss Travice occupied her place. Once or twice, when the winter parties were commencing, the fly came round as usual, and William walked; but Mildred, exceedingly tenacious of anything like intrusion, wholly declined this for the future, and refused the invitations, or went on foot, well cloaked, and escorted by Peter. William remonstrated, telling Mildred she was growing obstinate. Mildred answered that she would go out with them again when their visitor had returned to London.

But the visitor seemed in no hurry to return. She made a faint sort of pleading speech one day, that really she ought to go back for Christmas; she was sure Mr. and Mrs. Arkell must be tired of her: just one of those little pseudo moves to go, which, in politeness, cannot be accepted. Neither was it by Mr. and Mrs. Arkell: had the young lady remained with them a twelvemonth, in their proud and stately courtesy they would have pressed her to stay on longer. Mrs. Arkell had once or twice spoken of the primary object of her coming—the looking out for some desirable situation for her; but Miss Travice appeared to have changed her mind. She thought now she should not like to be in a country school, she said; but would get something in London on her return.

Mildred, naturally clear-sighted, felt convinced that Miss Travice was playing a part; that she was incessantly labouring to ingratiate herself into the good opinion of Mr. and Mrs. Arkell, and especially into that of William. "Oh, that they could see her as she really is!" thought Mildred; "false and false!" And Miss Travice took out her recreation tilting lance-shafts at Mildred.

"How is it you never learned music, Miss Arkell?" she was pleased to inquire one day, as she finished a brilliant piece, and gave herself a whirl round on the music-stool to speak.

"I can't tell," replied Mildred; "I did not learn it."

"Neither did you learn drawing?"

"No."

"Well, that's odd, isn't it? Mr. and Mrs. Dan Arkell must have been rather neglectful of you."

"I suppose they thought I should do as well without accomplishments as with them," was the composed answer. "To tell you the truth, Miss Travice, I dare say I shall."

"But everybody is accomplished now—at least, ladies are. I was surprised, I must confess, to find William Arkell a proficient in such things, for men rarely learn them. I wonder they did not have you taught music, if only to play with him. He has to put up with a stranger, you see—poor me."

Mildred's cheek burnt. "I have listened to him," she said; "hitherto he has found that sort of help enough, and liked it."

"He is very attractive," resumed Charlotte, throwing her bright eyes full at Mildred, a saucy expression in their depths; "don't you find him so?"

"I think you do," was Mildred's quiet answer.

"Of course I do. Haven't I just said it? And so, I dare say, do a great many others. Yesterday evening—by the way, you ought to have been here yesterday evening."

"Why ought I?"

"Mrs. Arkell meant to send for you, and told William to go; I heard her. He forgot it; and then it grew too late."

Mildred did not raise her eyes from her work. She was hemming a shirt-frill of curiously fine cambric—Mr. Arkell, behind the taste of his day, wore shirt-frills still. Mrs. Arkell rarely did any plain sewing herself; what her maid-servants did not do, was consigned to Mildred.

"Do you like work?" inquired Miss Charlotte, watching her nimble fingers, and quitting abruptly the former subject.

"Very much indeed."

Charlotte shrugged her shoulders with a spice of contempt. "I hate it; I once tried to make a tray-cloth, but it came out a bag; and mamma never gave me anything more."

"Who did the sewing at your house?"

"Betsey, of course. Mamma also used to do some, and groan over it like anything. I think ladies never ought—"

What Charlotte Travice was about to say ladies ought not to do was interrupted by the entrance of William. He had not been indoors since the early dinner, and looked pleased to see Mildred, who had come by invitation to spend a long afternoon.

"Which of you will go out with me?" he asked, somewhat abruptly; and his mother came into the room as he was speaking.

"Out where?" she asked.

"My father has a little matter of business at Purford to-day, and is sending me to transact it. It is only a message, and won't take me two minutes to deliver; but it is a private one, and must be spoken either by himself or me. I said I'd go if Charlotte would accompany me," he added, in his half-laughing, half-independent manner. "I did not know Mildred was here."

"And you come in and ask which of them will go," said Mrs. Arkell. "I think it must be Mildred. Charlotte, my dear, you will not feel offended if I say it is her turn? I like to be just and fair. It is you who have had all the drives lately; Mildred has had none."

Charlotte did not answer. Mildred felt that it was her turn, and involuntarily glanced at William; but he said not a word to second his mother's wish. The sensitive blood flew to her face, and she spoke, she hardly knew what—something to the effect that she would not deprive Miss Travice of the drive. William spoke then.

"But if you would like to go, Mildred? It is a long time since you went out, now I come to think of it."

Now I come to think of it! Oh, how the admission of indifference chilled her heart!

"Not this afternoon, thank you," she said, with decision. "I will go with you another opportunity."

"Then, Charlotte, you must make haste, or we shall not be home by dark," he said. "Philip is bringing the carriage round."

Mildred stood at the window and watched the departure, hating herself all the while for standing there; but there was fascination in the sight, in the midst of its pain. Would she win the prize, this new stranger? Mildred shivered outwardly and inwardly as the question crossed her mind.

She saw them drive away—Charlotte in her new violet bonnet, with its inward trimming of pretty pink ribbons, her prettier face raised to his—William bending down and speaking animatedly—sober old Philip, who had been in the family ten years, behind them. Purford was a little place, about five miles off, on the road to Eckford; and they might be back by dusk, if they chose. It was not much past three now, and the winter afternoon was fine.

Would she win him? Mildred returned to her seat, and worked on at the cambric frill, the question running riot in her brain. A conviction within her—a prevision, if you will—whispered that it would be a marriage particularly distasteful to Mr. and Mrs. Arkell. They did not yet dream of it, and would have been thankful to have their eyes opened to the danger. Mildred knew this; she saw it as clearly as though she had read it in a book; but she was too honourable to breathe it to them.

When the frill was finished, she folded it up, and told her aunt she would take her departure; Peter had talked of going out after banking hours with a friend, and her mother, who was not well, would be alone. Mrs. Arkell made but a faint resistance to this: Mildred came and went pretty much as she liked.

Peter, however, was at home when she got there, sitting over the fire in the dusk, in a thoughtful mood. On two afternoons in the week, Tuesdays and Thursdays, the bank closed at four; this was Thursday, and Peter had come straight home. Mildred took her seat at the table, against five o'clock should strike, the signal for their young maid-servant to bring the tea-tray in. It was quite dark outside, and the room was only lighted by the fire.

"What are you thinking of, Peter?" Mrs. Dan presently broke the silence by asking.

Peter took his chin from his hand where it had been resting, and his eyes from the fire, and turned his head to his mother. "I was thinking of a proposal Colonel Dewsbury made to me to-day," he answered; "deliberating upon it, in fact, and I think I have decided."

This was something like Greek to Mrs. Dan; even Mildred was sufficiently aroused from her thoughts to turn to him in surprise.

"The colonel wants me to go to his house in an evening, mother, and read the classics with his eldest son."

"Peter!"

"For about three hours, he says, from six till nine. He will give me a guinea a week."

"But only think how you slave and fag all day at that bank," said Mrs. Dan, who in her ailing old age thought work (as did Charlotte Travice) the greatest evil of life.

"And only think what a many additional comforts a guinea a week could purchase for you, mother," cried Peter in his affection; "our house would be set up in riches then."

"Peter, my dear," she gravely said, "I do not suppose I shall be here very long; and for comforts, I have as many as I require."

"Well, put it down to my own score, if you like," said Peter, with as much of a smile as he ever attempted; "I shall find the guinea useful."

"But if you thus dispose of your evenings, what time should you have for your books?" resumed Mrs. Arkell.

"I'll make that; I get up early, you know; and in one sense of the word, I shall be at my books all these three hours."

"How came Colonel Dewsbury to propose it to you?"

"I don't know. I met him as I was returning to the bank after dinner, and he began saying he was trying to find some one who would come in and read with Arthur. Presently he said, 'I wish you would come yourself, Mr. Arkell.' And after a little more talk I told him I would consider of it."

"I thought Arthur Dewsbury was to go into the army," remarked Mrs. Dan, not yet reconciled to the thing. "Soldiers don't want to be so very proficient in the classics."

"Not Arthur; he is intended for the church: the second son will be brought up for the army. Mildred, what do you say—should you take it if you were me?"

"I should," replied Mildred; "it appears to me to be a wonderfully easy way of earning money. But it is for your own decision entirely, Peter: do not let my opinion sway you."

"I think I had decided before I hung up my top-coat and hat on the peg at the bank," answered Peter. "Yes, I shall take it; I can but resign it later, you know, mother, if I find it doesn't work well."

The cathedral clock, so close to them, was chiming the quarters, and the first stroke of five boomed out; Peter rose and stretched himself with a relieved air. "It's always a weight off my mind when I get any knotty point decided," quoth he, rather simply; and in truth Peter was not good for much, apart from his Latin and Greek.

At the same moment, when that melodious college clock was striking, William Arkell was driving in at his own gates. He might have made more haste had he so chosen; and Mr. Arkell had charged him to be home "before dark;" but William had not hurried himself.

He was driving in quickly now, and stopped before the house-door. Philip left his seat and went to the horse's head, and William assisted out Miss Travice.

"Have you enjoyed your drive, Charlotte?" he whispered, retaining her hand in his, longer than he need have done; and there was a tenderness in his tone that might have told a tale, had anyone been there to read it.

"Oh! very, very much," she answered, in the soft, sweet, earnest voice she had grown to use when alone with William. "Stolen pleasures are always sweetest."

"Stolen pleasures?"

"This was a stolen one. You know I usurped the place of your cousin Mildred. She ought to have come."

"No such thing, Charlotte. She can go anytime."

"I felt quite sorry for her. I am apt to think those poor seamstresses require so much air. They—"

"Those what?" cried out William—and Miss Charlotte Travice immediately knew by the tone, that she had ventured on untenable ground. "Are you speaking of my cousin Mildred?"

"She is so kind and good; hemming cambric frills, and stitching wristbands! I wish I could do it. I was always the most wretched little dunce at plain sewing, and could never be taught it. My sister on the contrary—"

"I want to speak a word to you, Arkell."

William turned hastily, wondering who was at his elbow. At that moment the hall-door was thrown open, and the rays of the lamp shone forth, revealing the features of Robert Carr. Charlotte ran indoors, vouchsafing no greeting. She had taken a dislike to Robert Carr. He was free of speech, and the last time he and the young lady met, he had said something in her ear for which she would be certain to hate him for his life—"How was the angling going on? Had Bill Arkell bit yet?"

"Hallo!" exclaimed William as he recognised him. "I thought you were in London! I heard you went up on Tuesday night!"

"And came down last night. I want you to do me a favour, Arkell."

He put his arm within William's as he spoke, and began pacing the yard. William thought his manner unusual. There seemed a nervous restlessness about it—if he could have fancied such a thing of Robert Carr. William waited for him to speak.

"I have had an awful row with the governor to-day," he began at length. "I don't intend to stand it much longer."

"What about?"

"Oh! the old story—my extravagance. He was angry at my running up to town for a day, and called it waste of money and waste of time. So unreasonable of him, you know. Had I stayed a month, he'd not have made half the row."

"It does seem like waste, to go so far for only a day," said William, "unless you have business. That is a different thing."

"Well, I had business. I wanted to see a fellow there. You never heard any one make such a row about nothing. I have the greatest mind in the world to shake off the yoke altogether, and start for myself in life."

William could not help laughing. "You start?"

"You think I couldn't? If I do, rely upon it I succeed. I'm nearly sick of knocking about. I declare I'd rather sweep a crossing, and get ten shillings a week and keep myself upon it, than I'd continue to have my life bothered out by him. I shall tell him so one of these first fine days if he doesn't let me alone. Why doesn't he!"

"I suppose the fact is you continue to provoke him," remarked William.

"What about?" was the fierce rejoinder.

"Oh! you know, Carr. What I spoke to you of, before—though it is not any business of mine. Why don't you drop it?"

"Because I don't choose," returned Robert Carr, understanding the allusion. "I declare, before Heaven, that there's no wrong in it, and I don't choose to submit myself, abjectly, to the will of others. The thing might have been dropped at first but for the opposition that was raised. So long as fools continue that, I shall go there."

"For the girl's own sake, you should drop it. I presume you can't intend to marry her—"

"Marry her!" scoffingly interrupted Robert Carr.

"Just so. But she is a respectable girl, and—"

"I'd knock any man down that dared to say she wasn't," said Robert, quietly.

"But don't you know that the very fact of your continuing to go there must tend to damage her in public opinion? Edward Hughes must be foolish to allow it."

"Where's the wrong, or harm, of my going there?" demanded Robert, condescending to argue the question. "I like the girl excessively; I like talking to her. She has been as well reared as I have."

"Nonsense," returned William. "You can't separate her from her family; from what she is. I say you ought to drop it."

"What on earth has made you so squeamish all on a sudden? The society of that fine London lady, Miss Charlotte Travice?"

They were passing in a ray of light at the moment, thrown across the yard from one of the carriage lamps. Philip had left the carriage and the lamps outside, and was in the stable with the horse. Robert Carr saw his companion's face light up at the allusion, but William replied, without any symptom of anger—

"I will tell you what, people are beginning to talk of it from one end of the town to the other. I don't think you have any right to bring the scandal upon her. You bring it needlessly, as you yourself admit. A girl's good name, once lost, is not easy to regain, although it may be lost unjustly."

"I told you months ago, that there was nothing in it."

"I believe you; I believe you still. But now that the town has taken the matter up, and is passing its opinion upon it, I say that for the young girl's sake you should put a stop to it, and let the acquaintance cease."

"The town may be smothered for all I care—and serve it right!" was Robert Carr's reply. "But look here, Arkell, I didn't come to raise up this discussion, I have no time for it; and you may just take one fact into your note-book—that all you can say, though you talked till doomsday, would not alter my line of conduct by a hair's breadth. I came to ask you a favour."

"What is it?"

"Will you lend me the carriage for an hour or so to-morrow morning? It's to go to Purford."

"To Purford! Why that's where I have just been. I dare say you may have it. I will ask my father."

"But that is just what I don't want you to ask. I have to go there on a little private business of my own, and I don't wish it known that I have gone."

William hesitated. Only son, and indulged son though he was, he had never gone the length of lending out his father's carriage without permission; and he very much disliked the idea of doing so now. Robert Carr did not give him much time for consideration.

"You will be rendering me a service which I shan't forget, Arkell. If Philip will drive me over—"

"Philip! Do you want Philip with you?"

"Philip must go to bring back the carriage; I shan't return until the afternoon. Why, he will be there and home again almost before Mr. Arkell's up. I must go pretty early."

This, the going of Philip, appeared to simplify the matter greatly. To allow Robert Carr or anyone else to take the carriage off for a day without permission was one thing; for Philip to drive him to Purford early in the morning, and be back again directly, was another. "I think you may have it, Carr," he said; "but if my father misses the carriage and Philip—as he is sure to do—and asks where they are—"

"Oh, you may tell him then," interrupted Robert Carr.

"Very well. Shall Philip bring the carriage to your house?"

"No need of that; I'll come here and get up. I'd better speak to Philip myself. Don't stay out any longer in the cold, Arkell. Good night, and thank you."

William went indoors; and Robert Carr sought Philip in the stable to give him his instructions for the morning.

CHAPTER V

THE FLIGHT

In a quiet and remote street of the city was situated the house of Mr. Carr. Robert Carr walked towards it, with a moody look upon his face, after quitting William Arkell—a plain, dull-looking house, as seen from the street, presenting little in aspect beyond a dead wall, for most of the windows looked the other way, or on to the side garden—but a perfect bijou of a house inside, all on a small scale, with stained glass illuminating the hall, and statues and pictures ornamenting the rooms. The fretwork in the hall, and the devices on the windows—bright in colours when the sun shone through them, but otherwise dark and sombre—imparted the idea of a miniature chapel, when seen by a stranger for the first time. Old Mr. Carr had spent much time and money on his house, and was proud of it.

Robert swung himself in at the outer door in the wall, and then in at the hall door, which he shut with a bang; things, in fact, had arrived at a pitch of discomfort between him and his father hardly bearable by the temper of either. Neither would give way—neither would conciliate the other in the smallest degree. The disputes—arising, in the first place, from Robert's extravagance and unsteady habits—had continued for some years now; but during the past two or three months they had increased both in frequency and violence. Robert was idle—Robert spent—Robert did hardly anything that he ought to do, as member of a respectable community; these complaints made the basis of the foundation in all the disputes. But graver sins, in old Mr. Carr's eyes, of some special nature or other, cropped up to the surface from time to time. Latterly, the grievance had been this acquaintance of Robert's with Martha Ann Hughes; and it may really be questioned whether Robert, in his obstinate spirit, did not continue it on purpose to vex his father.

On the Tuesday (this was Thursday, remember) Robert had been, to use his father's expression, "swinging about all day"—meaning that Mr. Robert had passed it out of doors, nobody knew where, only going in to his meals. Their hours were early—as indeed was the general custom at Westerbury, and elsewhere, also, in those days—dinner at one o'clock, tea at five. About half-past four, on the Tuesday, Robert had gone in, ordered himself some tea made at once, and something to eat with it, and then went out again, taking a warm travelling rug, and telling the servant to say he was gone to London.

And he proceeded to the coach-office, took his seat in the mail, then on the point of starting, and departed.

Mr. Carr came in from the manufactory at five to his tea, and received the message—"Mr. Robert had gone to London by the mail." He was very wroth. It was an independent, off-hand mode of action, calculated to displease most fathers; but it was not the first time, by several, that Robert had been guilty of it. "He's gone off to spend that money," cried Mr. Carr, savagely; "and he won't come back until there's not a farthing of it left." Mr. Carr alluded to a hundred pounds which Robert had received not many days previously. A twelvemonth before, an uncle of Mr. Carr's and of Squire Carr's had died, leaving Robert Carr a legacy of a hundred pounds, and the same sum between the two sons of Mr. John Carr. This, of course, was productive of a great deal of heart-burning and jealousy in the Squire's family, that Robert should have the most; but it has nothing to do with our history just now. At the expiration of a year from the time of the death, the legacies were paid, and Robert had been in possession of his since the previous Saturday.

"He's gone to spend the money," Mr. Carr repeated. No very far-fetched conclusion; and Mr. Carr got over his wrath, or bottled it up, in the best way he could. He certainly did not expect Robert back again for a month at least; very considerably astonished, therefore, was he, to find Mr. Robert arrive back by the mail that took him, and walk coolly in to breakfast on the Thursday morning, having only stayed a few hours in London. A little light skirmishing took place then—not much. Robert said he had been to London to see a friend, and, having seen him, came back again; and that was all Mr. Carr could obtain. For a wonder, Robert spent the morning in the manufactory, but not in the presence of his father, who was shut in his private room. At dinner they met again, and before the meal was over the quarrel was renewed. It grew to a serious height. The old housekeeper, who had been in her place ever since the death of Mrs. Carr, years before, grew frightened, and stole to the door with trembling limbs and white lips. The clock struck three before it was over; and, in one sense, it was not over then. Robert burst out of the room in its very midst, an oath upon his lips, and strode into the street. Where he passed the time that afternoon until five o'clock could never be traced. Mr. Carr endeavoured afterwards to ascertain, and could not. Mr. Carr's opinion, to his dying day, was that he passed it at Edward Hughes's house; but Miss Hughes positively denied it, and she was by nature truthful. She stated freely that Robert Carr had called in that afternoon, and was for a few minutes alone with Martha Ann, she herself being upstairs at the time; but he left again directly. At five o'clock, as we have seen, he was with William Arkell, and then he went straight home.

Mr. Carr had nearly finished tea when he got in. The meal was taken in a small, snug room, at the end of the hall—a round room, whose windows opened upon the garden in summer, but were closed in now behind their crimson-velvet curtains.

Robert sat down in silence. He looked in the tea-pot, saw that it was nearly empty, and rang the bell to order fresh tea to be made for him. Whether the little assumption of authority (though it was no unusual circumstance) was distasteful to Mr. Carr, and put him further out of temper, cannot be told; one thing is certain, that he—he, the father—took up again the quarrel.

It was not a seemly one. Less loud than it had been at dinner-time, the tones on either side were graver, the anger more real and compressed. It seemed too deep for noise. An hour or so of this unhappy state of things, during which many, many bitter words were said by both, and then Robert rose.

"Remember," he said to his father, in a low, firm tone, "if I am driven from my home and my native place by this conduct of yours, I swear that I will never come back to it."

"And do you hear me swear," retorted Mr. Carr, in the same quiet, concentrated voice of passion, "if you marry that girl, Martha Ann Hughes, not one penny of my money or property shall you ever inherit; and you know that I will keep my word."

"I never said I had any thought of marrying her."

"As you please. Marry her; and I swear that I will leave all I possess away from you and yours. Before Heaven, I will keep my oath!"

And now we must go to the following morning, to the house of Mr. Arkell. These little details may appear trivial to the reader, but they bear their significance, as you will find hereafter; and they are remembered and talked of in Westerbury to this day.

The breakfast hour at Mr. Arkell's was nine o'clock. Some little time previous to it, William was descending from his room, when in passing his father's door he heard himself called to. Mr. Arkell appeared at his door in the process of dressing.

"William, I heard the carriage go out a short while ago. Have you sent it anywhere?"

Just the question that William had anticipated would be put. Being released now from his promise, he told the truth.

"Over to Purford! Why could he not have gone by the coach?"

"I don't know I'm sure," said William; and the same thought had occurred to himself. "I did not like to promise him without speaking to you, hut he made such a favour of it, and—I thought you would excuse it. I fancy he is on worse terms than ever with his father, and feared you might tell him."

"He need not have feared that: what should I tell him for?" was the rejoinder of Mr. Arkell as he retreated within his room.

Now it should have been mentioned that Mary Hughes was engaged to work that day at Mr. Arkell's. It was regarded in the town as a singular coincidence; and, perhaps, what made it more singular was the fact that Mrs. Arkell's maid, Tring (who had lived in the house ever since William was a baby, and was the only female servant kept besides the cook), had arranged with Mary Hughes that she should go before the usual hour, eight o'clock, so as to give a long day. The fact was, Mary Hughes's work this day was for the maids. It was Mrs. Arkell's custom to give them a gown apiece for Christmas, and the two gowns were this day to be cut out and as much done to them as the dressmaker, and Tring at odd moments, could accomplish. Mary Hughes, naturally obliging, and anxious to stand well with the servants in one of her best places, as Mrs. Arkell's was, arrived at half-past seven, and was immediately set to work in what Tring called her pantry—a comfortable little boarded room, a sort of offshoot of the kitchen.

Mr. Arkell spoke again at breakfast of this expedition of Robert Carr's. It wore to him a curious sound— first, that Robert could not have gone by the coach, which left Westerbury about the same hour, and had to pass through Purford on its way to London; and, secondly, why the matter of borrowing the carriage need have been kept from him. William could not enlighten him on either point, and the subject dropped.

Breakfast was over, and Mr. Arkell had gone into the manufactory, when the carriage came back. Philip drove at once to the stables, and William went out.

"Well," said he, "so you are back!"

"Yes, sir."

Philip began to unharness the horse as he spoke, and did not look up. William, who knew the man and his ways well, thought there was something behind to tell.

"You have driven the horse fast, Philip."

"Mr. Carr did, sir; it was he who drove. I never sat in front at all after we got to the three-cornered field. He drove fast, to get on pretty far before the coach came up."

"What coach?" asked William.

"The London coach, sir. He's gone to London in it."

"What! did he take it at Purford?"

"We didn't go to Purford at all, Mr. William. He ain't gone alone, neither."

"Philip, what do you mean?"

"Miss Hughes—the young one—is gone with him."

"No!" exclaimed William.

"It was this way, sir," began the man, disposing himself to relate the narrative consecutively. "I had got the carriage ready and waiting by a few minutes after eight, as he ordered me; but it was close upon half-past before he came, and we started. 'I'll drive, Philip,' says he; so I got in beside him. Just after we had cleared the houses, he pulls up before the three-cornered field, saying he was waiting for a friend, and I saw the little Miss Hughes come scuttering across it—it's a short cut from their house, you know, Mr. William—with a bit of a brown-paper parcel in her hand. 'You'll sit behind, Philip,' he says; and before I'd got over my astonishment, we was bowling along—she in front with him, and me behind. Just on this side Purford he pulled up again, and waited—it was in that hollow of the road near the duck-pond—and in two minutes up came the London coach. It came gently up to us, stopping by degrees; it was expecting him—as I could hear by the guard's talk, a saying he hoped he'd not waited long—and they got into it, and I suppose he's gone to London. Mr. William, I don't think the master will like this?"

William did not like it, either; it was an advantage that Robert Carr had no right to take. Had the girl forgotten herself at last, and gone off with him? Too surely he felt that such must be the case. He saw how it was. They had not chosen to get into the coach at Westerbury, fearing the scandal—fearing, perhaps, prevention; and Robert Carr had made use of this ruse to get her away. That there would be enough scandal in Westerbury, as it was, he knew—that Mr. Arkell would be indignant, he also knew; and he himself would come in for a large portion of the blame.

"Philip," he said, awaking from his reverie, "did the girl appear to go willingly?"

"Willingly enough, sir, for the matter of that, for she came up of her own accord—but she was crying sadly."

"Crying, was she?"

"Crying dreadfully all the way across the field as she came up, and along in this carriage, and when she got into the coach. He tried to persuade and soothe her; but it wasn't of any good. She hid her face with her veil as well as she could, that the outside passengers mightn't see her state as she got in; and there was none o' the inside."

William Arkell bit his lip. "Carr had no business to play me such a turn," he said aloud, in his vexation.

"Mr. William, if I had known what he was up to last night, I should just have told the master, in spite of the half-sovereign he gave me."

"Oh, he gave you one, did he?"

"He gave me one last evening, and he gave me another this morning; but, for all that, I should have told, if I'd thought she was to be along of him. I know what the master is, and I know what he'll feel about the business. And the two other Miss Hughes's are industrious, respectable young women, and it's a shabby thing for Mr. Carr to go and do. A fine way they'll be in when they find the young one gone!"

"They can't have known of it, I suppose," observed William, slowly, for a doubt had crossed his mind whether Robert could be taking the young girl away to marry her.

"No, that they don't, sir," impulsively cried the man. "I heard him ask her whether she had got away without being seen; and she said she had, as well as she could speak for her tears."

William Arkell, feeling more annoyed than he had ever felt in his life, not only on his own score, but on that of the girl herself, turned towards the manufactory with a slow step. The most obvious course now—indeed, the only honourable one—was to tell his father what he had just heard. He winced at having it to do, and a feeling of relief came over him, when he found that Mr. Arkell was engaged in his private room with some gentlemen, and he could not go in. There was to be also a further respite: for when they left Mr. Arkell went out with them.

William did not see him again until they met at dinner, for Mr. Arkell only returned just in time for it. Charlotte Travice was rallying William for being "absent," "silent," asking him where his thoughts had gone; but he did not enlighten her.

Barely had they sat down to dinner when Marmaduke Carr arrived—pale, fierce, and deeply agitated. Ignoring ceremony, he pushed past Tring into the dining-room, and stood before them, his lips apart, his words coming from them in jerks. Mr. Arkell rose from his seat in consternation.

"George Arkell, you and I have been friends since we were boys together. I had thought if there was one man in the whole town whom I could have depended on, it was you. Is this well done?"

"Why, what has happened?" exclaimed Mr. Arkell, rather in doubt whether Marmaduke Carr had suddenly gone deranged. "Is what well done?"

"So! it is you who have helped off my son."

"Helped him where? What is the matter, Carr?"

"Helped him where?" roared Mr. Carr, "why, on his road to London. He is gone off there with that—that—" Mr. Carr caught timely sight of the alarmed faces of Mrs. Arkell and Miss Travice, and moderated his tone—"that Hughes girl. You pretend to ask me where he's gone, when it was you sent him!—conveyed him half-way on his road."

"I protest I do not know what you mean," cried Mr. Arkell.

"Not know! Did your chaise and your servant take him and that girl to Purford, or did they not?"

For reply, Mr. Arkell cast a look on his son—a look of stern inquiry. William could only speak the truth now, and Mr. Arkell's brow darkened as he listened.

"And you knew of this—this elopement?"

"No, on my word of honour. If I had known of it, I should not have lent him the carriage. Robert"—he raised his eyes to Mr. Carr's—"was not justified in playing me this trick."

"I don't believe a word of your denial," roughly spoke Mr. Carr, in his anger; "you and he planned this escape together; you were in league with him."

It is useless to contend with an angry man, and William calmly turned to his father: "All I know of the matter, sir, I told you this morning. I never suspected anything amiss until Philip came back with the carriage and related what had occurred."

George Arkell knew that his son's veracity might be depended on, nevertheless he felt terribly annoyed at being drawn into the affair. Mrs. Arkell did not mend the matter when she inquired whither Robert had gone.

Mr. Carr answered intemperately, speaking out the truth more broadly than he need have done: his scamp of a son and the shameless Hughes girl had taken flight together.

Tring, who had stood aghast during the short colloquy, not at first understanding what was amiss, stole away to her pantry, where the dressmaking was going on. Tring sunk down in a chair at once, and regarded the poor seamstress with open mouth and eyes, in which pity and horror struggled together. Tring was of the respectable school, and really thought death would be a light calamity in comparison with such a flight.

"I have been obliged to cut your sleeves a little shorter than Hannah's, for the stuff ran short; but I'll put a deeper cuff, so you won't mind," said Miss Mary Hughes.

Surprised at receiving no answer, she looked up, and saw the expression on Tring's face. "Oh, Mary Hughes!"

There was so genuine an amount of pity in the tone, of some unnamed dread in the look, that Mary Hughes dropped her needle in alarm. "Is anybody took ill?" she asked.

"Not that, not that," answered Tring, subduing her voice to a whisper, and leaning forward to speak; "your sister, Martha Ann—I can't tell it you."

"What of her?" gasped Mary Hughes, a dreadful prevision of the truth rushing over her heart, and turning it to sickness.

"She has gone away with Mr. Robert Carr."

Mary Hughes, not of a strong nature, became faint. Tring got some water for her, and related to her as much as she had heard.

"But how is it known that she's gone? How did Mr. Carr learn it?" asked the poor young woman.

Tring could not tell how he learnt it. She gathered from the conversation that it was known in the town; and Mr. William seemed to know it.

"You'll spare me while I run home for a minute, Tring," pleaded Mary Hughes; "I can't live till I know the rights and the wrongs of it. I can't believe that she'd do such a thing. I'll be back as soon as I can."

"Go, and welcome," cried Tring, in her sympathy; "don't hurry back. What's our gowns by the side of this dreadful shock? Poor Martha Ann!"

"I can't believe she's gone; I can't believe it," reiterated the dressmaker, as she hastily flung on her cloak and bonnet; "there was never a modester girl lived than Martha Ann. It's some dreadful untruth that has got about."

The way in which Mr. Carr had learnt it so soon was this—one of the outside passengers of the coach, a young man of the name of Hart, had been only going as far as Purford, where the coach dropped him. He hurried over his errand there, and hurried back to Westerbury, big with the importance of what he had seen, and burning to make it known. Taking his course direct to Mr. Carr's, and only stopping to tell everybody he met on the way, he found that gentleman at home, and electrified him with the recital. From thence he ran to the house of Edward Hughes, and found Miss Hughes in a sea of tears, and her brother pacing the rooms in what Mr. Hart called a storm of passion. The young lady, it seems, had been already missed, and one of the gossips to whom Mr. Hart had first imparted his tale, had flown direct with it to the brother and sister.

"Why don't you go after her?" asked Hart; "I'd follow her to the end of the world if she was my sister. I'd take it out of him, too."

Ah, it was easy to say, why don't you go after her? But there were no telegraphs in those days, and there was not yet a rail from London to Westerbury. Robert Carr and the girl were half-way to London by that time; and the earliest conveyance that could be taken was the night mail.

"It's of no use," said Edward Hughes, moodily; "they have got too great a start. Let her go, ungrateful chit! As she has made her bed, so must she lie on it."

Mary Hughes got back to Mrs. Arkell's: she had found it all too true. Martha Ann had taken her opportunity to steal out of the house, and was gone. Mary Hughes, in relating this, could not sneak for sobs.

"My sister says she could be upon her Bible oath, if necessary, that at twenty-five minutes past eight Martha Ann was still at home. She called out something to her up the stairs, and Martha Ann answered her. She must have crept down directly upon that, and got off, and run all the way along the bank, and across the three-cornered field. She—she—" the girl could not go on for sobs.

Tring's eyes were full. "Is your sister much cut up?" she asked.

"Oh, Tring!"—and indeed the question seemed a bitter mockery to Mary Hughes—"I'm sure Sophia has had her death-blow. What a thing it is that I was engaged out to work to-day! If I had been at home, she might not have got away unseen."

Tring sighed. There was no consolation that she could offer.

"I was always against the acquaintance," Mary Hughes resumed, between her tears and sobs; "Sophia knows I was. I said more than once that even if Mr. Robert Carr married her, they'd never be equals. I'd have stopped it if I could, but I've no voice beside Sophia's, and I couldn't stop it. And now, of course, it's all over, and Martha Ann is lost; and she'd a deal better have never been born."

Nothing more satisfactory was heard or seen of the fugitives. They stayed a short time in London, and then went abroad, it was understood, to Holland. Those who wished well to the girl were in hopes that Robert Carr married her in London, but there appeared no ground whatever for the hope. Indeed, from certain circumstances that afterwards transpired, it was quite evident he did not. Westerbury gradually recovered its equanimity; but there are people living in it to this day who never have believed, and never will believe, but that William Arkell was privy to the flight.

CHAPTER VI

A MISERABLE MISTAKE

The time again went on—went on to March—and still Charlotte Travice lingered. It was some little while now that both Mr. and Mrs. Arkell had come to the conclusion within their own minds that the young lady's visit had lasted long enough, but they were of that courteous nature that shrunk not only from hinting such a thing to her, but to each other. She was made just as welcome as ever, and she appeared in no hurry to hasten her departure.

One afternoon Mildred, who had been out on an errand, was accosted by her mother before she had well entered.

"Whatever has made you so long, child?"

"Have I been so long?" returned Mildred. "I had to go to two or three shops before I could match the ribbon. I met Mary Pembroke, and she went with me; but I walked fast."

"It is past five."

"Yes, it has struck. But I did not go out until four, mother."

"Well, I suppose it is my impatience that has made me think you long," acknowledged Mrs. Dan. "Sit down, Mildred; I wish to speak to you. Mrs. George has been here."

"Has she?" returned Mildred, somewhat apathetically; but she took a chair, as she was told to do.

"She came to talk to me about future prospects. And I am glad you were out with that ribbon, Mildred, for our conversation was confidential."

"About her prospects, mamma?" inquired Mildred, raising her mild dark eyes.

"Hers!" repeated Mrs. Dan. "Her prospects, like mine, will soon be drawing to a close. Not that she's as old as I am by a good ten years. She came to speak of yours, Mildred."

Mildred made no rejoinder this time, but a faint colour arose to her face.

"Your Aunt George is very fond of you, Mildred."

"Oh, yes," said Mildred, rather nervously; and Mrs. Dan paused before she resumed.

"I think you must have seen, child, for some time past, that we all wanted you and William to make a match of it."

The announcement was, perhaps, unnecessarily abrupt. The blush on Mildred's face deepened to a glowing crimson.

"Mrs. George never spoke out freely to me on the subject until this afternoon, but her manner was enough to tell me that it was in their minds. I saw it coming as plainly as I could see anything."

Mildred made no remark. She had untied her bonnet, and began to play nervously with the strings as they hung down on either side her neck.

"But though I felt sure that it was in their minds," continued Mrs. Dan, "though I saw the bent of William's inclinations—always bringing him here to you—I never encouraged the feeling; I never forwarded it by so much as the lifting of a finger. You must have seen, Mildred, that I did not. In one sense of the word, you are not William's equal—"

Mrs. Dan momentarily arrested her words, the startled look of inquiry on her daughter's face was so painful.

"Do not misunderstand me, my dear. In point of station you and he are the same, for the families are one. But William will be wealthy, and William is accomplished; you are neither. In that point of view you may be said not to be on an equality with him; and there's no doubt that William Arkell might go a-wooing into families of higher pretension than his own, and be successful. It may be, that these considerations have withheld me and kept me neuter; but I have not—I repeat it, as I did twice over to Mrs. George just now—I have not forwarded the matter by so much as the lifting of a finger."

Mildred knew that.

"The gossiping town will, no doubt, cast ill-natured remarks upon me, and say that I have angled for my attractive nephew, and caught him; but my conscience stands clear upon the point before my Maker; and Mrs. George knows that it does. They have come forward of themselves, unsought by me; unsought, as I heartily believe, Mildred, by you."

"Oh, yes," was the eager, fervent answer.

"No child of mine would be capable, as I trust, of secret, mean, underhand dealing, whatever the prize in view. When I said this to Mrs. George just now, she laughed at what she called my earnestness, and said I had no need to defend Mildred, she knew Mildred just as well as I did."

Mildred's heart beat a trifle quicker as she listened. They were only giving her her due.

"But," resumed Mrs. Dan, "quiet and undemonstrative as you have been, Mildred, your aunt has drawn the conclusion—lived in it, I may say—that the proposal she made to-day would not be unacceptable to you. I agreed with her, saying that such was my conviction. And let me tell you, Mildred, that a more attractive and a bettor young man than William Arkell does not live in Westerbury."

Mildred silently assented to all in her heart. But she wondered what the proposal was.

"You are strangely silent, child. Should you have any objection to become William Arkell's wife?"

"There is one objection," returned Mildred, almost bitterly, as the thought of his intimacy with Charlotte Travice flashed painfully across her—"he has never asked me."

"But—it is the same thing—he has asked his mother for you."

A wild coursing on of all her pulses—a sudden rush of rapture in every sense of her being—and Mildred's lips could hardly frame the words—

"For me?"

"He asked for you after dinner to-day—I thought I said so—that is, he broached the subject to his mother. After Mr. Arkell went back to the manufactory, he stayed behind with her in the dining-room, and spoke to her of his plans and wishes. He began by saying he was getting quite old enough to marry, and the sooner it took place now, the better."

"Is this true?" gasped Mildred.

"True!" echoed the affronted old lady. "Do you suppose Mrs. George Arkell would come here upon such an errand only to make game of us? True! William says he loves you dearly."

Mildred quitted the room abruptly. She could not bear that even her mother should witness the emotion that bid fair, in these first moments, to overwhelm her. Never until now did she fully realize how deeply, how passionately, she loved William Arkell—how utter a blank life would have been to her had the termination been different. She shut herself in her bed-chamber, burying her face in her hands, and asking how she could ever be sufficiently thankful to God for thus bringing to fruition the half-unconscious hopes which had entwined themselves with every fibre of her existence. The opening of the door by her mother aroused her.

"What in the world made you fly away so, Mildred? I was about to tell you that Mrs. George expects us to tea. Peter will join us there by and by."

"I would rather not go out this evening, mamma," observed Mildred, who was really extremely agitated.

"I promised Mrs. George, and they are waiting tea for us," was the decisive reply. "What is the matter with you, Mildred? You need not be so struck at what I have said. Did it never occur to yourself that William Arkell was likely to choose you for his wife?"

"I have thought of late that he was more likely to choose Miss Travice," answered Mildred, giving utterance in her emotion to the truth that lay uppermost in her mind.

"Marry that fine fly-away thing!" repeated Mrs. Dan, her astonishment taking her breath away. "Charlotte Travice may be all very well for a visitor—here to-day and gone to-morrow; but she is not suitable for the wife of a steady, gentlemanly young man, like William Arkell, the only son of the first manufacturer in Westerbury. What a pretty notion of marriage you must have!"

Mildred began to think so, too.

"I shall not be two minutes putting on my shawl; I shan't change my gown," continued Mrs. Dan. "You can change yours if you please, but don't be long over it. It is past their tea-time."

Implicit obedience had been one of the virtues ever practised by Mildred, so she said no more. The thought kept floating in her mind as she made herself ready, that it had been more appropriate for William to visit her that evening than for her to visit him; and she could not help wishing that he had spoken to her himself, though it had been but a single loving hint, before the proposal could reach her through another. But these were but minor trifles, little worth noting in the midst of her intense happiness. As she walked down the street by her mother's side, the golden light of the setting sun, shining full upon her, was not more radiantly lovely than the light shining in Mildred Arkell's heart.

"I can't think what you can have been dreaming of, Mildred, to imagine that that Charlotte Travice was a fit wife for William Arkell," observed Mrs. Dan, who could not get the preposterous notion out of her head. "You might have given William credit for better sense than that. I don't like her. I liked her very much at first, but, somehow, she is one who does not gain upon you on prolonged acquaintance; and it strikes me Mr. and Mrs. George are of the same opinion. Mrs. George just mentioned her this afternoon—something about her being your bridesmaid."

"She my bridesmaid!" exclaimed Mildred, the very idea of it unpalatable.

"Mrs. George said she supposed she must ask Charlotte Travice to stay and be bridesmaid; that it would be but a mark of politeness, as she had been so intimate with you and William. It would not be a very great extension of the visit," she added, "for William seemed impatient for the wedding to take place shortly, now that he had made up his mind about it. It does not matter what bridesmaid you have, Mildred."

Ah! no; it did not matter! Mildred's happiness seemed too great to be affected by that, or any other earthly thing. Mrs. George Arkell kissed her fondly three or four times as she entered, and pressed her hand, as Mildred thought, significantly. Another moment, and she found her hand taken by William.

He was shaking it just as usual, and his greeting was a careless one—

"How d'ye do, Mildred? You are late."

Neither by word, or tone, or look, did he impart a consciousness of what had passed. In the first moment Mildred felt thankful for the outward indifference, but the next she caught herself thinking that he seemed to take her consent as a matter of course—as if it were not worth the asking.

When tea was over, and the lights were brought, Mr. and Mrs. Arkell and Mrs. Dan sat down to cribbage, the only game any of the three ever played at.

"Who will come and be fourth?" asked Mr. Arkell, looking over his spectacles at the rest. "You, Mildred?"

It had fallen to Mildred's lot lately to be the fourth at these meetings, for Miss Travice always held aloof, and William never played if he could help it; but on this evening Mildred hesitated, and before she could assent—as she would finally have done—Miss Travice sprang forward.

"I will, dear Mr. Arkell—I will play with you to-night."

"She knows of it, and is leaving us alone," thought Mildred. "How kind of her it is! I fear I have misjudged her."

"I say, Mildred," began William, as they sat apart, his tone dropped to confidence, his voice to a whisper, "did my mother call at your house this afternoon?"

Mildred looked down, and began to play with her pretty gold neckchain. It was one William had given her on her last birthday, nearly a year ago.

"My aunt called, I believe. I was out."

William's face fell.

"Then I suppose you have not heard anything—anything particular? I'm sure I thought she had been to tell you. She was out ever so long."

"Mamma said that Aunt George had been—had been—speaking to her," returned Mildred, not very well knowing how to make the admission.

William saw the confusion, and read it aright.

"Ah, Mildred! you sly girl, you know all, and won't tell!" he cried, taking her hand half-fondly, half-playfully, and retaining it in his.

She could not answer; but the blush on her cheek was so bright, the downcast look so tender, that William Arkell gazed at her lovingly, and thought he had never seen his cousin's face so near akin to perfect beauty. Mildred glanced up to see his gaze of fond admiration.

"Your cheek tells tales, cousin mine," he whispered; "I see you have heard all. Don't you think it is time I married?"

A home question. Mildred's lips broke into a smile by way of answer.

"What do you think of my choice?"

"People will say you might have made a better."

"I don't care if they do," returned Mr. William, firing up. "I have a right to please myself, and I will please myself. I am not taking a wife for other people, meddling mischief-makers!"

The outburst seemed unnecessary. It struck Mildred that he must have seriously feared opposition from some quarter, the tone of his voice was so sore a one. She looked up with questioning eyes.

"I have plenty of money, you know, Mildred," he added, more quietly. "I don't want to look out for a fortune with my wife."

"Very true," murmured Mildred.

"I wonder whether she has brought it out to my father?" resumed William, nodding towards his mother at the card-table. "I don't think she has; he seems only just as usual. She'll make it the subject of a curtain-lecture to-night, for a guinea!"

Mildred stole a glance at her uncle. He was intent on his cards, good old man, his spectacles pushed to the top of his ample brow.

"Do you know, Mildred, I was half afraid to come to the point with them," he presently said. "I dreaded opposition. I—"

"But why?" timidly interrupted Mildred.

"Well, I can't tell why. All I know is, that the feeling was there—picked up somehow. I dreaded opposition, especially from my mother; but, as I say, I cannot tell why. I never was more surprised than when she said I had made her happy by my choice—that it was a union she had set her heart upon. I am not sure yet, you know, that my father will approve it."

"He may urge against it the want of money," murmured Mildred; "it is only reasonable he should. And—"

"It is not reasonable," interposed William Arkell, in a tone of resentment. "There's nothing at all in reason that can be urged against it; and I am sure you don't really think there is, Mildred."

"And yet you acknowledge that you dreaded opening the matter to them?"

"Yes, because fathers and mothers are always so exacting over these things. Every crow thinks its own young bird the whitest, and many a mother with an only son deems him fit to mate with a princess of the blood-royal. I declare to you, Mildred, I felt a regular coward about telling my mother—foolish as the confession must sound to you; and once I thought of speaking to you first, and getting you to break it to her. I thought she might listen to it from you better than from me."

Mildred thought it would have been a novel mode of procedure, but she did not say so. Her cousin went on:—

"We must have the wedding in a month, or so; I won't wait a day longer, and so I told my mother. I have seen a charming little house just suitable for us, and—"

"You might have consulted me first, William, before you fixed the time."

"What for? Nonsense! will not one time do for you as well as another?"

Miss Arkell looked up at her cousin: he seemed to be talking strangely.

"But where is the necessity for hurrying on the wedding like this?" she asked. "Not to speak of other considerations, the preparations would take up more time."

"Not they," dissented Mr. William, who had been accustomed to have things very much his own way, and liked it. "I'm sure you need not raise a barrier on the score of preparation, Mildred. You won't want much beside a dress and bonnet, and my mother can see to yours as well as to Charlotte's. Is it orthodox for the bride and bridesmaid to be dressed alike?"

"Who was it fixed upon the bridesmaid?" asked Mildred. "Did you?"

"Charlotte herself. But no plans are decided on, for I said as little as I could to my mother. We can go into details another day."

"With regard to a bridesmaid, Mary Pembroke has always been promised—"

"Now, Mildred, I won't have any of those Pembroke girls playing a conspicuous part at my wedding," he interrupted. "What you and my mother can see in them, I can't think. Provided you have no objection, let it be as Charlotte says."

"I think Charlotte takes more upon herself than she has any cause to do," returned Mildred, the old sore feeling against Miss Travice rising again into prominence in her heart.

"I'll tell her if you don't mind, Mildred," laughed William. "But now I think of it, it was not Charlotte who mentioned it, it was my mother. She—"

"Mr. Peter Arkell."

The announcement was Tring's. It cut off William's sentence in the midst, and also any further elucidation that might have taken place. Peter came forward in his usual awkward manner, and was immediately pressed into the service of cribbage, in the place of Miss Travice, who never "put out" to the best advantage, and could not count. As Peter took her seat, he explained that his early appearance was owing to his having remained but an hour with Mr. Arthur Dewsbury, who was going out that evening.

Charlotte Travice sat down to the piano, and William got his flute. Sweet music! but, nevertheless, it grated on Mildred's ear. His whole attention became absorbed with Charlotte, to the utter neglect of Mildred. Now and then he seemed to remember that Mildred sat behind, and turned round to address a word to her; but his whispers were given to Charlotte. "It is not right," she murmured to herself in her bitter pain; "this night, of all others, it is not surely right. If she were but going back to London before the wedding!"

Supper came in, for they dined early, you remember; and afterwards Mrs. Dan and Mildred had their bonnets brought down.

"What a lovely night it is!" exclaimed Peter, as he waited at the hall door.

"It is that!" assented William, looking out; "I think I'll have a run with you. Those stars are enough to tempt one forth. Shall I go, Mildred?"

"Yes," she softly whispered, believing she was the attraction, not the stars.

But Mrs. Dan lingered. The fact was, Mrs. Arkell had drawn her to the back of the hall.

"Did you speak to her, Betty?"

"I spoke to her as soon as she came home. It was that that made us late."

"Well? She does not object to William?"

"Not she. I'll tell you a secret," continued Mrs. Dan; "I could see by Mildred's agitation when I told her to-day, that she already loved William. I suspected it long ago."

Mrs. Arkell nodded her head complacently. "I noticed her face when he was talking to her as they sat apart to-night; and I read love in it, if it ever was read. Yes, yes, it is all right. I thought I could not be mistaken in Mildred."

"I say, Aunt Dan, are you coming to-night or to-morrow?" called out William.

"I am coming now, my dear," replied Mrs. Dan; and she walked forward and took her son's arm. William followed with Mildred.

"Now, Mildred, don't you go and tell all the world to-morrow about this wedding of ours," he began; "don't you go chattering to those Pembroke girls."

"How can you suppose it likely that I would?" was the pained answer.

"Why, I know all young ladies are fond of gossiping, especially when they get hold of such a topic as this."

"I don't think I have ever deserved the name of gossip," observed Mildred, quietly.

"Well, Mildred, I do not know that you have. But it is not all girls who possess your calm good sense. I thought it might be as well to give even you a caution."

"William, you are scarcely like yourself to-night," she said, anxiously. "To suppose a caution in this case necessary for me!"

He had begun to whistle, and did not answer. It was a verse of "Robin Adair," the song Charlotte was so fond of. When the verse was whistled through, he spoke—

"How very bright the stars are to-night! I think it must be a frost."

Inexperienced as Mildred was practically, she yet felt that this was not the usual conversation of a lover on the day of declaration, unless he was a remarkably cool one. While she was wondering, he resumed his whistling—a verse of another song, this time.

Mildred looked up at him. His face was lifted towards the heavens, but she could see it perfectly in the light of the night. He was evidently thinking more of the stars than of her, for his eyes were roving from one constellation to another. She looked down again, and remained silent.

"So you like my choice, Mildred!" he presently resumed.

"Choice of what?" she asked.

"Choice of what! As if you did not know! Choice of a wife."

"How is it you play so with my feelings this evening?" she asked, the tears rushing to her eyes.

"I have not played with them that I know of. What do you mean, Mildred? You are growing fanciful."

She could not trust her voice to reply. William again broke into one of his favourite airs.

"I proposed that we should be married in London, amidst her friends," he said, when the few bars were brought to a satisfactory conclusion. "I thought she might prefer it. But she says she'd rather not."

"Amidst whose friends?" inquired Mildred, in amazement.

"Charlotte's. But in that case I suppose you could not have been bridesmaid. And there'd have been all the trouble of a journey beforehand."

"I bridesmaid!" exclaimed Mildred; and all the blood in her body seemed to rush to her brain as a faint suspicion of the terrible truth stole into it. "Bridesmaid to whom?"

William Arkell, unable to comprehend a word, stopped still and looked at her.

"You are dreaming, Mildred!" he exclaimed.

"What do you mean? Who is it you are going to marry?" she reiterated.

"Why, what have we been talking of all the evening? What did my mother say to you to-day? What has come to you, Mildred? You certainly are dreaming."

"We have been playing at cross purposes, I fear," gasped Mildred, in her agony. "Tell me who it is you are going to marry."

"Charlotte Travice. Whom else should it be?"

They were then turning round by what was called the boundary wall; the old elms in the dean's garden towered above them, and Mildred's home was close in sight. But before they reached it, William Arkell felt her hang heavily and more heavily on his arm.

Ah! how she was struggling! Not with the pain—that could not be struggled with for a long, long while to come—but with the endeavour to suppress its outward emotion. All, all in vain. William Arkell bent to catch a glimpse of her features under the bonnet—worn large in those days—and found that she was white as death, and appeared to be losing consciousness.

"Mildred, my dear, what ails you?" he asked, kindly. "Do you feel ill?"

She felt dying; but to speak was beyond her, then. William passed his arm round her just in time to prevent her falling, and shouted out, excessively alarmed—

"Peter! Aunt! just come back, will you? Here's something the matter with Mildred."

They were at the door then, but they heard him, and hastened back. Mildred had fainted.

"What can have caused it?" exclaimed Peter, in his consternation. "I never knew her faint in all her life before."

"It must have been that rich cream tart at supper," lamented Mrs. Dan, half in sympathy, half in reproof. "I have told Mildred twenty times that pastry, eaten at night, is next door to poison."

And so this was to be the ending of all her cherished dreams! Mildred lay awake in her solitary chamber the whole of that live-long night. There was no sleep, no rest, no hope for her. Desolation the most complete had overtaken her—utter, bitter, miserable desolation.

CHAPTER VII

A HEART SEARED

Mildred Arkell, in the midst of her agony, had the good sense to see that some extraordinary misapprehension had occurred, either on her mother's part or on Mrs. Arkell's; that William had not announced his wish of marrying her, but Charlotte Travice. From that time forward, Mildred would have a difficult part to play in the way of concealment. Her dearest feelings, her bitter mortification, her sighs of pain must be hidden from the world; and she prayed God to give her strength to go through her task, making no sign. The most embarrassing part would be to undeceive her mother; but she must do it, and contrive to do it without suspicion that she was anything but indifferent to the turn affairs had taken. Commonplace and insignificant as that little episode was—the partaking of a rich cream tart at Mrs. Arkell's supper-table—Mildred was thankful for it. Her mother, remarkably single-minded by nature, unsuspicious as the day, would never think of attributing the fainting fit to any other cause.

It may at once be mentioned that the singular misapprehension was on the part of Mrs. Arkell. She was so thoroughly imbued with the hope—it may be said with the notion—that her son would espouse Mildred, that when William broached the subject in a hasty and indistinct manner, she somehow fell into the mistake. The fault was probably William's. He did not say much, and his own fear of his mother's displeasure caused him to be anything but clear and distinct. Mrs. George Arkell caught at the communication with delight, believing it to refer to Mildred. She mentioned a word herself, in her hasty looking forward, about a bridesmaid. The names of Mildred and Charlotte, not either of them mentioned above once, got confused together, and altogether the mistake took place, William himself being unconscious of it.

William ran home that night, startling them with the news of the indisposition of Mildred. She had fainted in the street as they were going home. Mr. and Mrs. Arkell, loving Mildred as a daughter, were inexpressibly concerned; Charlotte Travice sat listening to the tale with wondering ears and eyes. "My aunt said it must be the effect of the cream tart at supper," he observed, "but I think that must be all rubbish. As if cream tart would make people faint! And Mildred has eaten it before."

"It was the agitation, my dear. It was nothing else," whispered Mrs. Arkell to her guest, confidentially, as she bid her good night in the hall. "A communication like that must cause agitation to the mind, you know."

"What communication?" asked Charlotte, in surprise. For Mrs. Arkell spoke as if her words must necessarily be understood.

"Don't you know? I thought William had most likely told you. It's about her marriage. But there, we'll talk of it to-morrow, I won't keep you now, Miss Charlotte, and I have to speak to Mr. Arkell."

Charlotte continued her way upstairs, wondering excessively; not able, as she herself expressed it, to make head or tail of what Mrs. Arkell meant. Mrs. Arkell returned to the dining-room, asked her husband to sit down again for a few minutes, for he was standing with his bed-candle in his hand, and she made the communication.

Elucidation was, however, near at hand, as it of necessity must be. On the following morning nothing was said at the breakfast-table; but on their going into the manufactory, Mr. Arkell took his son into his private room. Mr. Arkell sat down before his desk, and opened a letter that waited on it before he spoke. William stood by the fire, rather nervous.

"So, young sir! you are wanting, I hear, to encumber yourself with a wife! Don't you think you had better have taken one in your leading-strings?"

"I am twenty-five, sir," returned William, drawing himself up in all the dignity of the age. "And you have often said you hoped to see me settled before—"

"Before I died. Very true, you graceless boy. But you don't want me to die yet, I suppose?"

"Heaven forbid it!" fervently answered William.

"Well," continued the good man—and William had known from the first, by the tone of the voice, the twinkle in the eye, that he was pleased instead of vexed—"I cannot but say you have chosen worthily. I suppose I must look over her being portionless."

"Our business is an excellent one, and you have saved money besides, sir," observed William. "To look out for money with my wife would be superfluous."

"Not exactly that," returned Mr. Arkell, in his keen, emphatic tone. "But I suppose you can't have everything. Few of us can. She has been a good and affectionate daughter, William, and she will make you a good wife. I should have been better pleased though, had there been no relationship between you."

"Relationship!" repeated William.

"For I share in the popular prejudice that exists against cousins marrying. But I am not going to make it an objection now, as you may believe, when I tell you that I foresaw long ago what your intimacy would probably end in. Your mother says it has been her cherished plan for years."

William listened in bewilderment. "She is no cousin of mine," he said.

"No what?" asked Mr. Arkell, pushing his glasses to the top of his forehead, the better to stare at his son—for those glasses served only for near objects, print and writing—"is the thought of this marriage turning your head, my boy?"

"I don't understand what you are speaking of," returned William, perfectly mystified; "I only said she was not my cousin."

"Why, bless my heart, what do you mean?" exclaimed Mr. Arkell. "She has been your cousin ever since she was born; she is the daughter of my poor brother Dan; do you want to disown the relationship now?"

"Are you talking of Mildred Arkell?" exclaimed the astonished young man. "I don't want to marry her. Mildred is a very nice girl as a cousin, but I never thought of her as a wife. I want Charlotte Travice!"

"Charlotte Travice!"

The change in the tone, the deep pain it betrayed, struck a chill on William's heart. Mr. Arkell gazed at him before he again broke the silence.

"How came you to tell your mother yesterday that you wanted to marry Mildred?"

"I never did tell her so, sir; I told her I wished to marry Charlotte."

Mr. Arkell took another contemplative stare at his son. He then turned short away, quitted the manufactory by his own private entrance, walked across the yard, past the coach-house and stable, and went straight into the presence of his wife.

"A pretty ambassador you would make at a foreign court!" he began; "to mistake your credentials in this manner!"

Mrs. Arkell was seated alone, puzzling herself with a lap-fall of patchwork, and wishing Mildred was there to get it into order. Every now and then she would be taken with a sewing fit, and do about two stitches in a morning. She looked up at the strange address, the mortified tone.

"You told me William wanted to marry Mildred!"

"So he does."

"So he does not," was Mr. Arkell's answer. "He wants to marry your fine lady visitor, Miss Charlotte Travice."

Mrs. Arkell rose up in consternation, disregardful of the work, which fell to the ground. "You must be mistaken," she exclaimed.

"No; it is you who have been mistaken. William says he did not speak to you of Mildred; never thought of her as a wife at all; he spoke to you of Charlotte Travice."

"Dear, dear!" exclaimed Mrs. Arkell, a feeling very like unto faintness coming over her spirit; "I hope it is not so! I hope still there may be some better elucidation."

"There can be no other elucidation, so far, than this," returned Mr. Arkell, his tone one of sharp negation. "The extraordinary part of the affair is, how you could have misinterpreted his meaning, and construed Charlotte Travice into Mildred Arkell! I said we kept the girl here too long."

He turned away again with the last sentence on his tongue. He was not sufficiently himself to stay and talk then. Mrs. Arkell, in those first few minutes, was as one who has just received a blow. Presently she despatched a message for her son; she was terribly vexed with him; and, like we all do, felt it might be a relief to throw off some of her annoyance upon him.

"How came you to tell me yesterday you wanted to marry Mildred?" she began when he appeared, her tone quite as sharp as ever was Mr. Arkell's.

"I did not tell you so. My father has been saying something of the same sort, but it is a mistake."

"You must have told me so," persisted Mrs. Arkell; "how else could I have imagined it? Charlotte's name was never mentioned at all. Except—yes—I believe I said that she could be the bridesmaid."

"I understood you to say that Mildred could be the bridesmaid," returned William. "Mother, indeed the mistake was yours."

"We have made a fine mess of it between us," retorted Mrs. Arkell, in her vexation, as she arrived at length at the conclusion that the mistake was hers; "you should have been more explicit. What a simpleton they will think me! Worse than that! Do you know what I did yesterday?"

"No."

"I went straight to Mrs. Dan Arkell's as soon as you had spoken to me, and asked for Mildred to marry you."

"Mother!"

"I did. It is the most unpleasant piece of business I was ever mixed up in."

"Mildred will only treat it as a joke, of course?"

"Mildred treated it in earnest. Why should she not? When she came here last evening, she came expecting that she would shortly be your wife."

They stood looking at each other, the mother and son, their thoughts travelling back to the past night, and its events. What had appeared so strange in William's eyes was becoming clear; the cross-purposes, as Mildred had expressed it, in their conversation with each other, and Mildred's fainting-fit, when the elucidation came. He very much feared, now that he knew the cause of that fainting-fit—he feared that Mildred's love was his.

Mrs. Arkell's thoughts were taking the same course, and she spoke them:—"William, that fainting-fit must in some way have been connected with this. Mildred is not in the habit of fainting."

He made no reply at first. Loving Mildred excessively as a cousin, he would not have hurt her feelings willingly for the whole world. A half-wish stole over him that it was the fashion for gentlemen to cut themselves in half when two ladies were in the case, and so gallantly bestow themselves on both. Mrs. Arkell noted the mortification in his expressive face.

"What is to be done, William? Mrs. Dan told me she felt sure Mildred had been secretly attached to you for years."

Mrs. Arkell might not have spoken thus openly to her son, but for a hope, now beginning to dawn within her—that his choice might yet fall upon Mildred. William made no reply. He smoothed his hand over his troubled brow; he recalled more and more of the previous evening's scene; he felt deeply perplexed and concerned, for the happiness of Mildred was dear to him as a sister's. But the more he reflected on the case, the less chance he saw of mending it.

"You must marry Mildred," Mrs. Arkell said to him in a low tone.

"Impossible!" he hastily rejoined; "I cannot do that."

"But I made the offer for her to her mother! Made it on your part."

"And I made one for myself to Charlotte."

An embarrassed, mortified silence. Mrs. Arkell, an exceedingly honourable woman, did not see a way out of the double dilemma any more than William did.

"Do you know that I do not like her?" resumed Mrs. Arkell, in a voice hoarse with emotion. "That I have grown to dislike her? And what will become of Mildred?"

"Mildred will get over it in no-time," he answered, already beginning to reason himself into a satisfactory state of composure and indifference, as people like to do. "She is a girl of excellent common sense, and will see the thing in its proper light."

Strange perhaps to say, Mrs. Arkell fell into the same train of reasoning when the first moments of mortification had cooled down. She saw Mrs. Dan, and intimated that she had been under an unfortunate mistake, which she could only apologise for. Mrs. Dan, a sober-minded, courteous old lady, who never made a fuss about anything, and had never quarrelled in her life, said she hoped she had been mistaken as to Mildred's feelings. And when Mrs. Arkell next saw Mildred, the latter's manner was so quiet, so unchanged, so almost indifferent, that Mrs. Arkell repeated with complacency William's words to herself: "Mildred will get over it in no-time."

What mattered the searing of one heart? How many are there daily blighted, and the world knows it not! The world went on its way in Westerbury without reference to the feelings of Mildred Arkell; and poor Mildred went on hers, and made no sign.

The marriage went on—that is, the preparations for it. When a beloved and indulged son announces that he has fixed his heart upon a lady, and intends to make her his wife, consent and approval generally follow, provided there exists no very grave objection against her. There existed none against Miss Travice; and she made herself so pleasant and delightful to Mr. and Mrs. Arkell, when once it was decided she was to marry William, that they nearly fell in love with her themselves, and became entirely reconciled to the loss of Mildred as a daughter-in-law. The "charming little house" spoken of by William, was taken and furnished; and the wedding was to take place the end of April, Charlotte being married from Mr. Arkell's.

One item in the original programme was not carried out: Mildred refused to act as bridesmaid. Mrs. Arkell was surprised. The intimacy of the two families had been continued as before; for Mildred, in all senses of the word, had condemned herself to suffer in silence; and she was so quiet, so undemonstrative, that Mrs. Arkell believed the blow was quite recovered—if blow it had been. Mildred placed her refusal on the plea of her mother's health, which was beginning seriously to decline. Mrs. Arkell did not press it, for a half-suspicion of the true cause arose in her mind.

"Your sister must come down now, whether or not," she said to Charlotte.

Charlotte looked up hastily, a flush of annoyance on her bright cheek. Miss Charlotte had persistently refused Mrs. Arkell's proposal to invite her sister to the wedding; had turned a deaf ear to Mrs. Arkell's remonstrance that it was not fit or seemly this only sister should be excluded. Charlotte had carried her point hitherto; but Mrs. Arkell intended to carry hers now.

"Betsey can't bear visiting," she said, with pouting lips; "she would be sure to refuse if you did ask her."

"She would surely not refuse to come to her sister's marriage! You must be mistaken, Charlotte."

"She has never visited anywhere in all her life; has not been out, so far as I can call to mind, for a single day—has never drank tea away from home," urged Charlotte, who seemed strangely annoyed. "I have said so before."

"All the more reason that she should do so now," returned Mrs. Arkell. "Charlotte, my dear, don't be foolish; I shall certainly send for her."

"Then I shall write and forbid her to come," returned Charlotte; and she bit her lip for saying it as soon as the words were out.

"My dear!"

"I did not mean that, dear Mrs. Arkell," she pleaded, with a winning expression of repentance and a merry laugh; "but indeed it will not do to invite poor Betsey here."

"Very well, my dear."

But in spite of the apparently acquiescent "very well," Mrs. Arkell remained firm. Whether it was that she detected something false in the laugh, or that she chose to let her future daughter-in-law see which was mistress, or that she deemed it would not be right to ignore Miss Betsey Travice on this coming occasion, certain it was that Mrs. Arkell wrote a pressing mandate to the younger lady, and enclosed a five-pound note in the letter. And she said nothing to Charlotte of what she had done.

It was about this time that some definite news arrived in Westerbury of Robert Carr. He, the idle, roving, spendthrift spirit, had become a clerk in Holland. He had obtained a situation, he best knew how, in a merchant's house in Rotterdam, and appeared, so far, to have really settled down to steadiness. It would seem that the remark to William Arkell, "If I do make a start in life, rely upon it, I succeed," was likely to be borne out. He had taken this clerkship, and was working as hard as any clerk ever worked yet. Whether the industry would last was another thing.

Mr. John Carr, the squire's son, was the one to bring the news to Westerbury. Mr. John Carr appeared to be especially interested in his cousin's movements and doings: near as he was known to be in money matters, he had actually gone a journey to Rotterdam, to find out all about Robert. Mr. John Carr did not fail to remember, and hardly cared to conceal from the world that he remembered, that, failing Robert, who had been threatened times and again with disinheritance, he might surely look to be his uncle's heir. However it may have been, Mr. John Carr went to Rotterdam, saw Robert, stayed a few days in the place, and then came home again.

"Has he married the girl?" was Squire Carr's first question to his son.

"No," replied John, gloomily; for, of course it would have been to his interest if Robert had married her. Squire Carr and his son knew of Marmaduke's oath to disinherit Robert if he did marry Martha Ann Hughes; and they knew that he would keep his word.

"Is the girl with him still?"

"She's with him fast enough; I saw her twice."

"John, he may have married her in London."

"He did not, though. I said to Robert I supposed they had been married in London. He flew into one of his tempers at the supposition, and said he had never been inside a church in London in his life, or within fifty miles of it; and I am sure he was speaking the truth. He told me afterwards, when we were having a little confidential talk together, that he never should marry her, at any rate as long as his father lived; and she did not expect him to do it. He had no mind, he added, to be disinherited."

This news oozed out to Westerbury, and Mr. John was vexed, for he did not intend that it should ooze out. Amidst other ears, it reached that of Mr. Carr. "A cunning man in his own conceit," quoth he to a friend, alluding to his brother's son, "but not quite cunning enough to win over me. If Robert marries that girl, I'll keep my word, and not bequeath him a shilling of my money; but I'll not leave it to John Carr, or any of his brood."

Had this news touching Robert's life in Holland needed confirmation, such might have been supplied to it by a letter received from Martha Ann Hughes by her sister Mary. The shock to Mary Hughes had been, no doubt, very great, and she had written several letters since, begging and praying Martha Ann to urge Mr. Robert Carr to marry her, even now. For the first time Martha Ann sent an answer, just about the period that Mr. John Carr was in Holland. It was a long and very nicely-written letter; but to Mary Hughes's ear there was a vein of repentant sadness running throughout it. It was not likely Mr. Robert would marry her now, she said, and to urge it upon him would be worse than useless. She had chosen her own path and must abide by it; and she did not see that what she had done ought to cause people to reflect upon her sisters. Mary's saying that it did, must be all nonsense—or ought to be. Her sisters had done their part by her well; and if she had repaid them ill, that ought to be only the more reason for the world showing them additional kindness and respect: Mary would no doubt live to prove this. For herself she was not unhappy. Robert was quite steady, and had a good clerkship in a merchant's house. He was as kind to her as if they had been married twice over; and her position was not so unpleasant as Mary seemed to imagine, for nobody knew but what she was his wife—though, for the matter of that, they had made no acquaintances in the strange town.

Mary Hughes blinded her eyes with tears over this letter, and in her unhappiness lent it to anyone who cared to see it. And her strong-minded but more reticent sister, when she found out what she was doing, angrily called her a fool for her pains, and tore the letter to pieces before her face. But not before it had been heard of by Mr. Carr. For one, who happened to get hold of it, reported the contents to him.

CHAPTER VIII

BETSEY TRAVICE

They were grouped together in Mrs. Arkell's sitting-room, their faces half-indistinct in the growing twilight. Mrs. Arkell herself, doing nothing as usual; Mildred by her side, sewing still, although Mrs. Arkell had told her she was trying her eyes; Charlotte Travice, with a flush upon her face and a nervous movement of the restless foot—signs of anger suppressed, to those who knew her well; and a stranger, a young lady, whom you have not seen before.

Had anyone told you this young lady and Charlotte were sisters, you had disputed the assertion, so entirely dissimilar were they in all ways. A quiet little lady, this, of twenty years, with a smooth, fair face, somewhat insipid, for all its good sense; light blue eyes, truthful as Charlotte's were false; small features, and light hair, worn plainly. Perhaps what might have struck a beholder as the most prominent feature in Betsey Travice was her excessive natural meekness; nay, humility would be the better word. She was meek in mind, in temper, in look, in manner, in speech; humble always. She sat there at the fire, her black bonnet laid beside her, for the girl had felt cold after her journey, and the fire was more welcome to her than the going upstairs to array herself for attraction would have been to Charlotte. The weather was very cold for the close of April, and the coach—it was a noted circumstance in its usual punctuality—had been half an hour behind its time. She sat there, sipping the hot cup of tea that Tring had brought her, declining to eat, and feeling miserably uncomfortable, as she saw that, to one at least, she was not welcome.

That one was her sister. Mrs. Arkell had kept the secret well; and not until the evening of the arrival—but an hour, in fact, before the coach was expected in—was Charlotte told of it.

"Tring, or somebody, has been putting two pillows upon my bed," remarked Charlotte, who had run up to her bedroom to get a book. "I wonder what that's for."

"You are going to have a bedfellow to-night, my dear," said Mrs. Arkell.

"A bedfellow!" echoed Charlotte, in wonder. "Who is it?"

"Your sister."

"Who?" cried out Charlotte; and the sharp, passionate, uncontrolled tone struck on their ears unpleasantly.

"I told you I should have your sister down to the wedding," quietly returned Mrs. Arkell. "In my opinion it would have been unseemly and unkind not to do so. She is on her road now. Mildred has come in to help me welcome her. Betsey is Mrs. Dan's godchild, you know."

"And Mildred knew she was coming?" retorted Charlotte, as if that were a further grievance; and she spoke as fiercely as she dared, compatible with her present amiability as bride-elect.

"Mildred knew it from the first."

Of course there was no help for it now. Betsey was on her road down, as Mrs. Arkell expressed it, and it was too late to stop her, or to send her back again. Charlotte made the best of it that she could make, but never had her temper been nearer an explosion; and when Betsey arrived she took care to let her see that she had better not have come.

"And now, my dear, that you are warmed and refreshed a little, tell me if you were not glad to come," said Mrs. Arkell, kindly, as Betsey Travice put the empty cup on the table, and stretched out one small, thin hand to the blazing warmth.

"I was very glad, ma'am," was the reply, delivered in the humble, gentle, deprecatory tone which characterized Betsey Travice, no matter to whom she spoke. "I was glad to have the opportunity of seeing Charlotte, she had been gone away so long; and I shall like to see a wedding, for I have never seen one; and I was very glad to come also for another thing."

"What is that?" asked Mrs. Arkell, yearning to the pleasant, single-minded tone—to the truthful, earnest eyes.

"Well, ma'am, I'm afraid I was getting over-worked. Though it would have seemed ungrateful to kind Mrs. Dundyke to say so, and I never did say it. The children were heavy to carry about the kitchen, and up and down stairs; and the waiting on the lodgers was worse than usual. I used to have such a pain in my side and back towards night, that I did not know how to keep on."

Charlotte Travice was in an agony. It was precisely these revelations that she had dreaded in a visit from Betsey. That Betsey had to work like a horse at Mrs. Dundyke's, Charlotte thought extremely probable; but she had no mind that this state of things should become known at Mrs. Arkell's. In her embarrassment, she was unwise enough to attempt to deny the fact.

"Where's the use of your talking like this, Betsey?" she indignantly asked. "If you did attend a little to the children—as nursery governess—you need not have carried them about, making a slave of yourself."

"But you know how young they are, Charlotte! You know that they need to be carried. I would not have cared had it been only the children. There was all the house work and the waiting."

"But what had you to do with this, my dear?" asked Mrs. Arkell, a little puzzled, while Charlotte sat with an inflamed face.

Betsey Travice entered on the explanation in detail. Mrs. Dundyke cooked for her lodgers herself—and she generally had two sets of lodgers in the house—and kept a servant to wait upon them. Six weeks ago the servant had left—she said the place was too hard for her—and Mrs. Dundyke had not found one to her mind since. She got a charwoman in two or three times a week, and Betsey Travice had put herself forward to help with the work and the waiting. She had made beds and swept rooms, and laid cloths for dinner, and carried up dishes, and handed bread and beer at table, and answered the door; in short, had been, to all intents and purposes, a maid of all work.

To see her sitting there, and quietly telling this, was not the least curious portion of the tale. She looked a lady, she spoke as a lady—nay, there was something especially winning and refined in her voice; and she herself seemed altogether so incompatible with the work she confessed to have passed her later days in, that even Mildred Arkell gazed at her in fixed surprise.

"You are a fool!" burst forth Charlotte, between rage and crying. "If that horrible woman, that Mrs. Dundyke, thrust such degrading work upon you, you ought not to have done it."

"Oh! Charlotte, don't call her that! She is a kind woman; you know she is. If you please, ma'am, she's as kind as she can be," added Betsey, turning to Mrs. Arkell, in her anxiety for justice to be done to Mrs. Dundyke. "And for the work, I did not mind it. It's not as if I had never done any. I had to do all sorts of work in poor mamma's time, and I am naturally handy at it. I am sorry you should be angry with me, Charlotte."

"I don't think it was exactly the sort of work your friend Mrs. Dundyke should have put upon you," remarked Mrs. Arkell.

"But there was no help for it, ma'am," represented Betsey. "The work was there, and had to be done by somebody. That servant left us at a pinch. She had a quarrel with her mistress about some dripping that was missing, and she went off that same hour. I began to do what I could of myself, without being asked. Mrs. Dundyke did not like my doing it, any more than Charlotte does, but there was nobody else, and I could not bear to seem ungrateful. When Charlotte came here I had but sixpence left in my purse, and Mrs. Dundyke has bought me shoes and things that I have wanted since, from her own pocket."

A dead silence. Charlotte Travice felt as if she were going to have brain fever. Could the earth have opened then, and swallowed up Betsey, it had been the greatest blessing, in Charlotte's estimation, ever accorded her.

"What are your prospects for the future, Betsey?" quietly asked Mrs. Arkell.

"Prospects, ma'am? I have not any. At least"—and a sudden blush overspread the fair face—"not at present."

"But you cannot go on waiting on Mrs. Dundyke's lodgers. It is not a desirable position for yourself, nor a suitable one for your father's daughter."

"I shall not have to do that again. Mrs. Dundyke has engaged a good servant now; indeed, I could not else have come away; when I return, I shall only attend to the two children, and do the sewing."

"I think we must try and find you something better, Betsey."

"Oh, ma'am, you are very kind to interest yourself for me," was the reply; "but I have promised myself to Mrs. Dundyke for twelve months to come. I am very happy there; and when the work's over at night, we sit in her little parlour; she goes to sleep, and David does his accounts, and I darn the socks and stockings. You cannot think how comfortable and quiet it is."

"Who is David?" inquired Mrs. Arkell.

"Mrs. Dundyke's son. He is clerk in a house in Fenchurch-street, in the day; and he keeps books and that, for anybody who will employ him at night. Sometimes he has to bring them home to do. He is very industrious."

"What did you mean by saying you had promised yourself to Mrs. Dundyke for a twelvemonth?"

"It was when I was coming away. She cried at parting, and said she supposed she should never see me again, now I was coming to be with Charlotte and her grand acquaintances. I told her I should be sure to come back to her very soon, and I would stop a whole year with her, if she liked. She said, was it a promise; and I told her it was. Oh! ma'am, I would not be ungrateful to Mrs. Dundyke for the world! I should have had no home to go to when Charlotte came here, but for her. All our money was gone, and Mrs. Dundyke had been letting us stop on then, ever so long, without any pay. Besides, I shall like to be with her."

If Charlotte could have cut her sister's tongue out, she would most decidedly have done it. To own such a sister at all, was bad enough; but to be compelled to sit by while these revelations were made to her future mother-in-law, to her rival Mildred, was dreadful. If Charlotte had disliked Mildred before, she hated her now. The implied superiority of position which it had been her pleasure from the first to assume over Mildred, would now be taken for what it was worth. She flung her arms up with a gesture of passionate pain, and approached Mrs. Arkell. Had Betsey confessed to having passed her recent months in housebreaking, it had sounded less despicable to Charlotte's pretentious mind than this; and a dread had rushed over her, whether Mrs. Arkell might not, even at that eleventh hour, break off the union with her son.

"Mrs. Arkell, I pray you, do not notice this!" she said, her voice a wail of passion and despair. "It has, I am sure, not been as bad as Betsey makes it out; she could not have degraded herself to so great an extent. But you see how it is. She is but half-witted at best, and anyone might impose upon her."

Half-witted! Mrs. Arkell smiled at the look of surprise rising to Betsey's eyes at the charge. Charlotte's colour was going and coming.

"On the contrary, Charlotte, I should give your sister credit for a full portion of good plain sense. Why should you be angry with her? The sort of work was not suitable for her; but it seems she could not help herself."

"I'd rather hear that she had gone out and swept the crossings in the streets! I knew how it would be if you had her down! I knew she would disgrace me!"

Mrs. Arkell took Betsey's hand in hers. The young face was distressed; the blue eyes shone with tears. "I do not think you have disgraced anyone, Betsey; I think you have been a good girl. Charlotte," Mrs.

Arkell added, very pointedly, "I would rather see your sister what she is, than a fine lady, stuck up and pretentious."

Did Charlotte understand the rebuke? She made no sign. Tring came in with lights; it caused some little interruption, and while they were calming down again from the past excitement, Betsey Travice took the opportunity to approach Mrs. Arkell with a whisper.

"I don't know how to thank you for your kindness to me, ma'am, not only in inviting me here, but in sending me the money in the letter. If ever I have it in my power to repay it, you will not find me ungrateful. I do not mean the money; I mean the kindness."

"Hush, child!" said Mrs. Arkell, and patted her smooth fair hair.

"There was always something deficient in Betsey's mind," Charlotte was condescending to say to Mildred Arkell. "It is a great misfortune. Papa used to say times and again that Betsey was not a lady; never would be one. Will you believe me, that once, when she was about ten I think, she fell into a habit of curtseying to gentlepeople when she met them in the street, and we could hardly break her of it! Papa would have been quite justified, in my opinion, had he then put her into an asylum or a reformatory, or something of the kind."

"She does not strike me—as my aunt has just remarked—as being deficient in sense."

"In plain, rough, every-day sense perhaps she is not. But there's something wanting in her, for all that. Her notions are not those of a lady, if you can understand. You hear her speak of the work that horrid landlady has made her do—well, she feels no shame in it."

Before Mildred could answer, Mr. Arkell and William entered, big with some local news. They kindly welcomed the meek-looking young stranger, and then spoke it out.

Edward Hughes, the brother of the sisters so frequently mentioned, had bid adieu to Westerbury for ever. Whether he had at length become sick of the condemnatory comments the town had not yet forgotten to pass on Martha Ann, certain it was, that he had suddenly sold off his stock in trade, and gone away, en route for Australia. For some little time past he had said it was his intention to go; the two sisters also had spoken of it with a kind of dread; but it was looked upon by most people as idle talk. However, an opportunity arose for the disposing advantageously of his business and stock; he embraced it without an hour's delay and was already on his road to Liverpool to take ship. The town could hardly believe it, and concluded he was gone to escape the reflections on Martha Ann—although he had shown sufficient equanimity over them in general. People needn't bother him about it, he had been wont to say. They should talk to the one who had been the cause of the mischief, Mr. Carr's fine gentleman of a son.

"What a blow for the two sisters!" exclaimed Mildred. "What will they do?"

"Nay, my dear, they have their business," said Mr. Arkell. "I don't suppose their brother contributed at all to their support. On the contrary, people say he had been saving all he could to emigrate with."

"I don't know that I altogether alluded to money, Uncle George. It seems very sad for them to be left alone."

"It is sad for them," said Mrs. Arkell, agreeing with Mildred. "First Martha Ann, and now Edward!—it is a cruel bereavement. Tring says—and I have noticed it myself—that Mary Hughes has not been the same since that day's misfortune, three or four months ago."

"Ah," said Mr. Arkell, drawing a long breath, "I wish I had had the handling of Mr. Robert Carr that day!" The subject was a sore one with him, and ever would be. William believed, in his heart, that he had never been forgiven for having given the permission for the carriage that unlucky morning.

They continued to speak of the Hughes's and their affairs, and the interest of Betsey Travice appeared to be awakened. She had risen to go upstairs, but halted near the door, listening still.

"And now tell me," began Charlotte, when they were alone together in the chamber, "how you dared so to disgrace me!"

"Oh, Charlotte, how have I disgraced you? Do not be unkind to me. I wish I had not come."

"I wish it too with all my heart! Why did you come? How on earth could you think of coming? What possessed you to do it?"

"Mrs. Arkell wrote for me. She wrote to Mrs. Dundyke, asking her to see me off. I should, never else have thought of coming."

"Did I write for you, pray? Could you not have known that if you were wanted I should have written, and, failing that, you were not to come? You wicked girl!"

Betsey burst into tears. She had been domineered over in this manner, by Charlotte, all her life; and she took it with appropriate humility and repentance.

"Charlotte, you know I'd lay down my life to do you any good; why are you so angry with me?"

"And you do do me good, don't you!" retorted Charlotte. "Look at the awful disgrace you have this very evening brought upon me!"

"What disgrace?" asked Betsey, her blue eyes bespeaking compassion from the midst of her tears.

"Good heavens! what an idiot!" uttered the exasperated Charlotte. "She asks what disgrace! Did you not proclaim yourself before them a servant of all work—a scourer of rooms, a blacker of grates, a—"

"Stop, Charlotte; I have not done either of those things—Mrs. Dundyke would not let me. I made beds and waited on the drawing-room, and such-like light duties. I did this, but I did not black grates."

"And if you did do it, was there any necessity for your proclaiming it? Had you not the sense to know that for my sister to avow these things was to me the very bitterest humiliation? Not for your doing them," tauntingly added Charlotte, in her passion, "for you are worth nothing better; but because you are a sister of mine."

Betsey's sobs were choking her.

"Where did you get the money to come down?" resumed Charlotte.

"Mrs. Arkell sent it me, Charlotte. There was a five-pound note in her letter."

It seemed to be getting worse and worse. Charlotte sat down and poked the fire fiercely, Tring having lighted one in compassion to the young visitor's evident chilly state. Betsey checked her sobs, and bent down to kiss her sister's neck.

"Somehow I always offend you, Charlotte; but I never do it intentionally, as you know, and I hope you will forgive me. I so try to do what I can for everybody. I always hope that God will help me to do right. There was the work to be done at Mrs. Dundyke's, and it seemed to fall to me to do it."

Charlotte was not all bad, and the tone of the words could but conciliate her. Her anger was subsiding into fretfulness.

"The annoying thing is this, Betsey—that you feel no disgrace in doing these things."

"I should not do them by choice, Charlotte. But the work was there, as I say; the servant was gone, and there was nobody but me to do it."

"Well, well, it can never be mended now," returned Charlotte, impatiently. "Why don't you let it drop?"

Betsey sighed meekly. She would have been too glad to let it drop at first. Charlotte pointed imperiously to a chair near her.

"Sit down there. You have tried me dreadfully this evening. Don't you know that in a few days I shall be Mrs. William Arkell? His father is one of the largest manufacturers in Westerbury, and they are rolling in money. It was not pleasant, I can tell you, for my sister to show herself out in such a light. What do you think of him?"

"Oh, Charlotte! I think you must be so happy! I am so thankful, dear! Working, and all that, does not matter for me; but it would not have done for you. I never saw anyone so nice-looking."

"As I?"

"As Mr. William Arkell. How pleasant his manner is! And, Charlotte, who is that young lady down there? I did not quite understand. What a sweet face she has!"

"You never do understand. It is the cousin: Mildred. She thought to be Mrs. William Arkell," continued Charlotte, triumphantly. "The very first night I came here I saw it as plain as glass, and I took my resolution—to disappoint her. She has been loving William all her life, and fully meant him to marry her. I said I'd supplant her, and I've done it; and I know our marriage is just breaking her heart."

Betsey Travice—than whom one more generous-hearted, more unselfishly forgetful of self-interest, more earnestly single-minded, did not exist—felt frightened at the avowal. Had it been possible for her to recoil from her imperious sister, she had recoiled then.

"Oh, Charlotte!" was all she uttered.

"Why, you don't think I should allow so good a match to escape me, if I could help it! And, besides, I love him," added Charlotte, in a deeper voice.

"But if—oh, Charlotte! pardon me for speaking—I cannot help it—if that sweet young lady loved him before you came? had loved him for years?"

"Well?" said Charlotte, equably.

"It cannot be right of you to take him from her."

"Right or not right, I have done it," said Charlotte, with a passing laugh. "But it is right, for he loves me, and not her."

"What will she do?" cried Betsey, after a pause of concern; and it seemed that she asked the question of her own heart, not of Charlotte.

"Dwindle down into an old maid," was the careless answer: spoken, it is to be hoped, more in carelessness than heartlessness. "There, that's enough. Have you seen anything of Mrs. Nicholson?" resumed Charlotte.

"We have seen her a great many times, Charlotte; she has been very troublesome to Mrs. Dundyke. She wanted your address here: but for me, Mrs. Dundyke would have given it to her. She said—but, perhaps, I had better not tell it you."

"What who said? Mrs. Dundyke? Oh, you may tell anything she said. I know her delight was to abuse me."

"No, no, Charlotte; it never was. She only said it was not right of you to order so many new things when you were coming here, unless you could pay for them. I went to Mrs. Nicholson and paid her a sovereign off the account."

"How did you get the sovereign?"

"Mrs. Dundyke made me a present of it—as a little recompense for my work, she said. I did not so very much want anything for myself, for I had just had new shoes, and I had not worn my best clothes; so I took it to Mrs. Nicholson."

Did the young girl's generosity strike no chord of gratitude in Charlotte's heart? This money, owing to Mrs. Nicholson, a fashionable dressmaker, had been Charlotte's worry during her visit. She would soon have it in her power to pay now.

"I wonder what you'll do in future?" resumed Charlotte, looking at her sister. "You can't expect to find a home with me, you know. It would be entirely unreasonable. And you can't expect to marry, for I don't think you'd be likely to get anyone to have you. If—"

The exceedingly vivid blush that overspread the younger sister's cheek, the wondrous look of intelligence in the raised eyes, brought Charlotte's polite speech to a summary conclusion. "What's the matter?" she asked.

"Charlotte, if you would let me tell you," was the whispered answer. "Papa is dead, and mamma is dead, and there is no one left but you; and I suppose I ought to tell you. I have promised to marry David."

"Promised—what?" repeated Charlotte, in an access of consternation.

"To marry David Dundyke. Not yet, of course; not for a long while, I dare say. When he shall be earning enough to keep a wife."

For once speech failed Charlotte Travice, and she sat gazing at her sister. Her equanimity had received several shocks that evening; but none had been like this. She had seen but little of this David Dundyke; but, a vision of remembrance rose before her of an inferior, common young man, carrying coal-scuttles upstairs in his shirt-sleeves, who could not speak a word grammatically.

"Are you really mad, Betsey?"

"I feared you would not like it, Charlotte; and I know I can't expect to be as you are. But we shall be more than a hundred miles apart, so that it need not annoy you."

Betsey had unconsciously put the matter in the right light. It was not because Mr. Dundyke was unfit to be Betsey's husband, but because he was unfit to be her brother-in-law, that the matter so grated on the ear of Charlotte.

"I cannot expect much better, Charlotte; I have not been educated as you have. Perhaps if I had been—"

"But the man is utterly beneath you!" burst forth Charlotte. "He is a common man. He used—if I am not mistaken—to black the boots and shoes for the house at night, and carry up the coal before he went out in the morning!"

"But not as a servant, Charlotte; only to save work for his mother. Just as I helped with the rooms and waited, you know. He does it all still. They were very respectable once; but Mr. Dundyke died, and she had to struggle on, and she took this house in Upper Stamford-street. You have heard her tell mamma of it many a time."

"You can't think of marrying him, Betsey? You are something of a lady, at any rate; and he—cannot so much as speak like a Christian."

"He is very steady and industrious; he will be sure to get on," murmured Betsey. "Some of the clerks in the house he is in get a great deal of money."

"What house is it?" snapped Charlotte, beginning to feel cross again. "A public-house?—an eating-house?"

"It is a tea-house," said Betsey, mildly. "They are large wholesale tea-dealers; whole shiploads of tea come consigned to them from China. He went into it first of all as errand-boy, and—"

"You need not have told that, I think."

"And has got on by attention and perseverance to be a clerk. He is twenty-two now."

"If he gets on to be a partner—if he gets on to be sole proprietor—you cannot separate him from himself!" shrieked Charlotte. "Look here, Betsey; sooner than you should marry that low man, I'll have you to live with me. You can make yourself useful."

"Thank you kindly, Charlotte, all the same; but I could not come to you. You see, you and I do not get on together. It is my fault, I know, being so inferior; but I can't help it. Besides, I have promised David Dundyke."

Charlotte looked at her. "You do not mean to tell me that you have any love for this David Dundyke?"

Another bright blush, and Betsey cast down her pretty blue eyes. "We have seen so much of each other, Charlotte," she said, in a tone of apology; "he brings the books home nearly every evening now, instead of doing them out."

"Well, I shan't stop with you," concluded Charlotte, moving to the door. "I'm afraid to stop, for I truly believe you are going on for Bedlam. And you'd better make haste, if you want to do anything to yourself. Supper will be ready directly."

"One moment, Charlotte," said Betsey, detaining her—"I want to say only a word. They were speaking downstairs this evening of a family of the name of Hughes—a Mr. Edward Hughes, and some sisters."

"Well?" cried Charlotte.

"I think they are related to Mrs. Dundyke. She has relatives in Westerbury of that name; she has mentioned it several times since you came down. One or two of the sisters are dressmakers."

"Pleasant!" ejaculated Charlotte. "Are they intimate?"

"Not at all. I don't think they have met for years, and I am sure they never correspond. But when you were all speaking of the Hughes's to-night, I thought it must be the same. I did not like to say so."

"And it's well you did not," was Charlotte's comment. "Those Hughes people have not been in good odour in Westerbury since last December."

She went downstairs in a thoughtful mood, her brain at work upon the question of whether Betsey could be in her right mind. The revelation regarding Mr. David Dundyke caused her really to doubt it. She, Charlotte Travice, had a sufficiently correct taste—to give her her due—and it would have been simply impossible to her to have associated herself for life with anyone not possessing, outwardly at any rate, the attributes of a gentleman.

CHAPTER IX

DISPLEASING EYES

The wedding day of Mr. William Arkell and Miss Travice dawned. All had gone well, and was going on well towards completion. You who have learnt to like Mildred Arkell, may probably have been in hopes that some impediment might arise to frustrate the wedding—that the bride, after all, might be Mildred, not Charlotte. But it is in the chronicles of romance chiefly that this sort of poetical justice takes place. Weddings are not frustrated in real life; and when I told you at the beginning that this was a story of real life, I told you the truth. The day dawned—one of the finest the close of April has ever seen—and the wedding party went to church to the marriage, and came home again when it was over.

It was quite a noted wedding for those quiet days, and guests were bidden to it from far and near. That the bride looked charmingly lovely was indisputable, and they called William Arkell a lucky fellow.

A guest at the breakfast-table, but not in the church, was Mildred Arkell. She had wholly declined to be the bridesmaid; but it was next to impossible for her to decline to be at the breakfast. Put the case to yourselves, as Mildred had put it to herself in that past March night, that now seemed to be so long ago. Her resolve to pass over the affliction in silence; to bear, and make no sign, involved its consequences—and they were, that social life must go on just as usual, and she must visit at her uncle's as before. Worse than any other thought to Mildred, was the one, that the terrible blow to her might become known. She shrank with all the reticence of a pure-minded girl from the baring of her heart to others—shrank from it with a shivering dread—and Mildred felt that she would far rather die, than see her love suspected for one, who, as it now turned out, had never loved her. So she buried her misery within her, and went to Mr. Arkell's as before, not quite so frequently perhaps, but sufficiently so to excite no observation. She had joined in the plans and preparations for the wedding; had helped to fix upon the bride's attire, simply because she could not help herself. How she had borne it, and suppressed within her heart its own agony, she never knew. Charlotte's keen bright eyes would at times be fixed on hers, as if they could read her soul's secret; perhaps they did. William's rather seemed to shun her. But she had gone through it all, and borne it bravely; and none suspected how cruel was the ordeal.

And here was Mildred at the wedding-breakfast! There had been no escape for it. Peter went to church, but Mrs. Dan and Mildred arrived for breakfast only. Mildred, regarded and loved almost as a daughter of the house, had the place of honour assigned her next to William Arkell, his bride being on his other hand. None forgot how chaste and pretty Mildred looked that day; paler it may have been than usual, but that's expected at a wedding. She wore a delicate pearl-grey silk, and her gentle face, with its sweet, sad eyes, had never been pleasanter to look upon. "A little longer! a little longer!" she kept murmuring to her own rebellions heart. "May God help me to bear!"

Perhaps the one who felt the most out of place at that breakfast-table, was our young friend, Miss Betsey Travice. Miss Betsey had never assisted at a scene of gaiety in her life—or, as she called it, grandeur; and perhaps she wished it over nearly as fervently as another was doing. She wore a new shining silk of maize colour, the gift of Mrs. Arkell—for maize was then in full fashion for bridesmaids—and Betsey felt particularly stiff and ashamed in it. What if the young gentleman on her left, who seemed to partake rather freely of the different wines, and to be a rollicking sort of youth, should upset something on her beautiful dress! Betsey dared not think of the catastrophe, and she astonished him by suddenly asking him if he'd please to move his glasses to the other side.

For answer, he turned his eyes full upon her, and she started. Very peculiar eyes they were, round and black, showing a great deal of the white, and that had a yellow tinge. His face was sallow, but otherwise his features were rather fine. It was not the colour of the eyes, however, that startled Betsey Travice, but their expression. A very peculiar expression, which made her recoil from him, and it took its seat firmly thenceforth in her memory. A talkative, agreeable sort of youth he seemed in manner, not as old by a year or two, Betsey thought, as herself; but, somehow, she formed a dislike to him—or rather to his eyes.

"I beg your pardon—I did not catch what you asked me."

"Oh, if you please, sir," meekly stammered Betsey, "I asked if you would mind moving the wine glasses to the other side; all three of them are full."

"And you are afraid of your dress," he said, good-naturedly, doing what she requested. "Such accidents do happen to me sometimes, for I have a trick of throwing my arms about."

But, in spite of the good nature so evident on the surface, there was a hidden vein of satire apparent to Betsey's ear. She blushed violently, fearing she had done something dreadfully incongruous. "I wonder who he is?" she thought; amidst the many names of guests she had not caught his.

Later, when all had left, save the Arkell family, and the bride and bridegroom were some miles on their honeymoon tour, Betsey ventured to put the question to Mildred—Who was the gentleman who had sat next to her at breakfast?

Poor Mildred could not recollect. The breakfast was to her one scene of confused remembrance, and she knew nothing save that she and William Arkell sat side by side.

"I don't remember where you sat," she was obliged to confess to Betsey.

"Nearly opposite to you, Miss Arkell. He had great black eyes, and he talked loud."

"Oh, that was Ben Carr," interrupted Peter; "he did sit next to you. He is Squire Carr's grandson. Did you see an old gentleman with a good deal of white hair, at the end of the table, near my mother?"

"Yes, I did," said Betsey; "I thought what beautiful hair it was."

"That was Squire Carr. I wonder, by the way, what brought Ben at the breakfast. Aunt," added Peter, turning to Mrs. Arkell; "did you invite Benjamin Carr?"

"No, Peter, Benjamin was not invited," was the reply. "Squire Carr and his son were invited, but John declined. I don't much think he likes going out."

"Afraid of being put to the expense of a coat," interrupted Peter.

There was a general laugh, John Carr's propensity to closeness in expenditure was well known. Mrs. Arkell resumed—

"So when John Carr declined, your uncle asked for his eldest son, young Valentine, to come with the squire; it seems, however, the squire brought Benjamin instead."

"Report runs that the squire favours his younger grandson more than he does his elder," remarked Peter. "For that matter, I don't know who does like young Valentine; I don't, he is too mean-spirited. Why did you wish to know who it was, Miss Betsey?"

"Not for anything in particular, sir. What curious eyes he has got!"

It was late when Mrs. Dan and her children went home. The evening had been a quiet one; in no way different from the usual evenings at Mr. Arkell's. Mildred had borne up bravely, and been cheerful as the rest.

But, oh! the tension it had been to every nerve of her frame, every fibre of her heart! Not until she was shut up in the quiet of her own room, did she know the strain it had been. She took her pretty dress off, threw a shawl on her shoulders, and sat down; her brain battling with its misery, her hands pressed upon her throbbing temples.

How long she thus sat she could not tell. I believe—I honestly and truly believe—that no sorrow the world knows, can be of a nature more cruel than was Mildred's that night; certainly none could be more intensely felt. "How can I bear it?" she moaned, "how can I bear it? To see them come back here in their wedded happiness, and have to witness it, and live. Perhaps—after a time, if God will help me, I shall be—"

"What on earth are you doing, Mildred?"

She started from her chair with a scream. So entirely had she believed herself secure from interruption, that in the first confused moments it seemed as if her thoughts and anguish had been laid bare. Mrs. Dan stood there in her night-dress, a candle in her hand.

"You were moaning, Mildred. Are you ill?"

"I—I am quite well, mamma," stammered Mildred, her words confused, and her face a fiery red. "Do you want anything?"

"But how is it you are not undressed? I had been in bed ever so long."

"I suppose I had fallen into a train of thought, and let the time slip away," answered Mildred, beginning to undo her hair in a heap, as if to make up for the lost time. "Why have you come out of your bed, mamma?"

"Child, I don't feel myself, and I thought I'd come and call you. It is well, as it happens, that you are not undressed, for I think I should like a cup of tea made. If I drink it very hot, it may take away the pain."

"Where is the pain?" asked Mildred, beginning to put up her hair again, as hurriedly as she had undone it.

"I scarcely know where it is; I feel ill all over. The fact is, I never ought to go to these festivities," added Mrs. Dan, hastening back to her own room. "They are sure to upset me."

Alas! it was not the festivity that had "upset" Mrs. Dan; but that her time was come. Another hour, and she was so much worse, that Peter had to be aroused from his bed, and go for their doctor. Mrs. Daniel Arkell was in danger.

It may be deemed unfeeling, in some measure, to say it, but it was the best thing that could have happened for Mildred. It took her out of her own thoughts—away from herself. There was so much to do, even in that first night, which was only the commencement; and it all fell on Mildred. Peter, with his timid heart, and unpractised hands, was utterly useless in a sick room, as book-worms in general are; and their one servant, Ann, a young, inexperienced, awkward girl, was nearly as much so. Mustard poultices had to be got, steaming hot flannels, and many other things. Before Mildred had made ready one thing, another called for her. It was well it was so!

At seven o'clock, Peter started for his uncle's, and told the news there. Mr. Arkell went up directly; Mrs. Arkell a little later. Mrs. Dan's danger had become imminent then, and Mr. Arkell went himself, and brought back a physician.

Later in the morning, Mildred was called downstairs to the sitting-room. Betsey Travice was standing there. The girl came forward, a pleading light in her earnest eye.

"Oh, Miss Arkell! if you will only please to let me! I have come to ask to help you."

"To help me!" mechanically repeated Mildred.

"I am so good a nurse; I am indeed! Poor papa died suddenly, but I nursed mamma all through her last long illness; there was only me to do everything, and she used to say that I was as handy as if I had learnt it in the hospitals. Let me try and help you!"

"You are very, very kind," said Mildred, feeling inclined to accept the offer as freely as it was made, for she knew that she should require assistance if the present state of things continued. "How came you to think of it?"

"When Mrs. Arkell came home to breakfast this morning, she said how everything lay upon you, and that you would never be able to do it. I believe she was thinking of sending Tring; but I took courage to tell her what a good nurse I was, and to beg her to let me come. I said—if you will not think it presuming of me, Miss Arkell—that Mrs. Daniel was my Godmother, and I thought it gave me a sort of right to wait upon her."

Mildred, undemonstrative Mildred, stooped down in a sudden impulse, and kissed the gentle face. "I shall be very glad of you, Betsey. Will you stay now?"

There was no need of further words. Betsey's bonnet and shawl were off in a moment, and she stood ready in her soft, black, noiseless dress.

"Please to put me to do anything there is to do, Miss Arkell. Anything, you know. I am handy in the kitchen. I do any sort of rough work as handily as I can nurse. And perhaps your servant will lend me an apron."

Three days only; three days of sharp, quick illness, and Mrs. Daniel Arkell's last hour arrived. Betsey Travice had not boasted unwarrantably, for a better, more patient, ay, or more skilful nurse never entered a sick chamber. She really was of the utmost use and comfort, and Mildred righteously believed that Heaven had been working out its own ends in sending her just at that time to Westerbury.

It was somewhat singular that Betsey Travice should again be brought into the presence of the young gentleman to whose eyes she had taken so unaccountable a dislike. On that last day, when the final scene was near at hand, the maid came to the dying chamber, saying that Miss Arkell was wanted below; a messenger had come over from Mr. John Carr, and was asking to see her in person.

"I cannot go down now," was Mildred's answer; "you might have known that, Ann."

"I did know it, miss, and I said it; that is, I said I didn't think you could. But he wouldn't take no denial; he said Mr. Carr had told him not."

Giving herself no trouble as to who the "he" might be, Mildred whispered to Betsey Travice to go down for her, and mention the state of things.

Excessively to Betsey's discomfiture, she found herself confronted by the gentleman of the curious eyes, who held out his hand familiarly.

His errand was nothing particular, after all; but his father had expressly ordered him to see Miss Arkell, and convey to her personally his sympathy and inquiries as to her mother's state. For the news of Mrs. Dan's danger had travelled to Squire Carr's, and urgent business at home had alone prevented John Carr's coming over in person. As it was, he sent his son Ben.

Betsey, more meek than ever, thanked him, and told him how ill Mrs. Daniel was; that, in point of fact, another hour or two would bring the end. It was quite impossible Miss Arkell could, under the circumstances, leave the chamber.

"Of course she can't," he answered; "and I'm very sorry to hear it. My father will go on at me, I dare say, saying it was my fault, as he generally does when anything goes contrary to his orders. But he'd not have seen her any the more had he come himself. You will tell me who you are?" he suddenly continued to Betsey, without any break; "I sat by you at the breakfast, but I forget your name."

"If you please, sir, it is Betsey Travice," was the reply, and the girl quite cowered as she stood under the blaze of those black and piercing eyes.

"Betsey Travice! and a very pretty name, too. You'll please to say everything proper for us up there," jerking his head in the direction of the upper floors. "Oh! and I say, I forgot to add that my grandfather, the squire, intends to ride in to-morrow, and call."

He shook hands with her in the passage, and vaulted out at the front door, a tall, strong, fine young fellow. And those eyes, which had so unaccountably excited the disfavour of Miss Betsey, were generally considered the handsomest of the handsome.

Betsey stole upstairs again, and whispered the message into Mildred's ear. "It was that tall, dark young man, with the black eyes, that sat by me at Charlotte's wedding breakfast."

They waited on, in the hushed chamber: Peter, Mildred, Mr. and Mrs. Arkell, and Betsey Travice. And at two o'clock in the afternoon the shutters were put up to the windows, through which Mrs. Daniel Arkell would never look again.

CHAPTER X

GOING OUT AS LADY'S MAID

A week or two given to grief, and Mildred Arkell sat down to deliberate upon her plans for the future. It was impossible to conceal from herself, dutiful, loving, grieving daughter though she was, how wonderfully her mother's death had removed the one sole impediment to the wish that had for some little time lain uppermost in her heart. She wanted to leave Westerbury; it was misery to her to remain in it; but while her mother had lived, her place was there. All seemed easy now; and in the midst of her bitter grief for that mother, Mildred's heart almost leaped at the thought that there was no longer any imperative tie to bind her to her home.

She would go away from Westerbury. But how? what to do? For a governess Mildred had not been educated; and accomplishments were then getting so very general, even the daughters of the petty tradespeople learning them, that Mildred felt in that capacity she should stand but little chance of obtaining a situation. But she might be a companion to an invalid lady, might nurse her, wait upon her, and be of use to her; and that sort of situation she determined to seek.

Quietly, and after much thought, she arranged her plans in her own mind; quietly she hoped and prayed for assistance to be enabled to carry them out. Nobody suspected this. Mildred seemed to others just as she had ever seemed, quiet, unobtrusive Mildred Arkell, absorbed in the domestic cares of her own home, in thought for the comfort of her not at all strong brother. Mildred went now but very little to her aunt's. Betsey Travice had returned to London, to the enjoyments of Mrs. Dundyke's household, which she had refused to abandon; and William Arkell and his bride were not yet come home.

"Peter," she said, one late evening that they were sitting together—and it was the first intimation of the project that had passed her lips—"I have been thinking of the future."

"Yes?" replied Peter, absently, for he was as usual disputing some knotty point in his mind, having a Greek root for its basis. "What about it?"

"I am thinking of leaving home; leaving it for good."

The words awoke even Peter. He listened to her while she told her tale, listened without interrupting, he was so amazed.

"But I cannot understand why you want to go," he said at last.

"To be independent." Of course she was ready to assign any motive but the real one.

Peter could not understand this. She was independent at home. "I don't know what it is you are thinking of, Mildred! Our house will go on just the same; my mother's death makes no difference to it. I kept it before, and I shall keep it still."

"Oh yes, Peter, I know that. That is not it. I—in point of fact, I wish for a change of scene. I think I am tired of Westerbury."

"But what can you do if you go away from it?"

"I intend to ask Colonel and Mrs. Dewsbury: I suppose you have no objection. They have many influential friends in London and elsewhere, and perhaps they might help me to a situation."

"Why do you want to go to London?" rejoined Peter, catching at the word. "It's full of traps and pitfalls, as people say. I don't know; I never was there."

"I don't want to go to London, in particular; I don't care where I go." Anywhere—anywhere that would take her out of Westerbury, she had nearly added; but she controlled the words, and resumed calmly. "I would as soon go to London as to any other place, Peter, and to any other place as to London. I don't mind where it is, so that I find a—a—sphere of usefulness."

"I don't like it at all," said Peter, after a pause of deliberation. "There are only two of us left now, Mildred, and I think we ought to continue together."

"I will come and see you sometimes."

"But, Mildred—"

"Listen, Peter," she imperatively interrupted, "it may save trouble. I have made up my mind to do this, and you must forgive me for saying that I am my own mistress, free to go, free to come. I wished to go out in this way some time before my mother died; but it was not right for me to leave her, and I said nothing. I shall certainly go now. I heard somebody once speak of the 'fever of change,'" she added, with a poor attempt at jesting; "I suppose I have caught it."

"Well, I am sorry, Mildred: it's all I can say. I did not think you would have been so eager to leave me."

The ready tears filled her eyes. "I am not eager to leave you, Peter; it will be my greatest grief. And you know if the thing does not work well, and I get too much buffeted by the world, I can but come back to you."

It never occurred to Peter Arkell to interpose any sort of veto, to say you shall not go. He had not had a will of his own in all his life; his mother and Mildred had arranged everything for him, and had Mildred announced her intention of becoming an opera dancer, he would never have presumed to gainsay it.

The following morning Mildred called at Mrs. Dewsbury's. They lived in a fine house at the opposite side of the river; but only about ten minutes' walk distance, if you took the near way, and crossed the ferry.

One of the loveliest girls Mildred had ever in her life seen was in the drawing-room to which she was shown, to wait for Mrs. Dewsbury. It was Miss Cheveley, an orphan relative of Mrs. Dewsbury's, who had recently come to reside with her. She rose from her chair in courteous welcome to Mildred; and Mildred could not for a few moments take her eyes from her face—from the delicate, transparent features, the rich, loving brown eyes, and the damask cheeks. The announcement, "Miss Arkell," and the deep mourning, had no doubt led the young lady to conclude that it was the tutor's sister. Mrs. Dewsbury came in immediately.

"Lucy, will you go into the schoolroom," she said, as she shook hands with Mildred, whom she knew, though very slightly. "The governess is giving Maria her music lesson, and the others are alone."

As Miss Cheveley crossed the room in acquiescence, Mildred's eyes followed her—followed her to the last moment; and she observed that Mrs. Dewsbury noticed that they did.

"I never saw anyone so beautiful in my life," she said to Mrs. Dewsbury by way of apology.

"Do you think so? A lovely face, certainly; but you know face is not everything. It cannot compensate for figure. Poor Miss Cheveley!"

"Is Miss Cheveley's not a good figure?"

"Miss Cheveley's! Did you not notice? She is deformed."

Mildred had not noticed it. She had been too absorbed in the lovely face. She turned to Mrs. Dewsbury, apologized for calling upon her, told her errand, that she wished to go out in the world, and craved the assistance of herself and Colonel Dewsbury in endeavouring to place her.

"I know, madam, that you have influential friends in many parts of England," she said, "and it is this—"

"But in what capacity do you wish to go out?" interrupted Mrs. Dewsbury. "As governess?"

"I would go as English governess," answered Mildred, with a stress upon the word. "But I do not understand French, and I know nothing of music or drawing: therefore I fear there is little chance for me in that capacity. I thought perhaps I might find a situation as companion; as humble companion, that is to say, to make myself useful."

Mrs. Dewsbury shook her head. "Such situations are rare, Miss Arkell."

"I suppose they are; too rare, perhaps, for me to find. Rather than not find anything, I would go out as lady's maid."

"As lady's maid!" repeated Mrs. Dewsbury.

Mildred's cheek burnt, and she suddenly thought of what the town would say. "Yes, as lady's maid, rather than not go," she repeated, firm in her resolution. "I think I have not much pride; what I have, I must subdue."

"But, Miss Arkell, allow me to ask—and I have a motive in it—whether you would be capable of a lady's-maid's duties?"

"I think so," replied Mildred. "I would endeavour to render myself so. I have made my own dresses and bonnets, and I used to make my mother's caps until she became a widow; and I am fond of dressing hair."

Mrs. Dewsbury mused. "I think I have heard that you are well read, Miss Arkell?"

"Yes, I am," replied Mildred. "I am a thoroughly good English scholar; and my father, whose taste in literature was excellent, formed mine. I could teach Latin to boys until they were ten or eleven," she added, with a half smile.

"Do you read aloud well?"

"I believe I do. I have been in the habit of reading a great deal to my mother."

"Well now I will tell you the purport of my putting these questions, which I hope you have not thought impertinent," said Mrs. Dewsbury. "The last time Lady Dewsbury wrote to us—you may have heard of her, perhaps, Miss Arkell, the widow of Sir John?"

Mildred did not remember to have done so.

"Sir John Dewsbury was my husband's brother. But that is of no consequence. Lady Dewsbury, the widow, is an invalid; and the last time she wrote to us she mentioned in her letter that she was wishing to find some one who would act both as companion and maid. It was merely spoken of incidentally, and I do not know whether she is suited. Shall I write and inquire?"

"Oh, thank you, thank you!" cried Mildred, her heart eagerly grasping at this faint prospect. "I shall not care what I do, if Lady Dewsbury will but take me."

Mrs. Dewsbury smiled at the eagerness. She concluded that Mrs. Dan's death had made a difference in their income, hence the wish to go out. Mildred returned home, said nothing to anybody of what she had done, and waited, full of hope.

A short while of suspense, and then Mrs. Dewsbury sent for her. Lady Dewsbury's answer was favourable. She was willing to make the engagement, provided Miss Arkell could undertake what was required.

"First of all," said Mrs. Dewsbury to her, "Lady Dewsbury asks whether you can bear confinement?"

"I can indeed," replied Mildred. "And the better, perhaps, that I have no wish for aught else."

"Are you a good nurse in sickness?"

"I nursed my mother in her last illness," said Mildred, with tears in her eyes. "It was a very short one, it is true; but she had been ailing for years, and I attended on her. She used to say I must have been born a nurse."

"Lady Dewsbury is a great invalid," continued the colonel's wife, "and what she requires is a patient attendant; a maid, if you like to call it such; but who will at the same time be to her a companion and friend. 'A thoroughly-well-brought-up person,' she writes, 'lady-like in her manners and habits; but not a fine lady who would object to make herself useful.' I really think you would suit, Miss Arkell."

Mildred thought so too. "I will serve her to the very best of my power, Mrs. Dewsbury, if she will but try me;" and Mrs. Dewsbury noted the same eagerness that had been in her tone before, and smiled at it.

"She is willing to try you. Lady Dewsbury has, in fact, left the decision to the judgment of myself and the colonel. She has described exactly what she requires, and has empowered us to engage you, if we think you will be suitable."

"And will you engage me, Mrs. Dewsbury?"

"I will engage you now. The next question is about salary. Lady Dewsbury proposes to give at the rate of thirty pounds per annum for the first six months; after that at the rate of forty pounds; and should you remain with her beyond two years, it would be raised to fifty."

"Fifty!" echoed Mildred, in her astonishment. "Fifty pounds a year! For me!"

"Is it less than you expected?"

"It is a great deal more," was the candid answer. "I had not thought much about salary. I fancied I might be offered perhaps ten or twenty pounds."

Mrs. Dewsbury smiled. "Lady Dewsbury is liberal in all she does, Miss Arkell. I should not be surprised, were you to remain with her any considerable length of time, several years for instance, but she would double it."

But for the skeleton preying on Mildred Arkell's heart—the bitter agony that never left it by night or by day—she would have walked home, not knowing whether she trod on her head or her heels. The prospect of fifty pounds a-year to an inexperienced girl, who, perhaps, had never owned more than a few shillings at a time in her life, was enough to turn her head.

But it was not all to be quite plain sailing. Mildred had not disclosed the project to her aunt yet. Truth was, she shrunk from the task, foreseeing the opposition that would inevitably ensue. But it must no longer be delayed, for she was to depart for London that day week, and she went straight to Mrs. Arkells. As she had expected, Mrs. Arkell met the news with extreme astonishment and anger.

"Do you know what you are doing, child! Don't talk to me about being a burden upon Peter! You—"

"Aunt, hear me!" she implored: and be it observed, that to Mrs. Arkell, Mildred put not forth one word of that convenient plea of "seeing the world," that she had filled Peter with. To Mrs. Arkell she urged another phase of the reasoning, and one, in truth, which had no slight weight with herself—Peter's interests. "I ought not to be a burden upon Peter, aunt, and I will not. You know how his heart is set upon going to the university; but he cannot get there if he does not save for it? If I remain at home, the house must be kept up the same as now; the housekeeping expenses must go on; and it will take every shilling of Peter's earnings to do all this. Aunt, I could not live upon him, for very shame. While my mother was here it was a different thing."

"But—to go to Peter's own affairs for a moment," cried Mrs. Arkell, irascibly—"what great difference will your going away make to his expenses? Twenty pounds a year at most. Where's the use of your putting a false colouring on things to me?"

"I have not done so, aunt. Peter and I have talked these matters over since I resolved to go out, and I believe he intends to let his house."

"To let his house!"

"It is large for him now; large and lonely. He means to let it, if he can, furnished; just as it is."

"And take up his abode in the street?"

"He will easily find apartments for himself," said Mildred, feeling for and excusing Mrs. Arkell's unusual irritability. "And, aunt, don't you see what a great advantage this would be to him in his plans? Saving a great part of what he earns, receiving money for his house besides, he will soon get together enough to take him to college."

"I don't see anything, except that this notion of going away, which you have taken up, is a very wrong one. It cannot be permitted, Mildred."

"Oh! aunt, don't say so," she entreated. "Peter must put by."

"Let him put by; it is what he ought to do. And you, Mildred, must come to us. Be a daughter to me and to your uncle in our old age. Since William left it, the house is not the same, and we are lonely. We once thought—you will not mind my saying it now—that you would indeed have been a daughter to us, and in that case William's home and yours would have been here. He should never have left us."

"Aunt—"

"Be still, and hear me, Mildred. I do not ask you this on the spur of the moment, because you are threatening to go out to service; and it is nothing less. Child! did you think we were going to neglect you? To leave you alone with Peter, uncared for? Your uncle and I had already planned to bring you home to us, but we were willing to let you stay a short while with Peter, so as not to take everybody from him just at once. Why, Mildred, are you aware that your mother knew you were to come to us?"

Mildred was not aware of it. She sat smoothing the black crape tucks of her dress with her forefinger, making no reply. Her heart was full.

"A few days after I made that foolish mistake—but indeed the fault was William's, and so I have always told him—I went and had it all out with Mrs. Dan. I told her how bitterly disappointed I and George both were; but I said, in one sense it need make no difference to us, for you should be our daughter still, and come home to us as soon as ever—I mean, when the time came that you would no longer be wanted at home. And I can tell you, Mildred, that your mother was gratified at the plan, though you are not."

Mildred's eyes were swimming. She felt that if she spoke, it would be to break into sobs.

"Your poor mother said it took a weight from her mind. The house is Peter's, as you know, and he can't dispose of it, but the furniture was hers, left absolutely to her by your papa at his death. She had been undecided whether she ought not to leave the furniture to you, as Peter had the house; and yet she did not like to take it from him. This plan of ours provided for you; so her course was clear, not to divide the furniture from the house. As it turned out, she made no will, through delaying it from time to time; and in law, I suppose, the furniture belongs as much to you as to Peter. You must come home to us, Mildred."

"Oh, aunt, you and my uncle are both very kind," she sobbed. "I should have liked much to come here and contribute to your comforts; but, indeed—"

"Indeed—what?" persisted Mrs. Arkell, pressing the point at which Mildred stopped.

"I cannot—I cannot come," she murmured, in her distress.

"But why?—what is your reason?"

"Aunt! aunt! do not ask me. Indeed I cannot stop in Westerbury."

They were interrupted by the entrance of William, and Mildred literally started from her seat, her poor heart beating wildly. She did not know of their return—had been in hopes, indeed, that she should have left the town before it; but, as she now learnt, they came home the previous night.

"I can make nothing of Mildred," cried Mrs. Arkell to her son; and in her anger and vexation, she gave him an outline of the case. "It is the most senseless scheme I ever heard of."

Mildred had touched the hand held out to her in greeting, and dried her tears as she best could, and altogether strove to be unconcerned and calm. He looked well—tall, noble, good, as usual, and very happy.

"See if you can do anything to shake her resolution, William. I have tried in vain."

Mrs. Arkell quitted the room abruptly, as she spoke. Mildred passed her handkerchief over her pale face, and rose from her seat.

Knowing what he did know, it was not a pleasant task for William Arkell. But for the extreme sensitiveness of his nature, he might have given some common-place refusal, and run away. As it was, he advanced to her with marked hesitation, and a flush of emotion rose to his face.

"Is there anything I can urge, Mildred, that will induce you to abandon this plan of yours, and remain in Westerbury?"

"Nothing," she replied.

"Why should you persist in leaving your native place?—why have you formed this strange dislike to remain in it?" he proceeded.

She would have answered him; she tried to answer him—any idle excuse that rose to her lips; but as he stood there, asking WHY she had taken a dislike to remain in the home of her childhood—he, the husband of another—the full sense of her bitter sorrow and desolation came rushing on, and overwhelmed her forced self-control. She hid her face in her hands, and sobbed in anguish.

William Arkell, almost as much agitated as herself, drew close to her. He took her hand—he bent down to her with a whisper of strange tenderness. "If I have had a share in causing you any grief, or—or—disappointment, let me implore your forgiveness, Mildred. It was not intentionally done. You cannot think so."

She motioned him away, her sobs seeming as if they would choke her.

"Mildred, I must speak; it has been in my heart to do it since—you know when," he whispered hoarsely, in his emotion, and he gathered both her hands in his, and kept them there. "I have begun to think lately, since my marriage, that it might have been well for both of us had we understood each other better. You talk of going into the world, a solitary wanderer; and my path, I fear, will not be one of roses, although it was of my own choosing. But what is done cannot be recalled."

"I must go home," she faintly interrupted; "you are trying me too greatly." But he went on as though he heard her not.

"Can we not both make the best of what is left to us? Stay in Westerbury, Mildred! Come home here to my father and mother; they are lonely now. Be to them a daughter, and to me as a dear sister."

"I shall never more have my home in Westerbury," she answered; "never more—never more. We can bid each other adieu now."

A moment's miserable pause. "Is there no appeal from this, Mildred?"

"None."

"Will you always remember, then, that you are very dear to me? Should you ever want a friend, Mildred—ever want any assistance in any way—do not forget where I am to be found. I am a married man now, and yet I tell you openly that Westerbury will have lost one of its greatest charms for me, when you have left it."

"Let me go!" was all she murmured; "I cannot bear the pain."

He clasped her for a moment to his heart, and kissed her fervently. "Forgive me, Mildred—we are cousins still," he said, as he released her; "forgive me for all. May God bless and be with you, now and always!"

With her crape veil drawn before her face, with the cruel pain of desolation mocking at her heart, Mildred went forth; and in the court-yard she encountered Mrs. William Arkell, in a whole array of bridal feathers and furbelows, arriving to pay her first morning visit to her husband's former home. She held out her hand to Mildred, and threw back her white veil from her radiant face.

A confused greeting—she knew not of what—a murmured plea of being in haste—a light word of careless gossip, and Mildred passed on.

So there was to be no hindrance, and poor Mildred was to leave her home, and go forth to find one with strangers! But from that day she seemed to change—to grow cold and passionless; and people reproached her for it, and wondered what had come to her.

How many of these isolated women do we meet in the world, to whom the same reproach seems due! I never see one of them but I mentally wonder whether her once warm, kindly feelings may not have been crushed; trampled on; just as was the case with those of Mildred Arkell.

CHAPTER XI

MR CARR'S OFFER

Rare nuts for Westerbury to crack! So delightful a dish of gossip had not been served up to it since that affair of Robert Carr's. Miss Arkell was going out as lady's-maid!

Such was the report that spread, to the intense indignation of Mrs. Arkell. In vain that lady protested that her obstinate and reprehensibly-independent niece was going out as companion, not as lady's-maid; Westerbury nodded its head and knew better. It must be confessed that Mildred herself favoured the popular view: she was to be lady's-maid, she honestly said, as well as companion.

The news, indeed, caused real commotion in the town; and Mildred was remonstrated with from all quarters. What could she mean by leaving incapable Peter to himself?—and if people said true, Mr. and Mrs. Arkell would have been glad to adopt her. Mildred parried the comments, and shut herself up as far as she could.

But she could not shut herself up from all; she had to take the annoyances as they came. A very especial one arrived for her only the morning previous to her departure. It was not intended as an annoyance, though, but as an honour.

There came to visit her Mr. John Carr, the son and heir of the squire. He came in state—a phæton and pair, and his groom beside him. John Carr was a little man, with mean-looking features and thin lips; and there was the very slightest suspicion of a cross in his light eyes. Mildred was vexed at his visit; not because she was busy packing, but for a reason that she knew of. Some twelve months before, John Carr had privately made her an offer of his hand. She had refused it at once and positively, and she had never since liked to meet him. She could not escape now, for the servant said she was at home.

He had been shown upstairs to the drawing-room, an apartment they rarely used; and he stood there in top-boots and a rose in his black frock coat. Mildred saw at once what was coming—a second offer. She refused him before he had well made it.

"But you must have me, Miss Arkell, you must," he reiterated. "You know how much I have wished for you; and—is it true that you think of going out to service in London?"

"Quite true," said Mildred. "I am going as companion and maid to Lady Dewsbury."

"But surely that is not desirable. If there is no other resource left, you must come to me. I know you forbid me ever to renew the subject again; but—"

"I beg your pardon, Mr. Carr. Your premises are wrong. I am not going out because I have no other resource. I have my home here, if I chose to stay in it. I have one pressed urgently upon me with my aunt and uncle. It is not that. I am going because I wish to go. I wish for a change. It is very kind of you to renew your offer to me; but you must pardon my saying that I should have found it kinder had you abided by my previous answer."

"What is the reason you will not have me, Miss Arkell? I know what it is, though: it is because I have had two wives already. But if I have, I made them both happy while they lived. They—"

"Oh, pray, Mr. Carr, don't talk so," she interrupted. "Pray take my answer, and let the subject be at an end."

But Mr. Carr was one who never liked any subject to be at an end, so long as he chose to pursue it; and he was fond of diving into reasons for himself.

"I shall be Squire Carr after the old man's gone; the owner of the property. I can make a settlement on you, Miss Arkell."

"I don't want it, thank you," she said in her vexation. All Mildred's life, even when she was a little girl, she had particularly disliked Mr. John Carr.

"It's the children, I suppose," grumbled Mr. Carr. "But they need not annoy you. Valentine must stop at home; for it has not been the custom in our house to send the eldest son out. But Ben will go; I shall soon send him now. In fact, I did place him out; but he wouldn't stop, and came back again. Emma, I dare say, will be marrying; and then there's only the young children. You will be mistress of the house, and rule it as my late wife did. It is not an offer to be despised, Miss Arkell."

"I don't despise it," returned Mildred, wishing he would be said, and take himself away. "But I cannot accept it."

"Well, what is it, then? Do you intend never to marry?"

The question called up bitter remembrances, and a burning red suffused her cheeks.

"I shall never marry, Mr. Carr. At least, such is my belief now. Certainly I shall not marry until I have tried whether I cannot be happy in my life of dependence at Lady Dewsbury's."

Mr. John Carr's lucky star appeared not to be in the ascendant that day, and he went out considerably crest-fallen. Whipping his horses, he proceeded up the town to pay a visit to his uncle, Mr. Marmaduke Carr. None, save himself, knew how covetous were the eyes he cast to the good fortune his uncle had to bequeath to somebody; or that he would cast so long as the bequeathal remained in abeyance.

Lady Dewsbury lived in the heart of the fashionable part of London. Mildred went up alone. Mrs. Arkell had made a hundred words over it; but Mildred stood out for her independence: if she were not fit to take care of herself on a journey to London by day, she urged, how should she be fit to enter on the life she had carved out for herself? She found no trouble. Mr. Arkell had given instructions to the guard, and he called a coach for her at the journey's end. One of Mildred's great surprises on entering Lady Dewsbury's house was, to find that lady young. As the widow of the colonel's eldest brother—and the colonel himself was past middle age—Mildred had pictured in her mind a woman of at least fifty. Lady Dewsbury, however, did not look more than thirty, and Mildred was puzzled, for she knew there was a grown-up son, Sir Edward. Lady Dewsbury was a plain woman, with a sickly look, and teeth that projected very much; but the expression of her face was homely and kindly, and Mildred liked her at the first glance. She was leaning back in an invalid chair; a peculiar sort of chair, the like of which Mildred had never seen, and a maid stood before her holding a cup of tea. Mildred found afterwards that Lady Dewsbury suffered from an internal complaint; nothing dangerous in itself, but tedious, and often painful. It caused her to live completely the life of an invalid; going out very little, and receiving few visitors. The medical men said if she could live over the next ten years or so, she might recover, and be afterwards a strong woman.

Nothing could be more kind and cordial than her reception of Mildred. She received her more as an equal than an attendant. It relieved Mildred excessively. Reared in her simple country home, a Lady Dewsbury, or Lady anybody else, was a formidable personage to Mildred; one of the high-born and unapproachable of the land. It must be confessed that Mildred was at first as timid as ever poor humble Betsey Travice could have been; and nearly broke down as she ventured on a word of hope that "My lady," "her ladyship," would find her equal to her duties.

"Stay, my dear," said Lady Dewsbury, detecting the embarrassment—and smiling at it—"let us begin as we are to go on. I am neither my lady nor your ladyship to you, remember. When you have occasion to address me by name, I am Lady Dewsbury; but that need not be often. Mrs. Dewsbury said you were coming to be my maid, I think?"

"Yes," replied Mildred.

"I told her to say it, because I shall require many little services performed for me on my worst days that properly belong to a maid to perform; and I did not like to deceive you in any way. But can you understand me when I say that I do not wish you to do these things for me as a servant, but as a friend?"

"I shall be so happy to do them," murmured Mildred.

"I do not wish to keep two persons near me, a companion and a maid. I have tried it, and it does not answer. Until my sister married, she lived with me, my companion; and I had my maid. After my sister left, I engaged a lady to replace her, but she and the maid did not get on together; the one grew jealous of the other, and things became so unpleasant, that I gave both of them notice to leave. It then occurred to me that I might unite the two in one, if by good luck I could find a well-educated and yet domesticated lady, who would not be above waiting on an invalid. And I happened to mention this to Mrs. Dewsbury."

"I hope you will like me; I hope I shall suit," was Mildred's only answering comment.

"I like you already," returned Lady Dewsbury. "I am apt to take fancies to faces, and the contrary, and I have taken a fancy to yours. But I will go on with my explanation. You will not be regarded in the light of a servant, or ever treated as one. You will generally sit with me, and take your meals with me when I am alone. If I have visitors, you will take them in the little sitting-room appropriated for yourself. The servants will wait upon you, and observe to you proper respect. I have not told them you are coming here as my maid, but as my friend and companion."

Mildred felt overpowered at the kindness.

"In reality you will, as I have said, in many respects be my maid; that is, you will have to do for me a maid's duties," proceeded Lady Dewsbury. "You will dress me and undress me. You will sleep in the next room to mine, with the door open between, so as to hear me when I call; for I am sorry to say, my sufferings occasionally require sudden attendance in the night. As my companion, you will read to me, write letters for me, go with me in the carriage when I travel, help me with my worsted work, of which I am very fond, do my personal errands for me out of doors, give orders to the servants when I am not well enough, keep the housekeeping accounts, and always be—patient, willing, and good-tempered."

Lady Dewsbury said the last words with a laugh.

Mildred gave one of her sweet smiles in answer.

"I really mean it though, Miss Arkell," continued Lady Dewsbury. "Patience is absolutely essential for one who has to be with a sufferer like myself; and I could not bear one about me for a day who showed unwillingness or ill-temper. The trouble that I am obliged to give, is sufficiently present always to my own mind; but I could not bear to have the expression of it thrown back to me. The last and worst thing I must now mention; and that is, the confinement. When I am pretty well, as I am now, it is not so much; but it sometimes happens that I am very ill for weeks together; never out of my room, scarcely out of my bed: and not once perhaps during all that time will you be able to go out of doors."

"I shall not mind it indeed, Lady Dewsbury," Mildred said, heartily. "I am used to confinement. I told Mrs. Dewsbury so. Oh, if I can but suit you, I shall not mind what I do. I think it seems a very, very nice place. I did not expect to meet with one half so good."

"How old do you think I am?" suddenly asked Lady Dewsbury. "Perhaps Mrs. Dewsbury mentioned it to you?"

"It is puzzling me," said Mildred, candidly, quite overlooking the last question. "I could not take you to be more than thirty; but I—I had fancied—I beg your pardon, Lady Dewsbury—that you must be quite fifty. I thought Sir Edward was some years past twenty."

"Sir Edward?—what has that to do with—oh, I see! You are taking Sir Edward to be my son. Why, he is nearly as old as I am, and I am thirty-five. I was Sir John Dewsbury's second wife. I never had any children. Sir Edward comes here sometimes. We are very good friends."

Mildred's puzzle was explained, and Lady Dewsbury sent her away, happy, to see her room. It had been a gracious reception, a cordial welcome; and it seemed to whisper an earnest of future comfort, of length of service.

Lady Dewsbury was tolerably well at that period, and Mildred found that she might take advantage of it to pay an afternoon visit to Betsey Travice. She sent word that she was coming, and Betsey was in readiness to receive her; and Mrs. Dundyke, a stout lady in faded black silk, had a sumptuous meal ready: muffins, bread and butter, shrimps, and water-cress.

The parlour, on a level with the kitchen, was a very shabby one, and the bells of the house kept clanging incessantly, and Mrs. Dundyke went in and out to urge the servant to alacrity in answering them, and two troublesome fractious children, of eighteen months, and three years old, insisted on monopolizing the cares of Betsey; and altogether Mildred wondered that Betsey could or would stop there.

"But I like it," whispered Betsey, "I do indeed. Mrs. Dundyke is not handsome, but she's very kind-hearted, and the children are fond of me; and I feel at home here, and there's a great deal in that. And besides—"

"Besides—what?" asked Mildred, for the words had come to a sudden stand-still.

"There's David," came forth the faint and shame-faced answer.

"David?"

"Mrs. Dundyke's son. We are to be married sometime."

Mildred had the honour of an introduction to the gentleman before she left—for Mr. David came in—a young man above the middle height, somewhat free and confident in his address and manners. He was not bad-looking, and he was attired sufficiently well; for the house he was in, in Fenchurch-street, was one of the first houses of its class, and would not have tolerated shabbiness in any of its clerks. The shirt-sleeve episodes, the blacking-boot and carrying-up coal attire, so vivid in the remembrance of Charlotte Travice, were kept for home, for late at night and early morning. Of this, Mildred saw nothing, heard nothing.

"He has eighty pounds a year now," whispered Betsey to Mildred; "his next rise will be a hundred and fifty. And then, when it has got to that—," the blush on the cheeks, the downcast eyes, told the rest.

"Them there shrimps ain't bad; take some more of 'em."

Mildred positively started—not at the invitation so abruptly given to her, but at the wording of it. It was the first sentence she had heard him speak. Had he framed it in joke?

No; it was his habitual manner of speaking. She cast her compassionate eyes on Betsey Travice, just as Charlotte would have cast her indignant ones. But Betsey was used to him, and did not feel the degradation.

"Now, mother, don't you worry your inside out after that girl," he said, as Mrs. Dundyke, for the fiftieth time, plunged into the kitchen, groaning over the shortcomings of the servant. "You won't live no longer for it. Betsey, just put them two squalling chickens down, and pour me out a drop more tea; make yourself useful if you can till mother comes back. Won't you take no more, Miss Arkell?"

"Betsey," asked Mildred, in a low tone, as they were alone for a few minutes when Mildred was about to leave, "do you like Mr. David Dundyke?"

Betsey's face was sufficient answer.

"I think you ought not to be too precipitate to say you will do this or do the other. You are young, Mr. Dundyke is young, and—and—if you had had more experience in the world, you might not have engaged yourself to him."

"Thank you kindly; that is just as Charlotte says. But we are not going to marry yet."

"Betsey—you will excuse me for saying it: if I speak, it is for your own sake—do you consider Mr. Dundyke, with his—his apparently imperfect education, is suitable for you?"

"Indeed," answered Betsey, "his education is better than it appears. He has fallen into this odd way of speaking from habit, from association with his mother. She speaks so, you must perceive. He rather prides himself upon keeping it up, upon not being what he calls fine. And he is so clever in his business!"

Mildred could not at all understand that sort of "pride." Betsey Travice noticed the gravity of her eye.

"What education have I had, Miss Arkell? None. I learnt to read, and write, and spell, and I learnt nothing more. If I speak as a lady, it is because I was born to it, because papa and mamma and Charlotte so spoke, not from any advantages they gave me. I have been kept down all my life. Charlotte was made a lady of, and I was made to work. When I was only six years old I had to wait on mamma and Charlotte. I am not complaining of this; I like work; but I mention it, to ask you in what way, remembering these things, I am better than David Dundyke?"

In truth, Mildred could not say.

"What am I now but a burden on his mother?" continued Betsey. "In one sense I repay my cost; for, if I were not here, she would have to take a servant for the two little children. I have no prospects at all; I have nobody in the world to help me; indeed, Miss Arkell, it is generous of David to ask me to be his wife."

"You might find a home with your sister, now she has one. You ought to have it with her."

Betsey shook her head. "You don't know Charlotte," was all she answered.

Mildred dropped the subject. She took a ring from her purse, an emerald set round with pearls, and put it into Betsey's hand.

"It was my mother's," she said, "and I brought it for you. She had two of these rings just alike; one of them had belonged to a sister of hers who died. I wear the other—see! My mother was very poor, Betsey, or she might have left something worth the acceptance of you, her goddaughter."

Betsey Travice burst into tears, partly at the kind words, partly at the munificence of the gift, for she had never possessed so much as a brass ring in all her life.

"It is too good for me," she said; "I ought not to take it from you. I would not, but for your having one like it. What have I done that you should all be so kind to me? But I will never part with the ring."

And, indeed, the contrast between the kindness to her of the Arkells generally and the unfeeling behaviour of her sister Charlotte, could but mark its indelible trace on even the humble mind of Betsey Travice.

"Has Charlotte come home?" she asked.

"Have you heard from her?" exclaimed Mildred in astonishment. "She came home before I left Westerbury."

Betsey shook her head. "We are not to keep up any correspondence; Charlotte said it would not do; that our paths in life lay apart; hers up in the world, mine down; and she did not care to own me for a sister. Of course I know I am inferior to Charlotte, and always have been; but still—"

Betsey broke down. The grieved heart was full.

CHAPTER XII

MARRIAGES IN UNFASHIONABLE LIFE

The next twelvemonth brought little of event, if we except the birth of a boy to William Arkell and his wife. In the month of March, nearly a year after their marriage, the child was born; and its mother was so ill, so very near, as was believed, unto death, that Mrs. Arkell sent a despatch to bring down her sister, Betsey Travice. Had Charlotte been able to have a voice in the affair, rely upon it Betsey had never come.

But Charlotte was not, and Betsey arrived; the same meek Betsey as of yore. William liked the young girl excessively, and welcomed her with a warm heart and open arms. His wife was better then, could be spoken to, and did not feel in the least obliged to them for having summoned Betsey.

"I am glad to see you, Betsey," William whispered, "and so would Charlotte be, poor girl, if she were a little less ill. You shall stand to the baby, Betsey; he is but a sickly little fellow, it seems, and they are talking of christening him at once. If it were a girl, we would name it after you; we'll call it—can't we call it Travice? That will be after you, all the same, and it's a very pretty name."

Betsey shook her head dubiously. She had an innate fondness for children, and she kissed the little red face nestled in her arms.

"Charlotte would not like me to stand to it," she whispered.

"Not like it!" echoed William, who did not know his wife yet, and had no suspicion of the state of things. "Of course she would like it. Who has so great a right to stand to the child as you, her sister. Would you like it yourself?"

"Oh, very much; I should think it was my own little boy all through life."

"Until you have little boys of your own," laughed William, and Betsey felt her face glow. "All right, his name shall be Travice."

And so it was; the child was christened Travice George; and Betsey had become his godmother before Charlotte knew the treason that was agate. She was bitterly unkind over it afterwards to Betsey, reproaching her with "thrusting herself forward unwarrantably."

A very, very short stay with them, only until Charlotte was quite out of danger, and Betsey went back to London. "Do not, if you can help it, ever ask me down again, dear Mrs. Arkell," she said, with tears. "You must see how it is—how unwelcome I am; Charlotte, of course, is a lady, always was one, and I am but a poor working girl. It is natural she should wish us not to keep up too much intimacy."

"I call it very unnatural," indignantly remonstrated Mrs. Arkell.

Perhaps Betsey Travice yearned to this little baby all the more, from the fact that the youngest of the two children she had taken care of at Mrs. Dundyke's, had died a few months before. Fractious, sickly, troublesome as it had been, Betsey's fondness for it was great, and her sorrow heavy. There had been nobody to mourn it but herself; Mrs. Dundyke was too much absorbed in her household cares to spare time for grief, and everybody else, saving Betsey, thought the house was better without the crying baby than with it. These children were almost orphans; the mother, David's only sister, died when the last was born; the father, a merchant captain, given to spend his money instead of bringing it home, was always away at sea.

Death was to be more busy yet with the house of Mrs. Dundyke. A few months after Betsey's return from the short visit to Westerbury, when the hot weather set in for the summer, the other baby died. Close upon that, Mrs. Dundyke died—in a fit.

The attack was so sudden, the shock so great, that for a short time those left—David and Betsey—were stunned. David had to go to Fenchurch-street all the same; and Betsey quietly took Mrs. Dundyke's place in the house, and saw that things went on right. Duty was ever first with Betsey Travice; what her hand found to do, that she did with all her might; and the whole care devolved on her now. A clergyman and his wife were occupying the drawing-rooms, and they took great interest in the poor girl, and were very kind to her; but they never supposed but that she was some near relative of the Dundykes. David, who did not want for plain sense—no, nor for self-respect either—saw, of course, that the present state of things could not continue.

"Look here, Betsey," he said to her, one evening that they sat together in silence; he busy with his account books, and Betsey absorbed in trying to make out and remember the various items charged in the last week's butcher's bill; "we must make a change, I suppose."

She looked up, marking the place she had come to with her pencil. "What did you please to say, David?—make a change?"

"Well, yes, I suppose so, or we shall have the world about our ears. I mean to get rid of the house as soon as I can; either get somebody to come in and buy the good-will and the furniture; or else, if nobody won't do that, give up the house, and sell off the old things by auction, just keeping enough to furnish a room or two."

"It would be better to sell the good-will and the furniture, would it not?"

"Don't I say so? But I'm not sure of doing it, for houses is going down in Stamford-street: people that pay well for apartments, like to be fashionable, and get up to the new buildings westward. Any way, I'm afraid there won't be no more realized than will serve to pay what mother owed."

David stopped here and looked down on his accounts again. Betsey, who sat at the opposite side of the table, with the strong light of the summer evening lighting up its old red cloth, returned to hers. Before she had accomplished another item, David resumed—

"And all this will take time; three or four months, perhaps. And so, Betsey—if you don't mind being hurried into it—I think we had better be married."

"Be married!" echoed Betsey, dropping her book and her pencil. "Whatever do you mean?"

"I mean what I say," was David's sententious answer; "I don't mean nothing else. You and me must be married."

Betsey stared at him aghast. "Oh, David! how can you think of such a thing yet? It is not a month since your poor mother died."

"That's just it, her being dead," said David. "Don't you see, Betsey, neither you nor me can go out of the house until somebody takes to it, or till something's settled; and, in short, folks might get saying things."

Not for a full minute did she in the least comprehend his meaning. Then she burst into a passion of tears of anger; all her face aflame.

"Oh! David, how can you speak so? who would dare to be so cruel?"

"It's because I know the world better than you, and because I know how cruel it is, that I say it," added David. "Look here, Betsey, there's nobody left now to take care of you but me; and I shall take care of you, and I'm saying what's right. I shall buy a licence; it's a dreadful deal of money, when asking in church does as well, but that takes longer, and I'll spend the money cheerfully, for your sake. We'll go quietly to church next Sunday morning, and nobody need know, till it's all over, what we've been for. Unless you like to tell the servant, and the parson and his wife in the drawing-room. Perhaps you'd better."

"But, David—"

"Now, where's the good of contending?" he interrupted; "you don't want to give me up, do you?"

"You know I don't, David."

"Very well, then."

Betsey held out for some time longer, and it was only because she saw no other opening out of the dilemma—for, as David said, neither of them could leave the house if it was to go on—that she gave in at last. David at once entered upon sundry admonitions as to future economy, warning her that he intended they should live upon next to nothing for years and years to come. He did not intend to spend all his income, and be reduced to letting lodgings, or what not, when he should get old.

And a day or two after the marriage had really taken place, Betsey wrote a very deprecatory note to Charlotte, and another to Mrs. Arkell, with the news. But she did not give them an intimation of it beforehand. So that even had Charlotte wished to make any attempt to prevent it, she had not the opportunity. And from thenceforth she washed her hands of Betsey Dundyke, even more completely than she had done of Betsey Travice.

This first portion of my story is, I fear, rather inclined to be fragmentary, for I have to speak of the history of several; but it is necessary to do so, if you are to be quite at home with all our friends in it, as I always like you to be. The next thing we have to notice, was an astounding event in the life of Peter Arkell.

Peter Arkell was not a man of the world; he was a great deal too simple-minded to be anything of the sort. In worldly cunning, Peter was not a whit above Moses Primrose at the fair. Peter was getting on famously; he had let his house furnished, and the family who took it accommodated Peter with a room in it, and let him take his breakfast and dinner with them, for a very moderate sum. He worked at the bank, as usual, and he attended at Colonel Dewsbury's of an evening; that gentleman's eldest son had gone to college, but he had others coming on. Peter Arkell had also found time to write a small book, not in Greek, but touching Greek; it was excessively learned, and found so much favour with the classical world, that Peter Arkell grew to be stared at in his native city, as that very rare menagerie animal, a successful author; besides which, Peter's London publishers had positively transmitted him a sum of thirty pounds. I can tell you that the sum of thirty hundred does not appear so much to some people as that appeared to Peter. Had he gained thousands and thousands in his after life, they would have been to him as nothing, compared to the enraptured satisfaction brought to his heart by that early sum, the first fruits of his labours. Ask any author that ever put pen to paper, if the first guinea he ever earned was not more to him than all the golden profusion of the later harvest.

And so Peter, in his own estimation at any rate, was going on for a prosperous man. He put by all he could; and at the end of three years and a-half from Mildred's departure—for time is constantly on the wing, remember—Peter had saved a very nice sum, nearly enough to take him to Oxford, when he should find time to get there. For that, the getting there, was more of a stumbling block now than the means, since Peter did not yet see his way clear to resign his situation in the bank.

Meanwhile he waited, hoped, and worked. And during this season of patience, he had an honour conferred upon him by young Fauntleroy the lawyer: a gentleman considerably older than Peter, but called young Fauntleroy, in distinction to his father, old Fauntleroy the lawyer. Young Fauntleroy, who was as much given to spending as Peter was to saving, and had a hundred debts, unknown to the world, got simple Peter to be security for him in some dilemma. Peter hesitated at first. Four hundred pounds was a large sum, and would swamp him utterly should he ever be called upon to pay it; but upon young Fauntleroy's assuring him, on his honour, that the bank could not be more safe to pay its quarterly dividends than he was to provide for that obligation when the time came, Peter gave in. He signed his name, and from that hour thought no more of the matter. When a person promised Peter to do a thing he had the implicit faith of a child. And now comes the event that so astounded Westerbury.

You remember Lucy Cheveley, the young lady whose lovely face had so won on Mildred's admiration? How it came about no human being could ever tell, least of all themselves; but she and Peter Arkell fell in love with each other. It was not one of those ephemeral fancies that may be thrown off just as easily as they are assumed, but a passionate, powerful, lasting love, one that makes the bliss or the bane of a whole future existence. The chief of the blame was voted by the meddling town to Colonel and Mrs. Dewsbury. Why had they allowed Miss Cheveley to mix in familiar intercourse with the tutor? To tell the truth, Miss Cheveley had not been much better there than a governess. Her means were very small. She had only the pension of a deceased officer's daughter, and Mrs. Dewsbury, what with clothes and maintenance, was considerably out of pocket by her; therefore she repaid herself by making Miss Cheveley useful with the children. The governess was a daily one, and Lucy Cheveley helped the children at night to prepare their lessons for her. The study for both boys and girls was the same, and thus Lucy was in constant daily intercourse with Mr. Peter Arkell. Since the publication of Peter's learned book, and his consequent rise in public estimation, Colonel Dewsbury had once or twice invited him to dinner; and Miss Cheveley met him on an equality.

But the marvel was, how ever that lovely girl could have lost her heart to Peter Arkell—plain, shy, awkward Peter! But that such things have been known before, it might have been looked upon as an impossibility.

There was a fearful rumpus. The discovery came through Mrs. Dewsbury's bursting one night into the study in search of a book, when the children had left it, and she supposed it empty. Mr. Peter Arkell stood there with his arm round Lucy's waist, and both her hands gathered and held in his. For the first minute or so, Mrs. Dewsbury did not believe her own eyes. Lucy stood in painful distress, the damask colour glowing on her transparent cheek, and the explanation, as of right it would, fell to Peter.

These shy, timid, awkward-mannered men in every-day life, are sometimes the most collected in situations of actual embarrassment. It was so with Peter Arkell. In a calm, quiet way he turned to Mrs. Dewsbury, and told her the straightforward truth: that he and Miss Cheveley were attached to each other, and he had asked her to be his wife.

Mrs. Dewsbury was an excitable woman. She went back to the dining-room, shrieking like one in hysterics, and told the news. It aroused Colonel Dewsbury from his wine; and it was not a light thing in a general way that could do that, for the colonel was fond of it.

Then ensued the scene. Colonel and Mrs. Dewsbury heaped vituperation on the head of the tutor, asking what he could expect to come to for thus abusing confidence? Poor Peter, far more composed in that moment than he was in every-day matters, said honestly that he had not intended to abuse it; nothing would ever have been farther from his thoughts; but the mutual love had come to them both unawares, and been betrayed to each other without thought of the consequences.

All the abuse ever spoken would not avail to undo the past. Of course nothing was left now but to dismiss Mr. Peter Arkell summarily from his tutorship, and order Miss Cheveley never to hold intercourse by word or look with him again. This might have mended matters in a degree had Miss Cheveley acquiesced, and carried the mandate out; but, encouraged no doubt secretly by Mr. Peter, she timidly declined to do so—said, in fact, she would not. Colonel and Mrs. Dewsbury were rampant as two chained lions, who long to get loose and tear somebody to pieces.

For Mr. Peter Arkell was not to be got at. The law did not sanction his imprisonment; and society would not countenance the colonel in beating or killing him. Neither could Mrs. Dewsbury lock up Miss Lucy Cheveley, as was the mode observed to refractory damsels in what is called the good old time.

The next scene in the play was their marriage. Lucy, finding that she could never hope to obtain the consent of her protectors to it, walked quietly to church from their house one fine morning, met Peter there, and was married without consent. Peter had made his arrangements for the event in a more sensible manner than one so incapable would have been supposed likely to do. The friends who had occupied his house vacated it previously to oblige him; he had it papered and painted, and put into thoroughly nice order, spending about a hundred pounds in new furniture, and took Lucy home to it. Never did a more charming wife enter on possession of a home; and Westerbury, which of course made everybody's affairs its own, in the usual manner, was taken with a sudden fit of envy at the good fortune of Peter Arkell, when it had recovered its astonishment at Miss Cheveley's folly. One of her order marry poor Peter Arkell, the banker's clerk! The world must be coming to an end.

Colonel and Mrs. Dewsbury almost wished it was coming to an end, for the bride and bridegroom at any rate, in their furious anger. The colonel went to the bank, and coolly requested it to discharge Peter Arkell from its service. The bank politely declined, saying that Mr. Peter Arkell had done nothing to offend it, or of which it could take cognizance. Colonel Dewsbury threatened to withdraw his account, and carry it off forthwith to a sort of patent company bank, recently opened in the town. The bank listened with equanimity; it would be sorry of course, and hoped the colonel would think better of it; but, if he insisted, his balance (he never kept more than a couple of hundred pounds there) should then be handed to him. The colonel growled, and went out with a bang. He next wrote to Lady Dewsbury a peremptory letter, almost requiring her to discharge Miss Arkell from her service. Lady Dewsbury wrote word back that Mildred had become too valuable to her to be parted with; and that if Peter Arkell was like his sister in goodness, Lucy Cheveley had not chosen amiss.

Lucy had been married about a fortnight, and was sitting one evening in all her fragile loveliness, the red light of the setting sun flickering through the elm trees on her damask cheeks, when a tall elegant woman entered. This was Mrs. St. John, whose family had been intimate with the Cheveleys. The St. Johns inhabited that old building in Westerbury called the Palmery, of which mention has been made, but they had been away from it for the past two years. Mrs. St. John had just returned to hear the scandal caused by the recent disobedient marriage.

Though all the world abandoned Lucy, Mrs. St. John would not. She had not so many years been a wife herself, having married the widower, Mr. St. John, who was more than double her age, and had a grown-up son. Lucy started up, with many blushes, at Mrs. St. John's entrance; and she told the story of herself and Peter very simply, when questioned.

"Well, Lucy, I wish you happy," Mrs. St. John said; "but it is not the marriage you should have made."

"Perhaps not. I suppose not. For Mr. Arkell's family is of course inferior to mine—"

"Inferior! Mr. Arkell's family!" interrupted Mrs. St. John, all her aristocratic prejudices offended at the words. "What do you mean, Lucy? Mr. Arkell is of no family! They are tradespeople—manufacturers. We don't speak of that class as 'a family.' You are of our order; and I can tell you, the Cheveleys have had the best blood in their veins. It is a very sad descent for you; little less—my dear, I cannot help speaking—than degradation for life."

"If I had good family," spoke Lucy, "what else had I?"

"Beauty!" was Mrs. St. John's involuntary answer, as she gazed at the wondrously lustrous brown eyes, the bright exquisite features.

"Beauty!" echoed Lucy, in surprise. "Oh, Mrs. St. John! you forget."

"Forget what, Lucy."

"That I am deformed."

The word was spoken in a painful whisper, and the sensitive complexion grew carmine with the sense of shame. It is ever so. Where any defect of person exists, none can feel it as does its possessor; it is to the mind one ever-present agony of humiliation. Lucy Cheveley's spine was not straight; of fragile make and constitution, she had "grown aside," as the familiar saying runs; but at this early period of her life it was not so apparent to a beholder (unless the defect was known and searched for) as it afterwards became.

"You are not very much so, Lucy," was Mrs. St. John's answer. "And your face compensates for it."

Lucy shook her head. "You say so from kindness, I am sure. Do you know," she resumed, her voice again becoming almost inaudible, "I once heard Mrs. Dewsbury joking with Sir Edward about me. He was down for a week about a year ago, and she was telling him he ought to get married and settle down to a steady life. He answered that he could get nobody to have him, and Mrs. Dewsbury—of course you know it was only a jesting conversation on both sides—said, 'There's Lucy Cheveley, would she do for you?' 'She,' he exclaimed; 'she's deformed!' Mrs. St. John, will you believe that for a long while after I felt sick at having to go out, or to cross a room?"

"Yes, I can believe it," said Mrs. St. John, sadly, for she was not unacquainted with this sensitive phase in human misfortune. "Well, Lucy, you cannot be convinced, I dare say, that your figure is not unsightly, so we will let that pass. But I do not understand yet, how you came to marry Peter Arkell."

Lucy laughed and blushed.

"Ah! I see; you loved him. And yet, few, save you, would find Peter Arkell so lovable a man."

"If you only knew his worth, Mrs. St. John!"

"I dare say. But as a knight-errant he is not attractive. Of course, the chief consideration now, is—the thing being irrevocably done, and you here—what sort of a home will he be able to keep for you."

"I have no fear on that score; and I am one to be satisfied with so little. Colonel Dewsbury discharged him, but he soon found an evening engagement that is as good. He intends to go to Oxford when he can accomplish it, and afterwards take orders. When he is a clergyman, perhaps my friends, including you, Mrs. St. John, will admit that his wife can then claim to be in the position of a gentlewoman."

"But, meanwhile you must live."

Lucy smiled. "If you knew how entirely I trust and may trust to Peter, you would have no fear. We shall spend but little; we have begun on the most economical plan, and shall continue it. We keep but one servant—"

"But one servant!" echoed Mrs. St. John. "For you!"

"I did not bring Peter a shilling. I brought him but myself and the few poor clothes I possess, for my bit of a pension ceased at my marriage. You cannot think that I would run him into any expense not absolutely necessary. We have no need of more than one servant, for we shall certainly be free from visitors."

"How do you know that?"

"Peter has lived too retired a life to entertain any. And there's no fear that my friends will visit me. I have put myself beyond their pale."

"I cannot say that you have not. But how you will feel this, Lucy!"

"I shall not feel it. Mrs. St. John, when I chose my position in life as Peter Arkell's wife, I chose it for all time," she emphatically added. "Neither now, nor at any future period, shall I regret it. Believe me, I shall be far happier here, in retirement with him, although I have the consciousness of knowing that the world calls me an idiot, than I could have been had I married in what you may call my own sphere. For me there are not two Peter Arkells in the world."

And Mrs. St. John rose, and took her leave; deeply impressed with the fact, that though there might not be two Peter Arkells in the world, there was a great deal of infatuation. She could not understand how it was possible for one, born as Lucy Cheveley had been, to make such a marriage, and to live under it without repentance.

CHAPTER XIII

GOING ON FOR LORD MAYOR

The years rolled on, bringing their changes. Indeed, the first portions of this history are more like a panorama, where you see a scene here, and then go on to another scene there; for we cannot afford to relate these earlier events consecutively.

That good and respected man, Mr. George Arkell, had passed away with the course of time to the place which is waiting to receive us all. His wife followed him within the year. A handsome fortune, independently of the flourishing business at the manufactory, was left to our old friend William; and there was a small legacy to Mildred of a hundred pounds.

William Arkell had taken possession of all: of his father's place, his father's position, and his father's house. No son ever walked more entirely in his father's steps than did he. He was honoured throughout Westerbury, just as Mr. Arkell had been. His benevolence, his probity, his high character, were universally known and appreciated. And Mrs. William Arkell, now of course, Mrs. Arkell, was a very fine lady, but liked on the whole.

They had three children, Travice, Charlotte, and Sophia Mary. Travice bore a remarkable resemblance to his father, both in looks and disposition; the two girls were more like their mother. They were young yet; but no expense, even now, was spared upon them. Indeed, expense, had Mrs. Arkell had her way, would not have been spared in anything. Show and cost were not to William's taste; they were to hers: but he restrained it with a firm hand where it was absolutely essential.

Peter had not got to college yet, and Peter had not on the whole prospered. The great blow to him was the having to pay the four hundred pounds for which he had become security for Mr. Fauntleroy the younger. Mr. Fauntleroy the younger's affairs had come to a crisis; he went away for a time from Westerbury, and Peter was called upon to pay. There's no doubt that it was the one great blight upon Peter Arkell's life. He never recovered it. It is true that the money was afterwards refunded to him by degrees; but it seemed to do him no good; the blight had fallen.

He became ill. Whether it was the blow of this, that suddenly shattered his health, or whether illness was inherent in his constitution, Westerbury never fully decided; certain it was, that Peter Arkell became a confirmed invalid, and had to resign his appointment at the bank. But he had excellent teaching, and was paid well; and he brought out a learned book now and then, so that he earned a good living. He had two children, Lucy, and a boy some years younger.

Never since she quitted the place some ten or twelve years before, had Mildred Arkell paid a visit to Westerbury. She was going to do so now. Lady Dewsbury, whose health was better than usual, had gone to stay with her married sister, and Mildred thought she would take the opportunity of going to see her brother Peter, and to make acquaintance with his wife. It is probable that, without that tie, she would never have re-entered her native place. The pain of going now would be great; the pain of meeting William Arkell and his wife little less than it was when she first left it. But she made her mind up, and wrote to Peter to say she was coming.

It was on a windy day that Mildred Arkell—had anybody known her—might have been seen picking her way-through the mud of the streets of London. She went to a private house in the neighbourhood of Hatton Garden, rang one of its bells, and walked upstairs without waiting for it to be answered. Before she reached the third floor, a young woman, with a coarse apron on, and a quantity of soft flaxen hair twisted round her head, which looked like a lady's head in spite of the accompaniment of the apron, came running down it.

"Oh, Miss Arkell! if you had but sent me word you were coming!"

The tone was a joyous one, mixed somewhat with vexation; and Mildred smiled.

"Why should I send you word, Betsey? If you are busy, you need not mind me."

On the third floor of this house, in two rooms, Mr. and Mrs. David Dundyke had lived ever since their marriage. David himself had chosen it from the one motive that regulated most actions of his life—economy. The two lower floors of the house were occupied by the offices of a solicitor; the underground kitchen and attic by a woman who kept the house clean; and David had taken these two rooms, and got them very cheap, on condition that he should always sleep at home as a protection to the house. Not having any inducement to sleep out, David acceded readily; and here they had been for several years. It was, in one sense, a convenient arrangement for Betsey, for they kept no servant, and the woman occasionally did cleaning and other rough work for her, receiving a small payment weekly.

Will you believe me when I say that David Dundyke was ambitious? Never a more firmly ambitious man lived than he. There have been men with higher aims in life, but not with more pushing, persevering purpose. He wanted to become a rich man; he wanted to become one of importance in this great commercial city; but the highest ambition of all, the one that filled his thoughts, sleeping and waking, was a higher ambition still—and I hope you will hold your breath with proper deference while you read it—he aspired to become, in time, the LORD MAYOR!

He was going on for it. He truly and honestly believed that he was going on for it; slowly, it is true, but not less sure. Rome, as we all know was not built in a day; and even such men as the Duke of Wellington must have had a beginning—a first start in life.

Whatever David Dundyke's shortcomings might be, in—if you will excuse the word—gentility, he made up for it by a talent for business. Few men have possessed a better one; and his value in the Fenchurch-street tea-house, was fully known and appreciated. This wholesale establishment, which had tea for its basis, was of undoubted respectability. It took a high standing amidst its fellows, and was second in its large dealings to none. It was not one of your advertising, poetry-puffing, here-to-day and gone-to-morrow houses, but a genuine, sound firm, having real dealings with Chaney, as the respected white-haired head of the house was in the habit of designating the Celestial Empire. Mr. Dundyke sometimes presumed to correct the "Chaney," and hint to his indulgent master and head, that that pronunciation was a little antediluvian, and that nobody now called it anything but "Chinar."

David Dundyke had gone into this house an errand boy; he had risen to be a junior clerk. He was now not a junior one, but took rank with the first. Steady, taciturn, persevering, and industrious to an extent not often seen, thoroughly trustworthy, and in business dealings of strict honour, perhaps David Dundyke was one who could not fail to prosper, wherever he might have been placed. These qualities, combined with rare business foresight, had brought him into notice, and thence into favour. The faintest possible hint had been dropped to him by the white-haired old man, that perseverance, such as his, had been known to meet its reward in an association with the firm; a share in the business. Whether he meant anything, or whether it was but a casual remark, spoken without intention, David did not know; but he saw from thenceforth that one great ambition, of his, coming nearer and nearer. From that moment it was sure; it fevered his veins, and coloured his dreams; the massive gold chain of the Lord Mayor was ever dancing before his eyes and his brain; to be called "my lord" by the multitude, and to sit in that arm-chair, dispensing justice in the Mansion House, seemed to him a very heaven upon earth. Every movement of his mind had reference to it; every nerve was strained on the hope for it! For that he saved; for that he pinched; for that he turned sixpences into shillings, and shillings into pounds: for he knew that to be elected a Lord Mayor he must first of all be a rich man, and attain to the honour through minor gradations of wealth. He was judged to be a hard griping man by the few acquaintances he possessed, possessing neither sympathy for friends, nor pity for enemies; but he was not hard or griping at heart; it was all done to further this dream of ambition. For money in the abstract he really did not very much care; but as a stepping-stone to civic importance, it was of incalculable value.

He had four hundred pounds a year now, and they lived upon fifty. Betsey, the most generous heart in the world, saw but with his eyes, and was as saving and careful as might be, because it pleased him. Many and many a time he had taken home a red herring and made his dinner of it, giving his wife the head and the tail to pick for hers. Not less meek than of yore was Mrs. Dundyke, and felt duly thankful for the head and the tail.

Mrs. Dundyke had been at some household work when Mildred entered, but she soon put it aside and sat down with Mildred in the sitting-room, a cheerful apartment with a large window. Betsey was considerably over thirty years of age now, but she looked nearly as young as ever, as she sat bending her face a little down over her sewing while she talked, the stitching of a wristband; for she was one who thought it a sin to lose time. Mildred told her the news she had come to tell—that she was going on the morrow to Westerbury.

"Going to Westerbury!" echoed Mrs. Dundyke in great surprise; for it had seemed to her that Miss Arkell never meant to go to her native place again.

Mildred explained. She had a holiday for the first time since going to Lady Dewsbury's, and should use it to see her brother and his wife. "I came to tell you, Betsey," she added, "thinking you might have some message you would like me to carry to your sister."

A faint change, like a shadow, passed over Betsey Dundyke's face. "She would not thank you for it, Miss Arkell. But you may give my best love to her. She never came to see me, you know, when they were in London."

"When were they in London?" asked Mildred, quickly.

"Last year. Did you not know of it? Perhaps not, for you were in Paris with Lady Dewsbury at the time, and the reminiscence to me is not so pleasing as to make me mention it gratuitously. She came up with Mr. Arkell and their boy; they were in London about a week: he had business, I believe. The first thing he did was to come and see us, and he brought Travice; and he said he hoped I and my husband would make it convenient to be with them a good deal while they were in town, and would dine with them often at their hotel. Well, David, as you know, has no time to spare in the day, for business is first and foremost with him, but I went the next day to see Charlotte. She was very cool, and she let me unmistakably know in so many words that she could not make an associate of Mr. Dundyke. It was not nice of her, Miss Arkell."

"No, it was not. Did you see much of her?"

"I only saw her that once. William Arkell was terribly vexed, I could see that; and as if to atone for her behaviour, he came here often and brought Travice. Indeed, Travice spent nearly the whole of the time with us, and David would have let me keep him after they went home, but I knew it was of no use to ask Charlotte. He is the nicest boy! I—I know it is wrong to break the tenth commandment," she said, looking up and laughing through her tears, "but I envy Charlotte that boy."

It was an indirect allusion to the one great disappointment of Betsey Dundyke's life: she had no children. She was getting over the grief tolerably now; we get reconciled to the worst evil in time; but in the first years of her marriage she had felt it keenly. It may be questioned if Mr. Dundyke did. Children must have brought expense with them, so he philosophically pitted the gain against the loss.

"Why should Mrs. Arkell dislike to be on sisterly terms with you?" asked Mildred. "I have never been able to understand it."

"Charlotte has two faults—pride and selfishness," was Mrs. Dundyke's answer: "though I cannot bear to speak against her, and never do to David. When she first married, she feared, I believe, that I might become a burden upon her; and she did not like that I should be in the position I was at Mrs. Dundyke's; she thought it reflected in a degree upon her position as a lady. Now she shuns us, because she thinks we are altogether beneath her. Were we living in style, well established and all that, she would be glad to come to us; but we are in these two quiet rooms, living humbly, and Charlotte would cut off her legs before she'd come near us. Don't think me unkind, Miss Arkell; it is Charlotte who has forced this feeling upon me. I worshipped her in the old days, but I cannot be blind to her faults now."

David Dundyke came in. He shook hands cordially with Mildred, whom he was always glad to see. He had begun to dress like a city magnate now: in glossy clothes, and a white neckcloth; and a fine gold cable chain crossed on his waistcoat, in place of the modest silver one he used to wear. He had become more personable as he gained years, was growing portly, and altogether was a fine, gentlemanly-looking man. But his mode of speech! That had very little changed from the earlier style: perhaps David Dundyke was one who did not care to change it; or had no ear to catch the accents of others. If he had but never opened his mouth!

"I'm a little late, Betsey. Shouldn't ha' been, though, if I'd known who was here. Get us some tea, girl; and here's something to eat with it."

He pulled a paper parcel of shrimps out of his pocket as he spoke: a delicacy he was fond of. Some of them fell on the carpet in the process, and Betsey stooped to pick them up. David did not trouble himself to help her. He sat down and talked to Mildred.

"The last time you were here, I remember, something kept me out: extra work at the office, I think that was. I have been round now to Leifchild's. He is my stock-broker."

Mildred laughed. She supposed he was saying it for jest. But the keen look came over Mr. Dundyke's face that was usual to it when he spoke of money.

"Leifchild is a steady-going man; he's no fool, he isn't: There's not a steadier nor a keener on the stock exchange. I've knowed him since he was that high, for we was boys together; and, like me, he began from nothing. There was one thing kept him down—want of capital; if he had had that, he'd ha' been a rich man now, for many good things fell in his way, and he had to let 'em slip by him. I turned the risk over in my mind, Miss Arkell; for, and against; and I came to the conclusion to put a thousand pound in his hands, on condition—"

"A thousand pounds," involuntarily interrupted Mildred. "Had you so much—to spare?"

"Yes, I had that," said David Dundyke, with a little cough that seemed to say he might have found more, if he had cared to do so. "On condition that I went shares in whatsoever profit my thousand pound should be the means of realizing," he resumed where he had broken off. "And my thousand pound has not done badly yet."

Mildred could not help noting the significant satisfaction of the tone. "I should have fancied you too cautious to risk your money in speculating, Mr. Dundyke."

"And you fancied right. 'Tain't speculating: leastways not now. There might be some risk at first, but I knew Leifchild. In three months after that there thousand pound was in his hand, he had made two of it for me, and I took the one back from him, leaving him the other to go on with again. That hasn't done badly neither, Miss Arkell; it's paying itself over and over again. And I'm safe; for if he lost it all, I'm only where I was afore I began, and my first risked thousand is safe."

"And if failure should come, is there no risk to you?"

"Not a penny risk. Trust me for that. But failure won't come. My head's a pretty long one for seeing my way clear, and Leifchild lays every thing before me afore he ventures. It's better, this is, than your five per cent. investments."

"I think it must be," assented Mildred. "I wish I could employ a trifle in the same manner."

She spoke without any ulterior motive, but David Dundyke took the words literally. He had no objection to do a good turn where it involved no outlay to himself, and he really liked Mildred. He drew his chair an inch nearer, and talked to her long and earnestly.

"Let's say it's a hundred pound," he said. "Risk it. And when Leifchild has doubled that for you, take the first hundred back. If you lose the rest, it won't hurt; and if it multiplies its ones into tens, you'll be so much the better off."

It cannot be denied that Mildred was struck with the proposition. "But does Mr. Leifchild do all this for nothing?" she asked.

"In course he don't. Leifchild ain't a fool. He gets his percentage—and a good fat percentage too. The thing can afford it. Do as you like, you know, Miss Arkell; but if you take my advice, you mayn't find cause to be sorry for it in the end."

"Thank you," said Mildred, "I will think of it."

"Give Aunt Betsey's dear love to Travice," whispered Mrs. Dundyke, when Mildred was leaving, "and my best and truest regards to Mr. Arkell. And oh, Miss Mildred, if you could prevail upon them to let Travice come back with you to visit me, I should not know how to be happy enough! I have always so loved children; and David would like it, too."

"Is there any chance, think you?" returned Mildred.

"No, no, there is none; his mother would be indignant at the presumption of the request," concluded Betsey in her bitter conviction.

And she was not mistaken.

Mildred's heart ached with the changes; Peter was growing into a middle-aged man, his hair beginning to silver, his tall back bowed with care.

They were gathered in the old familiar sitting-room the night of her arrival at Westerbury. Peter and Mildred sat at the table, Mrs. Peter Arkell lay on her sofa; the children remained orderly on the hearth rug. Lucy was getting a great girl now; little Harry—a most lovely child, his face the counterpart of his mother's—was but three years old.

Never but once in her life had Mildred seen the exquisite face of Miss Lucy Cheveley; it had never left her memory. The same, same face was before her now, looking upwards from the sofa, not a whit altered—not a shade less beautiful. But Mildred had now become aware of a fact which she had not known previously—Peter had kept it from her in his letters—that the defect in Mrs. Peter Arkell's back had become more formidable, giving her pain nearly always. They had had a hard, reclining sofa made, a little raised at the one end; and here she had to lie a great deal, some days only getting up from it to meals.

"I am half afraid to encounter your wife," Mildred had said, as she walked home with Peter from the station—for there was a railway from London now, and the old coaching days had vanished for ever. "She is one of the Dewsbury family—of Mrs. Dewsbury's, at any rate—and I am but a dependent in it."

"Oh, Mildred! you little know my dear wife; but she is one in a thousand. She is very poorly this evening, and is so vexed at it; she says you will not think she welcomes you as she ought."

"What is it that is really the matter with her? Is it the spine? You did not tell me all this in your letters."

"It is the spine. She was never strong, you may be aware; and I believe there occurred some slight injury to it when the boy was born. The doctors think she will get stronger again; but I don't know."

"Is she in pain? Does she walk out?"

"She is not in pain when she lies, but it comes on if she exerts herself. Sometimes she walks out, but not often. She is so patient—so anxious to make the best of things; lying there, as she is often obliged to do, for hours, and going without any little thing she may want, because she will not disturb the servant from her work to get it. I don't think anyone was ever blessed with so patient and sweet a temper."

And when Mildred entered and saw the bright expectancy of the well-remembered face, the eager hands held out to welcome her, she knew that they were true sisters from that hour. The invalid drew down her face to her own flushed one.

"I am so grieved," she whispered, the tears rising in her earnest eyes; "this is one of my worst days, and I am unable to rise to welcome you."

"Do not think of it," answered Mildred; "I am glad to be here to wait upon you, I am used to nursing; I think it is my specialité," she added, with one of her old sunny smiles. "I will try and nurse you into health before I go back again."

"You shall make the tea, and do all those things, now you are here, Mildred," interposed Peter. "I am as awkward as an owl when I have to attempt anything, and Lucy lies and laughs at me."

"Which is to be my room?" asked Mildred. "I will go and take my things off, and come down to hear all the news of the old place."

"The blue room," said Mrs. Peter. "You will find little Lucy—"

"Your own old room, Mildred," interposed Peter. "Lucy, my dear, when Mildred left home the room was not blue, but a sort of dirty yellow."

Mildred went and came down again, bringing the children with her, little orderly things; steady Lucy quite like a mother to her baby brother. Mildred made acquaintance with them, and she and Peter gossiped away to their hearts' content; the one telling the news of the "old place," and its changes, the other listening.

"We think Lucy so much like you," Peter observed in the course of the evening, alluding to his little daughter.

"Like me!" repeated Mildred.

"It strikes us all. William never sees her but he thinks of you. He says we ought to have named her 'Mildred.'"

"His daughters are not named Mildred, either of them," she answered, hastily—an old sore sensation, that she had been striving so long to bury, becoming very rife within her.

"His wife chose their names—not he. She has a will of her own, and likes to exercise it."

"How do you get on with William's wife?"

"Not very well. She and Lucy did not take to each other at first, and I suppose never will. She is quite a fine lady now; and, indeed, always was, to my thinking; and William's wealth enables them to live in a style very different from what we can do. So Mrs. Arkell looks down upon us. We are invited to a grand, formal dinner there once a year, and that is about all our intercourse."

"A grand, formal dinner!" echoed Mildred. "For you!"

Peter nodded. "She makes it so on purpose, no doubt; a hint that we are not to be every-day visitors. She invites little Lucy there sometimes to play with Charlotte and Sophy; but I am sure the two girls despise the child just as their mother despises us."

"And does William despise you?" inquired Mildred, a touch of resentment in her usually gentle tone.

"How can you ask it, Mildred?" returned Peter, warmly. "I thought you knew William Arkell better than that. He grows so like his father—good, kindly, honourable. There's not a man in all Westerbury liked and respected as he is. He comes in sometimes in an evening; glad, I fancy, of a little peace and quietness. Between ourselves, Mildred, I fancy that in marrying Charlotte Travice, William found he had caught a Tartar."

"And so they are grand!" observed Mildred, waking out of a fit of musing, and perhaps hardly conscious of what she said.

"Terribly grand. She is. They keep their close carriage now. It strikes me—I may be wrong—but it strikes me that he lives up to every farthing of his income."

"My Uncle George did not."

"No, indeed! Or there'd not have been the fortune that there was to leave to William."

"But, Peter, I gather a good deal now and then from the local papers of the distress that exists in Westerbury, of the depressed state that the trade is falling into; more depressed even than it was when I left, and that need not be. Does not this state of things affect William Arkell?"

"It must affect him; though not, I conclude, to any great extent. You see, Mildred, he has what so many of the other manufacturers want—plenty of money, independent of his business. William has not to force his goods into the market at unfavourable moments; be his stock ever so large, he can hold it until the demand quickens. It is the being obliged to send their goods into the market at low prices, that swamps the others."

"Will the prosperity of the town ever come back to it, think you?"

"Never. And I am not sure that the worst has come yet."

Mildred sighed. She called Lucy to her and held her before her, pushing the hair from her brow as she looked attentively into her face. It was not a beautiful or a handsome face; but it was fair and gentle, the features pale, the eyes dark brown, with a sweet, sad, earnest expression: just such a face as Mildred's.

"Do you like your cousins, Charlotte and Sophia, Lucy?" asked Mildred.

"I like Travice best," was the little lady's unblushing answer. "Charlotte and Sophy tease me; they are not kind; but Travice won't let them tease me when he is there. He is a big boy, but he plays with me; and he says he loves me better than he does them."

"I really believe he does," said Peter, amused at the answer. "Travice is just like his father, as this child is like you—the same open, generous, noble boy that William himself was. When I see Travice playing with Lucy, I could fancy it was you and William over again—as I used to see you play in the old days."

"Heaven grant that the ending of it may not be as mine was!" was the inward prayer that went up from Mildred's heart.

"Travice is in the college school, I suppose, Peter?"

"Oh, yes. With a private evening tutor at home. The girls have a resident governess. William spares no money on their education."

"Would it not be a nice thing for Lucy if she could go daily and share their lessons?"

"Hush, Mildred! Treason!" exclaimed Peter, while Mrs. Peter Arkell burst into a laugh, her husband's manner was so quaint. "I have reason to know that William was hardy enough to say something of the same sort to his wife, and he got his answer. I and my wife, between us, teach Lucy. It is better so; for the child could not be spared from her mother. You don't know the use she is of, already."

"I am of use to mamma too, I am!" broke in a bold baby voice at Mildred's side.

She caught the little fellow on her knee: he thought no doubt he had been too long neglected. Mildred began stroking the auburn curls from his face, as she had stroked Lucy's.

"And I am like mamma," added the young gentleman. "Everybody says so. Mamma says so."

Indeed "everybody" might well say it. As the mother's was, so was the child's, the loveliest possible type of face. The same, the exquisite features, the refined, delicate look, the lustrous brown eyes and hair, the rose-flush on the cheeks. "No, I never did see two faces so much alike, allowing for the difference in age," cried Mildred, looking from the mother on the sofa to the child on her knee. "Tell me again what your name is."

"It's Harry Cheveley Arkell."

"Do you know," exclaimed Mildred, looking up at Mrs. Peter, "it strikes me this child speaks remarkably plain for his age."

"He does," was the answer. "Lucy did not speak so well when she was double his age. He is unusually forward and sensible in all respects. I fear it sometimes," she added in a lower tone.

"By why do you fear it?" quickly asked Mildred.

"Oh—you know the old saying, or superstition," concluded Mrs. Arkell, unable further to allude to it, for the boy's earnest eyes were bent upon her with profound interest.

"Those whom the gods love, die young," muttered Peter. "But the saying is all nonsense, Mildred."

Peter had been getting his books, and was preparing to become lost in their pages, fragrant as ever to him. Mildred happened to look to him and scarcely saved herself from a scream. He had put on a pair of spectacles.

"Peter! surely you have not taken to spectacles!"

"Yes, I have."

"But why?"

Peter stared at her. "Why does anybody take to them, Mildred? From failing sight."

"Oh, dear!" sighed Mildred. "We seem to have gone away altogether from youth—to be gliding into old age without any interregnum."

"But we are not middle-aged yet, Mildred," said Mrs. Peter.

A sudden opening of the door—a well-known form, tall, upright, noble, but from which a portion of the youthful elasticity was gone—and Mildred found herself face to face with her cousin William. How loved still, the wild beating of her heart told her! His simply friendly greeting, warm though it was, recalled her to her senses.

"What a stranger you have been to us, Mildred!" he exclaimed. "Never to come near Westerbury all these years! When my father was dying, he wished so much to see you."

"I would have come then had I been able, but Lady Dewsbury was very ill, and I could not leave her. Indeed, I wish I could have seen both my aunt and uncle once more."

"They felt it, I can tell you, Mildred."

"Not more than I did; not indeed so much. They could not: they had others with them nearer than I."

"Perhaps none dearer," he quietly answered. "My father's death was almost sudden at the last. The shock to me was great: I did not think to lose him so early."

"A little sooner or a little later!" murmured Mildred. "What does it matter, provided the departure be a hopeful one. As his must have been."

"As his was," said William. "Mildred, you are not greatly changed."

"Not changed!"

"I said, not greatly changed. It is still the same face."

"Ah, you will see it by daylight. My hair is turning grey."

"Mildred, which day will you spend with us?" he asked, when leaving. "To-morrow?"

Mildred evaded a direct reply. Even yet, though years had passed, she was scarcely equal to seeing the old home and its installed mistress; certainly not without great emotion. But she knew it must be overcome, and when Mr. Arkell pressed the question, she named, not the morrow, but the day following.

William Arkell went home, and had the nearest approach to a battle with his wife that he ever had had. Mrs. Arkell was alone in their handsome drawing-room; she did not keep it laid up in lavender, as the old people had done. She was as pretty as ever; and of genial manners, when not put out. But unfortunately she got put out at trifles, and the unpleasantness engendered by it was frequent.

"Charlotte, I have seen Mildred," he began as he entered. "She will spend the day with us on Friday, but I suppose you will call upon her to-morrow."

"No, I shan't," returned Mrs. Arkell. "She's nothing but a lady's-maid."

William answered sharply. Something to the effect that Mildred was a lady born and bred, a lady formerly, a lady still, and that he respected her beyond anyone on earth: in his passion, he hardly knew what he said. Mrs. Arkell was even with him.

"I know," she said—"I know you would have been silly enough to make her your wife, but for your better stars interposing and sending me to frustrate it. I don't suppose she has overcome the disappointment yet. Now, William, that's the truth, and you need not look as if you were going to beat me for saying it. And you need not think that I shall pay court to her, for I shall not. Whether as Mildred Arkell, your disappointed cousin, or as Mildred Arkell, Lady Dewsbury's maid, I am not called upon to do it."

William Arkell felt that he really could beat her. He did not answer temperately.

Mrs. Arkell could be aggravating when she chose; ay, and obstinate. She would not call on Mildred the following day, but three separate times did her handsome close carriage parade before the modest house of Mr. Peter Arkell, and never once, of all the three times, did she condescend to turn her eyes towards it, as she sat inside. Late that evening there arrived a formal note requesting the pleasure of Mr. and Mrs. Peter Arkell's accompanying Miss Arkell to dinner on the following day.

"She's going to do it grand, Peter," said Lucy to her husband with a laugh, in the privacy of their chamber at night. "She's killing two birds with one stone, impressing Mildred with her pomp, and showing her at the same time that she must not expect to be admitted to unceremonious intimacy."

Only Mildred went. Lucy said she was not well enough, and Peter had lessons to give. The former unpretentious and, for Mr. Arkell, convenient dinner hour of one o'clock had been long changed for a late one. Mildred, fully determined not to make a ceremony of the visit, went in about four o'clock, and found nobody to receive her. Mrs. Arkell was in her room, the maid said. She had seen Miss Arkell's approach, and hastened away to dress, not having expected her so early. Would Miss Arkell like to go to a dressing room and take her bonnet off? Miss Arkell replied that she would take it off there, and she handed it to the maid with her shawl.

The drawing-room had been newly furnished since old Mrs. Arkell's time, as Mildred saw at a glance. She was touching abstractedly some of its elegant trifles, musing on the changes that years bring, when the door flew open, and a tall, prepossessing, handsome boy entered, whistling a song at the top of his voice, and trailing a fishing line behind him. There was no need to ask who he was; the likeness was too great to the beloved face of her girlhood: it was the same manner, the same whistle; all as it used to be.

"You are Travice," she said, holding out her hand; "I should have known you anywhere."

"And you must be Mildred," returned the boy, impetuously taking the hand between both of his, and letting his cherished fishing line drop anywhere. "May I call you Aunt Mildred, as Lucy does?"

"Call me anything," was Mildred's answer. "I am so glad to see you at last. And to see you what you are! How like you are to your father!"

"All the world says that," said the boy with a laugh. "But how is it that nobody's with you? Where are they all? Where's mamma?"

Springing to the door he called out in the hall that there was nobody with Miss Arkell, that she was waiting in the drawing-room alone. His voice echoed to the very depths of the house, and two slender, pretty girls came running downstairs in answer to its sound. There was a slight look of William in both of them, but the resemblance to their mother was great, and Mildred's heart did not go out yearning to them as it had to Travice. She kissed them, and found them pleasant, lady-like girls; but with a dash of coquetry in their manner already.

"I hope I see you well, Miss Arkell."

Mildred was bending over the girls, and started at the well-remembered tones, so superlatively polite, but freezing and heartless. Charlotte was radiant in beauty and a blue silk dinner-dress, with flowing blue ribbons in her bright hair. Mildred felt plain beside her. Her rich black silk was made high, and its collar and cuffs were muslin, worked with black. Nothing else, save a gold chain; the pretty chain of her girlhood that William had given her; nothing in her hair. She was in mourning for a relative of Lady Dewsbury.

"You have made acquaintance with the children, I see, Miss Arkell."

"Yes; I am so glad to do it. Peter has sometimes mentioned them in his letters; and I have heard much of Travice from Betsey—Mrs. Dundyke. Your sister charged me to give you her best love, Mrs. Arkell. I saw her on Friday."

"She's very kind," coldly returned Mrs. Arkell; "but I don't quite understand how you can have heard much of my son from her; that is, how she can have had much to say. Mrs. Dundyke had not seen him since he was an infant, until we were in town last year."

"I think Travice has been in the habit of writing to her."

"In the habit of writing to Aunt Betsey,—of course I have been!" interposed Travice. "And she writes to me, too. I like Aunt Betsey. And I can tell you what, mamma, for all you go on against him so, I like Mr. Dundyke."

"Your likings are of very little consequence at present, Travice," was the languidly indifferent answer of his mother. "You will learn better as you grow older. My sister forfeited all claim on me when she married so low a man as Mr. Dundyke," continued Mrs. Arkell to Mildred; "and she knows that such is my opinion. I shall never change it. She married him deliberately, with her eyes open to the consequences, and of course she must take them. I said and did what I could to warn her, but she would not listen. And now look at the way in which they are obliged to live!"

"Mr. Dundyke earns an excellent income; in fact, I believe he is making money fast," observed Mildred. "Their living in the humble way they do is from choice, I think, not from necessity."

Mrs. Arkell shrugged her pretty shoulders with contempt.

"We will pass to another topic, Miss Arkell, that one does not interest me. What are the new fashions for the season? You must get them at first hand, from your capacity in Lady Dewsbury's household."

Mildred would not resent the hint.

"Indeed, Mrs. Arkell, if you only knew how little the fashions interest either Lady Dewsbury or me, you would perhaps laugh at us both," she answered. "Lady Dewsbury lives too much out of the world to need its fashions. She is a great invalid."

Peter's wife was right in her conjecture, for Mrs. Arkell had hastily summoned a dinner party. Mr. Arkell took his revenge, and faced his wife in a morning coat. Ten inclusive; and the governess and Travice were desired to sit down in the place of Mr. and Mrs. Peter. It may be concluded that Mildred was of the least consequence present, in social position; nevertheless, Mr. Arkell took her in to dinner, and placed her at his right hand. All were strangers to her, excepting old Marmaduke Carr. Squire Carr was dead, and his son John was the squire now.

It was not the quiet evening Mildred had thought to spend with them. She slipped from the drawing-room at ten, Mrs. Peter's health being the excuse for leaving early. Mr. Arkell had his hat on at the hall door waiting for her, just as it used to be in the days gone by.

"But, William, I do not wish to take you out," she remonstrated. "You have your guests."

"They are not my guests to-night," was his quiet answer, as he gave his arm to Mildred.

Travice came running out. "Oh, papa, let me go with you!"

"Get your trencher, then."

He stuck the college cap on his head and went leaping on, through the gates and up the street, just in the manner that college boys like to leap. Mr. Arkell and Mildred followed more soberly, speaking of indifferent things. Mildred began talking of Mr. Carr.

"How well he wears!" she said. "Peter tells me he has retired from business."

"These three or four years past. He did wisely. Those who keep on manufacturing, only do it at a loss."

"You keep it on, William."

"I know. But serious thoughts occur to me now and then of the wisdom of retiring. There are reasons against it, though. Were I to give up business, we should have to live in a very different style from what we do now; for my income would be but a small one, and that would not suit Mrs. Arkell. Besides, I really could not bear to turn my workmen adrift. There are too many unemployed already in the town; and I am always hoping, against my conviction, that times will mend."

"But if you only make to lose, how would the retiring from business lessen your income?"

William laughed. "Well, Mildred, of course I do get something still by my business; but in speaking of the bad times, we are all apt to make the worst of it. I dare say I make about half what we spend; but that you know, compared to the profits of old days, is as nothing."

"If you do make that, William, why think at all of giving up?"

"Because the doubt is upon me whether worse times may not come, and bring ruin with them to all who have kept on manufacturing. Were I as Marmaduke Carr is, a lonely man, I should give up to-morrow; but I have my wife and children to provide for, and I really do not know what to do for the best."

"What has become of Robert Carr? Has he ever been home?"

"Never. He is in Holland still for all I know. I have not heard his name mentioned for years in the town. Old Marmaduke never speaks of him; and others, I suppose, have forgotten him. You know that the old squire's dead?"

"Yes; and that John has succeeded him. Did John's daughter—Emma, I mean—ever marry?"

"She married very well indeed; a Mr. Lewis. Valentine, the son and heir, is at home with his father; steady, selfish, mean as his father was before him; but I fancy John Carr has trouble with the second, Ben."

"Ben promised to be a spendthrift, I remember," remarked Mildred. "What is Travice gazing at?"

Travice had come to a stand-still, and was standing with his face turned upwards. Mr. Arkell laughed.

"Do you remember my propensity for star-gazing, Mildred? Travice has inherited it. But with him it is more developed than it was with me. I should not be surprised at his turning out an astronomer one of these days."

Did she remember it! Poor Mildred fell into a reverie that lasted until William said good night to her at her brother's door.

She was not sorry when her visit to Westerbury came to an end. The town seemed to look cold upon her. Of those she had left in it, some had died, some had married, some had quitted the place for ever. The old had vanished, the middle-aged were growing old, the children had become men and women. It did not seem the same native place to Mildred; it never would seem so again. Some of the inhabitants of her own standing had dwindled down to obscurity; others who had not been of her standing, had gone up and become very grand indeed. These turned up their noses at Mildred, just as did Mrs. William Arkell; and thought it excessive presumption in a lady's maid to come amongst them as an equal. She had persisted in going out to service in defiance of all her friends, and the least she could do was to keep her distance from them.

Mildred did not hear these gracious comments, and would not have cared very much if she had heard them. She returned to her post at Lady Dewsbury's, and a few more years passed on.

CHAPTER XV

THE DEAN'S DAUGHTER

The tender green of early spring was on the new leaves of the cathedral elm trees. Not sufficient to afford a shade yet; but giving promise of its fulness ere the sultry days of summer should come.

The deanery of Westerbury was a queer old building to look at, especially in front. It had no lower windows. There were odd-looking patches in the wall where the windows ought to have been, and three or four doors. These doors had their separate uses. One of them was the private entrance of the dean and his family; one was used by the servants; one was allotted to official or state occasions, at the great audit time, for instance, when the dean and chapter held their succession of dinners for ever so many days running; and one (a little one in a corner) was popularly supposed to be a sham. But the windows above were unusually large, and so they compensated in some degree for the lack of them below.

Standing at the smallest of the windows on this spring day, was a young lady of some ten or twelve years old. She had a charming countenance, rather saucy, and great blue eyes as large as saucers. She wore a pretty grey silk frock, trimmed with black velvet—perhaps, as slight mourning—and her light brown hair fell on her neck in curls, that were apt to get untidy and entangled. It was Georgina Beauclerc, the only child of the Dean of Westerbury.

The window commanded a good view of the grounds, as the space here at the back of the cathedral was called—a large space; the green, inclosed promenade, shaded by the elm-trees, in the middle; well-kept walks outside; and beyond, all around, the prebendal and other houses. Opposite to the deanery, on the other side the walks, the elm-trees, and the grassy promenade, was the house of the Rev. Mr. Wilberforce, minor canon and sacrist of the cathedral, rector of St. James the Less, and head-master of the college school. Side by side with it was the quaint and small house once inhabited by the former rector of St. James the Less, an old clergyman, subject to gout, now dead and gone. The Rev. Wheeler Prattleton lived in the house now: he was also a minor canon, and chanter to the cathedral—that is, he held the office of what was called the chanter, which gave him the right to fix upon the services for the choir when the dean did not, but he only took his turn for chanting in rotation with the rest of the minor canons. On the other side the head-master's house was a handsome, good-sized dwelling, tenanted by a gentleman of the name of Lewis, who held a good and official position in connexion with the bishop, and had married the daughter of old Squire Carr, the sister to the present squire, and niece to Marmaduke. Beyond this, in a corner, was the quaintest house in the grounds, all covered with ivy, and seeming to have nothing belonging to it but a door; but the fact was, although the door was here, the house itself was built out behind, and could not be seen—its windows facing, some the river, some the open country, and catching a view of St. James the Less in the distance. Mr. Aultane, Westerbury's greatest lawyer, so far as practice went, though not perhaps in honour, lived here; and he held up his head and thought himself above the minor canons. In this one nook of the grounds a few private individuals congregated—it is not necessary to mention them all; but the rest of the houses were mostly occupied by the prebendaries and minor canons. In some lived the widows and families of prebendaries deceased.

Looking to the left, as Georgina Beauclerc stood at the deanery window, just beyond the gate that inclosed the grounds on that side, might be seen the tall red chimneys of the Palmery. It was, perhaps, inside, the worst of all the larger houses; but the St. John's came to it often because they owned it. They (the St. John's) were the best family in Westerbury, and held sway as such. Mr. St. John had died some years ago, leaving one son, about thirty years of age, greatly afflicted; and a young little son, by his second wife. But that young son was growing up now: time flies.

Georgina Beauclerc's great blue eyes, so clear and round, were fixed on one particular spot, and that appeared to be one rather difficult to see. She had her face and nose pressed against the glass, looking toward the college schoolroom, a huge building on the right of the deanery, just beyond the cloisters.

"They are late again!" she exclaimed, in a soliloquy of resentment. "I wish that horrid old Wilberforce was burnt!"

"Georgina!"

The tone of the reproof, more fractious than surprised, came from a recess in the large room, and Georgina turned hastily.

"Why, when did you come in, mamma? I thought you were safe in your bed room."

Mrs. Beauclerc came forward, a thin woman with a somewhat discontented look on her face, and a little nose, red at the tip. She had long given up all real rule of Georgina, but she had not given up attempting it. And Georgina, a wild, spoilt child, was in the habit of saying and doing very much what she liked. She made great friends of the college schoolboys, and had picked up many of their sayings; and this was particularly objectionable to the reserved Mrs. Beauclerc.

"What did you say about Mr. Wilberforce?"

"I said I wished he was burnt."

"Oh, Georgina!"

"I do wish he was scorched. It has struck one o'clock and the boys are not out! What business has he to keep them in? He did it once before."

"May I ask what business it is of yours, Georgina? But it has not struck one."

"I'm sure it has," returned Georgina.

"It has not, I tell you. How dare you contradict me? And allow me to ask why Miss Jackson quitted you so early to-day?"

"Because I dismissed her," returned the young lady, with equanimity. "I had the headache, mamma; and I can't be expected to attend to my studies when I have that."

"You have it pretty often," grumbled Mrs. Beauclerc; and indeed upon this plea, or upon some other, Georgina was perpetually contriving, when not watched, to get rid of her daily governess. "My opinion is, you never had the headache in your life."

"Thank you, mamma. That is just what Miss Jackson herself said yesterday afternoon. I paid her out for it. I sent her away with Baby Ferraday's kite fastened to her shawl behind."

"What?" exclaimed Mrs. Beauclerc.

"The kite was small, not bigger than my hand, but the tail was fine," continued the imperturbable Georgina. "You cannot imagine how grand the effect was as she walked along the grounds, and the wind took the tail and fluttered it. The college boys happened to come out of school at the moment; and they followed her, shouting out 'kites for sale; tails to sell.' Miss Jackson couldn't think what was the matter, and kept turning round. She'd have had it on till now, I hope, only Fred St. John went and tore it off."

Mrs. Beauclerc had listened in speechless amazement. When Georgina talked on in this rapid way, telling of her exploits—and to do the young lady justice, she never sought to hide them—Mrs. Beauclerc felt powerless for correction.

"What is to become of you?" groaned Mrs. Beauclerc.

"I'm sure I don't know, mamma; something good, I hope," returned the saucy girl. "Little Ferraday—I had called him up here to give him some cakes—could not think where his kite had vanished, and began to roar; so I found him sixpence and sent him into the town to buy another. I don't know whether he got lost or run over. The nurse seemed to think it would be one of the two, for she went into a fit when she found he had gone off alone."

"Georgina, I tell you these things cannot be permitted to continue. You are no longer a child."

The colloquy was interrupted by the entrance of the dean: a genial-looking man, with silver buckles in his shoes, and a face very much like Georgina's own. He had apparently just come in, for he had his shovel hat in his hand. The girl loved her father above everything on earth; to his slightest word she rendered implicit homage; though she waged hot war with all others in authority over her, commencing with Mrs. Beauclerc. She flew to the dean with a beaming face, and he clasped his arms round her with a gesture of the fondest affection. Mrs. Beauclerc left the room. She never cared to enter into a contest with her daughter before the dean.

"My Georgina!" came forth the loving whisper.

"Papa, is it one o'clock?"

"Not yet, my dear."

"I'm sure I heard the college clock strike."

"You thought you did, perhaps. It must have been the quarters."

"Oh, dear! I have been calling Mr. Wilberforce hard names for nothing."

"What has Mr. Wilberforce done to you, my Georgie?"

"I thought he was keeping the school in; and I want to speak to Frederick St. John."

They were interrupted. One of the servants appeared, and said a gentleman was asking permission to see the dean. The dean took the credential card handed to him: "Mr. Peter Arkell."

"Show Mr. Arkell up," said the dean. "Georgina, my dear, you can go to your mamma."

"I'd rather stay here, papa," she said, boldly.

One word of explanation as to this visit of Peter Arkell's. It had of course been his intention to get his son Henry entered at the college school, and to this end had the boy been instructed. Of rare capacity, of superior intellect, of sense and feeling beyond his years, it had been a pleasure to his teachers to bring him on: and they consisted of his father and mother. From the one he learnt the classics and figures; from the other music and English generally. Henry Arkell was apt at all things: but if he had genius for one thing more than another, it was certainly music. The sole luxury Mrs. Peter Arkell had retained about her, was her piano; and Henry was an apt pupil. Few boys are gifted with so rare a voice for singing, as was he; and his mother had cultivated it well: it was intended that he should enter the cathedral choir, as well as the school.

By the royal charter of the school, its number was confined to forty boys, king's scholars; of these, ten were chosen to be choristers: but the head master had the privilege of taking private pupils, who paid him handsomely. The dean had the right of placing in ten of these king's scholars, but he rarely exercised it; leaving it in the hands of the head master. Mr. Peter Arkell had applied several times lately to Mr. Wilberforce; and had received only vague answers from that gentleman—"when there was a vacancy to spare, he would think of his son"—but Peter Arkell grew tired. Henry was of an age to be in the school now, and he resolved to speak to the dean.

He came in, leading Henry by the hand. Georgina fell a little back, struck—awed—by the boy's wondrous beauty. The dean, one of the most affable men that ever exercised sway over Westerbury cathedral, shook hands with Peter Arkell, whom he knew slightly.

"I don't know that there's a vacancy," said the dean, when Mr. Arkell told his tale. "Your son shall have it, and welcome, if there is. I have left these things to Mr. Wilberforce."

At this juncture Miss Beauclerc threw the window up, and beckoned to some one outside. Had her mother been present she would have administered a reprimand, but the dean was absorbed with the visitors, and he was less particular than his wife. Georgina was but a child, he reasoned; she might be too careless in her manners now, but it would all come right with years. Better, far better see her genuine and truthful, if a little brusque, than false, mincing, affected, as young ladies were growing to be. And the dean checked her not.

"I know Mr. Wilberforce well, sir, and he has said he will do what he can," said Peter Arkell, in reply to the dean. "But I fear that I may have to wait an indefinite period. There are others in the town of far greater account than I, who are anxious to get their sons into the school; and who have, no doubt, the ear of Mr. Wilberforce. A word from you, Mr. Dean, would effect all, I am sure: if you would only kindly speak it in my behalf."

Dr. Beauclerc turned his head to see who was entering the room, for the door had opened. It was a handsome stripling, growing rapidly into manhood—Frederick, heir of the St. John's. He was already keeping his terms at Oxford; Mrs. St. John had sent him there too early; and in the intervals, when they were sojourning at Westerbury, he was placed in the college; not as an ordinary scholar; the private pupil, and the chief one too, of Mr. Wilberforce.

The dean gave him a nod, and took the hand of the eager, exquisite face turned to him. Like his daughter, he was a great admirer of beauty in the human face: it would often give him a thrill of intense pleasure.

"What is your name, my boy?"

"Henry Cheveley Arkell, sir."

The dean glanced at Peter Arkell with a half smile. He remembered yet the commotion caused in Westerbury when Miss Cheveley married the tutor, and the name brought it before him.

"How old are you?"

"Nearly ten, sir."

"If I could paint faces, I'd paint his," cried Georgina to young St. John, in a half whisper. "Why don't you do it?"

"I suppose you mean his portrait?"

"You know I do. But, Fred, is he not beautiful?"

"You may get sent away if you talk," was the gentleman's answer.

"Has he been brought on well in his Latin? Is he fit to enter as a king's scholar?" inquired the dean of Peter Arkell.

"He has been brought on well in all necessary studies, Mr. Dean; I may say it emphatically, well. I was in the college school myself, and know what is required. But learning has made strides of late, sir; boys are brought on more rapidly; and I can assure you that many a lad has quitted the college school in my days, his education finished, not as good a scholar as my son is now. I have taken pains with him."

"And we know what that implies from you, Mr. Arkell," said the dean, with a kindly smile. "You would like to be a king's scholar, my brave boy?"

"Oh yes, sir," said Henry, his transparent cheek flushing with hope.

"Then you shall be one. I will give you the first vacancy under myself."

They retired with many thanks; Frederick St. John giving Henry's bright waving hair a pull, as he passed him, by way of parting salutation.

"Papa! if you don't put that child into the college school, I will," began Georgina; her tone one of impassioned earnestness. "I will; though I have to beg it of old Wilberforce. I never saw such a face. I have fallen in love with it."

"I am going to put him in, Georgie. I like his face myself. But he can't go in until there's a vacancy. I must ask Mr. Wilberforce."

"There are two vacancies now, Dr. Beauclerc," spoke up Frederick St. John. "One of them is under you, I know."

"Indeed!"

"That is, there will be to-morrow. Those two West Indian boys, the Stantons, are sent for home suddenly: their mother's dying, or something of that. The master had the news this morning, and the school is in a commotion over it. If you do wish to fill the vacancy, sir, you should speak to Mr. Wilberforce at once, or he may stand it out that he has promised it," concluded Frederick St. John, with that freedom of speech he was fond of using, even to the dean.

"Stanton?" repeated the dean. "But were they not private pupils of the master's?"

"Oh dear no, sir, they are on the foundation. You might have seen them any Sunday in their surplices in college. They board at the master's house; that's all."

"Two dark boys, papa, the ugliest in the school," struck in Georgina, who knew a great deal more about the school than the dean did.

When Mr. Peter Arkell and Henry quitted the deanery, the former turned to the cloisters; for he had an errand to do in the town, and to go through the cloisters was the shortest way. He encountered some of the college boys in the cloisters, whooping, hallooing, shouting; their feet and their tongues a babel of confusion. Mr. Arkell looked back at them with strange interest. It did not seem so very long since he and his cousin William had been college boys themselves, and had shouted and leaped as merrily as these. Two or three of them touched their trenchers to Mr. Arkell: they were evening pupils of his.

Henry had turned the other way, towards his home. At the gate, when he reached it, the boundary of the cathedral grounds on that side, he found a meek donkey drawn up, the drawer of a sort of truck, holding a water barrel. A woman was in the habit of bringing this water every day from a famous spring outside the town, to supply some of the houses in the grounds. The water was drawn out by means of a contrivance called a spigot and faucet, and she was stooping over this, filling a can. Henry, boy like, halted to watch the process, for the water rushed out full force.

Putting in the spigot when the can was full, she was proceeding to carry it up the old stairs belonging to the gateway, above which lived one of the minor canons, when the first shout of the college boys broke upon her ear.

"Oh, mercy!" she screamed out, as if in abject fear; and Henry Arkell, who was then continuing his way, halted again and stared at her.

"Young gentleman," she said in a voice of appeal, "would you do me a charity?"

"What is it?" he asked. He was tall and manly for his years.

"If you would but stand by the barrel and guard it! The day afore yesterday, while my donkey and barrel was a stopped in this very spot, and I was a going up these here stairs with this very can, them wild young college gents came trooping by, and they pulled out the spigot and set the water a running. There warn't a drop left in the barrel when I got down. It was a loss to me I haven't over got."

"Go along," said Henry, "I'll guard it for you."

Unconscious boast! The boys came on in a roar of triumph, for they had caught sight of the water barrel. A young gentleman of the name of Lewis, a little older than Henry, was the first to get to the barrel, and lay his hand on the spigot.

"Oh, if you please, you are not to touch it," said Henry; "I am taking care of it."

"Halloa! what youngster are you? The donkey's brother?"

"Oh, don't take it out—don't!" pleaded Henry. "I promised the woman I'd guard it for her."

At this moment the woman's head was protruded through one of the small, deep, square loopholes of the ancient staircase; and she apostrophized the crew in no measured terms, and rather contradictory. They were a set of dyed villains, of young limbs, of daring pigs; and they were dear, good, young gentlemen, that she prayed for every night; and that she'd be proud to give a drink of the beautiful spring water to any thirsty day.

You know schoolboys; and may, therefore, guess the result of this. The derisive shouts increased; the woman was ironically cheered; and Henry Arkell had a struggle with Master Lewis for possession of the spigot, which ended in the former's ignominious discomfiture. He lay on the ground, the water pouring out upon him, when a tall form and authoritative voice dashed into the throng, and laid summary hands on Lewis.

"Now then, Mr. St. John! Please to let me alone, sir. It's no affair of yours."

"I choose to make it my affair, young Lewis. You help that boy up that you have thrown down."

Lewis rebelled. The rest of the boys had drawn back beyond reach of the splashing water. St. John stooped for the spigot, and put it in; and then treated Lewis to a slight shaking.

"You be quiet, Mr. St. John. If you cock it over us boys in school, it's no reason why you should, out."

Another instalment of the shaking.

"Help him up, I tell you, Lewis."

Perhaps as the best way of getting out of it, Lewis jerked himself forward, and did help him up. Henry had been unable to rise of himself, and for a few moments he could not stand: his knee was hurt. It was a curious coincidence that the first fall, when he was entering the school, and the last fall—But it may be as well not to anticipate.

"Now, mind you, Mr. Lewis: if you attempt a cowardly attack on this boy again—you are bigger and stronger than he is—I'll thrash you kindly."

Lewis walked away, leaving a mental word behind him—not spoken, he would not have dared that—for Frederick St. John. The woman came down wailing and lamenting at the loss of the water, and the boys scuttered off in a body. St. John threw the woman half-a-crown, and helped Henry home.

The dean held to his privilege for once, and gave Mr. Wilberforce notice that he had filled up the vacancy by bestowing it on the son of Mr. Peter Arkell. Mr. Wilberforce, privately believing that the world was about to be turned upside-down, could only bow and acquiesce. He did it with a good grace, and sent a courteous message for Henry to be there on the following Monday, at early school.

Accordingly, at seven o'clock, Henry was there. He did not like to troop in with the college boys, but waited until the head-master had come, and entered then. Mr. Wilberforce called him up, inscribed his name on the school-roll, put a few questions to him as to the state of his studies, and then assigned him his place.

The boy was walking to it with that self-consciousness of something like a thousand eyes being on him— so terrible to the mind of a sensitive nature, and his was eminently one—when the head-master's voice was heard.

"Arkell, junior."

Never supposing "Arkell, junior," could be meant for him, he went timidly on; but the voice rose higher.

"Arkell, junior."

It was so peremptory that Henry turned, and found it was meant for him. The sensitive crimson dyed his face deeper and deeper as he retraced his steps to the head-master's desk.

"Are you lame, Arkell, junior?"

"Oh, it's nothing, sir. It's nearly well."

"What's the matter, then?"

"I fell down last week, sir, and hurt my knee a little."

"Oh. Go to your desk."

"What a girl's face!" cried one, as Henry recommenced his promenade, for the indicated place was far down in the school.

"I'm blest if I don't believe it is the knight of the water-barrel!" exclaimed a big boy at the first desk. "Won't Lewis take it out of him! I hope he may get off with whole bones; but I'd not bet upon it."

"Lewis had better not try it on, or you either, Forbes," quietly struck in the second senior of the school, who was writing within hearing.

"Why, do you know him, Mr. Arkell?"

"Never you mind. I intend to take care of him."

The boys were trooping through the cloisters when school was over, and met the dean. Georgina was with him. She caught sight of Henry's face, and in her impulsive fashion dashed through the throng of boys to his side.

"Papa, he's here! Papa! he is here."

The dean, in his kindly manner, shook Henry by the hand. "Be a good boy, mind," he said. "Remember, you are under me."

"I'll try, sir," replied Henry.

"Do. I shall not lose sight of you." And, with a general nod to the rest, he departed, taking his daughter's hand.

For a full minute there was a dead silence. It was so entirely unusual a thing for the dean to shake hands familiarly with a college boy, that those gentry did not at first decide how to take it. Then one of them, more impudent than the rest, bowed his body down before the new junior with mock gravity.

"If you please, sir, wouldn't you be pleased to make yourself cock of the school after this, and cut out St. John?"

"Take care of your tongue, Marshall," admonished St. John, who made one of the throng.

"I am blowed, though!" returned Marshall. "Did anybody ever see such a go as this?"

"What's the row?" demanded Hennet, a fine youth, one of Mr. Wilberforce's private pupils, and who only now came up.

"Oh, my! you should have been here, Hennet," responded Marshall. "We have got a lord, or something else, among us. The Dean of Westerbury has been bowing down to worship him."

Hennet, not understanding, looked at St. John.

"No. Trash!" explained St. John. "Marshall is putting his tongue and his foot into it to-day. I'm off to breakfast."

The word excited anticipations of the meal, and all the rest were off to breakfast too—making the grounds echo with their shouts as they ran.

CHAPTER XVI

A CITY'S DESOLATION

Henry Arkell had been in the college school rather more than a year, and also in the choir—for he entered the two almost simultaneously, his fine voice obtaining him the place before any other candidate—when the rank and fashion of Westerbury found itself in a state of internal, pleasurable commotion, touching an amateur concert about to be given for the benefit of the distressed Poles.

Mrs. Lewis, the daughter of the late Squire Carr, Mrs. Aultane, and a few more of the lesser satellites residing near the cathedral clergy, suddenly found themselves, from some cause never clearly explained to Westerbury, aroused into a state of sympathy and compassion for that ill-starred country, Poland, and its ill-used inhabitants. Casting about in their minds what they could do to help those misérables— the French word slipped out at my pen's end—they alighted on the idea of an amateur morning concert, and forthwith set about organizing one. Painting in glowing colours the sufferings and hardships of this distant people, they contrived to gain the ear of the good-natured dean, and of Mrs. St. John of the Palmery, and the rest was easy. Canons and minor canons followed suit; all the gentry of the place took the concert under their especial patronage; and everybody with the slightest pretension to musical skill, intimated that they were ready to assist in the performances, if called upon. In fact, the miniature scheme grew into a gigantic undertaking; and no expense, trouble, or time was spared in the getting up of this amateur concert. Ladies of local rank and fashion were to sing at it; the mayor accorded the use of the guildhall; and Westerbury had not been in so delightful a state of excited anticipation for years and years.

But it is impossible to please everybody—as I dare say you have found out for yourselves at odd moments, in going through life. So it proved with this concert; and though it was productive of so much satisfaction to some, it gave great dissatisfaction to others. This arose from a cause which has been a bone of contention even down to our own days: the overlooking near distress, to assist that very far off. There are ill-conditioned spirits amidst us who protest that the dear little interesting black Ashantees should not be presented with nice fine warm stockings, while our own common-place young Arabs have to go without shoes. While the destitution in Westerbury was palpably great, crying aloud to Heaven in its extent and helplessness, it seemed to some inhabitants of the city—influential ones, too—that the movement for the relief of the far-off Poles was strangely out of place; that the amateur concert, if got up at all, ought to have been held for the relief of the countrymen at home. This opinion gained ground, even amidst the supporters of the concert. The dean himself was heard to say, that had he given the matter proper consideration, he should have advised postponement of this concert for the foreigners to a less inopportune moment.

You, my readers, may know nothing of the results following the opening of the British ports for the introduction of French goods, as they fell on certain local places. When the bill was brought into the House of Commons by Mr. Huskisson, these results—ruin and irrecoverable distress—were foreseen by some of the members, and urged as an argument against its passing. Its defenders did not deny the probable fact; but said that in all great political changes the FEW must be content to suffer for the good of the MANY. An unanswerable argument; all the more plain that those who had to discuss it were not of the few. That the few did suffer, and suffered to an extremity, none will believe who did not witness it, is a matter of appalling history. Ask Coventry what that bill did for it. Ask Worcester. Ask Yeovil. Ask other places that might be named. These towns lived by their staple trade; their respective manufactures; and when a cheaper, perhaps better article was introduced from France, so as to supersede, or nearly so, their own, there was nothing to stand between themselves and ruin.

Ah! my aged friends! if you were living in those days, you may have taken part in the congratulations that attended the opening of the British ports to French goods. The popular belief was, that the passing of the measure was as a boon falling upon England; but you had been awed into silence had you witnessed, but for a single day, the misery and confusion it entailed on these local isolated places. Take Westerbury: half the manufacturers went to total ruin, their downfall commencing with that year, and going on with the following years, until it was completed. It was but a question of the extent of private means. Those who had none to fly to, sunk at once in a species of general wreck; their stock of goods was sold for what it would fetch; their manufactories and homes were given up; their furniture was seized; and with beggary staring them in the face, they went adrift upon the cold world. Some essayed other means of making their living; essayed it as they best could without money and without hope, and struggled on from year to year, getting only the bread that nourished them. Others, more entirely overwhelmed with the blow, made a few poor efforts to recover themselves, in vain, in vain; and their ending was the workhouse. Honourable citizens once, good men, as respectable and respected as you are, who had been reared and lived in comfort, bringing up their families as well-to-do manufacturers ought; these were reduced to utter destitution. Some drifted away, seeking only a spot where they might die, out of sight of men; others found an asylum in their old age in the paupers' workhouse! You do not believe me? you do not think it could have been quite so bad as this? As surely as that this hand is penning the words, I tell you but the truth. For no fault of theirs did they sink to ruin; by no prudence could they have averted it.

The manufacturers who had private property—that is, property and money apart from the capital employed in their business—were in a different position, and could either retire from business, and make the best of what they had left, or keep on manufacturing in the hope that they should retrieve their losses, and that times would mend. For a very, very long time—for years and years—a great many cherished the delusive hope that the ports would be reclosed, and English goods again fill the markets. They kept on manufacturing; content, perforce, with the small profit they made, and drawing upon their private funds for what more they required for their yearly expenditure. How they could have gone on for so many years, hoping in this manner, is a marvel to them now. But the fact was so. There were but very few who did this, or who, indeed, had money to do it; but amidst them must be numbered Mr. Arkell.

But, if the masters suffered, what can you expect was the fate of the workmen? Hundreds upon hundreds were thrown out of employment, and those who were still retained in the few manufactories kept open, earned barely sufficient to support existence; for the wages were, of necessity, sadly reduced, and they were placed on short work besides. What was to become of this large body of men? What did become of them? God only knew. Some died of misery, of prolonged starvation, of broken hearts. Their end was pretty accurately ascertained; but those who left their native town to be wanderers on the face of the land, seeking for employment to which they were unaccustomed, and perhaps finding none—who can tell what was their fate? The poor rates increased alarmingly, little able as were the impoverished population to bear an increase; the workhouses were filled, and lamentations were heard in the streets. Poor men! They only asked for work, work; and of work there was none. Small bodies of famished wretches, deputations from the main body, perambulated the town daily, calling in timidly at the manufactories still open, and praying for a little work. How useless! when those manufactories had been obliged to turn off many of their own hands.

It will not be wondered at, then, if, in the midst of this bitter distress, the grand scheme for the relief of the Poles, which was turning the town mad with excitement, did not find universal favour. The workmen, in particular, persisted in cherishing all sorts of obstinate notions about it. Why should them there foreign Poles be thought of and relieved, while they were starving? Would the Polish clergy and the grand folks, over there, think of them, the Westerbury workmen, and get up a concert for 'em, and send 'em the proceeds? There was certainly rough reason in this. The discontent began to be spoken aloud, and altogether the city was in a state of semi-rebellion.

Some of the men were gathered one evening at a public-house they used; their grievances, as a matter of course, the theme of discussion. So many years had elapsed since the blow had first fallen on the city by the passing of the bill, almost a generation as it seemed, that the worn-out theme of closing the ports was used threadbare; and the men chiefly confined themselves to the hardships of the present time. Bad as the trade was at Westerbury, it was expected to be worse yet, for the more wealthy of the manufacturers were beginning to say they should be forced at last to close their works. The men lighted their pipes, and called for pints or half pints of ale. Those who were utterly penniless, and could, in addition, neither beg nor borrow money for this luxury, sat gloomily by, their brows lowering over their gaunt and famished cheeks.

"James Jones," said the landlord, a surly sort of man, speaking in reply to a demand for a half pint of ale, "I can't serve you. You owe five and fourpence already."

What Mr. James Jones might have retorted in his disappointment, was stopped by the entrance of several men who came in together. It was the "deputation;" the men chosen to go round the city that day and ask for work or alms. The interest aroused by their appearance overpowered petty warfare.

"Well, and how have ye sped?" was the eager general question, as the men found seats.

"We went round, thirteen of us, upon empty stomachs, and we left them at home empty too," replied a tidy-looking man with a stoop in his shoulders; "but we've done next to no good. Thorp, he has gone home; we gave him the money out of what we've collected for a loaf o' bread, for his wife and children's bad a-bed, and nigh clammed besides. The tale goes, too, that things are getting worse."

"They can't get worse, Read."

"Yes, they can; there was a meeting to-day of the masters. Did you hear of it?"

Of course the men had heard of it. Little took place in the town, touching on their interests, that they did not hear of.

"Then perhaps you've heard the measure that was proposed at it—to reduce the wages again. It was carried, too. George Arkell & Son's was the only firm that held out against it."

"Nobody has held out for us all along like Mr. Arkell," observed one who had not yet spoken. "He was a young man when these troubles first fell on the city, and he's middle-aged now, but never once throughout all the years has his voice been raised against us."

"True," said Read; "and when he speaks to us it is kindly and sympathizingly, like the gentleman he is, and as if we were fellow human beings, which they don't all do. Some of the masters don't care whether we starve or live; they are as selfish as they are high. Mr. Arkell has large means and an open hand; it's said he has the interests of us operatives at heart as much as he has his own; for my part, I believe it. His contribution to-day was a sovereign—more than twice as much as anybody else gave us."

"And why not!" broke in Mr. James Jones "If Arkells have got plenty—and it's well known they have—it's only right they should help us."

"As to their having such plenty, I can't say about that," dissented Markham—a superior man, and the manager of a large firm. "They have kept on making largely, and they must lose at times. It stands to reason, as things have been. Of course they had plenty of money to fall back upon. Everybody knows that; and Mr. Arkell has preferred to sacrifice some of that money—all honour to him—rather than turn off to destitution the men who have grown old in his service, and in his father's before him."

"It's true, it's true," murmured the men. "God bless Mr. William Arkell!"

"It's said that young Mr. Travice is to be brought up to the business, so things can't be very bad with them."

"Yah! bad with 'em!" roared a broad-shouldered old man. "It riles me to sit here and hear you men talk such foolery. Haven't he got his close carriage and his horses? and haven't he got his fine house and his servants? Things bad with the Arkells!"

"You should not cast blame to the masters," continued Markham. "How many of them are there who still keep on making, but whose resources are nearly exhausted!"

"No, no, 'taint right," murmured some of the more just-thinking of the men. "The masters' troubles must be ten-fold greater than ours."

"I should be glad to hear how you make that out?" grumbled a malcontent. "I have got seven mouths to feed at home, and how am I to feed 'em, not earning a penny? We was but six, but our Betsey, as was in service as nuss-girl at Mrs. Omer's, came home to-day. I won't deny that Mrs. Omer have been kind to her, keeping her on after they failed, and that; but she up and told her yesterday that she couldn't afford it any longer. I remember, brethren, when Mr. and Mrs. Omer held up their heads, and paid their way as respectable as the first manufacturer in Westerbury. Good people they was."

"Mr. Omer came to our place to-day," interrupted Markham, "to pray the governor to give him a little work at his own home, as a journeyman. But we had none to give, without robbing them that want it worse than he. I think I never saw our governor so cut up as he was, after being obliged to refuse him."

"Ay," returned the former speaker; "and our Betsey declares that her missis cried to her this morning, and said she didn't know but what they should come to the parish. Betsey, poor girl," he continued, "can't bear to be a burden upon us; but there ain't no help for it. There be no places to be had; what with so many of the girls being throwed out of employment, and the families as formerly kept two or three servants keeping but one, and them as kept one keeping none. There's nothing that she can do, brethren, for herself or for us."

"The Lord keep her from evil courses!" uttered a deep, earnest voice.

"If I thought as her, or any of my children, was capable of taking to them," thundered the man, his breast heaving as he raised his sinewy, lean arm in a threatening attitude, "I'd strike her flat into the earth afore me!"

"Things as bad with the masters as they be with us!" derisively resumed the broad-shouldered old man. "Yah! Some on you would hold a candle to the devil himself, though he appeared among ye horned and tailed! Why, I mind the time—I'm older nor some o' you be—when there warn't folks wanting to defend Huskisson! And I mind," he added, dropping his voice, "the judgment that come upon him for what he done."

"It's of no good opening up that again," cried Thomas Markham. "What Huskisson did, he did for his country's good, and he never thought it would bring the ill upon us that it did bring. I have told you over and over again of an interview our head governor—who has now been dead these ten years, as you know—had with Huskisson in London. It was on a Sunday evening in summer; and when the governor went in, Huskisson was seated at his library table, with one of the petitions sent up from Westerbury to the House of Commons, spread out before him. It was the one sent up in the May of that year, praying that the ports might be closed again—some of you are old enough to recollect it, my friends—the one in which our sufferings and wrongs were represented in truer and more painful colours than they were, perhaps, in any other of the memorials that went up. It was reported, I remember, that Mr. William Arkell had the chief hand in drawing out that petition: but I don't know how that might have been. Any way, it told on Mr. Huskisson; and the governor said afterwards, that if ever he saw remorse and care seated on a brow, it was on his."

"As it had cause to be!" was echoed from all parts of the room.

"Mr. Huskisson began speaking at once about the petition," continued the manager. "He asked if the sufferings described in it were not exaggerated; but the governor assured him upon his word of honour, as a resident in Westerbury and an eye-witness, that they were underdrawn rather than the contrary; for that no pen, no description, could adequately describe the misery and distress which had been rife in Westerbury ever since the bill had passed. And he used to say that, live as long as he would, he should never forget the look of perplexity and care that overshadowed Mr. Huskisson's face as he listened to him."

"It was repentance pressing sore upon him," growled a deep bass voice. "It's to be hoped our famished and homeless children haunted his dreams."

"The next September he met with the accident that killed him," continued Thomas Markham; "and though I know some of us poor sufferers were free in saying it was a judgment upon him, I've always held to my opinion that if he had foreseen the misery the bill wrought, he would never have brought it forward in the House of Commons."

"Here's Shepherd a coming in! I wonder how his child is? Last night he thought it was dying. Shepherd, how's the child?"

A care-worn, pale man made his way amid the throng. He answered quietly that the child was well.

"Well! why, you said last night that it was as bad as it could be, Shepherd! You was going off for the doctor then. Did he come to it?"

"One doctor came, from up there," answered Shepherd, pointing to the sky. "He came, and He took the child."

The words could not be misunderstood, and the room hushed itself in sympathy. "When did the boy die, Shepherd?"

"To-day, at one; and it's a mercy. Death in childhood is better than starvation in manhood."

"Could Dr. Barnes do nothing for him?" inquired a compassionate voice.

"He didn't try; he opened his winder to look out at me—he was undressing to go to bed—and asked whether I had got the money to pay him if he came."

"Hiss—iss—ss!" echoed from the room.

"I answered that I had not; but I would pay him with the very first money that I could scrape together; and I said he might take my word for it, for that had never been broken yet."

"And he would not come?"

"No. He said he knew better than to trust to promises. And when I told him that the boy was dying, and very precious to me, the rest being girls, he said it was not my word he doubted but my ability, for he didn't believe that any of us men would ever be in work again. So he shut down his winder and doused his candle, and I went home to my boy, powerless to help him, and I watched him die."

"Drink a glass of ale, Shepherd," said Markham, getting a glass from the landlord, and filling it from his own jug.

"Thank ye kindly, but I shall drink nothing to-night," replied Shepherd, motioning back the glass. "There's a sore feeling in my breast, comrades," he continued, sighing heavily; "it has been there a long while past, but it's sorer far to-day. I don't so much blame the surgeon, for there has been a deal of sickness among us, and the doctors have been unable to get their pay. Hundreds of us are nigh akin to starvation; there's scarcely a crust between us and death; we desire only to work honestly, and we can't get work to do. As I sat to-day, looking at my dead boy, I asked what we had done to have this fate thrust upon us?"

"What have we done? That's it!—what have we done?"

"But I did not come here to-night to grumble," resumed Shepherd, "I came for a specific purpose, though perhaps I mayn't succeed in it. I went down to Jasper, the carpenter, to-day, to ask him to come and take the measure for the little coffin. Well, he's like all the rest, he won't trust me; at last he said, if anybody would go bail he should be paid later, he'd make it; and I have come down to ye, friends, to ask who'll stand by me in this?"

A score of voices answered, each that he would—eager, sympathizing voices—but Shepherd shook his head. There was not one among them whose word the carpenter would take, for they were all out of work. In the silence that ensued, Shepherd rose to leave.

"Many thanks for the good-will, neighbours," he said. "And I don't grumble at my unsuccess, for I know how powerless many of ye are to aid me. But it's a bitter trial. I would rather my boy had never been born than that he should come to be buried by the parish. God knows we have heavy burdens to bear."

"Shepherd!" cried the clear voice of Thomas Markham, "I will stand by you in this. Tell Jasper I pass my word to see him paid."

Shepherd turned back and grasped the hand of Thomas Markham.

"I can't thank you as I ought, sir," he said; "but you have took a load from my heart. Though you were never repaid here, you would be hereafter; for I have come to feel a certainty that if our good deeds are not brought home to us in this world, they are only kept to speak for us in the next."

"I say, stop a minute, Shepherd," called out James Jones, as the man was again making his way to the door. "What made you go to Jasper? He's always cross-grained after his money, he is. Why didn't you go to White?"

"I did go to White first," answered Shepherd, turning to speak; "but White couldn't take it. He has got the job for all the new wooden chairs that are wanted for this concert at the town-hall, and hadn't time for coffins."

The mention was the signal for an outburst. It came from all parts of the room, one noise drowning another. Why couldn't a concert be got up for them? Weren't they as good as the Poles? Hadn't they bodies and souls to be saved as well as the Poles? Wasn't there a whole town of 'em starving under the very noses of them as had got up the concert? They could tell the company that French revolutions had growed out of less causes.

"And I'll tell ye what," roared out the old man with the broad shoulders, bringing his fist down on the table with such force that the clatter amidst the cups and glasses caused a sudden silence. "Every gentleman that puts his foot inside that there concert room, is no true man, and I'd tell him so to his face, if 'twas the Lord Lieutenant. What do our people want a fattening up of them there Poles, while we be starving? I wish the Poles was—"

"Hold your tongue, Lloyd," interposed Markham. "It's not the fault of the Poles, any more than it's ours; so where's the use of abusing them?"

"Yah!" responded Mr. Lloyd.

CHAPTER XVII

A DIFFICULTY ABOUT TICKETS

Amidst those who held a strong opinion on the subject of the concert—and it did not in any great degree differ from the men's—was Mr. Arkell. Mrs. Arkell knew of this, but never supposed it would extend to the length of keeping her away from it: or perhaps she wilfully shut her eyes to any suspicion of the sort.

On the morning preceding the concert, she was seated making up some pink bows, intended to adorn the white spotted muslin robes of her daughters, when the explanation came. She said something about the concert—really inadvertently—and Mr. Arkell took it up.

"You are surely not thinking of going to the concert?" he exclaimed.

"Indeed I am. I shall go and take Lottie and Sophy."

"Then, Charlotte, I desire that you will put away all thoughts of it," he said. "I could not allow my wife and daughters to appear at it."

"Why not? why not?" she asked in irritation.

"There is not the least necessity for my going over the reasons; you have heard me say already what I think of this concert. It is a gratuitous insult on our poor starving people, and neither I nor mine shall take part in it."

"All the influential people in the town are supporting it, and will be there."

"Not so universally as you may imagine. But at any rate what other people do is no rule for me. I should consider it little less than a sin to purchase tickets, and I will not do it, or allow it to be done."

Mrs. Arkell gave a flirt at the ribbon in her hand, and sent it flying over the table.

"What will Charlotte and Sophy say? Pleasant news this will be for them! These bows were for their white dresses. I might have spared myself the time and trouble of making them up. Travice goes to it," she added, resentfully.

"But Travice goes as senior of the college school. It has pleased Mr. Wilberforce to ask that the four senior boys shall be admitted; it has been accorded, and they have nothing to do but make use of the permission in obedience to his wishes. That is a different thing. If I had to buy a ticket for Travice, I assure you, Charlotte, the concert would wait long enough before it saw him there."

"Our tickets would cost only fifteen shillings," she retorted.

"I can't afford fifteen shillings," said Mr. Arkell, getting vexed. "Charlotte, hear me, once for all; if the tickets cost but one shilling each, I would not have you purchase them. Not a coin of mine, small or large, shall go to swell the funds of the concert. If you and the girls feel disappointed, I am sorry," he continued, in a kind tone. "It is not often that I run counter to your wishes; but in this one instance—and I must beg you distinctly to understand me—I cannot allow my decision to be disputed."

To say that Mrs. Arkell was annoyed, would be a very inadequate word to express what she felt. She had been fond of gaiety all her life; was fond of it still; she was excessively fond of dress; any project offering the one or the other was eagerly embraced by Mrs. Arkell. Though of gentle birth herself—if that was of any service to her—as the wife of William Arkell, the manufacturer, she did not take her standing in what was called the society of Westerbury—and you do not need, I presume, to be reminded what "society" in a cathedral town is; or are ignorant of its pretentious exclusiveness. There was not a more respected man in the whole city than Mr. Arkell; the dean himself was not more highly considered; but he was a manufacturer, the son of a manufacturer, and therefore beyond the pale of the visiting society. It never occurred to him to wish to enter it; but it did to his wife. To have that barrier removed, she would have sacrificed much; and now and again her reason would break out in private complaint against it. She could not see the justice of it. It is true her husband was a manufacturer; but he had been reared a gentleman; he was a brilliant scholar, one of the most accomplished men of his day. His means were ample, and their style of living was good. Mrs. Arkell glanced to some of the people revelling in the entrée of that society, with their poor pitiful income of a hundred pounds, or two, a year; their pinching and screwing; their paltry expedients to make both ends meet. Why should they be admitted and she excluded, was the question she often asked herself. But Mrs. Arkell knew perfectly well, in the midst of her grumbling, that one might as well try to alter the famed laws of the Medes and Persians, as the laws that govern society in a cathedral town: or indeed in any town. This concert she had looked forward to with more interest than usual, because it would afford her the opportunity of hearing some of the great ones of the county play and sing.

But she did not now see how to get to it; and her disappointment was bitter. It had fallen upon her as a blow. Mrs. Arkell had her faults, but she was a good wife on the whole; not one to run into direct disobedience. She generally enjoyed her own way; her husband rarely interfered to counteract it; certainly he had never denied her anything so positively as this. She sat, the image of discontent, listlessly tossing the pink bows about with her fingers, when her eldest daughter, a tall, elegant girl, came in.

"Oh, mamma! how lovely they are! won't they look well on the white dresses!"

"Well!" grunted Mrs. Arkell, "I might have spared myself the trouble of making them. We are not to go to the concert now."

"Not to go to the concert!" echoed Charlotte, opening her eyes in utter astonishment. "Does papa say so?"

"Yes; he will not allow tickets to be purchased. He does not approve of the concert. And he says, if the tickets cost but a shilling each, he should think it a sin to give it."

Charlotte sat down, the picture of dismay.

"Where will be the use of our new dresses now!" she exclaimed.

"Where will be the use of anything," retorted Mrs. Arkell. "Don't whirl your chain round like that, Charlotte, giving me the fidgets!"

Charlotte dropped her chain. A bright idea had occurred to her.

"If papa's objection lies in the purchase of tickets, let us ask Henry Arkell for his, mamma. Mrs. Peter is sure to be too ill to go."

One minute's pause of thought, and Mrs. Arkell caught at the suggestion, as a famished outcast catches at the bread offered to him. If a doubt obtruded itself, that their appearing at the concert at all would be almost as unpalatable to her husband as their spending money upon its tickets, she conveniently put it out of sight.

The gentlemen forming the choir of the cathedral, both lay-clerks and choristers, had been solicited to give their services to the concert; as an acknowledgment two tickets were presented to each of them, in common with the amateur performers. Henry Arkell had, of course, two with the rest, and these were the tickets thought of by Charlotte.

Not a moment lost Mrs. Arkell. Away went she to pay a visit to Mrs. Peter—a most unusual condescension; and it impressed Mrs. Peter accordingly, who was lying on her sofa that day, very poorly indeed. Mrs. Arkell at once proclaimed the motive of her visit; she did not beat about the bush, or go to work with crafty diplomacy, but she plunged into it with open frankness, telling of their terrible disappointment, through Mr. Arkell's objecting, on principle, to buy tickets.

"If you do not particularly wish to go yourself, Mrs. Peter—I know how unequal you are to exertion— and would give Henry's tickets to myself and Charlotte, I should feel more obliged than I can express."

There was one minute's hesitation on Mrs. Peter Arkell's part. She had really wished to go to this concert; she was nursing herself up to be able to go; and she knew how greatly Lucy, who had but few chances of any sort of pleasure, was looking forward to it. But the hesitation lasted the minute only; the next, the coveted tickets, with their pretty little red seal in the corner, were in the hand of Mrs. Arkell.

She went home as elated as though she had taken an enemy's ship at sea, and were sailing into port with it.

"Sophy must make up her mind to stay at home," she soliloquized. "It is her papa's fault, and I shall tell her so, if she's rebellious over it, as she is sure to be. This gives one advantage, however: there will be more room in the carriage for me and Charlotte. I wondered how we should all three cram in, with new white dresses on."

About the time that she was hugging this idea complacently to herself, the college clock struck one; and the college boys came pelting, pell-mell, down the steps of the schoolroom, their usual mode of egress. Travice Arkell, the senior boy of the school now—and the senior of that school possessed great power, and ruled his followers with an iron hand, more or less so according to his nature—waited, as he was obliged, to the last; he locked the door, and went flying across the grounds to leave the keys at the head master's. Travice Arkell was almost a man now, and would quit the school very shortly.

Bounding along as fast as he could go when he had left the keys—taking no notice of a knot of juniors who were quarrelling over marbles—Travice made a detour as he turned out of the grounds, and entered the house of Mrs. Peter Arkell. He was rather addicted to making this detour, but he burst in now at an inopportune moment. Lucy was in tears, and Mrs. Arkell was remonstrating against them in a reasoning, not to say a reproving tone. Henry, who had got in previously, was nursing his leg, a very blank look upon his face.

"What's the matter?" asked Travice, as Lucy made her escape.

"I thought Lucy had more sense," was the vexed rejoinder made by Mrs. Peter. "Don't ask, Travice. It is nothing."

"What is it, Harry, boy?" cried Travice, with scant attention to the "don't ask." "She can't be crying for nothing."

"It's about the concert," returned Henry, ruefully, his disappointment being at least equal to Lucy's. "Mamma has given away the tickets, and Lucy can't go."

"Whatever's that for?" asked Travice, who was as much at home at Mrs. Peter's as he was at his own house. "Who has got the tickets?"

"Mrs. Arkell."

"Mrs. Arkell!" shouted Travice, staring at the boy as if he questioned the truth of the words. "Do you mean my mother? What on earth does she want with your tickets?"

As he put the question he turned to Mrs. Peter, lying there with the sensitive crimson on her cheeks. She had certainly not intended to betray this to Travice: it had come out in the suddenness of the moment, and she strove to make the best of it now.

"I am glad it has happened so, Travice. I feel so weak to-day that I was beginning to think it would be imprudent, if not impossible, for me to venture to go to-morrow. To say the least, I am better away. As to Lucy, she is very foolish to cry over so trifling a disappointment. She'll forget it directly."

"But what does my mother want with your tickets?" reiterated Travice, unable to understand that point in the matter. "Why can't she buy tickets for herself?"

"Mr. Arkell has scruples, I believe. But, Travice, I am happy to—"

"Well, I shall just tell my mother what I think of this!" was the indignant interruption.

"Don't, Travice," said Mrs. Arkell. "If you only knew how glad I am to have the opportunity of rendering any little service to your home!" she whispered, drawing him to her with her gentle hand; "if you knew but half the kindness my husband and I receive from your father! I am only sorry I did not think to offer the tickets at first; I ought to have done so. It is all right; let us say no more about it."

Travice bent his lips to the flushed cheek: he loved her quite as much as he did his own mother.

"Take care, or you will get feverish; and that would never do, you know."

"My dear boy, I am feverish already; I have been a little so all day; and I am sure there could be no concert for me to-morrow, had I a roomful of tickets. It has all happened for the best, I say. I should only have been at the trouble of finding somebody to take Lucy."

As he was leaving the room he came upon Lucy in the passage, who was returning to it—the tears dried, or partially so; and if the long dark eye-lashes glistened yet, there was a happy smile upon the sweet red lips. Few could school themselves as did that thoughtful girl of fifteen, Lucy Arkell.

Travice stopped her as he closed the door.

"You'll trust me, will you not, Lucy?"

"For what?" she asked.

"To put this to rights. It—"

"Oh pray, pray don't!" she cried, fearing she hardly knew what. "Surely you are not thinking of asking for the tickets back again! I would not use them for the world. And they would be of no use to us now, for mamma says she shall not be well enough to go, and I don't think she will. I shall not mind staying at home."

Travice placed his two hands on her shoulders, and looked into her face with his sweet smile and his speaking eyes; she coloured strangely beneath the gaze.

"I'll tell you what it is, Lucy: you are just one of those to get put upon through life and never stand up for yourself. It's a good thing you have me at your side."

"You can't be at my side all through life," said Lucy, laughing.

"Don't make too sure of that, Mademoiselle." And the colour in her face deepened to a glowing crimson, and her heart beat wildly, as the significance of the tone made itself heard, in conjunction with his retreating footsteps.

He dashed home, spending about two minutes in the process, and dashed into the room where his mother was, her bonnet on yet, talking to Charlotte, and impressing upon her the fact that their going to the concert must be kept an entire secret from all, until the moment of starting arrived, but especially from papa and Sophy. Charlotte, in a glow of delight, acquiesced in everything.

"I say, mamma, what's this about your taking Mrs. Peter's tickets?"

He threw his trencher on the table, as he burst in upon them with the question, and his usually refined face was in a very unrefined glow of heat. The interruption was most unwelcome. Mrs. Arkell would have put him down at once, but that she knew, from past experience, Travice had an inconvenient knack of not allowing himself to be put down. So she made a merit of necessity, and told how Mr. Arkell had interdicted their buying tickets.

"Well, of all the cool things ever done, that was about the coolest—for you to go and get those tickets from Mrs. Peter!" he said, when he had heard her to an end. "They don't have so many opportunities of going out, that you should deprive them of this one. I'd have stopped away from concerts for ever before I had done it."

"You be quiet, Travice," struck in Charlotte; "it is no business of yours."

"You be quiet," retorted Travice. "And it is my business, because I choose to make it mine. Mother, just one question: Will you let Lucy go with you to the concert? Mrs. Peter fears she shall be too ill to go. I'm sure I don't wonder if she is," he continued, with a spice of impertinence; "I should be, if I had had such a shabby trick played upon me."

"It is like your impudence to ask it, Travice. When do I take out Lucy Arkell? She is not going to the concert."

"She is going to the concert," returned Travice, that decision in his tone, that incipient rebellion, that his mother so much disliked. "You have deprived them of their tickets, and I shall, therefore, buy them two in place of them. And when my father asks me why I spent money on the concert against his wish, I shall just lay the whole case before him, and he will see that there was no help for it. I shall go and tell him now, before I—"

"You will do no such thing, Travice," interrupted Mrs. Arkell, her face in a flame. "I forbid you to carry the tale to your father. Do you hear me? I forbid you;—and I am your mother. How dare you talk of spending your money on this concert? Buy two tickets, indeed!"

The first was a mandate that Travice would not break; the latter he conveniently ignored. Flinging his trencher on his head, he went straight off to buy the tickets, and carried them to Mrs. Peter Arkell's. There was not much questioning as to how he obtained them, for Mrs. St. John was sitting there. That they were fresh tickets might be seen by the numbers.

"My dear Travice," cried Mrs. Peter, "it is kind of you to bring these tickets; but we cannot use them. I shall be unable to go; and there is no one to take Lucy."

"Nonsense, there are plenty to take her," returned Travice. "Mrs. Prattleton would be delighted to take her; and I dare say," he added, in his rather free manner, as he threw his beaming glance into the visitor's face, "that Mrs. St. John would not mind taking charge of her."

"I will take charge of her," said Mrs. St. John—and the tone of the voice showed how genuinely ready was the acquiescence—"that is, if I go myself. But Frederick is ill to-day, and I am not sure that I can leave him to-morrow. But Lucy shall go with some of us. My niece, Anne, will be here, I expect, to-night. She is coming to pay a long visit."

"What is the matter with Frederick?" asked Travice, quickly.

"It appears like incipient fever. I suppose he has caught a violent cold."

"I'll go and see him," said Travice, catching up his trencher, and vaulting off before anyone could stop him.

Mrs. St. John rose, saying something final about the taking Lucy, and the arrangements for the morrow. She was the only one of the acquaintances of Miss Lucy Cheveley who had not abandoned Mrs. Peter Arkell. It is true the St. Johns were not very often at the Palmery, but when they were there, Mrs. St. John never failed to be found once a week sitting with the wife of the poor tutor, so neglected by the world.

And, after all, when the morrow came, Mrs. Peter Arkell was too ill to go. So she folded the spare ticket in paper, and sent it, with her love, to Miss Sophia Arkell.

CHAPTER XVIII

THE CONCERT

Never did there rise a brighter morning than the one on which the amateur concert was to take place. And Westerbury was in a ferment of excitement; carriages were rolling about, bringing the county people into the town; and fine dresses, every colour of the rainbow, crowded the streets.

Three parts of the audience walked to the concert, nothing loth, gentle and simple, to exhibit their attire in the blazing sunlight. It was certainly suspiciously bright that morning, had people been at leisure to notice it.

The Guildhall was filled to overflowing, when three ladies came in, struggling for a place. One was a middle-aged lady, quiet looking, and rather dowdy; the other was an elegant girl of seventeen, with clear brown eyes and a pointed chin; the third was Lucy Arkell.

There was not a seat to be found. The elder lady looked annoyed; but there was nothing for it but to stand with the mass. And they were standing when they caught—at least Lucy did—the roving eye of Travice Arkell.

Now, it happened that the four senior pupils of the college school—not the private pupils of Mr. Wilberforce, but the king's scholars—were being made of much account at this concert; and, by accident, or design, a side sofa, near to the orchestra—one of the best places—was assigned to them. Travice Arkell suddenly darted from his seat on it, and began to elbow his way down the room, for every avenue was choked. He reached Lucy at last.

"How late you are, Lucy! But I can get you a seat—a capital one, too. Will you allow me to pilot you to a sofa?" he courteously added to had the two ladies with her.

The elder lady turned at the address, and saw a tall, slender young man, with a pale, refined face. The college cap under his arm betrayed that he belonged to the collegiate school; otherwise, she had thought him too old for a king's scholar.

"You are very kind. In a few moments. But we ought to wait until this song that they are beginning is over."

It was not a song, but a duet—and a duet that had given no end of trouble to the executive management—for none of the ladies had been found suitable to undertake the first part in it. It required a remarkably clear, high, bell-like voice, to do it justice; and the cathedral organist, privately wishing the concert far enough—for he had never been so much pestered in all his life as since he undertook the arrangements—proposed Henry Arkell. And Mrs. Lewis, who took the second part, was fain to accept him: albeit, the boy was no favourite of hers.

"How singularly beautiful!" murmured the elder lady to Travice Arkell, as the clear voice burst forth.

"Yes, he has an excellent voice. The worst of him is, he is timid. He will out-grow that."

"I did not allude to the voice; I spoke of the boy himself. I never saw a more beautiful face. Who is he?"

Travice smiled. "It is Henry Arkell, Lucy's brother, and my cousin."

"Ah! I knew his mother once. Mrs. St. John was telling me her history last night. Anne, my dear, you have heard me speak of Lucy Cheveley: that is her son, and it is the same face. Then you," she continued, "must be Mr. Travice Arkell? Hush!"

For the duet was in full force just then, and Mrs. Lewis's rich contralto voice was telling well.

"Who is she?" asked Travice of Lucy in a whisper.

"Mrs. James. She's the governess," came the answer.

When the duet was over, Travice Arkell held out his arm to Mrs. James. "If you will do me the honour of taking it, the getting through the crowd may be easier for you," he said. But Mrs. James drew back, as she thanked him, and motioned him towards the younger lady with her. So Travice took the younger lady; not being quite certain, but suspecting who she was; and Mrs. James and Lucy followed as they best could.

And his reward was a whole host of daggers darted at him—if looks can dart them. The two ladies were complete strangers to the aristocracy of the grounds; and seeing Peter Arkell's daughter in their wake, the supposition that they belonged in some way to that renowned tutor, but obscure man, was not unnatural. Mrs. Lewis, who had come down to her sofa then, and Mrs. Aultane, who sat with her, were especially indignant. How dared that class of people thrust themselves at the top of the room amidst them?

"Travice," said Mrs. Arkell, bending forward from one of the cross benches, and pulling his sleeve as he passed on, "you are making yourself too absurd!"

"Am I! I am very sorry."

But he did not look sorry; on the contrary, he looked highly amused; and he bent his head now and again to say a word of encouragement to the fair girl on his arm, touching the difficulties of their progress. On, he bore, to the sofa he had quitted, and ordered the three seniors he had left on it to move off. In school or out, they did not disobey him; and they moved off accordingly. He seated the two ladies and Lucy on it, and stood near the arm himself; never once more sitting down throughout the concert. But he stayed with them the whole of the time, talking as occasion offered.

But, oh! that false morning brightness! Before the concert was over, the rain was coming down with fury, pelting, as the college boys chose to phrase it, cats and dogs. Very few had given orders for their carriages to be there; and they could only wait in hopes they would come, or send messengers after them. What, perhaps, rendered it more inconvenient was, that the concert was over a full half-hour earlier than had been expected.

The impatient company began to congregate in the lower hall; its folding doors of egress and its large windows looking to the street. Some one had been considerate enough to have a fire lighted at the upper end; and most inviting it was, now the day had turned to damp. The head master, who had despatched one of the boys to order his close carriage to be brought immediately, gave the fire a vigorous poke, and turned round to look about him. He was a little man, with silver-rimmed spectacles.

Two causes were exciting some commotion in the minds of the lesser satellites of the grounds. The one was the presuming behaviour of those people with Lucy Arkell, and the unjustifiable folly of Travice; the other was the remarkable absence of the Dean of Westerbury and his family from the concert. It, the absence, was put down to the dean's having at the last moment refused to patronize it, in consequence of its growing unpopularity; and Mrs. St. John's absence was attributed to the same cause. People knew later that the dean and Mrs. Beauclerc had remained at home in consequence of the death of a relative; but that is of no consequence to us.

"The dean is given to veering round," remarked Mrs. Aultane in an under tone to the head master. "Those good-natured men generally are."

The master cleared his throat, as a substitute for a reply. It was not his place to speak against the dean. And, indeed, he had no cause. He walked to the window nearest him, and looked out at the carriages and flies as they came tardily up.

Travice Arkell seemed determined to offend. He was securing chairs for those ladies now near the fire; and Mrs. Lewis put her glass to her eye, and surveyed them from head to foot. Her wild brother, Benjamin Carr, could not have done it more insolently.

"Who is that lady, Arkell?" demanded the master, of Travice, when he got the opportunity.

"It is a Mrs. James, sir."

"Oh. A friend of yours?"

"No, sir. I never saw her until to-day."

Mrs. Aultane bent her head. "Mrs. James? Who is Mrs. James? And the other one, too? I should be glad to know, Mr. Travice Arkell."

"I can't tell you much about them, Mrs. Aultane," returned Travice, suppressing the laugh of mischief in his eye. "I saw them for the first time in the concert-room."

"They came with your relative, Peter Arkell's daughter."

"Exactly so. That is, she came with them."

"Some people from the country, I suppose," concluded Mrs. Aultane, with as much hauteur as she thought it safe to put into her tone. "It is easy to be seen they have no style about them."

Travice laughed and went across the room. He was speaking to the ladies in question, when a gentleman of three or four-and-twenty came up and tapped him on the back.

"Won't you speak to me? It is Travice Arkell, I see, though he has shot up into a man."

One moment's indecision, and Travice took the hand in his. "Anderson! Can it be?"

"It can, and is. Captain Anderson, if you please, sir, now."

"No!"

"It's true. I have been lucky, and have got my company early."

"But what brings you here? I did not know you were in Westerbury."

"I arrived only this morning. Hearing of your concert when I got here, I thought I'd look in; but it was half over then, and I barely got inside the room. You don't mean to say that you are in the school still?"

Travice laughed, and held out the betraying cap. "It is a shame. I am too big for it. I have only a month or two longer to stay."

"But you must have been in beyond your time."

"I know I have."

"And who is senior?"

"Need you ask, looking at my size. This is Lucy; have you forgotten her?"

Captain Anderson turned. He had been educated in the college school, a private pupil of the head master's. Travice Arkell was only a junior in it when Anderson left; but Anderson had been intimate at the houses of both the Arkells.

"Miss Lucy sprung up to this! You were the prettiest little child when I left. And your sisters, Travice? I should like to see them."

Lucy laughed and blushed. Captain Anderson began talking to Mrs. James, and to the young lady who sat between her and Lucy.

"I can't stop," he presently said. "I see the master there. And that—yes, that must be Mr. and Mrs. Prattleton. There! the master is scanning me through his spectacles, wondering whether it's me or somebody else. I'll come back to you, Arkell."

He went forward, and was beset at once. People were beginning to recognise him. Anderson, the private pupil, had been popular in the grounds. Mrs. Aultane on one side, Mrs. Lewis on the other, took forcible possession of him, ere he had been a minute with the head master and his wife. It was hard to believe that the former somewhat sickly, fair-haired private pupil, who had been coddled by Mrs. Wilberforce with bark and flannel and beaten-up eggs, could be this fine soldierly man.

"Those ladies don't belong to you, do they?" cried Mrs. Aultane, beginning to fear she had made some mistake in her treatment of the ladies in question, if they did belong to Anderson.

"Ladies! what ladies?"

"Those to whom Travice Arkell is talking. He has been with them all day."

"They don't belong to me. What of them?"

"Nothing. Only these inferior people, strangers, have no right to push themselves amidst us, taking up the best places. We are obliged to draw a line, you know, in this manufacturing town; and none but strangers, ignorant of our distinctions, would dare to break it."

Captain Anderson laughed; he could not quite understand. "I don't think they are inferior," he said, indicating the two ladies. "Anything but that, although they may belong to manufacturers, and not be in your set. The younger one is charming; so is Lucy Arkell."

Mrs. Aultane vouchsafed no reply. It was rank heresy. The college boys were making a noise and commotion at the other end of the hall, and the master called out sharply—

"Arkell, keep those boys in order."

Travice sauntered towards them, gave his commands for silence, and returned to the place from whence he came. Henry Arkell came into the hall from the upper room, and there was a lull in the proceedings. The carriages came up but slowly.

"Don't you think we might walk home, Mrs. James?" inquired the younger lady. "I do not care to stay here longer to be stared at. I never saw people stare so in my life."

She said it with reason. Many were staring, and not in a lady-like manner, but with assuming manner and eye-glass to eye.

"They look just as though they thought we had no right to be here, Mrs. James."

"Possibly, my dear. It may be the Westerbury custom to stare at strangers. But I cannot allow you to walk home; you have thin shoes on. Mrs. St. John is certain to send your carriage, or hers."

"You did well, Harry," cried Travice Arkell, laying his hand on the young boy's shoulders. "Many a fair dame would give her price for your voice."

"And for something else belonging to you," added Mrs. James, taking the boy's hand and holding him before her as she gazed. "It is the very face; the very same face that your mother's was at your age."

"Did you know mamma then? Then, you must be a friend of hers," was Henry Arkell's eager answer.

"No, I never was her friend—in that sense. I was a governess in a branch of the Cheveley family, and Miss Lucy Cheveley and her father the colonel used to visit there. She had a charming voice, too; just as you have. Ah, dear me! speaking to you and your sister here, her children, it serves to remind me how time has flown."

"I am reminded of that, when I look at Captain Anderson here," said Travice Arkell, with a laugh. "Only the other day he was a schoolboy."

"If you want to be reminded of that, you need only look at yourself," retorted Anderson. "You have shot up into a maypole."

"Will you see me to the carriage, Travice, if you are not too much engaged?" cried out a voice which Travice knew well.

It was his mother's. She had seen the approach of her carriage from the windows of the upper hall, and was going down to it. Travice turned in obedience to the summons; and Captain Anderson sprang forward to renew his former friendship.

"You might set down Lucy on your way," said Travice, as they were stepping in. "I don't know how she'll get home through this pouring rain."

"And how would our dresses get on?" returned Mrs. Arkell, in hot displeasure. "Lucy, it seems, could contrive to get to the concert, and she must contrive to get from it. You can come in, Travice; you take up no room."

"Thank you, I'd not run the chance of damaging your dresses for all the money they cost."

As he returned to the hall, the boys, gathered round the door, were making a great noise, and Mr. Wilberforce spoke in displeasure.

"Can't you keep those boys in order, Mr. Arkell?"

Travice dealt out a very significant nod, one bespeaking punishment for the morrow, and the boys subsided into silence.

"Please, sir, your carriage is coming up the street," said Cockburn, junior, a little fellow of ten, to the head master, rather gratified possibly to be enabled to say it. "Somebody else's is coming too."

The windows became alive with heads. But the "somebody else's" proved to be of no interest, for it did not belong to any of the concert goers, and it went on past the Guildhall. Of course all the attention was then concentrated on the master's. It was a sober, old fashioned, rather shabby brown chariot; and it came up the street at a sober pace. The master, full of congratulation that the imprisonment was over, looked at it complacently. What then was his surprise to see another carriage dash before it, just as it was about to draw up, and usurp the place it had been confidingly driving to. A dashing vision of grandeur; an elegant yellow equipage bright as gold; its hammer-cloth gold also; its servants displaying breeches of gold plush, with powdered hair and gold-headed canes.

"Why, whose is it?" exclaimed the discomfited master, almost forgetting in his surprise the eclipse his own chariot had received.

"Whose can it be?" repeated the gazers in puzzled wonder. The livery was that of the St. John family; the colour was theirs; and, now that they looked closely, the arms were the St. Johns'. But the St. Johns' panels did not display a coronet! And there was not a single head throughout the hall, but turned itself in curiosity to await the announcement of the servant. He came in with his powder and his cane, and the college boys made way for him.

"The Lady Anne St. John's carriage."

She, Lady Anne, the fair girl of seventeen, looked at Travice Arkell, appearing to expect his arm as a matter of course. Travice gave it. Mrs. James tucked Lucy's arm within her own, in an old-fashioned manner, and followed them out.

They stepped into the carriage. Lady Anne waiting in her stately courtesy for Lucy to take the precedence; she followed; Mrs. James went last. And Travice Arkell lifted his trencher as they drove away.

The head master, smoothing his ruffled plumes, came out next, and Travice returned to the hall. Mrs. Aultane, feeling fit to faint, pounced upon him.

"Did you know that it was Lady Anne St. John?"

"Not at first," he answered, suppressing his laughter as he best could, for the whole thing had been a rich joke to him. "I guessed it: because I heard Mrs. St. John tell Mrs. Peter Arkell yesterday that Lady Anne was coming."

"And you couldn't open your mouth to say it! You could let us treat her as if—as if—she were a nobody!" gasped Mrs. Aultane. "If you were not so big, Travice Arkell, I could box your ears."

The next to come down from the upper hall was a group, of whom the most notable was Marmaduke Carr. A hale, upright man still, with a healthy red upon his cheeks: a few more years, and he would count fourscore. With him, linked arm in arm, was a mean little chap, looking really nearly as old as Marmaduke: it was Squire Carr. His eldest son, Valentine, was near him, a mean-looking man also, but well-dressed, with a red nose in his button-hole. Mrs. Lewis, the squire's daughter, came forward and joined them, putting her arm within her husband's, a big man with a very ugly face; and the squire's younger children, the second family, women grown now, followed. Old Marmaduke Carr—he was always open-handed—had treated every one of these younger children, six of them, and all girls, to the concert, for he knew the squire's meanness; and he was taking the whole party home to a sumptuous dinner. All the family were there except one, Benjamin, the second son. The Reverend Mr. Prattleton and his wife were of the group; the two families were on intimate terms; and if you choose to listen to what they are saying, you may hear a word about Benjamin.

The rain was coming down fiercely as ever, so there was nothing for it but to wait until some of the flies came back again. Mr. Prattleton, the squire, and Marmaduke Carr sought the embrasure of a window, where they could talk at will, and watch the approach of any vehicle that could be seized upon. Squire Carr was a widower still; he had never married a third wife. It may be, that the persistent rejection of Mildred Arkell in the days long gone by, had put him out of conceit of asking anybody else. Certain it was, he had not done it.

"And where is he now?" asked Mr. Prattleton of the squire, pursuing a conversation which had reference to Benjamin.

"Coming home," growled the squire; "so he writes us word. I thought how long this American fever would last."

"I never clearly understood what it was he went to do there," observed the clergyman.

"Nor I," said Squire Carr, drawing down the thin lips of his discontented mouth. "All I know is, it has cost me two hundred pounds, for he took a heap of things out there on speculation, which I have since paid for. He wrote word home that the things were a dead loss; that he sold them to a rogue who never paid him for them. That's six months ago."

"Then how has he lived since?" asked Mr. Prattleton.

"Heaven knows. I don't."

"Perhaps he has lived as he lived at Homberg, John," put in old Marmaduke, who had a trick of saying home truths to the squire, by no means palatable. "You know how he lived there, for two seasons."

"I don't know what he's doing, and I don't care," repeated the squire to Mr. Prattleton, completely ignoring Marmaduke's interruption. "I have tried to throw him off, but he won't be thrown off. He is coming home now, in the hope that I will put him into a farm; I know he is, though he has not said so. Pity but the ship would go cruizing round the world and never come back again."

"You did put him into a farm once."

"I put him into one twice, and had to take them on my own hands again, to save the land from being ruined," returned Squire Carr, wrathfully. "He—"

"But you know, John, Ben always said that the fault was partly yours," again put in old Marmaduke; "you would not allow proper money to be spent upon the land."

"It's not true. Ben said it, you say?—tush! it's not much that Ben sticks at. When he ought to have been over the farm in the early morning, he was in bed, tired out with his doings of the night. He was never home before daylight; gambling, drinking; evil knows what his nights would be spent in. The fact is, Ben Carr was born with an antipathy to work, and so long as he can beg or borrow a living without it, he won't do any."

"It is a pity but he had been put to some regular profession," said the minor canon.

"I put him to fifty things, and he came back from all," said the squire, tartly.

"He was never put regularly to anything, John," dissented Marmaduke. "You sent him to one thing—'Go and try whether you like it, Ben,' said you; Ben tried it for a week or two, and came back and said he didn't like it. Then you put him to another—'Try that, Ben,' said you; and Ben came back as before. The fact is, he ought to have been fixed at some one thing off hand, and my brother, the old squire, used to say it; not have had the choice of leaving it given him over and over again. 'You keep to that, Mr. Ben, or you starve,' would have been my dealings with him."

John Carr cast his thoughts back, and there was a sneer upon his thin lips; old Marmaduke had not dealt so successfully with his own son that he need boast. But John did not say it; for many years the name of Robert Carr had dropped out of their intercourse. Had he been dead—and, indeed, for all they heard of Robert, he might be dead—his name could not have been more completely sunk in silence. Marmaduke Carr never spoke of him, and the squire did not choose to speak: he had his reasons.

"It was the premium you stuck at, John. We can't put young men out without one, when they get to the age Ben was. There was another folly!—keeping the boy at home till he was twenty years of age, doing nothing except just idling about the land. But it's your affair, not mine; and Ben has certainly gone on a wrong tack this many a year now. I should have discarded him long ago, had he been my son."

"I should have felt tempted to do the same," observed the clergyman. "Benjamin has entailed so much trouble on you."

"And he'll entail more yet," was the consolatory prediction of old Marmaduke.

The squire made no reply. He had his arm on the window-frame supporting his chin, and looking dreamily out. His thoughts were with Benjamin. Why had he not yet discarded this scapegrace son—he, the hard man? Simply because there was a remote corner in his heart where Benjamin was cherished—cherished beyond all his other children. Petty, mean, hard as John Carr was, he had passionately loved his first wife; and Benjamin, in features, was her very image. His eldest son, Valentine, resembled him, the squire; Mrs. Lewis was like nobody but herself; his other children were by a different mother. He only cared for Benjamin. He did not care for Valentine, he did not care for the daughters, but he loved Benjamin; and the result was, that though Ben Carr brought home grief continually, and had done things for which Valentine, had he done them, would never have been pardoned, the squire, after a little holding out, was certain to take him into favour again, and give him another chance.

"When does George go out?" asked the squire of Mr. Prattleton, alluding to that gentleman's half-brother, who was nearly twenty years younger than himself.

"Immediately. And very fortunate we have been in getting him so good a thing. I hope the climate will agree with him."

"Grandpapa," said young Lewis, running up to the squire, "here are two flies coming down the street now. Shall I rush out and secure them first?"

"Ask Mr. Carr, my boy. He may like to stay longer, and give a chance to the rain to abate."

Mr. Carr, old Marmaduke, laughed. He knew John Carr of old, and his stingy nature. He would not order the flies to be retained lest the payment of them should fall to him.

"Go and secure them both, boy," said old Marmaduke; "and there's a shilling for your own trouble."

Young Lewis galloped out, spinning the shilling in his hand. "Don't I hope old Marmaduke will leave all his money to me!" quoth he, mentally. To say the truth, the whole family of the Carrs indulged golden dreams of this money more frequently than they need have done—apart from the squire, who was the most sanguine dreamer of all.

They were going out, to stow themselves in the two flies as they best could, when Marmaduke's eye fell on Travice Arkell. The old man caught his hand.

"Will you come home and dine with us, Travice? Five o'clock, sharp!"

"Thank you, sir—I shall be very glad," replied Travice, who liked good dinners as well as most schoolboys, and Mr. Carr's style of dinner, when he did entertain, was renowned.

"If you don't want these flies to be taken by somebody else, you had better come!" cried out young Lewis, putting his wet head in at the entrance door. "Mamma, I am stopping another for you."

Travice Arkell for once imitated the junior college boys, and splashed recklessly through the puddles of the streets, as fast as his legs would carry him, on his way to the Palmery, for he wanted to see Frederick St. John: he had just time. His nearest road led him past Peter Arkell's, and he spared a minute to look in.

"So you have got home safely, Lucy?"

"As if I could get home anything but safely, coming as I did!" returned Lucy, in merriment. "Such a commotion it caused when the carriage dashed up! The elm-trees became alive with rooks'-heads, not to speak of the windows. You should have seen the footman and his cane marshalling me to the door! But oh, Travice! when I got inside, the gilt was taken off the gingerbread!"

"How so?"

"You know how badly papa sees now without his spectacles. He did not happen to have them on, and he took it to be the old beadle of St. James the Less, with his laced hat and staff. He said he could not think what he wanted."

Travice laughed, laughed merrily, with Lucy. He stayed a minute, and then splashed on to the Palmery.

Frederick St. John was sitting up, but he had been really ill in the morning. Mrs. James and Lady Anne were giving him and Mrs. St. John the details of the concert. It was not surprising that no one had known Lady Anne. She had paid a long visit to Westerbury several years before, when she was a little girl; but growing girls alter, and her face was not recognised again. She had come for a long visit now, bringing, as before, her carriage and three or four servants—for she was an orphan, and had her own establishment.

"I say, Arkell, I'm glad you are come. Anne is trying to enlighten us about the grand doings this morning, and she can't do it at all. She protests that Mr. Wilberforce sang the comic song."

Lady Anne eagerly turned to Travice. "That little gentleman in silver spectacles, who was looking so impatiently for his carriage—who told you once or twice to pay attention to the college boys—was it not Mr. Wilberforce?"

"Undoubtedly."

"Well, did he not sing the comic song? I'm sure, if not, it was some one very like him."

Travice enjoyed the mistake. "It was little Poyns, the lay-clerk, who sang the comic song," he said, looking at Mrs. St. John and Frederick. "When Poyns gets himself up in black, as he did to-day, he looks exactly like a clergyman; and his size and spectacles do bear a resemblance to Mr. Wilberforce. But it was not Mr. Wilberforce, Lady Anne."

"Arkell," cried St. John, from his place on the sofa by the fire, Mrs. St. John being opposite to him, and the others dispersed as they chose about the small square room, glittering with costly furniture, "who was it came in unexpectedly and surprised you? Anne thinks it was one of the old college fellows."

"It was Anderson. Don't you remember him? He has got his company now."

"Anderson! I should like to see him. I hope he'll come and see me. Where's he stopping? I shall go out to-morrow."

"You'll do no such thing, Frederick," interposed Mrs. St. John.

"What a charming girl is Miss Lucy Arkell!" exclaimed Mrs. James to Travice. "She puts me greatly in mind of her mother, and yet she is not like her in the face. There is the same expression though, and she has the same gentle, sweet, modest manners. I like Lucy Arkell."

"So do I," cried Mr. St. John. "If my heart were not bespoken, I'm sure I should give it to her."

The words were uttered jestingly; nevertheless, Mrs. St. John glanced up uneasily. Frederick saw it. He knew in what direction his heart was expected to be given, and he stole a glance involuntarily at Lady Anne; but it passed from her immediately to rest upon his mother—a glance in which there was incipient rebellion to the wishes of his family; and Mrs. St. John had feared that it might be so, since the day when he had said, in his off-hand way, that Anne St. John was not the wife for his money.

Mrs. St. John's pulses were beating a shade quicker. There might be truth in his present careless assertion, that his heart was bespoken.

CHAPTER I

THE SCHOOL-BOY'S LOVE

A brilliant evening in July. The sun had been blazing all day with intense force, glittering on the white pavement of the streets, scorching the dry and thirsty earth; and it was not until his beams shone from the very verge of the horizon that the gay butterflies of humanity ventured to come forth.

Groups were wending their way to the Bishop's Garden: not the private garden of the respected prelate who reigned over the diocese of Westerbury, but a semi-public garden-promenade called by that name. In the years long gone by, a bishop of Westerbury caused a piece of waste land belonging to the grounds of his palace to be laid out as an ornamental garden. Broad sunny walks for the cold of winter, shady winding ones for the heat of summer, shrubberies and trees, flower-beds and grass-plots, miniature rocks and a fountain, were severally formed there; and then the bishop threw it open to the public, and it had ever since gone by the name of the Bishop's Garden. Not to the public indiscriminately—only to those of superior degree; the catering for the recreation of the public indiscriminately had not come into fashion then. It had always lain especially under the patronage of the residents of the grounds, and they took care—or the Cerberus of a gatekeeper did for them—that no inferior person should dare venture within yards of it: a tradesman might not so much as put his nose through the iron railings to take a peep in.

The garden was getting full when a college boy—he might be known by his trencher—passed the gate with a slow step. A party had just gone in whose movements his eyes had eagerly followed, but he was not near enough to speak. As he looked after them wistfully, his eye caught something glittering on the ground, and he stooped and picked it up. It was a small locket of gold, bearing the initials "G. B."

He knew to whom it belonged. He would have given half his remaining life, as it seemed, to go in and restore it to its owner. But that might not be; for the college boys, whether king's scholars or private pupils, were rigorously excluded by custom from the Bishop's Garden. And Williams, the gatekeeper, was stealing up then.

He was tall of his age, looking about sixteen, though he was not quite so much; tall enough to lean over the iron railings, which he did with intense eagerness; and never did woman's face betray more beauty, whether of form or colouring, than did his.

It was Henry Arkell. For the years have gone on, and the lovely boy of ten or eleven, has grown into this handsome youth. Other people and other things have grown with him.

"Now then! What be you doing here? You just please to take yourself off, young gentleman."

He quitted the railings in obedience; the college boys never thought of disputing the orders of the gatekeeper. Stepping backwards with a sort of spring, he stepped upon the foot of some one who was approaching the gate.

"Take care, Arkell."

He turned hastily and raised his trencher. The speaker was the good-natured Bishop of Westerbury; his widowed daughter on his arm.

"I beg your lordship's pardon."

"Too intent to see me, eh! You were gazing into the garden as if you longed to be there."

"I was looking for Miss Beauclerc, sir; I thought she might be coming near the gate. I have just picked up this, which she must have dropped going in."

"How do you know it is Miss Beauclerc's?" cried the bishop, glancing at the gold locket.

"I know it's hers, sir; and her initials are on it." But Henry turned his face out of sight, as he spoke. And lest any critic should set up a cavil at the bishop being addressed as "sir," it may be as well to mention that it was the custom with the college boys. Very few of them could bring their shy lips to utter any other title.

"Go in and give it to Miss Beauclerc, if it is hers," cried the bishop.

"The gatekeeper will not let me," said Henry, with a smile. "He tells us all that it is as much as his place is worth to admit a college boy."

"They ain't fit for such a place as this, nohow, my lord," spoke up the keeper. "Once let 'em in, and they'd be for playing at hare and hounds over the flower-beds."

"Nonsense!" said the bishop. "I don't see what harm there would be in admitting the seniors. You need not be so over-strict, Williams. Come in with me, Arkell, if you wish to find Miss Beauclerc; and come in whenever you like. Do you hear, Williams, I give this young gentleman the entrée of the garden."

The bishop laid his hand on Henry's shoulder, and they walked in together, all three, his daughter on his other side. Many a surprised eye-glass was lifted; many an indignant eye regarded them.

Never yet had a college boy—St. John always excepted—ventured within the pale of that guarded place. And if the bishop and his daughter had appeared accompanied by a fiery serpent, it could not have caused more inward commotion. But nobody dared betray it: the bishop was the bishop, and not to be interfered with.

"There's Miss Beauclerc, my lad."

And in a few minutes—Henry could not tell how, in his mind's tumultuous confusion—Georgina Beauclerc had turned into a side walk with him, and they were alone. Georgina was the same Georgina as ever—impulsive, wilful, and daringly independent. Everybody paid court to the dean's daughter.

"Did you drop this in coming in, Miss Beauclerc?"

"My locket! Of course I must have dropped it. Harry, I would not have lost it for the world."

His sensitive cheek wore a crimson flush at the words. He had given it to her on her last birthday, when she was eighteen. As she took it from him, their fingers touched. That touch thrilled through his veins, while hers were unconscious, or at best heedless of the contact.

It was the not uncommon tale; the tale that has been enacted many times in life, and which Lord Byron has made familiar to us as being his own heart's history—

"The maid was on the eve of womanhood: The boy had fewer summers; but his heart had far outgrown his years: And to his sight there was but one fair face on earth,   And that was shining on him."

It has been intimated that Georgina Beauclerc had inherited the dean's innate taste for what is called beauty, both human and statuesque. In the dean it was very marked. This, it may have been, that first drew forth her regard for Henry Arkell. Certain it was, she saw him frequently, and took no pains to disguise her admiration. He was a great favourite of the dean's—was often invited to the deanery. That he was no common boy, in nature, mind, or form, was apparent to the dean, as it was to many others, and Dr. Beauclerc evinced his regard openly. Georgina did the same. At first she had merely liked to patronize the young college boy; rather to domineer over him, looking upon him as a child in comparison with herself. But as they grew older, the difference in their years became less marked, and now they appeared nearly of the same age, for he looked older than he was, and Georgina younger. She was very pretty, with her large, rich blue eyes, and her small, fair features.

He had grown to love her; to love her with that impassioned love, which, pure and refined though it is, can only bring unhappiness. What did he think could be the ending? Did he reflect that it was utter madness in him to love the dean's daughter? It was nothing less than madness; and there were odd moments when the truth, that it was so, rose up in his mind, turning his whole soul to faintness.

And she, Georgina Beauclerc? She liked Henry Arkell very much indeed; she took pleasure in being with him, in talking with him, in flirting with him; she was conscious of a degree of pride when the handsome boy walked, as now, by her side; she encouraged his too-evident admiration for her; but she did not love him. She loved another too deeply to have any love left for him.

And she was so utterly careless of consequences. Had it been suggested to Miss Beauclerc that she was doing a wrong thing, bordering upon a wicked one, in thus trifling with that school-boy's heart, she would have laughed in very glee, and thought it fun. Though she must have known, if she ever took the trouble to glance forward, that in the years to come, did things continue as they were now, and Henry Arkell told his love to the ear, as well as to the eye and heart, the explosion must have place, and he would know how he had been deceived. What would her excuse be? that she liked him; that she liked his companionship; that she could not afford to reject his admiration? The gratification of the present moment was paramount with Georgina.

But what was Mrs. Beauclerc about, to suffer this? Mrs. Beauclerc! Had her daughter flirted with the whole forty king's scholars on a string, and the head master's private pupils to boot, she would never have seen it; no, nor understood it if pointed out to her. Her daughter was Miss Beauclerc, a young lady of high degree, and the college boys were inferior young animals with whom it was utterly impossible Georgina could possess anything in common.

"But how did you get in here, Harry?" began Miss Beauclerc, slipping the locket on her chain. "Has crusty old Williams gone to sleep this evening?"

"The bishop brought me in. He has given Williams orders that I am to be admitted here."

"Has he? What a glorious fellow! I'll give him ten kisses for that, as I used to do when I was a little girl. And now, pray, what became of you this afternoon? You said you should be in the cloisters."

"I know. I could not get out. I was doing Greek with my father."

"Doing Greek! It's always that. 'Doing Greek,' or 'doing Latin,' it's nothing else with you everlastingly. What a wretched pedant you'll be, Harry Arkell!"

"Never, I hope. But you know I must study; I have only my talents to depend upon for advancement in life; and my father, his heart is set on seeing me a bril—a good scholar."

"You are a brilliant scholar already," grumbled Georgina, bringing out the word which his modesty had left unspoken. "There's no reason why you should be at your books morning, noon, and night. I always said Mr. Peter Arkell was a martinet from the first hour he came to drill literature into me. Which he couldn't accomplish."

"The school meets in a week or two, you know, and—"

"Tiresome young reptiles!" interjected Miss Beauclerc. "We are quieter without them."

"And I must make the best use of my holidays for study," continued Henry. "They wish me to get to Oxford early."

"Goodness me! you might go now, if that's what you mean; you know enough. Harry, I do hope when you are ordained you'll get some high preferment."

"Such luck is not for me, Miss Beauclerc. I may never get beyond a curacy; or at most a minor canonry."

"Nonsense, and double nonsense! With the influential friends you may count even now! You know that everybody makes much of you. I should like to see you dean of this cathedral."

"And you—" Henry stopped in time. A tempting vision had mentally arisen, and for the moment led him out of himself. Did Georgina scent the treason, all but uttered? She resumed volubly, hastily—

"I have a great mind to tell you something; I think I will. But don't you let it go farther, Henry, for it is a secret as yet. There's going to be a school examination."

"No!" exclaimed Henry, some consternation in his tone.

"Why! are you afraid of it?"

"I am not. But I was thinking how very unfit the school is to stand it. What will Mr. Wilberforce say?"

"There's the fun," cried Georgina in glee. "When I heard papa talking of this, I said it would drive the head master's senses upside down. The dean and chapter are going to introduce all sorts of improvements into the school."

"What can have set them on to it!" exclaimed Henry, unable to recover his surprise and concern.

"The spelling, I think," said Georgina, pursing up her pretty mouth. "Jocelyn—and he'll be the senior boy this next half, you know—wrote a letter to his aunt; she rents her house and land under old Meddler, and knows the Meddlers—visits them, in fact. What should she do but take the letter to old Meddler, and asked him whether it was not a disgrace to any civilized community. Old Meddler kept the letter and brought it here, when he came into residence last week, and showed it to papa. There were not ten words spelt right in it. Altogether, there's going to be something or other done. But I'm sure you need not look so concerned over it, Henry Arkell; you are safe."

"I am safe. Yes, thanks to my father, I have enjoyed great advantages. But I am thinking of the others."

"Serve them right! They are a lazy set. Papa said, 'I should think Henry Arkell does not write like this!' I could have answered that, you know, had I chosen to bring out some of your letters."

There was a pause of silence. The tone had been significant, and his poor heart was beating wildly. "What a lovely rose!" he exclaimed, when the silence had become painful. "I wish I dare pluck it!"

"Dare! Nonsense! Pluck it if you wish."

"I thought it was forbidden to touch the flowers here!"

"So it is," said Georgina, snapping off the rose, one of the variegated species, and a great beauty. "But I do as I please. I would pluck all the flowers in the garden for two pins, just to see the old gardener's dismay."

"What would the visitors say to you?"

"Bow to me, and wish they dare perform such feats. Pshaw! I am the dean's daughter. Here, Harry, I will make you a present of it."

She threw the rose into his hand as she spoke, and she saw what the gift was to him.

"What shall you do with it, Harry?"

"Had I plucked the rose myself, I should have given it to my mother. I shall keep it now—keep it for ever. I may not," he added, lowering his tone, and speaking, as it were, to himself, "part with your gifts."

Georgina laughed lightly, an encouraging laugh.

Oh! it was wrong; wrong of her to act so. They reached the end of the shady walk and turned again.

"How long are you going to remain in that precious choir?" resumed Georgina, "wasting your time for the public benefit."

"Mr. St. John put the very same question to me this morning. He—"

"Mr. St. John!" she interrupted, in startling, nay, wild impulse, and her face became one glow of excitement. "But what do you mean?" she added, subsiding into calmness as recollection returned to her. "He is not in Westerbury."

The words, the emotion, told their own tale; and their true meaning flashed upon his brain. It was an era in the unhappy boy's life. How was it that he had been blind all these years?

"You take a strange interest in him, Miss Beauclerc," and there seemed to be no life left in his pale face, as he turned to her with the question.

"For another's sake," she evasively answered. "I told you some time ago Frederick St. John was in love with her."

He knew to whom she alluded. "Do you think it likely that he is, Miss Beauclerc?"

"If he's not in love with herself, he is in love with her beauty," said Georgina, with a laugh. "But you know what the popular belief is—that the heir of the St. Johns, whatever he may do with his love, may only give his hand to his cousin, Lady Anne."

"I hope it is so. She is the nicest girl, and he deserves a good wife. I used to sing duets with her when she was last at the Palmery."

"Oh!" said Georgina, turning her pretty nose into the air, "and so you fell in love with her."

"No," replied Henry; "my love was not mine to give."

Another pause. Georgina snatched a second flower—a carnation this time—and began pulling it to pieces.

"I suppose you heard from him this morning?"

"Yes."

"And where is he now?"

"In Spain. But he talks of coming home."

He stole a glance at her; at the loving light that shone in her bright blue eyes; at the soft glow, red as the carnation she was despoiling, on her conscious cheek. Why did he not read the signs in all their full meaning? Why did hope struggle with the conviction that would have arisen in his heart?

"Have you his letter?"

"Yes; you can read it if you like. There are no secrets. I have told him that Miss Beauclerc was fond of looking at his letters. He is enthusiastic, as usual, on the subject of pictures."

She closed her hand upon the foreign-looking letter which he took from his jacket pocket to give to her. "I will take it home with me, and return it to you to-morrow; I can't read it now. And, Harry, I am going back to my party, or perhaps they'll be setting the crier to work. Mind you don't breathe a word of that school examination: it would not do. But I tell things to you that I'd not tell to anybody else in the world."

She ran away up a side path, and Henry made his way to the more frequented part of the garden. It happened that he found himself again with the bishop; and the prelate laid his hand, as before, on the shoulder of the handsome boy, and kept him at his side.

Mrs. Peter Arkell had not grown better with years; on the contrary, the weakness in the back was greater, and her health in other ways began to fail. A residence of some weeks at the sea-side was deemed essential for her; absolutely necessary, said her medical attendant, Mr. Lane: and indeed it was not much less necessary for Peter Arkell himself, who was always ill now. His state of health told heavily upon them. He had been obliged to give up a great portion of his teaching; and but for his ever-ready friend and relative, Mr. Arkell, whose hand was always open, and for certain five-pound notes that came sometimes in Mildred's letters, Peter had not the remotest idea how he should have got along. This going to the sea-side would have been quite out of the question, but that they had met with a fortunate chance of letting their house for two months, to a family desirous of coming to Westerbury. Lucy, of course, would go with them; but the question was—what was to be done with Henry? Travice Arkell, in his impulsive good nature, said he must stop with them, and Mr. Arkell confirmed it. Henry supposed he must, but he felt sure it would not be palatable to Mrs. Arkell.

Travice Arkell was in partnership with his father now. At the time of his leaving school there had been a visible improvement in the prospects of the manufacturers, and Mr. Arkell yielded to his son's wish to join him, and hoped that the good times were coming back again. But the improvement had not lasted long; and Mr. Arkell was wont to say that Travice had cast in his lot with a sinking ship. The designation of the firm had never been altered; it was still "George Arkell and Son." Times fluctuated very much. Just now again there was a slight improvement; and altogether Mr. Arkell was still upon the balance, to give up business or not to give it up, as he had been for so many years.

Henry walked home from the Bishop's Garden, with the strange emotion displayed by Georgina Beauclerc, at the mention of Mr. St. John, telling upon his memory and his heart. Lucy met him at the door, her sweet face radiant.

"Oh, Henry! such news! News in two ways. I don't know which to tell you first. One part concerns you."

"Tell me that first, then," said he, laughing.

"You are not to be at Mr. Arkell's while we are away. You are to be at—guess where."

"I can't guess at all. I don't know anybody who'd have me."

"At the master's."

His eye lightened as he looked up.

"Am I? I am so glad! Is it true, Lucy?"

"It is quite true. Mr. Wilberforce saw mamma at the window, and came in to ask her how she was, and when she went, and all that. Mamma said how puzzled she had been what to do with you, but it was decided now you were to go to Mr. Arkell's. So then the master said he thought you had better go to him, and he should be most happy to invite you there for the time, no matter how long we remained away; and when mamma attempted to say something about the great kindness, he interrupted her, saying you had always been so good a pupil, and given him so little trouble, and did him altogether so much credit, that he should consider the obligation was on his side. So it is quite decided, Harry, and you are to go there."

"That's good news, then. And what's the other, Lucy?"

"Ah! the other concerns me. It is good, too."

"Are you going to be married?"

The question was but spoken in jest, and Henry wondered to see his sister's face change; but she only shook her head and laughed.

"Eva Prattleton is to accompany us to the sea-side."

"Eva Prattleton!"

"Mr. Prattleton came in just after the master left," resumed Lucy. "He said he had come with a petition: would mamma take charge of Eva to the sea-side, and let her go with us? He had intended—you know we heard of it, Harry—to take his two daughters to Switzerland this summer for a treat; but he begins to fear that Eva will not be equal to the travelling, for she's not strong, and a little thing fatigues her; and he thinks a month or two of quiet at the sea-side would do her more good. So that's arranged as well as the other."

"And what will Mary do?"

"Oh, she goes to Switzerland with her papa. He has not given up his journey. The two boys are to stay at home, and George Prattleton's to take care of them."

Henry laughed. The idea of Mr. George Prattleton's taking care of the boys struck him as being something ludicrous.

"But what do you think mamma says?" added Lucy, dropping her voice. "The terms hinted at by Mr. Prattleton for Eva were so liberal, that mamma feels sure he is doing this as much to make our sojourn there more easy to us, as for Eva's benefit; though she is not well, of course, and never has been since her mother's death; the grief then seemed to take such a hold upon her. How kind to us the Prattletons have always been!"

Henry mentally echoed the words—for they were true ones—all unconscious that a time was quickly approaching when he should have to repay this kindness with something very like ingratitude.

CHAPTER II

THE TOUR OF DAVID DUNDYKE, ESQUIRE

Perhaps of all the changes time had wrought, in those connected with our history, not one was more remarkable than that in Mr. and Mrs. Dundyke, in regard to their position in the world. They had changed in themselves of course; we all change; and were now middle-aged people of some five-and-forty years: Mr. Dundyke being red and portly; his wife, thin and meek as ever.

Little by little, step by step, had David Dundyke risen in the world. There had come a day when he was made a fourth partner in that famous tea-importing house, with which he had been so long connected. He was now the third partner, and his income was a large one. There had also come a day when he was elected a common councilman (I am not sure but this has been previously mentioned), and now the old longing, the height of his ambition, was really and truly dawning upon him. In the approaching autumn he was to be proposed for sheriff; and that, as we all know, leads in time to the civic chair.

You will readily understand that it was not at all consistent for a partner in a wealthy tea house, and a common councilman rising into note and attending the civic feasts, to remain the tenant of two humble rooms. Mr. Dundyke had made a change long ago. He and his wife, clinging still to apartments, as being less trouble, and also less expense on the whole, had moved into handsome ones; and there they remained for some years. But the prospect of the shrievalty demanded something more; and latterly Mr. Dundyke had taken a handsome villa at Brixton, had furnished it well, and set himself up there with two maid servants and a footman. In some degree his old miserly habits were on him still, and he rarely spent where he could save, or launched into any extravagance unless he had an end in view in doing it; but he had never very much loved money for its own sake alone, only as means to an end.

His great care, now that the glorious end was near, was to blazon forth his importance. He wanted the world (his little world) to forget what he had been; to forget the pinching and saving, the poor way of living, the red-herring dinners, and the past in general. He did what he could to blot out the past in the present. He looked out for correspondents to address him as "esquire;" and he took to wear a ring with a crest upon it.

In this very month of July, when you saw Henry Arkell and the dean's daughter walking in the Bishop's Garden—and a very hot July it was—Mr. Dundyke came to the decision of taking a tour. What first put it into his unfortunate head to do so, his wife never knew; though she asked herself the question afterwards many and many a time. He debated the point with himself, to go or not to go, some little while; balancing the advantages against the drawbacks. On the one hand, it would cost time and money; on the other, it would certainly be another stepping-stone in his advancing greatness, the more especially if he could get the Post or some other fashionable organ to announce the departure of "David Dundyke, Esquire, and Lady, on a Continental tour."

One sultry afternoon, when Mrs. Dundyke was sewing in her own sitting-room, he returned home somewhat earlier than usual.

"My mind is made up, Mrs. Dundyke," he said, before he had had time to look round, as he came in, wiping his hot brows. "I told you I thought I should go that tour; and I mean to start as soon as we have fixed upon our route. It must be somewhere foreign."

Mr. Dundyke's intellectual improvement had not advanced in an equal ratio with his fortunes; he called tour tower, and route rout. Indeed, he spoke almost exactly as he used to speak.

"Foreign!" echoed Mrs. Dundyke, somewhat aghast. Her geographical knowledge had always been imperfect and confused; the retired life she led, occupied solely in domestic affairs, had not tended to enlarge it; and the word "foreign" suggested to her mind extremely remote parts of the globe—the two poles and Cape Horn. "Foreign?"

"One can't travel anywhere now that's not foreign, Betsey," returned Mr. Dundyke, testily. "One can't humdrum up and down England in a stage-coach, as one used to do."

"True; but you said foreign. You don't mean America—or China—or any of those parts, do you, David?"

"It's never of no use talking to you about anything, Mrs. D.," said the common-councilman, in wrath. "Chinar! Why, it would be a life-journey! I shall go to Geneva."

"But, David, is not that very far?" she asked. "Where is it? Over in Greece, or Turkey, or some of those places."

"It is in Switzerland, Mrs. D. The tip-top quality go to it, and I mean to go. It will cost a good deal, I know; but I can stand that."

"And how shall we manage to talk Swiss?"

"There is no Swiss," answered Mr. Dundyke. "The language spoke there is French; the guide-book says so."

"It will be the same to us, David," she mildly said; "we cannot speak French."

"I know that 'we' means 'yes,' and 'no' means 'no.' We shall rub on well enough with that. So get all my stockings and shirts seen to, Betsey, and your own things; for the day after to-morrow I shall be off."

His wife looked up, not believing in the haste. But it proved true, nevertheless; for Mr. Dundyke had a motive in it. On the morning but one after, an excursion opposition steamer was advertised to start for Boulogne—fares, half-a-crown; return-tickets, four shillings. Of course David Dundyke could not let so favourable an opportunity slip; he still saved where he could.

Accordingly, on the said morning, which was very squally, they found themselves on the crowded boat. Such a sight! such a motley freight! Half London, as it seemed, had been attracted by the cheapness; but it was by no means a fashionable assemblage, nor yet a refined one.

"I hear somebody saying we shall have it rough, David," whispered Mrs. Dundyke, as they sat side by side, and the vessel passed Greenwich. "I hope we shall not be sea-sick."

"Pooh! sea-sick! we shan't be sea-sick!" imperiously cried the sheriff in prospective, as he turned his ring, now assumed for good, to the front of all beholders. "I don't believe in sea-sickness for my part. We did not feel sick when we went to Gravesend; you remember that, don't you, Betsey? It is more brag than anything else with people, talking about sea-sickness, that's my belief; a genteel way of letting out that they can afford to be travellers."

Excepting that one trip to Gravesend, of which he spoke, neither he nor his wife had ever been on the water in their lives. Neither of them had seen the sea. They had possessed really no inclination to stir from home; and saving had been, the ruling motive in David Dundyke's life.

The steamer went on. The river itself growing rough at Gravesend, the dead-lights were put in; and as they got nearer to the sea, the wind was freshening to a gale. Oh, the good steamer! will she ever live through it? The unbelieving common-councilman, to his horror and dismay, found sea-sickness was not a brag. He lay on the floor of the cabin, groaning, and moaning, and bewailing his ill fate in having come to sea.

"Heaven forgive me for having thought of this foreign tour! Steward! He stops up with them outsiders on deck! Heavens! Steward! Call him, somebody! Tell him it's for a common-councilman!"

Mrs. Dundyke was in the ladies' cabin—very ill, but very quiet. A dandy-looking man, impervious to the miseries of the passage, who had nothing to do but gape and yawn, took a sudden look in, by way of gratifying his curiosity, and, having done so, withdrew again—not, however, before one of the lady passengers had marked him. She took him for the captain.

"Capting! capting!" she called out; "if you please is that the capting?"

"Which?—where?" asked the steward's boy, to whom the question was addressed, turning round with a glass of brandy-and-water in his hand, which he was presenting to another lady, groaning up aloft in a berth.

"He came in at the door; he have got on tan kid gloves and shiny boots."

"That the captain!" cried the boy, gratified beyond everything at the lady's notion of a captain's rigging. "No, ma'am, he's up on deck."

"Just call the captain here, will you?" resumed the lady; "I know we are going down. I'm never ill aboard these horrid boats; but I'm worse, I'm dreadful timid."

"There ain't no danger, ma'am," said the boy.

"I know there is danger, and I know we are a going to be emerged to the bottom. If you'll call the capting down here, boy, I'll give you sixpence; and if you don't call him, I'll have you punished for insolence."

"Call him directly, ma'am," said the boy, rushing off with alacrity.

"I am the captain," exclaimed a rough voice, proceeding from a rough head, poking itself down the companion ladder; "what's wanted of me?"

"Oh! capting, we are going to the fishes fast! and some of us is dead of fright already. The vessel'll be in pieces presently! see how she rolls and pitches! and there's the sea dashing over the decks and against them boards at the windows, such as I never heard it; and all that awful crashing and cording, what is it?"

"There ain't no danger," shortly answered the commander, mentally vowing to punch the boy's head for calling him for nothing.

"Can't you put back, and land us somewhere, or take us into smooth water?" implored the petitioner; "we'd subscribe for a reward for you, capting, sir."

"Oh, yes, yes," echoed a faint chorus of voices; "any reward."

"There's no danger whatever, I tell ye, ladies," repeated the exasperated captain. "When we've got round this bit of headland, we shall have the wind at our starn, and go ahead as if the dickens druv us."

With this consolatory information, the rough head turned round and vanished. The grinning boy came out of a corner where he had hid himself, and appealed to the lady for his promised sixpence.

"I know we are going down!" she cried, as she fumbled in her bag for one. "That capting ought to lose his place for saying there's no danger; to me it's apparent to be seen. If he'd any humanity in him, he'd put back and land us somewhere, if 'twas only on the naked shore. Good mercy! what a lurch!—and now we're going to t'other side. No danger indeed! And all my valuable luggage aboard: my silk gownds, and my shawls, and my new lace mantle! Good gracious, ma'am, don't pitch out of your berth! you'll fall atop of me. Can't you hold on? What were hands made for?"

Some hours more yet, and then the steward, who had been whisking and whirling like one possessed, now on deck, now in the cabins, and now in his own especial sanctum, amid his tin jugs and his broken crockery, came whirling in once more to the large cabin, and said they were at the mouth of Boulogne harbour. "Just one pitch more, ladies and gentlemen—there it is—and now we are in the port, safe and sound."

"Don't talk to me about being in," cried poor Mr. Dundyke, from his place on the floor, not quite sure yet whether he was dead or alive, but rather believing he'd prefer to be the former. "Please don't step upon me, anybody. I couldn't stir yet."

All minor disasters of the journey overcome, the travellers reached Paris in safety. So far, Mr. Dundyke had found no occasion to rub on with his "we" and "no," for he encountered very few people who were not able to speak, or at least understand, a little English. But when they quitted Paris—and they remained in it but two days—then their difficulties commenced; and many were the distresses, and furious the fits of anger, of the common-councilman. It pleased Mr. Dundyke to travel by diligence on cross-country roads, rather than take the rail to Lyons—of which rail, and of all rails, he had a sort of superstitious dread—but this he found easy to do, though it caused him to be somewhat longer on the road. Here his tongue was at fault. He wanted to know the names of the towns and villages they passed through, the meaning of any puzzling object of wonder he saw on his way, and he could not ask; or, rather, he did ask repeatedly, but the answers conveyed to his ears only an unmeaning sound. It vexed him excessively.

"I don't think they understand you, David," Mrs. Dundyke said to him one day.

"And how should they understand, speaking nothing but heathen gibberish?" he returned. "It's enough to make a saint swear."

Another source of annoyance was the living. Those who have travelled by diligence in the more remote parts of France, and sat down to the tables-d'hôte at the road-side inns where the diligence halted, and remember the scrambling haste observed, may imagine the distresses of Mr. and Mrs. Dundyke. In common with their countrymen in general, they partook strongly of the national horror of frog-eating, and also of the national conviction that that delicate animal furnished the component parts of at least every second dish served up in France: so that it was little short of martyrdom to be planted down to a dinner, where half the dishes, for all the information they gave to the eye, might be composed of frogs, or something equally obnoxious. There would be the bouilli first, but Mr. Dundyke, try as he would, could not swallow it, although he had once dined on red-herrings; and there would be a couple of skinny chickens, drying on a dish of watercress, but before he could hope, in his English deliberation, to get at them, they were snapped up and devoured. Few men liked good living better than David Dundyke,— how else would he have been fit to become one of the renowned metropolitan body-corporate?—and when it was to be had at anybody else's cost, none enjoyed it more. At these tables-d'hôte, eat or not eat, he had to pay, and bitter and frequent were the heartburnings at throwing away his good money, yet rising up with an empty stomach. Not a tenth part of the cravings of hunger did he and his wife ever satisfy at these miserable tables-d'hôte. The very idea of but the minutest portion of a frog's leg going into their mouths, was more repulsive to their minds than that shuddering reminiscence of the steam-packet; and, what with this dread, and their inability to ask questions, Mr. and Mrs. Dundyke were nearly starved.

One day in particular it was very sad. They had halted at an inn in a good-sized town, not very far distant from Lyons. While the soup and bouilli were being devoured, the two unfortunates ate a stray radish or two, when up bustled the waiter with a funny-looking dish, its contents wonderfully like what a roast-beef eater might suppose cooked frogs to be, and presented it to Mr. Dundyke.

"What's this?" inquired Mr. Dundyke, delicately adventuring the tip of a fork towards the suspicious-looking compound, by way of indicating the nature of his question.

"Plait-il, monsieur?"

"This, this," rapping the edge of the dish with the fork; "what is it made of? what do you call it?"

"Une fricassée de petits pigeons, à l'oseille, monsieur," replied the discerning waiter.

Poor Mr. Dundyke pushed the dish away from him with a groan. "Une fricassée de petits pigeons, à l'oseille" in French, might be "Stewed frogs" in English.

"What was all that green mess in the dish?" asked his wife.

"The saints know," groaned the common-councilman. "Perhaps it's the fashion here to cook frogs in their own rushes."

Up came the waiter with another dish, that attentive functionary observing that the Monsieur Anglais ate nothing. A solid piece of meat, with little white ends sticking out of it, rising out of another bed of green. "Oseille" is much favoured in these parts of France.

"Whatever's this?" ejaculated the common-councilman, eyeing the dish with wondering suspicion. "It's as much like a porkipine as anything I ever saw. What d'ye call it?" rapping the edge of the dish as before.

"Foie-de-veau lardé, à l'oseille, monsieur."

The common-councilman was as wise as before, and sat staring at it.

"It can't be frogs, David, this can't," suggested Mrs. Dundyke, "it is too large and solid; and I don't think it's any foreign animal. It looks to me like veal. Veal, waiter?" she asked, appealingly.

"Oui, madame," was the answer, at a venture.

"And the green stuff round it is spinach, of course. Veal and spinach, my dear."

"That's good, that is, veal and spinach. I'll try it," said Mr. Dundyke.

He helped himself plentifully, and, pushing the dish to his wife, voraciously took the first mouthful, for he was fearfully hungry.

It was a rash proceeding. What in the world had he got hold of! Veal and spinach!—Heaven protect him from poison! It was some horrible, soft compound, sharp and sour; it turned him sick at once, and set his teeth on edge. He became very pale, and called faintly for the waiter.

But the garçon had long ago whisked off to other parts of the room, and there was Mr. Dundyke obliged to sit with that nauseous mystery underneath his very nose.

"Waiter!" he roared out at length, with all the outraged dignity of a common-councilman, "I say, waiter! For the love of goodness take this away: it's only fit for pigs. There's a dish there, with two little ducks upon it, and some carrots round 'em—French ducks I suppose they are: an Englishman might shut up shop if he placed such on his table. Bring it here."

"Plait-il, monsieur?"

"Them ducks—there—at the top, by the pickled cowcumbers. I'll take one."

The waiter ranged his perplexed eyes round and round the table. "Pardon, monsieur, plait-il?"

"I think you are an idiot, I do!" roared out Mr. Dundyke, unable to keep both his hunger and his temper. "That dish of ducks, I said, and it is being seized upon! They are tearing them to pieces! they are gone! Good Heavens! are we to famish like this?"

The waiter, in despair, laid hold of a slice of melon in one hand and the salt and pepper in the other, and presented them.

"The man is an idiot!" decided the exasperated Englishman. "What does he mean by offering me melon for dinner, and salt and pepper to season it?—that's like their putting sugar to their peas! I want something that I can eat," he cried, piteously.

"Qu'est-ce que c'est que je peux vous offrir, monsieur?" asked the agonized garçon.

"Don't you see we want something to eat," retorted the gentleman; "this lady and myself? We can't touch any of the trash on the table. Get us some mutton chops cooked."

"Pardon, monsieur, plait-il?"

"Some—mut—ton—chops," repeated the common-councilman, very deliberately, thinking that the slower he spoke, the better he should be understood. "And let 'em look sharp about it."

The waiter sighed and shrugged, and, after pushing the bread and butter and young onions within reach, moved away, giving up the matter as a hopeless job.

"Let's peg away at this till the chops come," cried Mr. Dundyke. And in the fallacious hope that the chops were coming, did the unconscious couple "peg" away till the driver clacked his long whip, and summoned his passengers to resume their seats in the diligence.

"I have had nothing to eat," screamed Mr. Dundyke. "They are doing me some mutton chops. I can't go yet."

"Deux diners, quatre francs, une bouteille de vin, trente sous," said the waiter in Mr. Dundyke's ear. "Fait cinq francs, cinquante, monsieur."

"Fetch my mutton chops," he implored; "we can't go without them: we can eat them in the diligence."

"Allons! dépêchons-nous, messieurs et dames," interrupted the conductor, looking in, impatiently. "Prenez vos places. Nous sommes en retard."

"They are swindlers, every soul of them, in this country," raved the common-councilman, passionately throwing down the money, when he could be made to comprehend its amount, and that there were no chops to come. "How dare you be so dishonest as charge for dinners we don't eat."

"I am faint now for the want of something," bewailed poor Mrs. Dundyke.

"If ever I am caught out of Old England again," he sobbed, climbing to his place in the diligence, "I'll give 'em leave to make a Frenchman of me, that's all."

CHAPTER III

A MEETING AT GRENOBLE

They arrived at Lyons; but here Mr. Dundyke's total ignorance of the language led him into innumerable misapprehensions and mishaps, not the least of which was his going from Lyons to Grenoble, thinking all the time that he was on the shortest and most direct road to Switzerland. This was in consequence of his rubbing on with "we" and "no." They had arrived at Lyons late in the evening, and after a night's rest, Mr. Dundyke found his way to the coach-office, to take places on to Switzerland. There happened to be standing before the office door a huge diligence, with the word "Grenoble" painted on it.

"I want to engage a place in a diligence; two places; direct for Switzerland," began Mr. Dundyke; "in a diligence like that," pointing to the great machine.

"You spoke French, von littel, sare?" asked the clerk, who could himself speak a very little imperfect English.

"We," cried Mr. Dundyke, eagerly, not choosing to betray his ignorance.

Accordingly, the official proceeded to jabber on in French, and Mr. Dundyke answered at intervals of hazard "we" and "no."

"Vous désirez aller à Grenoble, n'est-ce pas, monsieur?" remarked the clerk.

"We," cried out Mr. Dundyke at random.

"Combien de places, monsieur?"

"We," repeated the gentleman again.

"I do demande of the monsier how few of place?" said the official, suspecting his French was not understood quite so well as it might be.

"Two places for Switzerland," answered Mr. Dundyke. "I'm going on to Geneva, in a diligence like that."

"C'est ça. The monsier desire to go to Gren-haub; et encore jusqu'à Genève—on to Geneva."

"We," rapturously responded the common-councilman.

"I do comprends. Two place in the Gren-haub diligence. Vill the monsier go by dat von?" pointing to the one at the door. "She do go in de half hour."

"Not that one," retorted Mr. Dundyke, impatient at the clerk's obscure English. "I said in one like that, later."

"Yes, sare, I comprends now. You would partir by anoder von like her, the next one that parts. Vill you dat I retienne two place for Gren-haub?"

"We, we," responded Mr. Dundyke. "Two places. My wife's with me, Mrs. D.: I'm a common-councilman, sir, at home. Two places for Gren-haub. Corner ones, mind: in the interior."

"C'est bien, monsieur. She goes à six of de hours."

"She! Who?"

"The diligence, I do say."

"Oh," said the common-councilman to himself, "they call coaches 'she's' in this country. I wonder what they call women. Six hours you say we shall take going."

"Oui, monsieur," answered the clerk, without quite understanding the question, "il faut venir à six heures."

"And when does it start?"

"What you ask, sare?"

"She—the diligence—at what o'clock does it start for Gren-haub?"

"I do tell de sare at de six of de hours dis evening."

"We'll be here a quarter afore it then: never was late for anything in my life. Gren-haub's a little place, I suppose, sir, as it's not in my guide-book?"

"Comme ça," said the clerk, shrugging his shoulders. "She's not von Lyon."

"Who's she?" exclaimed the bewildered Mr. Dundyke; "who's not a lion?"

"Gren-haub, sare. I thought you did ask about her."

"The asses that these French make of themselves when they attempt to converse in English!" ejaculated the common-councilman. "Who's to understand him?"

He turned away, and went back to the hotel in glee, dreadfully unconscious that he had booked himself for Grenoble, and imagining that Gren-haub (as the word Grenoble in the Frenchman's mouth sounded to his English ears) must be the first town on the Swiss frontiers. "It's an awkward hour, though, to get in at," he deliberated: "six hours, that fellow said we should be, going: that will make it twelve at night when we get to the place. Things are absurdly managed in this country." This was another mistake of his: the anticipated six hours necessary, as he fancied, to convey him from Lyons to "Gren-haub," would prove at least sixteen.

At the appointed hour Mr. and Mrs. Dundyke took their seats in the diligence, which began its journey and went merrily on; at least as merrily as a French diligence, of the average weight and size, can be expected to go. Mr. Dundyke was merry, too, for him; for he had fortified himself with a famous dinner before starting: none of your frogs and rushes and "oseille," but rosbif saignant, and pommes de terre au naturel, specially ordered. Both the travellers had done it ample justice, and seasoned it with some hot brandy-and-water; Mr. Dundyke taking two glasses and making his wife take one. Therefore it was not surprising that both should sink, about nine o'clock, into a sound sleep. They had that compartment of the coach, called the intérieur, to themselves, and could recline almost at full length; and so comfortable were they, that all the various changing of horses and clackings of the whip failed to arouse them.

Not until six o'clock in the morning did Mr. Dundyke open his eyes, and then only partially. He was in the midst of the most delicious dream—riding in that coveted coach, all gilt and gingerbread, on a certain 9th of November to come, moving in stately dignity through Cheapside, amidst the plaudits of little boys, the crowding of windows, and the arduous exertions of policemen to preserve order in the admiring mob; sitting with the mace and sword-bearer beside him, his mace and sword-bearer! Mr. Dundyke had been pleased that his sleep, with such a dream, had lasted for ever, and he unwillingly aroused himself to reality.

It was broad daylight; the sun was shining with all the glorious beauty of a summer morning, shining right into the diligence, and roasting the face of the common-councilman. He rubbed his eyes and wondered where he was. Recollection began to whisper that when he had gone to sleep the previous evening it was dusk, and that ere that dusk had well subsided into the darkness of midnight he had expected to be at his destination, "Gren-haub;" whereas—was he asleep still, and dreaming it?—or was it really morning, and he still in the diligence?—or had some unexampled phenomenon of nature caused the sun to shine out at midnight? WHAT was it? In the greatest perturbation he tore his watch from his pocket, and found it was five minutes past six; but he knew that he was rather slower than French time.

A fine hubbub ensued. Mr. Dundyke startled his wife up in such a fright, that he nearly sent her into fits: he roared out to the coachman, he called for the conductor: he shook the doors, he knocked at the windows: he caused the utmost consternation amongst the quiet passengers in the rotonde and banquette, and woke up a deaf old gentleman in the coupé, who all thought he had gone suddenly mad. The diligence was stopped in haste, and out of the door rushed Mr. Dundyke.

"Where were they taking him to? Why had they not left him at Gren-haub? Did they know he was a common-councilman of the great city of London, a brother of the Lord Mayor and aldermen? How dared they run away with him and his wife in that style? Where were they carrying him to? Were they going to smuggle him off to Turkey or any of them heathen places to sell him for a slave? They must turn round forthwith, and drive him back to Gren-haub."

All this, and a great deal more of it, delivered in the English tongue and interspersed with not a few English expletives, was as Greek to the astonished lookers-on; and when they had sufficiently exercised their curiosity and stared at the enraged speaker, standing there without his hat, stamping his feet in the dust, and gesticulating more like a Frenchman than a stout specimen of John Bull, they all let loose their tongues together, in a jargon equally incomprehensible to the distressed Englishman. In vain did Mr. Dundyke urge their return to "Gren-haub," now with angry fury, now with tears, now with promises of reward; in vain the other side demanded to know what was the matter, and tried to coax him into the diligence. Not a word could one party understand of the other.

"Montez, monsieur; montez, mon pauvre monsieur. Dieu! qu'est-ce qu'il a? Montez, donc!"

Not a bit of it. Mr. Dundyke would not have mounted till now, save by main force. It took the conductor and three passengers to push and condole him in; and indeed they never would have accomplished it, but for the sudden dread that flashed over his mind of what would become of him if he were left there in the road, hatless, hopeless, and Frenchless, while his wife and his luggage and the diligence went on to unknown regions. Some of those passengers, if you could come across them now, would give you a dolorous history of the pauvre monsieur Anglais who went raving mad one summer's morning in the diligence.

There was little haste or punctuality in those old days of French posting—driver, conductor, passengers, and horses all liking to take their own leisure; and it was not far off twelve o'clock at noon, six hours after the morning's incomprehensible scene, and eighteen from the time of departure from Lyons, that the lazy old diligence reached its destination, and Mr. Dundyke discovered that he was in Grenoble. How he would ever have found his way out of it, and on the road to Switzerland, must be a question, had not an Englishman, a young man, apparently in delicate health, who was sojourning in the town, fortunately chanced to be in the diligence yard, and heard Mr. Dundyke's fruitless exclamations and appeals, as he alighted.

"Can I do anything for you?" asked the stranger, stepping forward. "I perceive we are countrymen."

Overjoyed at hearing once more his own language, the unhappy traveller seized the Englishman's hand with a rush of delight, and explained the prolonged torture he had gone through, and the doubt and dilemma he was still in—at least as well as he could explain what was to him still a mystery. "The savages cannot understand me," he concluded politely, "and of course I cannot be expected to understand them."

Neither could the stranger understand just at first; but with the conductor's tale on one side and Mr. Dundyke's on the other, he made out the difficulty, and set things straight for him, and went with him to the diligence office. No coach started for Chambéry, by which route they must now proceed, till the next morning at nine, so the stranger took two places for them in that.

"I'm under eternal obligations to you, sir," exclaimed the relieved traveller, "and if ever I should have it in my power to repay you, be sure you count on me. It's a common-councilman, sir, that you have assisted; that's what I am at home, and I'm going on to be Lord Mayor. You shall have a card for my inauguration dinner, sir, if you are within fifty miles of me. You will tell me your name, and where you live?"

"My name is Robert Carr," said the stranger. "I am a clergyman. I am from Holland."

The name struck on a chord of Mrs. Dundyke's memory. It took her back to the time when she was Betsey Travice, and on a certain visit at Westerbury. Though not in the habit of putting herself forward when in her husband's company, she turned impulsively to the stranger now.

"Have you relations at Westerbury, sir? Was your mother's name Hughes?"

"Yes," he said, looking very much surprised. "Both my father and mother were from Westerbury. I have a grandfather, I believe, living there still. My mother is dead."

"How very strange!" she exclaimed. "Can you come in this evening to us at the hotel for half-an-hour?"

"I would, with pleasure, but I leave Grenoble this afternoon," was the young clergyman's answer. "Can I do anything for you in London?"

"Nothing," said Mrs. Dundyke. "But my husband has given you our address; and if you will call and see us when we get home—"

"And you'll meet with a hearty welcome, sir," interrupted the common-councilman, shaking his hand heartily. "I'm more indebted to you this day than I care to speak."

Mrs. Dundyke watched him out of the yard. He might be about four-and-twenty; and was of middle height and slightly made, and he walked away coughing, with his hand upon his chest.

"David," she said to her husband, "I do think he must be a relative of yours! The Hughes's of Westerbury were related in some way to your mother."

"I'm sure I don't know," said David Dundyke. "I think I have heard her talk about them, but I am not sure. Any way I'm obliged to him; and mind, Betsey, if he does come to see us in London, I'll give him a right good dinner."

Ah, how little! how little do we foresee even a week or two before us! Never in this world would those two meet again.

And Mr. and Mrs. Dundyke proceeded under convoy to the Hôtel des Trois Dauphins, and made themselves as comfortable for the night as circumstances and the stinging gnats permitted.

Arriving at Geneva without further let or hindrance, David Dundyke, Esquire, and his wife, put up at the Hôtel des Bergues. And on the morning afterwards, when Mrs. Dundyke had dressed herself and looked about her, she felt like a fish out of water. The size of the hotel, the style pervading it, the inmates she caught chance glimpses of in the corridors, were all so different from anything poor humble Betsey Dundyke had been brought into contact with, that she began to feel her inferiority. And yet she looked like a lady, in her good and neat dress, and her simple cap half covering her fair and still luxuriant hair. Her face was red, tanned with the journey; but it was a pleasing and a nice face yet to look upon.

They descended to the great salle a little before ten. Many groups were breakfasting there at the long tables; most of them English, as might be heard by their snatches of quiet conversation. Some of them possessed an air of distinction and refinement that bespoke their standing in society. An English servant came in once and accosted his master as "my lord;" and a plain little body in a black silk gown and white net cap, was once spoken to as "Lady Jane." Mr. Dundyke had never, to the best of his knowledge, been in a room with a lord before; had never but once set eyes on a Lady Jane; and that was King Henry the Eighth's wife in waxwork; and, alive to his own importance though the common-councilman was, he felt unpleasantly out of place amidst them. In spite of his ambition his nature was a modest one.

Scarcely had he and his wife begun breakfast, when a lady and gentleman came in and took the seats next to him. The stranger was a tall, dark, rather handsome man; taller than Mr. Dundyke, who was by no means undersized, and approaching within three or four years to the same age. But while the common councilman was beginning to get rather round and puffy, just as an embryo alderman is expected to be, the stranger's form was remarkable for wiry strength and muscle: in a tussle for life or death, mark you, reader, the one would be a very child in the handling of the other.

Mr. Dundyke moved his chair a little to give more room, as they sat down, and the gentleman acknowledged it with a slight bow of courtesy. He spoke soon after.

"If you are not using that newspaper, sir," pointing to one that lay near Mr. Dundyke, "may I trouble you for it?"

"No use to me, sir," said the common-councilman, passing the journal. "I understand French pretty well when it's spoke, but am scarcely scholar enough in the language to read it."

"Ah, indeed," replied the stranger. "This, however, is German," he continued, as he opened the paper.

"Oh—well—they look sufficiently alike in print," observed the common-councilman. "Slap-up hotel, this seems, sir."

"Comfortable," returned the stranger, carelessly. "You are a recent arrival, I think."

"Got here last night, sir, by the diligence. We are travelling on pleasure; taking a holiday."

"There's nothing like an occasional holiday, a temporary relaxation from the cares of business," remarked the stranger, scanning covertly Mr. Dundyke. "As I often say."

"I am delighted to hear you say it, sir," exclaimed the common-councilman, hastily assuming a fact, from the words, which probably the speaker never thought to convey. "I am in business myself, sir, and this is the first holiday from it I have ever took: I gather that you are the same. Nothing so respectable as commercial pursuits: a London merchant, sir, stands as a prince of the world."

"Respectable and satisfactory both," joined in the stranger. "What branch of commerce—if you don't deem me impertinent—may you happen to pursue?"

"I'm a partner in a wholesale tea-house, sir," cried Mr. Dundyke, flourishing his hand and his ring for the stranger's benefit. "Our establishment is one of the oldest and wealthiest in Fenchurch-street; known all over the world, sir, and across the seas from here to Chinar. And as respected as it is known."

"Sir, allow me to shake hands with you," exclaimed the stranger, warmly. "To be a member of such a house does you honour."

"And I am a common-councilman," continued Mr. Dundyke, his revelations increasing with his satisfaction, "rising on fast to be a alderman and Lord Mayor. No paltry dignity that, sir, to be chief magistrate of the city of London, and ride to court in a gold and scarlet dress, and broidered ruffles! I suspect we have got some lords round about us here," dropping his voice to a still lower key, "but I'm blest, sir, if I'd change my prospects with any of them. I'm to be put up for sheriff in October."

"Ah," said the stranger, casting his deep black eyes around, "young scions with more debts than brains, long pedigrees and short purses, dealers in post obits and the like—they can't be put in comparison with a Lord Mayor of London."

"And what line are you in, sir?" resumed the gratified Lord Mayor in prospective. "From our great city, of course?"

The stranger nodded, but, before he answered, he finished his second cotelette, poured out some wine—for his breakfast disdained the more effeminate luxuries of tea and coffee—popped a piece of ice in, and drank it. "Have you heard of the house of Hardcastle and Co.?" he asked, in a tone meant only for Mr. Dundyke's ear.

"The East India merchants?" exclaimed the latter.

The stranger nodded again.

"Of course I have heard of them: who has not? A firm of incalculable influence, sir; could buy up half London. What of them?"

"Do you know the partners personally?"

"Never saw any of them in my life," replied Mr. Dundyke. "They are top-sawyers, they are; a move or two above us city tea-folks. Perhaps you have the honour of being a clerk in the house, sir?"

"I am Mr. Hardcastle," observed the stranger, smiling.

"Bless my soul, sir!" cried the startled Mr. Dundyke. "I'm sure I beg pardon for my familiarity. But stop—eh—I thought—"

"Thought what?" asked the stranger, for Mr. Dundyke came to a pause.

"That Mr. Hardcastle was an old man. In fact, the impression on my mind was, that he was something like seventy."

"Pooh, my dear sir! your thoughts are running on my uncle. He has been virtually out of the firm these ten years, though his name is still retained as its head. He is just seventy. A hale, hearty man he is too, and trots about the grounds of his mansion at Kensington as briskly as one of his own gardeners. But not a word here of who I am," continued the gentleman, pointing slightly round the room: "I am travelling quietly, you understand—incog., if one may say so—travelling without form or expense, in search of a little peace and quietness. I have not a single attendant with me, nor has my wife her maid. Mrs. Hardcastle," he said, leaning back, the better to introduce his wife.

The lady bowed graciously to Mr. and Mrs. Dundyke, and the former, in his flurry to acknowledge the condescension, managed to upset the coffee-pot. Mrs. Dundyke saw a stylish woman of thirty—at least, if a great deal of dress can constitute style. She had a handsome, but deadly pale face, with bold eyes, black as her husband's.

"I feel really glad to make your acquaintance," resumed Mr. Hardcastle. "Standing aloof, as I have purposely done, from the persons of condition staying in the hotel, I had begun to find it slow."

"Sir, I am sure I'm greatly flattered," said Mr. Dundyke. "Have you been long here, sir?"

"About three weeks or a month," replied the gentleman, carelessly. "We shall soon be thinking of going."

Mr. Dundyke did indeed feel flattered, and with reason, for the firm in question was of the very first consideration, and he was overwhelmed with the honour vouchsafed him. "A Lord Mayor might be proud to know him," he exclaimed to his wife, when they got upstairs from the breakfast. "I hope he'll give me his friendship when I am in the Chair."

"I think they have the next room to ours," observed Mrs. Dundyke. "I saw the lady standing at the door there this morning, when I was peeping out, wondering which was the way down to breakfast. Is it not singular they should be travelling in this quiet way, without any signs of their wealth about them?"

"Not at all singular," said the shrewd common-councilman. "They are so overdone with grandeur at home, these rich merchants, with their servants, and state, and ceremony, that it must be a positive relief to get rid of it altogether for a time, and live like ordinary people. I can understand the feeling very well."

It was more than Mrs. Dundyke could; and though, from that morning, the great merchant and his lady took pains to cultivate the intimacy thus formed, she never took to them so cordially as her husband. He, if one may use the old saying in such a sense, fell over head and ears in love with both, but Mrs. Dundyke never could feel quite at home with either. No doubt the sense of her own inferiority of position partly caused this: she felt, if her husband did not, that they were no society, even abroad, for the powerful Mr. and Mrs. Hardcastle. And, in her inmost heart, she did not like the lady. Her attire was ten times as costly and abundant as Mrs. Dundyke's, and she would wear more jewellery at one time than the latter had ever seen in all her life; and that was perhaps as it should be; but Mrs. Dundyke was apt to take likings and dislikings, and she could not like this lady, try as she would. She was certainly not a gentlewoman; and Mrs. Dundyke, with all her previous life's disadvantages of position, was that at heart, and could appreciate one. She decidedly wore rouge on her cheeks in an evening; she was not choice in her expressions at all times; and she was fond of wine, and did not object to brandy.

One morning Mrs. Dundyke happened to be in Mrs. Hardcastle's room, when the English waiter entered.

"My master's compliments, madam," he said, "and he hopes Mr. Hardcastle has some news for him this morning."

The lady's face went crimson, the first time Mrs. Dundyke had seen any natural colour on it, and she answered, in a haughty tone, that Mr. Hardcastle was not then in—when he was, the man could speak with him.

"For it is now a fortnight, madam, since he has daily promised to—"

"I have nothing to do with it," interrupted Mrs. Hardcastle, imperiously motioning the waiter from the room; "you must address yourself to my husband."

Mrs. Dundyke wondered what this little scene could mean. Had it been people of less known wealth than the Hardcastles, she might have thought it bore reference to the settlement—or non-settlement—of the bill. But that could scarcely happen with them.

"What are you thinking of, Betsey?" Mr. Dundyke asked her that same day, she sat so deep in thought.

"I was thinking of Mr. Hardcastle's eyes."

"Of Mr. Hardcastle's eyes!" echoed the common-councilman.

"Just then I was, David. The fact is, they puzzle me—they are always puzzling me. I feel quite certain I have seen them somewhere, or eyes exactly like them."

"They are as handsome eyes as ever I saw," was the answer.

"They may be handsome, but I don't like them. But that it is wrong to say it, I could almost say I hate them. They frighten me, David."

"That's just one of your foolish fancies," cried Mr. Dundyke, in wrath. "You are always taking them up, you know."

A day or two after this, Mr. Hardcastle came straight into the presence of Mr. Dundyke, some papers in his hand. "My dear sir," he said, "I want you to do me a favour."

The common-councilman jumped up and placed a chair for the great man, delighted at the prospect of doing him a favour.

"I wrote home a few days ago for them to send me a letter of credit on the bankers here. It came this morning, and just see what they have done!"

Mr. Hardcastle tossed, as he spoke, the letter of credit to Mr. Dundyke. Now the latter, shrewd man of business though he was amid his own chests of tea, knew very little of these foreign letters of credit, their forms, or their appearance. All he could make out of the present one was, that it was a sort of order to receive one hundred pounds.

"Don't you see the error?" exclaimed Mr. Hardcastle. "They have made it payable to my uncle, Stephen Hardcastle, instead of to me. My name's not Stephen, so it would be perfectly useless for me to present it. How the clerks came to make so foolish a mistake I cannot tell. Some one of them I suppose, in the pressure of business, managed to give unintelligible orders to the bankers, and so caused the error."

"Dear me!" said Mr. Dundyke.

"Now I want to know if you can let me have this sum. I shall write immediately to get the thing rectified, and if you can accommodate me for a few days, until the needful comes, I will then repay you with many thanks."

"But, dear me, sir!" exclaimed Mr. Dundyke,—"not but what I should be proud to do anything for you that I could, in my poor way—you don't suppose I've got a hundred pound here? Nor the half! nor the quarter of it!"

Mr. Hardcastle carelessly smiled, and played with his glittering cable watch-chain.

"I should not like to offer you what I have got, sir," continued the common-councilman, "but I am sure if you took it as no offence, and it would be of any temporary use to you—"

"Oh, thank you! No, it's not that," interrupted the great merchant. "Less than the hundred pounds would not be worth the trouble of borrowing. You have nothing like that sum, you say?"

Out came Mr. Dundyke's purse and pocket-book. He counted over his store, and found that, English and French money combined, he possessed twenty-two pounds, eleven shillings. The twenty pounds, notes and gold, he pushed towards Mr. Hardcastle, the odd money he returned to his pocket. "You are quite welcome, sir, for a few days, if you will condescend to make use of it."

"I feel extremely obliged to you," said Mr. Hardcastle; "I am half inclined to avail myself of your politeness. The fact is, Dundyke," he continued, confidentially, "my wife has been spending money wholesale, this last week—falling in love with a lot of useless jewellery, when she has got a cartload of it at home. I let her have what money she wanted, counting on my speedy remittances, and, upon my word, I am nearly drained. I will write you an acknowledgment."

"Oh no, no, sir, pray don't trouble to do that," cried the confiding common-councilman, "your word would be your bond all over the world." And Mr. Hardcastle laughed pleasantly, as he gathered up the money.

"Can you let me have five francs, David," said Mrs. Dundyke, coming in soon afterwards, when her husband was alone.

"Five francs! What for?"

"To pay our washing bill. It comes to four francs something; so far as I can make out their French figures."

"I don't know that you can have it, Mrs. D."

"But why?" she inquired, meekly.

"I have just lent most of my spare cash to Mr. Hardcastle. He received a hundred pound this morning from England, but there was a stupid error in the letter of credit, and he can't touch the money till the order has been back home to be rectified."

The information set Mrs. Dundyke thinking. She had just returned from a walk, and it was in coming up the stairs that a chambermaid had met her and given her the washing-bill. Not being accustomed to French writing and accounts, she could not readily puzzle it out, and, bill in hand, had knocked at Mrs. Hardcastle's door, intending to crave that lady's assistance. Mr. Hardcastle opened it only a little way.

"Is Mrs. Hardcastle at leisure, if you please, sir?" she asked.

"No; she's not in. I'll send her to you when she comes," was his reply, as he re-closed the door. And yet Mrs. Dundyke was almost certain she saw the tip of Mrs. Hardcastle's gown, as if she were sitting in the room on the right, the door opening to the left. And she also saw distinctly the person who had been once pointed out to her as the landlord of the hotel. He was standing at the table, counting money—a note or two, it looked, and a little gold. There was food in this to employ Mrs. Dundyke's thoughts, now she knew, or supposed, that very money was her husband's. A sudden doubt whether all was right—she afterwards declared it many times—flashed across her mind. But it left her as soon as thought: left her ashamed of doubting such people as the Hardcastles, even for a moment. She remained thinking, though.

"I know these foreign posts are uncertain," she observed, arousing herself, "and it will take, I suppose, eight or ten days before Mr. Hardcastle's remittance can reach him. Suppose it should not come when he expects, or that there should be another mistake in it?"

"Well?"

"Why—as we cannot afford to remain on here an indefinite period, waiting; at least, I suppose you would not like to do so, David; I was thinking it might be better for you to write home for more money yourself, and make certain."

"Just leave me to manage my own business, Betsey, will you: I am capable, I hope," was the common-councilman's ungracious answer. Nevertheless, he adopted his wife's suggestion.

Mr. and Mrs. Hardcastle continued all grace and smiles, pressing their champagne upon Mr. Dundyke and his wife at dinner, and hiring carriages, in which all the four drove out together. The common-councilman was rapidly overcoming his repugnance to a table-d'hôte, but the sumptuous one served in the hotel was very different from those he had been frightened with on his journey, and in the third week of his stay his wife had to let out all his waistcoats. The little excursions in the country he cared less for. The lovely country about Geneva was driven over again and again: Ferney, Coppet, the houses of Madame de Staël and Voltaire, all were visited, not much, it is to be feared, to the edification of the common-councilman. Thus three weeks from the time of their first arrival, passed rapidly away, and Mr. Dundyke and his wife felt they could not afford the time to linger longer in Geneva. They now only waited for the repayment of the twenty pounds from Mr. Hardcastle, and, strange to say, that gentleman's money did not arrive. He could not account for it, and gave vent to a few lordly explosions each morning that the post came in and brought him no advice of it.

"I'll tell you what it is!" he suddenly observed one morning—"I'll lay a thousand pounds to a shilling they have misunderstood my instructions, and have sent the money on to Genoa, whither we are bound after leaving here!"

"What a disaster!" uttered Mr. Dundyke. "Will the money be lost, sir?"

"No fear of that: nobody can touch it but myself. But look at the inconvenience it is causing, keeping me here! And you also!"

"I cannot remain longer," said Mr. Dundyke; "my time is up, and I may not exceed it. You can give me an order to receive the 20l. in London, sir: it will be all the same."

"But, my good fellow, how will you provide for the expenses of your journey to London?"

"I have managed that, sir," said the common-councilman. "I wrote home for thirty pounds."

"And is it come?" asked Mr. Hardcastle, turning his eye full upon the common-councilman with the startling rapidity of a flash of lightning. Mrs. Dundyke noticed, with astonishment, the look and the eager gesture: neither ever faded from her recollection.

"They came this morning," said the common-councilman. "I have them both safe here," touching the breast-pocket of his coat. "They were in them letters you saw me receive."

On rising from breakfast, Mr. Dundyke strolled out of the hotel, and found himself on the borders of the lake. The day was fearfully hot, and he began to think a row might be pleasant. A boat and two men were at hand, waiting to be hired, and he proceeded to haggle about the price, for one of the boatmen spoke English.

"I have spent a deal of money since I have been here, one way or another," he soliloquized, "and the bill I expect will be awful. But it won't be much addition, this row—as good be hung for a sheep as a lamb— so here goes."

He stepped into the boat, anticipating an hour's enjoyment. A short while after this, Mrs. Hardcastle, accompanied by Mrs. Dundyke, came on to Rousseau's Island. Mr. Dundyke was not so far off then, but that his wife recognised him. Mr. Hardcastle was the next to come up.

"What are you looking at? Why, who's that in a boat there? Surely not Dundyke! Give me the glass."

"Yes, it is," said Mrs. Dundyke.

"Where in the name of wonder is he off to, this melting day? To drown himself?"

The ladies laughed.

"Ah! I see; he can't stand it. The men are bearing off to the side—going to land him there. They had better put back."

Mrs. Dundyke sat down underneath the poplar trees, spreading a large umbrella over her head, and took out her work. Mrs. Hardcastle was never seen to do any work, but she seated herself under the shade of the umbrella; and the gentleman, leaving them to themselves, walked back again over the suspension bridge.

CHAPTER IV

A MYSTERY

Which of the three wore the deepest tint, the darkest blue—the skies, the hills, or the lake? Each was of a different shade, but all were blue and beautiful; and on all lay the aspect of complete repose. The two ladies, in that little garden near the Hôtel des Bergues, Rousseau's Island, as it is called, and which you who have sojourned in Geneva remember well, looking out over the lake at the solitary boat bearing away towards the right, noticed that no other object broke the prospect's stillness. It was scarcely a day for a row on Geneva's lake. Not a breath of air arose to counteract the vivid heat of the August sun; hot and shadeless he poured forth his overpowering blaze; and, lovely as the lake is, favoured by nature and renowned in poetry, it was more lovely that day to look at than to glide upon.

So thought the gentleman in that solitary boat, our friend Mr. David Dundyke—or, let us give him the title he had of late aspired to, David Dundyke, Esquire. He felt, to use his own words, "piping hot;" he sat on one side of the boat, and the sun burnt his back; he changed to the other, and it blistered his face; he tried the stern, and the sun seemed to be all round him. He looked up at the Jura, with a vain longing that they might be transported from their site to where they could screen him from his hot tormentor: he turned and gazed at the Alps, and wished he could see on them a shady place, and that he was in it; but, wherever he looked and turned, the sun seemed to blind and to scorch him. Some people, clayey mortals though the best of us are, might have found poetry, or food for it, in all that lay around; but David Dundyke had no poetry in his heart, still less in his head. He glanced, with listless, half-shut eyes, at the two men who were rowing him along; and began to wonder how any men could be induced to row, that burning day, even to obtain a portion of the world's idol—money. David Dundyke cared not, not he, for the scenery around; he never cared for anything in his life that was not substantial and tangible. What was the common scenery of nature to him, since it could not add to his wealth or enhance his importance?—and that was all the matter at his heart. He had never looked at it all the way from London to Geneva; he did not look at that around him now. Geneva itself, its lovely surrounding villas, its picturesque lake, the glorious chain of mountains on either side, even Mont Blanc in the distance, were as nothing to him. For some days after his arrival at Geneva, the mountain had remained obstinately enshrouded in clouds; but one evening that he and his wife were walking outside the town with Mr. Hardcastle, it was pointed out to him, standing proudly forth in all its beauty; and he had stared at it with just as much interest as he would have done at the hill in Greenwich Park covered with snow. He had seen the lovely colour, the dark, brilliant blue of the Rhone's waters, as they escaped from the lake to mingle with those of the thick, turbulent Arve; and he did not care to notice the contrast in the streams. There were no associations in his mind connected with that fair azure lake, whence coursed the one; he had no curiosity as to the never-changing glaciers that were the source of the other.

But, had Mr. Dundyke's soul been wholly given up to poetry and sentiment, it would have been lost that day in the overpowering heat. He bore it as long as he could, and then suddenly told the men to bear to the right and put him on shore. This movement had been observed by Mr. Hardcastle, from the little island, as you may remember. The men, not sorry perhaps to be off the lake themselves, inured though they were to Geneva's August sun, made speedily for a shady place, and landed him.

"Ah! this is pleasant," exclaimed Mr. Dundyke, throwing himself at full length on the cool and shady grass. "It is quite Heaven, this is, after that horrid burning lake." The two boatmen laid on their oars and rested.

"How thirsty it has made me!" he resumed, "I could drink the lake dry. What a luxury some iced wine would be now! And ice is so cheap and plentiful up at the hotel yonder. Suppose I send the boat back for Mr. Hardcastle, and the two women? And tell 'em it's Paradise, sitting here, in comparison with the hot hotel; and drop in a hint about the iced wine? He will be sure to take it, and be glad of the excuse. The women would find it rather of the ratherest for heat, coming across the lake, but charming when they got here. 'Tain't far, and their complexions are not of the spoiling sort. Mrs. D.'s ain't of no particular colour at all just now, except red; and t'other's is like chalk. Oh! let 'em risk it."

Taking out his silver pencil-case (as the men deposed to subsequently) he tore a leaf from his pocket-book, scribbled a few lines on it, and folding it, directed it to — Hardcastle, Esquire: and it had never occurred to Mr. Dundyke until that moment, and the fact struck him as a singular one, that he was ignorant of — Hardcastle, Esquire's Christian name. The men received the note and their orders, and then prepared to push off.

"We com back when we have give dis; com back for de jontilmans?" asked the one who spoke English.

"Come back! of course you are to come back," responded the common-councilman. "How am I to get home, else? But you are to bring the two ladies and the gentleman, and some ice and some wine; and to look sharp about it. Take care that the bottles don't get broke in the boat."

The men rowed away, leaving Mr. Dundyke lying there. They made good speed to the Hôtel des Bergues, according to orders, but were told that neither Mr. nor Mrs. Hardcastle was in. This caused a delay of two good hours. The boatmen lingered near the door of the hotel, waiting; and at last one of the waiters bethought himself that the ladies might be on Rousseau's Island. There they were found, and Mrs. Hardcastle read the note.

"What do you say?" she asked, tossing it to Mrs. Dundyke. "Shall we go?"

"But where is Mr. Hardcastle, ma'am?"

"Who's to know? He may be gone round to meet your husband. He saw the probable spot the boat was making for. We may as well go. Perhaps they are both waiting for us. Waiter," continued Mrs. Hardcastle, in her customary imperious manner, "let some wine be placed in the boat, and plenty of ice."

Under cover of umbrellas, the two ladies were rowed across the hot lake to the place where the men had left Mr. Dundyke. But no trace of that gentleman could now be seen; and they sat down in the shade to cool their heated faces, glad of the respite. Mrs. Hardcastle helped herself to some wine and ice, and Mrs. Dundyke presently took her work out of her pocket.

"How industrious you are!" exclaimed the idle woman. "What do you say the embroidery is for? A shirt front?"

Mrs. Dundyke displayed her work. It was for a shirt-front, and the embroidery was beautiful. She was doing two of them, she said. Her husband would require them during his shrievalty.

"I'd not take such trouble for my husband, though he were made king to-morrow," exclaimed Mrs. Hardcastle.

After making that remark she took some more wine, and subsequently dropped asleep. Mrs. Dundyke, engaged in her labour of love, for she loved both the work itself and him who was to wear it, let the time slip on unconsciously. It was only when the afternoon shadows struck on her view as becoming long, when the sun had changed his place from one part of the heavens to another, that a vague feeling of alarm stole over her.

"Where can he be? What is the time?"

She spoke aloud. Mrs. Hardcastle started at the words, and stared to see how the day had gone on. She, Mrs. Hardcastle, was the first to call out the name of Mr. Dundyke. She called it several times, and she had a loud, coarse, harsh voice; but only echo answered her. The boatmen woke up from their slumbers, and shouted in their patois, but there came no response from Mr. Dundyke. A sickening fear, whose very intensity made her heart cold, rushed over Mrs. Dundyke. Her hands shook; the red of her face turned to pallor.

"Why, you never mean to say you are alarmed!" exclaimed Mrs. Hardcastle, looking at her in surprise.

"No—no, ma'am, not exactly alarmed," returned poor Mrs. Dundyke, half ashamed to confess to the feeling. But her quivering lips gave the lie to her words. "I do think it strange he should go away, knowing he had sent for us. I was quite easy at first, thinking he had gone to sleep somewhere, overpowered with the heat. There is no danger, I suppose, that—that—anyone could fall into the water from this spot?"

There was certainly no danger of that: and the boatmen laughed at the notion, for the bank and the water were at that place nearly on a level.

"A man might walk in if he felt so inclined," observed Mrs. Hardcastle, jestingly, "but he could scarcely enter it in any other manner. And your husband is not one to cut short his life for pleasure."

Not he, indeed! Never a man less likely to make his own quietus than plain practical David Dundyke, with his future aspirations and his harmless ambition. His wife knew that the Lord Mayor's chair, shining in the distant vista, would alone have kept him from plunging head foremost into the most tempting lake that ever bubbled in the sunlight.

"There is no marvel about it," said Mrs. Hardcastle. "The boatmen were kept two hours at the hotel, remember, before we were found, and Mr. Dundyke naturally grew tired of waiting, and went away, thinking we should not come."

"But where can he be?" cried Mrs. Dundyke. "What has he done with himself?"

"He has gone back by land. There was no other course for him, if he thought—as he no doubt did think—that the boatman had misunderstood his orders and would not return."

"But, ma'am, he does not know his way back."

"Not know it! Instinct would tell it him. He has only to keep the lake on his right, and follow his nose; he would soon be in Geneva."

It was so probable a solution of the mystery, that Mrs. Dundyke had been unreasonable not to adopt it; indeed she was glad to do it; and they got into the boat, and were rowed back again, expecting Mr. Dundyke would be at the hotel. But they did not find him there. And it was nearly five o'clock then.

"That's nothing," said Mrs. Hardcastle. "The day is so hot he would take his time walking. My husband has not been in either, it seems. Rely upon it they have met and are together; they have turned into some cool café."

The ladies went upstairs together, each into her respective chamber: it has been said that the rooms joined. But that undefined dread, amounting to a positive agony, weighed still on the spirits of Mrs. Dundyke. She could not rest. Mrs. Hardcastle was attiring herself for dinner; not so Mrs. Dundyke; she stood at the door peeping out, hoping to see her husband appear in the long corridor. While thus looking, there came, creeping up the stairs, Mr. Hardcastle, stealing along, as it seemed to Mrs. Dundyke, to shun observation, his boots white, as if he had walked much in the dusty roads, his face scratched, and one of his fingers sprained (as she learnt afterwards) and bound up with a handkerchief.

"Oh, sir!" she cried, darting forward in high excitement, "where is he? where is Mr. Dundyke? What has happened to him?"

Mr. Hardcastle stood for a moment transfixed, and, unless Mrs. Dundyke was strangely mistaken, his face changed colour. She associated no suspicion with that pallor then; she but thought of her own ill manners in accosting him so abruptly.

"What of your husband?" he asked, rallying himself. "I don't know anything of him. Is he not in?"

Mrs. Dundyke explained. Mrs. Hardcastle, hearing their voices, came out of her room and helped her.

"Is that all?" exclaimed Mr. Hardcastle, when he had listened, and his tone was one of indifference. "Oh, he will soon be back. If he is not in, in time for dinner, Mrs. Dundyke, you can go down with us. Don't alarm yourself."

"But have you not seen him?—not been with him?" urged poor Mrs. Dundyke.

"I have never seen him since breakfast."

"We thought you might have walked round by the shore to join him, as you saw this morning where the boat was making for," remarked Mrs. Hardcastle.

He turned savagely upon her, his eyes glaring like a tiger's.

"No, madam," he said, with concentrated passion, "none save a fool would undertake such a walk to-day. I have been in the town, executing various commissions," he added, changing his tone, and addressing Mrs. Dundyke, "and a pretty accident I had nearly met with: in avoiding a restive horse on the dusty quays, I slipped down, with my face on some flint stones."

Mrs. Dundyke would not go down to dinner, but Mrs. Hardcastle fetched her into her own room afterwards, and ordered tea brought up, and they were both very kind to her, buoying up her spirits, and laughing at her fears. Her husband had only lost his way, they urged, and would be home fast enough by morning—a rare joke they would have with him about running away, when he did come.

It was eleven o'clock when Mrs. Dundyke wished them good night, and retired to her chamber, feeling like one more dead than alive. It is probable that few of us can form any adequate idea of her sensations. But for that horrible, mysterious dread, which seemed to have come upon her without sufficient cause, the mere absence of her husband ought not so very much to have alarmed her. She felt a conviction, sure and certain, that some dreadful fate had overtaken him; and, in that dread torture of suspense, she would have given her own life up the next moment, oh, how willingly, to see him return.

She stood at the open window of her room, leaning far out of it, hoping to see him come round the corner of the street, (stay, not so much hoping as wishing,) foot-sore and travel-worn, having lost his way and found it again. She wondered whether anyone was still up, to let him in, if he did come; if not, she would steal downstairs herself, and work at the door fastenings until she undid them. It was with great difficulty, exercising the very utmost self-control, that she stopped where she was, that she did not go out into the streets, searching for him.

While thus thinking, Mrs. Dundyke became aware that strange sounds were proceeding from the next room, though not at first had she heeded them. A fearful quarrel appeared to be taking place between Mr. and Mrs. Hardcastle, and Mrs. Dundyke drew back and closed her window in tremor. Its substance she could not hear, did not wish to hear; but wild sobs and reproaches seemed to come from the lady, and sharp words, not unmixed with oaths, from the gentleman. Twice Mrs. Dundyke heard her husband's name mentioned, or her own ("Dundyke"); and the quarrel seemed to have reference to him. One sentence of Mr. Hardcastle's came distinctly on her ear, apparently in answer to some threat or reproach; it was to the effect that Mrs. Hardcastle might leave him as soon as she pleased; might take her departure then, in the midnight hour. After awhile the anger appeared to subside, silence supervened, and Mrs. Dundyke watched through the live-long night. But her husband did not come.

With the morning Mrs. Hardcastle came to her. She said they had received letters which must cause them to depart for Genoa, where they found their remitted money had really been sent.

"But, ma'am," urged poor Mrs. Dundyke, "surely Mr. Hardcastle will not go and leave me alone in this dreadful uncertainty!"

"He intends to stay until the evening; he will not leave you a moment earlier than he is obliged. Perhaps your husband will make his appearance this morning."

In the course of the morning, Mr. Hardcastle went with the two boatmen to the place where they had landed Mr. Dundyke on the previous day, and a gentleman named by the proprietor of the hotel accompanied them; but not the slightest trace of him could be found, though some hours were spent in exploring. In the evening, by the six o'clock diligence, Mr. and Mrs. Hardcastle left Geneva, the former handing to Mrs. Dundyke an order upon the house in London, Hardcastle and Co., for the twenty pounds he had borrowed of her husband. He regretted, he said, his inability to furnish her, then, with any funds she might require, but he had barely sufficient to carry himself and wife to Genoa. If Mrs. Dundyke approved, he would, with the greatest pleasure, forward from that city any sum she chose to name; for, being known there, his credit was unlimited. Mrs. Dundyke declined his offer, with thanks: she reflected that, if her husband returned, he would have his money with him; and in the event of his mysterious absence being prolonged, she might as well write home for money as borrow it from Mr. Hardcastle at Genoa. She wondered, but did not presume to ask, how he had procured funds for his own journey, and to discharge his hotel bill, which he paid before starting.

"Keep up your spirits, Mrs. Dundyke," he cheeringly said as he shook hands with her at parting. "Depend upon it, your husband will come home, and bring some good reason for his absence; and if it were not that I am compelled—compelled by business—to go on to Genoa, I would not leave you."

She sat down as if some cold shiver had seized upon her heart. It was in her own room that this farewell was spoken; and in that one moment, as he released her hand, and his peculiar eyes rested on her in the parting, and then were lost sight of, it flashed into her mind where she had seen those eyes before. They were the eyes she had once so shrunk from at Westerbury; at least, they bore the same expression—Benjamin Carr's.

Mrs. Dundyke's pulses quickened, and she clasped her hands. For one single moment a doubt arose to her whether Mr. Hardcastle could be Mr. Hardcastle—whether he was not an impostor, Benjamin Carr, or any other, travelling under a false name; and a whole host of trifling incidents, puzzles to her hitherto, arose to her mind as if in confirmation. But the doubt did not last. That he was really anybody but the great Mr. Hardcastle—head, under his uncle, of the great house of Hardcastle and Co.—she did not believe. As to the resemblance in the eyes to those of Benjamin Carr, she concluded it must be accidental; and of Benjamin Carr's features she retained no recollection. She opened the order he had given her to receive the twenty pounds, and found it was signed "B. Hardcastle:" no Christian name in full. Mrs. Dundyke dismissed all doubts from her memory, and continued to believe implicitly in Mr. Hardcastle.

It was, perhaps, a somewhat curious coincidence—at least, you may deem it so, as events go on—that on this same evening an English clergyman should arrive at Geneva, and put up at the hotel. It was the Rev. Wheeler Prattleton, who was visiting Switzerland in pursuance of his intentions (as you once heard mention of), accompanied by his eldest daughter. The strange disappearance of Mr. Dundyke had caused some stir in the hotel, and the clergyman was told of it.

"It is an uncommon name, papa—Dundyke," observed Miss Prattleton. "Do you think it can be the Dundykes who are relatives of Mrs. Arkell's?"

"What Dundykes?" returned Mr. Prattleton, his memory on these points not so retentive as his daughter's. "Has Mrs. Arkell relatives of the name?"

"Oh, papa, you forget. Mrs. Arkell's sister is a Mrs. Dundyke. I have often heard Travice Arkell speak of her; he calls her Aunt Betsey. They live in London."

"We will ascertain, Mary," said Mr. Prattleton, his sympathies aroused. "If this lady should prove to be Mrs. Arkell's sister, we must do all we can for her."

It was very soon ascertained, for the clergyman at once sent up his card, and requested an interview with Mrs. Dundyke. Mr. Prattleton threw himself completely into the affair, and became almost painfully interested in it. He believed, as did all others, that nothing serious had occurred, but that from some unaccountable cause Mr. Dundyke remained absent—perhaps from temporary illness or accident; and every hour, as the days went on, was his return looked for. Mary Prattleton had the room vacated by the Hardcastles, Mr. Prattleton had one on the same floor; and their presence was of the very greatest comfort to poor, lonely, bereaved Mrs. Dundyke.

"Mary, I cannot tell you how I like her!" Mr. Prattleton impulsively exclaimed to his daughter. "She is a true lady; but so unobtrusive, so simple, so humble—there are few like her."

All the means they could think of were put in force to endeavour to obtain some clue to Mr. Dundyke, and to the circumstances of his disappearance. Mr. Prattleton took the conduct of the search upon himself. A Swiss peasant, or very small farmer, a man of known good character, and on whose word reliance might be placed, came forward and stated that on the day in question he had seen two gentlemen, whom he took to be English by their conversation, walking amicably together away from the lake, and about a mile distant from the spot of Mr. Dundyke's landing. The description he gave of these tallied with the persons of the missing man and Mr. Hardcastle. The stouter of the two, he said, who wore a straw hat and a narrow green ribbon tied round it, carried a yellow silk handkerchief, and occasionally wiped his face, which looked very red and hot. The other—a tall, dark man—had a cane in his hand with a silver top, looking like a dog's head, which cane he whirled round and round as he walked, after the manner of a child's rattle. All this agreed exactly. Mr. Dundyke's hat was straw, its ribbon green and narrow, and the handkerchief, which Mrs. Dundyke had handed him clean that morning, was yellow, with white spots. And again, that action of whirling his cane round in the air, was a frequent habit of Mr. Hardcastle's. The country was scoured in the part where this peasant had seen them, and also in the direction that they appeared to be going, but nothing was discovered. Mr. Prattleton reminded Mrs. Dundyke that there were more yellow silk handkerchiefs in the world than one, that straw hats and green ribbons were common enough in Geneva, and that many a gentleman, even of those staying at the hotel, carried a silver-headed cane, and might twirl it in walking. "Besides," added the clergyman, "if Mr. Hardcastle had been that day with Mr. Dundyke, what possible motive could he have for denying it?"

"True; most true," murmured the unhappy lady. She was still unsuspicious as a child.

One of Mr. Prattleton's first cares had been to write to London, asking for the number of the notes, forwarded by the house in Fenchurch-street to Mr. Dundyke. It had of course been lost with him; as also anything else he might have had in the shape of letters and papers, for they were all in his pocket-book, and he had it about him. When the answer was received by Mr. Prattleton, he made inquiries at the different money-changers, and traced the notes, a twenty-pound and a ten-pound. They had been changed for French money at Geneva, on the day subsequent to Mr. Dundyke's disappearance: the halves were in the shop still, and were shown to the clergyman. The money-changer could not recollect who had changed them, except that it was an Englishman; he thought a tall man: but so many English gentlemen came in to change money, he observed, that it was difficult to recollect them individually.

The finding of these notes certainly darkened the case very much, and Mr. Prattleton went home with a slow step, thinking how he could break the news to Mrs. Dundyke. She was sitting in his daughter's room, and he disclosed the facts as gently as possible.

Mrs. Dundyke did not weep; did not cry aloud: her quiet hands were pressed more convulsively together in her lap; and that was all.

"If my husband were living, how could anyone else have the notes to change?" she said. "Oh, Mr. Prattleton, there is no hope! It is as I have thought from the first: he fell into the lake and was drowned."

"Nay," said the clergyman, "had he been drowned the notes would have been drowned too. Indeed, I do not think there is even a chance that he was drowned: had he got into the lake accidentally, (which is next to impossible, unless he rolled in from the grass,) he could readily have got out again. But I find that more money was sent him than this thirty pounds, Mrs. Dundyke. The two halves of a fifty-pound note were sent as well. Do you know anything of it?"

"Nothing," she answered. "I knew he wrote home for thirty pounds; I knew of no more."

Mr. Prattleton gave her the letter, received that morning from Fenchurch-street, and she found it was as the clergyman said. Mr. Dundyke had written for fifty pounds, as well as the thirty; and it had been sent in two half notes, the whole of the notes in two separate letters: three half notes in one letter, and three in the other, and both letters had been dispatched by the same post. There could be no reasonable doubt therefore that all the money had been received by Mr. Dundyke.

"But I cannot trace the fifty," observed Mr. Prattleton, "and I have been to every money-changer's, and to every other likely place in Geneva. I went to the bank; I asked here at the hotel, but I can't find it. What do you want, Mary?"

Mary Prattleton had been for some few minutes trying to move a chest of drawers; the marble top made them heavy, and she desisted and looked at her father.

"I wish you would help me push aside these drawers, papa. My needle-book has fallen behind."

He advanced, and helped her to move the drawers from the wall. A chink, as of something falling, was heard, and a silver pencil-case rolled towards the feet of Mrs. Dundyke. She stooped mechanically to pick it up; and Miss Prattleton, who was stooping for her needle-book, was startled by a suppressed shriek of terror. It came from Mrs. Dundyke.

"It is my husband's pencil-case! it is my husband's pencil-case!"

"Dear, dear Mrs. Dundyke!" cried the alarmed clergyman, "you should not let the sight of it agitate you like this."

"You do not understand," she reiterated. "He had it with him on that fatal morning; he took it out with him. What should bring it back here, and without him? Where is he?"

Mr. Prattleton stood confounded; not able at first to take in quite the bearings of the case.

"How do you know he had it? He may have left it in the hotel."

"No, no, he did not. He went straight out from the breakfast-room, and, not a minute before, I saw him make a note with it on the back of a letter, and then return the pencil to the case in his pocket-book, where he always kept it, and put the pocket-book back into his pocket. How could he have written the note after the men landed him, telling us to join him there, without it?—he never carried but this one pencil. And now it is back in this room, and—oh, sir! the scales seem to fall from my eyes! If I am wrong, may Heaven forgive me for the thought!"

Her hands were raised, her whole frame was trembling; her livid face was quite drawn with the intensity of fear, of horror. Mr. Prattleton stood aghast.

"What do you say?" he asked, bending his ear, for the words on her lips had dropped to a low murmur. "WHAT?"

"He has surely been murdered by Mr. Hardcastle."

CHAPTER V

HOME, IN DESPAIR

The Reverend Mr. Prattleton literally recoiled at the words, and staggered back a few steps in his dismay. Not at first could he recover his amazement. The suggestion was so dreadful, so entirely, as he believed, uncalled for, that he began to doubt whether poor Mrs. Dundyke's trouble had not turned her brain.

"It surely, surely is so!" she impressively repeated. "He has been murdered, and by Mr. Hardcastle."

"Good heavens, my dear lady, you must not allow your imagination to run away with you in this manner!" cried the shocked clergyman. "A gentleman in Mr. Hardcastle's position of life—"

"Oh, stop! stop!" she interrupted; "is it his position of life? Is he indeed Mr. Hardcastle?"

And she began, in her agitation, to pour out forthwith the whole tale: the various half doubts of the Hardcastles, suppressed until now. Her conviction that Mrs. Hardcastle was certainly not a lady, their embarrassments for money, and other little items. Then there had been the long absence of Mr. Hardcastle on the day of the disappearance; his sneaking upstairs quietly on his return, hurt and scratched, warm and dusty, as if he had walked far; his sudden change of colour when she asked after her husband, and the angry look turned upon his wife when she suggested that he had possibly been with Mr. Dundyke. There was the description given by the Swiss peasant of the two gentlemen he had seen walking together that day, and the furious quarrel she had heard at night, when her husband's name was mentioned. All was told to Mr. Prattleton, what she knew, what she thought; all with an exception: the one faint suspicion that had crossed her as to whether Mr. Hardcastle could be Benjamin Carr. She did not mention that. Perhaps it had faded from her memory; and Benjamin Carr, a gentleman born, would be no more likely to commit a murder than the real Mr. Hardcastle. However it may have been, she did not mention it, then, or at any other time.

How could the pencil have got back to the hotel, and into that room, unless brought by Mr. Hardcastle? The testimony of the Swiss peasant, of the two gentlemen he had seen walking together, was terribly significant now. Mr. Prattleton, who had never been brought into contact with anything like murder in his life, felt as if he were on the eve of some awful discovery.

"It was so strange that people of the Hardcastles' position should be up here in one small room on the third floor of the hotel!" cried Mrs. Dundyke, mentioning the thought that had often struck her. "Mrs. Hardcastle said no other room was vacant when they came, and that may have been so; but would they not have changed afterwards?"

Mr. Prattleton went downstairs. He sought an interview with the host, and gleaned what information he could, not imparting a hint of these new suspicions. Could the host inform him who Mr. Hardcastle was?

The host supposed Mr. Hardcastle was—Mr. Hardcastle. Voilà tout! Although he did think that the name given in to the hotel at first was not so long as Hardcastle, but he was not quite sure; it had not been written down, only the number of the room they occupied. Monsieur and Madame had very much resented being put up on the third floor. It was the only room then vacant in all the hotel, and at first Madame said she would not take it, she would go to another hotel; but she was tired, and stopped, and the luggage, too, had been all brought in. Afterwards, when Madame was settled in it, she did not care to change. In what name were Monsieur's letters addressed—Hardcastle? Ma foi, yes, for all he knew; but Monsieur's letters stopped at the post-office, as did those of three parts of the company in the hotel, and Monsieur went for them himself. Money? Well, Monsieur did seem short of money at times;

but he had plenty at others, and he had paid up liberally at last. Other gentlemen sometimes ran short, when their remittances were delayed.

There was not a word in this that could tell really against Mr. Hardcastle. The host evidently spoke in all good faith; and Mr. Prattleton began to look upon Mrs. Dundyke's suspicions as the morbid fancies of a woman in trouble. He put another question to the landlord—what was his private opinion of this singular disappearance of Mr. Dundyke?

The landlord shook his head; he had had but one opinion upon the point for some days past. The poor gentleman, there was not the least doubt, had in some way got into the lake and been drowned. But the notes in his pocket-book? urged the clergyman—the money that had been changed at the money-changer's? Well, the fact must be, the host supposed, that his pocket-book was left upon the grass, or had floated on the water, and some thief had come across it and appropriated the contents.

Mr. Prattleton, after due reflection, became convinced that this must have been the case; and for the pencil-case, he believed that Mrs. Dundyke was in error in supposing her husband took it out with him.

Mrs. Dundyke was not so easily satisfied. She urged the strange fact of Mr. Hardcastle's appearance when he returned that day: his scratched face, his dusty clothes, his altogether disordered look, his sneaking up the stairs as if he did not want to be seen. But upon inquiry it was found that a gentleman, whose appearance tallied with the person of Mr. Hardcastle, did so fall on the dusty flint stones, in trying to avoid a restive horse, and his face was scratched and his hand hurt in consequence; and, as Mr. Prattleton observed, he really might be trying to avoid observation in coming up the hotel stairs, not caring to be met in that untidy state. The pencil-case was next shown to the boatmen; but they could not say whether it was the one the gentleman had written the note with. They were tired with the row in the hot sun, and did not take particular notice. One of them was certain that, whatever pencil the gentleman had used, he took it from his pocket; and he saw him tear the leaf out of the pocket-book to write upon.

Altogether it amounted to just this—that while Mr. Hardcastle might be guilty, he probably was innocent. Mr. Prattleton inclined to the latter belief; and as the days went on, Mrs. Dundyke inclined to it also. The points fraught with suspicion began to lose their dark hue, and when there arrived a stranger at the hotel, who happened to know that old Mr. Hardcastle's nephew was travelling on the continent, and was much inclined to spend money faster than he got it, though otherwise honourable, Mrs. Dundyke's suspicions faded, and she reproached herself for having entertained them.

But nothing further could be heard of Mr. Dundyke; nothing further was heard, and it became useless to linger on in Geneva. That he was in Geneva's lake, she never doubted, and the place became hateful to her.

She travelled towards home in company with Mr. Prattleton and his daughter. At Paris they parted; they remaining in it for a few days, she proceeding to London direct, which she reached in safety. Poor Mrs. Dundyke! As she sat alone in the dark cab which was to take her to her now solitary home at Brixton, she perhaps felt the loss, the dreadful circumstances of it altogether, more keenly than she had felt them yet. She sat with dry eyes, but a throbbing brain, feeling that life for her had ended; that she was left in a world whose happiness had died out.

It was a very pretty white villa, with a lawn before it, and encircled by carriage drive, with double gates. As the man drove in at one, and stopped before the entrance, and the door was thrown open to the light of the hall, Mrs. Dundyke became aware that some gentleman was standing there, behind the servant.

"Who is that, John?" she whispered.

"It's a stranger, ma'am; a gentleman who has just called. He seemed so surprised when I said you had not returned yet; but you drove up at the moment. And master, ma'am?"

Mrs. Dundyke did not answer. The servants knew that something was amiss; but she had not courage to explain then; in fact, she could scarcely suppress her emotion sufficiently to speak with composure. The stranger came forward to meet her, and she recognised the gentleman who had assisted them in Grenoble, and had given his name as Robert Carr.

"You see I have availed myself of your invitation to call," he said. "It is curious I should happen to come to-night when you are only returning. I fancied you did not intend to remain away so long. But where is Mr. Dundyke?"

She turned with him into one of the sitting-rooms—an elegant room of good proportions. The chandelier was lighted; a handsome china tea-service, interspersed with articles of silver, stood on the table; cold meats and other good things were ready; and altogether it was a complete picture of home comfort, of easy competency. The thought that he, who had been the many years partner of her life, would never come back to this again, combined with the home question of the Rev. Mr. Carr, struck out of her what little composure she had retained, and Mrs. Dundyke sank down in an easy chair, and burst into a storm of sobs.

To say that the young clergyman stood in consternation, would be saying little. He was not used to scenes, did not like them; and he felt inwardly uncomfortable, not knowing what he ought to say or do.

"Pray, forgive me," she murmured, when she had recovered sufficiently to speak. "You asked after my husband. He is lost—he is gone. He will never come home again."

"Lost!" repeated Robert Carr.

Mrs. Dundyke told her tale, and the young man listened in utter astonishment. He had never heard of such a thing in all his life; had never imagined anything so strange. It seemed that he could not be tired of asking questions—of hazarding conjectures. He wished he had been there, he said; he was sure that the search he would have instituted would have found him, dead or alive. And it was a somewhat remarkable fact that everybody, forthwith destined to hear the story, said the same. So prone are we to under-rate the exertions of other people, and over-rate our own.

But simple, courteous Mrs. Dundyke, could not forget the duties of hospitality amid her great sorrow. She went upstairs for a minute to take off her travelling things, and then quietly made tea for Robert Carr, asking him questions about himself as he drank it.

He had come straight to London from Grenoble, on business connected with an assistant ministry he expected to get in November, and then went to Holland. He had been back in London now about a week, but should soon be returning to Holland, as his wife was not in good health.

"His wife!" Mrs. Dundyke repeated in surprise. She thought he looked too young to have a wife.

Robert Carr laughed. He had a wife and two children, he said; he had married young.

Mrs. Dundyke told him that she thought they were connected—in fact, she knew they were, for old Mrs. Dundyke used to say so. "I do not quite remember how she made it out," continued Mrs. Dundyke; "I think she was a cousin in the second degree to the Miss Hughes's of Westerbury. They were—"

Mrs. Dundyke stopped short. None were more considerate than she of the feelings of others; and it suddenly struck her that the young clergyman before her, a gentleman himself, might not like to be reminded of these things.

"They were dressmakers, if you speak of my mother's sisters," he quietly said; "I have heard her say so. She was a lady herself in mind and manners; but her family were quite inferior."

Mrs. Dundyke did not feel her way altogether clear. She remembered hearing of the elopement; she remembered certain unpleasant subsequent rumours—that Martha Ann Hughes remained with Mr. Carr in Holland, although the ceremony of marriage had not passed between them. Always charitably judging, she supposed now that they must have been married at some subsequent period; and this, their eldest son, called himself Robert Carr. But it was not a topic that she felt comfortable in pursuing.

"You say that your mother is dead?" she resumed.

"She has been dead about five years. We are three of us: I; my brother Thomas, who was born two years after me; and my sister, Mary Augusta, who is several years younger. There were two other girls between my brother and Mary, but they died."

"Mr. Carr is in business in Rotterdam?"

"Yes; partner in a merchant's house there. He has saved money, and is well off."

Mrs. Dundyke faintly smiled; she was glad for a moment to make a semblance of forgetting her own woes. "Those random young men often make the most sober ones when they settle down. Your father was wild in his young days."

"Was he? I'm sure I don't know. You should see him now: a regular steady-going old Dutchman, fat and taciturn, who smokes his afternoons away in the summer-house. He has not been very well of late years; and I tell him he ought to spend his hours of recreation in taking exercise, not in sitting still and smoking."

"Does he keep up any intercourse with his relatives in Westerbury?" asked Mrs. Dundyke, for she had heard through Mildred Arkell that Westerbury never heard anything of its renegade son, Robert Carr, and did not know or care whether he was dead or alive—in fact, had forgotten all remembrance of him.

"Not any—not the least. I fancy my father and mother must have had some disagreement with their home friends, for they never spoke of them. I remember, when I was a little boy, my mother getting news of the death of a sister; but how it came to her I'm sure I don't know."

"She had two sisters, and she had a brother," said Mrs. Dundyke. "I heard that Mary died. Are the other sister and the brother living?"

"I really do not know. If we had possessed no relatives in the world, we could not have lived more completely isolated from them. I believe my grandfather is living, and in Westerbury—at least, I have not heard of his death."

"Have you lived entirely in Rotterdam?" she asked, her interest very much awakened, she scarcely knew why, for this young man. Perhaps it took its rise in the faint, sad thought, which would keep arising in spite of herself, that a terrible blow might be in future store for him, of whose possible existence he was evidently in utter ignorance.

"Our home has been in Rotterdam, but I and my brother have been educated in England. We were with a clergyman for some years in London, and then went to Cambridge. It would not have done for me to preach with a foreign accent," he added, with a smile.

"But you speak with a perfect accent," said Mrs. Dundyke; "as well as if you had never been out of England. Do you speak Dutch?"

"As a native; in fact, I suppose it may be said that I am a native. Dutch, English, German, and French—we speak them all well."

Poor Mrs. Dundyke heaved a bitter sigh. The words brought to her remembrance what her husband had said about their rubbing on with "we" and "no;" but she would not let it go on again to emotion. She observed the same delicate look on this young man that had struck her at Grenoble; and he coughed rather frequently, always putting his hand to his chest at the time, as if the cough gave him pain.

"Will you let me ask you if you are very strong?" she said. "I do not think you look so."

"I was strong," he replied, "no one more so, until I met with a hurt. In riding one day at Cambridge, the horse threw me, and kicked me here," touching his chest. "Since then, I have had a cough, more or less, and am sometimes in slight pain. My father despatched me on that tour, when I met you, with a view of making me strong."

"Was the injury great at the time?"

"No, I think not; the doctors said not. I believe some of the small arteries were ruptured. I spit blood for some time after it; and, do you know," he added, looking suddenly up at her, "the last day or two I have been spitting it a little again."

"You must take care of yourself," said Mrs. Dundyke, after a pause.

"So I do. I am going to a doctor to-morrow morning, for I want to get into duty again, and should be vexed if anything stopped it."

"Have you ever done duty?"

"Of course; for a twelvemonth. I had my title in the diocese of Ely. I am in full orders now, and hope to be at work in November."

A doubt came over Mrs. Dundyke as she looked at his slender hands and his hollow cheek, whether he would ever work again. Robert Carr rose to bid her good-bye.

"Can I be of any service to you in any way?" he said, in a low, earnest tone, as he held her hand in his. "You cannot tell what a strange impression this tale has made upon me; and I feel as if I should like to go to Geneva, and prosecute the search still."

"You are very kind," she said; "but indeed there is nothing else that can be done. The environs of Geneva were scoured, especially on the side where, as I have told you, two gentlemen were seen who bore the resemblance to my husband and Mr. Hardcastle."

"I don't like that Mr. Hardcastle," cried the young man; "no, I don't. He ought not to have gone away, and left you in the midst of your distress. It was an unfeeling thing to do."

"He could not help it. He said he had urgent business at Genoa."

"The business should have waited, had it been mine. Well, if I can do anything for you, Mrs. Dundyke, now or later, do let me. If what you say is correct—that we are related—I have a right to help you."

"Thank you very much. And remember," she added, in a voice almost as low as a whisper, "that should you ever be in—in—trouble, or distress, or need a friend in any way, you have only to come to me."

What was in Mrs. Dundyke's mind as she spoke? What made her say it? She was thinking of that shock which might be looming for him in the future, it was hard to say how near or how distant. And she felt that she could love this young man almost like a son.

"I will see you again, Mrs. Dundyke, before I leave town," were his last words.

But he did not. When he reached his lodgings that night, he found a telegraphic despatch awaiting him from Rotterdam, saying that his father was taken dangerously ill.

And the Reverend Robert Carr hastened to Dover by the first train, en route for Holland.

CHAPTER VI

NEWS FOR WESTERBURY

It cannot be denied that the present time, this first day after coming home, was one of peculiar pain to Mrs. Dundyke. She would have to go over the sad and strange story again and again, and there was no help for it. The chief partners in Fenchurch-street naturally required the particulars; the few friends she had, the household servants, wished to hear them, and there was only herself to tell the tale.

By ten o'clock, on the morning after her arrival, the second partner of the house, who wore rings and a moustache, and had altogether been an object of envy to the unfortunate common-councilman, was sitting with Mrs. Dundyke. She had not put on widow's weeds; she would not yet; she had said to Mary Prattleton, with a burst of grief, that a widow's cap would take the last remnant of lingering hope out of her. She wore a rich black silk gown, trimmed with much crape, but the cap and bonnet of the widow she assumed not.

Mr. Knowles, a kind-hearted man, who did not want for good sense, dandy though he was in dress, sat twirling his sandy moustache, the very gravest concern pervading his countenance. Mrs. Dundyke, who had never seen this gentleman more than once or twice, sat in humility, struggling with her grief. His social position was of a different standing from what poor Mr. Dundyke's had ever been.

"You see, Mrs. Dundyke, one hardly knows how to act, or what to be at," he remarked, after they had talked for some time, and she had related to him the details (always excepting any suspicion she might once have entertained of Mr. Hardcastle) as closely as she could. "Apart from the grief, the concern for your husband personally, it is altogether so awkward an affair, in a business point of view: we don't know whether we are to consider him as dead or alive."

She shook her head.

"There is little hope that he is alive, sir."

"Well, it would really seem like it. But what can have become of him?"

"There was the lake, you know."

"Yes."

A pause. Presently Mr. Knowles went on.

"When the letter came from that clergyman—Prattleton, wasn't his name?—saying that Mr. Dundyke was missing, and asking for the particulars of the money we had forwarded to him, we could not understand it. 'Missing!' cried old Mr. Knowles, who happened to have come to Fenchurch-street that day, 'one talks of a child being missing, but not of a man.' And when Mr. Prattleton's second letter came to us, giving some of the facts, I assure you we could with difficulty give credence to them."

"There is one little point I did not know of, sir; the sending to you for a fifty-pound note. My husband told me he was sending for the thirty pounds, but he did not say anything of the other. I cannot think why he sent for it."

Mr. Knowles took out his pocket-book.

"I happen to have Mr. Dundyke's letter, which was preserved quite accidentally, not being a strictly business one. You see, he only asks for the fifty pounds in a postscript, as if it were an afterthought. In fact, he says as much:" and Mrs. Dundyke's eyes filled as she looked on the well-known characters.

"P.S. Upon second thoughts, I doubt whether the 30l. will be enough for me. Be so good as to send me a 50l. note in addition to it; in halves as the other."

"Which accordingly we did," resumed Mr. Knowles, as Mrs. Dundyke returned him the letter. "And that note, you say, has not been traced?"

"No, sir, it has not."

"Well, it is altogether most strange. Of course whoever found the pocket-book (if the supposition that it was picked up on the bank of the lake be correct) may be keeping the fifty-pound note by him, but the probability is that he would have got rid of it at once, as he did the others."

"The most singular point to my mind throughout, sir, is the finding of the pencil-case in Mr. Hardcastle's room," said Mrs. Dundyke. "I can't get over that."

"Can't you? It appears to me easily explainable. The supposition that Mr. Dundyke took it out with him that morning must be a mistake. Mr. Hardcastle probably borrowed it from him at breakfast."

"I am quite sure, sir, he did not. I saw my husband put the pencil in its place in the pocket-book, and return the pocket-book to his pocket."

"Then he must have taken it out again when outside the room, and perhaps dropped it. Mr. Hardcastle may have picked it up, and carried it up to the chamber and forgotten it. There are many ways of accounting for that; but it is a pity the pencil was not found before Mr. Hardcastle's departure."

Mrs. Dundyke opened her lips to ask how then could her husband have written the pencilled note afterwards—that he never carried but that one; but she was weary with reiterating the same thing over and over again; and, after all, what Mr. Knowles said was possible. He might have dropped the pencil afterwards; Mr. Hardcastle might have picked it up and carried it to his room; and it certainly might have happened, it was not impossible, that her husband, contrary to custom, had a second pencil in his pocket.

"Shall we send the twenty-pound order to Hardcastle's house and get it cashed for you?" Mr. Knowles asked, when he was leaving. "I fancy that young Hardcastle is not very steady. He is a great deal on the continent, and I have heard he gambles."

Mrs. Dundyke thanked him and handed him the order. "Perhaps you would let the clerk inquire for Mr. Hardcastle's address at the same time, sir?" she said; "and whether he is still at Genoa. I should like to write and ask how he did find the pencil."

But when the order on Hardcastle and Co. was presented—as it was that same day—the house in Leadenhall-street declined to pay it, disclaiming all knowledge of the drawer. Upon the clerk's saying that it had been given by the nephew of Mr. Hardcastle, senior, to Mrs. Dundyke, in liquidation of money borrowed at Geneva, the firm shrugged their shoulders, and recommended the clerk to apply personally to that gentleman, at his residence at Kensington. This information was conveyed to Mrs. Dundyke, and she at once said she should like to go herself.

She went up to Mr. Hardcastle's the next day, and the old gentleman received her very courteously. He was a venerable man with white hair, and was walking up and down the room, which opened to a conservatory. Mrs. Dundyke did not state any particulars at first; she merely said that she had an order on the house in Leadenhall-street for twenty pounds, money borrowed by his nephew; that the house had declined to pay it, and had referred it to him.

"Borrowed money?" he repeated, in a sharp tone, as if the words visibly annoyed him.

"Yes, sir," he borrowed it of my husband; "his remittances did not arrive from England."

Mr. Hardcastle put on his spectacles, and she noticed that his hands trembled, she thought with agitation. "I have a nephew," he said, "who lives principally upon the continent; a thankless scapegrace he is, and has caused me a world of trouble. He has not been in England for eighteen months now, and I hope he will not come to it in a hurry; but he is always threatening it."

Mrs. Dundyke was surprised. "He told us, sir, that he had come from London recently; in fact, he said—he certainly implied—that he took a principal and active part in your house in Leadenhall-street."

"All boast, madam, all boast. He has not anything to do with it, and we would not let him have. I wonder he should say that, too! He is tolerably truthful, making a confession of his shortcomings, rather than hiding them."

"Is he at Genoa still, sir?"

"At where?" asked Mr. Hardcastle, looking at Mrs. Dundyke through his spectacles, which he had been all the time adjusting.

"He went on to Genoa, sir, from Geneva. I asked whether he was there still."

"He has not been at Geneva or at Genoa," said Mr. Hardcastle; "latterly, at any rate."

"Yes he has, sir; he was at Geneva when we got to it in July, and he stayed some time. He then went on to Genoa."

"Then he has deceived me," said Mr. Hardcastle, in a vexed tone. "I don't know why he should; it does not matter to me what place he is in. What is this, madam—the order? This is not his handwriting," hastily continued Mr. Hardcastle, at the first glance, as he unfolded the paper.

"I saw him write it, sir," said Mrs. Dundyke.

"Madam, it is no more like his writing than it is like yours or mine," was the testy answer. "And—what is this signature, B. Hardcastle? My nephew's name is Thomas."

There was a momentary silence. Mr. Hardcastle sat looking at the written order, knitting his brow in reflection.

"Madam, I do not think he could have been at Geneva when this was dated," he resumed; "I had a letter from him just about this time, written from Brussels. Stay, I will get it."

He opened a desk in the room and produced the letter. Singular to say, it bore date the 10th of August, the very day that the order was dated. The post-marks, both in Brussels and London, agreed with the date.

"It is impossible that it could have been he who wrote this order, madam, as you must perceive. Being in Brussels, he could not have been in Geneva. That this letter is in my nephew's handwriting, I assure you on my honour. You may read it; it is about family affairs, but that does not matter."

Mrs. Dundyke read the letter: it was not a long one. And then she looked in a dreamy sort of way at Mr. Hardcastle.

"Madam, I fear you must have been imposed upon."

"Have you two nephews, sir?"

"I never had but this one in my life, ma'am; and I have found him one too many."

"His wife is a showy woman, very pale, with handsome features," persisted Mrs. Dundyke, in a tone as dreamy as her gaze. Not that she disbelieved that venerable old man, but it all seemed so great a mystery.

"His wife! my nephew has no wife: I don't know who'd marry him. I tell you, ma'am, you have been taken in by some swindler who must have assumed his name. Though egad! my nephew's little better than a swindler himself, for he gets into debt with everybody who will let him."

Mrs. Dundyke sat silent a few moments, and she then told her tale—told everything that had occurred in connexion with her husband's mysterious fate. But when she came to hint her suspicions of Mr. Hardcastle's having been his destroyer, the old gentleman was visibly shocked and agitated.

"Good heavens! no! Spendthrift though he is, he is not capable of that awful crime. Madam, how do you suppose your husband lost his life? In a struggle? Did they quarrel?"

"I know nothing," answered poor Mrs. Dundyke.

"A quarrel and struggle it may have been. Mr. Hardcastle was a powerful man."

"A what? A powerful man, did you say, this Mr. Hardcastle?"

"Very powerful, sir; tall and strong. Standing nearly six feet high, and as dark as a gipsy."

"Thank Heaven for that relief!" murmured Mr. Hardcastle. "My nephew is one of the smallest men you ever saw, ma'am, short and slight, with fair curls: in fact, an effeminate dandy. There's his picture," added the old gentleman, throwing open the door of an inner room, "and when he next comes to England, and he is threatening it now, as you read in that letter, you shall see him. But, meanwhile, I will refer you to fifty persons, if you like, who will bear testimony that he is, in person, as I describe. There is no possible identity between them. Once more, thank Heaven!"

Mrs. Dundyke returned to her home. The affair seemed to wear a darker appearance than it had yet worn. And again her suspicions reverted to the man who had called himself Mr. Hardcastle.

We must now turn to Westerbury. That generally supine city was awakened out of its lethargy one morning, by hearing that Death had claimed Marmaduke Carr. On the very night that his grandson was at Mrs. Dundyke's, he was dying: and in the morning, Westerbury heard that he was dead.

On the same day, the instant the news was conveyed to them, Squire Carr and his son and heir came over with all the speed that the train could bring them, and went bustling to the house of the dead man. There they found Mr. Fauntleroy, the solicitor to the just deceased Mr. Carr. He was a tall, large man, this lawyer; a clever practitioner, a fast-living man, and, by the way, the same scapegrace who had done that injury, in the shape of money, to Peter Arkell. But Mr. Fauntleroy had settled down since then, and had made an enormous deal of money; and he held some sway in Westerbury.

"Here's a pretty go!" cried Mr. Fauntleroy, in his loud, blustering tones. "To think that he should die off like this, and nobody know of it!"

"I never knew he was ill," said the squire. "I should, of course, have come over if I had."

"Oh, he has been ill—that is to say, ailing—a good month now," returned the lawyer. "And when these aged healthy men begin to droop, their life is not worth much."

"Well, what's to be done now?" cried Squire Carr.

"Nothing of consequence until we hear from the son. I sent down to the carpenter this morning about the shell, but I shall do nothing more until we hear from Mr. Carr in Holland. I wrote a line to him the moment I heard what had happened, and was in time to get it off by the day mail. He will come over, there's no doubt."

"You knew his address, then?" cried Valentine. It was the first word he had spoken, and he had stood, with his little mean figure, rather behind his father, and his little mean light eyes furtively scanning the lawyer's countenance.

"I believe I know it," replied Mr. Fauntleroy. "There has been an address in our books as long as I have had anything to do with the office, 'Robert Carr, Messrs. something (I forget the name), Rotterdam.' I once asked Mr. Carr if it was his son's correct address, and he said it was, for all he knew. That is the address I have written to."

"Are you sure that the old man did not make a will?" asked the squire, alluding to his relative, Marmaduke.

"I am sure that I never made one for him," returned Mr. Fauntleroy. "Will? no, not he! The very mention of the subject used to anger him? Where was the use of his making a will, he said. His son would inherit just as well without a will as with one: he was heir-at-law."

Squire Carr's covetous heart gave vent to a resentful sigh. They were the very self-same words that Mr. Carr had used to him so many years ago, on the same topic. That old Marmaduke had not made a will, he felt as certain as that he should go to his own bed that night, but he could not help harping upon the contrary hope. As to Valentine, he could almost have found in his heart to forge one, had such doings not been unfashionable.

"Well, I must say Marmaduke might have remembered that he had other relatives besides that runagate son," grumbled the squire. "Had he been mine, I'd have cut him off with a shilling."

"Not a bit on't, Carr," laughed the lawyer, in his coarse way. "You'll not leave your chattels away from your own progeny; not even from the roving sheep, Ben."

Now it was a singular coincidence, amid the many small coincidences of this history, that Marmaduke Carr's son Robert should die at the same time as his father. But so it was. The exile of many, many years died without ever having seen his father, or sought for a word of reconciliation with him: he had died suddenly in a fit, before his father, but not above an hour or two; and without seeing one of his three children, for all were away from home when it occurred.

In reply to Mr. Fauntleroy's letter there arrived a short note, written by a lady who signed herself "Emma Carr, neé D'Estival." The language was English, and good English, too; but the handwriting was unmistakably French. In acknowledging the receipt of Mr. Fauntleroy's letter, it stated that "her husband" was from home; and it gave the information that Mr. Carr was dead—had died after a few hours' illness.

Nothing could exceed the commotion that this news excited at Squire Carr's. Robert Carr dead! then they were the heirs-at-law. They beset the office of Mr. Fauntleroy; they took the conduct of affairs into their own hands; they ordered the funeral, and they fixed the day of interment. Not by any means a remote day; scarcely decently so, according to English notions of keeping the dead. It was hot weather, Valentine remarked; and that was true: but Westerbury said they wanted to get the poor old man under ground that they might ransack the house, and see what valuables were in it. Mr. Fauntleroy was rather taken aback at these proceedings; at the summary wrestling of affairs out of his hands; and he had promised himself some nice little pickings out of all this, the funeral and the acting for Robert Carr, and one thing or another; but he did not see his way clear to hinder it. If Robert Carr was dead, and the old man had left no will, Squire Carr was undoubtedly the heir-at-law.

It was not, however, to be quite smooth sailing. On their return home from the funeral—and the only stranger invited to it was Mr. Arkell, he and Mr. Fauntleroy, with the two Carrs forming the mourners— Mr. Fauntleroy produced from his pocket a letter which he had received that morning. It was from the Reverend Robert Carr, the son of the deceased gentleman in Holland, requesting Mr. Fauntleroy to take all necessary arrangements upon himself for the interment of old Mr. Carr, his grandfather, and regretting that he was prevented journeying to attend it, in consequence of the melancholy circumstances already known to Mr. Fauntleroy. It desired that the style of the funeral should be handsome, in accordance with the fortune and position of the deceased. It was signed Robert Carr.

"Robert Carr!" contemptuously ejaculated the squire. "What a fool he must be to write in that strain to us!"

Mr. Fauntleroy chuckled over the letter; especially over that part of it ordering a suitable funeral. In his opinion, and in the opinion of Westerbury generally, the funeral of Mr. Carr had not been suitable. There were no mutes, no pall-bearers, no superfluous plumes, no anything: none but a mean-minded man would have ordered such a one.

Mr. Fauntleroy wrote back to the Reverend Robert Carr. He gave him a statement of the case in a dry, lawyery sort of way, and told him that Squire Carr being, under the apparent circumstances, heir-at-law, had taken possession of the affairs and property. This elicited a most indignant reply from Robert Carr. There could not be the slightest doubt that his father and mother were married, he said, and he should be in Westerbury as speedily as he could to maintain his own rights.

"Does he think he can impose upon us, this young fellow of a parson?" cried Squire Carr, when the letter was shown him. "He will be for making out next that his mother, that Hughes girl, was my cousin's wife. Let him prove it. Old birds are not caught with chaff."

And Squire Carr took out letters of administration.

CHAPTER VII

ROBERT CARR'S VISIT

Mrs. Arkell sat in her drawing-room with a visitor. She was listening to what struck her as being the very strangest tale she had ever heard or dreamt of. The Reverend Mr. Prattleton, who had reached home the previous night, had come this afternoon to tell her of the disappearance of Mr. Dundyke.

"Your sister wished me to give you the particulars as soon as I got home," he observed. "There was little, if any, acquaintance between you and Mr. Dundyke," he said, "but she felt sure you would feel concern for him, now he was dead, and would like to hear the details. It is a sad thing; I may say an awful thing."

"I never heard of such a thing," exclaimed Mrs. Arkell, forgetting her contempt for the Dundykes in the moment's interest. "It appears incredible that such a thing could happen. Do you really think he was murdered, Mr. Prattleton?"

"No, no; I don't think that," said the minor canon. "Of course there is the possibility; but I incline to the belief that he must have fallen into the lake, leaving his pocket-book on the shore. Indeed, I feel convinced of it, and I think Mrs. Dundyke felt so at last. In the first uncertainty and suspense, I hardly know what horrible things she did not fancy."

"But surely all proper search was made for him!"

"Of course it was. I am not sure that the police took so much interest in it, all of us being foreigners, and temporary sojourners in the town, as they would have done if a native had been missing. It was with difficulty they were persuaded to take a serious view of the case. The gentleman had only gone off somewhere else, they thought, without telling his wife. However, they did their best to find traces of him; but it proved useless."

"What could have taken them to Geneva?" exclaimed Mrs. Arkell.

"A desire for change and recreation, I suppose. The same that took me—that takes us all."

"But—those common working-people don't require change," had been on Mrs. Arkell's tongue; but she altered the words. Mrs. Dundyke was her sister, and unfortunately she could not deny it. "But—Geneva was very far to go."

"Not very, in these days of travelling. It is twenty years, Mrs. Arkell, since I was on the continent, and one seems to get about there ten times as quick as formerly. It's true I took the rail this time as much as I could; the Dundykes, on the contrary, preferred the old diligences, wherever they were to be had."

"Did you see Mr. Dundyke?"

"No," said the minor canon. "He had disappeared—is it not a strangely sounding word?—before we reached Geneva."

"What a mercy that it was not after it!" thought Mrs. Arkell, remembering the graces of manner of the ill-fated common-councilman. "Mrs. Dundyke has returned home, you say?"

"Oh, yes. When all hope was gone, we left Geneva. She went on home direct, but we stayed in Paris. I very much wished to call upon her as we came through London, but we had remained beyond our time, and I could not. I assure you, Mrs. Arkell, I do not know when I have met with anyone that so won on my regard and on Mary's, as your sister."

Mrs. Arkell raised her eyes in pure surprise. Her sister, humble Betsey Dundyke, win upon anybody's regard! It struck her that the clergyman must be saying it out of some notion of politeness; he could surely never mean it. The fact was, Mrs. Arkell had so long been accustomed to regard her sister in a disparaging point of view, that she could not look upon her in any other light.

"She was always a poor, weak sort of girl, between ourselves, Mr. Prattleton. Otherwise you know she never could have made such a marriage. The man was most inferior; dreadfully inferior."

"Indeed! Then I think he must have got on well," said Mr. Prattleton. "He was to have been one of the sheriffs, I believe, next year."

Mrs. Arkell superciliously drew down her still pretty lips. "A great many of those civic London people are quite inferior tradesmen," she said; "at least I have heard so. I only hope poor Betsey has enough left to keep her from want. When these business people die, it often happens that all they have dies with them, and—oh, William, Mr. Prattleton has brought us the strangest news! Mr. Dundyke—Betsey's husband, you know—is either murdered or drowned."

She had broken off thus on the entrance of her husband. Mr. Arkell, as he shook hands with the clergyman, listened in amazement little less great than his wife's, and asked question upon question, greatly interested. You see there was sufficient—what shall I say?—uncertainty, about the matter still, to make them look upon it more as an uncleared-up mystery, than a certain tragedy, and perhaps the chief feeling excited in all minds when they first heard it, was that of marvel. In the midst of Mr. Prattleton's explanations, the college clock struck three, and the bell rang out for afternoon service. It was the minor canon's signal.

"I must go," he said, as he rose; "it is my week for chanting. Mr. Wilberforce took the duty for me the two first days. I did intend to get home on Saturday last, but somehow the time slipped on."

Mr. Arkell was going into the town, and he walked with Mr. Prattleton as far as the large cathedral gates; for the minor canon went round to the front way that afternoon, as it lay in the road for Mr. Arkell. Lounging about in an idle mood, now against the contiguous railings, now against a post of the great doorway, in a manner not often seen at cathedral doors, and not altogether appropriate to them, was a rather tall, bilious-looking young man, with fair hair. He did not see them; his head was turned the other way.

"Can't you find anything better to do, George?"

The words came from the clergyman, and the young man turned with a start. It was George Prattleton, the half-brother of the minor canon, but very, very much younger. Mr. George held a good civil appointment in India, but he was now home on sick leave, and his days were eaten up with ennui. He made the Rev. Mr. Prattleton's his home, who good-naturedly allowed him to do it; but he was inclined to be what the world calls fast, and, except at the intervals (somewhat rare ones) when he had plenty of money in his pocket, he felt that the world was a wearisome sort of place, of no good to anybody. A good-natured, inoffensive young fellow on the whole; free from actual vice; but extravagant, incorrigibly lazy, and easily imposed upon. He generally called his brother "Mr. Prattleton." The difference in their ages justified it, and they had not been brought up together.

"I was deliberating whether I should go in to service this afternoon," said George—a sort of excuse for lounging against the door-post, as he shook hands with Mr. Arkell.

"By way of passing away the time!" cried the clergyman, some covert reproof in his tone.

"Well—yes," returned George, who was by no means unwilling to confess to his shortcomings. "It is a bore, having nothing to do."

"When you first came home you brought a cartload of books with you, red-hot upon studying Hindustanée. I wonder how many times you have opened them!"

Mr. Prattleton passed into the cathedral as he spoke. It was time he did, for the bell had been going twelve minutes. George pulled a rueful face as he thought of his Hindustanée.

"I tried it for six whole days after I came home, Mr. Arkell—I give you my word I did; but I couldn't get on at all by myself, and there is not a master to be had in the town. I shall set to it in right earnest before I go out again."

Mr. Arkell laughed. He rather liked the good-natured young man, and Travice he knew was fond of him.

"But, George, you should remember one thing," he said: "idleness does not get a man on in the world. You have a fine career before you out yonder, if you only take the trouble to secure it."

"I know that, Mr. Arkell; and I assure you not a fellow in all the three presidencies is steadier than I am, or works harder than I do, when I am there. It is only here, where I have no work before me, that I get into this dawdling way."

Mr. Arkell left him, passed out of the cathedral inclosure, and continued his way up the town. George Prattleton remained where he was, wondering what on earth he could do with himself. It was too late to go in to service, for the bell had ceased, the organ was pealing out, and he caught a glimpse, across the great body of the cathedral, of the white surplices of the dean and two of the chapter, as they whisked in at the cloister door. George Prattleton believed time must be given to mortals as a punishment for their sins. He had not a sixpence in his pocket; he owed so much at the billiard-rooms that he did not like to show his face there; he was in debt to all the tobacconists of the place; he had borrowed money from private friends; and altogether he rather wished for an earthquake, or something of that light nature, by way of a diversion to the general stagnation of the sultry afternoon.

Mr. Arkell meanwhile reached the house of lawyer Fauntleroy, for that was the place he was bound for. Mr. Fauntleroy was not his solicitor, but he had a question to ask him on a matter unconnected with professional business. As he was turning out of the office again, he nearly ran against a stranger in deep mourning, who was looking up, as though he wanted to find the number of the house. He was a slight, delicate-looking young man; and it instantly struck Mr. Arkell that he had seen his face before, or one like it.

"I beg your pardon," said the stranger, taking his hat more completely off than an Englishman generally does to one of his own sex, "can you tell me whether this is Mr. Fauntleroy's?"

"It is Mr. Fauntleroy's. I think—I think you are the son of Robert Carr!" impulsively cried Mr. Arkell, as the resemblance to the exiled and now dead friend of his boyhood flashed across his memory.

It was no other. The Reverend Robert Carr had hastened to Westerbury as soon as family arrangements and his own health permitted him. A few moments of conversation, and Mr. Arkell turned back with him to introduce him to Lawyer Fauntleroy, thinking at the same time that he had rarely seen anyone look so thin, so pale, so shadowy as Robert Carr.

It was a handsome house, this of Lawyer Fauntleroy's—and if you object to the term "Lawyer Fauntleroy," as old-fashioned, you must not blame me for using it. Westerbury rarely called him anything else; does not call him anything else now, if it has occasion to recal him or his doings. The offices were on either side of the door, as you entered; Mr. Fauntleroy's private room, a large, well fitted-up apartment, being on the right; a small ante-room led to it, generally the sanctum of the managing clerk.

Mr. Fauntleroy was at leisure, and the whole affair in all its details, past and present, was related to Robert Carr. Mr. Arkell remained also. It was not a pleasant office to have to seek to convince this young man of his own illegitimacy, never a doubt of which had arisen in his mind.

"My mother not married!" he repeated, a streak of suspicious crimson—suspicious when taken in conjunction with that hacking cough, those shadowy hands—"indeed you would not entertain such a thought had you known her. She was, I believe, of inferior family, but in herself she was a lady, and her children had cause to love and bless her. Not married! Why, are you aware, Mr. Fauntleroy, that my father was a partner in one of the first merchant's houses in Rotterdam, and that my mother held her own, and was visited, and respected as few are, so long as she lived?"

Lawyer Fauntleroy shook his head. He was a man who took practical views of most things, utterly scorning theoretical ones.

"I don't doubt your word, Mr. Carr, that your mother was a most estimable lady; I remember her myself, an uncommon pretty girl; but that does not prove that she was married."

Mr. Carr's eyes flashed. "Not prove it! Do you think, being what I tell you she was, a good, religious woman, that she would have lived with my father unless they had been married?"

"I have known such cases," cried the lawyer, with his dry practicalness, if there is such a word. "One of the first men in this city—if you except the clergy and that set—Haughton was his name, and plenty of money he had, and lived in style, as Mr. Arkell here can tell you, his sons sticking themselves above everybody, his wife and daughters setting the fashions—well, Mr. Carr, when he died, it was discovered that his wife was not his wife; that his children were nothing in the eyes of the law. Westerbury was electrified, I can tell you, and bestows hard names upon old Haughton to this day, for having so imposed upon them."

"You should not put such a case on a parallel with ours," said the young clergyman, in pained reproof.

"But, my good sir, it is on a parallel; so far, at all events. I tell you this family were looked upon as superior, as everything that was moral; not a word could be urged against the wife (as we'll call her for the argument's sake); she was respected and visited; and not until old Haughton died, and his will came to be read, did the secret ooze out. He left his money to them, but he could not leave it in the usual straightforward way. By the way," added the lawyer briskly, as a thought struck him; "in what manner was your father's will worded? How was your mother styled in it?"

"You forget that my mother has been dead for some time. The will was made only two years ago. It was a perfectly legally-drawn-up will, according to the Dutch laws; there can be no doubt of that."

"Do you remember how you are described in it, and your brothers and sisters?" persisted Mr. Fauntleroy.

"I have but one brother and one sister; we are described in what I suppose is the usual manner, by our Christian names, Robert, Thomas, and Mary Augusta, the sons and daughter of Robert Carr. It is something to that effect; I did not take particular notice of the wording."

"I wonder what the law is, over there, with regard to legitimacy?" mused Mr. Fauntleroy, his eyes seeing an imaginary Holland in the distance. "But, Mr. Carr, this is waste of time," he added, rousing himself; "the plain case round which the question will revolve, is not so much whether your father and mother were married, as whether it can be proved that they were. The law, in a case like this, requires proof actual—and very right that it should."

"I suppose there will not be the slightest difficulty in proving it," said Robert Carr, resenting the very suggestion.

"Can you prove it? Do you know where it took place?"

The young man shook his head. "I never heard where. It can be readily found out."

"Did you ever question your father upon the point?"

"No; it was not likely I should, seeing that my attention was never drawn to any doubt of the sort."

"Well, Westerbury has never entertained any doubt the other way," said the lawyer. "It is not agreeable to say these things to your face, Mr. Carr; but there's no help for it; and the sooner the question is set at rest for you, one way or the other, the better. I should not think there's a single person living still in Westerbury, who recollects the circumstances as they took place, that would believe your father married Miss Hughes after she went away with him."

"It is probable they were married before they did go away," spoke Robert Carr, hating more than he liked to show the being compelled to this discussion.

"That, I can answer for, they were not. When they left here she was Martha Ann Hughes."

"Mr. Fauntleroy is right so far," interposed Mr. Arkell. "They were not married when they left Westerbury: on that point there can be no mistake. The question that remains is, were they married subsequent to it?"

"They must have been," said Robert Carr.

"But there is no must in the case," dissented the lawyer. "The probabilities are that they were not: the belief is such."

"I do not see why you should persistently seek to cast this opprobrium on my father and mother, Mr. Fauntleroy!" exclaimed Robert Carr, his hollow face lighting up with reproach.

"Bless you, my good sir, I don't seek to cast it," said the lawyer, good-humouredly. "Facts are facts. If you can prove that Robert Carr married Miss Hughes, and your own legal birth with it, you will take the property; but if you can't prove it, Squire Carr must keep possession, and things will remain as they are. Where's the use of shutting our eyes to the truth?"

"There can be no doubt whatever of the marriage. I am sure of it; I would stake all my hopes upon it here and—I was going to say—hereafter."

"But you so speak only according to your belief, sir? You have no shadow of proof."

"True; but—"

"Just so," interrupted Mr. Fauntleroy, in his decisive and rather overbearing manner. "All the proofs lie on the other side—negative proofs, at any rate. They went away together without being married; that is certain—and, by the way, they hoaxed my friend here, William Arkell, into helping them off; and I believe his father never forgave him for it. Neither were there wanting subsequent proofs—negative ones, perhaps, as I say—that they remained unmarried; at any rate, for some years. Rely upon one thing, Mr. Robert Carr: that old Marmaduke, just dead, would have left his money away from his son unless he had been thoroughly certain that no marriage took place. He had sworn to disinherit his son if he married Miss Hughes, and he was a man to keep his word."

"Excuse me," said Robert Carr: "you do not perceive that this very fact may have been the motive that induced my father to keep his marriage a secret."

"I perceive it very well. But it is a great deal more probable that there never was a marriage. Weigh all the circumstances well, Mr. Carr; without prejudice: though, of course, it is difficult for you to do so. Over and over again your father was heard to say that he had no intention of marrying the girl—"

"You forget that you are speaking to me of my mother," interrupted Robert Carr.

"Well, yes, I did," acknowledged the lawyer. "It is difficult to speak to a son upon these things; but I think, Mr. Carr, you had better hear them. Mr. Arkell there, who was your father's intimate acquaintance, can testify how positively he disclaimed, even to him, any intention of marriage. Next came the—"

"Allow me," interposed the clergyman, his haughty tone bespeaking how painful all this was to him. "I presume no suspicion was cast upon my mother's name while she was in Westerbury?"

"Not a breath of it. Blame was cast, though, on her and her sisters for allowing the visits of Robert Carr: as is usual in all cases where there is much disparity in the social standing of the parties. Next came the elopement, I was about to say. They went direct to London, where they stayed together—"

"The marriage must have taken place there," again interrupted Robert Carr.

"I believe not," said Mr. Fauntleroy, dryly. "Marmaduke Carr took care to acquaint himself with particulars, and it was ascertained that they did not remain in London long enough to allow of it. The law, more particular then than it is now, required a residence of three weeks in a place, before a marriage could be solemnized, and they left for Holland ere the expiration of a fortnight. It was our house—my father then being its head—which sought out these particulars for old Marmaduke. No; rely upon it there was no marriage in London."

His tone plainly said, "Rely upon it there was no marriage, there or elsewhere." Mr. Carr was about to speak, but the lawyer raised his hand and continued.

"Some little time after they had settled in Rotterdam, John Carr—Squire Carr now—went over and saw them. There's no doubt his visit was a fishing one, hoping to find out that a marriage had taken place; for in that case, Marmaduke Carr would have wanted another heir than his son. I am sure that John, close-fisted as he was known to be, would have given a hundred pounds out of his pocket to be able to come back and report that they were married; but he could not. He was obliged to confess not only that his cousin and Miss Hughes were not married, but that Robert had told him he never should marry her. And, indeed, it was hardly to be supposed that he would then."

"But—"

"A moment yet, if you please, Mr. Carr. Some considerable time after this, and when I think there was one child born—which must have been you, sir—Mr. Carr got to see a letter written by Martha Ann Hughes to her sister Mary. I think he got the sight of it through you, Mr. Arkell?"

"Through my father. Mary Hughes was at work at our house, and Tring, our maid, brought the letter on the sly to my mother. My father, I remember, said he should like to show it to Marmaduke Carr; and he did so."

"Ay. Well, Mr. Carr, nothing could have been plainer than that letter. Mary Ann Hughes acknowledged that she had no hope of Robert's marrying her; but he was kind to her, she said, and she was as happy as anyone well could be under her unfortunate circumstances. Indeed, I fear you have no room for hope."

"Where is that letter?" asked the clergyman.

"It's impossible to say. Destroyed most likely long ago. None of your mother's family are remaining in Westerbury."

"Are they all dead?"

"Dead or dispersed. The brother went off to America or somewhere; and the second sister, Mary, died: it was said she grieved a great deal about her sister, your mother. The eldest sister married a young man of the name of Pycroft, and they also emigrated. Nothing has been heard of any of them for years."

"You must permit me to maintain my own opinion, Mr. Fauntleroy," pursued Robert Carr; "and I shall certainly not allow anyone to interfere with my grandfather's property. If the other branch of the family—Squire Carr and his sons—wish to put forth any pretensions to it, they must first prove their right."

Mr. Fauntleroy laughed. He was amused at the clergyman's idea of law.

"The proof lies with you, Mr. Carr," he said; "and not with them. They cannot prove a negative, you know; and they say that no marriage took place. It is for you to prove that it did. Failing that proof, the property will be theirs."

"And meanwhile? While we are searching for the proof?" questioned Robert Carr, after a pause.

"Meanwhile they retain possession. I understand that Mrs. Lewis has already come over and taken up her abode in the house."

"Who is Mrs. Lewis?" asked the clergyman.

"Squire Carr's widowed daughter. She has been living at home since her husband died. I was told this morning that she had come to the house with the intention of remaining."

Mr. Fauntleroy's information was correct. Mrs. Lewis had come to Marmaduke Carr's house, and was fully resolved to stop in it, fate and the squire permitting. Mr. Lewis had died about a year before, and left her not so well off as she could have wished. She had a competency; but she had not riches. She broke up her household in the Grounds, and went on a long visit to her father's, to save housekeeping temporarily; leaving her two boys, who were on the foundation of the college school, as boarders at the house of Mr. Wilberforce.

CHAPTER VIII

GOING OVER TO SQUIRE CARR'S

Mr. Arkell put his arm within Robert Carr's, as they walked away together. It would be difficult to express how very much he felt for this young man. His father's fault was not his, and Mr. Arkell, at least, would not be one to visit it upon him. For a few yards their steps were taken in silence; but the clergyman spoke at last, his eye dilating, his voice vehement.

"If they had only known my mother as I knew her, they would see how improbable is this tale that they are telling! I do not care what their suspicions are, what their want of proof; I know that my mother was my father's wife."

"Indeed I hope it will prove so," said Mr. Arkell, rather at a loss what else to say.

"She was modest, gentle, good, refined; she was respected as few are respected. There never was a trace of shame upon her brow. Could her children have been trained as she trained hers, if—if—I can hardly trust myself to speak of this. It is a cruel calumny."

Perhaps so. But, looking at it in its best light; allowing that they were really married; the calumny was alone the fault of this young man's father. If he could have removed the stigma, he should have done it. Did this poor young man begin to think so? Did unwilling doubts arise, even to him? Scarcely, yet. But the lines grew hard in his face as they walked along, and his troubled eyes looked out straight before him into space, seeing nothing.

"I wish you would give me the whole history of the past yourself, Mr. Arkell, now that I can listen quietly. I was hardly in a state to pay attention just now; somehow I distrusted that old lawyer."

"You need not have done that. He was your grandfather's man of business; and, though a little rough, he is sufficiently honest."

"Is he not acting for Squire Carr?"

"I think not. I am sure not."

"Will you give me the history of the past, quietly? as correctly as you can remember it."

Mr. Arkell did so; telling, with a half laugh, the ruse Robert Carr had exercised in getting his father's carriage to take them away, and the hot water he, William, got into in consequence. He told the whole affair from its earliest beginning to its ending, concealing nothing; he mentioned how Mary Hughes had happened to be at work at his mother's house that day; and the dreadful distress she experienced, as soon as the matter was made known to her; he even told how severe in its judgment on the fugitives was Westerbury.

"And were you severe upon them also?" asked Robert Carr.

"Just at first. That is, I believed the worst. But afterwards my opinion changed, and I thought it most likely that Robert married her in London. I thought that for some time. In fact, until I saw the letter that you heard Mr. Fauntleroy speak of, as having been written by your mother to her sister Mary."

"You saw that letter yourself, then?"

"Yes, my father showed it to me. Not in any gossiping spirit, but as a convincing proof that the opinion I had held was wrong, and his was right. He had been very greatly vexed at the whole affair, and would never listen to me when I said I hoped and thought they were married. It was, as Mr. Fauntleroy observed, a plain, convincing letter; and from the moment I saw it, I felt sure that there had been no marriage, and would be none. I am so grieved to tell you this, my dear young friend; but I might not be doing my duty if I were to suppress it."

Robert Carr's face turned a shade paler.

"I see exactly how it is," he said: "that it is next to impossible for you, or anyone else, to believe there was a marriage; all the circumstances telling against it. Nevertheless, I declare to you, Mr. Arkell, on my sacred word as a clergyman, that I am as certain a marriage did take place, as that there is a heaven above us."

Mr. Arkell did not think so, and there ensued a pause.

"Your father died rather suddenly, I believe," he said to Robert Carr.

"Very suddenly. He was taken with a sort of fit; I really cannot tell you its exact nature, for the medical men differed, but I suppose it was apoplexy. They agreed in one thing, that there was no hope from the first; and he never recovered consciousness. I was in London when they telegraphed to me, but when I got home he had been for some hours dead."

"I will send to the hotel for your portmanteau," said Mr. Arkell; "you must be our guest while you stay. My son will be delighted. He is about your own age."

"Thank you, no; you are very kind, but I would rather be alone just now," was Robert Carr's answer. "This is not a pleasant visit for me, and I am in poor health, besides. I shall not stay here long; I must enter upon a search for the register of the marriage. But I should like to pay a visit to the Carr's before I leave, and I am too fatigued to go back to-day."

"To pay a visit to the Carr's?" Mr. Arkell echoed.

"Yes. Why should I not? They are my relatives, and I do not see that there need be ill blood between us. As to the property, they have no real right to it whatever, and I hope I shall speedily produce proof that it is mine, and so put an end to any heartburning. I suppose," he added, reverting to the one subject, "that you are quite sure the marriage did not take place before they left Westerbury?"

"You may put that idea entirely aside," replied Mr. Arkell. "There's no doubt that their going away was in consequence of a bitter quarrel Robert had with his father; that it was unpremeditated until the night previous to their departure. In Westerbury they were not married, could not have been; but perhaps they were in London. It is true, I believe, they did not stay there anything like three weeks—and you heard what Mr. Fauntleroy said; but I suppose it is possible to evade the law, which exacts a residence of that length of time in a place, before the ceremony can be performed."

"Yes, there's no doubt they were married in London," concluded Robert Carr. "I must ascertain what parish they stayed in there; and the rest will be easy."

Not another word was said. Robert Carr walked on in silence, and Mr. Arkell did not interrupt it. Mr. Arkell took him into his house. In the dining-room, the old familiar room you have so often seen, sat a lady, languidly looking over a parcel of books just come in. By her side, leaning over her chair, grasping the books more eagerly than she, the stranger saw a young man of about his own age—tall, slender, gentlemanly—with a face of peculiar refinement, and a sweet smile.

"Now, I wonder what they mean by their negligence? The two books I ordered are not here. I wish they knew what it was to have these fine starry nights, and be without a book of reference; they—"

"Travice," interrupted Mr. Arkell, "I have brought you a visitor, the son of a once close friend of mine. My wife, Mrs. Arkell. Charlotte, this is Mr. Robert Carr, Mr. Carr's grandson."

Mrs. Arkell turned and received him with a curtsey and a dubious look. Always inclined to judge on the uncharitable side, she had had nothing but indifferent scorn to cast to the rumour that Robert Carr's children were going to lay claim to the property, just as she had scorned Robert Carr himself in the old days. She knew that this must be one of the children.

Travice went up at once and shook him warmly by the hand, his pleasant face smiling its own welcome. "I have often heard my father speak of yours," he said; "I am so pleased to see you."

Very little was said in the presence of Mrs. Arkell, touching the business that had brought Robert Carr to Westerbury; but one subject led to another, and Robert Carr told, as one of the strange occurrences of the world, that which had made so strong an impression on himself—the story of the disappearance of Mr. Dundyke. He told it as to strangers; and not, until he had related his own meeting with them at Grenoble, and his visit to Mrs. Dundyke on the night of her return to London, did he find that Mrs. Arkell was her sister. It was Travice Arkell's impetuosity that brought it out then; Mrs. Arkell had been better pleased that it should remain a secret.

"We have heard it all," said Travice; "and Mrs. Dundyke is my aunt and my godmother. She and my mother are sisters."

"I was not aware of it," said Robert Carr. "Is it not a strange tale?"

"Strange!" repeated Travice, "I never heard of anything half so strange. I have been waylaying Mr. Prattleton as he came out of college, wanting to hear more than my mother could tell me. I wish I had been at Geneva!"

"So do I," said Robert Carr.

Robert Carr remained to dinner. He still expressed a wish to make himself known to his relatives, the Carrs; and Mr. Arkell offered to drive him to Eckford on the following morning. A railway now went near the place; but the seven miles' drive was pleasanter than the ten of rail, and Squire Carr's house was a good mile and a half from the Eckford station. So it was arranged.

"Travice," said Mr. Arkell, as Robert Carr took his departure, "I was glad to see your reception of this gentleman. Be to him a friend in any way that you can. It may be, that he will not find too many of them in Westerbury."

Mrs. Arkell tossed her head. "I am rather surprised that you should bring him here, and introduce him on this familiar footing. The past history of the father is not a passport for the son. I should not have cared so much had Charlotte and Sophy been away."

"Charlotte and Sophy! He'll not poison them. What are you thinking of, Charlotte? He has been reared a gentleman; he is a clergyman of the Church of England. Whatever may have been the truth of the past, he is not to blame for it."

Travice Arkell was full of sympathy. "How ill he looks!" he exclaimed; "though he seems to think nothing of it, and says it is the result of a hurt. Is it not curious that he should have met with Mrs. Dundyke? He says his mother was in some way related to the Dundykes."

"There, that will do, Travice," interposed Mrs. Arkell. "I shall dream of that Geneva lake to-night, and of seeing dead men in it. But, William," she added in a lower tone to her husband, "what a misfortune it will be for Betsey, should she have nothing left to live upon! She would have to go out as a housekeeper, or something of that sort."

Squire Carr's residence was a low, rambling, red-brick building, with a quantity of outhouses lying around it, and an avenue of oaks leading almost up to the low-porched entrance door. Pacing before this porch, a clay pipe in his mouth, and his dark hair uncovered to the September sun, was Benjamin Carr. He seemed in a moody study, from which the sound of wheels aroused him, and he saw Mr. Arkell driving up in his open carriage, a stranger sitting with him, and the groom in the back seat. Benjamin Carr wore a short velveteen shooting-coat—it set off his tall form to advantage; and Robert Carr thought what a fine man he was.

"Why, Benjamin, I did not know you were at home."

"I got here a day or two ago," returned Benjamin, putting aside his pipe, and shaking hands with Mr. Arkell. "The squire's slice of luck brought me. One of the girls wrote me word of it; so I've come to see whether I can't drop in for a few of the pickings."

It was an awkward answer, considering that Robert Carr was listening; perhaps he did not understand it. Mr. Arkell made rather a bustle of getting out, and of standing aside for Robert, telling his groom to take the horse round to the stables. "Is your father in, Benjamin?" he asked.

"For all I know. I have seen none of them since breakfast. Valentine's gone over to Eckford, I believe; but—here's the squire."

The squire, attracted by the sounds of the arrival, was peeping forth from the house door. He wore a shabby old coat, and his poor shrunken clothes looked altogether too small even for his miserable little figure. Robert Carr was struck with the contrast to his fine son.

A word or two of explanation from Mr. Arkell, delivered in a low tone, a prolonged, astonished stare from Benjamin, and the squire, in a bewilderment of surprise, was shaking hands with Robert Carr.

"It is the first visit I have made to my father's native place, and though unpleasant circumstances have brought me, I do not see that they need be any reason for my shunning my relatives; I daresay we only wish, on both sides, all that is fair and right," began Robert Carr. "I expressed a wish to come and see you, sir, and Mr. Arkell kindly offered to drive me over."

Had the squire followed his first impulse, he might possibly have ordered Mr. Robert Carr off his premises again; for he could only look upon him as a secret enemy, who had very nearly wrested from him a brave inheritance. But his policy throughout life had been to conciliate, no matter at what expense of hypocrisy. It was the safest course, he held; and he pursued it now. Besides, if there was one man that the squire did not care to stand altogether a sneak before, it was William Arkell with his well-known uprightness.

The squire led the way to his study, turning over in his mind what secret end Robert Carr could hope to answer by coming over and spying into the enemy's quarters. That he had come as a spy, or in some character as base, it was out of the squire's nature to do other than believe. Benjamin followed, in a state of wonder. As they went along the stone passage, Robert Carr caught sight of some pretty girls peeping here and there like scared pheasants; but the squire raised his finger meaningly, and they scuttered away.

The visit was not a pleasant one, after all; and perhaps it was a mistake to have made it. The restraint was too visibly evident. Robert himself spoke of the inheritance—spoke openly, as one honourable, or we may as well say, indifferent, man would discuss it with another. There could be no possible doubt that his father and mother were married, he said; and he hoped the property of all sorts would be allowed to rest in abeyance until the fact was ascertained, which might be done in a week's time.

The squire was rather taken aback, especially at the easy, confident tone; not a boasting tone—one of quiet, calm surety. "Why, how do you think to ascertain it?" he asked.

"I shall search the registers of the London churches."

The squire burst into a laugh. Had Robert Carr told him he was going to search the moon, it could not have struck upon his ear as a more absurd proceeding. Squire Carr was as sure that there had been no marriage as that the sun was then shining on his visitor's head; he had been sure of it, to his cost, all these long years.

"Well," said he, "you'll do as you like, of course, but don't go to much expense over it."

"Why?"

"Because you will never find what you are looking for, and it's a sin to throw away good money. I asked your father myself whether he had been married to the girl in London, and he told me he had not, that he had never been inside a church in London in his life; he told me also that he never should marry her. He spoke on his honour, and therefore I know he spoke the truth."

There was an unpleasant silence. Robert Carr began to feel that the topic could not be pursued.

"Look here, Mr. Carr," resumed the squire, in his piping voice: "you, as a university man, must be in a degree a man of the world, and must know that what's fair for the goose is fair for the gander. Had Marmaduke Carr's son lived and come over here to take possession, he would have taken it, uninterfered with by us; it would have been his own, and we should have wished him joy. But he did not live, he died; he died, in the eyes of the law, childless, and I am the inheritor. As good tell me you lay claim to this house of mine here, as to the property I have just come into of my uncle Marmaduke's."

"You will not allow it to lie in abeyance for a while?"

"Most certainly not. Nobody else would: and you must be a very young man to ask it. I have the law on my side: you cannot in England act contrary to the law, Mr. Carr."

"Well, I daresay you think you are right," said Robert Carr in a tolerant spirit. "Let us drop the subject. I did not, I assure you, come here to enter upon it; I came to make acquaintance with you, my relatives, and to say, but in no spirit of anger or contention, that I intend to establish and maintain my rights. We need not be enemies, or speak as such."

"Very well," said the squire, "I'll ask you one thing, and then we'll drop it, as you say; and it was not I who began it, mind. How came you to think of advancing your claim to my uncle Marmaduke's property? What put it in your head?"

"I believe it to be my property—that I have succeeded to it, with my brother and sister, in consequence of the death of my father. You must understand, Squire Carr, it is only now, since this question arose, that I have heard there was any doubt cast upon our birth."

"I see. Robert kept it from you. He was a simpleton for his pains; and you must not mind my being plain enough to say it. Next to the wrong itself, the worst wrong that parents can inflict is the keeping it a secret from their children. And now let us go to luncheon. I told them to lay it. Never mind about its being early: you shall not go back without first taking something to eat."

"If you go away without partaking of our bread and salt, we shall think you bear us malice," said Benjamin, courteously, as he walked on to the dining-room with the clergyman.

Mr. Arkell was following, but the squire laid his finger on his arm to detain him. "Don't let him do it," he whispered.

"Do what?" asked Mr. Arkell.

"All this searching of registers and stuff that he talks of. Mind! I am not speaking in a selfish spirit, as I might if I were afraid of it,"—and for once the squire's earnest tones, and eyes, raised full in Mr. Arkell's face, proved that he was really speaking truth. "I am sorry for the young man; he is evidently a gentleman, and he looks sickly; and his father has done an ill part by him in letting this come upon him as a blow. There's not the smallest probability that they were married; I know what Robert said to me, and I would stake my life that they were not. If he searches every register in the three kingdoms, he'll never find its record; and it is a pity he should spend his money, and his time, and his hopes over it. Don't let him do it."

"That he will do it, I am quite certain," was the reply of Mr. Arkell. "He seems perfectly to reverence the memory of his mother; and it is as much to vindicate her fame that he will make the search, as for the sake of the inheritance. Robert Carr was grievously to blame to let it come to this. He ought to have set the question at rest, one way or the other, before his death."

"The fact is, Robert overreached himself," said Squire Carr. "I can see it plainly. He did not marry the girl, because it would have been the means of forfeiting his father's property—for old Marmaduke would have kept his word. He wanted to come into that property, and then to have made a will and left it to these children, relying on their foreign birth and residence to keep always the fact of their illegitimacy from them. But he died suddenly, you see, before he had come into it, and therefore the property goes from them. Robert overreached himself."

Mr. Arkell nodded his head. His opinion coincided with Squire Carr's.

CHAPTER IX

A STARTLED LUNCHEON-TABLE

The luncheon was laid in a low room, with a beam running across the ceiling; the walls, once bright with red flock paper and much gilding, were soiled and dull now, after the manner of a great many of our dining-rooms. Squire Carr took the head of the table. He apologised for the fare: cold veal, ham (which Benjamin, who sat at the foot of the table, carved), and salad. The squire's daughters did not appear at it. There were too many of them, he said to Robert; but Mrs. Lewis, who had just come over from Westerbury by the train, did. She was a big woman, with little eyes like the squire's, and a large face— the latter very red just now, through her mile-and-a-half walk in the sun from Eckford. She turned her back on the young clergyman when he said grace, as though he had no business there. Benjamin had whispered to her who he was, and the search of the marriage register books that was in prospect; and Mrs. Lewis resented it visibly. She had no mind to give up that bijou of a house just entered upon. She believed she should have trouble enough with her father to keep it, without another opponent coming into the field.

"What brings you over to-day, Emma?" asked the squire of Mrs. Lewis, as the meal proceeded. "Anything turned up?"

A rather ambiguous question, the latter one, to uninitiated ears; but the squire had been burning to put it, and Mrs. Lewis understood. He looked covertly at her for a moment with his blinking eyes, and then dropped them again.

"I only came over to see Ben, papa," she answered. "The news reached me this morning that he had come home. I have not had time to do anything yet."

Now, the fact was, Squire Carr had placed his daughter, knowing her admirable ferreting propensities, in Marmaduke Carr's house for one sole purpose—that of visiting its every hole and corner. "There may be a will," the squire had said to himself, in his caution, several times since the death. "I don't think there is; I could stake a great deal that there is not, for Marmaduke was not likely to make one; but it's as well to be on the safe side, and such things have been heard of as wills hid away in houses." And when the squire saw Mrs. Lewis, whom he had not expected that day, he began to fear that something of the sort had "turned up." The relief was great.

"Oh, to see Ben. You'll see enough of him, I expect, before he's off again."

"Are you going to make a long stay here, this time, Ben?" asked Mr. Arkell.

"Yes, I think I shall. Will you take some more ham, Emma?"

"Your name is the same as my wife's," observed the young clergyman, with a smile, as he passed Mrs. Lewis's plate for more ham: for it was Squire Carr's pleasure that servants did not wait at luncheon.

"Is it? It is a very ugly one," roughly replied Mrs. Lewis, who could not recover her equanimity in the presence of this gentleman. "I can't think how they came to give it me, for my part. I have a prejudice against the name 'Emma.' The woman bore it whom, of all the women I have known in the world, I most disliked."

"It was your mother's name, my dear," said the squire.

"And I think a charming name," said Robert Carr. "I am not sure but it was Emma D'Estival's name that first attracted me to her."

The squire looked up with a sort of start. He remembered the letter written by "Emma Carr, née D'Estival." Of course! she was this young man's wife.

"You look young to have a wife," was all the squire said.

"You look, to me, as if you had no business with one at all," added Mrs. Lewis with blunt plainness. "Sickly men should be cautious how they marry, lest they leave their wives widows. I have been so left. I threw aside my widow's cap only last week."

Robert Carr explained to them what his hurt had been, and how his chest had suffered at times since. He was aware he looked unusually ill just now, he said; but he had looked just as much so about a year and a half before—had coughed also. He should get well now, he supposed, like he did then. For one thing, speaking of his present looks, this matter was harassing him a good deal, and there had been his father's sudden death.

"Oh, by the way, Mr. Arkell, let me ask you something," exclaimed Mrs. Lewis suddenly. "I have heard the strangest thing. That a gentleman, a Mr. Dundas, or some such name, had been drowned or murdered, or something, at Geneva; a relative of your wife's. What is the truth of it?"

"That is the truth, as far as we can learn it," replied Mr. Arkell. "It was Mr. Dundyke, the husband of Mrs. Arkell's sister. You saw her once, I know, at my mother's house, a great many years ago; she was Miss Betsey Travice then—"

"But about the murder?" interrupted Mrs. Lewis. "Was he murdered? Roland ran home from Mr. Wilberforce's for a minute last night, and I heard it from him. I think he said the young Prattletons told him. I know he was quite up in arms about it. What is it?"

Mr. Arkell pointed to Robert Carr. "That gentleman can tell you better than I can," he said. "He heard the particulars from Mrs. Dundyke herself. I only heard them from Mr. Prattleton secondhand."

"I suppose you want me to tell the story, instead of yourself," said Robert Carr, with a glance and a smile at Mr. Arkell. "Mr. Prattleton was on the spot, and instituted the search, so his information cannot be secondhand."

They began it between them, but Mr. Arkell gradually ceased, and left it to Robert Carr. It appeared to take a singular hold on the squire's interest. He had just asked his son for more ham, but was too absorbed to send his plate for it. Ben held the slice between his knife and fork, and had to let it drop at last.

"Then he was not murdered!" exclaimed Mrs. Lewis. "It was only a case of drowning, after all!"

"Of drowning," assented Robert Carr. "At least that is the most probable supposition."

"It may rather be called at present a case of mysterious disappearance, as the sensational weekly papers would phrase it," interposed Mr. Arkell, speaking again. "Mrs. Dundyke at one time felt convinced that a murder had been committed, as Mr. Prattleton tells me, and afterwards modified her opinion. Now she feels her doubts renewed again."

"What a shocking thing!" exclaimed Mrs. Lewis. "And who does she think murdered him—if he was murdered?"

"The Mr. Hardcastle of whom mention has been made. Mrs. Dundyke has discovered that he was an impostor."

"Has she!" exclaimed Robert Carr.

"Mr. Prattleton heard from her by last evening's post, and he came in late, and showed me her letters," said Mr. Arkell. "This man, Hardcastle, had passed himself off as being a partner of the great Hardcastle house in Leadenhall-street—a nephew of its head and chief—whereas he turns out to be entirely unknown to them."

"And she thinks he did the murder?" quickly cried Mrs. Lewis, who was possessed of all a woman's curiosity on such subjects.

"She thinks the suspicions look very dark against him," said Mr. Arkell. "I confess I think the same."

"But I thought Mr. Carr, here, said she had completely exonerated this Mr. Hardcastle!" cried the squire. "Be quiet, Emma; you would let nobody speak but yourself, if you had your way."

"So I believe she did exonerate him," returned Mr. Arkell; "but in all cases the same facts wear so different an aspect, according to their attendant surroundings. When Mr. Hardcastle was supposed to be Mr. Hardcastle, one of the chief partners of the great East India house, the nephew of its many-years' chief, it was almost impossible to suppose that he could have committed the murder, however little trifling circumstances might seem to give point to the suspicion. But when we know that this man was not Mr. Hardcastle, but an impostor—probably a chevalier d'industrie, travelling about to see what prey he could bring down—those same trifling circumstances change into alarming facts, every one of which bears its own significance."

"I don't clearly understand what the facts were," said the squire. "He borrowed money, didn't he?"

"He borrowed money—twenty pounds; he would have borrowed a hundred, but Mr. Dundyke had it not with him. He, poor Mr. Dundyke, was utterly taken in by them from the first—never had a shadow of suspicion that anything was wrong; Mrs. Dundyke, on the contrary, tells Mr. Prattleton that she had. She feels quite sure that their running account at the hotel, for which she knows they were pressed, was paid with that twenty pounds, or part of it; and she says they—"

"In saying 'they,' of whom do you speak besides Mr. Hardcastle?" asked the squire.

"Of his wife. And Mrs. Dundyke did not like her. But let us come to the day of the disappearance. On that morning, as they sat at breakfast, Mr. Dundyke told Mr. Hardcastle that he was about to leave; and that some money he had written for, notes for thirty pounds, had come that morning—were inclosed in two letters which Mr. Hardcastle saw him receive and put in his pocket. Mrs. Dundyke says that she shall never forget the strangely eager glance—something like a wolf's when it scents prey—that he cast on Mr. Dundyke at mention of the thirty pounds. Mr. Dundyke went out alone, and hired a boat, as you have heard; and they afterwards saw him on the lake bearing away to the spot where he landed; Mr. Hardcastle saw him, and then walked away. Nothing more was seen of either of them until dinner-time, six o'clock, when Mr. Hardcastle returned; he came creeping into the house as if he wished to shun observation, travel-soiled, dusty, his face scratched, his hand hurt—just as if he had been taking part in some severe struggle; and Mrs. Dundyke is positive that his face turned white when she rushed up and asked where her husband was."

"Did she suspect him then?"

"Oh dear no; not with the faintest suspicion. That same night she heard a fearful quarrel between Mr. and Mrs. Hardcastle; weepings, lamentings, reproaches from Mrs. Hardcastle, ill-language from him; and twice she heard her husband's name mentioned. She told Mr. Prattleton subsequently that it was just as though the fact of the murder had been then disclosed to Mrs. Hardcastle, and she, the wife, had received it with a storm of horror and reproach. But the most suspicious circumstance was the pencil-case."

"What was that?" came the eager question from the squire and his daughter, for this had not yet been named.

"Well, what Mr. Prattleton tells me is this," said Mr. Arkell. "When Mr. Dundyke went out in the boat he had his pencil-case with him; Mrs. Dundyke saw him return it to his pocket-book the last thing before leaving the breakfast-room, and put the book in his pocket. It was the same pocket-book in which he had just placed the letters containing the bank-notes. The pencil-case was silver; it had been given to Mr. Dundyke by my cousin Mildred, and had his initials upon it; Mrs. Dundyke says he never carried any other—had not, she feels convinced, any other with him that morning. After he had landed on the opposite side of the lake, he must have made use of this pencil to write the note, which note he sent back to the hotel by the boatmen. So that it appears to be a pretty certain fact that, whatever evil overtook Mr. Dundyke, this pencil must have been about him. Do you follow me?"

"Yes, yes," answered the squire, testily. He did not like the narrative to be interrupted by so much as a thread.

"Good. But this same pencil-case was subsequently found in Mr. and Mrs. Hardcastle's room at the hotel."

"What!" exclaimed Benjamin Carr, looking up as if startled to sudden interest.

"The droll question is, how did it come there?" continued Mr. Arkell. "It was found in the room the Hardcastles had occupied at the hotel. They had left there some days; had gone on, they said, to Genoa. Mr. Prattleton's daughter was put in this room after their departure, and the silver pencil-case was picked up from behind the drawers. Mr. Prattleton and Mrs. Dundyke were in the chamber at the time, and the latter was dreadfully agitated; she quite startled him, he says, by saying that Mr. Hardcastle must have murdered her husband."

"Bless my soul!" exclaimed Squire Carr. "I see. The pencil-case which was lost with Mr. Dundyke reappeared in their room! How very strange! I should have had the man apprehended."

"The hypothesis of course is, that Mr. Hardcastle had in some manner possessed himself of the things the missing man had about his person," pursued Mr. Arkell. "Mr. Prattleton thought at the time that this could perhaps have been explained away. I mean the finding of the pencil-case—that Mr. Dundyke might have dropped it on going out from breakfast, and the other have picked it up; but since the arrival of Mrs. Dundyke's letter yesterday, he says he does not like the look of it at all."

"And the bank-notes that Mr. Dundyke had undoubtedly about his person were found to have been changed the subsequent day in Geneva," spoke up Robert Carr. "The money-changer thought they had been changed by a man whose appearance agreed with that of Mr. Hardcastle. And then there was the testimony of the Swiss peasant."

"What was the testimony?" asked the squire.

"A peasant, or small farmer, testified that he saw two gentlemen together walking away from the direction of the lake on the day of the disappearance; and in describing them, he exactly described the persons and dress of Mr. Hardcastle and Mr. Dundyke. I told Mrs. Dundyke," added the clergyman, "that I did not like her account of this Mr. Hardcastle; and she had expressed to me no suspicion of him then."

"And why did they not cause him to be apprehended?" asked the squire. "There could not well be a clearer case. I have committed many a man upon half the evidence. What sort of a man was he in person, this Hardcastle?"

"A tall, strong man, very dark; a fine man, Mrs. Dundyke says. I should think," added the clergyman, ranging his eyes around, lest haply he might find anyone in the present company to illustrate his meaning by ever so slight a likeness, as we are all apt to do in trying to describe a stranger—"I should think—"

Robert Carr stopped; his eyes were resting on the white face of Benjamin Carr. Those sallow, dark faces when they turn white are not pleasant to look upon.

"I should think," he continued, "that he must have been some such a man as your son here, sir. Yes, just such another; tall, strong, dark—"

"How dare you?" shouted Benjamin Carr, with a desperate oath. "How dare you point at me as the—the—as Mr. Hardcastle?"

The whole table bounded to their feet as if electrified. Benjamin had risen to his full height; his eyes glared on the clergyman; his fist was lifted menacingly to his face. Had he gone out of his senses? Some of them truly thought so. That he had momentarily allowed himself to lose his presence of mind, there could be no question.

"What on earth has taken you, Ben?"

The words came from Mrs. Lewis. Her brother's demeanour had been puzzling her. He had sat, with that one slight interruption mentioned, with his head down, looking sullen, as if he took no interest in the narrative; and she had seen his face grow whiter and whiter. She supposed it to be caused by the story; and said to herself, that she should not have thought Ben was chicken-hearted.

The squire followed suit. "Have you taken leave of your senses, sir? What's the matter with you? What is it, I say?"

"Your visitor offended me, sir," replied Benjamin Carr, slowly sitting down in his chair again, and beginning to recollect himself. "How dare he say that I bear a resemblance to this Hardcastle?"

"He never did say it," angrily returned the squire. "If you cause such a startling interruption at my table again, I shall request you to think twice before you sit down to it."

Mrs. Lewis was staring at her brother with a sort of wondering stare. Mr. Arkell could not make him out; and the young clergyman stood perfectly confounded. Altogether, Benjamin Carr was under a sea of keen eyes; and he knew it.

"I'm sure I beg your pardon if my words offended you," began Robert Carr. "I meant no offence. I only wished to convey an impression of what this Mr. Hardcastle was like—a tall, fine, dark man, as described to me. I never saw him. The same description would apply to thousands of men."

"I thought you did intend offence," said Benjamin Carr in a distinct tone. "Your words and manner implied it, at any rate."

"Don't show yourself a fool, Benjamin," cried out the squire. "I shall begin to think you are one. The clergyman no more meant to liken you to the man, than he meant to liken me; he was only trying to describe the sort of person. What has taken you? You must have grown desperately thin-skinned all on a sudden."

"Can't you let it drop?" said Benjamin, angrily. The squire sent up his plate as he spoke, for the ham that had been waiting all this while; perhaps by way of creating a divertissement; and Ben lifted the slice with a jerk, and then jerked the knife and fork down again. Mrs. Lewis, who had never come out of the prolonged stare, apparently arrived now at the solution of the problem.

"I know what it is, Ben," she quietly said. "This Hardcastle must be an acquaintance of yours. You know you do pick up all sorts of—"

"It is a lie," interrupted Ben, regardless of his good manners.

"Papa"—turning to the squire—"rely upon it I am right. Ben no doubt fell in with this Hardcastle on his travels, grew intimate with him, and now does not like to hear him aspersed."

"Be quiet, Emma," cried Ben, but his voice was lowered now, as if with concentrated passion, or policy. "You talk like a fool."

"Well, perhaps I do," retorted Mrs. Lewis, "but I think it is as I say for all that. You would not put yourself out like this for nothing. I dare say you did know the man; it was just the time that you were at Geneva."

"I was not at Geneva."

"You were at Geneva," she persisted. "You know you wrote home from thence."

"Why yes, of course you did, Ben," added the squire. "Valentine showed us the letter: you said you were hard up in it. But that's nothing new."

"I swear that I never saw this Hardcastle in my life," said Ben Carr, his white face turning to a dusky red. "What time did this affair happen?" he continued, suddenly addressing Mr. Arkell. "If I had been in Geneva at the time, I must have heard of it."

"I can tell you," said Robert Carr. "Mr. and Mrs. Dundyke went to Geneva the middle of July, and this must have happened about the second week in August."

Benjamin Carr poured himself out a glass of wine as he listened. He was growing cool and collected again.

"Ah, I thought I could not have been there. I went to Geneva the latter part of June. I and a fellow were taking a walking tour together. We stayed there a few days, and left it for Savoy the first week in July. I think I did write to Valentine while I was there. All these people, that you speak of, must have arrived afterwards."

"Then did you not see this Mr. Hardcastle, Ben?" asked his sister.

"I tell you, no! I never saw or heard of him in my life."

"Then why need you have flown out so?"

"Well, one does not like to be compared to a—murderer. Some of you had been calling him one."

No more was said. But the hilarity (if there had been any) of the meeting was taken away, and Robert Carr rose to leave. He had a little business to do in Westerbury yet, he said, and must go back that night to London. The squire was the only one who showed courtesy in the farewell. Benjamin was sullenly resentful still; Mrs. Lewis haughty and indifferent.

"Is he quite in his right mind?" Robert Carr asked of Mr. Arkell, as they drove out of the avenue.

"Who?—Benjamin Carr? Oh yes, he is right enough. He is as sharp as a needle."

"Then what could have caused him to break out in the manner he did? I never was so taken to in my life."

"I don't know," said Mr. Arkell; "it is puzzling me still. But for his very emphatic denial, I should assume it to be as Mrs. Lewis suggested—that he must have got acquainted with this Hardcastle, and did not like to hear any ill of him."

"Is he a married man?"

"No. Not any of the squire's children have married, except Mrs. Lewis. And she's a widow, as you heard her say."

"I suppose she is the daughter that has entered into possession of my grandfather's house?"

"She is. Hoping, no doubt, to stay there."

"Tell me, Mr. Arkell," resumed Robert Carr after a pause, for he could not forget the recent occurrence, "did you see anything offensive in my allusion?"

"Certainly not. Neither would anyone else. I say I cannot make out Benjamin Carr."

Before starting for London that night, Robert Carr paid a visit to Mr. Fauntleroy. It was after office hours, but that gentleman received him in his drawing-room. One of Mr. Fauntleroy's daughters, a buxom damsel on the same large scale as her father, was thumping through some loud piece on the piano. She satisfied her curiosity by a good look at the intruder, as all Westerbury would like to have done, for his name had been in men's mouths that day, and then retired with a good-humoured smile and nod, carrying her piece of music.

"Bab!" called out the lawyer.

Miss Fauntleroy came back. "Did you speak, pa?"

"Don't go strumming that in the next room. This gentleman has perhaps called to talk on matters of business."

She threw down the music with a laugh: gave another good-natured nod to Robert, and finally quitted the room.

"Mr. Fauntleroy, I have come—but I ought first to apologize for calling at this hour, but I am going off at once to London—I have come to ask if you will act for me as my legal adviser?"

Mr. Fauntleroy made a momentary pause. "Do you mean generally, or in any particular cause?"

"I mean in this, my cause. I require some solicitor to take it up at once, and serve a notice of ejectment on Squire Carr, from the possession of the property he has assumed. I suppose that would be the first legal step; but you will know what to do better than I. As the many years solicitor to my grandfather, I thought you might perhaps have no objection to become mine."

"I have no objection in the world," said Mr. Fauntleroy. "But, my good sir—and this, mind you, is disinterested advice—I would recommend you to pause before you enter on any such contest. There's not a shadow of chance that the property can be wrested from Squire Carr, so long as your father's marriage remains a doubt. It is his by law."

"I do not think there is a shadow of doubt that the proofs of the marriage will be found, and speedily. I go up to London to search. Meanwhile you will be so kind as act just as you would act were the proofs in your hand. I will not allow Squire Carr to retain, by ever so short a time, the property unmolested, or to fancy he retains it," continued the young man, in some emotion. "Every hour that he does so is a reflection on my mother's name."

"But—yes, that's all very well, very dutiful—but where's the use of entering on a contest certain to be lost?"

"It is certain to be gained; I know the proofs will be forthcoming."

"The most prudent plan will be to wait until they are," returned the lawyer. He was not usually so considerate for his clients; but this, as he looked upon it, was a hopeless case, one that nobody, many degrees removed from a fool, would venture upon.

"No," said Robert Carr, "I will not wait a day. Be so kind as take proper steps at once, Mr. Fauntleroy."

"Very well; if you insist upon it. It will cost money, you know."

"That shall be placed in your hands as soon as I can send the necessary instructions to Rotterdam. What sum shall you require?"

"Oh, suppose you let me have fifty pounds at first. Before that's expended, perhaps—perhaps some decision may have been come to."

Had Mr. Fauntleroy spoken the words on his tongue, they would have run, "perhaps you will have come to your senses."

"I will spare no expense on this cause; any money you want, you shall have, only my right must be maintained against the other branch of the family. Do you understand me, Mr. Fauntleroy?"

"I do; and I must ask you to understand me, and to remember later that I did not advise this. If the proofs of the marriage shall come to light, why, then of course the tables will be turned."

"By the way," said Robert Carr, "I have never asked what amount of money my grandfather has left?"

"Not much less than the value of twenty thousand pounds, taking it in the aggregate. He did not live up to his income, and it accumulated. There are several houses; the one he resided in is a beautiful little place. You have not been inside it?"

"No; I met Mrs. Lewis to-day, at the squire's, and I thought she might have invited me to see it," added Robert Carr. "But she did not."

"No danger; they'll keep you at arm's length, if they can. Well, Mr. Carr, you will not forget what I say, that I do not advise you to enter on this contest. And should you, after a day or two's reflection, think better of it, there's no harm done. Just drop me a line to say so, that's all. I won't charge you for my advice."

"You must think I am of a changeable nature," returned the young clergyman, half resentfully.

"I should think you a sensible man."

Robert could not smile, he was too serious. "And if you receive the money from me, instead of the letter you suggest, you will immediately commence this action; is that an understood thing between us, Mr. Fauntleroy?"

"It is," said Mr. Fauntleroy; "it will cost a mint of money, mind you, if it goes on to trial."

Robert Carr said no more; he was satisfied. As he went down the richly-carpeted stairs, two large female heads, and two coarsely-handsome, good-natured faces were propelled over the balustrades, to gaze after him: the heads and the faces of the Miss Fauntleroys.

CHAPTER X

A MISSIVE FOR SQUIRE CARR

Domestic relations did not progress very pleasantly at Squire Carr's. It was the old story; the old grievance; the one that had disturbed the internal economy of the home ever since Benjamin became a grown man: Benjamin required money, and the squire protested he had it not to give. Ben, he said, wanted to ruin him.

This time Ben had come home particularly out at elbows, metaphorically speaking; literally, he was, in regard to clothes, rather better off than usual. Ben had quitted his home the previous April, with a very fair sum of money in his pocket, drawn from the squire; where he had spent the time since was not very clear, unless he had been, as the squire expressed it, dodging about the continent; two or three letters having been received from him at long intervals, dated from different parts of it. Ben was not accustomed to be particularly communicative on the subject of his own wanderings; and all he said now was, that he had made a "pedestrian tour." One other thing was a vast deal more clear—that he had brought back empty pockets.

He was now worrying the squire to advance him funds for a visit to Australia, where he should be sure to make his fortune. Three or four fellows, whom he knew, were going, he said; they had a fine prospect before them, and he had the opportunity offered him of joining them. The worrying had begun on the very evening subsequent to the visit of Mr. Arkell and Robert Carr; a week or more had gone on since; and Ben systematically continued his importunities. The squire turned a stone-deaf ear. Ben had once before got money from him to make his fortune in Australia; and had come home after a two years' absence without a shirt to his back: Squire Carr must live to be an older man than he was now, before he forgot that. Valentine Carr put in his voice against it; he had for a long while been angrily resentful at these sums of money being advanced to Ben, far larger ones, he suspected, than the reigning powers allowed to come to his knowledge; and he was now raising his voice in opposition. He was the heir; and the estate, he said, was already impoverished too much.

One cloudy Saturday morning, close, hot, and unhealthy, Valentine Carr was mounting his horse to go to Westerbury. They had breakfasted early; breakfast was always taken early at the squire's, but especially so on Saturdays, the market day at Westerbury. Squire Carr was standing by his son, giving him various directions.

"You'll see how prices run to-day, Valentine; but mark you, I'll not sell a sheaf of the old corn if the market's flat. And the new you need not think of soliciting offers for, for I shall not sell yet awhile. The barley market ought to be brisk to-day; some of the maltsters, I hear, are already preparing to steep; and you may, perhaps, get rid of some loads. Have you the samples?"

Valentine Carr dived with one hand into his capacious pocket, by way of answer, and just showed some three or four little bags tied round with tape.

"You'll get first prices, mind, or you won't sell. Not a farmer in all the county can show better barley this year than ours. Do you hear?"

"I know," ungraciously returned Valentine. "I believe you think I'm a child still. I can't ride off to market without you, but you go on at me in this fashion: and it's nigh upon thirty years now since I went first."

"I know my own business better than anybody, and I can't afford to let things go below their value," rejoined the squire. "A halfpenny a bushel would make a difference to me now, and I should feel it. I'm shorter of money than I ought to be."

"Money goes in many ways that it ought not to go in," said Valentine, gathering up his bridle with a sniff. And the squire knew that it was a side-thrust at Ben. "Anything more?"

"You had better call on Emma, and ask whether she has made a list of the plate and pictures. If she has not, you may tell her that I shall come over next week and go over the things for myself. She might have sent it to me days ago. I'll not have so much as a plated spoon omitted, and so I told her. That's all."

Valentine Carr touched his horse and rode at a quick trot down the avenue. When the squire looked round, he found Benjamin—who had just got down to breakfast—at his side.

"We shall have a nasty, hot, muggy day, Ben!"

"Yes," said Ben, "we get these days sometimes in September. Father, if you won't let me have the two hundred, will you let me have one? I don't want to lose this chance, and my friends will have sailed. They are putting in three hundred each, but—"

"How many times are you going to tell me that?" interrupted the squire. "I don't believe it; no, I don't believe you have any friends who are possessed of three hundred to put. It is of no use your bothering, Ben; I haven't got the money to spare."

"Not got it to spare, when you have just come in to twenty thousand pounds!" returned Ben, not, however, venturing to speak in any tone but a conciliating one. "I only wish I had come in to a tithe of it! It was a slice of good luck that you never expected, squire, and you might be generous enough to help me once again."

In truth, the good luck had been so entirely unlooked for, that Squire Carr could not find in his heart to snub Ben for saying so, quite as fiercely as he might otherwise have done. "It was just a chance, Ben, Robert Carr's dying as he did."

"A very good chance for us. Look here, father: I can't stop on here, nagged at by Valentine, out of purse, out of your favour—"

"Whose fault is it that you are out of my favour?" interrupted the squire, taking off his old drab wide-awake to straighten a dent in the brim.

"Well, I suppose it's mine," acknowledged Ben. "What is a hundred pounds to the twenty thousand you have come into? A drop of water in the ocean."

"And if you got the hundred pounds and started with it, you'd be writing home in three months for another hundred! It has always been the case, Ben."

The words seemed to imply symptoms of so great a concession, compared to the positive refusal hitherto accorded him, that Ben Carr's hopes went up like a sky-rocket. He saw the hundred pounds in his possession and himself ploughing the deep waters, as vividly as though the picture had been presented to him in a magic mirror.

"It is a chance that I have never had, squire. These men are steady, industrious, practical fellows, who will keep me to my work, whether I will or not. They go out to make money, and I shall make some. Who knows but I may return home with a fortune to match this, just come to you?"

"Ben, you harp upon this money of Marmaduke's; but let me tell you that I don't know what I should have done without it. I have had nothing but drains upon me for years: you've been one of them."

"The old hypocrite!" thought Ben, "he's rolling in money, besides this new windfall. Well, sir," he said aloud, "I shall write—"

"Who's this?" interrupted the squire, who did not see so well as he once did.

It was the postman. Letters were not frequent at the squire's, as they are at many houses. The man was coming up the avenue, in the distance as yet. Squire Carr walked towards him and stretched out his hand for the letters.

The postman gave him two. One was a large, blue, formidable-looking packet, addressed to himself; the other was a perfumed, mignonne, three-cornered sort of missive, for Benjamin Carr, Esq.

"Here, Ben, I don't know who your correspondent may be," said the squire, tossing him the note. "She's an idiot, that's certain; nobody, above one, would think of sending a doll's thing like that through the post. It's a wonder it wasn't lost."

Benjamin Carr glanced at the handwriting and slipped the note into the pocket of his shooting coat. Sauntering to a little distance, while the squire was busy with his own letter, he there took it out, opened, and began to read it: a closely-written epistle, on thin foreign paper.

He was startled by something very like the bellow of a bull. Turning round, he saw the squire in a fine commotion, and the noise had come from him.

"Why, what is the matter?" exclaimed Ben, advancing.

"Matter!" ejaculated Squire Carr—"matter! They are mad; or else I am dreaming."

He held the formidable document before his eyes. He turned it, he gazed at it, he shook it, he pinched himself to see whether he was dreaming. If any man ever believed that his eyes played him false, Squire Carr believed his did then.

"What is it?" repeated the astonished Ben.

It was a notice from Mr. Fauntleroy that an action was entered upon—to eject him from the possession of that bijou of a house; to wrest from him the fortune; to give Marmaduke's money to Robert Carr; to forbid him to touch or remove so much (his own words just before to his son) as a plated spoon of the effects; to reduce him, in short, to a poor wretched non-inheriting beggar again. Not that all this, or the half of it, was stated; it was implied, and that was enough for the squire's vivid imagination.

"Ben, my boy, what does it mean?" he gasped.

"I'm sure I don't know," said Ben, considerably crestfallen.

"I'm not dreaming, am I?" asked the squire. "Mercy be good to us! What can they have found? Perhaps old Marmaduke made a will after all! They'd never enter an action without being justified. Get the horse into the dog-cart and drive me to the station, Ben. I must go over to see Fauntleroy. Hang him! the sly old villain! I should like to twist his neck."

"But you will promise me the hundred pounds, father?"

"Hundred pounds be shot!" shrieked the squire in a fury. "I've just got notice that I'm ruined, and he asks me for a hundred pounds! No, sir! nor a hundred pence. How can I afford money, now this inheritance is threatened?"

Benjamin Carr had a great mind to tell his father, that even if it were threatened and taken, he was as well off now as he had been a short while before. But it was not a time to press matters, and he drove the squire to the station in silence.

On that busy Saturday morning—and Saturdays were always busy days at the office of Mr. Fauntleroy—the clerks were amazed by the disturbed entrance of Squire Carr, pushing, agitated, restless; far more amazed than was perhaps their master, Mr. Fauntleroy. He had half expected it.

There ensued a hasty explanation; but the squire scarcely allowed himself to listen to it. Of all the blows that could have come upon him, this was the worst.

"And what do you think of yourself, pray, to be taking up a cause against the Carr family, when you have stuck by it for half a century, or it by you?"

"By old Marmaduke; by no others of it," returned Mr. Fauntleroy, who was secretly enjoying the squire's perplexity beyond everything.

"Why do you turn round against him now? I did not expect it of you, Fauntleroy."

"I don't understand you, squire."

"You are turning against the money he left, which is the same thing, wanting to make ducks and drakes of it."

"Marmaduke Curr's grandson came here and asked me if I would act for him as his solicitor, and I assented," said Mr. Fauntleroy. "In entering this action against you, I am but obeying his instructions."

"Marmaduke Carr's grandson!" scoffed the squire. "Who is he, the ill-born cur"—not but that the squire's words were somewhat plainer—"that he should presume to set himself up in his false pretences?"

"Ill-born or well-born, my clients are the same to me, provided their cause is good, and they pay me," coolly rejoined Mr. Fauntleroy.

"Well, is it a hoax?" asked the squire, coming nearer to the point, for Mr. Fauntleroy was taking a stealthy glance at his watch.

"If you mean is the action a hoax, most certainly it is not. Robert Carr looks upon it that he has the best right to his grandfather's money, and—"

"Why do you call him Robert Carr?" interposed the squire, in a flash of anger.

"What else can I call him? I wish you'd be a little cooler, and let me finish. And he has given me instructions to spare no pains, no expense, in maintaining this action against you."

"Is he a fool?" asked the squire. "It's one of two things: either he is a fool—for he must know that such an action can't be sustained under present circumstances, and so must you—or else he has got some secret information that I am in ignorance of. Has he got it? Is there a will of Marmaduke's found?"

"Of course there's not," said Mr. Fauntleroy, taken by surprise; "I should have heard of it, if there had been. As to any other information, I can't say; I don't know of any."

"Look here, Fauntleroy: if there is to be an action—not that I should think the fellow will be mad enough to go on with it—will you act for me?"

"I can't," said Mr. Fauntleroy; "I am acting for him."

"Turn him over. Who's he? I'd rather have you myself. And I must say you might have been neighbourly enough not to take this up against me."

"What does that signify? If I had not taken it up, somebody else would. And you have your own solicitors, you know, squire."

The squire growled. His solicitors were Mynn and Mynn, of Eckford—quiet, steady-going practitioners; but in so desperate a cause as this, the squire would have felt himself safer with a keen and not over-scrupulous man, such as Mr. Fauntleroy.

"You will not act for me, then?"

"I can't, squire."

"And you mean to carry it on to action?"

"I must do it. They are my positive instructions."

Squire Carr turned off in desperation, nearly upsetting Mr. Kenneth as he stamped through the outer office. As fast as he could, he stamped up to the railway station, and took the first train to Eckford, arriving at the office of Mynn and Mynn in a white heat.

Mynn and Mynn themselves were nearly myths, so far as their clients could get hold of them. Old Mynn had the gout perpetually; and the younger brother, George Mynn, had a chronic sort of asthma, and could not speak to people half his time. What business was absolutely necessary for a principal to do, George Mynn mostly did it. He made the journeys to London, he attended the sessions and assizes at Westerbury; but it very often happened that, when a client called at the office, neither would be there.

As it was, on this day. A young man of the name of Richards was head of the office just now, for the managing clerk had died, and Mynn and Mynn were looking out for another. A sharp, clever, unscrupulous man was this Richards, who, if he proved as clever when he got into practice for himself, would stand a fair chance of getting out of it again. He was alone when Squire Carr entered, and leaned over his desk to shake hands with him. He was a great friend of Valentine Carr's, and sometimes dined at the squire's on Sundays—a thin, weasely sort of man, not unlike Valentine himself, with a cast in one eye.

"Mr. George Mynn here to-day?"

"He is here to-day, squire; but he is not in just now. He's gone to Westerbury."

"I want to see him; I must see him," cried the squire, wiping his hot brows. "The most infamous thing has happened, Richards, that you ever heard of. They are going to try and wrest my Uncle Marmaduke's property from me."

"Who is?" asked Richards, in wonder.

"The son of that Robert Carr who went off with Martha Ann Hughes. It was before your time; but perhaps you have heard of it. There are children; and one of them has been down here, and has given Fauntleroy instructions to proceed against me and force me to give up the property."

"But I thought there was no marriage?" cried Richards. "Mr. Mynn was talking about it the other day."

"Neither was there."

Richards paused a moment, and then burst into a fit of laughter. To make pretensions of claiming property in such a case, amused him excessively.

"Well, they are doing it," said Squire Carr. "But I am astonished at Fauntleroy taking up such a cause. It's infamous, you know. They can do it only to annoy me; for they must be aware it's an action that will not lie."

"I say, squire, you must take care of one thing," said Richards, with the familiarity that characterised him, and which to some minds was exceedingly offensive—"mind they don't get up a false marriage."

"A false marriage! Why, the parties are dead."

"Oh, I mean proofs—false proofs. I've known such things done. When a fortune's at stake, you know, any means seem right ones."

"And I dare say they'd be capable of it," assented the squire. "Well, it must be seen to immediately. Here's what I had sent from Fauntleroy."

He drew out of his pocket the large letter, and Richards ran his eyes over it.

"They mean mischief," was his laconic remark.

"When can I see Mr. George Mynn?" asked the squire, the usual difficulties of getting at that gentleman striking upon his mind, especially after the last sentence, as a personal wrong. "Why doesn't he get a confidential clerk to do the outdoor work, so as to be in to see clients himself?"

"They are about engaging one, I believe," said Mr. Richards, alluding to the confidential clerk; "but he won't enter before December or January."

"Not before December or January!" retorted Squire Carr, as if that were another personal wrong.

"I heard George Mynn say we could do without one until then. So we can. The assize business is over, and there won't be much press for the next month or two. For my part, I wish they'd do without one for good. I could manage all they want done, if they'd let me."

"Well, look you here, Richards. I shall go on to the 'Bell' and get a bit of dinner at the ordinary, and then I shall come back here and wait till he comes in."

"He mayn't come in at all again to-day—sure not to, if he doesn't get back from Westerbury till late," was the satisfactory rejoinder of Richards; and Squire Carr felt that he should like to strike somebody in the dilemma, if he only knew whom.

"Then you will have to take my instructions," he said, sharply; "I shall be back in an hour."

"Very good," said Mr. Richards. "And we can talk this business over to-morrow, squire, as much as you like; for I am coming to your place for the day. I've promised Valentine, and I want to make the acquaintance of your second son."

For this Mr. Richards was but a clerk of some months standing at Mynn and Mynn's; to which situation he had come from a distance, and, therefore, had not yet enjoyed the honour of an introduction to Mr. Benjamin Carr.

Thus the great cause, "Carr versus Carr," was inaugurated. Those connected with it little dreamt of the strange excitement it was to create, ere the termination came.

CHAPTER XI

THE LAST OF ROBERT CARR

By a bright fire in her handsome and most comfortable drawing-room, in her widow's cap—assumed, now that all hope had died out—sat Mrs. Dundyke. The October wind was whistling without, the October rain was falling on the window panes; and there was a look of anxiety on her otherwise calm face, still so fair and attractive, as she listened to the storm. The summer and autumn, up to the close of September, had been remarkably warm and fine; but when October came in, it brought bad weather with it.

A gust and a patter, worse than any that had gone before, aroused Mrs. Dundyke from her seat. She laid her work—a woollen comforter, that she was knitting—on the small and beautiful table at her side, inlaid with mother-of-pearl, and walked to the window.

"I wonder whether he is out in it?" she said, as she watched the trees bending in the storm. "This anxiety is killing him. The very work is killing him. Abroad in all weathers; out of one damp church into another; getting heated with his weak state and the ardour of the pursuit, and then becoming chilled in some sudden storm such as this! He may find the record, perhaps, but he will never live to reap the benefit."

Need you be told that Mrs. Dundyke's soliloquy applied to Robert Carr? He was staying with her. When he went back to London from Westerbury, and sought Mrs. Dundyke, to deliver certain messages of the kindest nature sent by him from Mr. Arkell and Travice, she had insisted upon his making her house his home while he remained in London to pursue his search.

And he did so; and began his toilsome search of the London church marriage registers. What a wearying task it was, let those testify who may have been obliged to enter upon such. By dint of a great deal of trouble, and of correspondence with Mr. Fauntleroy, and recalled recollections from middle-aged people in Westerbury, who had been young men once and friends of the elder Robert Carr, he, the present Robert Carr, succeeded in ascertaining the place where his father and mother had sojourned that fortnight in London. It was in one of the quiet streets of the Strand, in the parish of St. Clement Danes. But when St. Clement Danes' register was examined, no entry of any such marriage could be found there; and for the first time since the blow fell, Robert Carr felt his heart sink with a vague fear that he dared not dwell upon.

It had seemed to him so easy! He had felt as sure a trust in his mother's marriage as he felt in Heaven. It was only to find out where they had stayed that fortnight in London, and search the parish church register; for there, and only there, Robert Carr argued, the marriage had taken place. But there, it was now evident, that it had not taken place, and he was all at sea.

He began with the other churches; he knew not what else to do. In Holland they could not have been married, from the want of legal papers, and other matters, necessary to foreigners united abroad. He searched the churches nearest to St. Clement Danes first, and then went on to others, and others, and others. He would go up after breakfast from his kind friend, who was nursing him like a mother, and begin his daily task; out of one church into another, as she had phrased it, in all weathers—rain, hail, storm—and go back at night again utterly wearied out.

Mrs. Dundyke stood at the window watching the rain. She fancied it was beginning to grow dusk; but it was not time just yet, and the afternoon was a dark one. He would not be home yet awhile, she was thinking. He stopped in those cold churches as long as there was a ray of light to see by. Mrs. Dundyke was turning from the window, when she saw an omnibus stop, and Robert Carr get out of it. He seemed worse than usual; weaker in strength, more tottering in frame; and as he looked up at her with a faint, sad smile, a conviction came over her that she should not be able to save the life of this poor young man; that all her care, all her comforts, all her ample income would not benefit him. And how very ample her income would for the future be, she had not known until that day. She was a rich lady for this world; she might ride in her carriage, if she chose, and be grand for all time.

"Oh! Robert!" she exclaimed, meeting him on the stairs—and she had taken to call him by the familiar name, as she might a son—"I fear you have got very wet! I am so glad you came home early!"

He walked unsteadily to the easy chair by the fire, and sunk in it. Mrs. Dundyke, with him daily, saw not the change that every hour was surely making in him; but she did notice how wan and ill he looked this evening.

"Have you not been well to-day, Robert?"

"Not very. I have been spitting so much of that blood again. And I felt so weary too; so sick of it all."

"There's no success, then, again!"

"None. Altogether, I thought I'd leave it for the day, and come back and take a rest."

He sighed as he spoke, but the sigh broke off with a moaning sound. Mrs. Dundyke glanced at him. She had resumed her knitting—which was a chest protector for himself—until the wine that she had rung for should be brought.

"Robert, are you losing heart?"

"No, I can never lose that. There was a marriage, if we could only find out where. You would be as sure of it as I am, dear Mrs. Dundyke, had you known my mother."

Mrs. Dundyke made no rejoinder. For herself, she had never fully believed in the marriage at all, but she was not cruel enough to say so. She sat watching him over her knitting: now bending forward with his thin hands spread out to the warmth of the fire; now suddenly bringing his hands to his chest as he coughed, choked; now lying back in the chair, panting, his thin nostrils working, his breath coming in great gasps; and there came in that moment over Mrs. Dundyke as she looked, a conviction—she knew not whence or why—that a very, very short period would bring the end.

She felt her face grow moist with a cold moisture. How was it that she had been so blind to the obvious truth? She knitted two whole rows of knitting before she spoke, and then she told him, with a calm voice, that she should write for his wife.

"How kind you are!" he murmured. "I shall never repay you."

Mrs. Dundyke laughed cheerfully.

"I don't want repayment. There is nothing to repay."

"Nothing to repay! No kindly friendship, no trouble, no cost! I wonder how much I cost you in wine alone?"

"Robert," she said, in a low, earnest tone—though she wondered whether he might not be jesting—"do you know what they tell me my future income will be? Mr. Littelby was here to-day, giving me an account of things, for I put my poor husband's affairs into his hands on my return. It will not be much less than two thousand a year."

The amount of the sum quite startled him.

"Two thousand a year!"

"It will indeed, as they tell me. By the articles of partnership I am allowed a handsome income from the house in Fenchurch-street; but the chief of the money comes from speculations my husband has been engaged in for many years, in connexion with a firm on the Stock Exchange. Safe speculations, and profitable; not hazardous ones. This money is realized, and put out in the Funds, in what they call the Five-per-Cents.; and I shall have nearly two thousand a year. I had no idea of it; and the puzzle to me now is, how I shall spend it. Don't you think I require a few kind visitors to help me?"

Before he could answer, there came on a violent fit of coughing, worse than any she had yet seen, and quite a little stream of blood trickled from his mouth. It was nothing particularly new, but that night Mrs. Carr was written for in haste.

"Tell her to bring the desk with her," said Robert; and Mrs. Dundyke wrote down the words just as he spoke them.

But he rallied again, and in a day or two was actually out as before, prosecuting his search amidst those hopeless churches. He confided what he called a secret to Mrs. Dundyke—namely, that he had not confessed to his wife that any suspicion was cast upon his birth. The honest truth was, Robert Carr shrunk from it; for he knew it would so alarm and grieve her. She was well connected; had fallen in love with the young Cambridge student during a visit she was paying in England; and when the time came that marriage was spoken of, her friends raised some objection because Robert Carr's father was not of gentle blood, but was in business as a merchant. What she would say when she came to know that he was suspected of not being even that merchant's legitimate son, Robert scarcely cared to speculate.

She arrived in an afternoon at Mrs. Dundyke's, having come direct to London Bridge by the steamer from Rotterdam. Robert was out in London, as usual; but Mrs. Dundyke was not alone: Mildred Arkell was with her. Perhaps of all people, next to his wife, Mildred had been most shocked at the fate of Mr. Dundyke. This was the first time she had seen his widow, for she had been away in the country with Lady Dewsbury.

A young, pretty woman, looking little more than a girl, with violet-blue eyes, dark hair, and a flush upon her cheeks. Mrs. Dundyke marvelled at her youth—that she should be a wife since three years, and the mother of two children.

"I wrote to you to be sure to bring the children," said Mrs. Dundyke.

"I know: it was very kind. But I thought, as Robert was ill, they might disturb him with their noise. They are but babies; and I left them behind."

Mrs. Dundyke was considering how she could best impart the news of the suspected birth to this poor, unconscious young lady. "If you could give her a hint of it yourself, should she arrive during my absence!" Robert Carr had said to Mrs. Dundyke that very morning, with the hectic deepening on his hollow cheeks. And Mrs. Dundyke began her task.

And a sad shock it proved to be. Mrs. Carr, accustomed to the legal formalities that attend a marriage in the country of her birth, and without which formalities the ceremony cannot be performed, could not for some time be led to understand how, if there was a marriage, it could have been kept a secret. There were many points difficult to make her, a foreigner, understand; but when she had mastered them, she grew strangely interested in the recital of the past, and Mildred Arkell, as a resident in Westerbury at the time, was called upon to repeat every little detail connected with the departure of her husband's father and mother from their native place. In listening, Mrs. Carr's cheek grew hectic as her husband's.

But she had her secret also, which she had been keeping from her husband. She told it now to Mrs. Dundyke. Something was wrong with affairs at Rotterdam. The surviving partners of the house, three covetous old Dutchmen, disputed their late partner's right (or rather that of his children) to draw out certain monies from the house; at the death of Robert Carr it lapsed to the house, they said. This was the account Mrs. Carr gave, but it was not a very clear one, neither did she seem to understand the case. The Carrs had in the house other money, about which there was no dispute, but even this the firm refused to pay out until the other matter was settled. The effect was, that the Carrs had no money to go on with; and there would probably be litigation.

"I did not tell Robert, because I was in hopes it would be comfortably decided without him," said Mrs. Carr. "By the way, you wrote me word that Robert said I was to bring over the desk. Which desk did he mean? his own or his father's?"

"I really don't know," replied Mrs. Dundyke; "he was very ill when he spoke, and I wrote the words down just as he spoke them."

"Well, I have brought both; I know he examined Mr. Carr's desk after his death, and he locked it up again, and has the key with him. His own desk also was at home; so, not knowing which was meant, I brought the two."

When Robert Carr came home that evening he looked awfully ill. The expression is not too strong a one; there was something in his attenuated face, its sunken eyes, its ghastly colour, and its working nostrils, that struck the beholder with awe. Mrs. Dundyke was alone in the dining parlour when he came in, and was shocked to see him. Whether it was the long day's work on his decreasing strength—for he had remained later than usual—she could not tell, but he had never looked so near death as this.

"Oh, Robert!" was her involuntary exclamation; "I had better go up and prepare your wife before she sees you."

He suffered her to put him in the great invalid chair she had surreptitiously had brought in a day or two before; he drank the restoring cordial she tendered him; he was passive in her hands as a child, in his great weakness. "I'm afraid I must have a week's rest," he said to her, as she busied herself taking off his gloves, and smoothing his poor damp hair. "My strength seems to be failing unaccountably; I don't know how I have got through the day."

"Oh yes, yes," she eagerly assented; "a little rest; that is what you want. You shall lie in bed all to-morrow."

"Has Emma brought the children?"

"No. They are quite well," she says; "I am going to send her down to you. And, Robert, she knows all, and says she'll help to search the registers herself."

Mrs. Dundyke spoke in a light-hearted tone, but before she went upstairs she sent an urgent message for the doctor.

And when the surgeon came, he said there was no further hope whatever, as, indeed, there had not been for some time now, and that a day or two would "decide."

Decide what? But that he did not say.

In one sense of the word, it may be said that death had come suddenly upon Robert Carr. Had he been less absorbed in that one point of worldly interest, he might have seen its approach more clearly. Not until the morning succeeding his wife's arrival, did he look it fully in the face; and then he found that it was upon the very threshold, was entering in at the opened door.

All the bustle, the anxiety as to temporal interests, the plans and provisions for the future for those to be left behind, ensued. Mrs. Dundyke hastily summoned a legal gentleman, Mr. Littelby. He was a solicitor of many years' standing, not in practice for himself, but conducting the business of an eminent legal firm. He was an old friend of the Dundykes, and Robert Carr had seen him several times; indeed his advice and assistance had been of much service in the search of the church registers. Mr. Littelby was about leaving his present situation, and was in negotiation with a firm in the country for another. Mrs. Dundyke sent up a hasty summons for him.

A handsome bedchamber, in which was every comfort, a bright fire in the hearth, a bed, on which lay a shadowy form, a pale shadowy face, a young weeping girl standing near, soon to be a widow, and you have almost the last scene in the short life of Robert Carr.

He was dying, poor fellow, with that secret, which he had no doubt shortened his life in endeavouring to trace, still unsolved; and he was dying with the conviction, that the proofs did exist somewhere, as fully upon him as it ever had been.

"Emma!"

She dried her eyes, and tried to hide that they had been wet, as she heard the call. The day was getting on.

"Is Littelby not come yet?"

"Yes, I think he is. Some one came a few minutes ago, and is downstairs with Mrs. Dundyke. I think I hear them coming up."

Mrs. Dundyke was coming into the room with a gentleman, a middle-aged man with a sharp nose and pleasant dark eyes. It was Mr. Littelby. They were left alone together—the lawyer and the dying man. But it was a very short and simple task, this will-making. Over almost as soon as begun.

"He asked me to tie you up with trustees, Emma," said the dying man; "but I have left all to you— children, and money, and all else. You will love them, won't you, when I am gone?"

"Oh, Robert, yes!" she said, with a burst of sorrow. "I wish I and they could go with you."

"And, Emma, mind that you prosecute this search. I have asked Littelby to help you, and he will. He says he expects to leave London at the end of the year, for he is in negotiation with another firm; but I dare say it will be found before then. Let that search be your first and greatest task."

She said it should be—she would have promised anything in that parting hour. She lay, with her pretty hair on the counterpane, and her wet eyes turned to him, devouring his last looks, listening to his last words. Almost literally the last in this world, for, before the close of the afternoon, Robert Carr fell into a lethargy, from which he did not awake alive.

And those two lone women were together in the house of the dead—widows indeed. The one deprived of her young husband almost on the threshold of life; the other bereft, she knew not how, of her many years' partner. Poor Mrs. Dundyke had hardly wanted more sorrow in her desolate home.

So far as ease in the future went, she was well off. The large income mentioned by her to Robert Carr would indeed be hers. It was chiefly the result of that first thousand pounds Mr. Dundyke had risked on the Stock Exchange. Fortune had favoured him in an unusual degree. You remember the nails in the horse-shoe, how they doubled and doubled: so it had seemed to be with the thousand pounds of Mr. Dundyke. But poor Mrs. Carr's future fortune was all uncertain. Whether she would have sufficient to keep her children in easy competency, or whether she would find herself, like so many more gentlewomen, obliged to do something for her bread in this world of changes, she did not know.

Even in this week that succeeded her husband's death, she was applied to for money, which she could not find. The application came from Mr. Fauntleroy. Lawyers have a peculiar facility for getting rid of money, as some of us have been obliged to know to our cost; and Mr. Fauntleroy had already disposed of the first fifty pounds advanced to him, and wanted more if he was to go on with the case.

Mrs. Carr had it not. Until affairs should be settled in Rotterdam, she had no such sum at her command. She could have procured it indeed from many friends, but she was sorely puzzled what to do for the best. On the one hand, there was the dying promise to her husband to pursue this cause; on the other, there was the extreme doubt whether there was any real cause to pursue. If there was no cause, why, then, how worse than foolish it would be to spend money over a chimera. Many and many were the anxious consultations she had with Mrs. Dundyke, even while her husband lay dead in the house.

On the day after the funeral—and there had been no mourner found to follow that poor young man to his last home, but one who had been fellow curate with him, and who was now in London—Mrs. Dundyke and her visitor were alone when a gentleman was shown in. A fine man yet, of middle age, but with a slight bend in the shoulders, as if from care, and grey threads mingling with his dark hair. It was not a time for Mrs. Carr to see strangers, and she rose to quit the drawing-room, after hurriedly replacing some papers in a desk she was examining. But there was something so noble, so pleasing, so refined, in the countenance of the man standing there, his hands held out to Mrs. Dundyke, and a sweet smile upon his lips, that she stopped involuntarily.

"Have you forgotten me, Betsey?"

For the moment she really had, for he was much changed; but the voice and the smile recalled her memory, and with a glad cry of recognition Mrs. Dundyke sprang forward, and received on her lips a sisterly kiss.

"Emma, don't go. This is your husband's friend, and my brother-in-law, William Arkell."

Mrs. Carr gladly held out her hand; her pretty face raised in its widow's cap. A shade came over William Arkell's at seeing that badge on one so young.

He had a little business in London, he explained, connected with the transfer of some of his property, and came up, instead of writing; came up—there was no doubt of it, though he did not say so—that he might have the opportunity of seeing Mrs. Dundyke.

Mrs. Carr left the room, and Mr. Arkell drew his chair nearer to his sister-in-law.

"You have heard nothing further, Betsey, of—of of your lost husband?"

She shook her head; she should never hear that again.

It was only natural that she should relate the circumstances to him, now that they met, although he had heard them so fully from Mr. Prattleton. Where much mystery exists, especially pertaining to undiscovered crime, it seems that we can never be tired of attempting to solve it. Human nature is the same all the world over, and these things do possess an irrepressible attraction for the human heart—very human it is, now and then. Mr. Arkell sat with his elbow on the arm of the chair, and his chin resting on his hand; he was looking dreamily into the fire as they talked.

"I should strongly suspect that Mr. Hardcastle, Betsey; should you know him if you saw him again?"

"Know him! know that same Mr. Hardcastle!" she repeated, wondering at what seemed so superfluous a question. "I should know him to the very end of my life. I should know him by his eyes, if by nothing else. They seem to be always before mine."

"Were they peculiar eyes, then?"

"Very. The first time I saw him, that morning at breakfast, his eyes seemed to strike upon my memory with a sort of repulsion. I felt sure I had seen eyes like them somewhere; and that the other eyes had caused me repulse likewise. All the time we were together at Geneva, his eyes kept puzzling me; it was like a word we have on the tip of the tongue, every moment thinking we must recollect it, but it keeps baffling us. So was it with Mr. Hardcastle's eyes; and it was only in the moment he was leaving for Genoa that I recollected whose they were like."

"And whose were they like?"

"A gentleman's I never saw but twice; once at your house, at your own wedding breakfast, and once in the week subsequent to it at Mrs. Daniel Arkell's: Benjamin Carr."

"Who?" exclaimed Mr. Arkell.

"Benjamin Carr, the present squire's son."

He sat with sudden uprightness in his chair, staring at her. The strange scene, when Robert Carr had likened Benjamin to the suspected murderer, was flashing into his mind. What did it mean, that agitation of Benjamin's? What did this likeness, now spoken of, mean? A wild doubt of horror came creeping over Mr. Arkell.

He opened his lips to speak, but recollected himself before the hasty impulse was put in force. Mrs. Dundyke noticed nothing unusual; her eyes and her thoughts were alike absorbed in the past.

"Will you describe this Mr. Hardcastle to me?" he asked presently, breaking the pause of silence: "as accurately and minutely as you can."

He noted every point that she gave in answer, every little detail. And he came to the conclusion that if Benjamin Carr was not Mr. Hardcastle, he might certainly have sat for his portrait.

"Unfortunately," said Mr. Arkell, speaking more to himself than to her, "were this man apprehended and punished, it could not bring poor Mr. Dundyke back to life."

"Alas no, it could not. I would almost rather let things remain as they are. If the man is guilty, his daily life must be one perpetual, ever-present punishment."

"Ay, indeed," murmured Mr. Arkell; "better leave him to it."

And he rather persistently, had her suspicions been awakened, led the conversation into other channels.

"Let me say to you what I chiefly came to say, Betsey," he whispered to Mrs. Dundyke in parting. "This has been a sudden and unexpected blow for you. I do not know how you may be left in regard to means; but if you have need of help, temporary or otherwise, you will let me know it. I have a right to give it, you know: you are Charlotte's sister."

The tears fell from her eyes on his hands as she pressed them gratefully in hers. She did not say how well she was left off, for her heart was full; she only thanked him, and intimated that she had enough.

Mr. Arkell went away in a sort of perplexed dream. Could that suspicion of Benjamin Carr be a true one? He would be silent; but it was nearly certain to come out in some other way: murder generally does. From Mrs. Dundyke's he went straight up to Lady Dewsbury's, and found that she and Miss Arkell had again gone out of town. It was a disappointment; he had not seen Mildred for years and years.

Mrs. Carr came back to the room, and resumed her occupation after he had gone—that of searching amid the papers in the desk of the late Robert Carr the elder. It had proved to be his own desk that her husband had wanted her to bring over—but that is of no consequence. She was searching for a very simple thing—merely a receipt for a small sum of money which she had herself paid for Mr. Carr just before he died, and had returned the receipt to him; but it is often upon the merest trifles that the great events of life turn. The claim for this small sum she heard was sent in again, and she thought perhaps she might find the receipt in the desk, where Mr. Carr had sometimes used to place such papers. She did not find that, but she found something else.

Mrs. Dundyke was sitting by, between the other side of the table and the fire. She was talking about the Arkells—the kindly generosity of William, the selfishness and persistent ill-will of Charlotte.

"And the children?" asked Mrs. Carr, as she stood, opening paper after paper. "Do they follow their father or mother in their treatment of you?"

"Of the daughters I know little; I may say nothing. They have never noticed me, even by a message. But the son—ah! you should know Travice Arkell! I cannot tell you how I love him. Will you believe that Charlotte—What is the matter?"

Emma Carr had come upon a sealed letter in an old blotting-book. The superscription was in the handwriting of her father-in-law, and ran as follows:—"To my son Robert. Not to be opened until after the death of my father, Marmaduke Carr."

She uttered the exclamation which had attracted the attention of Mrs. Dundyke, and sat down on her chair. With a prevision that this letter had something to do with the question of the marriage, she tore the letter open and sat gazing on it spellbound.

"Have you found the receipt, my dear?"

Not the receipt. With her cheeks flushing, her pulses quickening, her hands trembling, she laid the letter open before Mrs. Dundyke. "Robert was right; Robert was right! Oh! if he had but lived to read this! How could he have overlooked this, when he examined the desk after his father's death? It must have slipped between the leaves of the blotting-book, and been hidden there."

"MY DEAR SON ROBERT,—There may arise a question of your legitimacy when the time shall arrive for you to take possession of your grandfather's property. On the day I left Westerbury for ever, I married your mother, Martha Ann Hughes—she would not else have come with me. We were married in her parish church at Westerbury, St. James the Less, and you will find it duly entered in the register. This will be sufficient to prove your rights, so that there may be no litigation.

"Your affectionate father,
"RT. CARR."

And, scarcely knowing whether she was awake or dreaming, while Mrs. Dundyke, in vain attempted to recover her astonishment, Mrs. Carr wrote a line of explanation inside an envelope, and despatched the all-important document to Westerbury to Mr. Fauntleroy.

CHAPTER XII

MR RICHARDS' MORNING CALL

Mr. Fauntleroy was seated at breakfast, when this missive reached him. His two strapping daughters were with him: buxom, vulgar damsels, attired this morning in Magenta skirts and straw-coloured jackets. Mrs. Fauntleroy had been some years dead, and they ruled the house, and nearly ruled the lawyer. Strong-willed man though he was, carrying things out of doors with an iron hand, and sometimes a coarse one, he would yield to domestic tyranny; as many another has to do, if it were but known. It was fond tyranny, however, here; for whatever may have been the faults of the Miss Fauntleroys, they loved their father with a tender love. They were the only children of the lawyer—his co-heiresses—and to him they were as the apple of his eye.

The room they sat in faced the garden—a large fine garden at the back of the house. The leaves were red with the glowing tints of autumn, and as Mr. Fauntleroy looked up from his well-covered breakfast-table at the October sky, he made some remark upon the famous run the hounds would make; and a half sigh escaped his lips that his own hunting days were gone for ever.

"Would you be afraid to ride now, pa?"

"Look at my weight, Lizzy."

"I think some who ride are as heavy as you," was Miss Elizabeth's answer.

"Ah! but they are used to it; they have kept the practice up. Never a better follower than I in my younger days—always in at the death—but that's a long while ago now. I gave up hunting when I settled down. What d'ye call that, Bab?"

He was pointing with his fork to a dish apart. Miss Barbara looked at it critically, and did not recognise it. "I dare say it's some dish the new cook has sent up. It looks nice, pa."

"Hand some of it over, then," said Mr. Fauntleroy.

She helped him plentifully. The lawyer and his daughters were all fond of nice dishes, and liked good servings of them; as perhaps their large frames and their high colours testified. Miss Lizzy pushed up her plate.

"I'll take some, too, Bab."

"About that pic-nic, pa? Are we—"

"Oh! I don't know," interrupted the lawyer, with his mouth full. "You girls are always bothering for something of the sort. Get it up if you like, only don't expect me to go."

"The Arkells will join us, pa; Bab has asked them."

"Of course," said the lawyer with a loud laugh. "She'd not fail to ask them. How was Mr. Travice, Bab?"

"I shan't tell you, pa," answered Miss Bab, tossing her head in demonstrative indignation, though her whole face beamed with a gratified smile. "The idea! How should I know anything about Mr. Travice Arkell!"

"A good-looking young fellow," said the lawyer, significantly. "Perhaps others may be finding him so as well as you, Bab."

"Pa, then, you are a stupid! And I want to know who it is that's coming to dinner to-day?"

"Coming to dinner to-day, Bab? Nobody that I know of."

"You said last night you had invited somebody, but you went to sleep when I asked who."

"Oh! I remember. I met him yesterday, and he said he was going to call to-day. I told him to come in and dine, if he liked. It's Ben Carr."

"Oh!" said Miss Bab, with a depreciating sniff. "Only Ben Carr!"

"He's over here for a few days, stopping with Mrs. Lewis. He wants to be off to Australia or some place, but the squire turns crusty about advancing the funds. Ben and he came to an explosion over it, and Ben has made himself scarce at home in consequence. What's the time, Bab?"

Barbara Fauntleroy glanced over her father's head at the French clock behind him. "It's twenty-five minutes after nine, pa."

"Eh!" cried the lawyer, starting up. "Why, what a time I have been at breakfast! You girls should not keep me with your chatter."

He gathered up his letters, which lay in a stack beside him, and hastened into his office. The head clerk, Kenneth, was in the outer room, with one of the other clerks, a young man named Omer. Mr. Fauntleroy went in to ask a question.

"Have those deeds come in yet from the engrosser's, Kenneth?"

"No, sir."

"Not come! Why they promised them for nine o'clock this morning, and now it's half-past. Go for them yourself, Kenneth, at once, and give them a word of a sort. It's not the first time by many that they've been behindhand."

Mr. Kenneth took his hat and went out; and his master shut himself in his private room and began to open his letters. Sometimes he opened his letters at breakfast time, at others he carried them, as now, into the office.

Amidst these letters was the envelope despatched by Mrs. Carr, containing the important letter found in the desk. To describe Mr. Fauntleroy's astonishment when he read it, would be beyond mortal pen. To think that they should have been looking half over the world for this marriage record, when it was lying quietly under their very nose!

"By George!" exclaimed Mr. Fauntleroy. "A clever trick, though, of Robert Carr's—if he did so marry her. The secret was well kept. He would be sure we should suspect any place rather than Westerbury." "Omer!" he called out aloud.

The clerk came in, in answer, and stood before the table of Mr. Fauntleroy.

"Go down to St. James the Less, and look through the register. See if there's a marriage entered between Robert Carr and—what was the girl's Christian name?—Martha Ann Hughes. Stop a minute, I'll give you the date of the year. And—Omer—keep a silent tongue in your head."

Mr. Fauntleroy nodded significantly, and his clerk went out, knowing what that mandate meant, and that it might not be disobeyed. He came back after a while and went in to Mr. Fauntleroy.

"Well?" said the latter, looking up eagerly.

"It is there, sir."

"By George!" repeated the lawyer. "Only to think of that! That's all, Omer," he added, after a pause. "Mr. Kenneth wants you. And mind what I charged you as to a silent tongue."

"No fear, sir," said Omer, as he retired. And to give him his due there was no fear. One clerk had been discharged from Mr. Fauntleroy's office six months before, some tattling having been traced back to him; but Omer was of a silent nature, and cautious besides.

"I shall never be surprised at anything again," soliloquized Mr. Fauntleroy. "A week longer, and I should have thrown up the cause, unless the Holland Carrs had come forward with money. Won't I go on with it now! But—I suppose—" he continued more slowly, and in due deliberation, "the cause will be at an end now. Old Carr can't hold out in the face of this. Shall I tell of it? If I don't—and they don't else come to know of it—and the cause goes on, there'll be a pretty picking for both sides; and old Carr can afford it, for it's his pocket that will have to stand costs now. I'm not obliged to tell them; and I won't," concluded Mr. Fauntleroy.

But this little cunning plan of secrecy on the part of Mr. Fauntleroy was destined to be defeated. Mynn and Mynn, the solicitors of Eckford, were in negotiation with a gentleman in London to take the head of their office, and act as its chief during their own frequent absence. This gentleman, by one of those coincidences that arise in this world, to help our projects or baffle them, as the case may be, happened to be Mr. Littelby. The negotiation had been opened for some little time, and was only waiting for a personal interview for completion; Mr. Littelby himself being rather anxious for it, as it held out greater advantages than he enjoyed in his present post, one of which was a possible partnership. Mr. George Mynn made a journey to London to see him; and while he was gone, it chanced that the clerk, Richards, had occasion to see Mr. Fauntleroy.

He, Richards, arrived in Westerbury betimes on this same morning, and was told by Kenneth that he might go in to Mr. Fauntleroy. Richards found, however, that the room was empty; Mr. Fauntleroy having quitted it for an instant, leaving the inner door ajar.

The morning's letters, open, lay in a stack on the table, one upon another, faces upwards. Mr. Richards, a prying man, with a curiosity as sharp as his nose, and both were sharp as a needle, saw these letters, and took the liberty of bending his body forward from the spot where he stood, to bring his eyes within range of their contents. He read the first, which did him no good whatever; and then gently lifted it an inch slant-wise with his thumb and finger, and so came to the second. That likewise afforded him scant gratification; for it did not concern him at all, or any business with which he could possibly be connected, and he lifted it gingerly and came to the third. The third was the all-important letter of the deceased Robert Carr; and Mr. Richards read it with devouring eyes.

He did not care to go on now to the other letters. This was enough; and he regaled himself with a second perusal. A faint foot-fall in the passage warned him, and Mr. Richards stole away from danger.

Mr. Fauntleroy entered, coming bustling in by the door he had left ajar. Surprised perhaps to see the room tenanted which he had left empty, he glanced at his letters. Thought is quick. They were lying in the stack just as he had placed them, certainly undisturbed for any sign they gave; and the visitor was sitting yards off, in a remote chair behind the other door, his legs crossed and his hat held on his knees.

"Ah, Richards! you are here early this morning!"

"I was obliged to come early, sir, to get back in time," said Richards as he rose. "Mr. Mynn is ill, as usual, and Mr. George went to London yesterday afternoon; so the office is left to me."

"Gone to engage his new clerk, isn't he?" asked Mr. Fauntleroy, who had no more objection than Richards to hear somewhat of his neighbours' business.

"I believe so; gone to see him, at all events," replied Richards, speaking with scant ceremony; but it was in his nature so to do. "They want him to come next month, I hear."

"What's his name?"

"Littelton, or Littelby, or some such name. I heard them talking of him in their room. We are going to have a busy winter of it, Mr. Fauntleroy," continued the candid Richards, brushing a speck off his hat; "so the governors want the new man to come to us next month, or in December at latest. We have three causes already on hand for the spring assizes."

"That's pretty well for your quiet folks," returned Mr. Fauntleroy, as he sat down and placed a large weight on the stack of letters. "Whose are they?"

"Well, there's that old-standing cause of the Whitcombs, the remanet from last assizes; and there's a new one that I suppose I must not talk about: it's a breach of trust affair, and our side want it kept close, meaning to have a try at going in for a compromise, which they'll never get: and then there's your cause, Carr versus Carr. But, Mr. Fauntleroy, surely you'll never bring that into court! you can't win, you know."

Mr. Fauntleroy's eyes rested lovingly for a moment on the stack of letters. "If clients are sanguine without reasonable cause, we can't help it you know, Richards."

"Well, how those Holland Carrs can be sanguine bangs me hollow!" was the retort of Mr. Richards. "They've never had the ghost of a case from the first. I was dining at the old squire's on Sunday again, and we got talking of it. The old man was saying he thought the Carrs over in Holland must be mad, to persist risking their money in this way; and so they must be. There never could have been any marriage, Mr. Fauntleroy: I dare say you feel as sure of it as everybody else does."

Mr. Fauntleroy shrugged his huge shoulders. "The clergyman is dead; and the rest may not be so sanguine as he was. I confess I did think him a little mad. And now to your business, Richards. I suppose you have come about that tithe affair. Will Kenneth do for you? I am busy this morning."

"Kenneth won't do until I have had a word with yourself, and shown you a paper," replied Richards, taking out his letter-case. "Just look at that, Mr. Fauntleroy."

Mr. Fauntleroy unfolded the paper handed to him. It had nothing to do with our history; but he apparently found it so interesting or important, that Richards was not dismissed for nearly an hour. And at his departure, to make up for lost time, Mr. Fauntleroy set to work with a will: one of his first tasks being to drop a line to Mrs. Carr, acknowledging the receipt of the important letter, and cautioning her to keep the discovery a strict secret. All unconscious, as he was, that one had seen it in his own office.

Mr. Richards was scuttering along the street to the railway station, when he encountered Benjamin Carr. He could hardly stop to speak, for his own office really wanted him. In the past few weeks, since their first introduction, he and Benjamin Carr had been a great deal together, and the latter placed himself right in his path.

"I can't stay a minute, Ben,"—they had grown familiar, as you perceive,—"I shall lose the train."

Benjamin Carr turned, and stepped out alongside him, with a pace as quick. He began telling him, as they walked, of an outbreak he had had with the "old man," as he was pleased to call his father. "It was all about this money," exclaimed Ben. "He refuses to give me any until this affair is settled; persists in saying he may lose the inheritance: altogether we got in a passion, both of us. As if he could lose it!"

"I suppose it is within the range of possibility," said Richards.

"Nonsense!" replied Benjamin Carr. "You'll say there was a marriage next."

"There might have been."

"Pigs might fly."

"Suppose there was a marriage—and that it can be proved? What then?"

"Suppose there wasn't," wrathfully returned Ben Carr. "I'm not in a mood for joking, Richards."

They stepped on to the platform. The train was not in yet; was scarcely due: one of the porters remarked that "that there mid-day train didn't keep her time as well as some on 'em did." Richards familiarly passed his arm within Benjamin Carr's, and drew him beyond the platform. They turned sideways and halted before a dwarf wall, looking over it at the town, which lay beneath.

"You say you are not in a mood for joking, Ben: neither am I; and what I said to you I said with a meaning," began Richards in a low tone. "It has come to my knowledge—and you needn't ask me how or when or where, for I shan't tell you—that old Marmaduke's money, so far as you Eckford Carrs go, is imperilled. If the thing goes on to trial, you'll lose it: but I should think it won't go on to trial, for you'd never let it when you come to know what I know. The other side has got hold of a piece of evidence that would swamp you."

Benjamin Carr's great dark eyes turned themselves fiercely upon his companion: he saw that he was, in truth, not jesting. "It's not the record of the marriage, is it?" he asked, after a pause.

"Something like it."

Not a word was spoken for a couple of minutes. A little tinkling bell was heard in the station. Benjamin Carr broke the silence.

"Real, or forged?"

"Ah, I don't know. Real, I suppose. The man's dead you see, that young clergyman-fellow who came down, so he'd be hardly likely to get it up. I don't see how it could be done, either, in the present case. It's easier to suppress evidence of a marriage than it is to invent it. Still it may be on the cross."

"Can't you speak plain English, Richards."

"I hardly dare. But I suppose you could be silent, if I were to."

"I suppose I could. I have had secrets to carry in my lifetime weightier than this, whatever it may be."

Benjamin Carr lifted his hat, and wiped his brow with his handkerchief, as if the secrets were there and felt heavy still. Richards looked at him.

"You may speak out, Richards. You can't believe," he added, his tone changed to one of passionate pain, "that it is not safe with me."

"It must be kept safe for your own sake, for your family's sake. If any evidence has turned up, there's no cause to let the world know it before you are compelled. It would be damaging your cause irreparably."

Ben Carr nodded assent. "What is it?" he asked.

"Well, I think they have found out where the marriage was solemnized. I think so, mind; I am not positive. That is, I am not positive of the fact; only that they think it so."

"How did you hear it?"

"Now, Ben, you'll not get me to let out that. I've said so. Perhaps I dreamt it; perhaps a little bird told me: never mind. I mean to go over to your place to see Valentine to-night, and drop him a hint of the state of affairs. Shall you be at home?"

"I didn't mean to be at home for some days to come; but I'll meet you there. Take care of one thing: that you say nothing to the squire."

Mr. Richards gave a knowing nod sideways, as if to intimate that he knew just as well what to do and what not to do as Benjamin Carr. Just then the noise of a train was heard puffing up.

"Here it comes, Richards."

"Here it doesn't," was the reply. "It's coming the wrong way. This is the London train coming in."

The train came in, and stopped on the other side of the platform, while it discharged its passengers and any luggage pertaining to them. It then went puffing on, and the passengers crossed the line to this side, as they had to do before they could leave the station. Benjamin Carr and his friend stood still to look at them, and the former recognised in one of them Mr. Arkell.

"How d'ye do, Mr. Arkell," said Ben, holding out his hand. "Been out anywhere?"

But Mr. Arkell did not see the hand. What with the jostling crowd, what with a small portmanteau he was carrying, what with wondering who the stranger might be, hanging lovingly on Ben's arm, for Mr. Arkell had not the honour of knowing Mr. Richards by sight, he certainly did not appear to see the held-out hand. "Where have you been?" inquired Ben, inquisitively.

"I have been to London, Mr. Benjamin, as you wish to know. A short visit, though."

"Oh," said Ben, meaning to be jocular. "Seen any of my friends there?"

"I saw Mrs. Carr, the clergyman's young widow: I don't know whether you count her as one of your friends. And I saw Mrs. Dundyke."

There was a look in Mr. Arkell's face, not usual on it: a peculiar, solemn, penetrating look. Somehow Mr. Ben Carr's jocularity and his courage went out of him together.

"Mrs. Dundyke?" he repeated, vaguely, staring over the heads of the passing passengers. "Oh, ah, I remember, that connexion of yours. I don't know her."

"I got her to give me a description of the man, calling himself Hardcastle, who lies under the suspicion of knowing rather too clearly what became of Mr. Dundyke. Poor Robert Carr, just dead, attempted the description of him, you may remember, at your father's table."

"Ah; yes," said Ben, striving to be more vague than before: and his dark face perceptibly changed its hue.

"And I may tell you that this description of Mrs. Dundyke's has made a singular impression upon me, and a very disagreeable one. It is not my affair," he added, slowly and distinctly; "and for the present I shall not make it mine: but—"

"Here's your train, Richards. Got a return ticket?"

The two walked forward to meet it, Richards evidently pulled along by his companion. The train came dashing in too far, and had to be backed: porters ran about, departing passengers hustled each other. And altogether, in the general confusion, there was no more to be seen of Mr. Benjamin Carr.

CHAPTER XIII

A DISLIKE THAT WAS TO BEAR ITS FRUITS

The information, hinted at by Miss Beauclerc to Henry Arkell, had proved to be correct—the dean and chapter purposed to hold an examination of the college school.

To describe the consternation this caused would be difficult. It fell, not only upon the boys, but on the masters, like a clap of thunder: indeed the former cared for it the least. That the school was not in a state, in regard to its proficiency of study, to bear an examination, was a fact known to nearly everybody; and the head master, had it been possible, would have resisted the fiat of the dean.

In point of fact, the school had become notorious for its inefficiency. The old days of confining the boys' studies exclusively to Latin and Greek were over; but the additional branches inaugurated could scarcely be said to have begun. The masters, wedded to the old system, did not take to them kindly; the boys did not, of their own will, take to them at all. They could not spell; they knew nothing of English grammar, except what they could pick up of it through their acquaintance with the Latin; they hardly knew a single event in English, French, or modern history; and of geography they were intensively ignorant. What could be expected? For years and years, for many hours a day, had these boys been kept to work, always at the old routine work, Latin and Greek. Examine them in these classics, and Mr. Wilberforce would have no reason to complain of his pupils; but in all else a charity boy could beat them. Had one of those college boys been required to write a letter in English, every other word in it would have been spelled incorrectly. I am giving you a true account of the state of the school at that period: and I fear that you will scarcely believe it. A few of the boys, a very few, only some three or four, had been generally well educated; but these owed it to the care, the forethought, perhaps the means of their parents: home tutors were expensive.

As Miss Beauclerc had said, it was in consequence of a letter, written by one of the senior boys, that this trouble had come about. It was a disgraceful letter—speaking in reference to its spelling and composition—neither more nor less. The letter had been brought under the astonished eyes of one of the chapter, and he showed it to the dean. They awoke from their supineness, and much indignation at the young scholar was privately expressed. What did they expect? Did they think spelling came to the boys intuitively, as pecking at grain does to birds? It may be said that the boys ought to have been able to spell correctly before entering the school, and to have possessed some other general learning; that the parents ought to have taken care of that. But "ought" does not go for much in this world. Many of the boys were indulged children who had never been brought on at all, except in reading, and that was essential, or they could not be admitted; and, at that time, they entered young—nine years old. As they went in, little ignoramuses, so they remained, except in the classics. Many a boy has gone from that school to the university not educated at all, save in the dead languages.

Of course, when the innovation (as the masters regarded it) came in, a little stir was caused. A pretence was made of teaching the school foreign branches, such as spelling and geography; but whether it might be owing to the innate prejudice of their masters, or to their own stupidity, little, if any, progress was made. The boys remained lamentably deficient; and they thought it no shame to be so. Rather the contrary, in fact; for a feeling grew up in the school that these common branches of learning were not essential to them as gentlemen; that it was derogatory altogether to a foundation school to have them introduced. The masters had winked at this state of things, and they perhaps did not know how intensely ignorant some of their best classical scholars were.

It may be imagined, therefore, what the consternation was when the dean's announcement was received early in August. There was to be an examination held; but not until November; so the boys and the masters had three months to prepare. It's true you cannot convert ignorant boys into finished scholars in three months, however humble may be the attainments required; but you may do something towards it by means of drilling. So the boys, to their intense disgust, were drilled late and early—and that disgust did not render their apprehensions the quicker.

Amidst the very few who need not fear that, or any other examination, was Henry Arkell. He was not yet a senior boy (speaking of the four seniors), but he was by far the best scholar in the school. He owed this chiefly to his father. Mr. Peter Arkell was so finished a scholar himself, it had been strange indeed if he had not sought to render his son one; and Henry's abilities were of a most superior order. Indeed—but that a sort of prejudice exists against these clever lads, I could say a great deal more of his abilities, his attainments, than I mean to say—for this is no fictitious history. Intellectual, clever, good, refined, sensitive, Henry Arkell seemed to be one of those superior spirits not meant for this world. The event too often proves that they were not meant for it.

He was not a favourite in the school, except with a few. By the majority he was intensely disliked. The dislike arose from envy, and his own gifts excited it. His unusual beauty, his sensitive temperament, his refinement of manner, his ever-pervading sense of religion, his honourable nature, as seen in even the smallest action,—all and each of them were objectionable to the rough schoolboys. Most of these qualities he had inherited from his mother, and for any one of them, the school, as a whole, would have ridiculed and despised him. They would have been quite enough without his superior advancement; which put them to the shame, and called forth now and again some stinging comparison from the lips of the head master. When he first entered the school, he had unintentionally excited the ill-will of the two sons of Mrs. Lewis, and of their chosen companions, the two Aultanes. These boys longed above everything to thrash him every day of their lives; but he had been taken under the protection of Mr. St. John and Travice Arkell, and they dared not, and it did not increase their love for him.

But there was to arise a worse cause of enmity than any of these, as Henry grew older, and that was the favour shown him by the dean's daughter. To see him under the especial favour of the dean was aggravation enough; but that was as nothing compared to the intimacy accorded him by the dean's daughter. You know what these things are with schoolboys. Half the school believed themselves in love with this attractive girl, who condescended to freedom with them; the other half were in love with her. After their fashion, you know. It was not that serious love that makes or mars the heart for all time, though the boys might think it so. Lewis senior—his name was Roland, and he was one of the four senior boys—was especially envious of this favour of Miss Beauclerc's. He was very fond of her, and would have given all he possessed in the world for it to be accorded to him. He could only love and admire her at a distance; while Arkell might tell it to her face if he pleased—and Lewis felt sure he did. He hated Henry with a passionate hatred. He saw, with that intuition natural to these things, that Henry loved Georgina Beauclerc, and with no passing school-boy's love. He wished that the earth contained only their three selves, that he might set upon the fragile boy and kill him, and keep the young lady to himself ever afterwards—Adam and Eve in a second Paradise. Indeed, Mr. Lewis had got into a habit of indulging this train of thought rather more than was wholesome for him, and would have shot Henry Arkell in a duel with all the non-compunction in the world.

Not being able to do this—for the human race could not be exterminated so easily, and duels are not in fashion—he made up for the disappointment by rendering Henry Arkell's life as miserable as it is well possible for one boy to render another's. He excited the school against him; he openly derided the position and known poverty of his father, Peter Arkell; and he positively affected to rebel—he would have rebelled had he dared—when Henry came to reside temporarily in the head master's house. The scholars in that house had hitherto been gentlemen, he said, loudly. Indeed, but for one fortunate circumstance, Henry's life at the master's might have been rendered nearly unbearable; and this was, that he was in favour with the senior boy—an idle, gentlemanly fellow of the name of Jocelyn. So long as Jocelyn remained in the school, there could be no very undue open oppression put upon Henry Arkell. It was not that the head boy held Henry in any especial favour; but he was of too just a nature, too much the gentleman in ideas and habits, to permit cruelty or unfairness of any sort. But you have now heard enough to gather that Henry Arkell was not in favour with the majority of the college boys, his fellows; and you hear its causes.

The cramming that the boys were now subjected to, did not improve their temper. Unfortunately, the dean had not specified—perhaps purposely—what would be the branches chosen for examination. Mr. Wilberforce and the under masters presumed that it would chiefly lie in the classics, and, so far, were tolerably easy; but the result of this was, that the Latin and Greek lessons were increased, leaving less time for what they were pleased to consider inferior studies.

"Suppose," suggested the second master, one day, "it should be in those other studies that the dean purposes to examine them?"

Mr. Wilberforce turned purple.

"In those!—to the exclusion of the higher! Nonsense! It is not likely. The boys will cut a pretty figure if he should."

"The fact is, they are such a dull lot."

"Most of them: yes. I think, Mr. Roberts, you had better hold some dictation classes; and we'll get in a few conspicuous maps."

But all the studies that came in addition, whether dictation classes or the staring at maps, the boys resented wofully; and though they were obliged to submit, it did not, I say, improve their temper. One afternoon in October, when everything seemed to have gone wrong, and the school rather wished, on the whole, that they had never been born, or that books had not been invented, or that they were private pupils of the head master's (for they were not to be included in the examination, only the forty foundation boys, the king's scholars), the school was waiting impatiently to hear half-past four strike, for then only another half-hour must elapse before they would be released from school. The choristers had come in at four o'clock from service with the head master, whose week it was for chanting, and had settled down to their respective desks. Henry Arkell, who was at the first desk now, but nothing like its head, for promotion in the school was not attained by proficiency, but by priority of entrance, had come in with the rest; he was senior chorister now, and was seated bending over a book, his head half buried between his raised hands, and his elbows on the desk.

"What are you conning there so attentively, Mr. Arkell?"

The authoritative words came from Lewis. He was monitor that week, and therefore head of all the school, under the senior boy: his present position on the rolls was that of fourth senior.

"I'm reading Greek," replied Henry, without removing his hands or looking up. "I've done my lessons."

"Take your hands and elbows down. I should like to see."

Down went the hands and elbows, but he did not look up.

"I thought it might be an English comedy instead of a Greek tragedy," observed Lewis, satirically; "but it is Greek, I see. Boys, he's reading Greek! He's thinking to take the shine out of us at the examination. Preparing! Oh!"

"Not at all," said Henry, quietly. "I should have been as well prepared for the examination at a day's notice, as I am after nearly three months'. So might you have been if you'd chosen."

"You insolent young beggar! Do you mean to say I am not prepared?"

"I said nothing of the sort, Lewis."

"You implied it, though. You needn't think to get the prize—if it's true that the dean gives one."

"I don't think to get it. I wish you'd let me go on with my book."

"Oh yes, you do. You think to creep up the dean's sleeve, at second hand, through somebody that's a friend of yours; or that you are presumptuous enough to fancy is."

He understood the allusion, and suddenly raised his hands again, for the delicate hue of his transparent cheek changed to crimson. Lewis noted the movement.

"Now, by Jove, I'll put you up for punishment. I order your elbows off the desk, and you fling them on again in defiance. Wilberforce has flogged for less."

"Be quiet, Lewis," interposed Jocelyn. "Arkell's doing nothing that you need trouble him for. Just turn your attention to that second desk, and see what's going on there. They'll get Mr. Wilberforce's eyes upon them directly."

Lewis could have found in his heart to hang the senior boy. He was always interfering with him in this manner whenever he was monitor, to the detriment of his dignity as such. Lewis immediately struck up a wordy war, until the master's attention was excited and he commanded silence.

Oh, if this dislike of Henry Arkell had but died out at first! half this history would not then have been written. It might have done so under different circumstances; it might, perhaps, have done so but for the dean's daughter. From the very first hour that she knew him, Georgina Beauclerc made no secret of her liking. When she met the college boys, child though she was then, she would single him out from the rest, and stop talking to him. Her governess used to look defiance, but that made not the least impression on Miss Beauclerc. She invited him to the deanery; they never were allowed to put their noses inside it, except at those odd moments when they went to solicit the dean to allow them holiday from the cathedral; she would pass them sometimes without the slightest notice in the world, but she never so passed him.

If he had but been a dull, stupid, clumsy boy! Strange though it may seem, the rest hated him because he did his lessons. Their tasks were hurried over, imperfectly learnt at the best, if at all, and were generally concluded with a caning. His were always perfectly and efficiently done. They called him hard names for this; prig, snob, sneak; but, in point of fact, the boy was never allowed the opportunity of not doing them, for his father on that score was a martinet, and drilled him at home just as much as Mr. Wilberforce did at school. And, greatest of all advantages, his early education had been so comprehensive and sound. The horribly hard lessons, that were as death to the rest, seemed but play to him; and the natural consequence was, that the envy boiled over. Circumstances, in this point of view, were not favourable to him.

The long afternoon came to an end, five o'clock struck, and the boys clattered down the broad schoolroom steps, making the grounds and the old cloisters echo with their noise. There had been little time for play latterly; since the announcement of the forthcoming examination, the head and other masters had been awfully exacting on the subject of lessons, not to be trifled with. Henry Arkell, from the state of preparation in which he always was, had nearly as much time on his hands as usual, and had not ceased to take his lessons on the organ, or to practise on it twice a week, as was his custom. He learnt of the cathedral organist, Mr. Paul; for Mrs. Peter Arkell had deemed it well that Henry's great taste for music should continue to be cultivated. Another of the boys, named Robbins, a private pupil of the head master's, also learnt. The organist would not allow them to touch the noted cathedral instrument, save in his presence; and they were permitted by Mr. Wilberforce to practise in the church of St. James the Less, of which, as you may remember, he was the incumbent. One of the minor canons invariably held this living, for it was in the gift of the Dean and Chapter.

Henry was going there to practise this evening. He was at the house of the head master yet; his friends being still absent from Westerbury, for the family who had taken their house wished to remain in it until Christmas. The sea-side was doing Mrs. Peter Arkell a vast deal of good; her husband had obtained some teaching there, and Mr. Wilberforce had kindly intimated that Henry was welcome to remain with him a twelvemonth, if it suited their plans that he should; but the boy was beginning to long for them back with an intense longing.

He walked across the grounds to the master's house; put down his books, got his music, and went on towards the church of St. James the Less. It was a large, ancient church, with thick walls and little windows, and it stood all solitary by itself, in the midst of its churchyard, beyond the town on that side, but not many minutes' walk from the cathedral. The only house near it was the clerk's, and that not close to it: a poor, low, damp, aguish building, surrounded by grass as long as that in the neighbouring graveyard. The clerk was a bent, withered old man, always complaining of rheumatism; he had been clerk of that church now for many years.

Once beyond the grounds, Henry Arkell set off at his utmost speed. The evenings were growing dusk early, and Mr. Wilberforce allowed no light in the church, so he had to make the most of the daylight. He was flying past the palmery, when in making a dexterous spring to avoid a truck of apples standing there, he let his roll of music fly out of his hand; and it was in turning to pick up this that his eyes caught sight of a tall form at the palmery door; a distinguished, noble-looking young man, whose deep blue eyes were gazing at him in doubt. One moment's hesitation, on Henry's part, and he made but a step towards him.

"Oh, Mr. St. John! I did not know you were back."

"I thought it was certainly you, Harry, but your height puzzled me. How you have grown!"

Henry laughed. "They say I bid fair to be as tall as my cousin Travice. I hope I shan't be as tall as papa! When did you come home, Mr. St. John?"

"Now: an hour ago. I am going to look in at the deanery. Will you come with me, lest I should have forgotten the way?"

It was not often that Henry Arkell put aside duty for pleasure; he had been too well trained for that; but this temptation was irresistible. What would he not have put aside for the sake of seeing Georgina Beauclerc; and, it may be, that that wild suspicion of where Georgina's love was given, made him wish to witness the meeting.

A couple of minutes brought them to the deanery. St. John's joke of not finding the way might have some point in it, for he had been absent at least two years. In the room where you first saw her, gliding softly over the carpet with a waltzing step, was Georgina Beauclerc; and close to the window, listlessly looking out, sat a young lady of delicate beauty, one of the fairest girls it was ever Mr. St. John's lot to look upon. But this was not the first time he had seen her. It was the dean's niece, Sarah Beauclerc.

Henry was in the room first; St. John pushed him on, and followed him; he was in time therefore to see the momentary suspense, the start of surprise, the deep glow of crimson, of love, that rushed over the face of Georgina. Was it at himself, or at him? But never yet, so far as Henry saw, had that crimson hue dyed her face at his own approach.

One moment, and she had recovered herself. She went up to Mr. St. John with an outstretched hand, bantering words on her tongue.

"So you really are alive! We thought you had been buried in the Red Sea."

He made some laughing answer, and passed on to Sarah Beauclerc. He clasped both her hands in his; he bent over her with only a word or two of greeting, his low voice subdued to tenderness. What did it mean? Georgina's lips turned white as ashes, but she could not see her cousin's face.

"How is Mrs. Beauclerc?" asked St. John, turning, and beginning to talk generally; "Harry tells me that the dean is well, to the consternation of the college school, which has to prepare itself for an examination."

"Oh, that examination!" laughed Georgina; "it is turning some of their senses upside down. But now," she added, standing in front of Mr. St. John, "what am I to call you? Frederick?—Or am I to be formal, and say 'Mr. St. John?'"

"You used to call me Fred."

"But I was not a grown-up young lady then," making him a mock curtsey; "after all, I suppose I must call you Fred still, for I should be sure to lapse into it. Where have you been all this while? We have heard of you everywhere; in Paris, in Madrid, in Vienna, in Rome, in Antwerp, in—oh, all over the world."

"I think I have been nearly all over Europe," said Mr. St. John.

"Which of us has the most changed?" she abruptly asked, a curl of the finger indicating that she meant to speak of her cousin.

"Sarah has not changed," he answered, turning to Sarah Beauclerc, and an involuntary tenderness was again perceptible in his tone. "You have not changed either, Georgie, in manner," he added, with a laugh.

Georgina pouted. "You are not to call me 'Georgie' any longer, Mr. St. John."

"Very well, Miss Beauclerc, our careless times have gone for ever, I suppose; old age is creeping upon us."

"Don't be stupid," said Georgina. "Have you seen Lady Anne since your return?"

"Yes."

"You have!" she exclaimed, not expecting the answer.

"I saw her in London, as I came through it."

"Ah—yes—of course, I might have guessed that," was Georgina's rejoinder, spoken mysteriously. "Shall we have a battle royal?"

"What do you mean?" asked Mr. St. John.

"Between Lady Anne and another; you can't cut yourself in two, you know. Sarah, what's the matter with your face?"

It was a very conscious face just then, and a very haughty one. St. John knitted his brows, as if he divined Georgina's meaning, and was angered at it; and he began speaking hastily.

"Mine has been one of the pleasantest of tours. The galleries of paintings alone would have been worth—"

"Now, Fred, if you begin upon that everlasting painting theme, you'll never leave off," unceremoniously interrupted Georgiana. "Mrs. St. John says paintings will be your ruin."

"Does she?"

"Your purse has a hole at both ends, she says, where pictures are concerned, and she wishes you had only a tithe of the prudence of Mr. Isaac St. John."

Another slight knit of the brows. Sarah Beauclerc went to a side table and opened a book of views, taken in Spain, artistic sketches, exquisitely done. She turned her fair face to Mr. St. John.

"Will you kindly tell me if these are correct, Mr. St. John? That is, if you are personally acquainted with the spots."

He needed no second invitation. He did know the spots, and they bent over the views together, St. John growing eloquent. Henry Arkell, tolerably at home at the deanery, had drawn away from the group and was touching the keys of the piano; some sweet, extemporized melody, played so softly that it could scarcely be heard. Suddenly he found Georgina at his side.

"What did I tell you?" she abruptly said.

"What did you tell me?" he replied. "I'm sure I don't know what you mean, Miss Beauclerc."

"Go on with your playing; why do you stop? I don't care to be heard by the chairs and tables. Did I not tell you that he was in love either with her or with her beauty? You see, and hear."

"Are you sure he is not in love with somebody else?" asked Henry, his heart beating with that wild tumult that it mostly did when in the presence of Miss Beauclerc.

She understood his meaning, however it might please her to affect not to do so. He did not raise his eyes to look at her; and he continued the soft sweet playing, as she desired.

"Somebody else! Do you mean Lady Anne?"

"Oh, Miss Beauclerc! I was not thinking of Lady Anne."

"Perhaps you mean me, you stupid boy; perhaps you would like to insinuate that I am in love with him. You are stupid, Henry. Play a little louder. How I wish I played with half your taste. I should not get so much of old Paul's frownings and mamma's reproachings. Do you think I'd have Fred St. John? No, not though he were worth his weight in gold. We should never get along together; you might as well try to mix oil and water."

Oh, false words! But how many such are uttered daily, in the natural reticence of the shy heart, loving for the first time! Henry Arkell believed her at the moment, and his heart bounded on in its wild love, in spite of that ever present conviction that had taken up an abode within it. The strain changed to a popular love melody; but the playing was soft and sweet as before. Few have the charmed gift of playing as he played.

"I have been making something for you. I can't give it you now with those two pairs of eyes in the room. Lovers though they may be, I dare say they are watching; and Sarah's blue ones are very sharp. She might get telling mamma that I flirt with the college boys. And I won't give it you at all if you are stupid. What's Fred St. John to me, do you suppose? It's nothing really worth having, you know; but your vanity likes to be humoured, and—"

"Henry! how exquisitely you play!"

Mr. St. John was coming towards them with the remark, and the spell was broken. Henry rose from the piano, laughing carelessly in answer; and Frederick St. John wondered at the bright light in his eye, the flush of emotion on his cheek. But he did not read the signs correctly.

CHAPTER XIV

THE EXAMINATION

November came in. The nineteenth approached, and the travelling carriages of the different prebendaries bowled into Westerbury, as was customary at that season, bringing their owners to their residences in the Grounds. A great day in cathedral life was the nineteenth of November. It was the grand chapter day; the day when every member attached to the cathedral had to attend in the chapter-house after morning prayers, and answer to their names, as called over from the roll by the chapter clerk. The dean, the canons, the minor canons, the king's scholars, the organist, the lay-clerks, the sextons, the vergers, the bedesmen, and the two men-cooks officiating for the audit dinners at the deanery; all had to be there, health permitting. It was also the grand audit day; and the first day of the series of dinners held at the deanery; the dinner on this day being confined to the members of the cathedral: that is, the clergy, the choristers, and the lay-clerks. The rest of the boys, those who were only king's scholars, were not included, and very savage they were; but things were done in accordance with ancient custom. When the dean, at the conclusion of the ceremonies in the chapter-house, proffered an invitation to the "gentlemen choristers" to dine with him that evening at the deanery, and the gentlemen choristers bowed a gracious or a confused acquiescence, according to their state of nerves, the thirty king's scholars turned rampant with envy; and always wished either the choristers or the dean might come to some grief before the night arrived.

The great day came; an unusually great day, this, for the school, the examination having been fixed to take place on it by the dean. The morning service in the cathedral was at ten o'clock, the usual daily hour; and at eleven began the business in the chapter-house. Next came the examination. There had been some consultation between the dean and canons as to whether the examination should take place in the college hall, as the schoolroom was called, or the chapter-house; but they decided in favour of the college hall. As the boys were passing through the cloisters from the chapter-house on their way to it, walking orderly two and two in their surplices and trenchers, Georgina Beauclerc met them, her blue eyes smiling, the blue strings of her bonnet flying. The undaunted girl stopped to have a word, although the clergy, with the dean at their head, were actually coming out of the chapter-house, within view.

"There is to be a prize, boys," she whispered. "Good luck to whoever gets it. Will it be you, Jocelyn?"

"That it will not, Miss Beauclerc," was the reply of the senior boy. None knew better than he his own deficiencies, and that they chiefly arose through his own idleness.

"Whose will it be, then?"

"Well, if it turns upon general scholarship it ought to be Arkell's no doubt, Miss Beauclerc, only you see he is not a senior. If we are examined in Greek and Latin only, the merit may lie between him and Lewis senior."

Lewis senior, a great big hulky fellow, with hair as black as his uncle Ben's, sly eyes, and an ugly face, was standing close to Jocelyn. Taking the classics only, he was the best scholar in the school, Henry Arkell excepted; but he was more than a year older than Henry. Miss Beauclerc saw his countenance light up with triumph, and she threw back her pretty head. She detested Lewis, though perfectly conscious that he entertained more than a liking for her.

"You won't have much chance, Lewis, by the side of Arkell. Don't deceive yourself; don't faint with the disappointment."

She turned round and flew off, for the dean and clergy were close at hand. The boys continued their way to the college hall, Lewis's amiability not improved by the taunt. The general opinion in the school was, that if a prize was given, Lewis would gain it. He was a clever boy, though not popular; more clever than any one of the other seniors. Seniority went for everything in the college school, and for the dean to be guilty of the heterodoxy of awarding the prize to any except one of the four seniors had not occurred to the boys as being within the range of serious possibility.

The boys took their station in the school, and the dean proceeded to the examination. Two of the canons were with him, and the masters of the school, one of whom was the Rev. Mr. Prattleton; but he attended only twice a week for an especial branch of study. The clergy and boys all wore their surplices, and the dean and prebendaries retained their caps on their heads.

The examination proceeded smoothly enough, for the complaisant dean confined himself chiefly to the classics. He questioned the boys in the books and at the places put into his hands by the masters, and he winked metaphorically at the low promptings administered when the classes came to a full stop or a stammer. The masters recovered confidence, and were congratulating themselves inwardly at the dreaded event being well over, when, to their unspeakable dismay, the dean disbanded the classes, and, desiring the forty boys to stand indiscriminately before him, began to question them.

This was the real examination: some of the questions were simple, some difficult, embracing various subjects. But, simple or difficult, it was all one, for, taken by surprise, ill-educated, ill-grounded, the boys could not answer. One of them alone proved himself equal to the emergency. You need not be told that it was Henry Arkell. Not at a single question did he hesitate, till at length the dean told him, with a smile, not to answer, until the questions had gone the round of the school. Of all branches of education, save their rote of Latin and Greek, the boys were entirely ignorant, though some of the dean's questions were ludicrously simple.

"Can you make the square of a cube?"

Nobody answered, save by a prodigious deal of coughing, and Henry Arkell had once more to be appealed to.

"What is the difference between a right angle and an acute one?"

More coughing, and then a dead silence. The dean happened to be looking hard at one particular boy, or the boy fancied so, and his ears became as red as the head master's. "If you please, Mr. Dean, our desk is not in algebra."

"Who was Caligula?" continued the dean.

"King of France in the ninth century," was the prompt answer from one who thought he was in luck.

It was now the dean's turn to cough, as he replaced the question by another: "Can you tell me anything about Charles the Second?"

"He invented black lap-dogs with long ears."

The dean nearly choked.

"And was beheaded," added a timid voice.

"Was he?" retorted the dean. "Can you say anything about Charles the First, and the events of his reign?"

"Yes, sir. He found out the Gunpowder Plot, and was succeeded by Oliver Cromwell."

"Where are the Bahama Isles," asked the dean, in despair.

"In the Mediterranean," cried a tall boy.—"And they are very fertile," added another.

The dean paused a hopeless pause. "Can you spell 'Dutch?'"

"D-u-c-h." "D-u-t-s-h." "D-u-s-h-t," escaped from various tongues, drowning other novel phases of the word.

"Spell 'Cane,'" frowned the dean, though he was laughing inwardly.

"K-a-n-e," was the eager reply.

"Perhaps you can spell 'birch,'" roared Dr. Ferraday, an irascible prebendary.

They could: "B-u-r-c-h."

"What was the social condition of the Ancient Britons when their country was invaded by Julius Cæsar?" the dean asked, rubbing his face.

"They always went about naked, and never shaved, and their clothes were made of the skins of beasts."

"This is frightful," interrupted Dr. Ferraday. "The school reflects the greatest discredit upon—somebody," glaring through his spectacles at the purple and scarlet faces of the masters. "There's only one boy who is not a living monument of ignorance. He—what's your name, boy?"

"Arkell, sir."

"True; Arkell," assented Dr. Ferraday. He knew who he was perfectly well, but he was the proudest man of all the canons, and would not condescend to show that he remembered. "Sir, for your age you are a brilliant scholar."

"How is it?" puzzled Mr. Meddler, another of the prebendaries: "has Arkell superior abilities, and have all the rest none? Answer for yourself, Arkell."

The boy hesitated. Both in mind and manners he was so different from the general run of schoolboys; and he could not bear to be thus held out as a sort of pattern for the rest.

"It is not my fault, sir—or theirs. My father has always kept me to my studies so closely out of school hours, and attended to them himself, that I could not help getting on in advance of the school."

"Wilberforce," roughly spoke up Dr. Ferraday, in his overbearing manner, "how is it that this boy is not senior?"

"That post is attained by priority of entrance, sir," replied the master. "Arkell can only become senior boy when those above him leave."

"He ought to be senior now."

"We cannot act against the customs of the school, Dr. Ferraday," repeated the master. "Arkell is at the first desk, but he cannot be senior of the school out of his turn."

"Can you tell me whence England chiefly procures her supplies of cotton?" asked Mr. Meddler, mildly, of a mild-looking boy belonging to the third desk. "You, sir; Van Brummel, I think your name is."

Mr. Van Brummel, considerably taken-to at being addressed individually, lost his head completely. "From the signing of Magna Charta by King John."

"Why, what a stupid owl you must be!" snapped Dr. Ferraday, before Canon Meddler could speak. Mr. Van Brummel's face turned red; he was a timid boy, and he wondered whether they would order him to be flogged.

"Please, sir, I know that's the answer in the book," he earnestly said: "I learnt them over again this morning."

"It may be an answer to something, but not to my question," said Mr. Meddler, as he stepped apart to confer with his colleagues. "What is to be done, Mr. Dean? This state of things cannot be allowed to go on."

They talked for a few moments together, and then the dean turned to the boys.

"Stand forward, Arkell."

Henry Arkell advanced, a hot flush on his sensitive face; and the Dean threw round his neck a broad blue ribbon, suspending a medal of gold. "I have much pleasure in bestowing this upon you; never was reward more justly merited; and," he concluded, raising his voice high as he swept the room with his eyes, "I feel bound to declare publicly, that Henry Cheveley Arkell is an honour to Westerbury collegiate school."

"As all the rest of you are a disgrace to it," stormed Dr. Ferraday on the discomfited lot behind.

"You must let me have it back again to-morrow morning, that I may get your name inscribed on it," said the dean to Henry, in a low tone. "Wear it for to-day."

The boys were dismissed. They took off their surplices in the cloisters, not presuming to unrobe in the presence of the cathedral dignitaries, who prolonged their stay in the college hall: "to blow off at Wilberforce and the rest," one of the seniors irreverently surmised aloud. Some swung the surplices across their arms; some crammed them into bags; and an unusual silence pervaded the group. Lewis was bitterly disappointed. He was as good a classical scholar as Arkell, and thought he ought to have had the medal.

Miss Beauclerc was waiting at the deanery door. "Well, boys, and who has got it?" was her salutation before any of them were up.

"A sneaking young beggar," called out Lewis, thinking he might as well make the best of things to her, and answer first.

"Then you have not got it, Lewis; I told you you wouldn't," laughed the young lady; "though I heard that you made certain sure of it, and had ordered a glass case to keep it in."

Lewis nearly boiled over with rage.

"Arkell has gained it, Miss Beauclerc," said the senior boy.

"Of course; I knew he would. I was sure from the first that none of you could contend against him, provided there was a fair field and no favour."

"No favour!" scornfully echoed Lewis. "A bright eye and a girl's face, these are what we should covet now, to curry favour with the Dean and Chapter."

"Lewis, you forget yourself," reproved Miss Beauclerc; "and I'll inform against you if you talk treason of the dean," she laughingly continued.

"I beg your pardon, Miss Beauclerc," was the sullen apology of Lewis, delivered in a most ungracious tone.

"Arkell's merits alone have gained the prize, Lewis, and you know it," proceeded the young lady; "they must have gained it had he been as ugly as you."

"I am much obliged to you, Miss Beauclerc," foamed Lewis, with as much resentment as he dared show to the dean's daughter.

"Well, you are right about his merits, Miss Beauclerc," interrupted Jocelyn; "no question came amiss to him. By Jove! old Ferraday was not wrong in calling him a brilliant scholar; I had no idea he knew half as much. The dean said he was an honour to the school."

"That he has been a long while," she said, quietly. "You boys may sneer—you are sneering now, Aultane, but—"

"No, indeed, Miss Beauclerc," interrupted Aultane, "I would not do such a thing as sneer in your presence. Of course it couldn't be expected that he'd be anything but a good scholar, when his father's a schoolmaster."

"And teaches boys at half-a-crown an hour," put in Lewis junior. "He acknowledged to the dean, it was all through his father's cramming him."

Henry Arkell was coming up; Miss Beauclerc moved forwards and shook him by the hand.

"I congratulate you," she said, in a half whisper. "Why it looks like the ribbon of the Garter. You may win that some time, if you live; who knows? I knew you would get it, if you were only true to yourself; Frederick St. John said so too. Mind you write to-day to tell him."

She had taken the medal in her hand, and was looking at it. The rest pressed round as closely as they dared. Lewis only stood aside, a bitter expression on his ugly lips.

A little fellow ran up, all in a fright. "Oh! if you please, if you please, Miss Beauclerc, here comes the dean."

"What if he does?" retorted Miss Beauclerc; "he won't eat you. There, you may go, boys. Henry Arkell, you know you are expected at the deanery to-night."

"Yes, thank you, Miss Beauclerc," he replied, some hesitation, or surprise, visible in his tone.

"Ah, but I mean to us, after the dinner. Mamma has what she calls one of her quiet soirées. You'll be sure to come."

One glance from his brilliant eyes, beneath which her blue ones fell, and he drew away. The rest were already off. Georgina walked forward to meet the dean, and she put her arm within his in her loving manner.

"Oh, papa, the boys are so envious of the medal. I stopped them and made them show it me. That ugly Lewis is ready to cut his throat."

"Random-spoken as usual, my darling. Who's throat?"

"Henry Arkell's of course, papa. But I knew no one else would gain it. They are not fit to tie his shoes."

"In learning, they certainly are not. You can't imagine what a ludicrous display we have had! And some of them go soon to the university!"

"It's not the fault of the boys, papa. If they are never taught anything but Greek and Latin, how can they be expected to know anything else?"

"Very true, Georgie," mused Dr. Beauclerc. "Some of these old systems are stupid things."

The audit dinner in the evening went off as those dinners generally did. The boys dined at a table by themselves, and Henry, as their senior, had to exert firm authority over some, for the supply of wine was unlimited. Later in the evening, he passed through the gallery to the drawing-room, as invited by Miss Beauclerc. A few ladies were assembled: the canons' wives and daughters, Mrs. Wilberforce, and two or three other inhabitants of the Grounds; all very quiet, and what in these later days might have been called "slow:" Mrs. Beauclerc's parties mostly were so. They were talking of Frederick St. John when Henry went in, who was again absent from Westerbury, visiting somewhere with his mother and Lady Anne.

Henry wore his medal; the broad blue ribbon conspicuous. Some time was taken up examining that, and then he was asked to sing. It was a treat to hear him; and his voice as yet gave forth no token of losing its power and sweetness, though he was close upon sixteen.

He sang song after song—for they pressed for it—accompanying himself. One song that he was especially asked for, he could not remember without the music. Mrs. Wilberforce suggested that he should fetch it from home, but Georgina said she could play it for him, and sat down. It was that fine song called "The Treasures of the Deep," by Mrs. Hemans. It was found, however, that she could not play it; and after two or three attempts, she began a waltz instead; and the ladies, in the distance round the fire, forgot at length that they had wanted it.

Georgina wore an evening dress of white spotted muslin, a broad blue sash round her waist, and a bit of narrow blue velvet suspending a cross on her neck. She had taken off her bracelets to play, and her pretty white arms were bare. Her eyes were blue as the ribbon, and altogether she looked very attractive, very young, and she was that night in one of her wild and inexplicable humours.

What she really said, how he responded, will never be wholly known: certain it is, that she led him on, on, until he resigned himself wholly to the fascination and "told his love;" although he might have known that to do so was little less than madness. She affected to ridicule him; she intimated that her love was not for a college boy; but all the while her looks gave the lie to her words; her blue eyes spoke of admiration still; her flushed face of triumphant, gratified vanity. They were engaged round the fire, round the tables, anywhere; and Georgina had it all to herself, and played bars of music now and then, as if she were essaying different pieces.

"Let us put aside this nonsense," she suddenly said. "It is nonsense, and you know it, Harry. Here's a song," snatching the first that came to hand—"sing this; I'll play it for you."

"Do you think I can sing?—now? with your cold words blighting me. Oh, tell me the worst!" he added, his tone one of strange pain. "Tell me—"

"Goodness, Henry Arkell. If you look and talk in that serious manner, I shall think you have become crazy. Come; begin."

"I seem to be in a sort of dream," he murmured, putting his hands to his temples. "Surely all the past, all our pleasant intercourse, is not to be forgotten! You will not throw me away like this?"

"Where's the use of my playing this symphony, if you don't begin?"

"Georgina!—let me call you so for the first, perhaps for the last time—dear Georgina, you cannot forget the past! You cannot mean what you have just said."

"How unpleasant you are making things to-night!" she said, with a laugh. "I shall begin to think you have followed the example of those wretched little juniors, and taken plentifully of wine."

"Perhaps I have; perhaps it is owing to that that I have courage freely to talk to you now. Georgina, you know how I have loved you; you know that for years and years my life has been as one long blissful dream, filled with the image of you."

She stole a glance at him from her blue eyes; a smile hovered on her parted lips. He bent his head until his brown wavy curls mingled with her lighter hair.

"Georgina, you know—you know that you can be life or death to me."

He could not speak with consecutive smoothness; his heart was beating as if it would burst its bounds, his whole frame thrilled, his fingers were trembling.

"Tell me that it is not all to be forgotten!"

"Indeed, if you have been cultivating a wrong impression—I can only advise you to forget it. I have liked you;" her voice sank to the lowest whisper—"very much; I have been so stupid as to let you see it; but I never meant you to—to—presume upon it in this uncomfortable manner."

"One question!" he urged. "Only one. Is it that you have played with me, loving another?"

Her right hand was on the keys of the piano, striking chords continually; a false note grating now and then on the ear. Her left hand lay passive on her lap, as she sat, slightly turned to him.

"Stuff and nonsense! No, I have not. You will have them overhear you, Harry."

"Do not equivocate—dearest Georgina—let me hear the truth. It may be better for me; I can bear anything rather than deceit. Let me know the truth; I beseech it of you by all the hours we have passed together."

"Harry, you are decidedly beside yourself to-night. Don't suffer the world behind to get a notion of it."

"You are playing with me now," he said, quite a wail in his low voice. "Let me, one way or the other, be at rest. I never shall bear this suspense, and live. Give me an answer, Georgina; one that shall abide for ever."

"An answer to what?"

"Have you all this while loved another?"

She took her hand off the keys, and began picking out the treble notes of a song with her forefinger, bending her head slightly.

"The answer might not be palatable."

"No, it may not. Nevertheless, I pray you give it me. You are killing me, Georgina."

She looked up hastily; she saw that the bright, transparent complexion of the face had turned to a deadly whiteness; and, perhaps, in that one moment, Georgina Beauclerc's heart smote her with a slight reproach of cruelty. But she may have deemed it well to put an end to the suspense, and she bent her head again as she spoke.

"Even though I had loved another, what of that? I don't admit that I have; and I say that it is a question you have no right to ask me. Harry! be reasonable; though I had loved you, it could not come to anything; you know it could not; so what does it signify?"

"But you have not loved me?"

"Well—no. Not in that way. Here's the dean coming in; and here's pompous old Ferraday. You must sing a song; papa's sure to ask for one."

She hastened from the piano, as if glad to escape. The dean did ask for a song. But when they came to look for him who was to sing it, he was nowhere to be seen.

"Bless me!" cried the dean, "I thought Henry Arkell was here. Where is he?"

"I dare say he has gone home for the 'Treasures of the Deep,' papa," readily replied Georgina. "Somebody asked him to fetch it just now."

He had not gone for the "Treasures of the Deep;" and, as she guessed pretty accurately, he had no intention of returning. He was walking slowly towards the master's house, his temporary home; his head was aching, his brain was burning, and he felt as if all life had gone out of him for ever. That she had been befooling him; that she loved Frederick St. John with an impassioned lasting love, appeared to him as clear as the stars in a frosty sky.

But there were no stars then, and no frost; the fineness of the night had gone, and a drizzling rain was falling. He did not heed it; it might wet him if it would, might soak even that gay blue badge on his breast. Two people within view seemed to heed it as little; they were pacing together, arm-in-arm, in a dark part of the grounds, talking in an undertone. So absorbed were they, that both started when Henry came up; they were near a gaslight then, and he recognised George Prattleton. The other face, on which the light shone brightly, he did not know.

"How d'ye do?" said Henry. "Do you know whether Prattleton junior has got home yet?" Prattleton junior, the younger of the Reverend Mr. Prattleton's sons, was in the choir under Henry; and the senior chorister had had some trouble with that gentleman at the dinner-table on this, the audit-night.

"I don't know anything about Prattleton junior," returned George Prattleton in a testy tone, as if the question itself, or the being spoken to, had annoyed him.

Henry walked on, and round the corner came upon the gentleman in question, Prattleton junior, with another of the choristers, Mr. Wilberforce's son Edwin, each having taken as much as was good for him, both to eat and to drink.

"Who's that with George?" asked Henry—for it was somewhat unusual to see a stranger in the grounds at night.

"Oh, it's a Mr. Rolls," replied young Prattleton: "I heard my brother ask George. He meets him in the billiard rooms."

"Well, you be off home, now; you'll get wet. Wilberforce, I'm going in. You can come with me."

Young Mr. Prattleton appeared disposed to resist the mandate. He liked being in the rain, he persisted. But the arrival of his father at that moment from the deanery settled the matter.

And Henry Arkell, having happened to look back, saw George Prattleton draw the stranger into the shade, and remain in ambush while the minor canon passed.

The succeeding day to this was fine again, a charming day for the middle of November; and when the college school rushed down the steps at four o'clock, the upper boys were tempted to commence one of their noisy games. Nearly the only two who declined were the senior boy and Arkell. The senior of the school, whoever he might be for the time being, rarely, if ever, played, and the present one, Jocelyn, was also too idle. Both went quietly on to the master's, walking arm-in-arm. The school closed at four in the dead of winter. Henry came out again immediately, his music in his hand, and was running past the boys.

"I say, Arkell, we are going to cast lots for the stag. Where are you bolting to?"

"I can't join this evening—I'm off to practise. To-morrow is my lesson day, and I have not touched the organ this week."

"Cram! What's the good? It'll be night directly, and that mouldy old organ loft as dark as pitch."

"Oh, I shall see for ever so long to come—the sun has not set yet," returned Henry, without stopping. "Thank you, Lewis," he added, as a sharp stone struck his trencher. "That was from you, I saw. I shall not pay you back in kind."

There was a sting in the retort, from the very manner of giving it, so pointedly gentleman-like, for Henry Arkell had stopped a moment, and raised his trencher, as he might have done to the dean. Lewis saw that the boys were laughing at him, and he suddenly set upon seven juniors, and made the whole lot cry.

Active and swift, Henry soon gained the precincts of the church, St. James the Less. He pushed open the outer door of the clerk's house, and took the key of the church from its niche in the passage, close to the kitchen door. This he also opened, and looked in. It was a square room, the floor of red brick, and a bed, with a curtain drawn before it, was on one side against the wall. The old man, Hunt, sat smoking in the chimney corner.

"I am going in to play, Hunt. I have the key."

"Very well, sir."

"How's the missis?" he stopped to ask.

"She be bad in all her bones, sir, she be. I told her to lie down for half an hour: it's that nasty ague she have got upon her again. This be a damp spot to live in, so many low trees about," he continued, with a shrug of his shoulders.

Henry could not remember when the "missis" was not "bad in all her bones;" her ague seemed to be chronic. He proceeded on his way, passed the iron gates, walked up the churchyard, and unlocked the church door. Once in, he took the key from the outer lock, and placing it upon the bench inside, pushed the door to, but did not shut it. The taking out the key in this manner was by Mr. Wilberforce's orders: if they left it in the lock outside, some mischievous person might come and remove it, he had told the boys. Then he ascended to the organ-loft and commenced his practising. No blower was required, as certain pedals, touched with the feet, acted instead, something after the manner of a modern harmonium. His heart was in his task, in spite of the heavy care at it, for he loved music; and when it grew too dusk to see, he continued playing from memory.

The shades of evening were gathering outside, as well as in; and under cover of them a boy might have been seen stealing through the churchyard. It was Henry's rival, Lewis, whose mind had just been hatching a nice little revengeful plot. To say that Lewis had been half mad since the preceding day, would not be saying too much: he could have borne anything better than taunts from Miss Beauclerc; and for those taunts he would be revenged, the fates permitting, upon Henry Arkell. He did not quite see how, yet; but, as a little prologue, he intended to lock him in the church for the night, the idea of that having flashed into his mind after Henry had thanked him for throwing the stone.

Lewis gently pulled open the church door, looked for the key, saw it, and snatched it, locked the church door upon the unconscious boy, who was playing, and stole back again, key in hand. Beyond the gates of the churchyard he stopped to laugh, as though he had accomplished a great feat.

"Won't his crowing be cooled by morning! He'll be seeing ghosts all night, and calling out blue murder; but nobody can hear him, and there he must stop with them. What a jolly sell!"

He hid the key in his jacket pocket until he reached old Hunt's house. Lewis knew it was kept there, but did not know there was a niche or a nail for it in the passage. He did not care to be seen, and therefore must get the key in, in the best way he could.

The clerk and his ailing wife were sitting by their fire now, taking tea. A china saucer, containing some milk, had just been put down on the brick floor for the cat, a snarling, enormous yellow animal, but a particularly cherished one by both master and mistress. The cat had got her nose in it, and the old woman was lovingly regarding her, when the door opened about an inch, and the church key came flying in, propelled on to the cat's head and the saucer. The cat started away with a howl, the saucer flew in pieces, and the milk was scattered. In the midst of this the door closed again, and footsteps were heard scampering off.

"Mercy on us!" shrieked the old dame, startled out of her seven senses. "What be that?"

The clerk, recovering his consternation, rose and regarded the damage; the broken saucer, the wasted milk, and the scared cat—the genial animal standing with her back up in the farthest corner.

"That's the way they do it, is it?" he wrathfully cried, as he stooped to pick up the key, a difficult process, from his rheumatic loins. "My gentleman can't bring in the key and hang it up decently, but must shy it in, and do this mischief! I wonder the master lets 'em have the run of the organ! I wouldn't."

"It were that Robbins, I know," said the dame, shaking still.

"It were just the t'other, then—Arkell. Poor pussy! poor tit, tit, tit!"

"Arkell! Why he be always so quiet and perlite!"

"It's a perlite thing to fling the key in upon us after this fashion, ain't it?" growled the clerk.

"Come along then, titsey! Don't put its back up! Come to its missis!"

But the outraged cat wholly refused to be soothed. It snarled, and spit, and snarled again; making a spring finally into a pantry, and thence away through an open casement window.

The tea hour at the head master's was half-past five; and the boys sat down to it this evening as usual. They were accustomed to take that meal alone, and the absence of one or other of the boys at it had become, in consequence, rather general; therefore, Arkell's not appearing went really without notice. Lewis appeared to be in a flow of delight, and devoured Arkell's share of bread-and-butter as well as his own. There were in all, at this time, about ten boarders residing at the master's, some of them being his private pupils. The two Lewises were there still; but Mrs. Lewis had given notice of their removal at Christmas, as she intended to receive them into the house she had taken possession of—the late Marmaduke Carr's.

Now it happened, by good or by ill luck, as the reader may decide, that the master and Mrs. Wilberforce were abroad that evening. In his absence the senior boy had full authority, and the rest dared not disobey him. This might not have been well with some seniors; but Jocelyn was one in whom confidence could be placed. At supper—eight o'clock—Arkell was still absent, and Jocelyn now observed it. One of the others remarked that he was most likely at the deanery. This was Vaughan; a rather stupid boy, who had been nicknamed in consequence Bright Vaughan.

At nine o'clock, the man-servant brought in the book for prayers, read by the senior boy when the master himself was not there. Absence from prayers was never excused, unless under the especial permission of Mr. Wilberforce; and he would have severely punished any boy guilty of it. Another thing that he exacted was, that prayers should be read precisely to the hour. So Jocelyn read them, and the servant carried away the book.

"I say, though, where can Arkell be?" wondered the boys. "He's never out like this, unless he has leave."

"Perhaps he means to make a night of it?" suggested Lewis junior, opportunely enough, if he had but known it.

"Hold your tongue, Lewis junior," said Jocelyn. "He may have got leave from the master for the evening, and we not know it."

"I don't think he has, though," dissented young Wilberforce.

"We won't split upon him," eagerly spoke up Lewis—not the junior. "He has been a horrid sneak, especially in getting himself in with the dean's daughter; but it won't do to begin splitting one upon another."

"I should like to hear any of you attempting it," authoritatively spoke the senior boy. "I'd split you."

"We don't mean to. Don't be so sharp, Jocelyn."

"There's not the least doubt that he is at the deanery," decided Jocelyn. "I heard something said the other day about the master's having given him general leave to stop there, when asked, without coming home to say it."

"Who told you that, Jocelyn?" questioned Lewis, his ears turning red.

"I heard it, and that's enough. The master can depend upon Arkell, you know."

"Oh, can he though!" cried Lewis, ironically. "I'd lay a crown he's not at the deanery."

"Up to bed, boys," commanded Jocelyn.

The Lewises, senior and junior, and Henry Arkell slept in one room; the rest of the boys were divided into two others. The rooms in the quaint old house were not large. All had separate beds. Arkell's was in the corner behind the door. Marmaduke Lewis, the younger, was in bed immediately, schoolboy fashion, the process occupying about half-a-minute; but the elder did not seem inclined to be so quick to-night. He dawdled about the room, brushed his hair, held his mouth open to admire his teeth in the glass, tried how many different faces he could make, stuck pins in the candle, and, in short, seemed in anything but a bed humour. In the midst of this delay, he heard the voice of Mr. Wilberforce, speaking to one of the servants, as he ascended the stairs.

What Lewis did, in his consternation, he hardly knew. The first thing was to turn the candle upside down in the candlestick, and jam it well in; the next was to fling some of his brother's clothes on to his own chair; and the third to bolt into bed with his own clothes on, and draw the counterpane over his head. Mr. Wilberforce opened the door.

"Are you in bed, boys?"

Lewis put part of his face out.

"Yes, sir. Good night, sir."

"Good night," repeated Mr. Wilberforce, and closed the door upon the room.

Lewis breathed a blessing upon all propitious stars, that he had not looked behind the door at the vacant bed. Then his going to let out Arkell was impossible, now Mr. Wilberforce was in: which had been the indecisive project agitating his brain.

And now we must return to Henry Arkell. The church of St. James the Less struck a quarter past five when Henry took his fingers from the keys of the organ. "Only a quarter past five," he soliloquized; "how the evenings draw in! Last week was moonlight, and I did not notice it so much. I don't see how I shall get my practising here these winter months, unless I snatch an hour between morning and afternoon school."

He felt for his music, for it was too dark to see, rolled it up, and then felt his way down the narrow and nearly perpendicular staircase, dark even in daylight. When he reached the bench at the entrance, he placed his hand on the spot where he had put the key. He could not feel it: he only supposed he had missed the spot by an inch or two, and groped about with his hands. He turned to the door to pull it open, and let in the light.

The door was closed, was fast; and Henry Arkell felt his face grow hot as the truth burst upon him, that he was fastened up in the church. He concluded that the old clerk had done it in mistake. "I must ring the bell," thought he, "and let them know somebody's in the church."

But he was doomed to fresh disappointment, for, on groping his way to the belfry, he found it fastened: cords, bells, and all were locked up. Sometimes this door was locked, sometimes it was left open, just as the clerk remembered, or not, to fasten it.

"I can't stop here all night!" exclaimed he, his face growing more and more heated. "What in the world am I to do?"

What indeed? What would you have done, reader? Set on and shouted? But there was nobody to hear: the church was solitary, and its walls were thick. Thump at the door? But if you had nothing but your hands to thump with, little hope that any result would be obtained.

It was a novel and a disagreeable situation for the boy to be placed in—locked alone in the gloomy old church; gloomy in more than one sense of the word, and smelling of the dead. The small, confined windows were high up in the walls, and entirely inaccessible, and there was no other outlet. The vestry was only lighted by two panes of thick glass inserted into its roof; and, in short, the case was hopeless.

And the boy grew so. He shouted, and called, and thumped, just as you or I might have done, without any regard to its manifest inutility. He was a brave-spirited boy, owning a clear conscience; and he was a singularly religious boy, far more so than it is usual for those of his age to be, possessing an ever-present trust in God's good care and protection. Still, disagreeable thoughts would intrude: his lonely situation stood out in exaggerated force, and recollections of a certain ghostly tale, connected with that church, rose up before him. It was a tale which had gone the round of Westerbury the previous year, and the ghostly-inclined put firm faith in it. The old clerk was an obstinate believer in it, for he had seen it with his own eyes; the sexton had seen it with his, and two gravediggers had seen it with theirs. A citizen had died, and been buried in the middle aisle, not many yards from where Henry Arkell now stood. After his burial, suspicion arose that he had not come fairly to his end, and the coroner had issued his mandate for the disinterment of the body, and the sexton and two gravediggers proceeded to their task. They chose night to do it in, "not to be bothered with starers at 'em," they said; and the clerk chose to bear them company. At three o'clock in the morning the whole four rushed out of the church panic-stricken, made their way to the nearest street, and rose it with their frantic cries. Windows were thrown up in alarm, and nightcaps stretched out—what on earth was the matter? The buried man's ghost had appeared to them in a sea of blue flame, was the trembling tale they told, and which went forth to Westerbury. The blue flame was accounted for; the ghost, never. They had a basin full of gin with them, and, in lighting a pipe, they had managed to set light to the gin, which immediately ascended in a ghastly stream. The men, it was found, had a little gin on board themselves, as well as in the basin; and to that, no doubt, in conjunction with the blue flames, the ghost owed its origin.

Now a ghost in broad daylight, with all the bustle and reality of mid-day life about us, and a ghost fastened up with oneself in a church at night-time, bear two widely different aspects. Henry Arkell had heartily laughed at the story, had made merry over the consternation of the half-drunken men, but he did not altogether enjoy being so near the ghostly spot now; for though reason tried to be heard, imagination had got fast hold of the reins. He lifted his eyes, with a desperate effort, and looked round the church: he began to calculate which was the very spot, in the gloom of the middle aisle: he grasped the door of a pew near where he stood, and bent his face down upon it in an agony of terror.

"And I must be here until morning," his conviction whispered. "O God! keep this terror from me! Send thine Holy Spirit to come near and strengthen me! Oh, yes, yes," he resumed, after a pause; "I shall be all right if I do but trust in God. He is everywhere; He is with me now. I will go up to the organ again."

He groped his way up, sat down, and began to play as well as he could in the perfect darkness. He played some of the cathedral chants, and sang to them; it was a curious sound, echoing there in the dark and lonely night; and it was a positive fact that, in so doing, his superstitious alarm passed, from his mind.

But oh, how long the hours were! how long the quarters, as the slow clock gave them out! He still kept on playing, dreading to leave off lest the terror should come back again. When it struck nine, he could have thought it four in the morning, judging by the dreary time that seemed to have elapsed. "The boys will be going up to bed directly," he said, thinking of the master's; "oh, why don't they send out to look for me? But they'd never think of looking here!"

He kept on playing. About ten o'clock he knelt down to say his prayers, as if preparing to retire for the night, and then ensconced himself as comfortably as he could on the seat of the singers, which was well cushioned. "If I could but go to sleep, and sleep till daylight," thought he, "there would be no chance of that foolish terror coming back again. Foolish indeed! How very absurd I am!"

He fell into a train of thought; not happy thought: schoolboys have trouble as well as grown people: and Henry Arkell had plenty just then, as you know. The superstitious feeling did not come back, and at length he sank into sleep.

He did not know what roused him: something did. The first thing he heard distinctly was a scuffling noise, followed by a "hush-sh-sh!" breathed from a human voice. He felt a cramped sensation all over, but that arose from his inconvenient couch, and he could not for the life of him remember where he was.

He stretched out his hand, and it came in contact with the front of the gallery; it was close to him, for the singers' seat was very narrow: he raised himself to look over, still not remembering what had passed. He seemed to be in a church, for one of two male figures, walking up the aisle, carried a lighted taper, which threw its glimmering upon the pews, though the man shaded it with his hand. Whether Henry Arkell had been dreaming of robbers, certain it is, he judged these men to be such: they turned off to the vestry, which was on the side of the church, nearly at the top; and he rubbed his eyes, and full recollection returned to him.

"What has put robbers in my head?" he debated. "They are not robbers: they must be come to look for me. But they stole up as if they were robbers!" he added after a pause. "And why did they not call out to me?"

An impulse took him down from the gallery and up the church; he moved as silently as the men had done. The vestry door was open, and he stood outside on the matting and peeped in, secure of not being seen in the darkness. To his surprise, he recognised faces he knew—gentlemen's faces, not robbers'. One of them was George Prattleton; and the other was the stranger he had seen with him the previous night. What were they doing in the vestry at that hour?

"Now make haste about it, Rolls," George Prattleton was saying, as Henry gazed in. "I don't half like the work, and if I had not been more hard up than any poor devil ever was yet, you would never have got me on to it. There's the register."

George Prattleton had unlocked a safe and taken a book from it, which he put on the table. "Mind, Rolls, you are not to copy anything; that was the agreement."

"I don't want to copy anything: I gave you my word, didn't I?" was the reply of Mr. Rolls, who had seized upon the book. "I only want to see whether a certain entry is here, or whether it is not, and I give you 20l. for getting me the sight: and a deuced easy way it is of earning 20l., Prattleton."

Rolls had drawn a chair to the table, and was poring over the register, as he spoke, turning the leaves one by one. Prattleton stood by, and held the candle, not very steadily.

"I can't see, if you whiffle it like that, Prat," cried Mr. Rolls, taking the candlestick from his hand and setting it on the table.

"How long shall you be?"

"Why, I have hardly begun. Don't be impatient. Sit down on that other chair and take a nap, if you are tired."

Prattleton continued to stand at the table, but his impatience was evidently great. His back was to Henry Arkell, but the boy had full view of the countenance and movements of the other: his interest, in what was passing, was not less than his astonishment.

"You say you know the date, so where's the use of being so dilatory?" cried Mr. Prattleton. "You turn over the leaves as slow as if you were going to execution. Ah, you have it now, I think."

"No, I have not." And Rolls turned another leaf over as he spoke, and went on studying; but he stealthily placed his thumb to mark the page he left. Prattleton yawned, whistled, and yawned again, and finally turned away and began to look in the safe; anything to cover his impatience. Upon which, Henry Arkell distinctly saw Rolls turn back to the page where his thumb was, examine it intently, and then silently blow out the light.

"Halloa!" roared Prattleton, finding himself in darkness.

"What a beast of a candle!" indignantly uttered Mr. Rolls. "It's gone out!"

"What put it out?"

"How can I tell? The damp, I suppose: everything smells mouldy. Give us the matches, Prat."

"I have not got the matches. You took them."

"Did I? Then I'm blest if I have not left them on the bench at the door. Go for them, Prat, will you: if I lose my place in the book I shall have to begin all over again, and that will keep us longer than you'd like."

Mr. Prattleton—with a few expletives not often heard in churches—felt his way through the vestry door. Henry had not time to retreat, so he drew himself closely up against the wall, and Prattleton passed him. But, to Henry Arkell's surprise, a light almost immediately reappeared inside the vestry. He naturally looked in again.

Rolls had relighted the candle, and was inserting what looked like a thin board, behind one of the leaves of the register: he then drew a sharp penknife down it, close to the binding, and out came the leaf, leaving no trace. He folded the leaf, put it in his pocket with the board and the knife, and then blew out the light again. All was accomplished with speed, but with perfect coolness. "Nothing risk, nothing win," cried he, audibly: "I thought I could do him."

Prattleton soon came up the church with the box of matches, igniting some as he walked, by way of lighting his steps. Henry drew away against the wall, and crouched down beneath a dark mahogany pew.

"There go the three-quarters past one, Rolls; we have been in here five-and-twenty minutes. Don't let the light go out again."

"I shall soon have done. I am getting near the place where the entry ought to be—if it is in at all; but I told you there was a doubt. So much the better for us if it's not."

Prattleton sat down and drummed on the table. Rolls came to the end of the register.

"It's not in, Prattleton. Hurrah! It will be thousands of pounds in our pocket. When the other side brought forth the lame tale that there was such a thing, we thought it was a bag of moonshine. Here's your register. Put it up."

Henry stole silently towards the church door, hoping to get out: he dared not show himself to those two swindlers. He was fortunate: though the door was locked, the key was in, and he passed out, leaving it open. What he was to do with himself till morning, he knew not: he might sit down on the gravestones; but he had had enough of graves; he supposed he must pace the town.

The gentlemen set things straight in the vestry, and also came, in due course, to the door. They had left it locked, and now it was open! Each looked at the other in amazement.

"What possessed you to do that?" demanded Rolls, in a fiercer tone than was consistent with politeness.

"I do it! that's good," retorted Prattleton. "It was you locked it, or pretended to."

"I did lock it. You must have opened it when you came down for the matches."

"I wish we may be dropped upon if I did! I should be an idiot to open the door and give nightbirds a chance of scenting what we were up to."

"Psha!" impatiently uttered Rolls, "a locked door could not open of itself. But there's no harm done; so blow out the light, and let's get off."

Thus disputing—for in truth the open door had struck something like terror on the heart of both—George Prattleton and his friend quitted the church, leaving all secure. Mr. George had to carry the key home with him; he could not fling it into the clerk's house, as Lewis had done, for the house was fastened up; most houses are at two in the morning. He had successfully executed a little ruse to get the key, unsuspected by the clerk: watching his opportunity, he had arrived at the clerk's house when that official had gone out for his supper-beer, ostensibly to put a question in regard to the time that a funeral was to take place on the morrow; and while talking to the old dame, he managed to abstract the key, hanging one that outwardly resembled it in its place. The Reverend Mr. Prattleton often took the duty at St. James the Less for the head master; and George was tolerably familiar with its ways and places.

They went along with stealthy steps, their eyes peering fitfully into dark corners, lest any should be abroad and see them. Once in the more frequented streets it did not so much matter; they might be going home from some late entertainment, as Mr. George and his latch-key were not infrequently in the habit of doing. Rolls was in a glow of delight; and even an odd fear of detection now and then could not check it.

"I was as sure there was no entry there as sure can be. Our side was sure of it also; only it was well to look and see. I'm more glad than if anybody had put a hundred pounds in my hand."

"Who is your side?" asked George Prattleton. "You have not told me anything, you know, Rolls."

"Well, it would not be very interesting to you. It's an old dispute about a tithe cause; the name's Whiffam."

Not a very lucid explanation; but George Prattleton was tired and cross, and not really overcurious. At the corner of a street he and Rolls parted, and Mr. George went home and let himself in with his latch-key, deeming nobody the wiser for the night's exploit.

CHAPTER XVI

PERPLEXITY

Henry Arkell had ample leisure that night for reflection. He got into a newly-built house, whose doors were not yet in, glad of even that shelter. The precise object of what he had seen he did not presume to guess; but, that some bad deed had been transacted, there could be no doubt. And what ought to be his course in it?—it was that that was puzzling him. He could not go to Mr. Wilberforce, the incumbent of the church, and denounce George Prattleton—as he would have done had this stranger, Rolls, been the sole offender. Of all the people in Westerbury, that it should have been George Prattleton!—the brother of that kind man from whom his family had received so many obligations. Gratitude towards Mr. Prattleton seemed to demand his silence as to George; and Henry Arkell had an almost ultra sense of the sin of ingratitude.

There was no one of whom he could take counsel; his father was still absent, and he did not like to betray what he had seen to others. Once, the thought crossed him to ask Travice Arkell; but he knew how vexed George Prattleton would be; and he came to the final resolution of speaking to George himself. The mystery of locking him in seemed to be clear now. He supposed George had done it to get possession of the key, not knowing he was in the church.

With the first glimmering dawn of morning—not very early, you know, in November—Henry was hovering about the precincts of the clerk's house. He had no particular business there; but he was restless, and thought he might, by good luck, see or find out something, and he could not hope yet to get in at the master's. Hunt came out to fasten back his shutters.

"What's it you, sir?" exclaimed the old man, in surprise. "You be abroad betimes."

"Ay. How's the rheumatism?"

"Be you going to pay for that chaney saucer you broke?" asked Hunt, allowing the rheumatism to drop into abeyance.

"What saucer?"

"Why that chaney saucer. It was on the floor with the cat's milk, when you flung the key in last night and broke it. The missis is as vexed as can be—she have had it for years; and if it were cracked a bit, it did for our cat."

"I never broke it," returned Henry. "At least," he added, recollecting himself, and afraid of making some admission that might excite inquiries, "I did not know that I did."

"No, you weren't perlite enough to stop and see what damage you'd done; you made off as fast as your legs would take you. Here's the pieces on the dresser," added the clerk; "you can come and look at the smash you've made. The missis began a talking of getting 'em jined. 'Jine seven pieces,' says I; 'it would cost more nor a new one of the best chaney; and run out then.'"

He hobbled indoors as fast as he could for his lameness, and Henry followed him. The church key hung on its nail in the niche. Henry stared at it with open eyes; he did not expect to see it there. Had George Prattleton returned it to the clerk in the middle of the night? and was the old man an accomplice? But, as he gazed, his keen eye detected something not familiar in its aspect, and he raised his hand and turned the wards into the light. It was not the church key, though it closely resembled it.

He went into the kitchen: the old man was putting the broken pieces in a row. "There they be, sir; you can count 'em for yourself; and they ought to be replaced with a new one. A common delf would be better than none, for we be short of saucers, and the missis don't like a animal to drink out of the same as us Christians."

"You shall have a saucer," said Henry, somewhat dreamily. "Who threw in the key?"

"Who threw it in?" echoed the clerk.

"I meant to ask what time it was thrown in."

"Why, about five, or a little after: we was at tea. Didn't you know what time it was, yourself, with the clock going the quarters and the halves in your ears while you was at the organ? The missis—Who's that!"

The "who's that!" referred to a thumping at the house door, which Henry Arkell had closed when he came in. The clerk went and opened it. It was Lewis. Henry recognised his voice, and drew back out of sight.

Now, however uncomfortably Henry Arkell had passed the night, the author of his misfortune had passed it more so. Conscience, especially at the midnight hours, does indeed make cowards of us all, and it had made a miserable one of the senior Lewis. Not that he repented of what he had done, for the ill in itself, or from a better feeling towards his schoolfellow; but he feared the consequences. Suppose Henry Arkell, locked up with the dead, should die of fright, or turn mad? Lewis remembered to have heard of such things. Suppose he should, by a superhuman effort, reach one of the high and narrow windows, and, impelled by terror, propel himself through it and be killed? Why he, Lewis, would be hung; or, at the very least, transported for life. These flights of imagination, conveniently suppressing themselves during the evening, worked him into a state of indescribable dread and agitation, when alone at night. How he lay through it he could not tell, and as soon as the master's servants were astir, he got up and sneaked out of the house, with the intention of looking after Arkell, and what the night might have brought forth for him, administering first of all a preliminary beating to his brother as an instalment of what he would get, if he opened his mouth to tell of Arkell's absence.

"Why, what do you want?" uttered the clerk, when he saw Lewis. "We shall have the whole rookery of you college gents here presently."

Lewis paid no attention to what the words might imply; indeed, it may be questioned if he heard them, so great was his state of suspense and agitation. "Old fellow," said he, "I want the key of the church. Do lend it me: I'll bring it back to you directly."

"The key of the church!" returned the clerk; "you'll come and ask me for my house next. No, no, young master; I have not got the rector's orders to trust it to any but the two what practises. What do you want in the church?"

"Only to look after something that's left there. It's all right. I won't keep it five minutes."

"No, that you won't, sir, for you won't get it. If the master says you may have it, well and good; but you must get his orders first."

Lewis was desperate. He saw the key hanging in its place, rushed forward, took it from the hook, and made off with it in defiance.

"I won't have this," uttered the discomfited old man. "One a breaking our cat's saucer, and t'other a thieving off the key in my very face! I'll complain to Mr. Wilberforce. Sir, what do that senior Lewis want in the church? He looked as resolute as a lion, and his breath was a panting. What's he after?"

"It is beyond my comprehension," replied Henry, who was preparing to depart, more mystified than before. "If Lewis can get out, I can get in," he thought to himself, "and by dint of some great good luck, they may not have missed me."

Calling out a good morning to Hunt, he hastened away in the direction of the master's, wondering much what Lewis wanted in the church, but not believing it could have reference to his own incarceration.

The next actor on the scene was George Prattleton. He softly entered the clerk's passage, and stretched his hand up to the niche. But there he halted as if dumbfounded, and a key which he held he dropped back into his pocket again.

"What the mischief has been at work now?" muttered he. "How can the old man's eyes have been so quick? I must face the matter boldly, and persuade him his eyes are wrong. Hunt," cried he, aloud, pushing open the kitchen door, "where's the key of the church?"

"Where indeed, sir!" grumbled Hunt. "One of them senior college rebels have just been in and clawed it. But I promise him he won't do it twice: Mr. Wilberforce shall know the tricks they play me, now I'm old. Did you want it, sir?"

"No," returned George Prattleton, carelessly. "I saw it was not on its nail, that's all. I came to know the hour fixed for the funeral. Mr. Prattleton desired me to ascertain, and I looked in last evening, but you were out."

"The missis told me you had been, sir, but I had only just stepped out for our supper beer. Three o'clock to-day is the hour, sir: I thought the missis told you."

At this juncture, in came Lewis, very pale. "Hunt, this is not the key; it won't undo it; and—"

Lewis stopped in consternation, for his eyes had fallen on Mr. George Prattleton. The latter took the key from his unresisting hand.

"If Hunt is to let you college boys have the key at will, and you get tampering with the lock, no wonder it will not undo it. I had better keep it for him," he added, slipping it into his own pocket. "What did you want with the key, Lewis?"

Lewis did not answer.

"Here, Hunt, I'll give you up possession," continued Mr. Prattleton, putting the key on the hook; "but you know if any damage is done to the church, through your allowing indiscriminate entrance to these college gentlemen, you will be held responsible."

"I allow 'em!" returned the indignant clerk. "But Mr. Wilberforce shall settle it."

"That's not the church key," said Lewis, staring at the one just hung up.

Mr. Prattleton heard the assertion with equanimity, and began whistling a popular air as he left the house. Hunt just glanced upwards, and saw it was the veritable church key. "It is the key," he said. "What do you mean?"

"It must have been my shaking hand then," debated Lewis. "Old Hunt must know the key, and George Prattleton too. Hunt," he added, aloud, "you will lend me the key again for five minutes."

"No, sir," raved out the old clerk, "and I hope you'll be flogged for having took it in defiance, though you be a senior, and a'most six foot high."

He pushed Lewis out at the door as he spoke, fearing another act of defiance, and closed it.

Lewis stood in irresolution; his terror for the fate of Henry Arkell was strong upon him. He flew after George Prattleton.

"Will you do me a favour?" he panted, completely out of breath in his haste and agitation. "I want to get into the church, and Hunt has turned obstinate about the key. Will you get it from him for me?"

Mr. Prattleton stopped and gazed at him. "You cannot want anything in the church, Lewis. What are you up to?"

"Do get the key for me," he entreated, unable to help betraying his emotion. "I must go in; I must, Mr. Prattleton. It may be a matter of life or death."

"You are ill, Lewis; you are agitated. What is all this?"

"I am not ill. I only want to get into the church."

"For what purpose?"

"It's a little private matter of my own."

"You can tell me what it is."

"No, I cannot do that."

"Then I cannot help you."

Lewis was pushed to his wits' end. George Prattleton was walking on, but turned again and waited. He was not free from some inward wonder and agitation himself, remembering his own adventure of the past night.

"If I trust a secret to you, will you promise, on your honour, not to tell it again?" asked Lewis. "It's nothing much; only a lark, concerning one of us college boys."

"Oh, I'll promise," readily answered George Prattleton, who was rarely troubled with scruples of any sort, and used to be fond of "larks" himself; rather too much so.

"Well, then, I locked Harry Arkell in the church last night, and I want to go and see after him, for fear he should be dead of fright, or something of that, you know."

"In there all night? in the church all night?" stammered George Prattleton, as if he could not take in the meaning of the words.

"He went in to practise after school yesterday evening, and I turned the key upon him, and took it back to old Hunt's, and he has been in there ever since, fastened up with the ghosts. I did it only for a lark, you know."

George Prattleton's arms dropped powerless by his side, and his face turned of some livid colour between white and green. Would the previous night's exploit—his exploit—come out to the world through this miserable fellow's ill-timed "joke?" But all they could do now was to see after Henry Arkell.

They went back to the clerk's, and George Prattleton took the key from the hook.

"Something has been dropped in the church, Hunt," he carelessly said; "I'll go myself with Lewis, and see that he meddles with nothing."

"Something dropped in the church?" repeated the old man; "then, I suppose, that was what the other college gent has been after; though he didn't say nothing of it. He was here afore I had opened our shutters."

"Which of them was that?" asked George Prattleton, pausing, with the key in his hand.

"It were Mr. Arkell, sir; him what goes in to practise on the organ. He were in yesterday practising, and he flung the key back when he'd done, and broke our cat's chaney saucer, and then made off. I've been a showing him the mischief he went and done."

"Was that Mr. Arkell, do you say? Has Arkell been here this morning?"

"Why, it ain't two minutes since, sir. He cut up that way as if he was going straight home."

And as the man spoke, there flashed into George Prattleton's mind the little episode that had so startled him and his friend Rolls in the night—the finding of the church door open, when they had surely locked it. It must have been then that Henry Arkell got out of the church. How much had he witnessed of the scene in the vestry? had he recognised him, George Prattleton?

George Prattleton exchanged a look with Lewis, and hung the key up again, making some vague remark to the clerk, that Mr. Arkell had probably found what they were about to look for, if he had been to practise so recently as yesterday evening. Shutting the door behind him, he walked away with Lewis, whose senses were in a state of hopeless perplexity.

"He has got out, you hear, Lewis."

"But how could he get out?" returned Lewis. "He's not a fairy, to get through the keyhole, and he couldn't have got down from the windows! It's an impossibility."

"These apparent 'impossibilities' turn out sometimes to have been the most straightforward trifles in the world," observed George Prattleton, carelessly. "How do we know but old Hunt may have gone into the church himself last evening, to dust it, or what not? It is—"

"But then, Arkell would have come home," debated the perplexed Lewis, who truly thought some incomprehensible magic must have been at work.

"Well, Lewis, I don't think it much signifies how he got out, provided he is out; and were I you, I should not inquire too closely into particulars. You had better keep as quiet as you can in the matter; that's my advice to you; Mr. Wilberforce might not be disposed to treat your exploit as a 'joke,' should it come to his ears."

"But nobody knows it was me," said Lewis, eagerly.

"Just so: therefore your policy should be to keep still. As you please, though, of course."

"You won't tell of me, Mr. Prattleton?"

"Not I, faith! It's no affair of mine; but I'd not recommend you to attempt it again, Lewis. Good morning; I'm going into the town."

So early had they been abroad, and all this taken place, that it was not yet very much past seven, and when Henry Arkell reached the master's house, some of the boys were only going out of it for morning school. The hour for assembling was seven, but in the winter season some irregularity in arriving was winked at, for the best of all possible reasons, that the masters were late themselves; and it was often half past before the senior boy called over the roll. Henry went upstairs to give his face a wash; the man-servant saw him going up, but supposed he had only returned for something he might have forgotten. Neither of the Lewises was in the room, and he found his own bed tumbled as if he had slept in it. This of course had been Lewis's care; but Henry wondered at it. If Lewis had done it out of good nature, that his absence should not be observed, he must have changed greatly. It must be remembered that he knew nothing of Lewis's having locked him in the church; he supposed that must have been George Prattleton; but what he had seen tied his tongue from inquiring.

Jocelyn had done calling the roll when Henry got to the college hall. It was so unusual a thing for him to be marked late, that Jocelyn heaved his eyebrows in a sort of lazy surprise. Presently Jocelyn asked him in an undertone where he had been the previous evening.

"You missed me, then?" said Henry.

"Missed you!—we couldn't help missing you; you had not got back at bed-time. I suppose you were at the deanery—and got home at eleven? It's fine to be you! How's Miss Beauclerc?"

"As well as usual," replied Henry, with a nod and a laugh, to keep up the deception. Jocelyn's assumed idea was the most convenient one that could have been taken up.

Henry threw his eyes round the school in search of the Lewises. Surely they must know of his night's absence. The elder one he could not see; but the younger was at his desk with a red and sullen face, the effects of the private beating. He sat down to his lessons, with what courage he had, after his vigil; and presently, happening to look up, he saw Lewis senior.

Lewis senior was stealthily regarding him over the corner of a desk, with as much inward curiosity as though he had risen from the dead. Lewis was in a perplexed state of mystification yet. There Arkell was, sure enough; alive, and apparently well. He had not become an idiot; that, Lewis could see; he had not parted with his arms and legs. How had he got out? But the relief, to find him thus, was so great to Lewis's mind, that his spirits rose to a reckless height; and he was insolent to Jocelyn when the latter spoke to him about coming in after the roll was called.

At breakfast time Henry went in search of George Prattleton, but could not see him; the probability was that Mr. George had gone to bed again, and was taking out his night's rest by daylight. He sought him again at dinner-time, and then he had gone out; the two Prattleton boys thought to the billiard rooms. In the afternoon, however, as Henry was passing through the cloisters to the school, after service in the cathedral, he met him.

George Prattleton listened with an air of apparent incredulity to the tale; Henry had got locked up in the church, and seen him and a stranger go into the church at midnight, or thereabouts!—him, George Prattleton! Mr. George denied it in toto; and expressed his belief that Henry must have been dreaming.

"It's of no use talking like that, George Prattleton," said Henry, in a vexed tone. "You know quite well you were there. I saw the same man with you in the Grounds, the previous night, when I was going home after the audit-dinner."

"You must have seen double, then! I don't know whom you are talking of. Had you been drinking?"

"It won't do, George Prattleton. I was in full possession of both my sight and senses. You know whom I mean. His name's Rolls."

"Did he tell you his name?"

"No; but you did. I heard you call him by his name two or three times in the church last night. I want to know what I am to do about it."

"I don't know any Rolls; and I was not in the church last night; and my full persuasion is—if you really were locked in, as you say—that you fell asleep and dreamt this story."

"Now look you here, George Prattleton; if you persist in this line of denial, I shall be obliged to tell Mr. Wilberforce. I don't like to do it; your family and mine are intimate, and we have received many kindnesses from them, and I assure you I'd almost rather cut my tongue out than speak. But I can't let things go on at this uncertainty. Do you know what that Rolls did?"

"What did he do?" was the mocking rejoinder.

"He cut a leaf out of the register book."

"No?" shouted George Prattleton, the words scaring him to seriousness.

"I declare he did. When the candle went out, you thought it went out of itself, didn't you; well, he blew it out. I saw him blow it, and he called out, 'What a beast of a candle,' and said it was the damp put it out, and he got you to go for the matches. Was it not so?"

"Well?" said George Prattleton, too much alarmed to heed the half admission.

"Well, you had no sooner gone than he somehow got the candle alight again; I didn't see how, I suppose he had matches; and he took out a penknife, and put what looked like a thin board behind the leaf he was looking at, and cut it out. I say I'm not sure! but it's transportation for life to rob a church register."

George Prattleton wound his arm round one of the cloister pillars: face, heart, senses, alike scared. To give him his due, he would no more have countenanced a thing like this than he would have committed murder. All denial to Henry was over; and he felt half dead as he glanced forward to future consequences, and their effect upon his own reputation.

"You saw all this! Why on earth did you not pounce in upon him? or help me when I got back with the matches?"

"Because I was bewildered—frightened, if you will; and it all passed so quickly. I knew afterwards that it was what I ought to have done; but one can't do always the right thing at the right time."

"He put the leaf in his pocket, you say? It may not be destroyed. I—"

"Do you know what it related to?" interrupted Henry.

"Yes; to some old tithe cause—a dispute in a family he knows; people of the name of Whiffam," answered George Prattleton. "Some trifling cause, he said."

"Well, it's an awfully dangerous thing to do, let it relate to ever so trifling a cause," observed Henry. "Who is this Rolls? Do you know him well?"

"Three days back I did not know him from Adam," was the candid admission. "We met at the billiard rooms; and, somehow, we got thick directly. That night, when you saw us in the grounds, he was sounding me on this very thing—whether I could not get him a sight of the register."

"What's to be done about it?" asked Henry.

"I don't know," returned George Prattleton, flinging up his hands.

"It ought to be told to Mr. Wilberforce!"

"Be still, for heaven's sake! Would you ruin me? You must give me your promise, Henry Arkell, not to betray this; now, before we part."

"I don't wish to betray it; I'd do anything rather than bring trouble upon you. But it ought to be told."

"Nobody living may be the worse for what Rolls has done; nobody may ever hear of it more. Of course I shall charge him with his duplicity, and get the leaf back from him, if it is not destroyed, and replace it in the book. In that case, nobody can be the worse. Give me your promise."

Henry did not see what else he could do. If the leaf could be got back, and replaced, to speak of the abstraction might be productive of needless, gratuitous harm to George Prattleton. He put his hand into George's.

"You have my promise," he said; "but on one condition. I will never speak of this, so long as I am unaware of any urgent necessity existing for its disclosure. But should that necessity come, then I shall ask you to release me from my promise; and if you decline, I shall consider myself no longer bound by it."

"Very well; a bargain," said George Prattleton, after a pause. "And now I'm after that scoundrel Rolls. I'll tell you a secret before I go—tit for tat. Do you know how you got fastened in the church?"

"I suppose you did it, not knowing I was there."

"Not I. It was Lewis."

"Lewis!"

"Lewis senior. For a lark, he said, but I expect he owed you some grudge. By the way, though, I promised him I'd not speak of this; he told it me in confidence. I forgot that."

"I'll not speak of it. I can't, if I am to keep the other a secret. It was only the difficulty of accounting for my getting out of the church, that kept me from asking Hunt how I got locked in."

They parted. Mr. George Prattleton went in search of his friend Rolls, and Henry tore along the cloisters with all his might, anticipating he knew not what of reprimand from the head master for lingering on his way from college. It was close upon four o'clock, and his desk had some Greek to do yet; but the afternoon lessons were less regularly performed in winter than in summer.

CHAPTER XVII

A SHADOW OF THE FUTURE

On the second of December, Peter Arkell and his family came home, looking blooming. Eva Prattleton, who had stayed with them all the time, was blooming; as was Lucy; as was, for her, Mrs. Arkell. Even Peter himself looked quite a different man from the one who had gone away in July. Ah, my friends, there's nothing like running away from home to restore health and looks, if you can only leave care behind.

Quite a small crowd had assembled to meet them at the station. Nearly all the Prattleton family, including Mr. George, who was dreadfully in want just now of some distraction for his long hours. The two young Prattletons and Henry Arkell had rushed up, books in hand, just as they came out of school; and Travice Arkell, he was there. Handsome Travice! the best-looking young man in Westerbury when Frederick St. John was out of it.

"How have you been, Lucy?" he whispered, quietly coming near her, when he had done greeting the rest.

She shyly looked up at him as he took her hand. Scarcely a word was spoken. His head was bent for a moment over her blushing cheeks, and Travice looked as if he would very much have liked to take a kiss from the red ripe lips. It was impossible there; perhaps impossible elsewhere. Peter came up.

"Travice, I wish you'd see to the luggage, and that; and put my wife in a fly. There's enough of you here without me. I shall walk quietly on."

Just the same shy, awkward, incapable Peter Arkell as of yore. In usefulness his daughter Lucy was worth ten of him. He slipped out of the station by the least-frequented way, and walked on towards home. As he was going along, he met Kenneth, Mr. Fauntleroy's confidential clerk; and the latter stopped.

"I'm glad I met you," said Kenneth; "it will save me a journey to your house to-day, for we heard you'd be at home. How is it you have never sent us any money, Mr. Arkell?"

"Because I couldn't send it," returned Peter. "I wrote to Mr. Fauntleroy, telling him how impossible it was. I suppose he has managed it. He could if he liked, you know; it all lies in his hands."

"Ah, but he couldn't," answered Kenneth. "He had been too easy in one or two matters (I don't allude to your affairs), and had got involved in a good deal of expense through it; and the consequence is, he has been obliged to adopt a stricter policy in general."

"Mr. Fauntleroy knows how I was situated. In a strange place, you have to pay for everything as it comes in. I got a little teaching down there, and that helped; but it was not much."

"Well, Mr. Fauntleroy thought you ought to have sent him some money," persisted Kenneth. "And I'm not sure but he would have enforced it, had he not got it elsewhere."

"Got it elsewhere! On my account? What do you mean, Kenneth?"

"Mr. Arkell gave him ten pounds."

"Mr. Arkell gave him ten pounds!" almost shouted Peter. "How did that come about? Who said anything to Mr. Arkell?"

"I believe Mr. Fauntleroy happened to mention it accidentally. Or whether it was that he asked him for your exact address at the place, and said he was going to worry you for money, I'm not sure. I know Mr. Arkell said, better let you be quiet while you were there, and advanced the ten pounds."

"Mr. Fauntleroy had no right to speak to my cousin about it at all, Mr. Kenneth. I regard it as a breach of good faith. I wrote and asked Mr. Fauntleroy to wait, and he might have done so. As to the address, he knew that, for I gave it him."

"I'm in a hurry," said Mr. Kenneth. "I thought I'd speak to you, because I know Mr. Fauntleroy intended to send to you as soon as you came home. Here's another instalment due, now December's come in."

He went on his way. Peter Arkell looked after him for a minute, and then went on his. "Home to care! home to care!" he murmured with a sigh of pain.

Over and over again had Peter Arkell—not cursed, he was too good a man for that—but repented the day that placed him in the power of Mr. Fauntleroy. Some years previous to this, in a moment of great embarrassment, Peter Arkell had gone to Mr. Fauntleroy with his tale of woes. "Won't you help me?" he asked; "I once helped you." And Mr. Fauntleroy, entirely indifferent to his fellow-creature's woes though he was at heart, had not the face to refuse, with the recollection of that past obligation upon him. He helped him in this way. He advanced Peter Arkell two or three hundred pounds at a heavy rate of interest. It was not his own money, he said—he really had none to spare—it was the money of a client who had left it in his hands to make some profitable use of. Of course Peter Arkell understood it: at least he believed he did—that the money was Mr. Fauntleroy's own, and the plea of the client only put forth that the interest might be exacted—and his simple, honourable nature blushed for Mr. Fauntleroy. But he accepted it—he was too much in need of the assistance not to do it—and as the months and years went on he found himself unable to pay the interest. Things went on with some discomfort for a long time, and then Mr. Fauntleroy insisted on what he called some final arrangement being come to—that is, he said his client insisted upon it. The result was that Peter Arkell undertook to pay ten pounds every three months off the debt, interest, and costs, without the smallest notion how he could accomplish it. He had some learned book coming out, and if that turned up a trump card, he might be able to do it and more. But, when the book did come out it did not turn out a trump. The first ten pounds was due on the first of June last, and Peter had managed to pay it. The second ten was due on the first of September, and he wrote to Mr. Fauntleroy for grace. He now heard it had been paid by his cousin William Arkell. The third ten had been due the previous day, for this was the second of December. He would be able to pay this, for he had some money coming to him yet from the people who had rented his house, and, so far, that would be got rid of.

Peter might have paid it in another way. The first thing he saw on entering his home was a letter from his sister Mildred, and on opening it he found it contained a ten-pound note. These windfalls would come from Mildred now and then; and without them Peter had not an idea how he should have got along.

But not to his necessities did he appropriate this. The most prominent feeling swaying him then, was vexation that William Arkell should have been troubled about the matter—William, who had ever been so good to him—who had helped him out of more difficulties than the world knew of. In the impulse of the moment, without stopping to sit down, he went out again, carrying the note. He could not remember the day when he had been able to pay anything to his cousin, but at least he could do this.

Things were not prospering with the city, or with William Arkell. That the trade was going gradually down to ruin, to all but total extermination, he felt sure of now; and he bitterly regretted that Travice had cast in his lot with it. He had designed to send Travice to Oxford, to cause him to embrace one of the learned professions; but Travice had elected to follow his father, and Mr. Arkell had yielded—all just as it had been with himself in his own youth. None, save William Arkell himself, knew the care that was upon him, or how his property was dwindling down. Ever and anon there would come flashing a gleam of improvement in the trade, and rather large orders would come in, whispering hope for the future; but the orders and the hope soon faded again.

Peter entered the iron gates, and was turning to the left to the manufactory, when he saw Mr. Arkell at the dining-room window; so he went across to the house.

"No need to look for me abroad to-day, Peter," said his cousin, opening the dining-room door and meeting him in the hall. "I am not well enough to go out."

"What's the matter?" asked Peter.

"I don't know; I have had shivering fits all the morning—can do nothing but sit over this hot fire. Charlotte thinks it must be some sort of illness coming on; but I suppose it's only a cold. So you have got back at last?"

"Now, just," answered Peter, sitting down on the other side of the fire; "Travice said nothing about your illness; he was at the station."

"Was he? I did not know he had gone out. Oh, he thinks it's nothing, I dare say; I hope it will be nothing. What's this?"

Peter had handed him the ten-pound note. "It is what you paid to Mr. Fauntleroy while I was away; and bitterly vexed I am, to think he should have applied to you. I met Kenneth in leaving the station, and heard of it from him. But, William, I want to know why you paid it. Did Fauntleroy hold out any threats to you?"

"Something to that effect. He spoke of putting an execution into your house: it would not have done at all, you know, while strangers were in it. I never knew that he had got judgment."

"Oh yes, he did," said Peter, bitterly; "he took care of that. I am at his mercy any day, both in goods and person. He forgets, William, the service I rendered him, and my having to pay it: it is nothing but that that has kept me down in life. Put an execution in my house! I wonder where he expects to go to? Not to heaven, I should think?"

"He said his client pressed for the money—would not, in fact, wait."

"I dare say he did; it's just like him to say it. His client is himself."

"No?" exclaimed William Arkell, lifting his head.

"I firmly believe it to be so. He is pressing for another ten pounds now; it was due yesterday."

"Have you got it for him? If not, why do you give me this?"

"I have got it," said Peter; "I have to receive money to-day. Thank you a thousand times, William, for this and all else. How is business?"

"Don't ask. I feel too ill to fret over it just now. I'd give it up to-morrow but for Travice."

Certain words all but escaped Peter Arkell's lips, but they were suppressed again. He wondered—he had wondered long—why William Arkell continued to live at an expensive rate. That it was his wife's doings, not his, Peter knew; but he could not help thinking that, had he been a firm, clever man, as William was, he should not have yielded to her.

He met her in the hall as he went out. She wore a rich, trailing silk, and bracelets of gold. Peter stopped to shake hands with her; but she was never too civil to him, or to his daughter Lucy. In point of fact, Lucy had for some time haunted Mrs. Arkell's dreams in a very unpleasant manner, entailing a frequent nightmare, hideous to contemplate.

"What did Peter Arkell want here?" she asked of her husband, before she was well in the room; and her tone was by no means a gracious one.

"Not much," carelessly answered Mr. Arkell, who had drawn over the fire in another fit of shivering.

She took her seat in the chair Peter had vacated, and slightly lifted her rich dress, lest the scorching fire should mar its beauty.

"I suppose he came to borrow money," she said, no pleasant look upon her countenance.

"On the contrary, he came to pay me some."

"To pay you some! What for?"

"To repay me some, I should have said. I paid something for him during his absence—ten pounds—and he has now returned it."

For one single moment she felt inclined to doubt the words, and to say so. The next, she remembered how simply truthful was her husband.

"I want Travice," she said, presently. "I sent to the manufactory for him, but he was out. Will he be long, do you know?"

"I dare say not. Peter told me he was at the railway station. He went, I suppose, to meet them."

Mrs. Arkell lifted her head with a sort of start.

"Did you know he had gone?" she asked, sharply.

"I knew nothing at all of it. What are you so cross about?"

Mrs. Arkell bit her lips—her habit when put out.

"I have always objected to Travice's excessive intimacy with the Peter Arkells," she slowly said. "You know I have. But I might just as well have objected to the wind's blowing, for all the effect it has had. I hope it will not prove that I had cause."

"Cause! What cause? What do you mean, Charlotte?"

"Well, I think they are a mean, deceitful set. I think they are scheming to entrap Travice into an engagement with Lucy Arkell."

Ill as Mr. Arkell felt, he yet burst into a laugh. The notion of Peter's scheming to entrap anyone, or anything, was so ludicrous: simple, single-minded Peter, who had probably never given a thought to Lucy's marrying at all since she was in existence! and his wife was utterly above meanness of any sort—the very soul of openness and honour.

"Where did you pick up that notion?" he asked, when his laugh was over.

"I picked it up from observation and common sense," answered Mrs. Arkell, resentful of the laugh. "Travice used always to be there; and now that they are back, I suppose he will be again. He has lost no time in beginning, it seems."

"And if he is there, it does not follow that he goes for the sake of Lucy."

"It looks wonderfully like it, though."

"Nonsense, Charlotte! In the old days, when I was a young man, as Travice is, and Mildred was a girl like Lucy, quite as attractive—"

"Quite as what?" shrieked Mrs. Arkell. "I hope your taste does not put forward Lucy Arkell as attractive—or as Mildred's having been so before her. They are as like as two peas. A couple of uneducated, old-fashioned, old-maidish things, possessing not a single attraction."

"Opinions differ," said Mr. Arkell, quietly. "But if it be as you intimate, there's the less danger for Travice. What I was about to say was this—that in the old days I was in the habit of going to that house more than Travice goes to it now, and busy people, even my own mother, never believed but that I went for the sake of Mildred. I did not; neither did I marry her."

"The cases are different. You had no companion at home; Travice has his sisters. And it might have ended in your marrying Mildred, had I not come down on that long visit here, and saved you."

"Yes, it might." He was looking dreamily into the fire, his thoughts buried in the past; utterly oblivious to the present, and to the effect his remark might make. Mrs. Arkell felt particularly savage when she heard it.

"And a nice wife you'd have had! She is only fit for what she is—a lady's maid. Lucy will follow her example, perhaps, when old Peter's poverty has sent him into the grave. I always hated Lucy Arkell—it may be a strong term to use—but it's the truth. From the time that she was only as high as the elbow of that chair, and her mother, with the fine Cheveley notions, used to deck her out as a little court doll, I hated her!"

"And I have always thought her one of the sweetest and most loveable of children," quietly returned Mr. Arkell. "Opinions differ, I say, Charlotte. But why should you have hated her?"

"Because—I think it must have been" (and Mrs. Arkell looked into the fire also in reflection, and for once spoke her true sentiments)—"I think it must have been because you and Travice made so much of her. I only know it has been."

"I'd not cherish it, Charlotte."

"You would not, I know. Tell me," she added, with quite a gust of passion in voice and eye, "would you like to see your fine, attractive, noble son, thrown away upon Lucy Arkell?"

"My head is as bad as it can be, Charlotte; I wish you'd not worry me. I think I must be going to have some fever."

"He might marry half Westerbury. With his good looks, his education, his fine prospects—"

"Yes, do put in them," interrupted Mr. Arkell. "Very fine they are, in the present aspect of affairs."

"Affairs will get good again. I don't believe the half that's said about the badness of trade. You have made a good thing of it," she added significantly.

"Pretty well; I and my father before me. But those times have gone by for ever."

"I don't believe it; I believe the trade will revive again and be as lucrative as before; and Travice will be able to maintain a home such as we have maintained. It is a fine prospect, I don't care how you may deny it in your gloom; and I say that Travice, enjoying it, might marry half the desirable girls in Westerbury."

"He'd be taken up for bigamy if he did."

"Can't you be serious?" she angrily asked. "Whereas, if he got enthralled by that bane, Lucy Arkell, and— Good patience, here she is!" broke off Mrs. Arkell, as her eyes fell on the courtyard. "The impudence of that! Not half an hour in the town, and to come here!"

Lucy, in her grey travelling cloak, and fresh straw bonnet, came staggering in under a load: a flower-pot, with a great plant in bloom. She looked well. In moments of excitement, there was something of her mother's loveliness in her face; in the lustre of the soft and sweet dark eyes, in the rose bloom of the delicate cheeks, and at those times she was less like Mildred. Lucy put her load on the table, and turned to offer her hand to Mrs. Arkell. Mrs. Arkell touched the tips of the fingers, but Mr. Arkell took her in his arms and kissed her twice; and then recollected himself and fell into proper repentance.

"I ought not to have done it, Lucy; I forgot myself. But, my dear, in the joy of seeing you, and seeing you so pretty, I quite lost sight of precaution. I am shivering with cold and illness, Lucy, and may be going to have I don't know what."

Lucy laughed. She was not afraid, and said so.

"Mamma made me bring this down at once for your conservatory," she said, addressing Mrs. Arkell. "It is a wax plant, and a very beautiful one. The last time we were here, you were regretting you had not a nice one, and when mamma saw this, she thought of you. She sends her very kind regards, Mrs. Arkell, and hopes you will accept it. And now that's my message, and there's my load, and I have delivered both," concluded Lucy, merrily.

In the face of the present—and it was really a beautiful one of its nature—Mrs. Arkell could not maintain her utter ungraciousness. She unbent a very little: unwillingly thanked Lucy for the plant, and inquired how Mrs. Peter Arkell was.

"I think we had better send our girls to the sea-side, if they could come back improved as Lucy has," remarked Mr. Arkell; and the remark aggravated his wife. "Are those roses on your cheeks real, Lucy, or have you learnt the use of that fashionable cosmetic, rose-powder?"

"They are quite real," answered Lucy, the cheeks blushing their own testimony to the answer. "It has done us all so much good! Mr. Prattleton said he should not have known mamma, had he met her in a strange place, she is looking so different. But I am warm just now. It was coming through the streets with that: everybody stared at me."

"Could not Travice have brought it?" asked Mr. Arkell.

"He did offer; but mamma said I should bring it more carefully than he, and she sent me off with it at once. She had been taking care of it herself all the way."

"Where is Travice?" inquired Mrs. Arkell, the sharp tone perceptible in her voice again, more especially to Mr. Arkell's ears.

"He was helping mamma indoors when I came. Papa had gone somewhere: he left us at the station."

Mr. Arkell did not say that he had been there. He was looking very poorly just then, and his hands, quite trembling with cold, were blue as he stretched them out to the fire. Lucy, an admirable sick nurse from her training, the being with her ailing mother, threw back her grey cloak, knelt down, and took them into her own warm hands to chafe them.

It was what one of Mr. Arkell's own daughters would not, or could not, have done. He looked down on the pretty upturned face, every line of which spoke of a sweet goodness. She was more lovely, more attractive than Mildred had been—or was it that his eyes had then had a film before them?—and he felt that—were he in Travice's place—

"I wonder you liked to stay so long away, leaving Henry to himself!" interrupted Mrs. Arkell.

"He was at Mr. Wilberforce's, you know," replied Lucy. "He was very well there; very happy."

"I suppose he comes home to-day."

"No, not until the college school breaks up for Christmas. Mr. Wilberforce thinks he had better not disturb himself before. Have you heard of the gold medal? But of course you have. I hope I shall not grow too proud of my brother. But oh, Mrs. Arkell! pray tell me! What do you think of that dreadful thing, the loss of Mr. Dundyke? Will he ever come back again?"

"Ever come back again!" repeated Mrs. Arkell, believing that Lucy was putting on an affectation of childishness. "How can a murdered man come back?"

"Was he murdered? I thought they supposed he was drowned, but were not certain what it was. Was he murdered?" she repeated, looking at Mr. Arkell, for Mrs. Arkell did not appear inclined to answer her.

"I fear he was, Lucy."

"Oh, what a dreadful thing! Mrs. Arkell, what will Mrs. Dundyke do?"

"Oh, she has enough to live upon, I believe."

"I did not quite mean it in that light," said Lucy, gently, as Mrs. Arkell's remark jarred upon her ear. "And old Marmaduke Carr has died," she resumed, "and there's going to be a law-suit about the property. What a great many things seem to have happened since we went away! Mr. Arkell, which side do you think has the most right to gain the law-suit?"

"The most right? Well, there's a great deal to be said on both sides, Lucy. If there was no marriage, of course the property does belong to the Carrs of Eckford; if there was a marriage, they have no right to it whatever. In any case, the blame lies with Robert Carr; and his descendants suffer."

"Do you think there was a marriage?" continued Lucy.

Mr. Arkell shook his head.

"I don't, my dear, now. Had there been one, some traces of it would have been found ere this."

"Then young Mrs. Carr will lose the law-suit!"

"Undoubtedly. It appears very strange to me that Fauntleroy should go on with it."

The hands were warm now, and Lucy rose.

"You have done me good, Lucy," said Mr. Arkell, as she was putting on her gloves to leave; "good in all ways. A bright face and a cheering manner! my dear, in sickness, they are worth their weight in gold."

Making the best of her way home, she found Travice alone. Henry was upstairs with his mother, uncording boxes.

"What a time you have been, Lucy!" was the salutation; for it had seemed very long to him.

"Have I? I did not once sit down. Mr. Arkell says I look well after my sojourn, but I told him he should see mamma."

"So he should. But I must be going, Lucy. Do you look well?"

He took both her hands in his, and stood before her, his face a little bent, regarding her intently. Lucy blushed violently under the gaze. Suddenly, without any warning, his lips were on hers; and he took the first kiss that he had taken from Lucy since her childhood.

"Don't be angry with me, Lucy! Think it a cousin's kiss, if you will."

As he went out, the large shadow of a large, gaily-dressed woman, passing between him and the setting sun, was cast upon Travice Arkell. The shadow of Barbara Fauntleroy. If he could but have foreseen the type it was of the terrible shadow that was to fall upon him in the future!

VOLUME III

CHAPTER I

DIAMOND CUT DIAMOND—A SURPRISE

It happened on that same second of December that Mr. Littelby took his place for the first time as conductor of the business of Mynn and Mynn. He had arrived at Eckford the previous day, as per agreement, but was not installed formally in the office until this. Old Mynn, not in his gout now, had come down early, and was brisk and lively; George Mynn was also there.

He was an admitted solicitor just as much as were Mynn and Mynn; he was to be their confidential locum tenens; the whole management and conduct of affairs was, during their absence, to fall upon him; he was, in point of fact, to be practically a principal, not a clerk, and at the end of a year, if all went well, he was to be allowed a share in the business, and the firm would be Mynn, Mynn, and Littelby.

It was not, then, to be wondered at, that the chief of the work this day was the inducting him into the particulars of the various cases that Mynn and Mynn happened to have on hand, more especially those that were to come on for trial at the Westerbury assizes, and would require much attention beforehand. They were shut up betimes, the three, in the small room that would in future be Mr. Littelby's—a room which had hitherto been nobody's in particular, for the premises were commodious, but which Mr. Richards had been in the habit of appropriating as his own, not for office purposes, but for private uses. Quite a cargo of articles belonging to Mr. Richards had been there: coats, parcels, pipes, letters, and various other items too numerous to mention. On the previous day, Richards had received a summary mandate to "clear it out," as it was about to be put in order for the use of Mr. Littelby. Mr. Richards had obeyed in much dudgeon, and his good feeling towards the new manager—his master in future—was not improved. It had not been friendly previously, for Mr. Richards had a vague idea that his way would not be quite so much his own as it had been.

He sat now at his desk in the public office, into which clients plunged down two steps from the landing on the first flight of stairs, as if they had been going into a well. His subordinate, a steady young man named Pope, who was browbeaten by Richards every hour of his life, sat at a small desk apart. Mr. Richards, ostensibly occupied in the perusal of some formidable-looking parchment, was, in reality, biting his nails and frowning, and inwardly wishing he could bring the ceiling down on Mr. Littelby's head, shut up in that adjoining apartment; and could he have invented a decent excuse for sending out Pope, in the teeth of the intimation Mr. George Mynn had just given, that Pope was to stop in, for he should want him, Mr. Richards would have had his own ear to the keyhole of the door.

Mr. Littelby and Mr. Mynn sat at the square table, some separate bundles of papers before them, tied up with red string; Mr. George Mynn stood with his back to the fire. Never was there a keener or a better man of business than Mynn the elder, when his state of health allowed him a respite from pain.

He had been well for two or three weeks now, and the office found the benefit of it. He was the one to explain matters to Mr. Littelby; Mr. George only put in a word here and there. In due course they came to a small bundle of papers labelled "Carr," and Mr. Mynn, in his rapid, clear, concise manner, gave an outline of the case. Before he had said many words, Mr. Littelby raised his head, his face betokening interest, and some surprise.

"But I thought the Carr case was at an end," he observed. "At least, I supposed it would naturally be so."

"Oh dear no," said old Mynn; "it's coming on for trial at the assizes—that is, if the other side are so foolish as to go on to action. I don't myself think they will be."

"The other side? You mean the widow of Robert Carr the clergyman?" asked Mr. Littelby, scarcely thinking, however, that Mr. Mynn could mean it.

"The widow and the brother—yes. Fauntleroy, of Westerbury, acts for them. But he'll never, as I believe, bring so utterly lame a case into court."

Mr. Littelby wondered what his new chief could mean; he did not understand at all.

"I should have supposed the case would have been brought to an end by you," he observed. "From the moment that the marriage was discovered to have taken place, your clients, the Carrs of Eckford, virtually lost their cause."

"But the marriage has not been discovered to have taken place," said Mr. Mynn.

"Yes, it has. Is it possible that you have not had intimation of it from Mr. Fauntleroy?"

Mr. Mynn paused a moment. Mr. George, who had been looking at his boots, raised his head to listen.

"Where was it discovered?—who discovered it?" asked Mr. Mynn, with the air of a man who does not believe what is being said to him.

"The widow, young Mrs. Carr, found the notice of it. In searching her late father-in-law's desk, she discovered a letter written by him to his son. It was the week subsequent to her husband's death. The letter had slipped between the leaves of an old blotting-book, and lain there unsuspected. While poor Robert Carr the clergyman was wearing away his last days of life in those fruitless searchings of the London churches, he little thought how his own carelessness had forced it upon him. He examined this very desk when his father died, for any papers there might be in it, and must have examined it imperfectly, for there the letter must have been."

"But what was in the letter?" asked George Mynn, speaking for the first time since the topic arose.

"It stated that he had married the young lady who went away with him, Martha Ann Hughes, on the morning they left Westerbury—married her at her own parish church, St.—St.—I forget the name."

"Her parish church was St. James the Less," said Mr. Mynn, speaking very fast.

"Yes, that was it; I remember now. It struck me at the time as being a somewhat uncommon appellation. That is where the marriage took place, on the morning they left Westerbury."

Mr. Mynn sat down; he had need of some rest to recover his consternation. Mr. George never spoke: he said afterwards, that the thought flashed upon him, he could not tell how or why, that the letter was a fraud.

"How did you know of this?" was Mr. Mynn's first question.

Mr. Littelby related how: that Mrs. Carr had informed him of it at the time of the discovery: and, it may be observed, that he was unconscious of breaking any faith in repeating it. Mrs. Carr, attaching little importance to Mr. Fauntleroy's request of keeping it to herself, had either forgotten or neglected to caution Mr. Littelby, to whom it had at once been told. Mr. Littelby, on his part, had never supposed but the discovery had been made known to Mynn and Mynn and the Carrs of Eckford, by Mr. Fauntleroy, and that the litigation had thus been brought to an end.

"And you say this is known to Mr. Fauntleroy?" asked old Mynn.

"Certainly. Mrs. Carr forwarded the letter to him the very hour she discovered it."

"Then what can possess the man not to have sent us notice of it?" he exclaimed. "He'd never be guilty of the child's play of concealing this knowledge until the cause was before the court, and then bringing it forward as a settler! Fauntleroy's sharp in practice; but he'd hardly do this."

"Is it certain that the marriage did take place there?" quietly put in Mr. George Mynn.

They both looked at him; his quiet tone was so full of significance: and Mr. Mynn had to turn round in his chair to do it.

"It appears to me to be a very curious story," continued the younger man. "What sort of a woman is this Mrs. Carr?"

A pause. "You are not thinking that she is capable of—of—concocting any fraud, are you?" cried Mr. Littelby.

"I should be sorry to say it. I only say the thing wears a curious appearance."

"She is entirely incapable of it," returned Mr. Littelby, warmly. "She is quite a young girl, although she has been a wife and mother. Besides, the letter, remember, only stated where the marriage took place, and where its record might be found. I remember she told me that the words in the letter were, that the marriage would be found duly entered in the register."

Mr. Mynn was leaning back in his chair; his hands in his waistcoat pockets, his eyes half closed in thought.

"Did you see this letter, Mr. Littelby?" he inquired, rousing himself.

"No. Mrs. Carr had sent it off to Mr. Fauntleroy. She told me its contents, I daresay nearly word for word."

"Because I really do not think the marriage could have taken place as described. It would inevitably have been known if it had: some persons, surely, would have seen them go into the church; and the parson and clerk must have been cognisant of it! How was it that these people kept the secret? Besides, the parties were away from the town by eight o'clock, or thereabouts."

"I don't know anything about the details," said Mr. Littelby; "but I do know that the letter, stating what I have told you, was found by Mrs. Carr, and that she implicitly believes in it. Would the letter be likely to assert a thing that a minute's time could disprove? If the record of the marriage is not on the register of St. James the Less, to what end state that it is?"

"If this letter stated what you say, Mr. Littelby, rely upon it that the record is there. There have been such things known, mind you"—and old Mynn lowered his voice as he spoke—"as frauds committed on registers; false entries made. And they have passed for genuine, too, to unsuspicious eyes. But, if this is one, it won't pass so with me," he added, rising. "Not a man in the three kingdoms has a keener eye than mine."

"It is impossible that a false entry can have been made in the register!" exclaimed Mr. Littelby, speaking slowly, as if debating the question in his own mind.

"We shall see. I assure you I consider it equally impossible for the marriage to have taken place, as stated, without detection."

"But—assuming your suspicion to be correct—who can have been wicked enough to insert the entry?" cried Mr. Littelby.

"That, I can't tell. The entry of the marriage would take the property from our clients, the Carrs of Eckford, therefore they are exempt from the suspicion. I wonder," continued Mr. Mynn in a half-secret tone, "whether that young clergyman got access to the register when he was down here?"

"That young clergyman was honest as the day," emphatically interrupted Mr. Littelby. "I could answer for his truth and honour with my life. The finding of that letter would have sent him to his grave easier than he went to it."

"There's another brother, is there not?"

"Yes. But he is in Holland, looking after the home affairs, which are also complicated. He has not been here at all since his father's death."

"Ah, one doesn't know," said old Mynn, glancing at his watch. "Hundreds of miles have intervened, before now, between a committed fraud and its plotter. Well, we will say no more at present. I'll tell you more when I have had a look at this register. It will not deceive me."

"Are you going over now?" asked Mr. George.

"At once," replied old Mynn, with decision; "and I'll bring you back my report and my opinion as soon as may be."

But Mr. Mynn was away considerably longer than there appeared any need that he should be. When he did arrive he explained that his delay arose from the effectual and thorough searching of the register.

"I don't know what could have been the meaning or the use of that letter you told us of, Mr. Littelby," he said, as he took off his coat; "there is no entry of the marriage in the church register of St. James the Less."

"No entry of it!"

"None whatever."

Mr. Littelby did not at once speak: many thoughts were crowding upon his mind. He and old Mynn were standing now, and George Mynn was sitting with his elbow on the table, and his aching head leaning on his hand. The least excitement out of common, sometimes only the sitting for a day in the close office, would bring on these intolerable headaches.

"I have searched effectually—and I don't suppose the old clerk of the church blessed me for keeping him there—and I am prepared to take an affidavit, if necessary, that no such marriage is recorded in the book," continued the elder lawyer. "What could have been the aim or object of that letter, I cannot fathom."

"Mr. Carr will not come into the money, then?" said Mr. Littelby.

"Of course not, so far as things look at present. I thought it was very strange, if such a thing had been there, that Fauntleroy did not let it be known," he emphatically added.

"You are sure you have fully searched?"

"Mr. Littelby, I have fully searched," was the reply; and the lawyer was not pleased at being asked the question after what he had said. "There is no such marriage entered there; and rely upon it no such marriage ever was entered there. I might go farther and say, with safety in my opinion, that there never was such marriage entered anywhere."

"Then why should Robert Carr, the elder, have written the letter?"

"Did he write it? It may be a question."

"No, he never wrote it," interposed George Mynn, looking up. "There was some wicked plot concocted—I don't say by whom, and I can't say it—of which this letter was the prologue. Perhaps the epilogue—the insertion of the marriage in the register—was frustrated; possibly this letter was found before its time, and the despatching it to Mr. Fauntleroy marred the whole. How can we say?"

"We can't say," returned old Mynn. "One thing I can say and affirm—that there's no record; and had the letter been a genuine one, the entry would be there now."

"I wonder if Mr. Fauntleroy believes the entry to be there?" cried Mr. Littelby. "I am nearly sure that he has not given notice of the contrary to Mrs. Carr. She would have told me if he had."

"If Fauntleroy has been so foolish as to take the information in the letter for granted, without sending to see the register, he must put up with the consequences," said old Mynn; "I shall not enlighten him."

He spoke as he felt—cross. Mr. Mynn was not pleased at having spent the best part of the day over what he had found to be a fool's errand; neither did he like to have been startled unnecessarily. He sat down and drew the papers before him, saying something to the effect that perhaps they could attend to their legitimate business, now that the other was disposed of. Mr. Littelby caught the cue, and resolved to say no more in that office of Carr versus Carr.

And so, it was a sort of diamond cut diamond. Mr. Fauntleroy had said nothing to Mynn and Mynn of his private information; and Mynn and Mynn would say nothing to Mr. Fauntleroy of theirs.

Christmas drew on. Mrs. Dundyke, alone now, for Mr. Carr had gone back to Holland, was seated one afternoon by her drawing-room fire, in the twilight, musing very sadly on the past. The servants were at tea in the kitchen, and one of them had just been up to ask her mistress if she would take a cup, as she sometimes did before her late dinner, and had gone down again, leaving unintentionally the room door unlatched.

As the girl entered the kitchen, the sound of laughter and merriment came forth to the ears of Mrs. Dundyke. It quite jarred upon her heart. How often has it occurred to us, bending under the weight of some secret trouble that goes well-nigh to break us, to envy our unconscious servants, who seem to have no care!

The kitchen door closed again, and silence supervened—a silence that soon began to make itself felt, as it will in these moments of gloom. Mrs. Dundyke was aroused from it in a remarkable manner; not violently or loudly, but still in so strange a way, that her mouth opened in consternation as she listened, and she rose noiselessly from her chair in a sort of horror.

She had distinctly heard the latch-key put into the street-door lock; just as she had heard it many a time when her husband used to come home from business in the year last gone by. She heard it turned in the lock, the peculiar click it used to give, and she heard the door quietly open and then close again, as if some one had entered. Not since they went abroad the previous July had she heard those sounds, or had the door thus been opened. There had been but that one latch-key to the door, and Mr. Dundyke, either by chance or intention, had carried it away with him in his pocket. It had been in his pocket during the whole period of their travels, and been lost with him.

What could it mean? Who had come in? Footsteps, slow, hesitating footsteps were crossing the hall; they seemed to halt at the dining-room, and were now ascending the stairs. Mrs. Dundyke was by far too practical a woman to believe in ghosts, but that anything but the ghost of her husband could open the door with that latch-key and be stealing up, was hard to believe.

"Betsey!"

If ever she felt a wish to sink into the wall, or through the floor, she felt it then. The voice which had called out the familiar home name, was her husband's voice; his, and yet not his. His, in a manner; but querulous, worn, weakened. She stood in horror, utterly bewildered, not daring to move, her arms clasping a chair for protection, she knew not from what, her eyes strained on the unlatched door. That it could be her husband returned in life, her thoughts never so much as glanced at.

He pushed open the door, and came in without any surprise in his face or greeting on his tongue; came in and went straight to the fire, and sat down in a chair before it, just as though he had not been gone away an hour—he who had once been David Dundyke. Was it David Dundyke still—was it? He looked thin and shabby, and his hair was cut close to his head, and he was altogether altered. Mrs. Dundyke was gazing at him with a fixed, unnatural stare, like one who has been seized with catalepsy.

He saw her standing there, and turned his head, looking at her for a full minute.

"Betsey!"

She went forward then; it was her husband, and in life. What the mystery could have been she did not know yet—did not glance at in that wild moment—but she fell down at his knees and clasped him to her, and wept delirious tears of joy and agony.

It seemed—when the meeting was over, and the marvelling servants had shaken hands with him, and he had been refreshed with dinner, and the time came for questions—that he could not explain much of the mystery either. He had evidently undergone some great change, physically and mentally, and it had left him the wreck of what he was, with his faculties impaired, and a hesitating speech.

More especially impaired in memory. He could recollect so little of the past; indeed, their sojourn at the hotel at Geneva seemed to have gone from his mind altogether. Mrs. Dundyke saw that he must have had some sort of brain attack; but, what, she could not tell.

"David, where have you been all this while?" she said, soothingly, as he lay on the sofa she had drawn to the fire, and she sat on a stool beneath and clasped his hand.

"All this while? I came back directly."

She paused. "Came back from where?"

"From the bed."

"The bed!" she repeated; and her heart beat with a sick faintness as she felt, for the twentieth time, that henceforth he could only be questioned as a child. "From the bed you lay in when you were ill?"

"Yes."

"Were you ill long?"

"No. I lay in it after I got well: my head and my legs were not strong. They turned. It was the bed in the kitchen with the large white pillows. They slept in the back room."

"Who did?"

"Paul and Marie. She's his wife."

"Did they take care of you?"

"Yes, they took care of me. Little Paul used to fetch the water. He's seven."

"Do you remember—" (she spoke the words with trembling, lest the name should excite him) "Mr. Hardcastle?"

It did in some degree. He lay looking at his wife, his face and thoughts working. "Hardcastle! It was him that—that—was with me when I fell down."

"Where did you fall?" she asked, as quietly as she could.

"In the sun. We walked a long, long way, and he gave me something to drink out of a bottle, and I was giddy, and he told me to go to sleep."

"Did he stay with you?"

Mr. Dundyke stared as though he did not understand the question.

"I went giddy. He took my pocket-book; he took out the letters, and put it back to me again. Paul found it. I went to sleep in the sun."

"When did Paul find it?"

David Dundyke appeared unable to comprehend the "when." "In his cart," he said; "he found me too."

"David, dear, try and recollect; did Paul take you to his cottage?"

David looked puzzled, and then nodded his head several times, as if wishing to convince himself of the fact.

"And I suppose you were ill there?"

"I suppose I was ill there; they said so. Marie spoke English; she had been at—at—at sea."

This was not very perspicuous, but Mrs. Dundyke did not care for minor details.

"How did you come home?" she asked. And she glanced suddenly down at his boots; an idea presenting itself to her, that she might see them worn and travel-stained. But they were not. They were the same boots that he had on that last morning in Geneva, and they appeared to have been little worn.

"How did I come home?" he repeated. "I came. Marie said I was well enough. Paul changed the note."

"What note?" she asked.

"The note from England. He didn't see that when he took the others."

"He" evidently meant Mr. Hardcastle. She began to comprehend a little, and put her questions accordingly.

"Mr. Hardcastle must have robbed you, David."

"Mr. Hardcastle robbed me."

She found he had a habit of repeating her words. She had noticed the same peculiarity before, in cases of decaying intellect.

"The bank note that he did not find was the one you had written for over and above what you wanted. Why did you write for it, David?"

This was a back question, and it took a great many others before David could answer. "He might have wanted to borrow more," he said at length; "I'd have lent him all then."

Poor man! That he should have had such blind faith in Mr. Hardcastle as to send for money in case he should "want to borrow more!" Mrs. Dundyke had taken this view of the case from the first.

"You don't believe in him now, David?"

"I don't believe in him now. He has got my bank notes; and he left me in the sun. Paul, put me in the cart when it came by."

"David, why did you not write to me?"

David stared. "I came," he said. And she found afterwards, that he could not write; she was to find that he never attempted to write again.

"Did you send to Geneva?—to me?"

"To Geneva?—to me?"

"To me—me, David; not to you. Did you send to Geneva?"

He shook his head, evidently not knowing what she meant, and seemed to think. Mrs. Dundyke felt nearly sure that he must have lain long insensible, for weeks, perhaps months; that is, not sufficiently conscious to understand or remember; and that when he grew better, Geneva and its doings had faded from his remembrance.

"How did you come home, David?" she asked again. "Did you come alone?"

"Did you come alone—yes, in the diligences, and rail, and sea. I told them all to take me to England; Paul got the money for me; he took the note and brought it back."

Paul had changed it into French money; that must be the meaning of it. Mr. Dundyke put his hand in his pocket and pulled out sundry five-franc pieces.

"Marie's got some. I gave her half."

Mrs. Dundyke hoped it was so. She could hardly understand yet, how he could have found his way home alone; even with the help of "I told them all to take me to England."

"David!" she whispered, "David! I don't know how I shall ever be thankful enough to God!"

"I'd like some porter."

It was a contrast that grated on her ear; the animal want following without break on the spiritual aspiration. She was soon to find that any finer feeling he might ever have possessed, had gone with his mind. He could eat and drink still, and understand that; but there was something wrong with the brain.

"How did you come down here to-night, David?"

"How did I come down here to-night? There was the omnibus."

The questions began to pain her. "He is fatigued," she thought; "perhaps he will answer better to-morrow." The porter was brought to him, and he fell asleep immediately after drinking it. She rose from her low seat, and sat down in a chair opposite to him.

It was like a dream; and Mrs. Dundyke all but pinched herself to see whether she was awake or asleep. She believed that she could tell pretty accurately what the past had been. Mr. Hardcastle had followed her husband to the side of the lake that morning, had in some way induced him to go away from it; had taken him a long, long way into the cross country—and it must have been at that time that the Swiss peasant, who gave his testimony at Geneva, had seen them. At the proper opportunity, Mr. Hardcastle must have, perhaps, given him some stupefying drink, and then robbed him and left him; but Mrs. Dundyke inclined to the opinion that the man must have believed Mr. Dundyke insensible, or he surely would never have allowed him to see him take the notes. He must then have lain, it was hard to say how long, before Paul found him; and the lying thus in the sun probably induced the fit, or sun-stroke, or brain fever, whatever it was, that attacked him. He spoke of a cart: and she concluded that Paul must have been many miles out of the route of his home, or else the search instituted would surely have found him, had he been within a few miles of Geneva. Why these people had kept him, had not declared him to the nearest authorities, it was hard to say. They might have kept him from benevolent motives; or might have seen the bank note in his pocket-book, and kept him from motives of worldly interest. However it might be, they had shown themselves worthy Christian people, and she should ever be deeply grateful. He had evidently no idea of the flight of time since; perhaps—

"What do you wear that for?"

He was lying with his eyes open, and pointing to the widow's cap. She rose and bent over him, as she answered—

"David! David, dear! we have been mourning you as dead."

"Mourning me as dead! I am not dead."

No, he was not dead, and she was shedding happy tears for it, as she threw the cap off from the braids of her still luxuriant hair.

As well, perhaps, almost that he had been dead! for the best part of his life, the mind's life, was over. No more intellect; no more business for him in Fenchurch-street; no more ambitious aspirations after the civic chair!—it was all over for ever for poor David Dundyke.

But he had come home. He who was supposed to be lying dead—murdered—had come home. It was a strange fact to go forth to the world: one amidst the extraordinary tales that now and then arise to startle it almost into disbelief.

CHAPTER II

A DOUBTFUL SEARCH

On the 3rd of February the college boys reassembled for school, after the Christmas holidays. Rather explosive were the choristers at times at getting no holidays—as they were pleased to regard it; for they had to attend the cathedral twice daily always. Strictly speaking, the boys had assembled on the previous day, the 2nd of February, and those who lived at a distance, or had been away visiting, had to be back for that day. It is Candlemas Day, as everybody knows, and a saint's day; and on saints' days the king's scholars had to attend the services.

On the 3rd the duties of the school began, and at seven in the morning the boys were clattering up the steps. It was not a propitious morning: snow and sleet doing battle, one against the other. Jocelyn had left, and the eldest of the two Prattletons had succeeded him as senior. Cookesley was second senior, Lewis third, and the eldest of the Aultanes was fourth.

The boys were not assembling in any great amount of good feeling. Lewis, who with his brother had passed the holidays at the house of the late Marmaduke Carr, and consequently had been in Westerbury, did not forget the grudge he owed to Henry Arkell. It had been Mr. Lewis's pleasure to spend his leisure-hours (time, possibly, hanging somewhat heavily on his hands) in haunting the precincts of the cathedral. Morning, noon, and night had he been seen there; now hovering like a ghost in one of the cloister quadrants, now playing at solitary pitch-and-toss in the grounds, and now taking rather slow, meditative steps past the deanery. He had thus made himself aware that Henry Arkell and Miss Beauclerc not unfrequently met; whether by accident or design on the young lady's part, she best knew. Four times each day had Henry Arkell to be in the grounds and cloisters on his way to and from college; and, at the very least, on two of those occasions, Miss Beauclerc would happen to be passing. She always stopped. Lewis had seen him sometimes walking on with only a lift of the trencher, and Miss Beauclerc would not have it, but stopped as usual. There was no whispering, there were apparently few secrets; the talking was open and full of gaiety on the young lady's part, if her laughter was anything to judge by; but Lewis was not the less savage. When he met her, she would say indifferently, "How d'ye do, Lewis?" and pass on. Once, Lewis presumed to stop her with some item of news that ought to have proved interesting, but Miss Beauclerc scarcely listened, made some careless remark in answer, and continued her way: the next minute she met Henry Arkell, and stayed with him. That Lewis was in love with the dean's daughter, he knew to his sorrow. How worse than foolish it had been on his part to suffer himself to fall in love with her, we might say, but that this passion comes to us without our will.

Lewis believed that she loved Henry Arkell; he believed that but for Henry Arkell being in the field, some favour might be shown to him; and he had gone on hating him with a fierce and bitter hatred. One day, Henry had come springing down the steps of the cathedral, and encountered Miss Beauclerc close to him. They stood there on the red flagstones of the cloisters, no gravestone being in that particular spot, Georgina laughing and talking as usual. Lewis was in the opposite quadrant of the cloisters, peeping across stealthily, and a devout wish crossed his heart that Arkell was buried on the spot where he then stood. Lewis was fated not to forget that wish.

How he watched, day after day, none save himself saw or knew. He was training for an admirable detective in plain clothes. He suspected there had been some coolness between Henry and Miss Beauclerc, and that she was labouring to dispel it; he knew that Arkell did not go to the deanery so much as formerly, and he heard Miss Beauclerc reproach him for it. Lewis had given half his life for such a reproach from her lips to be addressed to him.

There were so many things for which he hated Henry Arkell! There was his great progress in his studies, there was the brilliant examination he had undergone, and there was the gold medal. Could Lewis have conveniently got at that medal, it had soon been melted down. He had also taken up an angry feeling to Arkell on account of the doings of that past November night—the locking up in the church of St. James the Less. Lewis had grown to nourish a very strange notion in regard to it. After puzzling his brain to torment, as to how Arkell could have got out, and finding no solution, he arrived at length at the conclusion that he had never been in. He must have left the church previously, Lewis believed, and he had locked up an empty church. It is true he had thought he heard the organ going, but he fully supposed now that he heard it only in fancy. Arkell's silence on the point contributed to this idea: it was entirely beyond Lewis's creed to suppose a fellow could have such a trick played him and not complain of it. Arkell had never given forth token of cognisance from that hour to this, and Lewis assumed he had not been in.

It very much augmented his ill feeling, especially when he remembered his own night of horrible anticipation. Mr. Lewis had come to the final conclusion that Arkell had been "out on the spree;" and but for a vague fear that his own share in the night's events might be dragged to light, he would certainly have contrived that it should reach the ears of Mr. Wilberforce. He and his brother were to be for another half year boarders at the master's house. Cookesley acted there as senior; the senior boy, Prattleton, living at home.

The boys trooped into the schoolroom, and Prattleton stood with the roll in his hand. Lewis had not joined on the previous day; he had obtained grace until this, for he wanted to spend it at Eckford. As he came in now, he made rather a parade of shaking hands with Prattleton, and wishing him joy of his honours. Most of the boys liked to begin by being in favour with a new senior, however they might be fated to end, and Lewis and Prattleton were great personal friends—it may be said confidants. Lewis had partially trusted Prattleton with the secret of his love for Miss Beauclerc; and he had fully entrusted him with his hatred of Henry Arkell. Scarcely a minute were they together at any time, but Lewis was speaking against Arkell; telling this against him, telling that. Constant dropping will wear away a stone; and Prattleton listened until he was in a degree imbued with the same feeling. Personally, he had no dislike to Arkell himself; but, incited by Lewis, he was quite willing to do him any ill turn privately.

The roll was called over when Henry Arkell entered. He put down a load of books he carried, and went up to Prattleton to shake hands, as Lewis had done; being a chorister, he had not gone into the schoolroom on the previous day; and he wished him all good luck.

"I am sorry to have to mark you late on the first morning, Arkell," Prattleton quietly said as he shook hands with him. "The school has a superstition, you know—that anyone late on the first morning will be so, as a rule, through the half."

"I know," answered Henry. "It is no fault of mine. Mr. Wilberforce desired me to tell you that he detained me, therefore I am to be marked as having been present."

"Did he detain you?"

"For ten minutes at least. I met him as I was coming in, and he caused me to go back with him to his house and bring in these books. He then gave me the message to you."

"All right," said Prattleton, cheerfully: and he erased the cross against Arkell's name, and marked him as present.

Even this little incident exasperated Lewis. His ill feeling rendered him unjust. No other boy, that he could remember, had been marked as present, not being so. He was beginning to say something sarcastic upon the point, when the entrance of the master himself shut up his tongue for the present.

But we cannot stop with the college boys just now.

On this same day, later, when the sun, had there been any sun to see, was nearing the meridian, Lawyer Fauntleroy sat in his private office, deep in business. Not a more clever lawyer than he throughout the town of Westerbury; and to such men business flocks in. His table stood at a right angle with the fireplace, and the blazing fire burning there, threw its heat upon his face, and his feet rested on a soft thick mat of wool. Mr. Fauntleroy, no longer young, was growing fonder and fonder of the comforts of life, and he sat there cosily, heedless of the hail that beat on the window without.

The door softly opened, and a clerk came in. It was Kenneth. "Are you at home, sir?"

Mr. Fauntleroy glanced up from the parchment he was bending over—a yellow-looking deed, and his brow looked forth displeasure. "I told you I did not care to be interrupted this morning, Kenneth, unless it was for anything very particular. Who is it?"

"A lady, sir. 'Mrs. Carr' was the name she gave in."

"Carr—Carr?" debated Mr. Fauntleroy, unable to recal any lady of the name amidst his acquaintance. "No. I have no leisure for ladies to-day."

Kenneth hesitated. "It's not likely to be the Mrs. Carr in Carr v. Carr; the lady you have had some correspondence with, is it, sir?" he waited to ask. "She is a stranger, and is dressed as a widow."

"The Mrs. Carr in Carr v. Carr!" repeated Mr. Fauntleroy. "By Jupiter, I shouldn't wonder if she's come to Westerbury! But I thought she was in Holland. Show her in."

Mr. Kenneth retired, and came back with the visitor. It was Mrs. Carr. Mr. Fauntleroy pushed aside the deed before him, and rose to salute her, wondering at her extreme youth. She spoke English fluently, but with a foreign accent, and she entered at once upon the matter which had brought her to Westerbury.

"A circumstance has occurred to renew the old anxiety about this cause," she said to Mr. Fauntleroy. "Should we lose it, I shall lose all I have at present to look forward to, for our affairs in Holland are more complicated than ever. It may turn out, Mr. Fauntleroy, that my share of this inheritance will be all I and my little children will have to depend upon in the world."

"But the cause is safe," returned Mr. Fauntleroy. "The paper you found and forwarded to me last October—or stay, November, wasn't it—"

"Would you be so kind as let me see that paper?" she interrupted.

Mr. Fauntleroy rose and brought forward a bundle of papers labelled "Carr." He drew out a letter, and laid it open before his visitor. It was the one you saw before; the letter written by Robert Carr the elder to his son, stating that the marriage had been solemnized at the church of St. James the Less, and that the entry of it would be found there.

"And there the marriage is entered, as I subsequently wrote you word," observed Mr. Fauntleroy. "It is singular how your husband could have overlooked that letter."

"It had slipped between the leaves of the blotting-book, or else been placed there purposely by Mr. Carr," she answered; "and my husband may not have been very particular in examining the desk, for at that time he did not know his legitimacy would be disputed. Are you sure it is in the register, sir?" she continued, some anxiety in her tone.

"Quite sure," replied Mr. Fauntleroy. "I sent to St. James's to search as soon as I got this letter, glad enough to have the clue at last; and there it was found."

"Well—it is very strange," observed Mrs. Carr, after a pause. "I will tell you what it is that has made me so anxious and brought me down. But, in the first place, I must observe that I concluded the cause was at an end. I cannot understand why the other side did not at once give up when that letter was discovered."

Knowing that he had kept the other side in ignorance of the letter, Mr. Fauntleroy was not very explanatory on this point. Mrs. Carr continued—

"My husband had a friend of the name of Littelby, a solicitor. He was formerly the manager of an office in London, but about two months since he left it for one in the country, Mynn and Mynn's—"

"Mynn and Mynn," interrupted Mr. Fauntleroy; "that's the firm who are conducting the case for your adversaries—the Carrs, of Eckford. Littelby? Yes, it is the name of their new man, I remember."

"Well, sir, last week Mr. Littelby was in London, and he called at Mrs. Dundyke's, where I had been staying since I came over from Holland, a fortnight before. The strangest thing has happened there! Mr. Dundyke—but you will not thank me to take up your time, perhaps, with matters that don't concern you. Mr. Littelby spoke to me upon the subject of the letter that I had found, and he said he feared there was something wrong about it, though he could not conceive how, for that there had been no marriage, so far as could be discovered."

"He can say the moon's made of green cheese if he likes," cried Mr. Fauntleroy.

"He said that the opinion of Mynn and Mynn was, that the pretended letter had been intended as a ruse—a false plea, written to induce the other side to give up peaceably; but that most positively there was no truth in the statement of the marriage being in the register. Sir, I am sure Mr. Littelby must have had good cause for saying this," emphatically continued Mrs. Carr "He is a man incapable of deceit, and he wishes well to me and my children. The last advice he gave me was, not to be sanguine; for Mynn and Mynn were clever and cautious practitioners, and he knew they made sure the cause was theirs."

"Sharp men," acquiesced Mr. Fauntleroy, nodding his head with a fellow-feeling of approval; "but we have got the whip hand of them in your case, Mrs. Carr."

"I thought it better to tell you this," said she, rising. "It has made me so uneasy that I have scarcely slept since; for I know Mr. Littelby would not discourage me without cause."

"Without fancying he has cause," corrected Mr. Fauntleroy. "Be at ease, ma'am: the marriage is as certain as that oak and ash grow. Where are you staying in Westerbury?"

"In some lodgings I was recommended to in College-row," answered she, producing a card. "Perhaps you will take down the address—"

"Oh, no need for that," said Mr. Fauntleroy, glancing at it, "I know the lodgings well. Mind they don't shave you."

Mrs. Carr was shown out, and Mr. Fauntleroy called in his managing clerk. "Kenneth," said he, "let the Carr cause be completed for counsel; and when the brief's ready, I'll look over it to refresh my memory. Send Omer down to St. James the Less, to take a copy of the marriage."

"I thought Omer brought a copy," observed Mr. Kenneth.

"No; I don't think so. It will save going again if he did. Ask him."

Mr. Kenneth returned to the clerks' office. "Omer, did you bring a copy of the marriage in the case, Carr v. Carr, when you searched the register at St. James's church?" he demanded.

"No," replied Omer.

"Then why did you not?"

"I had no orders, sir. Mr. Fauntleroy only told me to look whether such an entry was there."

"Then you must go now—What's that you are about? Winter's settlement? Why, you have had time to finish that twice over."

"I have been out all the morning with that writ," pleaded Omer, "and could not get to serve it at last. Pretty well three hours I was standing in the passage next his house, waiting for him to come out, and the wind whistling my head off all the time."

Mr. Kenneth vouchsafed no response to this; but he would not disturb the clerk again from Winter's deed. He ordered another, Mr. Green, to go to St. James's church for the copy, and threw him half-a-crown to pay for it.

Young Mr. Green did not relish the mission, and thought himself barbarously used in being sent upon it, inasmuch as that he was an articled clerk and a gentleman, not a paid nobody. "Trapesing through the weather all down to that St. James's!" muttered he, as he snatched his hat and greatcoat.

It struck three o'clock before he came back. "Where's Kenneth?" asked he, when he entered.

"In the governor's room. You can go in."

Mr. Green did go in, and Mr. Kenneth broke out into anger. "You have taken your time!"

"I couldn't come quicker," was Mr. Green's reply. "I had to look all through the book. The marriage is not there."

"It is thrift to send you upon an errand," retorted Mr. Kenneth. "You have not been searching."

"I have done nothing else but search since I left. If the entry had been there, Mr. Kenneth, I should have been back in no time. It is not exactly a day to stop for pleasure in a mouldy old church that's colder than charity, or to amuse oneself in the streets."

Mr. Fauntleroy looked up from his desk. "The entry is there, Green: you have overlooked it."

"Sir, I assure you that the entry is not there," repeated Mr. Green. "I looked very carefully."

"Call in Omer," said Mr. Fauntleroy. "You saw the entry of Robert Carr's marriage to Martha Ann Hughes?" he continued, when Omer appeared.

"Yes, sir."

"You are sure of it?"

"Certainly, sir. I saw it and read it."

"You hear, Mr. Green. You have overlooked it."

"If Omer can find it there, I'll do his work for a week," retorted young Green. "I will pledge you my veracity, sir—"

"Never mind your veracity," interrupted Mr. Fauntleroy; "it is a case of oversight, not of veracity. Kenneth, you have to go down to Clark's office about that bill of costs; you may as well go on to St, James's and get the copy."

"Two half-crowns to pay instead of one, through these young fellows' negligence," grumbled Mr. Kenneth. "They charge it as many times as they open their vestry."

"What's that to him? it doesn't come out of his pocket," whispered Green to Omer, as they returned to their own room. "But if they find the Carr marriage entered there, I'll be shot in two."

"And I'll be shot in four if they don't," retorted Omer. "What a blind beetle you must have been, Green!"

Mr. Kenneth came back from his mission. He walked straight into the presence of Mr. Fauntleroy, and beckoning Omer in after him, attacked him with a storm of reproaches.

"Do you drink, Mr. Omer?"

"Drink, sir!"

"Yes, drink. Are the words not plain enough?"

"No, sir, I do not," returned Omer, in astonishment.

"Then, Mr. Omer, I tell you that you do. No man, unless he was a drunken man, could pretend to see things which have no place. When you read that entry of Robert Carr's marriage in the register, you saw double, for it never was anywhere but in your brain. There is no entry of the marriage in St. James's register," he added, turning to Mr. Fauntleroy.

Mr. Fauntleroy's mouth dropped considerably. "No entry!"

"Nothing of the sort!" continued Mr. Kenneth. "There's no name, and no marriage, and no anything—relating to Robert Carr."

"Bless my heart, what an awful error to have been drawn into!" uttered Mr. Fauntleroy, who was so entirely astounded by the news, that he, for the moment, doubted whether anything was real about him. "All the expense I have been put to will fall upon me; the widow has not a rap, certain; and to take her body in execution would bring no result, save increasing the cost. Mr. Omer, are you prepared to take these charges on yourself, for the error your carelessness has led us into? I should not have gone on paying costs myself but for that alleged entry in the register."

Mr. Omer looked something like a mass of petrifaction, unable to speak or move.

"But for the marriage being established—as we were led to suppose—we never should have gone on to trial. Mrs. Carr must have relinquished it," continued Mr. Fauntleroy.

"Of course we should not," chimed in the managing clerk.

"I thought there must be some flaw in the wind; I declare I did, by the other side's carrying it on, now that I find Mynn and Mynn knew of the alleged marriage," exclaimed Mr. Fauntleroy. "I shall look to you for reimbursement, Omer. And, Mr. Kenneth, you'll search out some one in his place: we cannot retain a clerk in our office who is liable to lead us into ruinous mistakes, by asserting that black is white."

Mr. Omer was beginning to recover his senses. "Sir," he said, "you are angry with me without cause. I can be upon my oath that the marriage of Robert Carr with Martha Ann Hughes is entered there: I repeated to you, sir, the date, and the names of the witnesses: how could I have done that without reading them?"

"That's true enough," returned Mr. Fauntleroy, his hopes beginning to revive.

"Here's a proof," continued the young man, taking out a worn pocket-book. "I am a bad one to remember Christian names, so I just copied the names of the witnesses here in pencil. 'Edward Blisset Hughes,' and 'Sophia Hughes,'" he added, holding it towards Mr. Fauntleroy.

"They were her brother and sister," remarked Mr. Fauntleroy, in soliloquy, looking at the pencilled marks. "Both are dead now; at least, news came of her death, and he has not been heard of for years: she married young Pycroft."

"Well, sir," argued Omer, "if these names had not been in the register, how could I have taken them down? I did not know the names before, or that there ever were such people."

The argument appeared unanswerable, and Mr. Fauntleroy looked at his head clerk. The latter was not deficient in common sense, and he was compelled to conclude that he had himself done what he had accused Mr. Green of doing—overlooked it.

"Allow me to go down at once to St. James's, sir," resumed Omer.

"I will go with you," said Mr. Fauntleroy. The truth was, he was ill at ease.

They proceeded together to St. James's church, causing old Hunt to believe that Lawyer Fauntleroy and his establishment of clerks had all gone crazy together. "Search the register three times in one day!" muttered he; "nobody has never done such a thing in the memory of man."

But neither Omer nor his master, Mr. Fauntleroy, could find any such entry in the register.

CHAPTER III

DETECTION

Afternoon school was over. Mr. Wilberforce had been some time at home, and was bestowing a sharp lecture on his son Edwin for some delinquency, when he was told that Lawyer Fauntleroy waited in his study. The master brought his anger to a summary conclusion, and went into the presence of his visitor.

"My business is not of a pleasant nature," he premised. "I must tell you in confidence, Mr. Wilberforce, that after all the doubt and discredit cast upon the affair, Robert Carr was discovered to have married that girl at St. James's—your church now—and the entry was found there."

"I know it," said Mr. Wilberforce. "I saw it in the register."

The lawyer stared. "Just repeat that, will you?" said he, putting his hand to his ear as if he were deaf.

"I heard it was to be found there, and the first time afterwards that I had occasion to make an entry in the register, I turned back to the date, out of curiosity, and read it."

"Now I am as pleased to hear you say that as if you had put me down a five-hundred pound note," cried Mr. Fauntleroy. "I daresay you'll not object, if called upon, to bear testimony that the marriage was registered there."

"The register itself will be the best testimony," observed Mr. Wilberforce.

"It would have been," said the lawyer; "but that entry has been taken out of the register."

"Taken out!" repeated Mr. Wilberforce.

"Taken out. It is not in now."

"Stuff and nonsense!" cried the master.

"So I said, when my clerks brought me word to-day that it was not in. The first sent, Green—you know the young dandy; it's but the other day he was in the college school—came back and said it was not there. Kenneth gave him a rowing for carelessness, and went himself. He came back and said it was not there. Then I thought it was time to go; and I went, and took Omer with me, who saw the entry in the book last November, and copied part of it. Green was right, and Kenneth was right; there is no such entry there."

"This is an incredible tale," exclaimed Mr. Wilberforce.

The old lawyer drew forward his chair, and peered into the rector's face. "There has been some devilry at work—saving your calling."

"Not saving it at all," retorted Mr. Wilberforce, as hot as when he had been practically demonstrating of what birch is made in the college schoolroom. "Devilry has been at work, in one sense or another, and nothing short of devilry, if it be as you say."

"It has not only gone, but there's no trace of it's going, or how it went. The register looks as smooth and complete as though it had never been in any hands but honest ones. But now," added the lawyer, "there's another thing that is puzzling me almost as much as the disappearance itself; and that is, how you got to know of it."

"I heard of it from Travice Arkell."

"From Travice Arkell!"

"Yes, I did. And the way I came to hear of it was rather curious," continued the master. "One of my parishioners was thought to be dying, and I was sent for in a hurry, out of early school. Mr. Prattleton generally attends these calls for me, but this poor man had expressed a wish that I myself should go to him. It was between eight and nine o'clock, and Travice Arkell was standing at their gates as I passed, reading a letter which the postman had just delivered to him. It was from Mrs. Dundyke, with whom the Carrs were stopping—"

"When was this?" interrupted Mr. Fauntleroy.

"The beginning of November. Travice Arkell stopped me to tell of the strange news that the letter conveyed to him; that a paper had been found in Robert Carr the elder's writing, stating that the marriage had taken place at St. James the Less, the morning he and Miss Hughes left Westerbury, and it would be found duly entered in the register. The news appeared to me so excessively improbable, that I cautioned Travice Arkell against speaking of it, and recommended him to keep it to himself until the truth or falsehood of it should be ascertained."

"What made you give him this caution?"

"I tell you; I thought it so improbable that any such marriage should have taken place. I thought it a hoax, set afloat out of mischief, probably by the Carrs of Eckford; and I did not choose that my church, or anything in it, should be made a jest of publicly. Travice Arkell agreed with my view, and gave me his promise not to mention it. His father was away at the time."

"Where?"

"I really forget. I know he had come home only the day before from a short visit to London, and went out again, somewhere the same day. Travice said he did not expect him back that second time for some days."

"Well?" said Mr. Fauntleroy, in his blunt manner, for the master had stopped, in thought.

"Well, the next morning Travice Arkell called upon me here. He had had a second letter from Mrs. Dundyke, begging him not to mention to anyone what she had said about the marriage, for Mrs. Carr had received a hasty letter from Mr. Fauntleroy, forbidding her to speak of it to anyone. So, after all, that caution that I gave to Travice might have been an instinct."

"And do you think he had not mentioned it?"

"I feel sure that he has never allowed it to escape his lips. He has too great a regard for his aunt, Mrs. Dundyke. She feared she had done mischief, and was most anxious. On the following Sunday, when I was marrying a couple in my church before service, and had got the register out, I looked back to the date, and there, sure enough, was the marriage duly entered."

"And you have not spoken of it?"

"I have not. If, as you say, the marriage is no longer there, it is a most strange thing; an incredible thing. But I'll see into it."

"Somebody must see into it," returned the lawyer, as he departed. "A parish register ought to be kept as sacred as the crown jewels."

Mr. Wilberforce—a restless man when anything troubled him—started off to Clark Hunt's, disturbing that gentleman at his tea. "Hunt, follow me," said he, as he took the key from its niche, "and bring some matches and a candle with you. I want to examine the register."

"If ever I met with the like o' this!" cried Hunt, when the master had walked on. "Register, register, register! my legs is aching with the tramping back'ards and for'ards, to that vestry to-day."

He walked after Mr. Wilberforce as quickly as his lameness would allow. The latter was already in the vestry. He procured the key of the safe (kept in a secret place which no one knew of save himself, the clerk, and the Reverend Mr. Prattleton) opened it, and laid the book before him. Mr. Wilberforce knew, by the date, where the entry ought to be, where it had been, and he was not many minutes ascertaining that it was no longer there.

"Gone and left no trace, as Fauntleroy said," he whispered to himself. "How can it have been done? The leaf must have been taken out! oh yes, it's as complete a thing as ever I saw accomplished: and how is it to be proved that it's gone? This comes of their careless habit of not paging their leaves in those old days: had they been paged, the theft would have been evident. Hunt," cried he, aloud, raising his head, "this register has been tampered with."

"Law, sir, that's just what that great lawyer, Fauntleroy, wanted to persuade me on. He has been a-putting it into your head, maybe; but don't you be frighted with any such notion, sir. 'Rob the register!' says I to him; 'no, not unless they robs me of my eyesight first. It's never touched, nor looked at,' says I, 'but when I'm here to take care on it.'"

"A leaf has been taken out. Who has had access here?"

"Not a soul has never had access to this vestry, sir, unless I have been with 'em, except yourself or Mr. Prattleton," persisted the old register keeper. "It's not possible, sir, that the book has been touched."

"Now don't argue like that, Hunt," testily returned Mr. Wilberforce, "I tell you that the register has been rifled, and it could not have been done without access being obtained to it. To whom have you entrusted the key of the church?"

"Never to nobody, save the two young college gents, what comes to play the organ," said the clerk, stoutly.

"And they could not get access to the register. Some one else must have had the key."

The old man sat down on a chair, opposite Mr. Wilberforce; placing his two hands on his knees, he stared very fixedly on vacancy. Mr. Wilberforce, who knew his countenance, fancied he was trying to recall something.

"I remember a morning, some time ago," cried he, slowly, "that one of them senior college gents—but that couldn't have had nothing to do with the register."

"What do you remember?" questioned Mr. Wilberforce.

"Your asking if anybody had had the key, put me in mind of it, sir. One of them college seniors; Lewis, it was; came to my house soon after I got up. A rare taking he seemed to be in; with fright, or something like it; and wanted me to lend him the key of the church. 'No, no, young gent,' says I, 'not without the master's orders.' He was a panting like anything, and looked as resolute as a bear, and when he heard that, he snatched the key, and tore off with it. Presently, back he comes, saying it was the wrong key and wouldn't undo the door. Mr. George Prattleton had come round then: Mr. Prattleton had told him to ask about the time fixed for a funeral—which, by token, I remember was Dame Furbery's—and he took the key from Mr. Lewis, and hung it up, and railed off at me for trusting it to the college gents. Lewis finding he couldn't get it from me, went after Mr. George Prattleton, and they came back, and Mr. George took the key from the hook to go to the church with Lewis. What it was Lewis had said to him, I don't pertend to guess, but they was both as white as corpses—as white I know, as ever was dead Dame Furbery in her coffin: which was just about then a being screwed down. After all, they hung the key up again, and didn't go into the church."

"When was this?" asked Mr. Wilberforce.

"It was the very day, sir, after our cat's chaney saucer was done for; and that was done for the day after the grand audit dinner at the deanery. Master Henry Arkell, after going into the church to practise, couldn't be contented to bring the key back and hang it up, like a Christian, but must dash it on to the kitchen floor, where it split the cat's chaney saucer to pieces, and scattered the milk, a-frighting the cat, who had just got her nose in it, a'most into fits, and my missis too. Well, sir, when I opened my shutters the next morning, who should be a standing at the gate but Arkell, so I fetched him in to see the damage he had done; and it was while he was in the kitchen, a-counting the pieces, that Lewis came to the door."

"But this must have been early morning," cried Mr. Wilberforce.

"Somewhere about half after six, sir: it was half moonlight and half twilight. I remember what a bright clear morning it was for November."

"Why, at that hour both Lewis and Arkell must have been in their beds, asleep, at my house."

"Law, sir, who can answer for schoolboys, especially them big college gents? When they ought to be a-bed, they're up; and when they ought to be up, they're a-bed. They was both at my house that morning."

Mr. Wilberforce could not make much of the tale, except that two of his boarders were out when he had deemed them safe in bed; and he left the church. It was dusk then. As he was striding along, in an irascible mood, he met Henry Arkell. He touched his cap to the master, and was passing on.

"Not so fast, Mr. Arkell. I want a word with you."

Arkell stopped and stood before Mr. Wilberforce, his truthful eye and open countenance raised fearlessly.

"I gave you credit for behaving honourably, and as a gentleman ought, during the time you were residing in my house, but I find I was deceived. Who gave you leave, pray, to sneak out of it at early morning, when everybody else was in bed?"

"I never did, sir," replied Henry.

"Take care, Arkell. If there's one fault I punish more than another, it is a falsehood; and that you know. I say that you did sneak out of my house at untoward and improper hours."

"Indeed, sir, I never did," he replied with respectful earnestness.

The master raised his forefinger, and shook it at his pupil. "You were down at Hunt's one morning last November, by half-past six, perhaps earlier; you must have gone down by moonlight—Ah, I see," added the master, in an altered tone, for a change flashed over Henry Arkell's features, "conscience is accusing you of the falsehood."

"No, sir, I told no falsehood. I don't deny that I was at Hunt's one morning."

"Then how can you deny that you stole out of my house to get there? Perhaps you will explain, sir."

What was Henry Arkell to do? Explain, in the full sense of the word, he could not; but explain, in a degree, he must, for Mr. Wilberforce was not one to be trifled with. He was a perfectly ingenuous boy, both in manner and character, and Mr. Wilberforce had hitherto known him for a truthful one: indeed, he put more faith in Arkell than in all the rest of the thirty-nine king's scholars.

"Perhaps you will dare to tell me that you stopped out all night, instead of sneaking out in the morning?" pursued the master.

"Yes, sir, I did; but it was not my fault: I was kept out."

"Where were you, and who kept you out?"

"Oh, sir, if you would be so kind as not to press me—for indeed I cannot tell. I was kept out, and I could not help myself."

"I never heard so impudent an avowal from any boy in my life," proceeded Mr. Wilberforce, when he recovered his astonishment. "What was the nature of the mischief you were in? Come; I will know it."

"I was not in any mischief, sir. If I might tell the truth, you would say that I was not.'"

"This is most extraordinary behaviour," returned the master. "What reason have you for not telling the truth?"

"Because—because—well, sir, the reason is, that I could not speak without getting others into trouble. Indeed, sir," he earnestly added, "though I did stop out from your house all night, I did no wrong; I was in no mischief, and it was no fault of mine."

Strange perhaps to say, the master believed him: from his long experience of the boy, he could believe nothing but good of Harry Arkell, and if ever words bore the stamp of truth, his did now.

"I am in a hurry at present," said the master, "but don't flatter yourself this matter will rest."

Henry touched his cap again, and the master strode on to the residence of the Reverend Mr. Prattleton, and entered it without ceremony. Mr. Prattleton was seated with his two sons, and with George.

"Send the boys away for a minute, will you?" cried the master to his brother clergyman.

The boys went away, exceedingly glad to be sent. "You can go on with your Greek in the other room," said their father. But to that suggestion they were conveniently deaf, preferring to take an evening gallop through some of the more obscure streets, where they knocked furiously at all the doors, and pulled out a few of the bell-wires.

"An unpleasant affair has happened, Prattleton," began the master. "The register at St. James's has been robbed."

"The register robbed!" echoed Mr. Prattleton. "Not the book taken?"

"Not the book itself. A leaf has been taken out of it."

"How?"

"We must endeavour to find out how. Hunt protests that nobody has had access to it but ourselves, save in his presence."

"I do not suppose they have," returned Mr. Prattleton. "How could they? When was it taken?"

"Sometime since the beginning of November. And there'll be a tremendous stir over it, as sure as that we are sitting here: it was wanted for—for—some trial at the next assizes," concluded the master, recollecting that Mr. Fauntleroy had cautioned him still not to speak of it. "Fauntleroy's people went to-day to take a copy of it, and found it gone; so Fauntleroy came on to me."

"You are sure it is gone?" continued Mr. Prattleton. "An entry is so easily overlooked."

"I am sure it is not in the book now: and I read it there last November."

"Well, this is an awkward thing. Have you no suspicion?—no clue?"

"Not any. Hunt was telling a tale—By the way," added Mr. Wilberforce, turning to George Prattleton, who had moved himself to a polite distance, as if not caring to hear, "you were mixed up in that. He says, that last November you and Lewis had some secret between you, about the church. Lewis went down to his house one morning by moonlight, got the key by stratagem, and brought it back, saying it was the wrong one: and you then went to the church with him, and both of you were agitated. What was it all about? What did he want in the church?"

"Oh—something had been left there, I think he said, when one of the college boys had gone in to practise. That was nothing, Mr. Wilberforce. We did not go into the church, after all."

George Prattleton spoke with eagerness, and then hastened from the room, but not before Mr. Wilberforce had caught a glimpse of his countenance.

"What is the matter with George?" whispered he.

Mr. Prattleton turned, and looked at the door by which he had gone out. "With George?" he repeated: "nothing that I know of. Why?"

"He turned as pale as my cravat: just as Hunt describes him to have been when he went into the church with Lewis. I shall begin to think there is a mystery in this."

"But not one that touches the register," said Mr. Prattleton. "I'll tell you what that mystery was, but you must not bring in me as your informant; and don't punish the boy, now it's over, Wilberforce; though it was a disgraceful and dangerous act. It seems that young Arkell—what a nice lad that is! but he comes of a good stock—went into St. James's one evening to practise, and Lewis, who owed him a grudge, stole after him and locked him in, and took back the key to Hunt's, where he broke some heirloom of the dame's, in the shape of a china saucer, Hunt and his wife taking it to be Arkell. Arkell was locked in the church all night."

"Locked in the church all night!" repeated the amazed Sir. Wilberforce. "Why the fright might have turned him—turned him—stone blind!"

"It might have turned him stone dead," rejoined Mr. Prattleton. "Lewis, it appears, got terrified for the consequences, and as soon as your servants were up, he went to Hunt's to get the key and let Arkell out. Hunt would not give it him, and Lewis appealed to George. That's what has sent George out of the room, pale, as you call it; he was afraid lest you should question him too closely, and he passed his word to Lewis not to betray him."

"What a villanous rascal!" uttered the master. "I never liked Lewis, but I would not have given him credit for this. Did George tell you?"

"Not he; he is not aware I know it. Lewis, some days afterwards, imparted the exploit to my boy, Joe. Joe, in his turn, imparted it to his brother, under a formidable injunction of secrecy, and I happened to overhear them, and became as wise as they were."

"You ought to have told me this," remarked Mr. Wilberforce, his countenance bearing its most severe expression.

"Had one of my own boys been guilty of it, I would have brought him to you and had him punished in the face of the school; but as no harm had come of it, I did not care to inform against Lewis: though I don't excuse him; it was a dastardly action."

"Well, this explains what Lewis wanted in the church, but it brings us no nearer the affair of the register. I think I shall offer a reward for the discovery."

Mr. Wilberforce proceeded home, and into the study where his boarders were assembled, some half dozen of the head boys. One of them, a great tall fellow, stood on his head on a table, his feet touching the wall. "Who's that?" uttered the master. "Is that the way you prepare your lessons, sir?"

Down clattered the head and the feet, and the gentleman stood upright on the floor. It was Lewis senior. Mr. Wilberforce took a seat, and the boys held their breath: they saw something was wrong.

"Vaughan."

"Yes, sir."

"Did you lock Henry Arkell up in St. James's Church, and compel him to pass a night there?"

Mr. Vaughan opened all the eyes he possessed.

"I, sir! I have not locked him up, sir. I don't think Arkell is locked up," added Vaughan, in the confusion of his ideas. "I saw him talking to you, sir, just now, in Wage-street."

Lewis pricked up his ears, which had turned of a fiery red; then Arkell had been locked in! Mr. Wilberforce sharply seized upon Vaughan's words.

"What brought you in Wage-street, pray?"

"If you please, sir," coughed Vaughan, feeling he had betrayed himself, "I only went out for an exercise book. I finished mine last night, sir, and forgot it till I went to do my Latin just now. I didn't stop anywhere a minute, sir; I ran there and back as quick as lightning. Here's the book, sir."

Believing as much of this as he chose, Mr. Wilberforce did not pursue the subject. "Then which of you gentlemen was it who did shut up Arkell?" asked he, gazing round. "Lewis, senior, what is the matter with you, that you are skulking behind? Did you do it?"

Lewis saw that all was up. "That canting hound has been peaching at last," quoth he to himself. "I laid a bet with Prattleton he'd do it."

"It is the most wicked and cowardly action that I believe ever disgraced the college school," continued Mr. Wilberforce, "and it depends upon how you meet it, Lewis, whether or not I shall expel you. Equivocate to me now, if you dare. Had it come to my knowledge at the time, you should have been flogged till you could not stand, and ignominiously expelled. Flogged you will be, as it is. Do you know, sir, that he might have died through it?"

Lewis hung his head, wishing Arkell had died; and then he could not have told the master.

"I think the best punishment will be, to lock you up in St. James's all the night, and see how you will like it," continued Mr. Wilberforce.

Lewis wondered whether he was serious; and the perspiration ran down him at the thought. "He was not locked in all night," he said, sullenly, by way of propitiating the master. "When we went to open the church, he was gone."

"Gone! What do you mean now?"

"He had got out somehow, sir, for Hunt said he had just seen him, and when I ran back to morning school, he was in the college hall. Mr. George Prattleton advised me not to make a stir, to know how he had got out, but to let it drop."

As Lewis spoke, Mr. Wilberforce suddenly remembered that Hunt said Henry Arkell was in his kitchen, when Lewis came, frightened, and thumping for the key. It occurred to him now, for the first time, to wonder how that could have been.

"When you locked Arkell in, what did you do with the key?"

"I took it to Hunt's, sir."

"And gave it to Hunt?"

"Yes, sir. That is," added Lewis, thinking it might be as well to be correct, "I pushed it into the kitchen, where Hunt was."

"And broke Dame Hunt's saucer," retorted Mr. Wilberforce. "When did you have the key again. Speak up, sir?"

"I didn't have it again, sir," returned Lewis. "The key I took from the hook, next morning, would not fit into the lock, and I took it back. Hunt said it was the right key, and George Prattleton said it was the key; but I am sure it was not, although George Prattleton called me a fool for thinking so."

The master revolved all this in his mind, and thought it very strange. He was determined to come to the bottom of it, and despatched Vaughan to Arkell's house to fetch him. The two boys came back together, and Mr. Wilberforce, without circumlocution, addressed the latter.

"When this worthy companion of yours," waving his hand contemptuously towards Lewis, "locked you in the church, how did you get out?"

Henry Arkell glanced at Lewis, and hesitated in his answer. "I can't tell, sir."

"You can't tell!" exclaimed Mr. Wilberforce. "Did you walk out of it in your sleep? Did you get down from a window?—or through the locked door? How did you get out, I ask?"

Before there was time for any reply, the master's servant entered, and said the Rev. Mr. Prattleton was waiting to speak to the master immediately. Mr. Wilberforce, leaving the study door open, went into the opposite room. Mr. Prattleton, who stood there, came forward eagerly.

"Wilberforce, a thought has struck me, and I came in to suggest it. When the boy passed the night in the church, did he get playing with the register?"

"He would not do it; Arkell would not," spoke the master, in the first flush of thought.

"Not mischievously; but he may have got fingering anything he could lay his hands upon—and it is the most natural thing he would do, to while away the long hours. A spark may have fallen on the leaf, and—"

"How could he get a light?—or find the key of the safe?" interrupted Mr. Wilberforce.

"Schoolboys can ferret out anything, and he may have found its hiding-place. As to a light, half the boys keep matches in their pockets."

Mr. Wilberforce mused upon the suggestion till it grew into a probability. He called in Arkell, and shut the door.

"Now," said he, confronting him, "will you speak the truth to me, or will you not?"

"I have hitherto spoken the truth to you, sir," answered Arkell, in a tone of pain.

"Well; I believe you have: it would be bad for you now, if you had not. It is about that register, you know," added Mr. Wilberforce, speaking slowly, and staring at him.

There was but one candle on the table, and Henry Arkell pulled out his handkerchief and rubbed it over his face: between the handkerchief and the dim light, the master failed to detect any signs of emotion.

"Did you get fingering the register-book in St. James's, the night you were in the church?"

"No, sir, that I did not," he readily answered.

"Had you a light in the church?"

"You boys have a propensity for concealing matches in your clothes, in defiance of the risk you run," interrupted Mr. Prattleton. "Had you any that night?"

"I had no matches, and I had no light," replied Henry. "None of the boys keep matches about them except those who"—smoke, was the ominous word which had all but escaped his lips—"who are careless."

"Pray what did you do with yourself all the time?" resumed the master.

"I played the organ for a long while, and then I lay down on the singers' seat, and went to sleep."

"Now comes the point: how did you get out?"

"I can't say anything about it, sir, except that I found the door open towards morning, and I walked out."

"You must have been dreaming, and fancied it," said the master.

"No, sir, I was awake. The door was open, and I went out."

"Is that the best tale you have got to tell?"

"It is all I can tell, sir. I did get out that way."

"You may go home for the present," said Mr. Wilberforce, in anger.

"Are you satisfied?" asked Mr. Prattleton, as Arkell retired.

"I am satisfied that he is innocent as to the register; but not as to how he escaped from the church. Allowing it to be as he says—and I have always found him so strictly truthful—that he found the door open in the middle of the night, how did it come open? Who opened it? For what purpose?"

"It is an incomprehensible affair altogether," said the Rev. Mr. Prattleton. "Let us sit down and talk it over."

As Arkell left the room, Lewis, senior, appeared at the opposite door, propelling forth the fire-tongs, a note held between them.

"This is for you," cried he, rudely, to Arkell, who took the note. Lewis flung the tongs back in their place. "My hands shouldn't soil themselves by touching yours," said he.

When Arkell got out, he opened the letter under a gas-lamp, and read it as well as he could for the blots. The penmanship was Lewis, junior's.

"Mr. ARKELL,—Has you have chozen to peech to the master, like a retch has you ar, we give you notise that from this nite you will find the skool has hot has the Inphernal Regeons, a deal to hot for you. And my brother don't care a phether for the oisting he is to get, for he'll serve you worce. And if you show this dockiment to any sole, you'l be a dowble-died sneek, and we will thresh your life out of you, and then duck you in the rivor."

Henry Arkell tore the paper to bits, and ran home, laughing at the spelling. But it was a very fair specimen of the orthography of Westerbury collegiate school.

CHAPTER IV

ASSIZE SATURDAY

To attempt to describe the state of Mr. Fauntleroy would be a vain effort. It was the practice of that respected solicitor never to advance a fraction of money out of his pocket for any mortal client, unless the repayment was as safe and sure as the Bank of England. He had deemed the return so in the case of Mrs. Carr, and had really advanced a good bit of money; and now there was no marriage recorded in the register.

How had it gone out of it? Mr. Fauntleroy's first thought, in his desperation, was to suspect Mynn and Mynn, clean-handed practitioners though he knew them to be, as practitioners went, of having by some sleight of hand spirited the record away. But for the assertion of Mr. Wilberforce, that he had read it, the lawyer would have definitely concluded that it had never been there, in spite of Mr. Omer and his pencilled names. He went tearing over to Mynn and Mynn's in a fine state of excitement, could see neither Mr. Mynn nor Mr. George Mynn, hired a gig at Eckford, and drove over to Mr. Mynn's house, two miles distant. Mr. Mynn, strong in the gout, and wrapped up in flannel and cotton wool in his warm sitting-room, thought at first his professional brother had gone mad, as he listened to the tale and the implied accusation, and then expressed his absolute disbelief that any record of any such marriage had ever been there.

"You must be mad, Fauntleroy! Go and tamper with a register!—suspect us of stealing a page out of a church's register! If you were in your senses, and I had the use of my legs, I'd kick you out of my house for your impudence. I might just as well turn round and tell you, you had been robbing the archives of the Court of Chancery."

"Nobody knew of the record's being there but you, and I, and the rector," debated Mr. Fauntleroy, wiping his great face. "You say you went and saw it."

"I say I went and didn't see it," roared the afflicted man, who had a dreadful twinge just then. "It seems—if this story of yours is true—that I never heard it was there until it was gone. Don't be a simpleton, Fauntleroy."

In his heart of hearts, of course Mr. Fauntleroy did not think Mynn and Mynn had been culpable, only in his passion. His voice began to cool down to calmness.

"I'm ready to accuse the whole world, and myself into the bargain," he said. "So would you be, had you been played the trick. I wish you'd tell me quietly what you know about the matter altogether."

"That's where you should have begun," said old Mynn. "We never heard of any letter having been found, setting forth that the record of the marriage was in the register of St. James's, never thought for a moment that there had been any marriage, and I don't think it now, for the matter of that," he added, par parenthèse, "until the day our new manager, Littelby, took possession, and I and George were inducting him a little into our approaching assize and other causes. We came to Carr versus Carr, in due course, and then Littelby, evidently surprised, asked how it was that the letter despatched to you—to you, Mr. Fauntleroy, and which letter it seems you kept to yourself, and gave us no notice of—had not served to put an end to the cause. Naturally I and my brother inquired what letter Mr. Littelby alluded to, and what were its contents, and then he told us that it was a letter written by Robert Carr, of Holland, stating that the marriage had taken place at the church of St. James the Less, and that its record would be found entered on the register. My impression at the first moment was—and it was George's very strongly—that there had been nothing of the sort; no marriage, and consequently no record; but immediately a doubt arose whether any fraud had been committed by means of making a false entry in the register. I went off at once to Westerbury, fully determined to detect and expose this fraud—and my eyes are pretty clear for such things—I paid my half-crown, and went with the clerk and examined the register, and found I had my journey for nothing. There was no such record in the register—no mention whatever of the marriage. That is all I know of the affair, Mr. Fauntleroy."

Had Mr. Fauntleroy talked till now, he could have learnt no more. It evidently was all that his confrère knew; and he went back to Westerbury as wise as he came, and sought the house of Mr. Wilberforce. The record must have been taken out between the beginning of November and the 2nd of December, he told the master. Omer, and the master himself, had both seen it at the former time; old Mynn searched on the 2nd of December, and it was gone.

This information did not help Mr. Wilberforce in his perplexity, as to who could have tampered with it. It was impossible but that his suspicion should be directed to the night already spoken of, when Arkell was locked up in the church, and seemed to have got out in a manner so mysterious nobody knew how. Arkell adhered to his story: he had found the door open in the night, and walked out; and that was all that could be got from him. The master took him at his word. Had he pressed him much, he might have heard more; had he only given him a hint that he knew the register had been robbed, and that both trouble and injustice were likely to arise from it, he might have heard all; for Henry fully meant to keep his word with George Prattleton, and declare the truth, if a necessity arose for it. But it appeared to be the policy of both the master and Mr. Fauntleroy to keep the register out of sight and discussion altogether. Not a word of the loss was suffered to escape. Mr. Fauntleroy had probably his private reasons for this, and the rector shrank from any publicity, because the getting at the register seemed to reflect some carelessness on him and his mode of securing it.

Meanwhile the public were aware that some internal commotion was agitating the litigants in the great cause Carr versus Carr. What it was, they could not penetrate. They knew that a young lady, Mrs. Carr the widow, was stopping in Westerbury, and had frequent interviews with Mr. Fauntleroy; and they saw that the renowned lawyer himself was in a state of ferment; but not a breath touching the register in any way had escaped abroad, and George Prattleton and Henry Arkell were in ignorance that there was trouble connected with it. George had ventured to put a question to the Reverend Mr. Prattleton, regarding Mr. Wilberforce's visit in connection with it, and was peremptorily ordered to mind his own business.

And the whole city, ripe for gossip and for other people's affairs, as usual, lived in a perpetual state of anticipation of the assizes, and the cause that was to come on at them.

It is probable that this blow to Mr. Fauntleroy—and he regarded it in no less a light—rendered him more severe than customary in his other affairs. On the first of March, another ten pound was due to him from Peter Arkell. The month came in, and the money was not paid; and Mr. Fauntleroy immediately threatened harsh measures: that he would sell him up for the whole of the debt. He had had judgment long ago, and therefore possessed the power to do it; and Peter Arkell went to him. But the grace he pleaded for, Mr. Fauntleroy refused longer to give; refused it coarsely and angrily; and Peter was tempted to remind him of the past. Never yet had he done so.

"Have you forgotten what I did for you?" he asked. "I saved you once from what was perhaps worse than debt."

"And what if you did?" returned the strong-minded lawyer—not to speak more plainly. "I paid you back again."

"Yes; but how? In driblets, which did me no good. And if you did repay me, does that blot out the obligation? If any one man should be lenient to another, you ought to be so to me, Fauntleroy."

"Have I not been lenient?"

"No. It is true, you have not taken the extreme measures you threaten now, but what with the sums you have forced me to pay, the costs, the interest, I know not what all, for I have never clearly understood it, you have made my life one of worry, hardship, and distress. But for that large sum I had to pay suddenly for you I might have done differently in the world. It was my ruin; yes, I assert it, for it is the simple truth, the finding of that sum was my ruin. It took from me all hope of prosperity, and I have been obliged ever since to be a poor, struggling man."

"I paid you, I say; what d'ye mean?" roughly spoke Mr. Fauntleroy.

Peter Arkell shook his head. He had said his say, and was too gentle-minded, too timid-mannered to contend. But the interview did him no good: it only served to further anger Mr. Fauntleroy.

A few days more, and Assize Saturday came in—as it is called in the local phraseology. The judges were expected in some time in the afternoon to open court, and the town was alive with bustle and preparation. On this bright day—and it was one of the brightest March ever gave us—a final, peremptory, unmistakable missive arrived for Peter Arkell from Mr. Fauntleroy. And yet the man boasted in it of his leniency of giving him a few hours more grace; it even dared to hint that perhaps Mr. Arkell, if applied to, might save his home. But the gist of it was, that if the ten pounds were not paid that afternoon by six o'clock, at Mr. Fauntleroy's office, on Monday morning he should proceed to execution.

It was not a pleasant letter for Mrs. Peter Arkell. She received it. Peter was out; and she lay on the sofa in great agitation, as might be seen from the hectic on her cheeks, the unnatural brightness of her eyes. How lovely she looked as she lay there, a lace cap shading her delicate features, no description could express. The improvement so apparent in her when they returned from the sea-side had not lasted; and for the last few weeks she had faded ominously.

The cathedral clock chimed out the quarter to three, and the bell rang out for service. It had been going some time, when Henry, who had been hard at his studies in the little room that was once exclusively his father's, came in. The great likeness between mother and son was more apparent than ever, and the tall, fine boy of sixteen had lost none of his inherited beauty. It was the same exquisite face; the soft, dark eyes, the transparent complexion, the pure features. Perhaps I have dwelt more than I ought on this boy's beauty; but he is no imaginary creation; and it was of that rare order that enchains the eye and almost enforces mention whenever seen, no matter how often. It is still vivid in the remembrance of Westerbury.

"I am going now, mamma."

"You will be late, Henry."

Something in the tone of the voice struck on his ear, and he looked attentively at his mother. The signs of past emotion were not quite obliterated from her face.

"Mamma, you have been crying."

It was of no use to deny it; indeed the sudden accusation brought up fresh tears then. Painful matters had been kept as much as possible from Henry; but he could not avoid knowing of the general embarrassments: unavoidable, and, so to speak, honourable embarrassments.

"What is it now?" he urgently asked.

"Nothing new; only the old troubles over and over again. Of course, the longer they go on, the worse they get. Never mind, dear; you cannot mend matters, so there's no necessity for allowing them to trouble you. There is an invitation come for you from the Palmers'. I told Lucy to put the note on the mantel-piece."

He saw a letter lying there and opened it. His colour rose vividly as he read, and he turned to look at the direction. It was addressed "Mr. Peter Arkell;" but Henry had read it then.

"You see, they want you to spend Monday with them at Heath Hall, and as it will be the judges' holiday, you can get leave from college and do so."

"Mother," he interrupted—and every vestige of colour had forsaken his sensitive face—"what does this letter mean?"

Mrs. Arkell started up and clasped her hands. "Oh, Henry! what have you been reading? What has Lucy done? She has left out the wrong letter. That was not meant for you."

"Does it mean a prison for papa?" he asked, controlling his voice and manner to calmness, though his heart turned sick with fear. "You must tell me all, mother, now I have read this."

"Perhaps it does, Henry. Or else the selling up of our home. I scarcely know what myself, except that it means great distress and confusion."

He could hardly speak for consternation. But, if he understood the letter aright, a sum of ten pounds would for the present avert it. "It is not much," he said aloud to his mother.

"It is a great deal to us, Henry; more than we know where to find."

"Papa could borrow it from Mr. Arkell."

"I am sure he will not, let the consequences be what they may. I don't wonder. If you only knew, my dear, how much, how often, he has had to borrow from William Arkell—kind, generous William Arkell!— you could hardly wish him to."

"But what will be done?" he urged.

"I don't know. Unless things come to the crisis they have so long threatened. Child," she added, bursting into tears, "in spite of my firmly-seated trust, these petty anxieties are wearing me out. Every time a knock comes to the door, I shiver and tremble, lest it should be people come to ask for money which we cannot pay. Henry, you will be late."

"Plenty of time, mamma. I timed myself one day, and ran from this to the cloister entrance in two minutes and a half. Are you being pressed for much besides this?" he continued, touching the letter.

"Not very much for anything else," she replied. "That is the worst: if that were settled, I think we might manage to stave off the rest till brighter days come round. If we can but retain, our home!—several times it would have gone, but for Mr. Arkell. But I was wrong to speak of this to you," she sighed: "and I am wrong to give way, myself. It is not often that I do. God never sent a burden, but He sent strength to bear it: and we have always, hitherto, been wonderfully helped. Henry, you will surely be late."

He slowly took his elbow from the mantel-piece, where it had been leaning. "No. But if I were, it would be something new: it is not often they have to mark me late."

Kissing his mother, he walked out of the house in a dreamy mood, and with a slow step; not with the eager look and quick foot of a schoolboy, in dread of being marked late on the cathedral roll. As he let the gate swing to, behind him, and turned on his way, a hand was laid upon his shoulder. Henry looked round, and saw a tall, aristocratic man, looking down upon him. In spite of his mind's trouble, his face shone with pleasure.

"Oh, Mr. St. John! Are you in Westerbury?"

"Well, I think you have pretty good ocular demonstration of it. Harry, you have grown out of all knowledge: you will be as tall as my lanky self, if you go on like this. How is Mrs. Arkell?"

"Not any better, thank you. I am so very pleased to see you," he continued: "but I cannot stop now. The bell has been going ten minutes."

"In the choir still? Are you the senior boy?"

"Senior chorister as before, but not senior boy yet. Prattleton is senior. Jocelyn went to Oxford in January. Did you come home to-day?"

"Of course. I came in with the barristers."

"But you are not a barrister?" returned Henry, half puzzled at the words.

"I a barrister! I am nothing but my idle self, the heir of all the St. Johns. How is your friend, Miss Beauclerc?"

"She is very well," said Henry; and he turned away his head as he answered. Did St. John's heart beat at the name, as his did, he wondered.

"Harry, I must see your gold medal."

"Oh, I'll fetch it out in a minute: it is only in the parlour."

He ran in, and came out with the pretty toy hanging to its blue ribbon. Mr. St. John took it in his hand.

"The dean displayed taste," was his remark. "Westerbury cathedral on one side, and the inscription to you on the other. There; put it up, and be off. I don't want you to be marked late through me."

There was not another minute to be lost, so Henry slipped the medal into his jacket-pocket, flew away, and got on to the steps in his surplice one minute before the dean came in.

There was a bad practice prevailing in the college school, chiefly resorted to by the senior boys: it was that of pledging their goods and chattels. Watches, chains, silver pencil-cases, books, or anything else available, were taken to Rutterley, the pawnbroker's, without scruple. Of course this was not known to the masters. A tale was told of Jones tertius having taken his surplice to Rutterley's one Monday morning; and, being unable to redeem it on the Saturday, he had lain in bed all day on the Sunday, and sent word to the head master that he had sprained his ankle. On the Monday, he limped into the school, apparently in excruciating pain, to the sympathy of the masters, and intense admiration of the senior boys. Henry Arkell had never been guilty of this practice, but he was asking himself, all college time, why he should not be, for once, and so relieve the pressure at home. His gold watch, the gift of Mr. Arkell, was worth, at his own calculation, twenty pounds, and he thought there could be no difficulty in pledging it for ten. "It is not an honourable thing, I know," he reasoned with himself; "but the boys do it every day for their own pleasures, and surely I may in this dreadful strait."

Service was over in less than an hour, and he left the cathedral by the front entrance. Being Saturday afternoon, there was no school. The streets were crowded; the high sheriff and his procession had already gone out to meet the judges, and many gazers lingered, waiting for their return. Henry hastened through them, on his way to the pawnbroker's. Possessed of that sensitive, refined temperament, had he been going into the place to steal, he could not have felt more shame. The shop was partitioned off into compartments or boxes, so that one customer should not see another. If Henry Arkell could but have known his ill-luck! In the box contiguous to the one he entered, stood Alfred Aultane, the boy next below him in the choir, who had stolen down with one of the family tablespoons, which he had just been protesting to the pawnbroker was his own, and that he would have it out on Monday without fail, for his godfather the counsellor was coming in with the judges, and never failed to give him half a sovereign. But that disbelieving pawnbroker obstinately persisted in refusing to have anything to do with the spoon, for he knew the Aultane crest; and Mr. Alfred stood biting his nails in mortification.

"Will you lend me ten pounds on this?" asked Henry, coming in, and not suspecting that anybody was so near.

"Ten pounds!" uttered Rutterley, after examining the watch. "You college gentlemen have got a conscience! I could not give more than half."

"That would be of no use: I must have ten. I shall be sure to redeem it, Mr. Rutterley."

"I am not afraid of that. The college boys mostly redeem their pledges; I will say that for them. I will lend you six pounds upon it, not a farthing more. What can you be wanting with so large a sum?"

"That is my business, if you please," returned Henry, civilly.

"Oh, of course. Six pounds: take it, or leave it."

A sudden temptation flashed across Henry's mind. What if he pledged the gold medal? But for his having it in his pocket, the thought would not have occurred to him. "But how can I?" he mentally argued—"the gift of the dean and chapter! But it is my own," temptation whispered again, "and surely this is a righteous cause. Yes: I will risk it: and if I can't redeem it before, it must wait till I get my money from the choir. So he put the watch and the gold medal side by side on the counter, and received two tickets in exchange, and eight sovereigns and four half-sovereigns.

"Be sure keep it close, Mr. Rutterley," he enjoined; "you see my name is on it, and there is no other medal like it in the town. I would not have it known that I had done this, for a hundred times its worth."

"All right," answered Mr. Rutterley; "things left with me are never seen." But Alfred Aultane, from the next box, had contrived both to hear and see.

Henry Arkell was speeding to the office of Mr. Fauntleroy, when he heard sounds behind him "Iss—iss—I say! Iss!"

It was Aultane. "What became of you that you were not at college this afternoon?" demanded Henry, who, as senior chorister, had much authority over the nine choristers under him.

"College be jiggered! I stopped out to see the show; and it isn't come yet. If Wilberforce kicks up a row, I shall swear my mother kept me to make calls with her. I say, Arkell, you couldn't do a fellow a service, could you?"

Henry was surprised at the civil, friendly tone—never used by some of the boys to him. "If I can, I will," said he. "What is it?"

"Lend me ten bob, in gold. I must get it: it's for something that can't wait. I'll pay you back next week. I know you must have as much about you."

"All the money I have about me is wanted for a specific purpose. I have not a sixpence that I can lend: if I had, you should be welcome to it."

"Nasty mean wretch!" grunted Aultane, in his heart. "Won't I serve him out!"

The cathedral bells had been for some time ringing merrily, giving token that the procession had met the judges, and was nearing the city, on its return. Just then a blast was heard from the trumpets of the advancing heralds, and Aultane tore away to see the sight.

CHAPTER V

ASSIZE SUNDAY

The next day was Assize Sunday. A dense crowd collected early round the doors of the cathedral, and, as soon as they were opened, rushed in, and took possession of the edifice, leaving vacant only the pulpit, the bishop's throne, and the locked-up seats. It was the custom for the bishop (if in Westerbury), the dean and chapter, and the forty king's scholars, to assemble just inside the front entrance and receive the judges, who were attended in state to the cathedral, just as they had been attended into Westerbury the previous afternoon, the escort being now augmented by the mayor and corporation, and an overflowing shoal of barristers.

The ten choristers were the first to take up their standing at the front entrance. They were soon followed by the rest of the king's scholars, the surplices of the whole forty being primly starched for the occasion. They had laid in their customary supply of pins, for it was the boys' pleasure, during the service on Assize Sunday, to stick pins into people's backs, and pin women's clothes together; the density of the mob permitting full scope to the delightful amusement, and preventing detection.

The thirty king's scholars bustled in from the cloisters two by two, crossed the body of the cathedral to the grand entrance, and placed themselves at the head of the choristers. Which was wrong: they ought to have gone below them. Henry Arkell, as senior chorister, took precedence of all when in the cathedral; but not when out of it, and that was a somewhat curious rule. Out of the cathedral, Arkell was under Prattleton; the latter, as senior boy, being head of all. He told Prattleton to move down.

Prattleton declined. "Then we must move up," observed Henry. "Choristers."

He was understood: and the choristers moved above the king's scholars.

"What do you mean by that?" demanded Prattleton. "How dare you disobey me, Mr. Arkell?"

"How dare you disobey me?" was Henry Arkell's retort, but he spoke civilly. "I am senior here, and you know it, Prattleton." It must be understood that this sort of clashing could only occur on occasions like the present: on ordinary Sundays and on saints' days the choristers and king's scholars did not come in contact in the cathedral.

"I'll let you know who's senior," said Prattleton. "Choristers, move down; you juniors, do you hear me? Move down, or I'll have you hoisted to-morrow."

"If Mr. Arkell tells us, please, sir," responded a timid junior, who fancied Mr. Prattleton looked particularly at him.

The choristers did not stir, and Prattleton was savage. "King's scholars, move up, and shove."

Some of the king's scholars hesitated, especially those of the lower school. It was no light matter to disobey the senior chorister in the cathedral. Others moved up, and proceeded to "shove." Henry Arkell calmly turned to one of his own juniors.

"Hardcast, go into the vestry, and ask Mr. Wilberforce to step here. Should he have gone into college, fetch him out of the chanting-desk."

"Remain where you are, Hardcast," foamed Prattleton. "I dare you to stir."

Hardcast, a little chap of ten, was already off, but he turned round at the word. "I am not under your orders, Mr. Prattleton, when the senior chorister's present."

A few minutes, and then the Reverend Mr. Wilberforce, in his surplice and hood, was seen advancing. Hardcast had fetched him out of the chanting-desk.

"What's all this? what hubbub are you boys making? I'll flog you all to-morrow. Arkell, Prattleton, what's the matter?"

"I thought it better to send for you, sir, than to have a disturbance here," said Arkell.

"A disturbance here! You had better not attempt it."

"Don't the king's scholars take precedence of the choristers, sir?" demanded Prattleton.

"No, they don't," returned the master. "If you have not been years enough in the college to know the rules, Mr. Prattleton, you had better return to the bottom of school, and learn them. Arkell, in this place, you have the command. King's scholars move down, and be quick over it: and I'll flog you all round," concluded Mr. Wilberforce, "if you strike up a dispute in college again."

The master turned tail, and strode back as fast as his short legs would carry him: for the dean and chapter, marshalled by a verger and the bedesmen, were crossing the cathedral; and a flourish of trumpets, outside, told of the approach of the judges. The Reverend Mr. Wilberforce was going to take the chanting for an old minor canon whose voice was cracked, and he would hardly recover breath to begin.

The choristers all grinned at the master's decision, save Arkell and Aultane, junior: the latter, though second chorister, took part with Prattleton, because he hated Arkell; and as the judges passed in their flowing scarlet robes with the trains held up behind, and their imposing wigs, so terrible to look at, the bows of the choristers were much more gracious than those of the king's scholars. The additional mob, teeming in after the judges' procession, was unlimited; and a rare field had the boys and their pins that day.

The hubbub and the bustle of the morning passed, and the cathedral bell was again tolling out for afternoon service. Save the dust, and there was plenty of that, no trace remained of the morning's scene. The king's scholars were already in their seats in the choir, and the ten choristers stood at the choir entrance, for they always waited there to go in with the dean and chapter. One of them, and it was Mr. Wilberforce's own son, had made a mistake in the morning in fastening his own surplice to a countrywoman's purple stuff gown, instead of two gowns together; and, when they came to part company, the surplice proved the weakest. The consequence was an enormous rent, and it had just taken the nine other choristers and three lay-clerks five minutes and seventeen pins, fished out of different pockets, to do it up in any way decent. Young Wilberforce, during the process, rehearsing a tale over in his mind, for home, about that horrid rusty nail that would stick out of the vestry door.

The choristers stood facing each other, five on a side, and the dean and canons would pass between them when they came in. They stood at an equidistance, one from the other, and it was high treason against the college rules for them to move an inch from their places. Arkell headed one line, Aultane the other, the two being face to face. Suddenly a college boy, who was late, came flying from the cloisters and dashed into the choir, to crave the keys of the schoolroom from the senior boy, that he might procure his surplice. It was Lewis junior; so, against the rules, Prattleton condescended to give him the keys; almost any other boy he would have told to whistle for them, and marked him up for punishment as "absent." Prattleton chose to patronise him, on account of his friendship with Lewis senior. Lewis came out again, full pelt, swinging the keys in his hand, rather vain of showing to the choristers that he had succeeded in obtaining them, just as two little old gentlemen were advancing from the front entrance.

"Hi, Lewis! stop a moment," called out Aultane, in a loud whisper, as he crossed over and went behind Arkell.

"Return to your place, Aultane," said Arkell.

Mr. Aultane chose to be deaf.

"Aultane, to your place," repeated Henry Arkell, his tone one of hasty authority. "Do you see who are approaching?"

Aultane looked round in a fluster. But not a soul could he see, save a straggler or two making their way to the side aisles; and two insignificant little old men, arm-in-arm, close at hand, in rusty black clothes and brown wigs. Nobody to affect him.

"I shall return when I please," said he, commencing a whispered parley with Lewis.

"Return this instant, Aultane. I order you."

"You be—"

The word was not a blessing, but you are at liberty to substitute one. The little old men, to whom each chorister had bowed profoundly as they passed him, turned, and bent their severe yellow faces upon Aultane. Lewis junior crept away petrified; and Aultane, with the red flush of shame on his brow, slunk back to his place. They were the learned judges.

They positively were. But no wonder Aultane had failed to recognise them, for they bore no more resemblance to the fierce and fiery visions of the morning, than do two old-fashioned black crows to stately peacocks.

"What may your name be, sir?" inquired the yellower of the two. Aultane hung his head in an agony: he was wondering whether they could order him before them on the morrow and transport him. Wilberforce was in another agony, lest those four keen eyes should wander to his damaged surplice and the pins. Somebody else answered: "Aultane, my lord."

The judges passed on. Arkell would not look towards Aultane: he was too noble to add, even by a glance, to the confusion of a fallen enemy: but the other choristers were not so considerate, and Aultane burst into a flow of bad language.

"Be silent," authoritatively interrupted Henry Arkell. "More of this, and I will report you to the dean."

"I shan't be silent," cried Aultane, in his passionate rage. "There! not for you." Beside himself with anger, he crossed over, and raised his hand to strike Arkell. But one of the sextons, happening to come out of the choir, arrested Aultane, and whirled him back.

"Do you know where you are, sir?"

In another moment they were surrounded. The dean's wife and daughter had come up; and, following them, sneaked Lewis junior, who was settling himself into his surplice. Mrs. Beauclerc passed on, but Georgina stopped. Even as she went into college, she would sometimes stop and chatter to the boys.

"You were quarrelling, young gentlemen! What is the grievance?"

"That beggar threatened to report me to the dean," cried Aultane, too angry to care what he said, or to whom he spoke.

"Then I know you deserved it; as you often do," rejoined Miss Beauclerc; "but I'd keep a civil tongue in my head, if I were you, Aultane. I only wonder he has not reported you before. You should have me for your senior."

"If he does go in and report me, please tell the dean to ask him where his gold medal is," foamed Aultane. "And to make him answer it."

"What do you mean?" she questioned.

"He knows. If the dean offered him a thousand half-crowns for his medal, he could not produce it."

"What does he mean?" repeated Miss Beauclerc, looking at Henry Arkell.

He could not answer: he literally could not. Could he have dropped down without life at Georgina's feet, it had been welcome, rather than that she should hear of an act, which, to his peculiarly refined temperament, bore an aspect of shame so utter. His face flushed a vivid red, and then grew white as his surplice.

"He can't tell you," said Aultane; "that is, he won't. He has put it into pawn."

"And his watch too," squeaked Lewis, from behind, who had heard of the affair from Aultane.

Henry Arkell raised his eyes for one deprecating moment to Miss Beauclerc's face; she was struck with their look of patient anguish. She cast an annihilating frown at Lewis, and, raising her finger haughtily motioned Aultane to his place. "I believe nothing ill of you," she whispered to Henry, as she passed on to the choir.

The next to come in was Mr. St. John. "What's the matter?" he hurriedly said to Henry, who had not a vestige of colour in his cheeks or lips.

"Nothing, thank you, Mr. St. John."

Mr. St. John went on, and Lewis skulked to his seat, in his wake. Lewis's place was midway on the bench on the decani side, seven boys being above him and seven below him. The choristers were on raised seats in front of the lay-clerks, five on one side the choir, five opposite on the other; Arkell, as senior, heading the five on the decani side.

The dean and canons came in, and the service began. While the afternoon psalms were being sung, Mr. Wilberforce pricked the roll, a parchment containing the names of the members of the cathedral, from the dean downwards, marking those who were present. Aultane left his place and took the roll to the dean, continuing his way to the organ-loft, to inquire what anthem had been put up. He brought word back to Arkell, 'The Lord is very great and terrible. Beckwith.' Aultane would as soon have exchanged words with the yellow-faced little man sitting in the stall next the dean, as with Arkell, just then, but his duty was obligatory. He spoke sullenly, and crossed to his seat on the opposite side, and Arkell rose and reported the anthem to the lay-clerks behind him. Mr. Wilberforce was then reading the first lesson.

Now it happened that there was only one bass at service that afternoon, he on the decani side, Mr. Smith; the other had not come; and the moment the words were out of Arkell's mouth, "The Lord is very great. Beckwith," Mr. Smith flew into a temper. He had a first-rate voice, was a good singer, and being inordinately vain, liked to give himself airs. "I have a horrid cold on the chest," he remonstrated, "and I cannot do justice to the solo; I shan't attempt it. The organist knows I'm as hoarse as a raven, and yet he goes and puts up that anthem for to-day!"

"What is to be done?" whispered Henry.

"I shall send and tell him I can't do it. Hardcast, go up to the organ-loft, and tell—Or I wish you would oblige me by going yourself, Arkell: the juniors are always making mistakes. My compliments to Paul, and the anthem must be done without the bass solo, or he must put up another."

Henry Arkell, ever ready to oblige, left his stall, proceeded to the organ-loft, and delivered the message. The organist was wroth: and but for those two little old gentlemen, whom he knew were present, he would have refused to change the anthem, which had been put up by the dean.

"Where's Cliff, this afternoon?" asked he, sharply, alluding to the other bass.

"I don't know," replied Henry. "He is not at service."

The organist took up one of the anthem books with a jerk, and turned over its leaves. He came to the anthem, "I know that my Redeemer liveth," from the Messiah.

"Are you prepared to do justice to this?" he demanded.

"Yes, I believe I am," replied Henry. "But—"

"But me no buts," interrupted the organist, who was always very short with the choristers. "'I know that my Redeemer liveth. Pitt.'"

As Henry Arkell descended the stairs, Mr. Wilberforce was concluding the first lesson. So instead of giving notice of the change of anthem to Mr. Wilberforce and the singers on the cantori side, he left that until later, and made haste to his own stall, to be in time for the soli parts in the Cantate Domino, which was being sung that afternoon in place of the Magnificat. In passing the bench of king's scholars, a foot was suddenly extended out before him, and he fell heavily over it, striking his head on the stone step that led to the stalls of the minor canons. A sexton, a verger, and one or two of the senior boys, surrounded, lifted, and carried him out.

The service proceeded; but his voice was missed in the Cantate; Aultane's proved but a poor substitute.

"I wonder whether the anthem's changed?" debated the bass to the contre tenor.

"Um—no," decided the latter. "Arkell was coming straight to his place. Had there been any change, he would have gone and told Wilberforce and the opposites. Paul is in a pet, and won't alter it."

"Then he'll play the solo without my accompaniment," retorted the bass, loftily.

Henry Arkell was only stunned by the fall, and before the conclusion of the second lesson, he appeared in the choir, to the surprise of many. After giving the requisite notice of the change in the anthem to Mr.

Wilberforce and Aultane, he entered his stall; but his face was white as the whitest marble. He sang, as usual, in the Deus Misereatur. And when the time for the anthem came, Mr. Wilberforce rose from his knees to give it out.

"The anthem is taken from the burial service."

The symphony was played, and then Henry Arkell's voice rose soft and clear, filling the old cathedral with its harmony, and the words falling as distinctly on the ear as if they had been spoken. "I know that my Redeemer liveth, and that he shall stand at the latter day upon the earth. And though after my skin worms destroy this body, yet in my flesh I shall see God: whom I shall see for myself, and mine eyes shall behold, and not another." The organist could not have told why he put up that particular anthem, but it was a remarkable coincidence, noticed afterwards, that it should have been a funeral one.

But though Henry Arkell's voice never faltered or trembled, his changing face spoke of bodily disease or mental emotion: one moment it was bright as a damask rose, the next of a transparent whiteness. Every eye was on him, wondering at the beauty of his voice, at the marvellous beauty of his countenance: some sympathised with his emotion; some were wrapt in the solemn thoughts created by the words. When the solo was concluded, Henry, with an involuntary glance at the pew of Mrs. Beauclerc, fell against the back of his stall for support: he looked exhausted. Only for a moment, however, for the chorus commenced.

He joined in it; his voice rose above all the rest in its sweetness and power; but as the ending approached, and the voices ceased, and the last sound of the organ died upon the ear, his face bent forward, and rested without motion on the choristers' desk.

"Arkell, what are you up to?" whispered one of the lay-clerks from behind, as Mr. Wilberforce recommenced his chanting.

No response.

"Nudge him, Wilberforce; he's going to sleep. There's the dean casting his eyes this way."

Edwin Wilberforce did as he was desired, but Arkell never stirred.

So Mr. Tenor leaned over and grasped him by the arm, and pulled him up with a sudden jerk. But he did not hold him, and the poor head fell forward again upon the desk. Henry Arkell had fainted.

Some confusion ensued: for the four choristers below him had every one to come out of the stall before he could be got out. Mr. Wilberforce momentarily stopped chanting, and directed his angry spectacles towards the choristers, not understanding what caused the hubbub, and inwardly vowing to flog the whole five on the morrow. Mr. Smith, a strong man, came out of his stall, lifted the lifeless form in his arms, and carried it out to the side aisle, the head, like a dead weight, hanging down over his shoulder. All the eyes and all the glasses in the cathedral were bent on them; and the next to come out of his stall, by the prebendaries, and follow in the wake, was Mr. St. John, a flush of emotion on his pale face.

The dean's family, after service, met Mr. St. John in the cloisters. "Is he better?" asked Mrs. Beauclerc. "What was the matter with him the second time?"

"He fainted; but we soon brought him to in the vestry. Young Wilberforce ran and got some water. They are walking home with him now."

"What caused him to fall in the choir?" continued Mrs. Beauclerc. "Giddiness?"

"It was not like giddiness," remarked Mr. St. John. "It was as if he fell over something."

"So I thought," interrupted Georgina. "Why did you leave your seat to follow him?" she continued, in a low tone to Mr. St. John, falling behind her mother.

"It was a sudden impulse, I suppose. I was unpleasantly struck with his appearance as I went into college. He was looking ghastly."

"The choristers had been quarrelling: Aultane's fault, I am sure. He lifted his hand to strike Arkell. Aultane reproached him with having"—Georgina Beauclerc hesitated, with an amused look—"disposed of his prize medal."

"Disposed of his prize medal?" echoed Mr. St. John.

"Pawned it."

St. John uttered an exclamation. He remembered the tricks of the college boys, but he could not have believed this of his favourite, Henry Arkell.

"And his watch also, Lewis junior added," continued Georgina. "They gave me the information in a spiteful glow of triumph. Henry did not deny it: he looked as if he could not. But I know he is the soul of honour, and if he has done anything of the sort, those beautiful companions of his have over-persuaded him: possibly to lend the money to them."

"I'll see into this," mentally spoke Mr. St. John.

CHAPTER VI

PEACHING TO THE DEAN

Mr. St. John went at once to Peter Arkell's. Henry was alone, lying on his bed.

"After such a fall as that, how could you be so imprudent as to come back and take the anthem?" was his unceremonious salutation.

"I felt equal to it," replied Henry. "The one, originally put up, could not be done."

"Then they should have put up a third, for me. The cathedral does not lack anthems, I hope. Show me where your head was struck."

Henry put his hand to his ear, then higher up, then to his temple. "It was somewhere here—all about here—I cannot tell the exact spot."

As he spoke, a tribe of college boys was heard to clatter in at the gate. Henry would have risen, but Mr. St. John laid his arm across him.

"You are not going to those boys. I will send them off. Lie still and go to sleep, and dream of pleasant things."

"Pleasant things!" echoed Henry Arkell, in a tone full of pain. Mr. St. John leaned over him.

"Henry, I have never had a brother of my own; but I have almost loved you as such. Treat me as one now. What tale is it those demons of mischief have got hold of, about your watch and medal?"

With a sharp cry, Henry Arkell turned his face to the pillow, hiding its distress.

"I suppose old Rutterley has got them. But that's nothing; it's the fashion in the school: and I expect you had some urgent motive."

"Oh, Mr. St. John, I shall never overget this day's shame: they told Georgina Beauclerc! I would rather die this moment, here, as I lie, than see her face again."

His tone was one of suppressed anguish, and Mr. St. John's heart ached for him: though he chose to appear to make light of the matter.

"Told Georgina Beauclerc: what if they did? She is the very one to glory in such exploits. Had she been the dean's son, instead of his daughter, she would have been in Rutterley's sanctum three times a week. I don't think she would stand at going, as it is, if she were hard up."

"But why did they tell her! I could not have acted so cruelly by them. If I could but go to some far-off desert, and never face her, or the school, again!"

"If you could but work yourself into a brain fever, you had better say! that's what you seem likely to do. As to falling in Georgina Beauclerc's opinion, which you seem to estimate so highly (it's more than I do), if you pledged all you possess in a lump, and yourself into the bargain, she would only think the better of you. Now I tell you so, for I know it."

"I could not help it; I could not, indeed. Money is so badly wanted—"

He stopped in confusion, having said more than he meant: and St. John took up the discourse in a careless tone.

"Money is wanted badly everywhere. I have done worse than you, Harry, for I am pawning my estate, piecemeal. Mind! that's a true confession, and has never been given to another soul: it must lie between us."

"It was yesterday afternoon when college was over," groaned Henry. "I only thought of giving Rutterley my watch: I thought he would be sure to let me have ten pounds upon it. But he would not; only six: and I had the medal in my pocket; I had been showing it to you. I never did such a thing in all my life before."

"That is more than your companions could say. How did it get to their knowledge?"

"I cannot think."

"Where's the—the exchange?"

"The what?" asked Henry.

"How dull you are!" cried Mr. St. John. "I am trying to be genteel, and you won't let me. The ticket. Let me see it."

"They are in my jacket-pocket. Two." He languidly reached forth the pieces, and Mr. St. John slipped them into his own.

"Why do you do that, Mr. St. John?"

"To study them at leisure. What's the matter?"

"My head is beginning to ache."

"No wonder, with, all this talking. I'm off. Good-bye. Get to sleep as fast as you can."

The boys were in the garden and round the gate still, when he went down.

"Oh, if you please, sir, is he half killed? Edwin Wilberforce says so."

"No, he is not half killed," responded Mr. St. John. "But he wants quiet, and you must disperse, that he may have it."

"My brother, the senior boy, says he must have fallen down from vexation, because his tricks came out," cried Prattleton junior.

Mr. St. John ran his eyes over the assemblage. "What tricks?"

"He has been pawning the gold medal, Mr. St. John," cried Cookesley, the second senior of the school. "Aultane junior has told the dean: Bright Vaughan heard him."

"Oh, he has told the dean, has he?"

"The dean was going into the deanery, sir, and Miss Beauclerc was standing at the door, waiting for him," explained Vaughan to Mr. St. John. "Something she said to Aultane put him in a passion, and he took and told the dean. It was his temper made him do it, sir."

"Such a disgrace, you know, Mr. St. John, to take the dean's medal there," rejoined Cookesley. "Anything else wouldn't have signified."

"Oh, been rather meritorious, no doubt," returned Mr. St. John. "Boys!"

"Yes, Mr. St. John."

"You know I was one of yourselves once, and I can make allowance for you in all ways. But when I was in the school, our motto was, Fair play, and no sneaking."

"It's our motto still," cried the flattered boys.

"It does not appear to be. We would rather, any one of us, have pitched ourselves off that tower," pointing to it with his hand, "than have gone sneaking to the dean with a private complaint."

"And so we would still, in cool blood," cried Cookesley. "Aultane must have been out of his mind with passion when he did it."

"How does Aultane know that Arkell's medal is in pawn?"

"He does not say how. He says he'll pledge his word to it."

"Then listen to me, boys: my word will, I believe, go as far with you as Aultane's. Yesterday afternoon I met Henry Arkell at the gate here; I asked to see his medal, and he brought it out of the house to show me. He is in bed now, but perhaps if you ask him to-morrow, he will be able to show it to you. At any rate, do not condemn him until you are sure there's a just reason. If he did pledge his medal, how many things have you pledged? Some of you would pledge your heads if you could. Fair play's a jewel, boys— fair play for ever!"

Off came the trenchers, and a shout was being raised for fair play and Mr. St. John; but the latter put up his hand.

"I thought it was Sunday. Is that the way you keep Sunday in Westerbury? Disperse quietly."

"I'll clear him," thought Mr. St. John, as he walked home. "Aultane's a mean-spirited coward. To tell the dean!"

Indeed, the incautious revelation of Mr. Aultane was exciting some disagreeable consternation in the minds of the seniors; and that gentleman himself already wished his passionate tongue had been bitten out before he made it.

The following morning the college boys were astir betimes, and flocked up in a body to the judges' lodgings, according to usage, to beg what was called the judges' holiday. The custom was for the senior judge to send his card out and his compliments to the head master, requesting him to grant it; and the boys' custom was, as they tore back again, bearing the card in triumph, to raise the whole street with their shouts of "Holiday! holiday!"

But there was no such luck on this morning. The judges, instead of the card and the request, sent out a severe message—that from what they had heard the previous day in the cathedral, the school appeared to merit punishment rather than holiday. So the boys went back, dreadfully chapfallen, kicking as much mud as they could over their trousers and boots, for it had rained in the night, and ready to buffet Aultane junior as the source of the calamity.

Aultane himself was in an awful state of mind. He felt perfectly certain that the affair in the cathedral must now come out to the head master, who would naturally inquire into the cause of the holiday's being denied; and he wondered how it was that judges dared to come abroad without their gowns and wigs, deceiving unsuspicious people to perdition.

Before nine, Mr. St. John was at Henry Arkell's bedside. "Well," said he, "how's the head?"

"It feels light—or heavy. I hardly know which. It does not feel as usual. I shall get up presently."

"All right. Put on this when you do," said Mr. St. John, handing him the watch. "And put up this in your treasure place, wherever that may be," he added, laying the gold medal beside it.

"Oh, Mr. St. John! You have—"

"I shall have some sport to-day. I have wormed it all out of Rutterley; and he tells me who was down there and on what errand. Ah, ah, Mr. Aultane! so you peached to the dean. Wait until your turn comes."

"I wonder Rutterley told you anything," said Henry, very much surprised.

"He knew me, and the name of St. John bears weight in Westerbury," smiled he who owned it. "Harry, mind! you must not attempt to go into school to-day."

"It is the judges' holiday."

"The judges have refused it, and the boys have sneaked back like so many dogs with their tails scorched."

"Refused it! Refused the holiday!" interrupted Henry. Such a thing had never been heard of in his memory.

"They have refused it. Something must be wrong with the boys, but I am not at the bottom of the mischief yet. Don't you attempt to go near school or college, Harry: it might play tricks with your head. And now I'm going home to breakfast."

Henry caught his arm as he was departing. "How can I ever thank you, Mr. St. John? I do not know when I shall be able to repay you the money; not until—"

"You never will," interrupted Mr. St. John. "I should not take it if you were rolling in gold. I have done this for my own pleasure, and I will not be cheated out of it. I wonder how many of the boys have got their watches in now. Good-bye, old fellow."

When Mr. Wilberforce came to know of the refused holiday, his consternation nearly equalled Aultane's. What could the school have been doing that had come to the ears of the judges? He questioned sharply the senior boy, and it was as much as Prattleton's king's scholarship was worth to attempt to disguise by so much as a word, or to soften down, the message sent out from the judges. But the closer the master questioned the rest of the boys, the less information he could get; and all he finally obtained was, that some quarrel had taken place between the two head choristers, Arkell and Aultane, on the Sunday afternoon, and that the judges overheard it.

Early school was excused that morning, as a matter of necessity; for the master—relying upon the holiday—did not emerge from his bed-chamber until between eight and nine; and you may be very sure that the boys did not proceed to the college hall of their own accord. But after breakfast they assembled as usual at half-past nine, and the master, uneasy and angry, went in also to the minute. Henry Arkell failed to make his appearance, and it was remarked upon by the masters.

"By the way," said Mr. Wilberforce, "how came he to fall down in college yesterday? Does anybody know?"

"Please, sir, he trod upon a surplice," said Vaughan the bright. "Lewis junior says so."

"Trod upon a surplice!" repeated Mr. Wilberforce. "How could he do that? You were standing. Your surplices are not long enough to be trodden upon. What do you mean by saying that, Lewis junior?"

Lewis junior's face turned red, and he mentally vowed a licking to Bright Vaughan, for being so free with his tongue; but he looked up at the master with an expression as innocent as a lamb's.

"I only said he might have trodden on a surplice, sir. Perhaps he was giddy yesterday afternoon, as he fainted afterwards."

The subject dropped. The choristers went into college for service at ten o'clock, but the master remained in his place. It was not his week for chanting. Before eleven they were back again; and the master had called up the head class, and was again remarking on the absence of Henry Arkell, when the dean and Mr. St. John walked into the hall. Mr. Wilberforce rose, and pushed his spectacles to the top of his brow in his astonishment.

"Have the goodness to call up Aultane," said the dean, after a few words of courtesy, as he stood by the master's desk.

"Senior, or junior, Mr. Dean?"

"The chorister."

"Aultane, junior, walk up," cried the master. And Aultane, junior, walked up, wishing himself and his tongue and the dean, and all the rest of the world within sight and hearing, were safely boxed up in the coffins in the cathedral crypt.

"Now, Aultane," began the dean, regarding him with as much severity as it was in the dean's nature to regard anyone, even a rebellious college boy, "you preferred a charge to me yesterday against the senior chorister; that he had been pledging his gold medal at Rutterley's. Have the goodness to substantiate it."

"Oh, my heart alive, I wish he'd drop through the floor!" groaned Aultane to himself. "What will become of me? What a jackass I was!"

"I did not enter into the matter then," proceeded the dean, for Aultane remained silent. "You had no business to make the complaint to me on a Sunday. What grounds have you for your charge?"

Aultane turned red and white, and green and yellow. The dean eyed him closely. "What proof have you?"

"I have no proof," faltered Aultane.

"No proof! Did you make the charge to me, knowing it was false?"

"No, sir. He has pledged his medal."

"Tell me how you know it. Mr. St. John knows he had it in his own house on Saturday."

Aultane shuffled first on one foot, and then on the other; and the dean, failing explanation from him, appealed to the school, but all disclaimed cognizance of the matter. "If you behave in this extraordinary way, you will compel me to conclude that you have made the charge to prejudice me against Arkell; who, I hear, had a serious charge to prefer against you for ill-behaviour in college," continued the dean to Aultane.

"If you will send to the place, you will find his medal is there, sir," sullenly replied Aultane.

"The shortest plan would be to send to Arkell's, and request him to dispatch his medal here, if the dean approves," interposed Mr. St. John, speaking for the first time.

The dean did approve, and Cookesley was despatched on the errand. He brought back the medal. Henry was not in the way, but Mrs. Arkell had found it and given it to him.

"Now what do you mean by your conduct?" sternly asked the dean of Aultane.

"I know he pledged it on Saturday, if he has got it out to-day," persisted the discomfited Aultane, who was in a terrible state, between wishing to prove his charge true, and the fear of compromising himself.

"I know Henry Arkell could not be guilty of a despicable action," spoke up Mr. St. John; "and, hearing of this charge, I went to Rutterley's to ask him a few questions. He informed me there was a college boy at his place on Saturday, endeavouring to pledge a table-spoon, but he knew the crest, and would not take it in—not wishing, he said, to encourage boys to rob their parents. Perhaps Aultane can tell the dean who that was?"

There was a dead silence in the school, and the look of amazement on the head-master's face was only matched by the confusion of Aultane's. The dean, a kind-hearted man, would not examine further.

"I do not press the matter until I hear the complaint of the senior chorister against Aultane," said he aloud, to Mr. Wilberforce. "It was something that occurred in the cathedral yesterday, in the hearing, unfortunately, of the judges. But a few preliminary tasks, by way of present punishment, will do Aultane no harm."

"I'll give them to him, Mr. Dean," heartily responded the master, whose ears had been so scandalised by the mysterious allusions to Rutterley's, that he would have liked to treat the whole school to "tasks" and to something else, all round. "I'll give them to him."

"You see what a Tom-fool you have made of yourself!" grumbled Prattleton senior to Aultane, as the latter returned to his desk, laden with work. "That's all the good you have got by splitting to the dean."

"I wish the dean was in the sea, I do!" madly cried Aultane, as he savagely watched the retreat of that very reverend divine, who went out carrying the gold medal between his fingers, and followed by Mr. St. John. "And I wish that brute, St. John was hung! He—"

Aultane's words and bravery alike faded into silence, for the two were coming back again. The master stood up.

"I forgot to tell you, Mr. Wilberforce, that I have recommended Henry Arkell to take a holiday for a day or two. That was a violent fall yesterday; and his fainting afterwards struck me as not wearing a favourable appearance."

"Have you seen him, Mr. Dean?"

"I saw him an hour ago, just before service. I was going by the house as he came out of it, on his way to college, I suppose. It is a strange thing what it could have been that caused the fall."

"So it is," replied the master. "I was inquiring about it just now, but the school does not seem to know anything."

"Neither does he, so far as I can learn. At any rate, rest will be best for him for a day or two."

"No doubt it will, Mr. Dean. Thank you for thinking of it."

They finally went out, St. John casting a significant look behind him, at the boys in general, at Aultane junior in particular. It said as plainly as looks could say, "I'd not peach again, boys, if I were you;" and Aultane junior, but for the restraining presence of the head master, would assuredly have sent a yell after him.

How much St. John told of the real truth to the dean, that the medal had been pledged, we must leave between them. The school never knew. Henry himself never knew. St. John quitted the dean at the deanery, and went on to restore the medal to its owner: although Georgina Beauclerc was standing at one of the deanery windows, looking down expectantly, as if she fancied he was going in.

Travice was at that moment at Peter Arkell's, perched upon a side-table, as he talked to them. Henry leaned rather languidly back in an elbow-chair, his fingers pressed upon his head; Lucy was at work near the window; Mrs. Peter, looking very ill, sat at the table. Travice had not been at service on the previous afternoon, and the accident had been news to him this morning.

"But how did you fall?" he was asking with uncompromising plainness, being unable to get any clear information on the point. "What threw you down?"

"Well—I fell," answered Henry.

"Of course you fell. But how? The passage is all clear between the seats of the king's scholars and the cross benches; there's nothing for you to strike your foot against; how did you fall?"

"There was some confusion at the time, Travice; the first lesson was just over, and the people were rising for the cantate. I was walking very fast, too."

"But something must have thrown you down: unless you turned giddy, and fell of your own accord."

"I felt giddy afterwards," returned Henry, who had been speaking with his hand mostly before his eyes, and seemed to answer the questions with some reluctance. "I feel giddy now."

"I think, Travice, he scarcely remembers how it happened," spoke Mrs. Arkell. "Don't press him; he seems tired. I am so glad the dean gave him holiday."

At this juncture, Mr. St. John came in with the medal. He stayed a few minutes, telling Harry he should take him for a drive in the course of the day, which Mrs. Arkell negatived; she thought it might not be well for the giddiness he complained of in the head. St. John took his leave, and Henry went with him outside, to hear the news in private of what had taken place in the college hall. Mrs. Arkell had left the room then, and Travice took the opportunity to approach Lucy.

"Does it strike you that there's any mystery about this fall, Lucy?"

"Mystery!" she repeated, raising her eyes. "In what way?"

"It is one of two things: either that he does not remember how he fell, or that he won't tell. I think it is the latter; there is a restraint in his manner when speaking of it: an evident reluctance to speak."

"But why should he not speak of it?"

"There lies what I call the mystery. A sensational word, you will say, for so slight a matter. I may be wrong—if you have not noticed anything. What's that you are so busy over?"

Lucy held it up to the light, blushing excessively at the same time. It was Harry's rowing jersey, and it was getting the worse for wear. Boating would soon be coming in.

"It wants darning nearly all over, it is so thin," she said. "And the difficulty is to darn it so that the darn shall be neither seen nor suspected on the right side."

"Can't you patch it?" asked Travice.

She laughed out loud. "Would Harry go rowing in a patched jersey? Would you, Travice?"

He laughed too. "I don't think I should much mind it."

"Ah, but you are Travice Arkell," she said, her seriousness returning. "A rich man may go about without shoes if he likes; but a poor one must not be seen even in mended ones."

"True: it's the way of the world, Lucy. Well, I should mend that jersey with a new one. Why, you'll be a whole day over it."

"I dare say I shall be two. Travice, there's Mr. St. John looking round for you. He was beckoning. Did you not see him.

"No, I only saw you," answered Travice, in a tone that was rather a significant one. "I see now; he wants me. Good-bye, Lucy."

He took her hand in his. There was little necessity for it, seeing that he came in two or three times a day. And he kept it longer than he need have done.

CHAPTER VII

CARR VERSUS CARR

It was two o'clock in the afternoon, and a crowd of busy idlers was gathered round the Guildhall at Westerbury, for the great cause was being brought on—Carr versus Carr.

That they could not get inside, you may be very sure, or they would not have been round it. In point of fact, the trial had not been expected to come on before the Tuesday; but in the course of Monday morning two causes had been withdrawn, and the Carr case was called on. The Nisi Prius Court immediately became filled to inconvenience, and at two o'clock the trial began.

It progressed equably for some time, and then there arose a fierce discussion touching the register. Mr. Fauntleroy's counsel, Serjeant Wrangle, declaring the marriage was there up to very recently; and Mynn and Mynn's counsel, Serjeant Siftem, ridiculing the assertion. The judge called for the register.

It was produced and examined. The marriage was not there, neither was there any sign of its having been abstracted. Lawrence Omer was called by Serjeant Wrangle; and he testified to having searched the register, seen the inscribed marriage, and copied the names of the witnesses to it. In proof of this, he tendered his pocket-book, where the names were written in pencil.

Up rose Serjeant Siftem. "What day was this, pray?"

"It was the 4th of November."

"And so you think you saw, amidst the many marriages entered in the register, that of Robert Carr and Martha Ann Hughes?"

"I am sure I saw it," replied Mr. Omer.

"Were you alone?"

"I looked over the book alone. Hunt, the clerk of the church, was present in the vestry."

"It must appear to the jury as a singular thing that you only, and nobody else, should have seen this mysterious entry," continued Serjeant Siftem.

"Perhaps nobody else looked for it; they'd have seen it if they had," shortly returned the witness, who felt himself an aggrieved man, and spoke like one, since Mynn and Mynn had publicly accused him that day of having gone down to St. James's in his sleep, and seen the entry in a dream alone.

"Does it not strike you, witness, as being extraordinary that this one particular entry, professed to have been seen by your eyes, and by yours alone, should have been abstracted from a book safely kept under lock and key?" pursued Serjeant Siftem. "I am mistaken if it would not strike an intelligent man as being akin to an impossibility."

"No, it does not strike me so. But events, hard of belief, happen sometimes. I swear the marriage was in the book last November: why it is not there now, is the extraordinary part of the affair."

It was no use to cross-examine the witness further; he was cross and obstinate, and persisted in his story. Serjeant Siftem dismissed him; and Hunt was called, the clerk of the church, who came hobbling in.

The old man rambled in his evidence, but the point of it was, that he didn't believe any abstraction had been made, not he; it must be a farce to suppose it; a crotchet of that great lawyer, Fauntleroy; how could the register be touched when he himself kept it sure and sacred, the key of the safe in a hiding-place in the vestry, and the key of the church hanging up in his own house, outside his kitchen door? His rector said it had been robbed, and in course he couldn't stand out to his face as it hadn't, but he were upon his oath now, and must speak the truth without shrinking.

Serjeant Wrangle rose. "Did the witness mean to tell the court that he never saw or read the entry of the marriage?"

"No, he never did. He never heard say as it were there, and he never looked."

"But you were present when the witness Omer examined the register?" persisted Serjeant Wrangle.

"Master Omer wouldn't have got to examine it, unless I had been," retorted Hunt to Serjeant Wrangle. "I was a-sitting down in the vestry, a-nursing of my leg, which were worse than usual that day; it always is in damp weather, and—"

"Confine yourself to evidence," interrupted the judge.

"Well, sir, I was a-nursing of my leg whilst Master Omer looked into the book. I don't know what he saw there; he didn't say; and when he had done looking I locked it safe up again."

"Did you see him make an extract from it?" demanded Serjeant Wrangle.

"Yes, I saw him a-writing' something down in his pocket-book."

"Have you ever entrusted the key of the safe to strange hands?"

"I wouldn't do such a thing," angrily replied the witness. "I never gave it to nobody, and never would; there's not a soul knows where it is to be found, but me, and the rector, and the other clergyman, Mr. Prattleton, what comes often to do the duty. I couldn't say as much for the key of the church, which sometimes goes beyond my custody, for the rector allows one or two of the young college gents to go in to play the organ. By token, one on 'em—the quietest o' the pair, it were, too—flung in that very key on to our kitchen floor, and shivered our cat's beautiful chaney saucer into seven atoms, and my missis—"

"That is not evidence," again interrupted the judge.

Nothing more, apparently, that was evidence, could be got from the witness, so he was dismissed.

Call the Reverend Mr. Wilberforce.

The Reverend Mr. Wilberforce, rector of St. James the Less, minor canon and sacrist of Westerbury Cathedral, and head-master of the collegiate school, came forward, and was sworn.

"You are the rector of St. James the Less?" said Serjeant Wrangle.

"I am," replied Mr. Wilberforce.

"Did you ever see the entry of Robert Carr's marriage with Martha Ann Hughes in the church's register."

"Yes, I did." Serjeant Siftem pricked up his ears.

"When did you see it?"

"On the 7th of last November."

"How do you fix the date, Mr. Wilberforce?" inquired, the judge, recognising him as the minor canon who had officiated in the chanter's desk the previous day in the cathedral.

"I had been marrying a couple that morning, my lord, the 7th. After I had entered their marriage, I turned back and looked for the registry of Robert Carr's, and I found it and read it."

"What induced you to look for it?" asked the counsel.

"I had heard that his marriage was discovered to have taken place at St. James's, and that it was recorded in the register;" and Mr. Wilberforce then told how he had heard it. "Curiosity induced me to turn back and read it," he continued.

"You both saw it and read it?" continued Serjeant Wrangle.

"I both saw it and read it," replied Mr. Wilberforce.

"Then you testify that it was undoubtedly there?"

"Most certainly it was."

"The reverend gentleman will have the goodness to remember that he is upon his oath," cried Serjeant Siftem, impudently bobbing up.

"Sir!" was the indignant rebuke of the clergyman. "You forget to whom you are speaking," he added, amidst the dead silence of the court.

"Can you remember the words written?" resumed Serjeant Wrangle.

"The entry was properly made; in the same manner that the others were, of that period. Robert Carr and Martha Ann Hughes had signed it; also her brother and sister as witnesses."

"You have no doubt that the entry was there, then, Mr. Wilberforce?" observed the judge.

"My lord," cried the reverend gentleman, somewhat nettled at the question, "I can believe my own eyes. I am not more certain that I am now giving evidence before your lordship, than I am that the marriage was in the register."

"It is not in now?" said the judge.

"No, my lord; it must have been cleverly abstracted."

"The whole leaf, I presume?" said Serjeant Wrangle.

"Undoubtedly. The marriage entered below Robert Carr's was that of Sir Thomas Ealing: I read that also, with its long string of witnesses: that is also gone."

"Can you account for its disappearance?" asked Serjeant Wrangle.

"Not in the least. I wish I could: and find out the offenders."

"The incumbent of the parish at that time is no longer living, I believe?" observed Serjeant Wrangle.

"He has been dead many years," replied Mr. Wilberforce. "But it was not the incumbent who married them: it was a strange clergyman who performed the ceremony, a friend of Robert Carr's."

"How do you know that?" snapped Serjeant Siftem, bobbing up again.

"Because he signed the register as having performed it," replied Mr. Wilberforce, confronting the Serjeant with a look as undaunted as his own.

What cared Serjeant Siftem for being confronted? "How do you know he was a friend of Robert Carr's?" went on he.

"In that I speak from hearsay. But there are many men of this city, older than I am, who remember that the Reverend Mr. Bell and Robert Carr were upon exceedingly intimate terms: they can testify it to you, if you choose to call them."

Serjeant Siftem growled, and sat down; but was up again in a moment. "Who was clerk of the parish at that time?" asked he.

"There was no clerk," replied the witness. "The office was in abeyance. Some of the parishioners wanted to abolish it; but they did not succeed in doing so."

"Allow me to ask you, sir," resumed Serjeant Wrangle, "whether the entrance of the marriage there is not a proof of its having taken place?"

"Most assuredly," replied Mr. Wilberforce. "A proof indisputable."

But courts of justice, judges, and jury require ocular and demonstrative proof. It is probable there was not a soul in court, including the judge and Serjeant Siftem, but believed the evidence of the Reverend Mr. Wilberforce, even had they chosen to doubt that of Lawrence Omer; but the register negatively testified that there had been no marriage, and upon the register, in law, must rest the onus of proof. Had there been positive evidence, not negative, of the abstraction of the leaf from the register, had the register itself afforded such, the aspect of affairs would have been very different. Mr. Mynn testified that on the 2nd day of December he had looked and could find no trace of the marriage in the register: it was certainly evident that it was not in now. When the court rose that night, the trial had advanced down to the summing-up of the judge, which was deferred till morning: but it was felt by everybody that that summing-up would be dead against the client of Mr. Fauntleroy, and that Squire Carr had gained the cause.

The squire, and his son Valentine, and Mynn and Mynn, and one or two of the lesser guns of the bar, but not the great gun, Serjeant Siftem, took a late dinner together, and drank toasts, and were as merry and uproarious as success could make them: and Westerbury, outside, echoed their sentiments—that 'cute old Fauntleroy had not a leg to stand upon.

'Cute old Fauntleroy—'cute enough, goodness knew, in general—was thinking the same thing, as he took a solitary chop in his own house: for he did not get home until long past the dinner-hour, and his daughters were out. After the meal was finished, he sat over the fire in a dreamy mood, he scarcely knew how long, he was so full of vexation.

The extraordinary revelation, that the disputed marriage had taken place at St. James the Less, and lain recorded all those years unsuspiciously in the register, with the still more extraordinary fact that it had been mysteriously taken out of it, electrified Westerbury. The news flew from one end of the city to the other, and back again, and sideways, and everywhere.

But not until late in the evening was it carried to Peter Arkells. Cookesley, the second senior of the school, went in to see Henry, and told it; and then, for the first time, Henry found that the abstraction of the leaf had reference to the great cause—Carr versus Carr.

"Will Mrs. Carr lose her verdict through it?" he asked of Cookesley.

"Of course she will. There's no proof of the leaf's having been taken out. If they could only prove that, she'd gain it; and very unjust it will be upon her, poor thing! We had such a game in school!" added Cookesley, passing to private interests. "Wilberforce was at the court all the afternoon, giving evidence; and Roberts wanted to domineer over us upper boys; as if we'd let him! He was so savage."

Cookesley departed. Henry had his head down on the table: Mrs. Arkell supposed it ached, and bade him go to bed. He apparently did not hear her; and presently started up and took his trencher.

"Where are you going?" she asked, in surprise.

"Only to Prattleton's. I want to speak to George."

"But, Henry—"

Remonstrance was useless. He had already gone. Prattleton senior came to the door to him.

"George? George is at Griffin's; Griffin has got a bachelor's party. Whatever do you want with him? I say, Arkell, have you heard of the row in school this morning? The dean came in about that medal business—what a fool Aultane junior was for splitting!—and St. John spoke about one of the fellows having been at Rutterley's on Saturday, trying to pledge a spoon with the Aultane crest upon it: he didn't say actually the crest was the Aultanes', or that the fellow was Aultane, but his manner let us know it. Wasn't Aultane in a way! He said afterwards that if he had had a pistol ready capped and loaded, he should have shot himself, or the dean, or St. John, or somebody else. Serve him right for his false tongue! There'll be an awful row yet. I know I'd shoot myself, before I'd go and peach to the dean!"

But Prattleton was wasting his words on air. Henry had flown on to Griffin's—the house in the grounds formerly occupied by Mr. and Mrs. Lewis. The Reverend Mr. Griffin was the old minor canon, with the cracked voice, and it was his son and heir who was holding the bachelor's party. George Prattleton came out.

There ensued a short, sharp colloquy—Henry insisting upon being released from his promise; George Prattleton, whom the suggestion had startled nearly out of his senses, refusing to allow him to divulge anything.

"She'll not get her cause," said Henry, "unless I speak. It will be awfully unjust."

"You'll just keep your tongue quiet, Arkell. What is it to you? The Carr folks are not your friends or relatives."

"If I were to let the trial go against her, for the want of telling the truth, I should have it on my conscience always."

"My word!" cried George Prattleton, "a schoolboy with a conscience! I never knew they were troubled with any."

"Will you release me from my promise of not speaking?"

"Not if you go down on your knees for it. What a green fellow you are!"

"Then I shall speak without."

"You won't," cried Prattleton.

"I will. I gave the promise only conditionally, remember; and, as things are turning out, I am under no obligation to keep it. But I would not speak without asking your consent first, whether I got it or not."

"I have a great mind to carry you by force, and fling you into the river," uttered Prattleton, in a savage tone.

"You know you couldn't do it," returned Henry, quietly: "if I am not your equal in age and strength, I could call those who are. But there's not a moment to be lost. I am off to Mr. Fauntleroy's."

Henry Arkell meant what he said: he was always resolute in right: and Prattleton, after a further confabulation, was fain to give in. Indeed he had been expecting nothing less than this for the last hour, and had in a measure prepared himself for it.

"I'll tell the news myself," said George Prattleton, "if it must be told: and I'll tell it to Mr. Prattleton, not to Fauntleroy, or any of the law set."

"I must go to Mr. Prattleton with you," returned Henry.

"You can wait for me out here, then. We are at whist, and my coming out has stopped the game. I shan't be more than five minutes."

George Prattleton retreated indoors, and Henry paced about, waiting for him. He crossed over towards the deanery, and came upon Miss Beauclerc. She had been spending an hour at a neighbouring house, and was returning home, attended by an old man-servant. Muffled in a shawl and wearing a pink silk hood, few would have known her, except the college boy. His heart beat as if it would burst its bounds.

"Why, it's never you!" she cried. "Thank you, Jacob, that will do," she added to the servant. "Don't stand, or you'll catch your rheumatism; Mr. Arkell will see me indoors."

The old man turned away with a bow, and she partially threw back her pink silk hood to talk to Henry, as they moved slowly on to the deanery door.

"Were you going to call upon us, Harry?"

"No, Miss Beauclerc. I am waiting for George Prattleton. He is at Griffin's."

"Miss Beauclerc!" she echoed; "how formal you are to-night. I'd not be as cold as you, Henry Arkell, for the whole world!"

"I, cold!"

He said no more in refutation. If Georgina could but have known his real feelings! If she could but have divined how his pulses were beating, his veins coursing! Perhaps she did.

"Are you better? What a fall you had! And to faint after it!"

"Yes, I think I am better, thank you. It hurt my head a little."

"And you had been annoyed with those rebellious school boys! You are not half strict enough with the choristers. I hope Aultane will get a flogging, as Lewis did for locking you up in St. James's Church. I asked Lewis the next day how he liked it: he was so savage. I think he'd murder you if he could: he's jealous, you know."

She laughed as she spoke the last words, and her gay blue eyes were bent on him; he could discern them even in the dark, obscure corner where the deanery door stood. Henry did not answer: he was in wretched spirits.

"Harry, tell me—why is it you so rarely come to the deanery? Do you think any other college boy would dare to set at nought the dean's invitations—and mine?"

"Remembering what passed between us one night at the deanery—the audit night—can you wonder that I do not oftener come?" he inquired.

"Oh, but you were so stupid."

"Yes, I know. I have been stupid for years past."

Miss Beauclerc laughed. "And you think that stopping away will cure you?"

"It will not cure me; years will not cure me," he passionately broke forth, in a tone whose anguish was irrepressible. "Absence and you alone will do that. When I go to the university—" He stopped, unable to proceed.

"When you go to the university you will come back a wise man. Henry," she continued, changing her manner to seriousness, "it was the height of folly to suffer yourself to care for me. If I—if it were reciprocated, and I cared for you, if I were dying of love for you, there are barriers on all sides, and in all ways."

"I am aware of it. There is the barrier between us of disparity of years; there is a wide barrier of station; and there is the greatest barrier of all, want of love on your side. I know that my loving you has been nothing short of madness, from the first: madness and double madness since I knew where your heart was given."

"So you will retain that crotchet in your head!"

"It is no crotchet. Do you think my loving eyes—my jealous eyes, if you so will it—have been deceived? You must be happy, now that he has come back to Westerbury."

"Stupid!" echoed Miss Beauclerc.

"But it has been your fault, Georgina," he resumed, reverting to himself. "I must reiterate it. You saw what my feelings were becoming for you, and you did all you could to draw them on; you may have deemed me a child then in years; you knew I was not, in heart. They might have been checked in the onset, and repressed: why did you not do it? why did you do just the contrary, and give me encouragement? You called it flirting; you thought it good sport: but you should have remembered that what is sport to one, may be death to another."

"This estrangement makes me uncomfortable," proceeded Miss Beauclerc, ignoring the rest. "Papa keeps saying, 'What is come to Henry Arkell that he is never at the deanery?' and then I invent white stories, about believing that your studies take up your time. I miss you every day; I do, Henry; I miss your companionship; I miss your voice at the piano; I miss your words in speaking to me. But here comes your friend George Prat, for that's the echo of old Griffin's door. I know the different sounds of the doors in the grounds. Good night, Harry: I must go in."

She bent towards him to put her hand in his, and he—he was betrayed out of his propriety and his good manners. He caught her to his heart, and held her there; he kissed her face with his fervent lips.

"Forgive me, Georgina," he murmured, as she released herself. "It is the first and the last time."

"I will forgive you for this once," cried the careless girl; "but only think of the scandal, had anybody come up: my staid mamma would go into a fit. It is what he has never done," she added, in a deeper tone. "And why your head should run upon him I cannot tell. Mine doesn't."

Henry wrung her hand. "But for him, Georgina, I should think you cared for me. Not that the case would be less hopeless."

Miss Beauclerc rang a peal on the door-bell, and was immediately admitted—whilst Henry Arkell walked forward to join George Prattleton, his heart a compound of sweet and bitter, and his brain in a mazy dream.

But we left Mr. Fauntleroy in a dream by the side of his fire, and by no means a pleasant one. He sat there he did not know how long, and was at length interrupted by one of his servants.

"You are wanted, sir, if you please."

"Wanted now! Who is it?"

"The Rev. Mr. Prattleton, sir, and one or two more. They are in the drawing-room, and the fire's gone out."

"He has come bothering about that tithe case," grumbled Mr. Fauntleroy to himself. "I won't see him: let him come at a proper time. My compliments to Mr. Prattleton, Giles, but I am deep in assize business, and cannot see him."

Giles went out and came in again. "Mr. Prattleton says they must see you, sir, whether or no. He told me to say, sir, that it is about the cause that's on, Carr and Carr."

Mr. Fauntleroy proceeded to his drawing-room, and there he was shut in for some time. Whatever the conference with his visitors may have been, it was evident, when he came out, that for him it had borne the deepest interest, for his whole appearance was changed; his manners were excited, his eyes sparkling, and his face was radiant.

They all left the house together, but the lawyer's road did not lie far with theirs. He stopped at the lodgings occupied by Serjeant Wrangle, and knocked. A servant-maid came to the door.

"I want to see Serjeant Wrangle," said Mr. Fauntleroy, stepping in.

"You can't sir. He is gone to bed."

"I must see him for all that," returned Mr. Fauntleroy.

"Missis and master's gone to bed too," she added, by way of remonstrance. "I was just a-going."

"With all my heart," said Mr. Fauntleroy. "I must see the serjeant."

"'Tain't me, then, sir, that'll go and awaken him," cried the girl. "He's gone to bed dead tired, he said, and I was not to disturb him till eight in the morning."

"Give me your candle," replied Mr. Fauntleroy, taking it from her hand. "He has the same rooms as usual, I suppose; first floor."

Mr. Fauntleroy went up the stairs, and the girl stood at the bottom, and watched and listened. She did not approve of the proceedings, but did not dare to check them; for Mr. Fauntleroy was a great man in Westerbury, and their assize lodger, the serjeant, was a greater.

Tap—tap—tap: at Serjeant Wrangle's door.

No response.

Tap—tap—tap, louder.

"Who the deuce is that?" called out the serjeant, who was only dignified in his wig and gown. "Is it you, Eliza? what do you want? It's not morning, is it?"

"'Tain't me, sir," screamed out Eliza, who had now followed Mr. Fauntleroy. "I told the gentleman as you was dead tired and wasn't to be woke up till eight in the morning, but he took my light and would come up."

"I must see you, Serjeant," said Mr. Fauntleroy.

"See me! I'm in bed and asleep. Who the dickens is it?"

"Mr. Fauntleroy. Don't you know my voice? Can I come in?"

"No; the door's bolted."

"Then just come and undo it. For, see you, I must."

"Can't it wait?"

"If it could I should not have disturbed you. Open the door and you shall judge for yourself."

Serjeant Wrangle was heard to tumble out of bed in a lump, and undo the bolt of the door. Eliza concluded that he was in his night attire, and modestly threw her apron over her face. Mr. Fauntleroy entered.

"The most extraordinary thing has turned up in Carr versus Carr," cried he. "Never had such a piece of luck, just in the nick of time, in all my practice."

"Do shut the door," responded Serjeant Wrangle; "I shall catch the shivers."

Mr. Fauntleroy shut the door, shutting out Eliza, who forthwith sat down on the top stair, and wished she had ten ears. "Have you not a dressing-gown to put on?" cried he to the serjeant.

"I'll listen in bed," replied the serjeant, vaulting into it.

A whole hour did that ill-used Eliza sit on the stairs, and not a syllable could she distinguish, listen as she would, nothing but an eager murmuring of voices. When Mr. Fauntleroy came out, he put the candle in her hand and she attended him to the door, but not in a gracious mood.

"I thought you were going to stop all night, sir," she ventured to say. "Dreadful dreary it was, sitting there, a-waiting."

"Why did you not wait in the kitchen?"

"Because every minute I fancied you must be coming out. Good night, sir."

"Good night," returned Mr. Fauntleroy, putting half-a-crown in her hand. "There; that's in case you have to wait on the stairs for me again."

Eliza brightened up, and officiously lighted Mr. Fauntleroy some paces down the street, in spite of the gas-lamp at the door, which shone well. "What a good humour the old lawyer's in!" quoth she. "I wonder what his business was? I heard him say something had arose in Carr and Carr."

CHAPTER VIII

THE SECOND DAY

Tuesday morning dawned, and before nine o'clock the Nisi Prius court was more densely packed than on the preceding day: all Westerbury—at least, as many as could push in—were anxious to hear his lordship's summing up. At twenty-eight minutes after nine, the javelins of the sheriff's men appeared in the outer hall, ushering in the procession of the judges.

The senior judge proceeded to the criminal court; the other, as on the Monday, took his place in the Nisi Prius. His lordship had his notes in his hand, and was turning to the jury, preparatory to entering on his task, when Mr. Serjeant Wrangle rose.

"My lord—I must crave your lordship's permission to state a fact, bearing on the case, Carr versus Carr. An unexpected witness has arisen; a most important witness; one who will testify to the abstraction from the register; one who was present when that abstraction was made. Your lordship will allow him to be heard?"

Serjeant Siftem, and Mynn and Mynn, and Squire Carr and his son Valentine, and all who espoused that side, looked contemptuous daggers of incredulity at Serjeant Wrangle. But the judge allowed the witness to be heard, for all that.

He came forward; a remarkably handsome boy, at the stage between youth and manhood. The judge put his silver glasses across his nose and gazed at him: he thought he recognised those beautiful features.

"Swear the witness," cried some official.

The witness was sworn.

"What is your name?" demanded Serjeant Wrangle.

"Henry Cheveley Arkell."

"Where do you reside?"

"In Westerbury, near the cathedral."

"You are a member of the college school and a chorister, are you not?" interposed the judge, whose remembrance had come to him.

"A king's scholar, my lord, and senior chorister."

"Were you in St. James's Church on a certain night of last November?" resumed Serjeant Wrangle.

"Yes. On the twentieth."

"For how long? And how came you to be there?"

"I went in to practise on the organ, when afternoon school was over, and some one locked me in. I was there until nearly two in the morning."

"Who locked you in?"

"I did not know then. I afterwards heard that it was one of the senior boys."

"Tell the jury what you saw."

Henry Arkell, amidst the confused scene, so unfamiliar to him, wondered which was the jury. Not knowing, he stood as he had done before, looking alternately at the examining counsel and the judge.

"I went to sleep on the singers' seat in the organ-gallery, and slept until a noise awoke me. I saw two people stealing up the church with a light; they turned into the vestry, and I went softly downstairs and followed them, and stood at the vestry door looking in."

"Who were those parties?"

"The one was Mr. George Prattleton; the other a stranger, whose name I had heard was Rolls. George Prattleton unlocked the safe and gave Rolls the register, and Rolls sat down and looked through it: he was looking a long while."

"What next did you see?"

"When George Prattleton had his back turned to the table, I saw Rolls blow out the light. He pretended it had gone out of itself, and asked George Prattleton to fetch the matches from the bench at the entrance door. As soon as George Prattleton had gone for them, a light reappeared in the vestry, and I saw Rolls place what looked to be a piece of thick pasteboard behind one of the leaves, and then draw a knife down it and cut it out. He put the leaf and the board and the knife into his pocket, and blew out the candle again.

"Did George Prattleton see nothing of this?"

"No. He was gone for the matches, and when he came back the vestry was in darkness, as he had left it. 'Nothing risk, nothing win; I thought I could do him,' I heard Rolls say to himself."

"After that?"

"After that, when Mr. George Prattleton came back with the matches, Rolls lighted the candle and continued to look over the register, and George Prattleton grumbled at him for being so long. Presently Rolls shut the book and hurrahed, saying that it was not in, and Mr. Prattleton might put it up again."

"Did you understand what he meant by 'it.' Can you repeat the words he used?"

"I believe I can, or nearly so, for I have thought of them often since. 'It's not in the register, Prattleton,' he said. 'Hurrah! It will be thousands of pounds in our pockets. When the other side brought forth the lame tale that there was such an entry, we thought it a bag of moonshine.' I think that was it."

"What next happened?"

"I saw Rolls hand the book to George Prattleton, and then I went down the church as quietly as I could, and found the key in the door and got out. I hid behind a tombstone, and I saw them both come from the church, and Mr. George Prattleton locked it and put the key in his pocket. I heard them disputing at the door, when they found it open; Rolls accused George Prattleton of unlocking the door when he went to get the matches; and George Prattleton accused Rolls of having neglected to lock it when they entered the church."

"Meanwhile it was you who had unlocked it, to let yourself out?"

"Yes. And I was in too great a hurry, for fear they should see me, to shut it after me."

"A very nicely concocted tale!" sneered Serjeant Siftem, after several more questions had been asked of Henry, and he rose to cross examine. "You would like the court and jury to believe you, sir?"

"I hope all will believe, who hear me, for it is the truth," he answered, with simplicity. And he had his wish; for all did believe him; and Serjeant Siftem's searching questions, and insinuations that the fancied George Prattleton and Rolls were nothing but ghosts, failed to shake his testimony, or their belief.

The next witness called was Roland Carr Lewis, who had just come into court, marshalled by the second master. A messenger, attended by a javelin man, had been despatched in hot haste to the college schoolroom, demanding the attendance of Roland Lewis. Mr. Roberts, confounded by their appearance, and perplexed by the obscure tale of the messenger, that "two of the college gentlemen, Lewis and another, was found to have had som'at to do with the theft from the register, though not, he b'lieved, in the way of thieving it theirselves," left his desk and his duties, and accompanied Lewis. The head master had been in court all the morning.

"You are in the college school," said Serjeant Wrangle, after Lewis was sworn, and had given his name.

"King's scholar, sir, and third senior," replied Lewis, who could scarcely speak for fright; which was not lessened when he caught sight of the Dean of Westerbury on the bench, next the judge.

"Did you shut up a companion, Henry Cheveley Arkell, in the church of St. James the Less, one afternoon last November, when he had gone in to practise on the organ?"

Lewis wiped his face, and tried to calm his breathing, and glared fearfully towards the bench, but never spoke.

"You have been sworn to tell the truth, the whole truth, and nothing but the truth, sir, and you must do so," said the judge, staring at his ugly face, through his glasses. "Answer the question."

"Y—es."

"What was your motive for doing so?" asked Serjeant Wrangle.

"It was only done in fun. I didn't mean to hurt him."

"Pretty fun!" ejaculated one of the jury, who had a timid boy of his own in the college school, and thought how horrible might be the consequences should he get locked up in St. James's Church.

"How long did you leave him there?"

"I don't know. I took back the key to the clerk's, and the next morning, when we went to let him out, he was gone."

"Who is 'we?' Who was with you?" cried Serjeant Wrangle, catching at the word.

"Mr. George Prattleton. He was at the clerk's in the morning, and I told him about it, and asked him to get the key, for Hunt would not let me have it. So he was coming with me to open the church; but Hunt happened to say that Arkell had just been to his house. He had got out somehow."

When this witness, after a good deal of badgering, was released, Serjeant Siftem, a bright thought having occurred to him, desired that the Reverend Mr. Wilberforce might get into the witness-box. The Reverend Mr. Wilberforce did so; and the serjeant began, in an insinuating tone:

"The witness, Henry Cheveley Arkell, is under your tuition in the collegiate school, I assume?"

"He is," sternly replied Mr. Wilberforce, who had not forgotten Serjeant Siftem's insult of the previous day.

"Would you believe him on his oath?"

"On his oath, or without it."

"Oh, you would, would you?" retorted the Serjeant. "Schoolboys are addicted to romancing, though."

"Henry Arkell is of strict integrity. His word may be implicitly trusted."

"I can bear testimony to Henry Arkell's honourable and truthful nature," spoke up the dean, from his place beside the judge. "His general conduct is exemplary; a pattern to the school."

"Henry Cheveley Arkell," roared out the undaunted Serjeant Siftem, drowning the dean's voice. "I have done with you, Mr. Wilberforce." So the master left the witness-box, and Henry re-entered it.

"I omitted to put a question to you, Mr. Chorister," began Serjeant Siftem. "Should you know this fabulous gentleman of your imagination, this Rolls, if you were to see him?"

"Yes," replied Henry. "I saw him this morning as I came into court."

That shut up Serjeant Siftem.

"Where did you see him?" inquired the judge.

"In the outer hall, my lord. He was with Mr. Valentine Carr. But I am not sure that his name is Rolls," added the witness. "When I pointed him out to Mr. Fauntleroy, he was surprised, and said that was Richards, Mynn and Mynn's clerk."

The judge whispered a word to somebody with a white wand, who was standing near him, and that person immediately went hunting about the court to find this Rolls or Richards, and bring him before the judge. But Rolls had made himself scarce ere the conclusion of Henry Arkell's first evidence; and, as it transpired afterwards, decamped from the town. The next witness put into the box was Mr. George Prattleton.

"You are aware, I presume, of the evidence given by Henry Cheveley Arkell," said Serjeant Wrangle. "Can you deny that part of it which relates to yourself?"

"No, unfortunately I cannot," replied George Prattleton, who was very down in the mouth—as his looks were described by a friend of his in court. "Rolls is a villain."

"That is not evidence, sir," said the judge.

"He is a despicable villain, my lord," returned the witness, giving way to his injured feelings. "He came to Westerbury, pretending to be a stranger, and calling himself Rolls, and I got acquainted with him; that is, he scraped acquaintance with me, and we were soon intimate. Then he began to make use of me; he asked if I would do him a favour. He wanted to get a private sight of the register in St. James's Church. So I consented, I am sorry to say, to get him a private sight; but I made the bargain that he should not copy a single word out of it, and of course I meant to be with him and watch him."

"Did you know that his request had reference to the case of Carr versus Carr?" inquired Serjeant Wrangle.

"No, I'll swear I did not," retorted the witness, in an earnest tone, forgetting, probably, that he was already on his oath. "He never told me why he wanted to look. He would go in at night: if he were seen entering the church in the day, it might be fatal to his client's cause, was the tale he told; and I am ashamed to acknowledge that I took him in at night, and suffered him to look at the register. I have heard to-day that his name is Richards."

"You knew where the key of the safe was kept?"

"Yes; I was one day in the church with the Reverend Mr. Prattleton, and saw him take it from its place."

"Did you see Rolls (as we will call him) abstract the leaf?"

"Of course I did not," indignantly retorted the witness. "I suddenly found the vestry in darkness, and he got me to fetch the matches, which were left on the bench at the entrance door. It must have been done then. Soon after I returned he gave me back the register, saying the entry he wanted was not there, and I locked it up again. When we got to the church door we were astonished to find it open, but—"

"But did you not suspect it was opened by one who had watched your proceedings," interrupted the judge.

"No, my lord. Rolls left the town the next morning early; when I went to find him he was gone, and I have never been able to see him since. That's all I know of the transaction, and I can only publicly repeat my deep regret and shame that I should have been drawn into such a one."

"Drawn, however, without much scruple, as it appears," rebuked the judge, with a severe countenance. "Allow me to ask you, sir, when it was you first became acquainted with the fact that a theft had been perpetrated on the register?"

Mr. George Prattleton did not immediately answer. He would have given much not to be obliged to do so: but the court wore an ominous silence, and the judge waited his reply.

"The day after it took place, Arkell, the college boy, came and told me what he had seen, but—"

"Then, sir, it was your duty to have proclaimed it, and to have had steps taken to arrest your confederate, Rolls," interrupted the stern judge.

"But, my lord, I did not believe Arkell. I did not indeed," he added, endeavouring to impart to his tone an air of veracity, and therefore—as is sure to be the case—imparting to it just the contrary. "I could not believe that Rolls, or any one else in a respectable position, such he appeared to occupy, would be guilty of so felonious an action."

"The less excuse you make upon the point, the better," observed the judge.

For some few minutes Serjeant Siftem and his party had been conferring in whispers. The serjeant, at this stage, spoke.

"My lord, this revelation has come upon my instructors, Mynn and Mynn, with, the most utter surprise, and—"

"The man, Rolls, or Richards, is really clerk to Mynn and Mynn, I am informed," interrupted the judge, in as significant a tone as a presiding judge permits himself to assume.

"He was, my lord; but he will not be in future. They discard him from this hour. In fact, should he not make good his escape from the country, which it is more than likely he is already endeavouring to effect, he will probably at the next assizes find himself placed before your lordship for judgment, should you happen to come this circuit, and preside in the other court. But Mynn and Mynn wish to disclaim, in the most emphatic manner, all cognizance of this man's crime. They—"

"There is no charge to be brought against Mynn and Mynn in connexion with it, is there?" again interposed the judge.

"Most certainly not, my lord," replied the counsel, in a lofty tone, meant to impress the public ear.

"Then, Brother Siftem, it appears to me that you need not take up the time of the court to enter on their defence."

"I bow to your lordship's opinion. Mynn and Mynn and their client, Squire Carr, are not less indignant that so rascally a trick should have been perpetrated than the public must be. But this evidence, which has come upon them in so overwhelming a manner, they feel they cannot hope to confute. I am therefore instructed to inform your lordship and the jury, that they withdraw from the suit, and permit a verdict to be entered for the other side."

"Very good," replied the judge.

And thus, after certain technicalities had been observed, the proceedings were concluded, and the court began to empty itself of its spectators. For once the RIGHT had prospered. But Westerbury held its breath with awe when it came to reflect that it was the revengeful act of Roland Carr Lewis, that locking up in the church, which had caused his family to be despoiled of the inheritance they had taken to themselves!

The Reverend Mr. Wilberforce laid hold of Henry Arkell, as he was leaving the Guildhall. "Tell me," said he, but not in an angry tone, "how much more that is incomprehensible are you keeping secret, allowing it to come out to me piecemeal?"

Henry smiled. "I don't think there is any more, sir."

"Yes, there is. It is incomprehensible why you should not have disclosed at the time all you had been a witness to in the church. Why did you not?"

"I could not speak without compromising George Prattleton, sir; and if I had, he might have been brought to trial for it."

"Serve him right too," said Mr. Wilberforce.

Presently Henry met the dean, his daughter, Frederick St. John, and Lady Anne. The dean stopped him.

"What do you call yourself? A lion?"

Henry smiled faintly.

"I think you stand a fair chance of being promoted into one. Do you know what I wished to-day, when you were giving your evidence?"

"No, sir."

"That you were my own son."

Henry involuntarily glanced at Georgina, and she glanced at him: her face retained its calmness, but a flush of crimson came over his. No one observed them but Mr. St. John.

"I want you at the deanery to-night," continued the dean, releasing Henry. "No excuse about lessons now: your fall on Sunday has given you holiday. You will come?"

"Yes, sir."

"I mean to dinner—seven o'clock. The judges will be there. The one who tried the cause said he should like to meet you. Go and rest yourself until then."

"Thank you, sir. I will come."

Georgina's eyes sparkled, and she nodded to him in triumph a dozen times, as she walked on with the dean.

Following in the wake of the dean's party came the Rev. Mr. Prattleton. Henry approached him timidly.

"I hope you will forgive me, sir. I could not help giving my evidence."

"Forgive you!" echoed Mr. Prattleton; "I wish nobody wanted forgiveness worse than you do. You have acted nobly throughout. I have recommended Mr. George to get out of the town for a while; not to remain in it in idleness and trouble my table any longer. He can join his friend Rolls on the continent if he likes: I understand he is most likely off thither."

The fraud was not brought home to the Carr family. It was indisputably certain that the squire himself had known nothing whatever of it: had never even been aware that the marriage was entered on the register of St. James the Less. Whether his sons Valentine and Benjamin were equally guiltless, was a matter of opinion. Valentine solemnly protested that nothing had ever been told to him; but he did acknowledge that Richards came to him one evening, and said he thought the cause was likely to be imperilled by "certain proceedings" that the other side were taking. He, Valentine Carr, authorized him to do what he could to counteract these proceedings (only intending him to act in a fair manner), and gave him carte blanche in a moderate way for the money that might be required. He acknowledged to no more: and perhaps he had no more to acknowledge: neither did he say how much he had paid to Richards. Benjamin treated the whole matter with contempt. The most indignant of all were Mynn and Mynn. Really respectable practitioners, it was in truth a very disagreeable thing to have been forced upon them; and could they have got at their ex-clerk, they would willingly have transported him.

And Mr. Fauntleroy, in the flush of his great victory, in the plenitude of his gratitude to the boy whose singular evidence had caused him to win the battle, went down that same day to Peter Arkell's and forgave him the miserable debt that had so long hampered him. For once in his life, the lawyer showed himself generous. People used to say that such was his nature before the world hardened him.

So, taking one thing with another, it was a satisfactory termination to the renowned cause, Carr versus Carr.

It was a large state dinner at the deanery. But the chief thing that Henry Arkell saw at it was, that Mr. St. John sat by Georgina Beauclerc. The judges—who did not appear in their wigs and fiery gowns, to the relief of private country individuals of wide imaginations, that could not usually separate them—were pleasant men, and their faces did not look so yellow by candle-light. They talked to Henry a great deal, and he had to rehearse over, for the general benefit, all the scene of that past night in St. James's Church. Mrs. Beauclerc, usually so indifferent, was aroused to especial interest, and would not quit the theme; neither would Lady Anne St. John, now visiting at the Palmery, and who was present with Mrs. St. John.

But Georgina—oh, the curious wiles of a woman's heart!—took little or no notice of Henry. They had been for some time in the drawing-room before she came near him at all—before she addressed a word to him. At dinner she had been absorbed in Mr. St. John: gay, laughing, animated, her thoughts, her words, were all for him. Sarah Beauclerc, conspicuous that night for her beauty, sat opposite to them, but St. John had not the opportunity of speaking to her, beyond a passing word now and again. In the drawing-room, no longer fettered—though perhaps the fetters had been willing ones—St. John went at once to Sarah, and he did not leave her side. Ah! Henry saw it all: both those fair girls loved Frederick St. John! What would be the ending?

Georgina sat at a table apart, reading a new book, or appearing to read it. Was she covertly watching that sofa at a distance? It was so different, this sitting still, from her usual restless habits of flitting everywhere. Suddenly she closed her book, and went up to them.

"I have come to call you to account, Fred," she began, speaking in her most familiar manner, but in a low tone. "Don't you see whose heart you are breaking?"

He had been sitting with his head slightly bent, as he spoke in a whisper to his beautiful companion. Her eyes were cast down, her fingers unconsciously pulled apart the petals of some geranium she held; her whole attitude bespoke a not unwilling listener. Georgina's salutation surprised both, for they had not seen her approach. They looked up.

"What do you say?" cried St. John. "Breaking somebody's heart? Whose? Yours?"

She laughed in derision, flirting some of the scent out of a golden phial she had taken up. "Sarah, you should have more consideration," she continued. "It is all very well when Lady Anne's not present, but when she is—There! you need not go into a flaming fever and fling your angry eyes upon me. Look at Sarah's face, Mr. St. John."

Mr. St. John walked away, as though he had not heard. Sarah caught hold of her cousin.

"There is a limit to endurance, Georgina. If you pursue this style of conversation to me—learnt, as I have repeatedly told you, from the housemaids, unless it is inherent," she added, in deep scorn—"I shall make an appeal to the dean."

"Make it," said Georgina, laughing. "It was too bad of you, Sarah, with his future wife present. She'll go to bed and dream of jealousy."

Quitting her cousin, she went straight up to Henry Arkell. "Why do you mope like this?" she cried.

"Mope!" he repeated.

He had been at another table leaning his head upon his hand. It was aching much: and he told her so.

"Oh, Harry, I am sorry; I forgot your fall. Will you sing a song?"

"I don't think I can to-night."

"But papa has been talking to the judges about it. I heard him say your singing was worth listening to. I suppose he had been telling them all about you, and the whole romance, you know, of Mrs. Peter Arkell's marriage, for one of them—it was the old one—said he used to be intimate with her father, Colonel Cheveley. Here comes the dean! that's to ask you to sing."

He sat down at once, and sang a song of the day. Then he went on to one that I dare say you all know and like—"Shall I, wasting in despair." At its conclusion one of the judges—it was the old one, as Georgina irreverently called him—came to him at the piano, and asked if he could sing Luther's Hymn.

A few chords by way of prelude, lasting some few minutes, probably played to form a break between the worldly song and the sacred one—for if anyone was ever endowed with an innate sense of what was due to sacred things, it was Henry Arkell—and then the grand old hymn, in all its beautiful simplicity, burst upon their ears. Never had it been done greater justice to than it was by that solitary college boy. The room was hushed to stillness; the walls echoed with the sweet sounds; the solemn words thrilled on the listeners' hearts, and the singer's whole soul seemed to go up with them. Oh, how strange it was, that the judge should have called for that particular, sacred song!

The echoes of it died away in the deepest stillness. It was broken by Henry himself; he closed the piano, as if nothing else must be allowed to come after that; and the tacit mandate was accepted, and nobody thought of inquiring how he came to assume the liberty in the dean's house.

Gradually the room resumed its humming and its self-absorption, and Georgina Beauclerc, under cover of it, went up to him.

"How could you make the excuse that your head was aching? None, with any sort of sickness upon them, could sing as you have just done."

"Not even with heart sickness," he answered.

"Now you are going to be absurd again! What do you mean?"

"To-night has taught me a great deal, Georgina. If I have been foolish enough—fond enough, I might say—to waver in my doubts before, that's over for ever."

"So much the better; you will be cured now."

She had spoken only lightly, not meaning to be unkind or unfeeling; but she saw what she had done, by his quivering lip. Leaning across him as he stood, under cover of showing him something on the table, she spoke in a deep, earnest tone.

"Henry, you know it could never be. Better that you should see the truth now, than go on in this dream of folly. Stay away for a short while if you will, and overget it; and then we will be fast friends as before."

"And this is to be the final ending?"

She stole a glance round at him, his voice had so strange a sound in it. Every trace of colour had faded from his face.

"Yes; it is the only possible ending. If you get on well and become somebody grand, you and I can be as brother and sister in after life."

She moved away as she spoke. It may be that she saw further trifling would not do. But even in the last sentence, thoughtlessly though she had spoken it, there was an implied consciousness of the wide difference in their social standing, all too prominent to that sensitive ear.

A minute afterwards St. John looked round for him, and could not see him.

"Where's Henry Arkell?" he asked of Georgina.

She looked round also.

"He is gone, I suppose," she answered. "He was in one of his stupid moods to-night."

"That's something new for him. Stupid?"

"I used the word in a wide sense. Crazy would have been better."

"What do you mean, Georgina?"

"He is a little crazy at times—to me. There! that's all I am going to tell you: you are not my father confessor."

"True," he said; "but I think I understand without confession. Take care, Georgina."

"Take care of what?"

"Of—I may as well say it—of exciting hopes that are most unlikely to be realized. Better play a true part than a false one."

She laughed a little saucy laugh.

"Don't you think I might turn the tables and warn you of that? What false hopes are you exciting, Mr. St. John?"

"None," he answered. "It is not in my nature to be false, even in sport."

Her laugh changed to one of derision; and Mr. St. John, disliking the sound, disliking the words, turned from her, and joined the dean, who was then deep in a discussion with one of the judges.

CHAPTER IX

THE SHADOW OF DEATH

The days went on; and the dull, heavy pain in the head, complained of by Henry Arkell, increased in intensity. At first his absence from his desk at school, his vacant place at college, excited comment, but in time, as the newness of it wore off, it grew to be no longer noticed. It is so with all things. On the afternoon of the fall, the family surgeon was called in to him: he saw no cause for apprehension, he said;

the head only required rest. It might have been better, perhaps, had the head (including the body and brain) been able to take the recommended rest; but it could not. On the Monday morning came the excitement of the medal affair, as related to him by Mr. St. John, and also by many of the school; in the evening there occurred the excitement of that business of the register; the interview with the Prattletons, and subsequently with Mr. Fauntleroy. On the next day he had to appear as a witness; and then came the deanery dinner in the evening and Georgina Beauclerc. All sources of great and unwonted excitement, had he been in his usual state of health: what it was to him now, never could be ascertained.

As the days went on, and the pain grew no better, but worse, and the patient more heavy, it dawned into the surgeon's mind that he possibly did not understand the case, and it might be as well to have the advice of a physician. The most clever the city afforded was summoned, and he did not appear to understand it either. That there was some internal injury to the head, both agreed; but what it might be, it was not so easy to state. And thus more days crept on, and the doctors paid their regular visits, and the pain still grew worse; and then the half-shadowed doubt glided into a certainty which had little shadow about it, but stern substance—that the injury was rapidly running on to a fatal issue.

He did not take to his bed: he would sit at his chamber window in an easy chair, his poor aching-head resting on a pillow. "You would be better in bed," everybody said to him. "No, he thought he was best up," he answered; "it was more change: when he was tired of the chair and the pillow, he could lie down outside the bed." "It is unaccountable his liking to be so much at the window," Mrs. Peter Arkell remarked to Lucy. To them it might be; for how could they know that a sight of one who might pass and cast a glance up to him, made his day's happiness?

That considerable commotion was excited by the opinion of the doctors, however cautiously intimated, was only to be expected. Mr. Arkell heard of it, and brought another physician, without saying anything beforehand at Peter's. But it would seem that this gentleman's opinion did not differ in any material degree from that of his brethren.

The Reverend Mr. Wilberforce sat at the head of his dinner-table, eating his own dinner and carving for his pupils. His face looked hot and angry, and his spectacles were pushed to the top of his brow, for if there was one thing more than another that excited the ire of the master, it was that of the boys being unpunctual at meals, and Cookesley had this day chosen to be absent. The second serving of boiled beef was going round when he made his appearance.

"What sort of behaviour do you call this, sir?" was the master's salutation. "Do you expect to get any dinner?"

"I am very sorry to be so late, sir," replied Cookesley, eyeing the boiled beef wishfully, but not daring to take his seat. "I went to see Arkell, and—"

"And who is Arkell, pray, or you either, that you must upset the regulations of my house?" retorted the master. "You should choose your visiting times better, Mr. Cookesley."

"Yes, sir. I heard he was worse; that's the reason I went; and when I got there the dean was with him. I waited, and waited, but I had to come away without seeing Arkell, after all."

"The dean with Arkell!" echoed Mr. Wilberforce, in a disbelieving tone.

"He is there still, sir. Arkell is a great deal worse. They say he will never come to school or college again."

"Who says so, pray?"

"Everybody's saying it now," returned Cookesley. "There's something wrong with his head, sir; some internal injury caused by the fall; but they don't know whether it's an abscess, or what it is. It will kill him, they think."

The master's wrath had faded: truth to say, his anger was generally more fierce in show than in reality. "You may take your seat for this once, Cookesley, but if ever you transgress again—Hallo!" broke off the master, as he cast his eyes on another of his pupils, "what's the matter with you, Lewis junior? Are you choking, sir?"

Lewis junior was choking, or gasping, or something of the sort, for his face was distorted, and his eyes were round with seeming fright. "What is it?" angrily repeated the master.

"It was the piece of meat, sir," gasped Lewis. A ready excuse.

"No it wasn't," put in Vaughan the bright, who sat next to Lewis junior. "Here's the piece of meat you were going to eat; it dropped off the fork on to your plate again; it couldn't be the meat. He's choking at nothing, sir."

"Then, if you must choke, you had better go and choke outside, and come back when it's over," said the master to Lewis. And away Lewis went; none guessing at the fear and horror which had taken possession of him.

The assize week had passed, and the week following it, and still Henry Arkell had not made his appearance in the cathedral or the school. The master could not make it out. Was it likely that the effects of a fall, which broke no bones, bruised no limbs, only told somewhat heavily upon his head, should last all this while, and incapacitate him from his duties? Had it been any other of the king's scholars, no matter which of the whole thirty-nine Mr. Wilberforce would have said that he was skulking, and sent a sharp mandate for him to appear in his place; but he thought he knew better things of Henry Arkell. He did not much like what Cookesley said now—that Arkell might never come out again, though he received the information with disbelief.

Mr. St. John was a daily visitor to the invalid. On the day before this, when he entered, Henry was at his usual post, the window, but standing up, his head resting against the frame, and his eyes strained after some distant object outside. So absorbed was he, that Mr. St. John had to touch his arm to draw his attention, and Henry drew back with a start.

"How are you to-day, Harry? Better?"

"No, thank you. This curious pain in my head gets worse."

"Why do you call it curious?"

"It is not like an ordinary pain. And I cannot tell exactly where it is. I cannot put my hand on any part of my head and say it is here or it is there. It seems to be in the centre of the inside—as if it could not be got at."

"What were you watching so eagerly?"

"I was looking outside," was Henry's evasive reply. "They had Dr. Ware to me this morning; did you know it?"

"I am glad of that!" exclaimed Mr. St. John. "What does he say?"

"I did not hear him say much. He asked me where my head was struck when I fell, but I could not tell him—I did not know at the time, you remember. He and Mr.—"

Henry's voice faltered. A sudden, almost imperceptible, movement of the head nearer the window, and a wild accession of colour to his feverish cheek, betrayed to Mr. St. John that something was passing which bore for him a deep interest. He raised his own head and caught a sufficient glimpse: Georgina Beauclerc.

It told Mr. St. John all: though he had not needed to be told; and Miss Beauclerc's mysterious words, and Henry's past conduct became clear to him. So! the boy's heart had been thus early awakened—and crushed.

"The heart that is soonest awake to the flowers
Is always the first to be touched by the thorns,"

whistled Mr. St. John to himself.

Ay, crushing is as sure to follow that early awaking, as that thorns grow on certain rose-trees. But Mr. St. John said nothing more that day.

On the following day, upon going in, he found Henry in bed.

"Like a sensible man as you are," quoth Mr. St. John, by way of salutation. "Now don't rise from it again until you are better."

Henry looked at him, an expression in his eyes that Mr. St. John did not like, and did not understand. "Did they tell you anything downstairs, Mr. St. John?" he inquired.

"I did not see anyone but the servant. I came straight up."

"Mamma is lying down, I dare say; she has been sitting with me part of the night. Then I will tell it you. I shall not be here many days," he whispered, putting his hand within Mr. St. John's.

Mr. St. John did not take the meaning: that the case would have a fatal termination had not yet crossed his mind. "Where shall you be?" cried he, gaily, "up in the moon?"

Henry sighed. "Up somewhere. I am going to die."

"Going to what?" was the angry response.

"I am dying, Mr. St. John."

Mr. St. John's pulses stood still. "Who has been putting that rubbish in your head?" cried he, when he recovered them sufficiently to speak.

"The doctors told my father yesterday evening, that as I went on, like this, from bad to worse, without their being able to discover the true nature of the case, they saw that it must terminate fatally. He knew that they had feared it before. Afterwards mamma came and broke it to me."

"Why did she do so?" involuntarily uttered Mr. St. John, in an accent of reproach. "Though their opinion may be unfavourable—which I don't believe, mind—they had no right to frighten you with it."

"It does not frighten me. Just at first I shrank from the news, but I am quite reconciled to it now. A faint idea that this might be the ending, has been running through my own mind for some days past, though I would not dwell on it sufficiently to give it a form."

"I am astonished that Mrs. Arkell should have imparted it to you!" emphatically repeated Mr. St. John. "What could she have been thinking of?"

"Oh, Mr. St. John! mamma has striven to bring us up not to fear death. What would have been the use of her lessons, had she thought I should run in terror from it when it came?"

"She ought not to have told you—she ought not to have told you!" was the continued burden of Mr. St. John's song. "You may get well yet."

"Then there is no harm done. But, with death near, would you have had me, the only one it concerns, left in ignorance to meet it, not knowing it was there? Mamma has not waited herself for death—as she has done, you know, for years—without learning a better creed than that."

Mr. St. John made no reply, and Henry went on: "I have had such a pleasant night with mamma. She read to me parts of the Revelation; and in talking of the glories which I may soon see, will you believe that I almost forgot my pain? She says how thankful she is now, that she has been enabled to train me up more carefully than many boys are trained—to think more of God."

"You are a strange boy," interrupted Sir. St. John.

"In what way am I strange?"

"To anticipate death in that tone of cool ease. Have you no regrets to leave behind you?"

"Many regrets; but they seemed to fade into insignificance last night, while mamma was talking with me. It is best that they should."

"Henry, it strikes me that you have had your griefs and troubles, inexperienced as you are," resumed Mr. St. John.

"Oh yes, I have," he answered, betrayed into an earnestness, incompatible with cautious reserve. "Some of the college boys have not suffered me to lead a pleasant life with them," he continued, more calmly; "and then there has been my father's gradually straitening income."

"I think there must have been some other grief than these," was Mr. St. John's remark.

"What other grief could there have been?"

"I know but of one. And you are over young for that."

"Of course I am; too young," was the eager answer.

"That is enough," quietly returned Mr. St. John; "I did not tell you to betray yourself. Nay, Henry, don't shrink from me; let me hear it: it will be better and happier for you that I should."

"There is nothing—I don't know what you mean—what are you talking of, Mr. St. John?" was the incoherent answer.

"Harry, my poor boy, I know almost as much as you," he whispered. "I know what it is, and who it is. Georgie Beauclerc. There; you cannot tell me much, you see."

Henry Arkell laid his hand across his face and aching eyes; his chest was heaving with emotion. Mr. St. John leaned over him, not less tenderly than a mother.

"You should not have wasted your love upon her: she is a heartless girl. I expect she drew you on, and then turned round and said she did not mean it."

"Oh yes, she did draw me on," he replied, in a tone full of anguish; "otherwise, I never—But it was my fault also. I ought to have remembered the many barriers that divided us; the—"

"You ought to have remembered that she is an incorrigible flirt, that is what you ought to have remembered," interrupted Mr. St. John.

"Well, well," sighed Henry, "I cannot speak of these things to you: less to you than to any one."

"Is that an enigma? I should think you could best speak of them to me, because I have guessed your secret, and the ice is broken."

Again Henry Arkell sighed. "Speaking of them at all will do no good; and I would now rather think of the future than of the past. My future lies there," he added, pointing to the blue sky, which, as seen from his window, formed a canopy over the cathedral tower. "She has, in all probability, many years before her here: Mr. St. John, if she and you spend those years together, will you sometimes talk of me? I should not like to be quite forgotten by you—or by her."

"Spend them together!" he echoed. "Another enigma. What should bring me spending my years with Georgina Beauclerc?"

Henry withdrew his hands from his eyes, and turned them on Mr. St. John. "Do you think she will never be your wife?"

"She! Georgina Beauclerc! No, thank you."

Henry Arkell's face wore an expression that Mr. St. John understood not. "It was for your sake she treated me so ill. She loves you, Mr. St. John. And I think you know it."

"She is a little simpleton. I would not marry Georgie Beauclerc if there were not another English girl extant. And as to loving her—Harry, I only wish, if we are to lose you, that I loved you but one tenth part as little."

"Sorrow in store for her! sorrow in store for her!" he murmured, as he turned his face to the pillow. "I must send her a message before I die: you will deliver it for me?"

"I won't have you talk about dying," retorted Mr. St. John. "You may get well yet, I tell you."

Henry opened his eyes again to reply, and the calm peace had returned to them. "It maybe very soon; and it is better to talk of death than to shrink from it." And Mr. St. John grumbled an ungracious acquiescence.

"And there is another thing I wish you would do for me: get Lewis junior here to-day. If I send to him, I know he will not come; but I must see him. Tell him, please, that it is only to shake hands and make friends; that I will not say a word to grieve him. He will understand."

"It's more than I do," said Mr. St. John. "He shall come."

"I should like to see Aultane—but I don't think my head will stand it all. Tell him from me, not to be harsh with the choristers now he is senior—"

"He is not senior yet," interposed Mr. St. John in a husky tone.

"It will not be long first. Give him my love, and tell him, when I sent it, I meant it fully; and that I have no angry feeling towards him."

"Your love?"

"Yes. It is not an ordinary message from one college boy to another," panted the lad, "but I am dying."

After Mr. St. John left the house, he encountered the dean. "Dr. Beauclerc, Henry Arkell is dying."

The dean stared at Mr. St. John. "Dying! Henry Arkell!"

"The inward injury to the head is now pronounced by the doctors to be a fatal one. They told the family last night there was little, if any, more hope. The boy knows it, and seems quite reconciled."

The dean, without another word or question, turned immediately off to Mr. Arkell's, and Westerbury as immediately turned its aristocratic nose up. "The idea of his condescending to enter the house of those poor Arkells! had it been the other branch of the Arkell family, it would not have been quite so lowering. But Dr. Beauclerc never did display the dignity properly pertaining to a dean."

Dr. Beauclerc, forgetful as usual of a dean's dignity, was shown into Mrs. Arkell's parlour, and from thence into Henry Arkell's chamber. The boy's ever lovely face flushed crimson, from its white pillow, when he saw the dean. "Oh, sir! you to come here! how kind!"

"I am sorry for this, my poor lad," said the dean, as he sat down. "I hear you are not so well: I have just met Mr. St. John."

"I shall never be well again, sir. But do not be sorry. I shall be better off; far, far happier than I could be here."

"Do you feel this, genuinely, heartily?" questioned the dean.

"Oh yes, how can I do otherwise than feel it? If it is God's will to take me, I know it must be for my good."

"Say that again," said the dean. "I do not know that I fully caught your meaning."

"I am in God's hands: and if He takes me to Him earlier than I thought to have gone, I know it must be for the best."

"How long have you reposed so firm a trust in God?"

"All my life," answered Henry, with simplicity: "mamma taught me that with my letters. She taught me to take God for my guide; to strive to please Him; implicitly to trust in Him."

"And you have done this?"

"Oh no, sir, I have only tried to do it. But I know that there is One to intercede for me."

"Have you sure and certain trust in Christ?" returned the dean, after a pause.

"I have sure and certain trust in Him," was the boy's reply, spoken fervently: "if I had not, I should not dare to die. I wish I might have received the Sacrament," he whispered; "but I have not been confirmed."

"Henry," said the dean, in his quick manner, "I do believe you are more fitted for it than are some who take it. Would it be a comfort to you?"

"It would indeed, sir."

"Then I will come and administer it. At seven to-night, if that hour will suit your friends. I will ascertain when I go down."

"Oh, sir, you are too good," he exclaimed, in his surprise: "mamma thought of asking Mr. Prattleton. I am but a poor college boy, and you are the Dean of Westerbury."

"Just so. But when the great King of Terrors approaches, as he is now approaching you, it makes us remember that in Christ's kingdom the poor college boy may stand higher than the Dean of Westerbury. Henry, I have watched your conduct more than you are aware of, and I believe you to have been as truly good a boy as it is in human nature to be: I believe that you have continuously striven to please God, in little things as in great."

"If I could but have done it more than I have!" thought the boy.

It was during this interview that Mr. Cookesley arrived; and, as you have seen, nearly lost his dinner. As soon as the boys rose from table, they, full of consternation, trooped down to Arkell's, picking up several more of the king's scholars on their way, who were not boarders at the house of Mr. Wilberforce. The dean had gone then, but Mr. St. John was at the door, having called again to inquire whether there was any change. He cast his eyes on the noisy boys, as they approached the gate, and discerned amongst them Lewis junior. Mr. St. John stepped outside, and pounced upon him, with a view to marshal him in. But Lewis resisted violently; ay, and shook and trembled like a girl.

"I will not go into Arkell's, sir," he panted. "You have no right to force me. I won't! I won't!"

He struggled on to his knees, and clasped a deep-seated stone in the Arkells' garden for support. Mr. St. John, not releasing his collar, looked at him with amazement, and the troop of boys watched the scene over the iron railings.

"Lewis, what is the meaning of this?" cried Mr. St. John. "You are panting like a coward; and a guilty one: What are you afraid of?"

"I'm afraid of nothing, but I won't go into Arkell's. I don't want to see him. Let me go, sir. Though you are Mr. St. John, that's no reason why you should set up for master over the college boys."

"I am master over you just now," was the significant answer. "Listen: I have promised Arkell to take you to him, and I will do it: you may have heard, possibly, that the St. Johns never break their word. But Arkell has sent for you in kindness: he appeared to expect this opposition, and bade me tell it you: he wants to clasp your hand in friendship before he dies. Walk on, Lewis."

"You are not master over us boys," shrieked Lewis again, whose opposition had increased to sobs.

But Mr. St. John proved his mastership. Partly; by coaxing, partly by authoritative force, he conducted Mr. Lewis to the door of Henry's chamber. There Lewis seized his arm in abject terror; he had turned ghastly white, and his teeth chattered.

"I cannot fathom this," said Mr. St. John, wondering much. "Have I not told you there is nothing to fear? What is it that you do fear?"

"No; but does he look very frightful?" chattered Lewis.

"What should make him look frightful? He looks as he has always looked. Be off in; and I'll keep the door, if you want to talk secrets."

Mr. St. John pushed him in, and closed the door upon them. Henry held out his hand, and spoke a few hearty words of love and forgiveness; and Lewis put his face down on the counterpane and began to howl.

"Lewis, take comfort. It was done, I know, in the impulse of the moment, and you never thought it would hurt me seriously. I freely forgive you."

"Are you sure to die?" sobbed Lewis.

"I think I am. The doctors say so."

"O-o-o-o-o-o-h!" howled Lewis; "then I know you'll come back and haunt me with being your murderer: Prattleton junior says you will. He saw it done, so he knows about it. I shall never be able to sleep at night, for fear."

"Now, Lewis, don't be foolish. I shall be too happy where I am, to come back to earth. No one knows how it happened: you say Prattleton does, but he is your friend, and it is safe with him. Take comfort."

"Some of us have been so wicked and malicious to you!" blubbered Lewis. "I, and my brother, and Aultane, and a lot of them."

"It is all over now," sighed Henry, closing his heavy eyes. "You would not, had you foreseen that I should leave you so soon."

"Oh, what a horrid wretch I have been!" sobbed Lewis, rubbing his smeared face on the white bedclothes, in an agony. "And, if it's found out, they might try me next assizes and hang me. And it is such a dreadful thing for you to die!"

"It is a happy thing, Lewis; I feel it is, and I have told the dean I feel it. Say good-bye to the fellows for me, Lewis; I am too ill to see them. Tell them how sorry I am to leave them; but we shall meet again in heaven."

Lewis grasped his offered hand, and, with a hasty, sheepish movement, leaned forward and kissed him on the cheek: then turned and burst out of the room, nearly upsetting Mr. St. John, and tore down the stairs. Mr. St. John entered the chamber.

"Well, is the conference satisfactorily over?"

Again Henry reopened his heavy eyes. "Is that you, Mr. St. John?"

"Yes, I am here."

"The dean is coming here this evening at seven, for the sacrament. He said my not being confirmed was no matter in a case like this. Will you come?"

"Henry, no," was the grave answer. "I am not good enough."

"Oh, Mr. St. John!" The ready tears filled his eyes. "I wish you could!" he beseechingly whispered.

"I wish so too. Are you distressed for me, Henry? Do not look upon me as a monster of iniquity: I did not mean to imply it. But I do not yet think sufficiently of serious things to be justified in partaking of that ordinance without preparation."

"It would have seemed like a bond of union between us—a promise that you will some time join me where I am going," pleaded the dying boy.

"I hope I shall: I trust I shall: I will not forget that you are there."

As Mr. St. John left the house, he made his way to the grounds, in a reflective mood: the cathedral bell was then ringing for afternoon service, and, somewhat to his surprise, he saw the dean hurrying from the college; not to it.

"I'm on my way back to Arkell's! I'm on my way back to Arkell's!" he exclaimed, in an impetuous manner; and forthwith he began recounting a history to Mr. St. John; a history of wrong, which filled him, the dean, with indignation.

"I suspected something of the sort," was Mr. St. John's quiet answer; and the dean strode on his way, and Mr. St. John stood looking after him, in painful thought. When the dean came out of Mr. Peter Arkell's again, he was too late for service that afternoon. Although he was in residence!

Just in the unprepared and sudden manner that the news of Henry Arkell's approaching death must have fallen upon my readers, so did it fall upon the town. People could not believe it: his friends could not believe it: the doctors scarcely believed it. The day wore on; and whether there may have lingered any hope in the morning, the evening closed it, for it brought additional agony to his injured head, and the most sanguine saw that he was dying.

All things were prepared for the service, about to take place, and Henry lay flushed, feverish, and restless, lest he should become delirious ere the hour should arrive: he had become so rapidly worse since the forepart of the day. Precisely as the cathedral clock struck seven, the house door was thrown open, and the dean placed his foot on the threshold:

"PEACE BE UNTO THIS HOUSE, AND TO ALL THAT DWELL WITHIN IT!"

The dean was attended to the chamber, and there he commenced the office for the Visitation of the Sick, omitting part of the exhortation, but reading the prayer for a soul on the point of departure. Then he proceeded with the Communion.

When the service was over, all, save Mrs. Arkell and the dean, quitted the room. Henry's mind was tranquil now.

"I will not forget your request," whispered the dean.

"Near to the college door, as we enter," was Henry's response.

"It shall be done as you wish, my dear."

"And, sir, you have promised to forgive them."

"For your sake. You are suffering much just now," added the dean, as he watched his countenance.

"It gets more intense with every hour. I cannot bear it much longer. Oh, I hope I shall not suffer beyond my strength!" he panted; "I hope I shall be able to bear the agony!"

"Do not fear it. You know where to look for help!" whispered the dean; "you cannot look in vain. Henry, my dear boy, I leave you in peace, do I not?"

"Oh yes, sir, in perfect peace. Thank you greatly for all."

CHAPTER X

THE GRAVESTONE IN THE CLOISTERS

It was the brightest day, though March was not yet out, the first warm, lovely day of spring. Men passed each other in the streets, with a congratulation that the winter weather had gone, and the college boys, penned up in their large schoolroom, gazed aloft through the high windows at the blue sky and the sunshine, and thought what a shame it was that they should be held prisoners on such a days instead of galloping over the country at "Hare and Hounds."

"Third Latin class walk up," cried Mr. Wilberforce.

The third Latin class walked up, and ranged itself in front of the master's desk. "Who's top of this class?" asked he.

"Me, sir," replied the gentleman who owned that distinction.

"Who's 'me' sir?"

"Me, sir."

"Who is 'me,' sir?" angrily repeated the master, his spectacles bearing full on his wondering pupil.

"Charles Van Brummel, sir," returned that renowned scholar.

"Then go down to the bottom for saying 'me.'"

Mr. Van Brummel went down, considerably chopfallen, and the master was proceeding to work, when the cathedral bell tolled out heavily, for a soul recently departed.

"What's that?" abruptly ejaculated the master.

"It's the college death-bell, sir," called out the up class, simultaneously, Van Brummel excepted, who had not yet recovered his equanimity.

"I hear what it is as well as you," were all the thanks they got. "But what can it be tolling for? Nobody was ill."

"Nobody," echoed the boys.

"Can it be a member of the Royal Family?" wondered the master—the bishop and the dean he knew were well. "If not, it must be one of the canons."

Of course it must! for the college bell never condescended to toll for any of the profane vulgar. The Royal Family, the bishop, dean, and prebendaries, were the only defunct lights, honoured by the notice of the passing-bell of Westerbury Cathedral.

"Lewis junior," said the master, "go into college, and ask the bedesmen who it is that is dead."

Lewis junior clattered out. When he came back he walked very softly, and looked as white as a sheet.

"Well?" cried Mr. Wilberforce—for Lewis did not speak.

"It's tolling for Henry Arkell, sir."

"Henry Arkell!" uttered the master. "Is he really dead? Are you ill, Lewis junior? What's the matter?"

"Nothing, sir."

"But it is an entirely unprecedented proceeding for the cathedral bell to toll for a college boy," repeated Mr. Wilberforce, revolving the news. "The old bedesmen must be making some mistake. Half of them are deaf, and the other half are stupid. I shall send to inquire: we must have no irregularity about these things. Lewis junior."

"Yes, sir."

"Lewis junior, you are ill, sir," repeated the master, sharply. "Don't say you are not. Sit down, sir."

Lewis junior humbly sat down. He appeared to have the ague.

"Van Brummel, you'll do," continued Mr. Wilberforce. "Go and inquire of the bedesmen whether they have received orders; and, if so, from whom: and whether it is really Arkell that the bell is tolling for."

Van Brummel opened the door and clattered down the stairs, as Lewis junior had done; and he clattered back again.

"The men say, sir, that the dean sent them the orders by his servant. And they think Arkell is to be buried in the cathedral."

"In—deed!" was the master's comment, in a tone of doubt. "Poor fellow!" he added, after a pause, "his has been a sudden and melancholy ending. Boys, if you want to do well, you should imitate Henry Arkell.

I can tell you that the best boy who ever trod these boards, as a foundation scholar, has now gone from among us."

"Please, sir, I'm senior of the choir now," interposed Aultane junior, as if fearing the master might not sufficiently remember that important fact.

"And a fine senior you'll make," scornfully retorted Mr. Wilberforce.

It was Mr. St. John who had taken the news of his death to the dean, and the latter immediately sent to order the bell to be tolled. St. John left the deanery, and was passing through the cloisters on his way to Hall-street, when he saw in the distance Mrs. and Miss Beauclerc, just as the cathedral bell rang out. Mrs. Beauclerc was startled, as the head master had been: her fears flew towards her aristocratic clergy friends. She tried the college door, and, finding it open, entered to make inquiries of the bedesmen. Georgina stopped to chatter to Mr. St. John.

"Fancy, if it should be old Ferraday gone off!" cried she. "Won't the boys crow? He has got the influenza, and was sitting by his study fire yesterday in a flannel nightcap."

"It is the death-bell for Henry Arkell, Georgina."

A vivid emotion dyed her face. She was vexed that it should be apparent to Mr. St. John, and would have carried it off under an assumption of indifference.

"When did he die? Did he suffer much?"

"He died at a quarter past eleven; about twenty minutes ago. And he did not suffer so much at the last as was anticipated."

"Well, poor fellow, I hope he is happy."

"That he is," warmly responded Mr. St. John. "He died in perfect peace. May you and I be as peaceful, Georgina, when our time shall come."

"What a blow it must be to Mrs. Arkell!"

"I saw her as I came out of the house just now, and I could not help venturing on a word of entreaty, that she would not grieve his loss too deeply. She raised her beautiful eyes to me, and I cannot describe to you the light, the faith, that shone in them. 'Not lost,' she gently whispered, 'only gone before.'"

Georgina had kept her face turned from the view of Mr. St. John. She was gazing through her glistening eyes at the graveyard, which was enclosed by the cloisters.

"What possesses the college bell to toll for him?" she exclaimed, carelessly, to cover her emotion. "I thought," she added, with a spice of satire in her tone, "that there was an old curfew law, or something as stringent, against its troubling itself for anybody less exalted than a sleek old prebendary."

Mr. St. John saw through the artifice: he approached her, and lowered his voice. "Georgina, he sent you his forgiveness for any unkindness that may have passed. He sent you his love: and he hopes you will sometimes recal him to your remembrance, when you walk over his grave, as you go into college."

Surprise made her turn to Mr. St. John: but she wilfully ignored the first part of the sentence. "Over his grave! I do not understand."

"He is to be buried in the cloisters, near to this entrance-door, near to where we are now standing. There appears to be a vacant space here," cried Mr. St. John, looking down at his feet: "I dare say it will be in this very spot."

"By whose decision is he to be buried in the cloisters?" quickly asked Georgina.

"The dean's, of course. Henry craved it of him."

"I wonder papa did not tell me! What a singular fancy of Henry's!"

"I do not think so. It was natural that he should wish his last resting-place to be amidst old associations, amidst his old companions; and near to you, Georgina."

"There! I knew what you were driving at," returned Georgina, in a pouting, wilful tone. "You are going to accuse me of breaking his heart, or some such obsolete nonsense: I assure you I never—"

"Stay, Georgina; I do not care to hear this. I have delivered his message to you, and there let it end."

"You are as stupid and fanciful as he was," retorted Miss Beauclerc.

"Not quite so stupid in one respect, for he was blind to your faults; I am not. And never shall be," he added, in a tone of significance which caused the life-blood at Georgina's heart to stand still.

But she could not keep it up—the assumption of indifference, the apparent levity. The death was telling upon her, and she burst into hysterical tears. At that moment, Lewis junior passed them, and swung in at the cathedral door, on the master's errand, meeting Mrs. Beauclerc, who was coming out.

"Tell mamma I'm gone home," whispered Georgina to Mr. St. John, as she disappeared in the opposite direction.

"Arkell is dead, Mr. St. John," observed Mrs. Beauclerc. "The bell is tolling for him. I wonder the dean ordered the bell to toll for him: it will cause quite a commotion in the city to hear the college death-bell."

"He is to be buried here, in the cloisters, Mrs. Beauclerc."

"Really! Will the dean allow it?"

"The dean has decided it."

"Oh, indeed. I never understand half the dean does."

"So your companion is gone, Lewis junior," observed Mr. St. John, as the boy came stealing out of the college with his information. But Lewis never answered: and though he touched his forehead (he had no cap on) to the dean's wife, he never raised his eyes; but sneaked on, with his ghastly face, and his head bent down.

Those of the college boys who wished it went to see him in his coffin. Georgina Beauclerc also went. She told the dean, in a straightforward manner, that she should like to see Henry Arkell now he lay dead; and the dean saw no reason for refusing. The death had sobered Miss Beauclerc; but whatever feeling of remorse she might be conscious of, was hidden within her.

"You will not be frightened, I suppose, Georgina?" said the dean, in some indecision. "Did you ever see anybody dead?"

"I saw that old gardener of ours that died at the rectory, papa. I was frightened at him; a frightful old yellow scarecrow he looked. Henry Arkell won't look like that. Papa, I wish those wicked college boys who were his enemies could be hung!"

"Do you, Georgina?" gravely returned the dean. "He did not wish it; he forgave and prayed for them."

"They were so very—"

She could not finish the sentence. The reference to the schoolboys brought too vividly the past before her, and she rushed away to her own room, bursting with the tears she had to suppress until she got there.

It seemed that her whole heart must burst with grief, too, as she stood in the presence of the corpse. She had asked St. John to go with her; and the two were alone in the room. Save for the ashy paleness, Henry looked just as beautiful as he had been in life: the marble lids were closed over the brilliant eyes, never to open again in this life; the once warm hands lay cold and useless now. Some one—perhaps his mother—had placed in one of the hands a sprig of pink hyacinth; some was also strewed on the breast of the flannel shroud. The perfume came all-powerfully to their senses; and never afterwards did Georgina Beauclerc come near the scent of that flower, death-like enough in itself, but it brought all-forcibly to her memory the death-chamber of Henry Arkell.

She stood, leaning over the side of the coffin, sobbing painfully. The trestles were very low, so that it was much beneath her as she stood. St. John stood opposite, still and calm.

"He loved you very much, Georgina—as few can love in this world. You best know how you requited him."

Perhaps it was a harsh word to say in the midst of her grief; but St. John could not forgive her for the past, whatever Henry had done. She bent her brow down on the coffin, and sobbed wildly.

"Still, you made the sunshine of his life. He would have lived it over again, if he could, because you had been in it. You had become part of his very being; his whole heart was bound up in you. Better, therefore, that he should be lying there, than have lived on to the future, to the pain that it must, of necessity, have brought."

"Don't!" she wailed, amid her choking sobs.

Not another word was spoken. When she grew calm, Mr. St. John quitted the room to descend—for she motioned to him to pass out first. Then—alone—she bent down her lips to the face that could no longer respond; and she felt, in the moment's emotion, as if her heart must break.

"Oh! Henry—my darling! I was very cruel to you! Forgive—forgive me! But I did love you—though not as I love him."

Mr. St. John was waiting for her below, on the landing, near the drawing-room door. "You must pardon the family for not receiving you, Georgina. Mrs. Arkell mentioned it to me this morning; but they are overwhelmed with grief. It has been so unexpected, you see. Lucy is the worst. Mrs. Arkell"—he compelled his voice to a lower whisper—"has an idea that she will not be long behind him."

The burial day of Henry Arkell arrived. The dean had commanded a holiday from study, and that the king's scholars should attend the funeral. Just before the hour appointed for it, half-past eleven, some of them took up their station in the cloisters, in silent order, waiting to join the procession when it should come, a bow of black crape being attached to the left shoulder of their surplices. Sixteen of the king's scholars had gone down to the house, as they were appointed to do. Mrs. Beauclerc, her daughter, and the families of the prebendaries were already in the cathedral; with some other spectators, who had got in under the pretext of attending morning prayers, and who, when the prayers were over, had refused to quit their seats again: of course the sextons could not decently turn them out. Half a dozen ladies took up their station in the organ-loft, to the inward wrath of the organist, who, however, had to submit to the invasion with suavity, for one of them was the dean's daughter. It was the best viewing place, commanding full sight of the cathedral body and the nave on one side, and of the choir on the other. The bell tolled at intervals, sending its deep, gloomy boom over the town; and the spectators patiently waited. At length the first slow and solemn note of the organ was sounded, and Georgina Beauclerc shrank into a corner, contriving to see, and yet not be seen.

From the small door, never used but upon the rare occasion of a funeral, at the extremity of the long body of the cathedral, the procession advanced at last. It was headed by the choristers, two and two, the lay clerks, and the masters of the college school. The dean and one of the canons walked next before the coffin, which was borne by eight of the king's scholars, and the pall by eight more. Four mourners followed the coffin—Peter Arkell, his cousin William, Travice, and Mr. St. John; and the long line was brought up by the remainder of the king's scholars. So slow was their advance, as to be almost imperceptible to the spectators, the choir singing:

"I am the resurrection and the life, saith the Lord: he that believeth in me, though he were dead, yet shall he live: and whosoever liveth and believeth in me shall never die.

"I know that my Redeemer liveth, and that he shall stand at the latter day upon the earth. And though after my skin worms destroy this body, yet in my flesh shall I see God; whom I shall see for myself, and mine eyes shall behold, and not another."

The last time those words were sung in that cathedral, but some three weeks past, it was by him over whom they were now being sung; the thought flashed upon many a mind. At length the choir was reached, and the coffin placed on the trestles; Georgina Beauclerc's eyes—she had now come round to the front of the organ—being blinded with tears as she looked down upon it. Mr. St. John glanced up, from his place by the coffin, and saw her. Both the psalms were sung, and the dean himself read the lessons; and it may as well be here remarked, that at afternoon service the dean desired that Luther's hymn should be sung in place of the usual anthem; some association with the last evening Henry had spent at his house no doubt inducing it.

The procession took its way back to the cloisters, to the grave, Mr. Wilberforce officiating. The spectators followed in the wake. As the coffin was lowered to its final resting-place—earth to earth, ashes to ashes, dust to dust—the boys bowed their heads upon their clasped hands, and some of them sobbed audibly; they felt all the worth of Henry Arkell now that he was gone. The grave was made close to the cloister entrance to the cathedral, in the spot where had stood Mr. St. John and Georgina Beauclerc; where had once stood Georgina and Henry Arkell, the day that wretched Lewis had wished him buried there. An awful sort of feeling was upon Lewis now, as he remembered it. A few minutes, and it was over. The dean turned into the chapter-house, the mourners moved away, and the old bedesmen, in their black gowns, began to shovel in the earth upon the coffin. Mr. Wilberforce, before moving, put up his finger to Aultane, and the latter advanced.

"You choristers are not to go back to the vestry now, but to come into the hall in your surplices."

Aultane wondered at the order, but communicated it to those under him. When they entered the college hall, they found the king's scholars ranged in a semicircle, and they fell in with them according to their respective places in the school. The boys' white surplices and the bows of crape presenting a curious contrast.

"What are we stuck out like this for?" whispered one to the other. "For show? What does Wilberforce want? He's sitting still, as if he waited for somebody."

"Be blest if I know," said Lewis junior, whose teeth were chattering. "Unless it is to wind up with a funeral lecture."

However, they soon did know. The dean entered the hall, wearing his surplice, and carrying his official four-cornered cap. Mr. Wilberforce rose to bow the dean into his own seat, but the dean preferred to stand. He looked steadily at the circle before he spoke; sternly, some of them thought; and they did not feel altogether at ease.

"Boys!" began the dean. And there he stopped; and the boys lifted their heads to listen to what might be coming.

"Boys, our doings in this world bear a bias generally to good or to evil, and they bring their consequences with them. Well-doing brings contentment and inward satisfaction; but ill-doing as certainly brings its day of retribution. The present day must be one of retribution to some of you, unless you are so hardened in wickedness as to be callous to conscience. How have—"

The dean was interrupted by the entrance of Mr. St. John and Travice Arkell. They took off their hats; and their streaming hatbands swept the ground, as they advanced and stood by the dean.

"Boys," he resumed, "how have you treated Henry Arkell? I do not speak to all; I speak to some. Lewis senior, does your conscience prick you for having fastened him in St. James's Church, in the dark and lonely night? Aultane junior, does yours sting you for your insubordination to him on Assize Sunday, when you exposed yourself so disgracefully to two of the judges of the land, and for your malicious accusation of him to Miss Beauclerc, followed by your pitiful complaint to me? Prattleton, have you, as senior of the school, winked at the cabal against him?"

The three boys hung their heads and their red ears: to judge by their looks, their consciences were pricking them very sharply.

"Lewis junior," resumed the dean, in a sudden manner, "of what does your conscience accuse you?"

Lewis junior turned sick, and his hair stood on end. He could not have replied, had it been to save him from hanging.

"Do you know that you are the cause of Henry Arkell's death?" continued the dean, in a low but distinct accent, which penetrated the room. "And that you might, in justice, be taken up as a murderer?"

Lewis junior burst into a dismal howl, and fell down on his knees and face, burying his forehead on the ground, and sticking up his surpliced back; something after the manner of an ostrich.

"It was the fall in the choir on Assize Sunday that killed Henry Arkell," said the dean, looking round the hall; "that is, he has died from the effects of the fall. You gentlemen are aware of it, I believe?"

"Certainly they are, Mr. Dean," said the head master, wondering on his own account, and answering the dean because the "gentlemen" did not.

"He was thrown down," resumed the dean; "wilfully thrown down. And that is the one who did it," pointing with his finger at Lewis junior.

Two or three of the boys had been cognisant of the fact, as might be seen from their scarlet faces; the rest wore a look of timid curiosity; while Mr. Wilberforce's amazed spectacles wandered from the dean's finger to the prostrate and howling Lewis.

"Yes," said the dean, answering the various looks, "the author of Henry Arkell's death is Lewis junior. You had better get up, sir."

Lewis junior remained where he was, shaking his back as if it had been a feather-bed, and emitting the most extraordinary groans.

"Get up," cried the dean, sternly.

There was no disobeying the tone, and Lewis raised himself. A pretty object he looked, for the dye from his new black gloves had been washed on to his face.

"He told me he forgave me the day before he died; he said he had never told any one, and never would," howled Lewis. "I didn't mean to hurt him."

"He never did tell," replied the dean: "he bore his injuries, bore them without retaliation. Is there another boy in the school who would do that?"

"No, that there is not," put in Mr. Wilberforce.

"When you locked him in the church, Lewis senior, did he inform against you? When you came to me with your cruel accusation, Aultane, did he revenge himself by telling me of a far worse misdemeanour, which you had been guilty of? Did he ever inform against any who injured him? No; insults, annoyances, he bore all in silence, because he would not bring trouble and punishment upon you. He was a noble boy," warmly continued the dean: "and, what's more, he was a Christian one."

"He said he would not tell of me," choked Lewis junior, "and now he has gone and done it. O-o-o-o-o-o-h!"

"He never told," quietly repeated the dean. "During the last afternoon of his life, it came to my knowledge, subsequent to an interview I had had with him, that Lewis junior had wilfully thrown him down, and I went back to Arkell and taxed him with its being the fact. He could not deny it, but the whole burden of his admission was, 'Oh, sir, forgive him! do not punish him! I am dying, and I pray you to forgive him for my sake! Forgive them all!' Do you think you deserve such clemency?" asked the dean, in an altered tone.

Lewis only howled the louder.

"On his part, I offer you all his full and free forgiveness: Lewis junior, do you hear? his full and free forgiveness. And I believe you have also that of his parents." The dean looked at Travice Arkell, and waited for him to speak.

"A few hours only before Henry died, it came to Mr. Peter Arkell's knowledge—"

"I informed him," interrupted the dean.

"Yes," resumed Travice. "The dean informed Mr. Arkell that Henry's fall had not been accidental. But—as he had prayed the dean, so he prayed his father, to forgive the culprit. Lewis junior, I am here on the part of Mr. Arkell to offer his forgiveness to you."

"I wish I could as easily accord mine," said the dean. "No punishment will be inflicted on you, Lewis junior: not because no punishment, that I or Mr. Wilberforce could command, is adequate to the crime, but that his dying request, for your pardon, shall be complied with. If you have any conscience at all, his fate will lie upon it for the remainder of your life, and you will bear its remembrance about with you."

Lewis bent down his head on the shoulder nearest to him, and his howls changed into sobs.

"One word more, boys," said the dean. "I have observed that not one in the whole school—at least such is my belief—would be capable of acting as Henry Arkell did, in returning good for evil. The ruling principle of his life, and he strove to carry it out in little things as in great, was to do as he would be done by. Now what could have made him so different from you?"

The dean obtained no reply.

"I will tell you. He loved and feared God. He lived always as though God were near him, watching over his words and his actions; he took God for his guide, and strove to do His will: and now God has taken him to his reward. Do you know that his death was a remarkably peaceful one? Yes, I think you have heard so. Holy living, boys, makes holy dying; and it made his dying holy and peaceful. Allow me to ask, if you, who are selfish and wicked and malignant, could meet death so calmly?"

"Arkell's mother is often so ill, sir, that she doesn't know she'll live from one day to another," a senior ventured to remark in the general desperation. "Of course that makes her learn to try not to fear death, and she taught him not to."

"And she now finds her recompense," observed the dean. "A happy thing for you, if your mothers had so taught you. Dismiss the school, Mr. Wilberforce. And I hope," he added, turning round to the boys, as he and the other two gentlemen left the hall, "that you will, every one, go home, not to riot on this solemn holiday, but to meditate on these important thoughts, and resolve to endeavour to become more like Henry Arkell. You will attend service this afternoon."

And that was the ending. And the boy, with his talents, his beauty, and his goodness, was gone; and nothing of him remained but what was mouldering under the cloister gravestone.

HENRY CHEVELEY ARKELL.
Died March 24th, 18—,
Aged 16. Not lost, but gone before.

CHAPTER XI

THOUGHTLESS WORDS

This is the last part of our history, and you must be prepared for changes, although but little time—not very much more than a year—has gone by.

Death has been busy during that period. Mrs. Peter Arkell survived her son so short a time, that it is already twelve months since she was laid in the churchyard of St. James the Less. It is a twelvemonth also since Mr. Fauntleroy died, and his daughters are the great heiresses of Westerbury.

Westerbury had need of heiresses, or something else substantial, to keep up its consequence; for it was dwindling down lower (speaking of its commercial importance) day by day. The clerical party (in contradistinction to the commercial) rose and flourished; the other fell.

Amidst those with whom it was beginning to be a struggle to keep their heads above water was Mr. Arkell. The hope that times would mend; a hope that had buoyed up for years and years other large manufacturers in Westerbury, was beginning to show itself what it really was—a delusive one. A deplorable gloom hung over the brow of Mr. Arkell, and he most bitterly repented that he had not thrown this hope to the winds long ago, and given up business before so much of his good property was sacrificed. He had in the past year made those retrenchments in his expenditure, which, in point of prudence, ought to have been made before; but his wife had set her face determinately against it, and to a peaceable-dispositioned man like Mr. Arkell, the letting the ruin come is almost preferable to the contention the change involves. Those of my readers who may have had experience of this, will know that I only state what is true. But necessity has no law: and when Mr. Arkell could no longer drain himself to meet these superfluous expenses, the change was made. The close carriage was laid down; the household was reduced to what it had been in his father's time—two maids, and a man for the horse and garden, and he admonished his wife and daughters that they must spend in dress just half what they had spent. But with all the retrenchment, Mr. Arkell saw himself slowly drifting downwards. His manufactory was still kept on; but it had been far better given up. It must surely come to it, and Travice would have to seek a different channel of obtaining a living. Not only Travice: the men who had grown old in William Arkell's service, they must be turned adrift. There's not the least doubt that this last thought helped, more than all else, to keep Mr. Arkell's decision on the balance.

And Peter Arkell? Peter was in worse plight than his cousin. As it had been all their lives, the contrast in their fortunes marked, so it was still; so it would be to the end. William still lived well, and as a gentleman; he had but lopped off superfluities; Peter was a poor, bowed, broken man, obliged to be careful how he laid out money for even the common necessaries of life. But for Mildred's never-ceasing forethought, those necessaries might not always have been bought. The death of his wife, the death of his gifted son, had told seriously upon Peter Arkell: and his health, never too good, had since been ominously breaking up.

His good and gentle daughter, Lucy, had care upon her in many ways. The little petty household economies it was necessary to practise unceasingly, wearied her spirit; the uncertainty of how they were to live, now that her father could no longer teach or write—and his learned books had brought him in a trifle from time to time—chilled her hope. Not yet had she recovered the shock, the terrible heart-blow brought to her by the death of Henry; and her mother's death had followed close upon it. It seemed to have cast a blight upon her young spirit: and there were times when Lucy, good and trusting girl though she was, felt tempted to think that God was making her path one of needless sorrow. The sad, thoughtful look was ever in her countenance now, in her sweet brown eyes; and her fair features, not strictly beautiful, but pleasant to look upon, grew more like what Mildred's were after the blight had fallen upon her. But no heart-blight had as yet come to Lucy.

One evening an old and confidential friend of Peter Arkell's dropped in to sit an hour with him. It was Mr. Palmer, the manager and cashier of the Westerbury bank, and the brother to Mr. Palmer of Heath Hall. As the two friends talked confidentially on this evening, deploring the commercial state of the city, and saying that it would never rise again from its distress, Mr. Palmer dropped a hint that the firm of George Arkell and Son had been effecting another mortgage on their property. Mr. Peter Arkell said nothing then; but Lucy, who went into the room on the departure of their guest, noticed that he remained sunk in melancholy silence; and she could not arouse him from it.

Travice Arkell came in. Travice was in the habit of coming in a great deal more than one of the ruling powers at home had any idea of. Travice would very much have liked to make Lucy his wife; but there were serious impediments in more ways than one, and he was condemned to silence, and to wait and see what an uncertain future might bring forth.

The romance that had been enacted in the early days of William Arkell and Mildred was being re-enacted now. But with a difference. For whereas William, as you have seen, forsook the companion of his boyhood, and cast his love upon a stranger, Travice's whole hopes were concentrated upon Lucy. And Lucy loved him with all the impassioned ideality of a first and powerful passion, with all the fervour of an imaginative and reticent nature. It was impossible but that each should detect, in a degree, the feelings of the other, though they might not be, and had not been, spoken of openly.

Travice reached the chess-board from a side-table where it was kept, took his seat opposite Peter, and began to set out the men. Of the same kind, considerate nature that his father was before him, he compassionated the lonely man's solitary days, and was wont to play a game at chess with him sometimes in an evening, to while away one of his weary hours. But Peter, on this night, put up his hand in token of refusal.

"Not this evening, Travice. I am not equal to it. My spirits are low."

"Do you feel ill?" asked Travice, beginning to put the pieces in the box again.

"I feel low; out of sorts. Mr. Palmer has been here talking of things, and he gives so deplorable a state of private affairs generally, consequent upon the long-continued commercial depression, that it's hard to say who's safe and whose tottering. He has especial means of ascertaining, you know, so there's no doubt he's right."

"Well, what of that?" returned Travice. "It cannot affect you; you are not in business."

"True. I was not thinking of myself."

"A game at chess will divert your thoughts."

"Not to-night, Travice; I'd rather not play to-night."

"Will you have a game, Lucy?"

She looked up from her sewing to smile a negative. "That would be leaving papa quite to his thoughts. I think we had better talk to him."

"Travice," Peter Arkell suddenly said, "I am sure this depression must seriously affect your father."

"Of course it does," was the ready answer. "He has just now had to borrow more money again."

"Then Palmer was right," thought Peter Arkell. "Will he keep on the business?" he asked aloud.

"I should not, were I in his place," said Travice. "He would have given up long ago, I believe, but for thinking what's to become of me. Of course if he does give up, I am thrown on the world, a wandering Arab."

His tone was as much one of jest as of gravity. The young do not see things in the same light as the old. To his father and to Peter Arkell, his being thrown out of the business he had embraced as his own, appeared an almost irrecoverable blight in life; to Travice himself it seemed but a very slight misfortune. The world was before him, and he had honour, education, health, and brains; surely he could win his way in it!

"It is not well to throw down one calling and take up another," observed Peter, thoughtfully. "It does not always answer."

"But if you are forced to it!" argued Travice. "There's no help for it then, and you must do the best you can."

"It is a pity but you had gone to Oxford, Travice, and entered into some profession!"

"I suppose it is, as things seem to be turning out. Thrown out of the manufactory, I should seem a sort of luckless adventurer, not knowing which way to turn to prey upon the public."

"It would be just beginning life again," said Peter, his grave tone bearing in it a sound of reproach to the lighter one.

He rose, and went to the next room—the "Peter's study" of the old days—to get something from his desk there. Travice happened to look at Lucy, and saw her eyes fixed upon him with a troubled, earnest expression. She blushed as he caught their gaze.

"What's the matter, Lucy?"

"I was wondering whatever you would do, if Mr. Arkell does give up."

"I think I should be rather glad of it? I could turn astronomer."

"Turn astronomer! But you don't really mean that, Travice?"

He laughed.

"I should mean it, but for one thing."

"What is that one thing?"

"That it might not find me in bread and cheese. Perhaps they'd make me honorary star-gazer at the observatory royal. The worst is, one must eat and drink; and the essentials necessary for that don't drop from the clouds, as the manna once did of old. Very convenient for some of us if it did."

"I wish you'd be serious," she rejoined, the momentary tears rising to her eyes. She was feeling wretchedly troubled, she could not tell why, and his light mood jarred upon her.

It changed now as he looked at her. Travice Arkell's face changed to an expression of deep, grave meaning, of troubled meaning, and he dropped his voice to a low tone as he rose and stood near Lucy, looking down upon her.

"I wish I could be serious; I have wished it, Lucy, this long while past. Other men at my age are thinking of forming those social ties that man naturally expects to form; of gathering about him a home, and a wife, and children. I must not; for what I can see at present, they must be denied to me for good and all; unless—unless—"

He broke off abruptly. Lucy, suppressing the emotion that had arisen, glanced up at him, as she waited for the conclusion. But the conclusion did not come.

"You see now, Lucy, why I cannot be serious. Perhaps you have seen why before. In the uncertain state that our business is, not knowing but the end of it may be bankruptcy—"

"Oh, Travice!" she involuntarily exclaimed, in the shock that the word brought to her.

"I do assure you it has crossed my mind now and then, that such may be the final ending. It would break my father's heart, I know, and it would half break mine for his sake; but others in the town have succumbed, who were once nearly as rich as we were, and the fate may overtake us. I wish I could be serious; serious to a purpose; but I cannot."

"I wanted to show you a prospectus, Travice, that was left here to-day," interrupted Peter Arkell, coming back to the room. "I wonder what next they'll be getting up a company over? I put it into my desk, but I can't find it. Lucy, look about for it, will you?"

She got up to obey, and Travice caught a sight of the raised face, whose blushes had been hidden from him; blushes called forth by his words and their implied meaning. She had understood it.

But she had not understood the sentence at whose conclusion Travice Arkell had broken down. "That the ties of wife and children must be denied to him for good and all, unless—"

Unless what? Unless he let them sacrifice him, would be the real answer. Unless he sacrificed himself, his dearest hopes, every better feeling that his heart possessed, at a golden shrine. But Travice Arkell would have a desperate fight first.

The Miss Fauntleroys, co-heiresses of the wealthy old lawyer—who might have died worth more but for his own entanglements in early life—had become intimate and more intimate at the house of William Arkell. Ten thousand pounds were settled on each, and there was other money to divide between them, which was not settled. How Lawyer Fauntleroy had scraped together so much, Westerbury could not imagine, considering he had been so hampered with old claims. Strapping, vulgar, good-humoured damsels, these two, as you have before heard; with as little refinement in looks, words, and manner as their father had possessed before them. Their intimacy had grown, I say, with the Arkell family. Mrs. Arkell courted them to her house; the young ladies were quite eager to frequent it without courting; and it had come to be whispered all over the gossiping town, that Mr. Arkell's son and heir might have either of them for the asking.

Perhaps not quite true this, as to the "either," perhaps yes. It was indisputable that both liked him very much; but any hope the younger might have felt disposed to cherish had long been merged in the more recognised claim to him of the elder; recognised by the young ladies only, mind you, in the right, it may be, of her seniorship. Nothing in the world could have been more satisfactory to Mrs. Arkell than this union. She overlooked their want of refinement, and their many other wants of a similar nature—of refinement, indeed, she may have deemed that Travice possessed enough for himself and for a wife too—she thought of the golden hoard in the bank, the firm securities in the three per cent consols, and she pertinaciously cherished the hope and the resolve that Barbara Fauntleroy should become Barbara Arkell.

It is well to say "pertinaciously." That Travice had set his resolve against it, she tacitly understood; and once when she went so far as to put her project before him in a cautious hint, Travice had broken out with the ungallant assertion that he would "as soon marry the deuce." But he might have to give in at last. The constant dropping of water on a stone will wear it away; and the constant, unceasing tongue of a woman has been known to break the iron walls of man's will.

Another suitor had recently sprung up for Miss Lizzie Fauntleroy. No less a personage than Benjamin Carr. The reappearance of Mr. Dundyke upon the scene of the living world had considerably astonished many people; possibly, amidst others, Ben Carr himself. In the great relief it brought to the mind of Mr. Arkell, distorted, you may remember, with a certain unpleasant doubt, he almost forgot to suspect him at all; and he buried the past in silence, and in a measure, took luckless Ben into favour again; that is, he did not forbid him his house.

Ben, in fact, had come out apparently nourishing from all past escapades suspected and unsuspected, and was residing with his father, and dressing like a gentleman. No more was heard of his wish to go abroad. Squire Carr had made him a half promise to put him into a farm; and while Ben waited for this, he paid court to Lizzie Fauntleroy. At first she laughed in his face for an old fool, next she began to giggle at his soft speeches, and now she listened to him. Ben Carr had some attraction yet, in spite of his four-and-forty years.

In the course of the following morning, Peter Arkell suddenly announced his intention of going out, to the great surprise of Lucy. It was a most unfit day, rainy, and bleak for the season; and he had not stepped over the threshold for weeks and weeks.

"Papa! You cannot go out to-day. It is not fit for you."

"Yes, I shall go. I want particularly to speak to my cousin William: you can help me thither with your arm, Lucy. Get my old cloak down, and air it at the fire; I can wrap myself in that."

Lucy ventured no further remonstrance. When her papa took a thing into his head, there was no turning him.

They started together through the bad weather to the house of William Arkell. The dear old house! where Peter had spent so many pleasant evenings in his youthful days. He crossed the yard at once to the manufactory, telling Lucy to go indoors and wait for him. William Arkell was alone in his private room, and was not a little surprised at the visit.

"Why Peter!" he exclaimed, rising from his desk, and placing an arm-chair by the fire, "What has brought you out such a day as this? Sit down."

Before Peter did so, he closed the door, so that they should be quite alone. He then turned and clasped his cousin by the hand.

"William," he began, emotion mingling with his utterance, "I have come to you, a poor unhappy man. Conscious of my want of power to do what I ought—fearing that there is less chance of my doing it, day by day."

"What do you mean?" inquired Mr. Arkell.

"Amidst the ruin that has almost universally fallen on the city, you have not escaped, I fear your property is being seriously drawn upon?"

"And, unless things mend, it will soon be drawn to an end, Peter."

"Heaven help me!" exclaimed Peter. "And to know that I am in your debt, and cannot liquidate it! It is to speak of this, that I am come out to-day."

"Nay, now you are foolish!" exclaimed Mr. Arkell. "What matters a hundred pounds or two, more or less, to me? The sum would cut but a poor figure by the side of what I am now habituated to losing. Never think of it, Peter: I never shall. Besides, you had it from me in driblets, so that I did not miss it."

"When I had used to come to you for assistance in my illnesses, for I was ashamed to draw too much upon Mildred," proceeded the poor man, "I never thought but that I should, in time, regain permanent strength, and be able to return it. I never meant to cheat you, William."

"Don't talk like that, Peter!" interrupted Mr. Arkell. "If the money were returned to me now, it would only go the way that the rest is going. I have always felt glad that it was in my power to render you assistance in your necessities: and if I stood this moment without a shilling to turn to, I should not regret it any more than I do now."

They continued in converse, but we need not follow it. Lucy meanwhile had entered the house, and went about, looking for some signs of its inhabitants. The general sitting-room was empty, and she crossed the hall and opened the door of the drawing-room. A bouncing lady in fine attire was coming forth from it, talking and laughing loudly with Mr. Arkell; it was Barbara Fauntleroy.

Shaking hands with Lucy in her good-humoured manner as she passed her, she talked and laughed her way out of the house. Lucy was in black silk and crape still; Miss Fauntleroy was in the gayest of colours; and Mrs. Peter Arkell had been dead longer than Mr. Fauntleroy. They had worn their black a twelvemonth and then quitted it. It was not fashionable to wear mourning long now, said the Miss Fauntleroys.

Charlotte Arkell, with scant ceremony, sat down to the piano, giving Lucy only a nod. Nothing could exceed the slighting contempt in which she and her sister held Lucy. They had been trained in it. And they were highly accomplished young ladies besides, had learnt everything there was to be taught, from the harp and oriental tinting, down to Spanish, German, and chenille embroidery. Lucy's education had been solid, rather than ornamental: she spoke French well, and played a little; and she was more skilled in plain sewing than in fancy. They never allowed their guarded fingers to come into contact with plain work, and had just as much idea of how anything useful was done, as of how the moon was made. So these two fine young ladies despised Lucy Arkell, after the fashion of the fine young ladies of the present day. Charlotte also was great in the consciousness of other self-importance, for she was soon to be a wife. That Captain Anderson whom you once saw at a concert, had paid a more recent visit to Westerbury; and he left it, engaged to Charlotte Arkell.

Charlotte played a few bars, and then remembered to become curious on the subject of Lucy's visit. She whirled herself round on the music stool: it had been a favourite motion of her mother's in the old days.

"What have you come for, Lucy?"

"Papa wanted to see Mr. Arkell, and I walked with him. He is gone into the manufactory."

"I thought your papa was too ill to go out."

"He is very ailing. I think he ought not to have come out on a day like this. Do not let me interrupt your practising, Charlotte."

"Practising! I have no heart to practise!" exclaimed Charlotte. "Papa is always talking in so gloomy a way. He was in here just now: I was deep in this sonata of Beethoven's, and did not hear him enter, and he began saying it would be better if I and Sophy were to accustom ourselves to spend some of our time usefully, for that he did not know how soon we might be obliged to do it. He has laid down the carriage; he has made fearful retrenchments in the household: I wonder what he would have! And as to our buying anything new, or subscribing to a concert, or anything of that sort, mamma says she cannot get the money from him. I wish I was married, and gone from Westerbury! I am thankful my future home is to be far away from it!"

"Things may brighten here," was all the consolation that Lucy could offer.

"I don't believe they ever will," returned Charlotte. "I see no hope of it. Papa looks sometimes as if his heart were breaking."

"How soon the Miss Fauntleroys have gone out of mourning!" observed Lucy.

"Oh, I don't know. They wore it twelve months; that's long enough for anything. Let me give you a caution, Lucy," added Charlotte, laughing: "don't hint at such a thing as that Barbara Fauntleroy's not immaculate perfection: it would not do in this house."

"Why?" exclaimed Lucy, wondering at her words and manner.

"She is intended for its future head, you know, when the present generation of heads shall—shall have passed away. I'm afraid that's being poetical; I didn't mean to be."

Lucy sat as one in a maze, wondering WHAT she might understand by the words. And Charlotte whirled round on her stool again to the sonata, with as little ceremony as she had whirled from it.

While Miss Fauntleroy was there, Mrs. Arkell had sent a private message to Travice that she wanted him; but Travice did not obey the summons until the young lady was gone. He came then: and Mrs. Arkell attacked him for not coming before; she was attacking him now, while Charlotte and Lucy were talking.

"Why did you not come in at once?" asked Mrs. Arkell, in the cross tone which had latterly become habitual; "Barbara Fauntleroy was here."

"That was just the reason," returned Travice, in his usual candid manner; "I waited until she should be gone."

If there was one thing that vexed Mrs. Arkell worse than the fact itself, it was the open way in which her son steadily resisted the hints to him on the subject of Miss Fauntleroy. She felt at times that she could have beaten him; she was feeling so now. Her temper turned acrid, her face flushed, her voice rose.

"Travice, if you persist in this systematic rudeness—"

"Pardon me, mother. I wish you would refrain from bringing up the subject of Miss Fauntleroy to me. I do not care to hear of her in any way; she—Who's that? Why, I do believe it's Lucy's voice!"

The colloquy with Mrs. Arkell had taken place in the hall. Travice made one bound to the drawing-room. The sudden flush on the pale face, the glad eagerness of the tone, struck dismay to the heart of Mrs. Arkell. She quickly followed him, and saw that he had taken both of Lucy's hands in greeting.

"Oh, Lucy! are you here this morning? I know you have come to stay the day! Take your things off."

Lucy laughed—and Mrs. Arkell had the pleasure of seeing that her cheeks wore an answering flush. She shook her head and drew her hands from Travice, who seemed as if he could have kept them for ever.

"Do I spend a day here so often that you think I can come for nothing else? I only came with papa, and I am going back with him soon."

But Travice pressed the point of staying. Charlotte also—feeling, perhaps, that even Lucy was a welcome break to the monotony the house had fallen into—urged it. Mrs. Arkell maintained a marked silence; and in the midst of it the two gentlemen came in. Mr. Arkell kissed Lucy, and said she had better stop.

But Peter settled it the other way. Lucy must go home with him then, he said; but if she liked to come down in the afternoon, and stay for the rest of the day, she could. It was so settled, and they took their departure. Mr. Arkell walked with Peter across the court-yard, talking. Travice, in the very face and eyes of his mother, gave his arm to Lucy.

"Why did you not stay?" he whispered, as they arrived at the gates. "Lucy, do you know that to part with you is to part with my life's sunshine?"

Mrs. Arkell was standing at the door as he turned, and beckoned to him from the distance.

"I wish to speak with you," she said, as he approached.

She led the way into the dining-room, and closed the door on them, as if for some formidable interview. Travice saw that she was in a scarcely irrepressible state of anger, and he perched himself on a vacant side-table—rather a favourite way of his. He began humming a tune; gaily, but not disrespectfully.

"What possesses you to behave in this absurd manner to Lucy Arkell?" she began, in passion.

"What have I done now?" asked Travice.

"You are continually, in some way or other, contriving to thrust that girl's company upon us! I will not permit it, Travice; I have borne with it too long. I—"

"Why, she is not here twice in a twelvemonth," interrupted Travice.

"Don't say absurd things. She is. And she is not fit society for your sisters."

"If they were only half as worthy of her society as she is superior to them, they would be very different girls from what they are," spoke Travice, with a touch of his father's old heat. "If there's one thing that Lucy is, pre-eminently, it's a gentlewoman. Her mother was one before her."

Mrs. Arkell grew nearly black in the face. While she was trying to speak, Travice went on.

"Ask my father what his opinion of Lucy is. He does not say she is here too much."

"Your father is a fool in some things, and so are you!" retorted Mrs. Arkell, a sort of scream in her voice. "How dare you oppose me in this way, Travice?"

"I am very sorry to do so," returned the young man; "and I beg your pardon if I say more than you think I ought. But I cannot join in your unjust feeling against Lucy, and I will not tolerate it. I wish you would not bring up this subject at all: it is one we never can agree upon."

"You requested me just now not to 'bring up' the subject of Miss Fauntleroy to you," said Mrs. Arkell, in a tone of irony. "How many other subjects would you be pleased to interdict?"

"I don't want to hear even the name of those Fauntleroys!" burst out Travice, losing for a moment his equanimity. "Great brazen milkmaids!"

"No! you'd rather hear Lucy's!" screamed Mrs. Arkell. "You'd—"

"Lucy! Don't name them with Lucy, my dear mother. They are not fit to tie Lucy's shoes! She has more sense of propriety in her little finger, than they have in all their great overgrown bodies!"

This was the climax. And Mrs. Arkell, suppressing the passion that shook her as she stood, spoke with that forced calmness that is worse than the loudest fury. Her face had turned white.

"Continue your familiar intercourse with that girl, if you will; but, listen!—you shall never make a wife of anyone so paltry and so pitiful! I would pray Heaven to let me follow you to your grave, Travice, rather than see you marry Lucy Arkell."

She spoke the words in her blind rage, never reflecting on their full import; never dreaming that a day was soon to come, when their memory would return to her in her extremity of vain and hopeless repentance.

CHAPTER XII

MISCONCEPTION

"It shall be put a stop to! it shall be put a stop to!" murmured Mrs. Arkell to herself, as she sat alone when Travice had left her, trying to recover her equanimity. "Once separated from that wretched Lucy, he would soon find charms in Barbara Fauntleroy."

There was no time to be lost; and that same afternoon, when Lucy arrived, according to promise, crafty Mrs. Arkell began to lay the foundation stone. Lucy found her in the drawing-room alone.

"I will take my bonnet upstairs," said Lucy. "Shall I find Charlotte and Sophy anywhere?"

"No," replied Mrs. Arkell, in a very uncompromising tone. "They have gone out with the Miss Fauntleroys."

"I was unwilling to come this afternoon," observed Lucy, as she returned and sat down, "for papa does not seem so well. I fear he may have taken cold to-day; but he got to his books and writing after dinner, as usual."

"Does he think of bringing out a new book?" asked Mrs. Arkell; and Lucy did not detect the irony of the question.

"Not yet. He is about half through one. Is there any meeting to-day, do you know, Mrs. Arkell?" she resumed. "I met several gentlemen hurrying up the street as I came along."

"I thought everybody knew of it," replied Mrs. Arkell. "A meeting of the manufacturers was convened at the Guildhall for this afternoon. Mr. Arkell and Travice have gone to it."

"Their meetings seem to bring them no redress," returned Lucy, sadly. "The English manufacturers have no chance against the French now."

"I don't know what is to become of us," ejaculated Mrs. Arkell. "Charlotte, thank goodness, will soon be married and away; but there's Sophy! Travice will have enough to live upon, without business."

"Will he?" exclaimed Lucy, looking brightly up. "I am so glad to hear it! I thought your property had diminished until it was but small."

"Our property is diminishing daily," replied Mrs. Arkell. "Which makes it the more necessary that Travice should secure himself by his marriage."

Lucy did not answer; but her heart throbbed violently, and the faint colour on her cheek forsook it. Mrs. Arkell, without looking towards her, rose to poke the fire, and continued talking as she leaned over the grate, with her back to Lucy.

"It is intended that Travice shall marry Barbara Fauntleroy."

The sense of the words was very decided, carrying painful conviction to Lucy's startled ear. She could not have answered, had her life depended on it.

"Lucy, my dear," proceeded Mrs. Arkell, speaking with unwonted affection, and looking Lucy full in the face, "I am speaking to you in entire confidence, and I desire you will respect it as such. Do not drop a hint to Travice or the girls; they would not like my speaking of it."

Lucy sat quiet; and Mrs. Arkell quite devoured the pale face with her eyes.

"At first he did not care much for Barbara; and in truth he does not care for her now, as one we intend to marry ought to be cared for. But that will all come in time. Travice, like many other young men, may have indulged in a little carved-out romance of his own—I don't know that he did, but he may—and he has the good sense to see that his romance must yield to reality."

"Yes!" ejaculated Lucy, feeling that she was expected to say something in answer.

"There is our property dwindling down to little; there's the business dwindling down to nothing; and suppose Travice took it into his head to many a portionless girl, what prospect would there be before him? Why, nothing but poverty and self-reproach; nothing but misery. And in time he would hate her for having brought him to it."

"True! true!" murmured Lucy.

"And now," added Mrs. Arkell, "that he is on the point of consenting to marry Miss Fauntleroy, it is the duty of all of us, if we care for his future happiness and welfare, to urge his hopes to that point. You see it, Lucy, I should think, as well as we do."

There was no outward emotion to be observed in Lucy. A transiently white cheek, a momentary quiver of the lip, and all that could be seen was over. Like her aunt Mildred, it was her nature to bear in silence; but some of us know too well that that is the grief which tells. There was a slight shiver of the frame, visible to those keen eyes watching her, and she compelled herself to speak as with indifference.

"Has he consented?"

"My dear Lucy, I said he was on the point of consenting. And there's no doubt he is. I had an explanation with Travice this morning; he seemed inclined to shun Miss Fauntleroy, for I sent for him while she was here, and he did not come. After you left, I spoke to him; I pointed out the state of the case, and said what a sweet girl Miss Fauntleroy was, what a charming wife she would make him; and I hope I brought him to reason. You see, Lucy, how advantageous it will be in all ways, their union. Not only does it provide for Travice, but it will remove the worst of the great care hanging over the head of Mr. Arkell, and which I am sure, if not removed, will shorten his life. Do you understand?"

"I—think so," replied Lucy, whose brain was whirling in spite of her calm manner.

Mrs. Arkell drew her chair nearer to Lucy, and dropped her voice.

"Our position is this, my dear. A very great portion of Mr. Arkell's property is locked up in his stock, which is immense. I should not have kept on manufacturing as he has done; and I believe it has been partly for the sake of those rubbishing workmen. Unless he can get some extraneous help, some temporary assistance, he will have to force his stock to sale at a loss, and it would just be ruin. Miss Fauntleroy proposes to advance any sum he may require, as soon as the marriage has taken place, and there's no doubt he will accept it. It will be only a temporary loan, you know; but it will save us a great, a ruinous loss."

"She proposes to advance it?" echoed Lucy, struck with the words, in the midst of her pain.

"She does. She is as good hearted a girl as ever lived, and proposed it freely. In fact, she would be ready and willing to advance it at once, for of course she knows it would be a safe loan, but Mr. Arkell will not hear of it. She knows what our wishes are upon the subject of the marriage, and she sees that Travice has been holding back; and but for her very good-natured disposition she might not have tolerated it. However, I hope all will soon be settled now, and she and Travice married. Lucy, my dear, I rely upon you for Mr. Arkell's sake, of whom you are so fond, for Travice's own sake, to forward on this by any little means in your power. And, remember, the confidence I have reposed in you must not be broken."

Lucy sat cold and still. In honour she must no longer think of a possible union with Travice—must never more allow word or look from him seeming to point to it.

"For Mr. Arkell's sake," she kept repeating to herself, as if she were in a dream; "for Travice's own sake!" She saw the future as clearly as though it had been mapped out before her eyes in some prophetic vision: Travice would marry Barbara Fauntleroy and her riches. She almost wished she might never see him more; it could only bring to her additional misery.

Charlotte Arkell came in with Barbara Fauntleroy. Sophy had gone home with the other one for the rest of the day. An old aunt, bed-ridden three parts of her time, had lived with the young ladies since the death of their father. But they were not so very young; and they were naturally independent. Barbara was quite as old as Travice Arkell.

"How shall I bear to see them together?" thought Lucy, as Barbara Fauntleroy sat down opposite to her, in her rustling silk of many colours, and no end of gold trinkets jingling about her. "I wonder why I was born? But for papa, I could wish I had died as Harry did!"

For that first evening, however, she was spared. Their little maid arrived in much commotion, asking to see Miss Lucy. Her papa was feeling worse than when she left home, was the word she brought, and he thought if Lucy did not mind it, he should like her to go back to him at once.

Lucy hastened home. She found her father very poorly; feverish, and coughing a great deal. It was the foreshadowing of an illness from which he was destined never to recover.

Whether his allotted span of life had indeed run out, or whether his exposure to the weather that unlucky morning helped to shorten it, Lucy never knew. A week or two of uncertain sickness—now a little better, now a little worse, and it became too evident that hope of recovery for Peter Arkell was over. A bowed, broken man in frame and spirit, but comparatively young in years, Peter was passing from the world he had found little else than trouble in. Lucy wrote in haste and distress for her Aunt Mildred, but a telegram was received in reply, announcing the death of Lady Dewsbury. She had died somewhat suddenly, Mildred said, when a letter came by the next morning's post, in which she gave particulars.

It was nearly impossible for her to come away before the funeral: nothing short of imminent danger in her brother's state would bring her. She had for a long while been almost sole mistress of the household; Lady Dewsbury was ever her kind friend and protectress; and she could not reconcile it to her feelings to abandon the house while she lay dead in it, unless her brother's state absolutely demanded that she should. Lucy was to write, or telegraph, as necessity should require.

There was no immediate necessity for her to come, and Lucy wrote accordingly. Lucy stayed on alone with the invalid, shunning as much as was possible the presence of Travice, when he made his frequent visits: that presence which had hitherto been to her as a light from heaven. Mrs. Arkell, paying a ceremonious call of condolence one day, whispered to Lucy that Travice was becoming quite "reconciled," quite "fond" of Barbara Fauntleroy.

On the evening of the day after Lady Dewsbury was interred, Mildred arrived in Westerbury. Lucy did not know she was coming, and no one was at the station to meet her. Leaving her luggage to be sent after her, she made her way to her brother's house on foot: it was but a quarter of an hour's walk, and Mildred felt cramped with sitting in the train.

She trembled as she came in sight of it, the old home of her youth, fearing that its windows might be closed, as those had been in the house just quitted. As she stood before the door, waiting to be admitted, remembrances of her childhood came painfully across her—of her happy girlhood, when those blissful dreams of William Arkell were mingled with every thought of her existence.

"And oh! what did they end in!" she cried, clasping her hands tightly together and speaking aloud in her anguish. "What am I now? Chilled in feeling; worn in heart; old before my time."

A middle-aged woman, with a light in her hand, opened the door. Mildred stepped softly over the threshold.

"How is Mr. Arkell?"

The woman—she was the night nurse—stared at the handsomely attired strange lady, whose deep mourning looked so fresh and new, coming in that unceremonious manner at the night-hour.

"He is very ill, ma'am; nearly as bad as he can be," she replied, dropping a low curtsey. "What did you please to want?"

"He is in his old chamber, I suppose," said Mildred, turning towards the staircase. The woman, quite taken aback at this unceremonious proceeding, interposed her person.

"Goodness, ma'am, you can't go up to his chamber!" she cried out in amazement. "The poor gentleman's dying. I'll call Miss Lucy."

"I am Miss Arkell," said Mildred quietly, passing on up the staircase.

She laid aside her sombre bonnet, with its deep crape veil, her heavy shawl, and entered the chamber softly. Lucy was at a table, measuring some medicine into a tea-cup. A pale, handsome young man stood by the fire, his elbow resting on the mantel-piece. Mildred glanced at his face, and did not need to ask who he was.

Near the bed was Mr. William Arkell; but oh! how different from the lover of Mildred's youth! Now he was a grey-haired man, stooping slightly, looking older than his actual years—then tall, handsome, attractive, as Travice was now. And did William Arkell, at the first view, recognise his cousin? No. For that care-worn, middle-aged woman, whose hair was braided under a white net cap, bore little resemblance to the once happy Mildred Arkell. But the dying man, lying panting on the raised pillows, knew her instantaneously, and held out his feeble hands with a glad cry.

It was a painful meeting, and one into which we have little right to penetrate. Soon, very soon, Peter spoke out the one great care that was lying at his heart. He had not touched upon it till then.

"I am leaving my poor child alone in the world," he panted. "I know not who will afford her shelter—where she will find a home?"

"I would willingly promise you to take her to mine, Peter," said Mr. Arkell. "Poor Lucy should be as welcome to a shelter under my roof as are my own girls; but, heaven help me! I know not how long I may have a home for any of them."

"Leave Lucy to me, Peter," interposed Miss Arkell. "I shall make a home for myself now, and that home shall be Lucy's. Let no fear of her welfare disturb your peace."

Travice listened half resentfully. He was standing against the mantel-piece still, and Lucy, just then stirring something over the fire, was close to him.

"They need not think about a home for you, Lucy," he whispered, taking the one disengaged hand into his. "That shall be my care."

Lucy coldly drew her hand away. Her head was full of Barbara Fauntleroy—of the certainty that that lady would be his wife—for she believed no earthly event would be allowed to set aside the marriage: her spirit rebelled against the words. What right had he to breathe such to her—he, the engaged husband of another?

"I shall never have my home with you," she said, in the same low whisper. "Nothing should induce me to it."

"But, Lucy—"

"I will not hear you. You have no right so to speak to me. Aunt! aunt!"—and the tears gushed forth in all their bitter anguish—"let me find a home with you!"

Mildred turned and clasped fondly the appealing form as it approached her. Travice, hurt and resentful, quitted the room.

The death came, and then the funeral. A day or two afterwards, Mrs. Arkell condescended to pay a stately visit of ceremony to Mildred, who received her in the formerly almost-unused drawing-room. Lucy did not appear. Miss Arkell, her heart softened by grief, by much trial, was more cordial than perhaps she had ever been to Mrs. Arkell, before her marriage or after it.

"What a fine young man Travice is!" she observed, in a pause of their conversation.

"The finest in Westerbury," said Mrs. Arkell, with all the partiality of a mother. "I expect he will be thinking of getting married shortly."

"Of getting married! Travice! To whom? To Lucy?"

The question had broken from her in her surprise, in association with an idea that had for long and long floated through her brain—that Travice and Lucy were attached to each other. Mildred knew not whence it had its origin, unless it was in the frequent mention of Travice in Lucy's letters. Mrs. Arkell heard, and tossed her head indignantly.

"I beg your pardon, Miss Arkell—to Lucy, did you say? Travice would scarcely think of wedding a portionless bride, under present circumstances. You must have heard of the rich Fauntleroy girls? It is one of them."

Mildred—calm, composed, quiet Mildred—could very nearly have boxed her own ears. Never, perhaps, had she been more vexed with herself—never said an inadvertent thing that she so much wished recalled. How entirely Lucy was despised, Mrs. Arkell's manner and words proclaimed; and the fact carried its sting to Mildred's heart.

"I had no reason to put the question," she said, only caring how she could mend the matter; "I dare say Lucy would not thank me for the idea. Indeed, I should fancy her hopes may lie in quite a different direction. Young Palmer, the lawyer, the son of her father's old friend, has been here several times this past week, inquiring after our health. His motives may be more interested ones."

This was a little romance of Mildred's, called forth by the annoyance and vexation of the moment. It is true that Tom Palmer frequently did call; he and Lucy had been brought up more like brother and sister than anything else; but Miss Arkell had certainly no foundation for the supposition she had expressed. And Mrs. Arkell knew she could have none; but she chose to believe it.

"It would be a very good match for Lucy," she replied. "Tom Palmer has a fine practice for so young a man; there are whispers, too, that he will be made town-clerk whenever the vacancy occurs."

Home went Mrs. Arkell; and the first of the family she happened to come across was Travice.

"Travice, come to me for an instant," she said, taking his arm to pace the court-yard; "I have been hearing news at Peter Arkell's. Lucy's a sly girl; she might have told us, I think. She is engaged—but I don't know how long since. Perhaps only in these few days, since the funeral."

"Engaged in what?"

"To be married. She marries Tom Palmer."

"It is not true," broke forth Travice. "Who in the world has been telling you that falsehood?"

"Not true!" repeated Mrs. Arkell. "Why don't you say it is not true that I am talking to you—not true that this is Monday—not true that you are Travice Arkell? Upon my word! You are very polite, sir."

"Who told it you?" reiterated Travice.

"They told me. Mildred Arkell told me. I have been sitting there for the last hour, and we have been talking that and other affairs over. I can tell you what, Travice—it will be an excellent match for Lucy; a far superior one to anything she could have expected—and they seem to know it."

Even as she spoke, there shot a remembrance through Travice Arkell's heart, as an icebolt, of the night he had stood with Lucy in the chamber of her dying father, and her slighting words, in answer to his offer of a home: "I shall never have my home with you; nothing should induce me to it." She would not hear him; she told him he had no right so to speak to her. She had been singularly changed to him during the whole period of her father's illness; had shunned him by every means in her power; had been cold and distant when they were brought into contact. Before that, she was open and candid as the day. This fresh conduct had been altogether inexplicable to Travice, and he now asked himself whether it could have arisen from any engagement to marry Tom Palmer. If so, the change was in a degree accounted for; and it was certainly not impossible, if Tom Palmer had previously been wishing to woo her, that Mr. Peter Arkell, surprised by his dangerous illness, should have hurried matters to an engagement.

The more Travice Arkell reflected on this phase of probabilities, the more he became impressed with it: he grew to look upon it as a certainty; he felt that all chance for himself with Lucy was over. Could he blame her? As things were with him and his father, he saw no chance of his marrying her; and, in a worldly point of view, Lucy had done well—had done right. It's true he had never thought her worldly, and he had thought that she loved him; he believed that Tom Palmer had never been more to her than a wind that passes: but why should not Lucy have grown self-interested, as most other girls were? And to Travice it was pretty plain she had.

He grew to look upon it as a positive certainty; he believed, without a shadow of doubt, that it must be the fact: and how bitterly and resentfully he all at once hated Tom Palmer, that gentleman himself would have been surprised to find. It was only natural that Travice should feel it as a personal injury inflicted on himself—a slight, an insult; you all know, perhaps, what this feeling is: and in his temper he would not for some days go near Lucy. It was only when he heard the news that Mildred was returning to London, and would take her niece with her, that he came to his senses.

That same evening he took his way to the house. Mildred, it should be observed, was equally at cross-purposes. She hastened to speak to Lucy the day of Mrs. Arkell's visit, asking her if she had heard that Travice was engaged to Miss Fauntleroy; and Lucy answered after the manner of a reticent, self-possessed maiden, and made light of the thing, and was altogether a little hypocrite.

"Known that! O dear, yes! for some time," she said. "It would be a very good thing for Travice."

And so Mildred put aside any slight romance she had carved out for them, as wholly emanating from her imagination; but the sore feeling—that Lucy was despised by the mother, perhaps by the son—clung to her still.

She was sitting alone when Travice entered. He spoke for some time on indifferent subjects—of the news of the town; of her journey to London; of her future plans. They were to depart on the morrow.

"Where's Lucy?" he suddenly asked; and there was a restlessness in his manner throughout the interview that Mildred had never observed before.

"She is gone to spend the evening with Mrs. Palmer. I declined. Visiting seems quite out of my way now."

"I should have thought it would just now be out of Lucy's," spoke Travice, in a glow of resentment.

"Ordinary visiting would be," returned Miss Arkell, speaking with unnecessary coldness, and conscious of it. "Mrs. Palmer was here this afternoon; and, seeing how ill Lucy looked, she insisted on taking her home for an hour or two. Lucy will see no one there, except the family."

"What makes her look ill?"

Miss Arkell raised her eyes at the tone. "She is not really ill in body, I trust; but the loss of her father has been a bitter grief to her, and it is telling upon her spirits and looks. He was all she had in the world; for I—comparatively speaking—am a stranger."

There was a pause. Travice was leaning idly against the mantel-piece, in his favourite position, twirling the seals about that hung to his chain, his whole manner bespeaking indifference and almost contemptuous unconcern. Had anyone been there who knew him better than Mildred did, they could have told that it was only done to cover his real agitation. Mildred stole a glance at the fine young man, and thought that if he resembled his father in person, he scarcely resembled him in courtesy.

"Does Lucy really mean to have that precious fool of a Tom Palmer?" he abruptly asked.

Miss Arkell felt indignant. She wondered how he dared to speak in that way; and she answered sharply.

"Tom Palmer is a most superior young man. I have not perceived that he has any thing of the fool about him, and I don't think many others have. Whenever he marries, he will make an excellent husband. Why should you wish to set me against him? Let me urge you not to interfere with Lucy's affairs, Travice; she is under my protection now."

Oh, if Mildred could but have read Travice Arkell's heart that night!—if she had but read Lucy's! How different things might have been! Travice moved to shake hands with her.

"I must wish you good evening," he said. "I hope you and Lucy will have a pleasant journey to-morrow. We shall see you both again some time, I suppose."

He went out with the cold words upon his lips. He went out with the conviction, that Lucy was to marry Tom Palmer, irrevocably seated on his heart. And Travice Arkell thought the world was a miserable world, no longer worth living in.

CHAPTER XIII

THE TABLES TURNED

Mildred had to go back for a time to Lady Dewsbury's. That lady's house and effects now lapsed to Sir Edward; but Sir Edward was abroad with his wife and children, and he begged Miss Arkell to remain in it, its mistress, until they could return. This was convenient for Mildred's plans. It afforded a change of scene for Lucy; and it gave the opportunity and time for the house in Westerbury to be renovated; in which she intended now to take up her abode. The house was Mildred's now: it came to her on the death of her brother, their father having so settled it; but for this settlement, poor Peter had disposed of it in his necessities long ago.

Charlotte Arkell married, and departed with her husband, Captain Anderson, for India, taking Sophy with her. The paying over her marriage portion of a thousand pounds—a very poor portion beside what she once might have expected—further crippled the resources of Mr. Arkell; and things seemed to be coming to a crisis.

And Travice? Travice succumbed. Hardly caring what became of him, he allowed himself to be baited—badgered—by his mother into offering himself to one of the "great brazen milkmaids." From the hour of Lucy's departure from the city, she let him have no peace, no rest.

One day—and it was the last feather in the scale, the little balance necessary to weigh it down—Mr. Arkell summoned his son to a private interview. It was only what Travice had been expecting.

"Travice, what is your objection to Miss Fauntleroy?"

"I can't bear the sight of her," returned Travice, curling his lips contemptuously. "Can you, sir?"

Mr. Arkell smiled. "There are some who would call her a fine woman, Travice: she is one."

"A fine vulgar woman," corrected Travice, with a marked stress upon the word. "I always had an instinctive dread of vulgar people myself. I certainly never could have believed I should voluntarily ally myself with one."

"Never marry for looks, my boy," said Mr. Arkell in an eager whisper. "Some, who have done so before you, have awoke to find they had made a cruel mistake."

"Most likely, sir, if they married for looks alone."

Mr. Arkell glanced keenly at his son. "Travice, have I your full confidence? I wish you would give it me."

"In what way?" inquired Travice. "Why do you ask that?"

"Am I right in suspecting that you have cherished a different attachment?"

The tell-tale blood dyed Travice Arkell's brow. Mr. Arkell little needed other answer.

"My boy, let there be no secrets between us. You know that your welfare and happiness—your happiness, Travice—lie nearest to my heart. Have you learnt to love Lucy Arkell?"

"Yes," said Travice; and there was a whole world of pain in the simple answer.

"I thought so. I thought I saw the signs of it a long while ago; but, Travice, it would never do."

"You would object to her?"

"Object to her!—to Lucy!—to Peter's child! No. She is one of the sweetest girls living; I am not sure but I love her more than I do my own: and I wish she could be my real daughter and your wife. But it cannot be, Travice. There are impediments in the way, on her side and on yours; and your own sense must tell you this as well as I can."

He could not gainsay it. The impediments were all too present to Travice every hour of his life.

"You cannot take a portionless wife. Lucy has nothing now, or in prospect, beyond any little trifle that may come to her hereafter at Mildred's death; but I don't suppose Mildred can have saved much. It is said, too, that Lucy is likely to marry Tom Palmer."

"I know she is," bitterly acquiesced Travice.

"Lucy, then, for both these reasons, is out of the question. Have you not realized to your own mind the fact that she is?"

"Oh yes."

"Then, Travice, the matter resolves itself into a very small compass. It stands alone; it has no extraneous drawbacks; it can rest upon its own merits or demerits. Will you, or will you not, marry Miss Fauntleroy?"

Travice remained silent.

"It will be well for me that you should, for the temporary use of money that would then be yours would save us, as you know, from a ruinous loss; but, Travice, I would not, for the wealth of worlds, put that consideration against your happiness; but there is another consideration that I cannot put away from me, and that is, that the marriage will make you independent. For your sake, I should like to see you marry Miss Fauntleroy."

"She—"

"Wait one moment while I tell you why I speak. I do not think you are doing quite the right thing by Miss Fauntleroy, in thus, as it were, trifling with her. She expects you to propose to her, and you are keeping her in suspense unwarrantably long. You should either make her an offer, or let it be unmistakably known that there exists no such intention on your part. It would be a good thing in all ways, if you can only make up your mind to it; but do as you please: I do not urge you either way."

"I may as well do it," muttered Travice to himself. "She has chosen another, and it little matters what becomes of me: look which way I will, there's nothing but darkness. As well go through life with Bab Fauntleroy at my side, like an incubus, as go through it without her."

And Travice Arkell—as if he feared his resolution might desert him—went out forthwith and offered himself to Miss Fauntleroy. Never, surely, did any similar proposal betray so much hauteur, so much indifference, so little courtesy in the offering. Barbara happened to be alone; she was sitting in a white muslin dress, looking as big as a house, and waiting in state for any visitors who might call. He spoke out immediately. She probably knew, he said, that he was a sort of bankrupt in self, purse, and heart; little worth the acceptance of any one; but if she would like to take him, such as he was, he would try and do his duty by her.

The offer was really couched in those terms; and he did not take shame to himself as he spoke them. Travice Arkell could not be a hypocrite: he knew that the girl was aware of the state of things and of his indifference; he believed she saw through his love for Lucy; and he hated her with a sort of resentful hatred for having fixed her liking and her hopes upon him. He had been an indulged son all his life—a sort of fortune's pet—and the turn that things had taken was an awful blow.

"Will she say she'll have me?" he thought as he concluded. "I don't believe any other woman would." But Barbara Fauntleroy did say she would have him; and she put out her hand to him in her hearty good-natured way, and told him she thought they should get on very well together when once they had "shaken down." Travice touched the hand; he shook it in a gingerly manner, and then dropped it; but he never kissed her—he never said a warmer word than "thank you." Perhaps Miss Fauntleroy did not look for it: sentiment is little understood by these matter-of-fact, unrefined natures, with their loud voices, and their demonstrative temperaments. Travice would have to kiss her some time, he supposed; but he was content to put off the evil until that time came.

"How odd that you should have come and made me an offer this morning, Mr. Travice," she said, with a laugh. "Lizzie has just had one."

"Has she?" languidly returned Travice. His mind was so absorbed in the thought just mentioned, that he had no idea whether the lady meant an offer or a kiss that her sister had received, and he did not trouble himself to ask. It was quite the same to Travice Arkell.

"It's from Ben Carr," proceeded Miss Fauntleroy. "He came over here this morning, bringing a great big nosegay from their hot-house, and he made Liz an offer. Liz was taken all of a heap; and I think, but for me, she'd have said yes then."

"I dare say she would," returned Travice, and then wished the words recalled. They and their haughty tone had certainly been prompted by the remembrance of the "yes," just said to him by another.

"Liz came flying into the next room to me, asking what she should do; he was very pressing, she said, and wanted her answer then. I'm certain she'd have given it, Mr. Travice, if I had not been there to stop her. I went into the room with her to Ben Carr, and I said, 'Mr. Ben, Liz won't say anything decided now, but she'll think of it for a few days; if you'll look in on Saturday, she'll give you her answer, yes or no.' Ben Carr stared at me angry enough; but Liz backed up what I had said, and he had to take it."

"Does she mean to accept him?" asked Travice.

"Well, she's on the waver. She does not dislike him, and she does not particularly like him. He's too old for her; he's twenty years older than Liz; but it's her first offer, and young women are apt to think when they get that, they had better accept it, lest they may never get another."

"Your sister need not fear that. Her money will get her offers, if nothing else does."

He spoke in the impulse of the moment; but it occurred to him instantly that it was not generous to say it.

"Perhaps so," said Miss Fauntleroy. "But Lizzie and I have always dreaded that. We would like to be married for ourselves, not for our money. Sometimes we say in joke to one another we wish we could bury it, or could have passed ourselves off to the world as being poor until the day after we were married, and then surprised our husbands by the news, and made them a present of the money."

She spoke the truth; Travice knew she did. Whatever were the failings of the Miss Fauntleroys, genuine good nature was with both a pre-eminent virtue.

"Ben Carr is not the choice I should make," remarked Travice. "Of course, it's no business of mine."

"Nor I. I don't much like Ben Carr. Liz thinks him handsome. Well, she has got till Saturday to make up her mind—thanks to me."

Travice rose, and gingerly touched the hand again. The thought struck him again that he ought to kiss her; that he ought to put an engagement-ring on one of those fair and substantial fingers; ought to do many other things. But he went out, and did none of them.

"I'll not deceive her," he said to himself, as he walked down the street, more intensely wretched than he had ever in his life felt. "I'll not play the hypocrite; I couldn't do it if it were to save myself from hanging. She shall see my feeling for her exactly as it is, and then she'll not reproach me afterwards with coldness. It is impossible that I can ever like her; it seems to me now impossible that I can ever endure her; but if she does marry me in the face of such evident feelings, I'll do my best for her. Duty she shall have, but there'll be no love."

A very satisfactory state in prospective! Others, however, besides Travice Arkell, have married to enter on the same.

Some few months insensibly passed away in London for Miss Arkell and Lucy, and when they returned to Westerbury the earth was glowing with the tints of autumn. They did not return alone. Mrs. Dundyke, a real widow now beyond dispute, came with them. Poor David Dundyke, never quite himself after his return, never again indulging in the yearning for the civic chair, which had made the day-dream of his industrious life, had died calmly and peacefully, attended to the last by those loving hands that would fain have kept him, shattered though he was. He was lying now in Nunhead Cemetery, from whence he would certainly never be resuscitated as he had been from his supposed grave in Switzerland. Mrs. Dundyke grieved after him still, and Mildred pressed her to go back with them to Westerbury, for a little change. She consented gladly.

But Mrs. Dundyke did not go down in the humble fashion that she had once gone as Betsey Travice. She sent on her carriage and her two men servants. That there was a little natural feeling of retaliation in this, cannot be denied. Charlotte had despised her all her life; but she should at least no longer despise her on the score of poverty. "I shall do it," she said to Mildred, "and the carriage will be useful to us. It can be kept at an inn, with the horses and coachman; and John will be useful in helping your two maids."

It was late when they arrived at Westerbury; Miss Arkell did not number herself amid those who like to start upon a journey at daybreak; and Lucy looked twice to see whether the old house was really her home: it was so entirely renovated inside and out, as to create the doubt. Miss Arkell had given her private orders, saying nothing to Lucy, and the change was great. Various embellishments had been added; every part of it put into ornamental repair; a great deal of the furniture had been replaced by new; and, for its size, it was now one of the most charming residences in Westerbury.

"Do you like the change, Lucy?" asked Miss Arkell, when they had gone through the house together, with Mrs. Dundyke.

"Of course I do, Aunt Mildred;" but the answer was given in a somewhat apathetic tone, as Lucy mostly spoke now. "It must have cost a great deal."

"Well, is it not the better for it? I may not remain in Westerbury for good, and I could let my house to greater advantage now than I could have done before."

"That's true," listlessly answered Lucy.

"Lucy," suddenly exclaimed Miss Arkell, "what is it that makes you appear so dispirited? I could account for it after your father's death; it was only reasonable then; but it seems to me quite unreasonable that it should continue. I begin to think it must be your natural manner."

Lucy's heart gave a bound of something like terror at the question. "I was always quiet, aunt," she said.

None had looked on with more wonder at the expense being lavished on the house than Mrs. Arkell. "So absurd!" she exclaimed, loftily. "But Mildred Arkell was always pretentious, for a lady's maid."

William Arkell called to see Mildred the morning after her arrival. Very much surprised indeed, was he, to see also Mrs. Dundyke. He carried the news home to his wife.

"Betsey down here!" she answered. "Why, what has brought her?"

"She told me she had accompanied Mildred for a little change. She is coming in to see you by-and-by, Charlotte."

"I hope she's not coming begging!" tartly responded Mrs. Arkell.

"Begging?"

"Yes; begging. It's a question whether she's left with enough to live upon. I'm sure we have none to spare, for her or for anybody else; and so I shall plainly tell her if she attempts to ask."

That they had none to spare, was an indisputable fact. Mrs. Arkell had done all in her power to hurry the marriage on with Miss Fauntleroy, but Travice held back unpardonably. His cheek grew bright with hectic, his whole time was spent in what his mother called "moping;" and he entered but upon rare occasions the house of his bride elect. Mr. Arkell would not urge him by a single word; but, in the delay, he had had to sacrifice another remnant of his property.

The first use that Mrs. Dundyke put her carriage to in Westerbury, was that of going in it to William Arkell's. Mildred declined to accompany her, and Lucy was obliged to go with her; Lucy, who would have given the whole world not to go. But she could not say so.

Mrs. Arkell was in the dining-room, when the carriage drove in at the court-yard gates. She wondered whose it was. A nice close carriage, the servants attending it in mourning. She did not recognise it as one she knew.

She heard the visitors shown into the drawing-room, and waited for the cards with some curiosity. But no cards came in. Mrs. Dundyke, the servant brought word, and she was with Miss Lucy Arkell.

Mrs. Dundyke! Wondering what on earth brought Betsey in that carriage, and where she had picked it up, Mrs. Arkell took a closer view of it through the window. It was too good a carriage to be anything but a private one, and those horses were never hired; and there were the servants. She looked at the crest. But it was not a crest. Only an enclosed cipher, D.D.

It did not lessen her curiosity, and she went to the drawing-room, wondering still; but she never once glanced at the possibility that it could be Mrs. Dundyke's; the thought occurred to her that it must belong to some member of the Dewsbury family, and had been lent to Mildred.

It was a stiff meeting. Mrs. Arkell, fully imbued with the persuasion that her sister was left badly off, that she was the same poor sister of other days, was less cordial than she might have been. She shook hands with her sister; she shook hands with Lucy; but in her manner there was a restraint that told. They spoke of general subjects, of Mr. Dundyke's strange adventure in Switzerland, and his subsequent real death; of Lucy's sojourn in London; of Charlotte's recent marriage; of the departure of Sophy with her for India—just, in fact, as might have been the case with ordinary guests.

"Travice is soon to be married, I hear," said Mrs. Dundyke.

"Yes; but he holds back unpardonably."

Had Mrs. Arkell not been thinking of something else, she had never given that tart, but true answer. She happened just then to be calculating the cost of Mrs. Dundyke's handsome mourning, and wondering how she got it.

"Why does he hold back?" quickly asked Mrs. Dundyke.

"Oh, I don't know," said Mrs. Arkell, with a gay, slighting laugh. "I suppose young men like to retain their bachelor liberty as long as they can. Does your aunt purpose to settle down in Westerbury, Lucy?"

"For the present."

"Does she think of going out again?"

"Oh no."

"Perhaps she has saved enough to keep herself without? She could not expect to find another such place as Lady Dewsbury's."

It was not a pleasant visit, and Mrs. Dundyke did not prolong it. As they were going out they met Travice.

"Oh, Aunt Betsey! How glad I am to see you!"

But he turned coldly enough to shake hands with Lucy. He cherished resentment against her in his heart. She saw he did not look well; but she was cold as he was. As he walked across the hall with his aunt, Mrs. Arkell drew Lucy back into the drawing-room. Her curiosity had been on the rack all the time.

"Whose carriage is that, Lucy? One belonging to the Dewsburys'?"

"It is Mrs. Dundyke's."

"Mrs.—what did you say? I asked whose carriage that is that you came in," added Mrs. Arkell, believing that Lucy had not heard aright.

"Yes, I understood. It is Mrs. Dundyke's. She sent it on, the day before yesterday, with her servants and horses."

"But—does—she—keep a carnage and servants?" reiterated Mrs. Arkell, hardly able to bring out the words in her perplexed amazement.

"Oh, yes."

"Then she must be left well off?"

"Very well. She is very rich. I believe her income is close upon two thousand a year."

"Two thou—" Mrs. Arkell wound up with a shriek of astonishment. Lucy had to leave her to recover it in the best way she could, for Mrs. Dundyke had got into the carriage and was waiting for her.

The poor, humble Betsey, whom she had so despised and slighted through life! Come to this fortune! While hers and her husband's was going down. How the tables were turned!

Yes, Mrs. Arkell. Tables always are on the turn in this life.

CHAPTER XIV

A RECOGNITION

When the first vexation was overcome, the most prominent thought that remained to Mrs. Arkell was, what a fool she had been, not to treat Betsey better—one never knew what would turn up. All that could be done was, to begin to treat her well now: but it required diplomacy.

Mrs. Arkell began by being gracious to Mildred, by being quite motherly in her behaviour to Lucy; this took her often to Miss Arkell's, and consequently into the society of Mrs. Dundyke. Sisterly affection must not be displayed all at once; it should come by degrees.

As a preliminary, Mrs. Arkell introduced to her sister and Mildred as many of her influential friends in Westerbury as she could prevail upon them to receive. This was not many. Gentle at heart as both were, neither of them felt inclined to be patronized by Mrs. Arkell now, after her lifetime of neglect. They therefore declined the introductions, allowing an exception only in the persons of the Miss Fauntleroys, who were so soon, through the marriage of Travice and Barbara, to be allied to the family. Mrs. Dundyke was glad to renew her acquaintance with Mr. Prattleton and his daughter.

Both the Miss Fauntleroys were making preparations for their marriage, for the younger one had accepted Mr. Benjamin Carr. The old squire, so fond of money, was in an ecstacy at the match his fortunate son was going to make, and Ben had just now taken a run up to Birmingham to look at some furniture he had seen advertised. Ben had a good deal of the rover in his nature still, and was glad of an excuse for taking a run anywhere.

The Miss Fauntleroys grew rather intimate at Mildred's. Their bouncing forms and broad good-natured faces, were often to be seen at the door. They began rather to be liked there; their vulgarity lessened with custom, their well-meaning good humour won its own way. They invited Miss Arkell, her niece, and guest, to spend a long afternoon with them and help them with some plain work they were doing for the poor sewing-club—for they were adepts in useful sewing, were the Miss Fauntleroys—and to remain to dinner afterwards. Lucy would have given the whole world to refuse: but she had no ready plea; and she had not the courage to make one. So she went with the rest.

She was sitting at one of the windows of the large drawing-room with Lizzie Fauntleroy, both of them at work at the same article, a child's frock, when Travice Arkell entered. Lucy's was the first face he saw: and so entirely unexpected was the sight of it to him, that, for once in his life, he nearly lost his self-possession. No wonder; with the consciousness upon him of the tardy errand that had taken him there—that of asking his future bride to appoint a time for their union. Once more Mr. Arkell had spoken to his son: "You must not continue to act in this way, Travice; it is not right; it is not manly. Marry Miss Fauntleroy, or give her up; do which you decide to do, but it must be one or the other." And he came straight from the conference, as he had on the former occasion, to ask her when the wedding day should be. He could not sully his honour by choosing the other alternative.

A hesitating pause, he looking like one who has been caught in some guilty act, and then he walked on and shook hands with Miss Fauntleroy. He shook hands with them all in succession; with Lucy last: that is, he touched the tips of her fingers, turning his conscious face the other way.

"Have you brought me any message from Mrs. Arkell?" asked Miss Fauntleroy, for it was so unusual a thing for Travice to call in the day that she concluded he had come for some specific purpose.

"No. I—I came to speak to you myself," he answered. And his words were so hesitating, his manner so uncertain, that they looked at him in surprise; he who was usually self-possessed to a fault. Miss Fauntleroy rose and left the room with him.

She came back in about a quarter of an hour, giggling, laughing, her face more flushed than ordinary, her manner inviting inquiry. Lizzie Fauntleroy, with one of those unladylike, broad allusions she was given to use, said to the company that by the looks of Bab, she should think Mr. Travice Arkell had been asking her to name the day. There ensued a loud laugh on Barbara's part, some skirmishing with her sister, and then a tacit acknowledgment that the surmise was correct, and that she had named it. Lucy sat perfectly still: her head apparently as intent upon her work as were her hands.

"Liz may as well name it for herself," retorted Barbara. "Ben Carr has wanted her to do it before now."

"There's no hurry," said Lizzie. "For me, at any rate. When one's going to marry a man so much older than oneself, one is apt not to be over ardent for it."

They continued to work, an industrious party. Accidentally, as it seemed, the conversation turned upon the strange events which had occurred at Geneva: it was through Mrs. Dundyke's mentioning some embroidery she had just given to Mary Prattleton. The Miss Fauntleroys, who had only, as they phrased it, heard the story at second-hand, besought her to tell it to them. And she complied with the request.

They suspended their work as they listened. It is probable that not a single incident was mentioned that the Miss Fauntleroys had not heard before; but the circumstances altogether were of that nature that bear hearing—ay, and telling—over and over again, as most mysteries do. Their chief curiosity turned— it was only natural it should—on Mr. Hardcastle, and they asked a great many questions.

"I would have scoured the whole country but what I'd have found him," cried Barbara. "Genoa! Rely upon it, he and his wife turned their faces in just the contrary direction as soon as they left Geneva. A nice pair."

"Do you think," asked Lucy, in her quiet manner, raising her eyes to Mrs. Dundyke, "that Mr. Hardcastle followed him for the purpose of attacking and robbing him?"

"Ah, my dear, I cannot tell. It is a question that I often ask myself. I feel inclined to think that he did not. One thing I seem nearly sure of—that he did not intend to injure him. I have not the least doubt that Mr. Hardcastle was at his wit's end for money to pay his hotel bill, and that the thirty pounds my poor husband mentioned as having received that morning, was an almost irresistible temptation. There's no doubt he followed him to the borders of the lake; that he induced him, by some argument, to walk away with him, across the country; but whether he did this with the intention of—"

"Did Mr. Dundyke not clear this up after his return?" interrupted Lizzie Fauntleroy.

"Never clearly; his recollections remained so confused. I have thought at times, that the crime only came with the opportunity," continued Mrs. Dundyke, reverting to what she was saying. "It is possible that the heat of the day and the long walk, though why Mr. Hardcastle should have caused him to take that long walk, unless he had ulterior designs, I cannot tell—may have overpowered my husband with a faintness, and Mr. Hardcastle seized the opportunity to rifle his pocket-book."

"You seem to be more lenient in your judgment of Mr. Hardcastle than I should be," observed Lizzie Fauntleroy.

"I have thought of it so long and so often, that I believe I have grown to judge of the past impartially," was Mrs. Dundyke's answer. "At first I was very much incensed against the man; I am not sure but I thought hanging too good for him; but I grew by degrees to look at it more reasonably."

"And the pencil?"

"He must have taken it from the pocket-book in his hurry, when he took the money. That he did it all in haste, the not finding the two half-notes for fifty pounds proves."

"Suppose Mr. Dundyke had returned to Geneva the next day and confronted him. What then?"

"Ah, I don't know. Mr. Hardcastle relied, perhaps, upon being able to make good his own story, and he knew that David had the most unbounded faith in him."

"Well, take it in its best light—that Mr. Dundyke fainted from the heat of the sun—the man must have been a brute to leave him alone," concluded Lizzie Fauntleroy.

"Yes," was the answer, as a faint colour rose to Mrs. Dundyke's cheek; "that I can never forgive."

The afternoon and the work progressed satisfactorily, and dinner time arrived. Miss Fauntleroy had invited Travice to come and partake of it, but he said he had an engagement—which she did not half believe. The nearly bed-ridden old aunt came down to it, and was propped up to the table in an invalid chair. Miss Fauntleroy took the head; Miss Lizzie the foot. It was a well-spread board: Lawyer Fauntleroy's daughters liked good dinners. Their manners were more free at home than abroad, rather scaring Mildred. "How could Travice have chosen here?" she mentally asked.

"There's no gentlemen present, so I don't see why I should not give you a toast," suddenly exclaimed Lizzie Fauntleroy, as the servant was pouring out the first glass of champagne. "The bridegroom and bride elect. Mr. Travice Ar—"

Lizzie stopped in surprise. Peeping in at the door, in a half-jocular, half-deprecatory manner, as if he would ask pardon for entering at the unseasonable hour, was Mr. Benjamin Carr. His somewhat dusty appearance, and his over-coat on his arm, showed that he had then come from the station after his Birmingham journey. Lizzie, too hearty to be troubled with superfluous reticence or ceremony of any kind, started up with a shout of welcome.

Of course everything was dis-arranged. The visitors looked up with surprise; Barbara turned round and gave him her hand. Ben began an apology for sitting down in the state he was, and had handed his coat to a servant, when he found a firm hand laid upon his arm. He wheeled round, wondering who it was, and saw a widow's cap, and a face he did not in the first moment recognise.

"Mr. Hardcastle!"

With the words, the voice, the recognition came to him, and the past scenes at Geneva rose before his startled memory as a vivid dream. He might have brazened it out had he been taken less utterly by surprise, but that unnerved him: his face turned ashy white, his whole manner faltered. He looked to the door as if he would have bolted out of it; but somebody had closed it again.

Mrs. Dundyke turned her face to the amazed listeners, who had risen from their seats. But that it had lost its colour also, there was no trace in it of agitation: it was firm, rigid, earnest; and her voice was calm even to solemnity.

"Before heaven, I assert that this is the man who in Geneva called himself Mr. Hardcastle, who did that injury—much or little, he best knows—to my husband! He—"

"But this is Benjamin Carr!" interrupted the wondering Miss Fauntleroy.

"Yes; just so; Benjamin Carr," assented Mrs. Dundyke, in a tone that seemed to say she expected the words. "I recognised you, Benjamin Carr, on the last day of your stay in Geneva, when you were giving me that false order on Leadenhall Street. From the moment I first saw you, the morning after we arrived at Geneva, your eyes puzzled me. I knew I had seen them somewhere before, and I told my poor husband so; but I could not recollect where. In the hour of your leaving, the recollection came to me; and I knew that the eyes were those of Benjamin Carr, or eyes precisely similar to his. I thought it must be the latter; I could not suppose that Squire Carr's son, a gentleman born and reared—"

But here a startling interruption intervened. It suddenly occurred to Miss Lizzie Fauntleroy, amidst the general confusion outward and inward, that the Mr. Hardcastle who had figured in the dark and disgraceful story, was said to have been accompanied by a wife. Considering that he was now designing to confer that honour upon her, the reflection was not agreeable. Miss Lizzie came to a hasty conclusion, that the real Mrs. Carr must be lying perdue somewhere, while he prosecuted his designs upon herself and her money, conveniently ignoring the result of what he might be running his head wholesale into—a prosecution for bigamy. She went butting at him, her voice raised to a shriek, her nails out, alarmingly near to his face.

"You false, desperate, designing villain! You dare to come courting me as a single man! You nearly drew me into a marriage! Where's your wife? Where's your wife, villain?"

This charge was a mistaken one, and Ben Carr somewhat rallied his scared senses. "It is false," he said. "I swear on my honour that I have no wife; I swear that I never have had one."

"You had your wife with you in Geneva," said Mrs. Dundyke.

"She was not my wife. Lizzie Fauntleroy, can't you believe me? I have never married yet. I never thought of marrying until I saw you."

"It's all the same now," said Lizzie, with equanimity. "I don't like tricks played me. Better that I should have discovered this before marriage than after."

"It is false, on my honour. You will not allow it to make any difference to our—"

"Not allow it to make any difference," interposed Lizzie, imperiously cutting short his words. "Do you take me for a fool, Ben Carr? You've seen the last of me, I can tell you that; and if pa were living still, he should prosecute you for getting my consent to a marriage under false pretences."

"If I do not prosecute you, Benjamin Carr," resumed Mrs. Dundyke, "you owe it partly to my consideration for your family, partly to the unhappy fact that it could not bring my poor husband back to life. It could not restore to him the mental power he lost, the faculties that were destroyed. It could not bring back to me my lost happiness. How far you may have been guilty, I know not. It must rest with your conscience, and so shall your punishment."

He stood something like a stag at bay—half doubting whether to slink away, whether to turn and beard his pursuers. Barbara Fauntleroy threw wide the door.

"You had better quit us, I think, Mr. Carr."

"I see what it is," said he, at length, to the Miss Fauntleroys. "You are just now too prejudiced to listen to reason. The tale that woman has been telling you of me is a mistaken one; and when you are calm, I will endeavour to convince you of it."

"Calm, man!" cried Barbara, with a laugh. "I'm calm enough. It isn't such an interlude, as this, that could take any calmness away from me. It has been as good to me as a scene at the play."

But the gentleman did not wait to hear the conclusion. He had escaped through the open door. Those left stared at one another.

"Come along," said Lizzie, with unruffled composure; "don't let the dinner get colder than it is. I dare say I'm well rid of him. Where's our glasses of champagne? A drop will do us all good. Oh dear, Mrs. Dundyke! Pray don't suffer it to trouble you!"

She had sat down in a far corner, poor woman, with her face hidden, drowned in a storm of silent tears.

The event, quickly though it had transpired—over, as it were, in a moment—exercised a powerful influence on the spirits of Mrs. Dundyke. It brought the old trouble so vividly before her, that she could not rally again as the days went on; and she told Mildred that she should go back to London, but would come to her again at a future time. The resolution was a sudden one. Mrs. Arkell happened to call the same day, and was told of it.

"Going back to London to-morrow!" repeated Mrs. Arkell in consternation; and she hastened to her sister's room.

Mrs. Dundyke had her drawers all out, and her travelling trunk open, beginning to put things together. Mrs. Arkell went in, and closed the door.

"Betsey, you are going back, I hear; therefore I must at once ask the question that I have been intending to ask before your departure. It may sound to you somewhat premature: I don't know. Will you forget and forgive?"

"Forget and forgive what?"

"My coldness during the past years."

"I am willing to forgive it, Charlotte, if that will do you any good. To forget it is an impossibility."

Mrs. Dundyke spoke with civil indifference. She was wrapping different toilet articles in paper, and she continued her occupation. Mrs. Arkell, in a state of bitter vexation at the turn things had taken, terribly self-repentant that she should have pursued a line of conduct so inimical to her own interests, sat down on a low chair, and fairly burst into tears.

"Why, what's the matter, Charlotte?"

"You are a rich woman now, and therefore you despise us. We are growing poor."

"How can you talk such nonsense!" exclaimed Mrs. Dundyke, screwing down the silver stopper of a scent-bottle. "If I became as rich and as grand as a duke, it could never cause me to make the slightest difference in my conduct to anybody, high or low."

"Our intercourse has been so cold, so estranged, during this visit!"

"And, but that you find I am a little better off than you thought for, would you have allowed it to be otherwise than cold and estranged?" returned Mrs. Dundyke, putting down the scent-bottle, and facing her sister.

There was no reply. What, indeed, could there be?

"Charlotte," said Mrs. Dundyke, dropping her voice to earnestness, as she went close to her sister, "the past wore me out. Ask yourself what your treatment of me was—for years, and years, and years. You know how I loved you—how I tried to conciliate you by every means in my power—to be to you a sister; and you would not. You threw my affection back upon myself; you prevented Mr. Arkell and your children coming to me; you heaped unnecessary scorn upon my husband. I bore it; I strove against it; but my patience and my love gave way at last, and I am sorry to say resentment grew in its place. Those feelings of affection, worn out by slow degrees, can never grow again."

"It is as much as to say that you hate me!"

"Not so. We can be civil when we meet; and that can be as often as circumstances bring us into the same locality. But I do not think there can ever be cordiality between us again."

"I had thought you were of a forgiving disposition, Betsey."

"So I am."

"I had thought—" Mrs. Arkell paused a moment, as if half ashamed of what she was about to say—"I had thought to enlist your sisterly feelings for me; that is, for my daughters. You are rich now; you have plenty of money to spare; and their patrimony has dwindled down to nothing—nothing compared to what it ought to have been. They—"

"Stay, Charlotte. We may as well come to an understanding on this point at once; it will serve for always. Your daughters have never condescended to recognise me in their lives; it was perhaps your fault, perhaps theirs: I don't know. But the effect upon me has not been a pleasant one. I shall decline to help them."

Mrs. Arkell's proud spirit was rising. What it had cost thus to bend herself to her life-despised sister, she alone knew. She beat her foot upon the hearth-rug.

"I don't know how they'll get along. But for Mr. Arkell's having kept on the business for Travice, we should be rich still. He has always been a fool in some things."

"Don't disparage your husband before me, Charlotte; I shall not listen calmly; you were never worthy of him. I love Mr. Arkell for his goodness, and I love your son. If you asked me for help for Travice, you should have it; never for your daughters."

"Very kind, I'm sure! when you know he does not want it," was the provoking and angry answer. "Travice is placed above requiring your help, by marriage with Miss Fauntleroy."

And Mrs. Arkell gave her head a scornful toss as she went out, and banged the chamber-door after her.

CHAPTER XV

MILDRED'S RECOMPENSE

The consent of Travice once obtained, the necessary word spoken to Miss Fauntleroy, Mrs. Arkell hurried the marriage on in earnest. So long as Travice had only made the offer, and given no signs of wishing for the ceremony to take place, not much could be done; but he had now said to Barbara, "Fix your own day."

There was no trouble needed in regard to a house; at least, there had not hitherto been. The house that the Miss Fauntleroys lived in was their own, and Barbara wished to continue in it. It was supposed that her sister would be moving to a farm in the parish of Eckford. That was now frustrated. "Never mind," said Barbara, in her easy way, "Lizzie can stop on with us; Travice won't mind it, and I shall like it. If we find afterwards that it does not answer, different arrangements can be made."

The Miss Fauntleroys were generous in the matter of Benjamin Carr. Those others who had been present were generous, even Mrs. Dundyke. The identification of the gentleman with the Mr. Hardcastle, of Geneva memory, was not allowed to transpire: they all had regard to the feelings of the squire and his family. It was fortunate that the only servant in the room had gone from it with Benjamin Carr's over-coat, and Barbara had had the presence of mind to slip the bolt of the door. Mr. Ben Carr, however, thought it well to take a tour just at this time, and he did not show his face in Westerbury previous to his departure.

Lucy Arkell was solicited to be one of the bridesmaids; but Lucy declined. Mildred remembered a wedding which she had declined to attend as bridesmaid. How little, how little did she think that the same cruel pain was swaying the motives of Lucy!

Lucy and her aunt saw but little now of the Arkells. Travice never called; Mr. Arkell, full of trouble, confined himself to his home; and Mrs. Arkell had not entered the house since the rebuff given her by Mrs. Dundyke. Lucy held aloof from them; and Mildred certainly did not go there of her own accord. It therefore came to pass that they heard little news of the doings there, except what might be dropped by chance callers-in.

And now, as if Mildred had really been gifted with prevision, Tom Palmer made an offer of his hand and heart to Lucy. Lucy's response was by no means a dignified one—she burst out crying. Mildred, in surprise, asked what was the matter, and Lucy said she had not thought her old friend Tom could have been so unkind. Unkind! But the result was, that Lucy refused him in the most positive manner, then and for always. Mildred began to think that she could not understand Lucy.

There was a grand party given one night at Mrs. Arkell's, and they went to that. Mildred accepted the invitation without consulting Lucy. The Palmers were there; and Travice treated Tom very cavalierly. In fact, that word is an appropriate one to characterise his general behaviour to everybody throughout the evening. And, so far as anybody saw, he never once went near Miss Fauntleroy, with the exception that he took her into the supper room. Mr. Arkell did not appear until quite late in the evening. It was said he had an engagement. So he had, with men of business; while the revelry was going on in doors, he was in his counting-house, endeavouring to negotiate for a loan of money, in which he was not successful. Little heart had he at ten o'clock to go in and dress himself and enter upon that scene of gaiety. Mildred exchanged but a few sentences with him, but she thought he was in remarkably low spirits.

"Are you not well, William?" she asked.

"I have a headache, Mildred."

It was a day or two after this, and but a few days previous to the completion of the wedding, when unpleasant rumours, touching the solvency of the good old house of George Arkell and Son, reached the ears of Miss Arkell. They were whispered to her by Mr. Palmer, the old friend of the family.

"It is said their names will be in the Gazette the day after to-morrow, unless some foreign help can come to them."

Miss Arkell sat, deeply shocked; and poor Lucy's colour went and came, showing the effect the news had upon her.

"I had no idea that they were in embarrassment," said Mildred.

"It is so. You see, this wedding of young Travice Arkell's, that is to bring so much money into the family, has been delayed too long," observed Mr. Palmer. "It is said now that Travice, poor fellow, has an unconquerable antipathy to his bride, and though he consented to the alliance to save his family, he has been unable to bring his mind to conclude it. While the grass grows, the steed starves, you know."

"Miss Fauntleroy was willing that her money should be sacrificed."

"It would not have been sacrificed, not a penny of it; but the use of it would have enabled the house to redeem its own money, and bring its affairs to a satisfactory close. Had there been any risk to the money, William Arkell would not have agreed to touch it: you know his honourable nature. However, through the protracted delay—which Travice will no doubt reflect sharply upon himself for—the marriage and the money will come too late to save them."

Mr. Palmer departed, and Lucy sat like one in a dream. Her aunt glanced at her, and mused, and glanced again. "What are you thinking of, Lucy?" she asked.

Lucy burst into tears. "Aunt, I was thinking what a blight it is to be poor! If I had thousands, I would willingly devote them all to save Mr. Arkell. Papa told me, when he lay dying, how his cousin William had helped him from time to time; had saved his home more than once; and had never been paid back again."

"And suppose you had money—attend to me, Lucy, for I wish a serious answer—suppose you were in possession of money, would you be really willing to sacrifice a portion of it, to save this good friend, William Arkell?"

"All, aunt, all!" she answered, eagerly, "and think it no sacrifice."

"Then put on your bonnet, Lucy, child," returned Miss Arkell, "and come with me."

They went forth to the house of Mr. Arkell; and as it turned out, the visit was opportune, for Mrs. Arkell was away, dining from home. Mr. Arkell was in a little back parlour, looking over accounts and papers, with his son. The old man—and he was looking an old man that evening, with trouble, not with years—rose in surprise when he saw who were his visitors, and Travice's hectic colour went and came. Mildred had never been in the room since she was a young woman, and it called up painful recollections. It was the twilight hour of the evening: that best hour, of all the twenty-four, for any embarrassing communication.

"William," began Miss Arkell, seating herself by her cousin, and speaking in a low tone, "we have heard it whispered that your affairs are temporarily involved. Is it so?"

"The world will soon know it, Mildred, above a whisper."

"It is even so then! What has led to it?"

"Oh, Mildred! can you ask what has led to it, when you look at the misery and distress everywhere around us? Search the Gazette for the past years, and see how many names you will find in it, who once stood as high as ours! The only wonder is, that we have not yet gone with the stream. It is a hard case, Mildred, when we have toiled all our lives, that the labour should come to nothing at last," he continued; "that our closing years, which ought to be given to thoughts of another world, must be distracted with the anxious cares of this."

"Is your difficulty serious, or only temporary?" resumed Miss Arkell.

"It ought to be only temporary," he replied; "but the worst is, I cannot, at the present moment, command my resources. We have kept on manufacturing, hoping for better times; and, to tell you the truth, Mildred, I could not reconcile it to my conscience to turn off my old workmen to beggary. There was Travice, too. I have a heavy stock of goods on hand; to the amount of some thousands; and this locks up my diminished capital. I am still worth what would cover my business liabilities twice over—and

I have no others—but I cannot avail myself of it for present emergencies. I have turned every stone, Mildred, to keep my head above water: and I believe I can struggle no longer."

"What amount of money would effectually relieve you?" asked Miss Arkell.

"About three thousand pounds," he replied, answering the question without any apparent interest.

"Then to-morrow morning vouchers for that sum shall be placed in the Westerbury bank at your disposal. And for double that sum, if you require it."

Mr. Arkell looked up in astonishment; and finally addressed to her the very words which he had once before done, in early life, upon a far different subject.

"You are dreaming, Mildred!"

She remembered them; had she ever forgotten one word said to her on that eventful night? and sighed as she replied:

"This money is mine. I enjoyed, as you know, a most liberal salary for seven or eight-and-twenty years; and the money, as it came in, was placed out from the first to good interest; later, a part of it to good use. Lady Dewsbury also bequeathed me a munificent sum by her will; so that altogether I am worth—"

His excessive surprise could not let her continue. That Mildred had saved just sufficient to live upon, he had deemed probable; but not more. She had been always assisting Peter. He interrupted her with words to this effect.

Mildred smiled. "I could place at your disposal twelve thousand pounds, if needs must," she said. "I had a friend who helped me to lay out my money to advantage. It was Mr. Dundyke. William, how can I better use part of this money than by serving you?"

William Arkell shook his head in deprecation. Not all at once, in the suddenness of the surprise, could he accept the idea of being assisted by Mildred. Peter had taken enough from her.

"Peter did not take enough from me," she firmly said. "It is only since Peter's death that I have learnt how straitened he always was—he kept it from me. I have been taking great blame to myself, for it seems to me that I ought to have guessed it—and I did not. But Peter is gone, and you are left. Oh, William, let me help you!"

"Mildred, I have no right to it from you."

She laid her hand upon his arm in her eagerness. She bent her gentle face, with its still sweet expression, near to him, and spoke in a whisper.

"Let me help you. It will be a recompense for the past pain of my lonely life."

His eyes looked straight into hers for the moment. "I have had my pain, too, Mildred."

"But this loan? you will take it. Lucy, speak up," added Miss Arkell, turning to her niece. "This money is willed to you, and will be yours sometime. Is it not at your wish that I come this evening, as well as at my own?"

"Oh, sir," sobbed Lucy to Mr. Arkell, "take it all. Let my aunt retain what will be sufficient for her life, but keep none for me; I am young and healthy, and can go out and work for my living, as she has done. Take all the rest, and save the credit of the family."

William Arkell turned to Lucy, the tears trickling down his cheeks. She had taken off her bonnet on entering, and he laid his hand fondly on her head.

"Lucy, child, were this money exclusively your aunt's, I would not hesitate to make use of sufficient of it now to save my good name. In that ease, I should wind up my affairs as soon as would be conveniently possible, retire from business, and see how far what is left to me would go towards a living. It would be enough; and my wife would have to bring her mind to think it so. But this sum that your aunt offers me—that you second—may be the very money she has been intending to hand over with you as a marriage portion. And what would your husband say at its being thus temporarily appropriated?"

"My husband!" exclaimed Lucy, in amazement; "a marriage portion for me! When I take the one, it will be time enough to think of the other." Miss Arkell, too, looked up with a questioning gaze, for she had quite forgotten the little romance—her romance—concerning young Mr. Palmer.

"I shall never marry," continued Lucy, in answer to Mr. Arkell's puzzled look. "I think I am better as I am."

"But, Lucy, you are going to marry. You are going to marry Tom Palmer."

Lucy laughed. She could not help it, she said, apologetically. She had laughed ever since he asked her, except just at the time, at the very idea of her marrying Tom Palmer, the little friend of her girlhood. Tom laughed at it himself now; and they were as good friends as before. "But how did you hear of it?" she exclaimed.

Travice came forward, his cheek pale, his lip quivering. He laid his fevered hand on Lucy's shoulder.

"Is this true, Lucy?" he whispered. "Is it true that you do not love Tom Palmer?"

"Love him!" cried Lucy, indignantly, sad reproach in her eye, as she turned it on Travice. "You have seen us together hundreds of times; did you ever detect anything in my manner to induce you to think I 'loved' him?"

"I loved you," murmured Travice, for he read that reproach aright, and the scales which had obscured his eyes fell from them, as by magic. "I have long loved you—deeply, passionately. My brightest hopes were fixed on you; the heyday visions of all my future existence represented you by my side, my wife. But these misfortunes and losses came thick and fast upon my father. They told me at home here, he told me, that I was poor and that you were poor, and that it would be madness in us to think of marrying then, as it would have been. So I said to myself that I would be patient, and wait—would be content with loving you in secret, as I had done—with seeing you daily as a relative. And then the news burst upon me that you were to marry Tom Palmer; and I thought what a fool I had been to fancy you cared for me; for I knew that you were not one to marry where you did not love."

The tears were coursing down her cheeks. "But I don't understand," she said. "It is but just, as it were, that Tom has asked me; and you must be speaking of sometime ago."

The fault was Mildred's. Not quite all at once could they understand it; not until later.

"I shall never marry; indeed I shall never marry," murmured Lucy, as she yielded for the moment to the passionate embrace in which Travice clasped her, and kissed away her tears of anguish. "My lot in life must be like my aunt's now, unloving and unloved."

"Oh, is there no escape for us!" exclaimed Travice, wildly, as all the painful embarrassment of his position rushed over his mind. "Can we not fly together, Lucy—fly to some remote desert place, and leave care and sorrow behind us? Ere the lapse of many days, another woman expects to be my wife! Is there no way of escape for us?"

None; none. The misery of Travice Arkell and his cousin was sealed: their prospects, so far as this world went, were blighted. There were no means by which he could escape the marriage that was rushing on to him with the speed of wings: no means known in the code of honour. And for Lucy, what was left but to live on unwedded, burying her crushed affections within herself, as her aunt had done?—live on, and, by the help of time, strive to subdue that love which was burning in her heart for the husband of another, rendering every moment of the years that would pass, one continued, silent agony!

"The same fate—the same fate!" moaned Mildred Arkell to herself, whilst Lucy sunk into a chair and covered her pale face with her trembling hands. "I might have guessed it! Like aunt, like niece. She must go through life as I have done—and bear—and bear! Strange, that the younger brother's family, throughout two generations, should have cast their shadow for evil upon that of the elder! A blight must have fallen upon my father's race; but, perhaps in mercy, Lucy is the last of it. If I could have foreseen this, years ago, the same atmosphere in which lived Travice Arkell should not have been breathed by Lucy. The same fate! the same fate!"

Lucy was sobbing silently behind her hands. Travice stood, the image of despair. Mildred turned to him.

"Then you do not love Miss Fauntleroy?"

"Love her! I hate her!" was the answer that burst from him in his misery. "May Heaven forgive me for the false part I shall have to play!"

But there was no escape for him. Mildred knew there was not; Mr. Arkell knew it; and his heart ached for the fate of this, his dearly-loved son.

"My boy," he said, "I would willingly die to save you—die to secure your happiness. I did not know this sacrifice was so very bitter."

Travice cast back a look of love. "You have done all you could for me; do not you take it to heart. I may get to bear it in time."

"Get to bear it!" What a volume of expression was in the words! Mildred rose and approached Mr. Arkell.

"We had better be going, William. But oh! why did you let it come to this? Why did you not make a confidante of me?"

"I did not know you could help me, Mildred; indeed I did not."

"I will tell you who would have been as thankful to help you as I am—and that is your sister-in-law, Betsey Dundyke. She could have helped you more largely than I can."

"But not more lovingly. God bless you, Mildred!" he whispered, detaining her for a moment as she was following Travice and Lucy out.

Her eyes swam with tears as she looked up at him; her hands rested confidingly in his.

"If you knew what the happiness of serving you is, William! If you knew what a recompence this moment is for the bitter past!"

"God bless you, Mildred!" he repeated, "God bless you for ever."

She drew her veil over her face to pass out, just as she had drawn it after that interview, following his marriage, in the years gone by.

And so the credit of the good and respected old house was saved; saved by Mildred. Had it taken every farthing she had amassed; so that she must have gone forth again, in her middle age, and laboured for a living, she had rejoiced to do it! William Arkell had not waited until now, to know the value of the heart he had thrown away.

And the marriage day drew on. But before it dawned, Westerbury knew that it would bring no marriage with it. Miss Fauntleroy knew it. For the bridegroom was lying between life and death.

Of a sensitive, nervous, excitable temperament, the explanation of that evening, taken in conjunction with the dreadful tension to which his mind had been latterly subjected, far greater than any one had suspected, was too much for Travice Arkell. Conscious that Lucy Arkell passionately loved him; knowing now that she had the money, without which he could not marry, and that part of that money was actually advanced to save his father's credit; knowing also, that he must never more think of her, but must tie himself to one whom he abhorred; that he and Lucy must never again see each other in life, but as friends, and not too much of that, he became ill. Reflection preyed upon him: remorse for doubting Lucy, and hastening to offer himself to Miss Fauntleroy, seated itself in his mind, and ere the day fixed for his marriage arrived, he was laid up with brain fever.

With brain fever! In vain they tried their remedies: their ice to his head; their cooling medicines; their blisters to his feet. His unconscious ravings were, at moments, distressing to hear: his deep love for Lucy; his impassioned adjurations to her to fly with him, and be at peace; his shuddering hatred of Miss Fauntleroy. On the last day of his life, as the doctors thought, Lucy was sent for, in the hope that her presence might calm him. But he did not know her: he was past knowing any one.

"Lucy!" he would utter, in a hollow voice, unconscious that she or any one else was present—"Lucy! we will leave the place for ever. Have you got your things ready? We will go where she can't find us out, and force me to her. Lucy! where are you? Lucy!"

And Mrs. Arkell! She was the most bitterly repentant. Many a sentence is spoken lightly, many an idle threat, many a reckless wish; but the vain folly is not often brought home to the heart, as it was to Mrs. Arkell.

"I would pray Heaven to let me follow you to your grave, Travice, rather than see you marry Lucy Arkell." He was past feeling or remembering the words; but they came home to her. She cast herself upon the bed, praying wildly for forgiveness, clinging to him in all the agony of useless remorse.

"Oh, what matters honour; what matters anything in comparison with his precious life!" she cried, with streaming eyes. "Tell him, Lucy,—perhaps he will understand you—that he shall indeed marry you if he will but set his mind at rest, and get well; he shall never again see Miss Fauntleroy. Lucy! are there no means of calming him? If this terrible excitement lasts, it will kill him. Tell him it is you he shall marry, not Barbara Fauntleroy."

"I cannot tell him so," said Lucy, from the very depth of her aching heart. "It would not be right to deceive him, even now. There can be no escape, if he lives, from the marriage with Miss Fauntleroy."

A few more hours, and the crisis came. The handsome, the intelligent, the refined Travice Arkell, lay still, in a lethargy that was taken to be that of death. It went forth to Westerbury that he was dead; and Lucy took her last look at him, and walked home with her aunt Mildred—to a home, which, however well supplied it was now with the world's comforts, could only seem to her one of desolation. Lucy Arkell's eyes were dry; dry with that intensity of anguish that admits not of tears, and her brain seemed little less confused than his had done, in these last few days of life.

Mildred sat down in her home, and seemed to see into the future. She saw herself and her niece living on in their quiet and monotonous home; her own form drooping with the weight of years, Lucy's approaching middle life. "The old maids" they would be slightingly termed by those who knew little indeed of their inward history. And in their lonely hearts, enshrined in its most hidden depths, the image that respectively filled each in early life, the father and son, William and Travice Arkell, never, never replaced by any other, but holding their own there so long as time should last.

Seated by her fire on that desolate night, she saw it as in a vision.

CHAPTER XVI

MISS FAUNTLEROY LOVED AT LAST

But Travice Arkell did not die. The lethargy that was thought to be death proved to be only the exhaustion of spent nature. When the first faint indications of his awaking from it appeared, the physicians said it was possible that he might recover. He lay for some days in a critical state, hopes and fears about equally balancing, and then he began to get visibly stronger.

"I have been nearly dead, have I not?" he asked one day of his father, who was sitting by the bed.

"But you are better now, Travice. You will get well. Thank God!"

"Yes, the danger's over. I feel that, myself. Dear father! how troubled you have been!"

"Travice, I could hardly have borne to lose you," he murmured, leaning over him. "And—thus."

"I shall soon be well again; soon be strong. Be stronger, I hope," and Travice faintly pressed the hand in which his lay, "to go through the duties that lie before me, than I was previously."

Mr. Arkell sighed from the very depths of his heart. If his son could but have looked forward to arise to a life of peace, instead of pain!

Mildred was with the invalid often. Mrs. Dundyke, who, concerned at the imminent danger of one in whom she had always considered that she held a right, had hastened to Westerbury when the news was sent to her, likewise used to go and sit with him. But not Lucy. It was instinctively felt by all that the sight of Lucy could only bring the future more palpably before him. It might have been so different!

Mrs. Dundyke saw Mr. Arkell in private.

"Is there no escape for him?" she asked; "no escape from this marriage with Miss Fauntleroy? I would give all I am worth to effect it."

"And I would give my life," was the agitated answer. "There is none. Honour must be kept before all things. Travice himself knows there is none; neither would he accept any, were it offered out of the line of strict honour."

"It is a life's sacrifice," said Mrs. Dundyke. "It is sacrificing both him and Lucy."

"Had I possessed but the faintest idea of the sacrifice it really was, even for him, it should never have been contemplated, no matter what the cost," was Mr. Arkell's answer.

"And there was no need of it. If you had but known that! My fortune is a large one now, and the greater portion of it I intended for Travice."

"Betsey!"

"I intended it for no one else. Perhaps I ought to have been more open in expressing my intentions; but you know how I have been held aloof by Charlotte. And I did not suppose that Travice was in necessity of any sort. If he marries Miss Fauntleroy, the half of what I die possessed of will be his; the other half will go to Lucy Arkell. Were it possible that he could marry Lucy, they'd not wait for my death to be placed above the frowns of the world."

"Oh Betsey, how generous you are! But there is no escape for him," added Mr. Arkell, with a groan at the bitter fact. "He cannot desert Miss Fauntleroy."

It was indisputably true. And that buxom bride-elect herself seemed to have no idea that anybody wanted to be off the bargain, for her visits to the house were frequent, and her spirits were unusually high.

You all know the old rhyme about a certain gentleman's penitence when he was sick; though it may not be deemed the perfection of good manners to quote it here. It was a very apt illustration of the feelings of Mrs. Arkell. While her son lay sick unto death, she would have married him to Lucy Arkell; but no sooner was the danger of death removed, and he advancing towards convalescence, than the old pride—avarice—love of rule—call it what you will—resumed sway within her; and she had almost been ready to say again that a mouldy grave would be preferable for him, rather than desertion of Miss Fauntleroy. In fine, the old state of things was obtaining sway, both as to Mrs. Arkell's opinions and to the course of events.

"When can I see him?" asked Miss Fauntleroy one day.

Not the first time, this, that she had put the question, and it a little puzzled Mrs. Arkell to answer it. It was only natural and proper, considering the relation in which each stood to the other, that Miss Fauntleroy should see him; but Mrs. Arkell had positively not dared to hint at such a visit to her son.

"Travice sits up now, does he not?" continued the young lady.

"Yes, he has sat up a little in the afternoon these two days past. We call it sitting up, Barbara, but, in point of fact, he lies the whole time on the sofa. He is not strong enough to sit up."

"Then I'm sure I may see him. It might not have been proper, I suppose, to pay him a visit in bed," she added, laughing loudly; "but there can't be any impropriety now. I want to see him, Mrs. Arkell; I want it very particularly."

"Of course, Barbara; I can understand that you do. I should, in your place. The only consideration is, whether it may not agitate him too much."

"Not it," said Barbara. "I wish you'd go and ask him when I may come. I suppose he is up now?"

Mrs. Arkell had no ready plea for refusal, and she went upstairs there and then. Travice was lying on the sofa, exhausted with the exertion of getting to it.

"My dear, I think you look better," Mrs. Arkell began, not altogether relishing her task; and she gently pushed the bits of brown hair, now beginning to grow again, from the damp, white forehead. "Do you feel so?"

He drew her fingers for a moment into his, and held them there. He was always ready to respond to his mother's little tokens of affection. She had opposed him in the matter of Lucy Arkell, but he was ever generous, ever just, and he blamed circumstances more than he blamed her.

"I feel a great deal better than I did a week ago. I shall get on now."

Mrs. Arkell paused. "Some one wants to see you, Travice."

The hectic came into his white face as she spoke—a wild rush of crimson. Was it possible that he thought she spoke of Lucy? The idea occurred, to Mrs. Arkell.

"My dear, it is Barbara. She has asked to see you a great many times. She is downstairs now."

Travice raised his thin hand, and laid it for a moment over his face, over his closed eyes. Was he praying for help in his pain?—for strength to go through what must be gone through—his duty in the future; and to do it bravely?

"Travice, my dear, but for this illness she would now have been your wife. It is only natural that she should wish to come and see you."

"Yes, of course," he said, removing his hand, and speaking very calmly; "I have been expecting that she would."

"When shall she come up? Now?"

He did not speak for a moment.

"Not now; not to-day; the getting up seemed to tire me more than it has done yet. Tell her so from me. Perhaps she will take the trouble to call again to-morrow, and come up then."

The message was carried to Miss Fauntleroy, and she did not fail in the appointment. Mrs. Arkell took her upstairs without notice to her son; possibly she feared some excuse again. The sofa was drawn near the fire as before, and Travice lay on it; had he been apprised of the visit, he might have tried to sit up to receive her.

She was very big as usual, and very grand. A rich watered lilac silk dress, looped up above a scarlet petticoat; a velvet something on her arms and shoulders, of which I really don't know the name, covered with glittering jet trimmings; and a spangled bonnet with fancy feathers. As she sailed into the room, her petticoats, that might have covered the dome of St. Paul's, knocked over a little brass stand and kettle, some careless attendant having left them on the carpet, near the wall. There was no damage, except noise, for the kettle was empty.

"That's my crinoline!" cried the hearty, good-humoured girl. "Never mind; there's worse misfortunes at sea."

"No, Travice, you had better not rise," interposed Mrs. Arkell, for he was struggling into a sitting position. "Barbara will excuse it; she knows how weak you are."

"And I'll not allow you to rise, that's more," said Barbara, laying her hand upon him. "I am not come to make you worse, but to make you better—if I can."

Mrs. Arkell, not altogether easy yet upon the feelings of Travice as to the visit, anxious, as we all are with anything on our consciences, to get away, invited Barbara to a chair, and hastened from the room. Travice tried to receive her as he ought, and put out his hand with a wan smile.

"How are you, Barbara?"

There was no reply, except that the thin hand was taken between both of hers. He looked up, and saw that her eyes were swimming in tears. A moment's struggle, and they came forth, with a burst.

"There! it's of no good. What a fool I am!"

Just a minute or two's indulgence to the burst, and it was over. Miss Fauntleroy rubbed away the traces, and her broad face wore its smiles again. She drew a chair close, and sat down in front of him.

"I was not prepared to see you look like this, Travice. How dreadfully it has pulled you down!"

She was gazing at his face as she spoke. Her entrance had not called up anything of colour or emotion to illumine it. The transparent skin was drawn over the delicate features, and the refinement, always characterizing it, was more conspicuous than it had ever been. No two faces, perhaps, could present a greater contrast than his did, with the broad, vulgar, hearty, and in a sense, handsome one of hers.

"Yes, it has pulled me down. At one period there was little chance of my life, I believe. But they no doubt told you all at the time. I daresay you knew more of the different stages of the danger than I did."

"And what was it that brought it on?" asked Miss Fauntleroy, untying her bonnet, and throwing back the strings. "Brain fever is not a common disorder; it does not go about in the air!"

There was a slight trace of colour now on the thin cheeks, and she noticed it. Travice faintly shook his head to disclaim any knowledge on his own part.

"It is not very often that we know how these illnesses are brought on. My chief concern now"—and he looked up at her with a smile—"must be to find out how I can best throw it off."

"I have been very anxious for some days to see you," she resumed, after a pause. "Do you know what I have come to say?"

"No," he said, rather languidly.

"But I'll tell you first what I heard. When you were lying in that awful state between life and death—and it is an awful state, Travice, the danger of passing, without warning, to the presence of one's Maker—I heard that it was I who had brought on the fever."

His whole face was flushed now—a consciousness of the past had risen up so vividly within him. "You!" he uttered. "What do you mean?"

"Ah! Travice, I see how it has been. I know all. You have tried to like me, and you cannot. Be still, be calm; I do not reproach you even in thought. You loved Lucy Arkell long before anybody thought of me, in connection with you; and I declare I honour the constancy of your heart in keeping true to her. Now, if you are not tranquil I shall get my ears boxed by your doctors, and I'll not come and see you again."

"But—"

"You just be quiet. I'm going to do the talking, and you the listening. There, I'll hold your hands in mine, as some old, prudent spirit might, to keep you still—a sister, say. That's all I shall ever be to you, Travice."

His chest was beginning to heave with emotion.

"I have a great mind to run away, and leave you to fancy you are going to be tied to me after all! Pray calm yourself. Oh! Travice, why did you not tell me the truth—that you had no shadow of liking for me; that your love for another was stronger than death? I should have been a little mortified at first, but not for long. It is not your fault; you did all you could; and it has nearly killed you—"

"Who has been telling you this?" he interrupted.

"Never mind. Perhaps somebody, perhaps nobody. It's the town's talk, and that's enough. Do you think I could be so wicked and selfish a woman as to hold you to your engagement, knowing this? No! Never shall it be said of Barbara Fauntleroy, in this or in aught else, that she secured her own happiness at the expense of anybody else's."

"But Barbara—"

"Don't 'Barbara' me, but listen," she interrupted playfully, laying her finger on his lips. "At present you hate me, and I don't say that your heart may not have cause; but I want to turn that hatred into love. If I can't get it as a wife, Travice, I may as a friend. I like you very much, and I can't afford to lose you quite. Heaven knows in what way I might have lost you, had we been married; or what would have been the ending."

He lay looking at her, not altogether comprehending the words, in his weakness.

"You shall marry Lucy as soon as you are strong enough; and a little bird has whispered me a secret that I fancy you don't know yet—that you'll have plenty and plenty of money, more than I should have brought you. We'll have a jolly wedding; and I'll be bridesmaid, if she'll let me."

Barbara had talked till her eyes were running down with tears. His lashes began to glisten.

"I couldn't do it, Barbara," he whispered; "I couldn't do it."

"Perhaps not; but I can, and shall. Listen, you difficult old fellow, and set your mind and your conscience at rest. Before that great and good Being, who has spared you through this death-sickness, and has spared me, perhaps, a life of unhappiness, I solemnly swear that I will not marry you! I don't think I have much pride, but I've some; and I am above stooping to accept a man that all the world knows hates me like poison. I'd not have you now, Travice, though there were no Lucy Arkell in the world. A pretty figure I should cut on our wedding day, if I did hold you to your bargain! The town might follow us to church with a serenade of marrowbones and cleavers, as they do the butchers. I'll not leave you until you tell me all is at an end between us—on your side as on mine."

"It is not right, Barbara. It is not right that I should treat you so."

"I'll not leave you until you tell me all is at an end."

"I can't tell it you."

"I'll not leave you until you tell me all is at an end," she persistently repeated. "No, not if I have to stop in the room all the blessed night, as your real sister might. What do I care for their fads and their punctilios? Here I'll stop."

He looked up in her face with a smile. It had more of love in it than Barbara had ever seen expressed to her from him. She bent down and kissed his lips.

"There! that's an earnest of our new friendship. Not that I shall be giving you kisses in future, or expect any from you. Lucy might not like it, you know, or you either. I don't say I should, for I may be marrying on my own score. We might have been an estranged man and wife, Travice, wishing each other dead and buried and perhaps not gone to heaven, every day of our lives. We will be two firm friends. You don't reject me, you know; I reject you, and you can't help yourself."

"We will be friends always, Barbara," he said, from the depths of his inmost heart, as he held her warm hand on his breast. "I am beginning to love you as one already."

"There's a darling fellow! Yes, I should call you so though Lucy were present. Oh, Travice! it's best as it is! A little bit of smart to get over—and that's what I have been doing the past week or so—and we begin on a truer basis. I never was suited to you, and that's the truth. But we can be the best friends living. It won't spoil my appetite, Travice; I'm not of that flimsy temperament. Fancy me getting brain-fever through being crossed in love!"

She laughed out loud at the thought—a ringing, merry laugh. It put Travice at ease on the score of the "smart."

"And now I'm going into the manufactory to tell Mr. Arkell that you and I are two. If he asks for the cause, perhaps I shall whisper to him that I've found out you won't suit me and I prefer to look out for somebody that will; and when Mrs. Arkell asks it me, 'We've split, ma'am—split' I shall tell her. Travice! Travice! did you really think I could stand, knowing it, in the way of anybody's life's happiness?"

He drew her face down to his. He kissed it as he had never kissed it before.

"Friends for life! Firm, warm friends for life, you and I and Lucy! God bless you, Barbara!"

"Mind! I stand out for a jolly ball at the wedding! Lizzie and I mean to dance all night. Fancy us!" she added, with a laugh that rang through the room, "the two forlorn damsels that were to have been brides ourselves! Never mind; we shan't die for the lack of husbands, if we choose to accept them. But it's to be hoped our second ventures will turn out more substantial than our first."

And Travice Arkell, nearly overcome with emotion and weakness, closed his eyes and folded his hands as she went laughing from the room, his lips faintly moving.

"What can I do unto God for all the benefits that He hath done unto me?"

It was during this illness of Travice Arkell's that a circumstance took place which caused some slight degree of excitement in Westerbury. Edward Blissett Hughes, who had gone away from the town between twenty and thirty years before, and of whom nobody had heard much, if any, tidings of since, suddenly made his appearance in it again. His return might not have given rise to much comment, but for the very prominent manner in which his name had been brought forward in connexion with the assize cause; and perhaps no one was more surprised than Mr. Hughes himself when he found how noted he had become.

It matters not to tell how the slim working man of three or four-and-thirty, came back a round, comfortable, portly gentleman of sixty, with a smart, portly wife, and well to do in the world. Well to do?—nay, wealthy. Or how he had but come for a transitory visit to his native place, and would soon be gone again. All that matters not to us; and his return needed not to have been mentioned at all, but that he explained one or two points in the past history, which had never been made quite clear to Westerbury.

One of the first persons to go to see him was William Arkell; and it was from that gentleman Mr. Hughes first learnt the details of the dispute and the assize trial.

Robert Carr had been more malin—as the French would express it—than people gave him credit for. That few hours' journey of his to London, three days previous to the flight, had been taken for one sole purpose—the procuring of a marriage licence. Edward Hughes, vexed at the free tone that the comments of the town were assuming in reference to his young sister, made a tardy interference, and gave Robert Carr his choice—the breaking off the acquaintance, or a marriage. Robert Carr chose the latter alternative, stipulating that it should be kept a close secret; and he ran up to town for the licence. Whether he really meant to use it, or whether he only bought it to appease in a degree the aroused precautions of the brother, cannot be told. That he certainly did not intend to make use of it so soon, Edward Hughes freely acknowledged now. The hasty marriage, the flight following upon it, grew out of that last quarrel with his father. From the dispute at dinner-time, Robert went straight to the Hughes's house, saw Martha Ann, got her consent, and then sought the brother at his workshop, as Edward Hughes still phrased it, and arranged the plans with him for the following morning. Sophia Hughes was of necessity made a party to the scheme, but she was not told of it until night; and Mary they did not tell at all, not daring to trust her. Brother and sister bound themselves to secrecy, for the sake of the fortune that Robert Carr would assuredly lose if the marriage became known; and they suffered the taint to fall on their sister's name, content to know that it was undeserved, and to look forward to the time when all should be cleared up by the reconciliation between father and son, or by the death of Mr. Carr. They were anxious for the marriage, so far beyond anything they could have expected, and, consequently, did not stand at a little sacrifice. Human nature is the same all the world over, and ambition is inherent in it. Robert Carr, on his part, risked something—the chance that, with all their precautions, the fact of the marriage might become known. That it did not, the event proved, as you know; but circumstances at that moment especially favoured them. The rector of St. James the Less was ill; the Reverend Mr. Bell was Robert Carr's firm friend and kept the secret, and there was no clerk. They stole into the church one by one on the winter's morning. Mr. Bell was there before daylight, got it open, and waited for them. The moment Mary Hughes was out of the house, at half-past seven, in pursuance of her engagement at Mrs. Arkell's, Martha Ann was so enveloped in cloaks and shawls that she could not have been readily recognised, had anybody met her, and sent off alone to the church. Her brother and sister followed by degrees. Robert Carr was already there; and as soon as the clock struck eight, the service was performed. One circumstance, quite a little romance in itself, Mr. Hughes mentioned now; and but for a fortunate help in the time of need, the marriage might, after all, not have been completed. Robert Carr had forgotten the ring. Not only Robert, but all of them. That important essential had never once occurred to their thoughts, and none had been bought. The service was arrested midway for the want of it. A few moments' consternation, and then Sophia Hughes came to the rescue. She had been in the habit of wearing her mother's wedding-ring since her death, and she took it from her finger, and the service was completed with it. The party stole away from the church by degrees, one by one, as they had gone to it, and escaped observation. Few people were abroad that dark, dull morning; and the church stood in a lonely, unfrequented part. The getting away afterwards in Mr. Arkell's carriage was easy.

"Ah," said Mr. Arkell now to the brother, "I did not forgive Robert Carr that trick he played upon me for a long while, it so vexed my father. He thought the worst, you know; and for your sister's sake, could not forgive Robert Carr. Had he known of the marriage, it would have been a different thing."

"No one knew of it—not a soul," said Mr. Hughes. "Had we told one, we might as well have told all. I and Sophia knew that we could keep our own counsel; but we could not answer beyond ourselves—not even for Mary."

"Could you not trust her?"

"Trust her!" echoed Mr. Hughes. "Her tongue was like a sieve: it let out everything. She missed mother's ring off Sophia's finger. Sophia said she had lost it—she didn't know what else to say—and before two days were out, the town-crier came to ask if she'd not like it cried. Mary had talked of the loss high and low."

"Did she never know that there had been a marriage?" asked Mr. Arkell.

"Quite at the last, when she had but a day or two left of life. Sophia told her then; she had grieved much over Martha Ann, and was grieving still. Sophia told her, and it sent her easy to her grave. Soon after she died, Sophia married Jem Pycroft, and they came out to me. She's dead now. So that there's only me left out of the four of us," added the returned traveller, after a pause.

"And Martha Ann's eldest son became a clergyman, you say; and he died! I should like to see the other two children she left. Do they live in Rotterdam?"

"I am not sure; but you would no doubt hear of them there. They sold off Marmaduke Carr's property when they came into it, after the trial. It's not to be wondered at: they had no pleasant associations connected with Westerbury."

Edward Hughes burst into a laugh. "What a blow it must have been for stingy John Carr!"

"It was that," said Mr. Arkell. "He is always pleading poverty; but there's no doubt he has been saving money ever since the old squire died and he came into possession. That can't be far short of twenty years now."

"Twenty years! How time flies in this world, sir!" was the concluding remark of Mr. Hughes.

There was no drawback thrown in the way of this marriage of Travice Arkell's, by himself, or by anybody else; and the day for it was fixed as soon as he became convalescent. Mrs. Arkell had to reconcile herself to it in the best way she could; and if she found it a pill to swallow, it was at least a gilded one: Mrs. Dundyke's money would go to him and Lucy—and there was Miss Arkell's as well. They would be placed above the frowns of the world the hour they married, and Travice could turn amateur astronomer at will.

On the day before that appointed for the ceremony, Lucy, in passing through the cloisters with Mrs. Dundyke, from some errand in the town, stopped as she came to that gravestone in the cloisters. She bent her head over it, for she could hardly read the inscription—what with the growing dusk, and what with her blinding tears.

"Oh, Aunt Betsey"—she had caught the name from Travice—"if he had but lived! If he could but be with us to-morrow!"

Aunt Betsey touched with her gentle finger the sorrowing face. "He is better off, Lucy."

"Yes, I know. But in times of joy it seems hard to remember it. I wonder—I hope it is not wrong to wonder it—whether he and mamma are always with me in spirit? I have grown to think so."

"The thinking it will not do you harm, Lucy."

"Oh, was it not a cruel thing, Aunt Betsey, for that boy Lewis to throw him down! He was forgiven by everybody at the time; but in my heart—I won't say it. But for that, Henry might be alive now. They left the college school afterwards. Did you know that?"

"The Lewises? Yes; I think I heard it."

"A reaction set in for Henry after he died, and the boys grew shy and cool to the two Lewises. In fact, they were sent to Coventry. They did not like it, and they left. The eldest went up to be in some office in London, and the youngest has gone to a private school."

"It is strange that the two great inflicted evils in your family and in mine, should have come from the Carrs!" exclaimed Mrs. Dundyke. "But, my dear, do not let us get into a sorrowful train of thought to-day. And, all the sorrow we can give, cannot bring back to us those who are gone."

"I wish you could have seen him!" murmured Lucy. "He was so beautiful! he—"

"Here are people coming, my dear."

Lucy turned away, drying her eyes. A clerical dignitary and a young lady were advancing through the cloisters. As they met, the young lady bowed to Lucy, and the gentleman raised his shovel hat—not so much as to acquaintances, as because they were ladies passing through his cloisters.

"Who are they?" whispered Mrs. Dundyke, when the echo of their footsteps had died away.

"The dean and Miss Beauclerc. Aunt Betsey, she knew Henry so well! She came to see him in his coffin."

They were at Mr. Arkell's house, in the evening—Lucy, her aunt, and Mrs. Dundyke. The breakfast in the morning was to be given in it, Miss Arkell's house being small, and the carriages would drive there direct from St. James-the-Less. Mrs. Arkell, gracious now beyond everything, had sent for them to spend the last evening, and see the already laid-out table in the large drawing-room. She could not spare Travice that last evening, she said.

Oh, how it all came home to Mildred! She had gone to that house the evening before a wedding in the years gone by, taken to it perforce, because she dared make no plea of refusal. She had seen the laid-out table in the drawing-room then, just as she was looking down upon it now.

"Lucy's destiny is happier!" she unconsciously murmured.

"Did you speak, Mildred?"

She raised her eyes to the questioner by her side, William Arkell. She had not observed that he was there.

"I?—Yes; I say Lucy's will be a happy destiny."

"Very happy," he assented, glancing at a group at the end, who were engaged in a hot and laughing dispute, as to the placing of the guests, Travice maintaining his own opinion against Aunt Betsey and Lucy. Travice looked very well now. His hair was long again; his face, delicate still—but it was in the nature of its features to be so—had resumed its hue of health. Lucy was radiant in smiles and blue ribbons, under the light of the chandelier.

"I begin to think that destinies are more equally apportioned than we are willing to imagine; that where there are fewer flowers there are fewer thorns," Mr. Arkell observed in a low tone. "There is a better life, Mildred, awaiting us hereafter."

"Ah, yes. Where there shall be neither neglect, nor disappointment, nor pain; where—"

"Here you are!" broke out a loud, hearty, laughing voice upon their ears. "I knew it was where I should find you. Lucy, I have been to your house after you. Take my load off me, Travice."

Need you be told that the voice was Barbara Fauntleroy's? She came staggering in under the load: a something held out before her, nearly as tall as herself.

A beautiful epergne for the centre of the table, of solid silver. Travice was taking it from her, but awkwardly—he was one of the incapable ones, like poor Peter Arkell. Miss Fauntleroy rated him and pushed him away, and lifted it on the table herself, with her strong hands.

"It's our present to you two, mine and Lizzie's. You'll accept it, won't you, Lucy?"

Kindness invariably touched the chord of Lucy Arkell's feelings, perhaps because she had not been in the way of having a great deal of it shown to her in her past life. The tears were in her earnest eyes, as she gently took the hands of Miss Fauntleroy.

"I cannot thank you as I ought. I—"

"Thank me, child! It's not so much to thank me for. Doesn't it look well on the table, though? Mrs. Arkell must allow it to stand there for the breakfast."

"For that, and for all else," whispered Lucy, with marked emotion, retaining the hands in her warm clasp. "You must let us show our gratitude to you always, Barbara."

Barbara Fauntleroy bent her full red lips on Lucy's fair forehead. "Our bargain—his and mine—was, that we were all three to be firm and fast friends through life, you know. Lucy, there's nobody in the world wishes you happier than I do. Jolly good luck to you both!"

"Thank you, Barbara," said Travice, who was standing by.

"And now, who'll come and release Lizzie?" resumed Miss Fauntleroy. "We shall have her rampant. She's in a fly at the door, and can't get out of it."

"Not get out of it!" repeated Mr. Arkell.

"Not a bit of it. It's filled with flower-pots from our hot-house. We thought perhaps you'd not have enough for the rooms, so we've brought a load. But Lizzie got into the fly first, you see, to pack them for bringing steadily, and she can't get out till they are out. I took care of the epergne, and Lizzie of the pots."

With a general laugh, everybody rushed to get to the imprisoned Lizzie. Lucy lingered a moment, ostensibly looking at the epergne, really drying her tears away. Travice came back to her.

He took her in his arms; he kissed the tears from her cheeks; he whispered words of the sweetest tenderness, asking what her grief was.

"Not grief, Travice—joy. I was thinking of the past. What would have become of us but for her generosity?"

"But for her generosity, Lucy, I should have been her husband now. I should never have held my darling in my arms. Yes, she was generous! God bless her always! I'll never hate anybody again, Lucy."

Lucy glanced up shyly at him, a smile parting her lips at the last words. And she put her hand within the arm of him who was soon to be her husband, as they went out in the wake of the rest, to rescue the flower-pots and Miss Lizzie Fauntleroy.

And Mr. St. John and the dean's daughter? Ah! not in this place can their after-history be given. But you may hear it sometime.

MRS HENRY WOOD (aka ELLEN WOOD) – A CONCISE BIBLIOGRAPHY

Danesbury House (1860)
East Lynne (1861)
The Elchester College Boys (1861)

A Life's Secret (1862)
Mrs. Halliburton's Troubles (1862)
The Channings (1862)
The Foggy Night at Offord: A Christmas Gift for the Lancashire Fund (1863)
The Shadow of Ashlydyat (1863)
Verner's Pride (1863)
Lord Oakburn's Daughters (1864)
Oswald Cray (1864)
Trevlyn Hold; or, Squire Trevlyn's Heir (1864)
William Allair; or, Running away to Sea (1864)
Mildred Arkell: A Novel (1865)
The Argosy (1865)
Elster's Folly: A Novel (1866)
St. Martin's Eve: A Novel (1866)
Lady Adelaide's Oath (1867)
Orville College: A Story (1867)
The Ghost of the Hollow Field (1867)
Anne Hereford: A Novel (1868)
Castle Wafer; or, The Plain Gold Ring (1868)
The Red Court Farm: A Novel (1868)
Roland Yorke: A Novel (1869)
Bessy Rane: A Novel (1870)
George Canterbury's Will (1870)
Dene Hollow (1871)
Within the Maze: A Novel (1872)
The Master of Greylands (1872)
Johnny Ludlow (1874)
Bessy Wells (1875)
Told in the Twilight: Containing 'Parkwater' and nine short stories (1875)
Adam Grainger: A Tale (1876)
Edina (1876)
Our Children (1876)
Parkwater: With four other tales (1876)
Pomeroy Abbey (1878)
Lady Adelaide (1879)
Johnny Ludlow, Second Series (1880)
A Tale of Sin and Other Tales (1881)
Court Netherleigh: A Novel (1881)
About Ourselves (1883)
Johnny Ludlow. Third Series (1885)
Lady Grace and Other Stories (1887)
The Story of Charles Strange (1888)
Featherston's Story. A Tale by Johnny Ludlow (1889)
The Unholy Wish and Other Stories (1890)
The House of Halliwell. A Novel (1890)
Ashley and Other Stories (1897)
Victor Serenus (1898)
Johnny Ludlow. Fifth series (1899)

Johnny Ludlow. Sixth series (1899)

Translations
Les Channing. Traduit de l'Anglais par Mme Abric-Encontre (1864)
Les Filles de Lord Oakburn: Roman traduit de l'anglais par L. Bochet (1876)
La Gloire des Verner: Roman traduit de l'anglais par L. de L'Estrive (1878)
Le Serment de Lady Adelaïde: Roman traduit de l'anglais par Léon Bochet (1878)

www.ingramcontent.com/pod-product-compliance
Lightning Source LLC
Chambersburg PA
CBHW060218030726
47499CB00004B/1094